ORIGINAL SIN

G.D. Burkhead

Acknowledgements

I started writing this book in 2012. Crucially, I didn't work on this story with anything like regularity during all that time — there were years where it sat untouched in a folder somewhere while more pressing things and more polished stories happened — but the fact remains that, on the year this book finally releases, Chapter 1 turns 13 years old. It and I have had a lot of help in that long timespan, so let's get to it. I'll try and keep this to a single page — lord knows this thing's long enough as it is.

Thank you to the writing professors at Lindenwood University whose classes I was in when this story first began: George Hickenlooper, Spencer Hurst, Ann Canale, and Rift Fournier, all of whom helped me figure out my narrative voice, even if they didn't always jive with it.

Thank you to Jonathan French, of *Autumn's Fall* and *Grey Bastards* fame, who graciously took time out of his own indie author journey to pass on what he'd learned to my wife and I, who helped workshop the first chapters of this book when it was in its early stages, and who told me he'd find me and end me if I never saw it through to completion. It remains one of the most flattering threats I've ever received, and I remembered it fondly whenever the motivation waned.

Thank you to the staff at Boba Mocha in Duluth, Georgia, where a lot of the first draft of this thing got written. I did a lot of lurking and loitering at the corner tables there, drank a lot of tea, probably weirded some of the staff out a bit by being awkward in public, but the vibes were immaculate, what can I say?

Thank you to my family for raising me to be weird and instilling a love of reading and fantasy in me from a young age. I think some of you will like this one, but I know even those of you who think this is some weird nonsense will still be proud of me for making it happen.

And thank you to Manda, the first and biggest fan of this story, especially during those periods where I was convinced I was wasting my time with it. Thank you for letting me bounce ideas off of you, and for the initial reading and course corrections, and for cheering me on and keeping me going when I needed it most, and for all that sappy marriage stuff in general. Love you, baby.

Contents

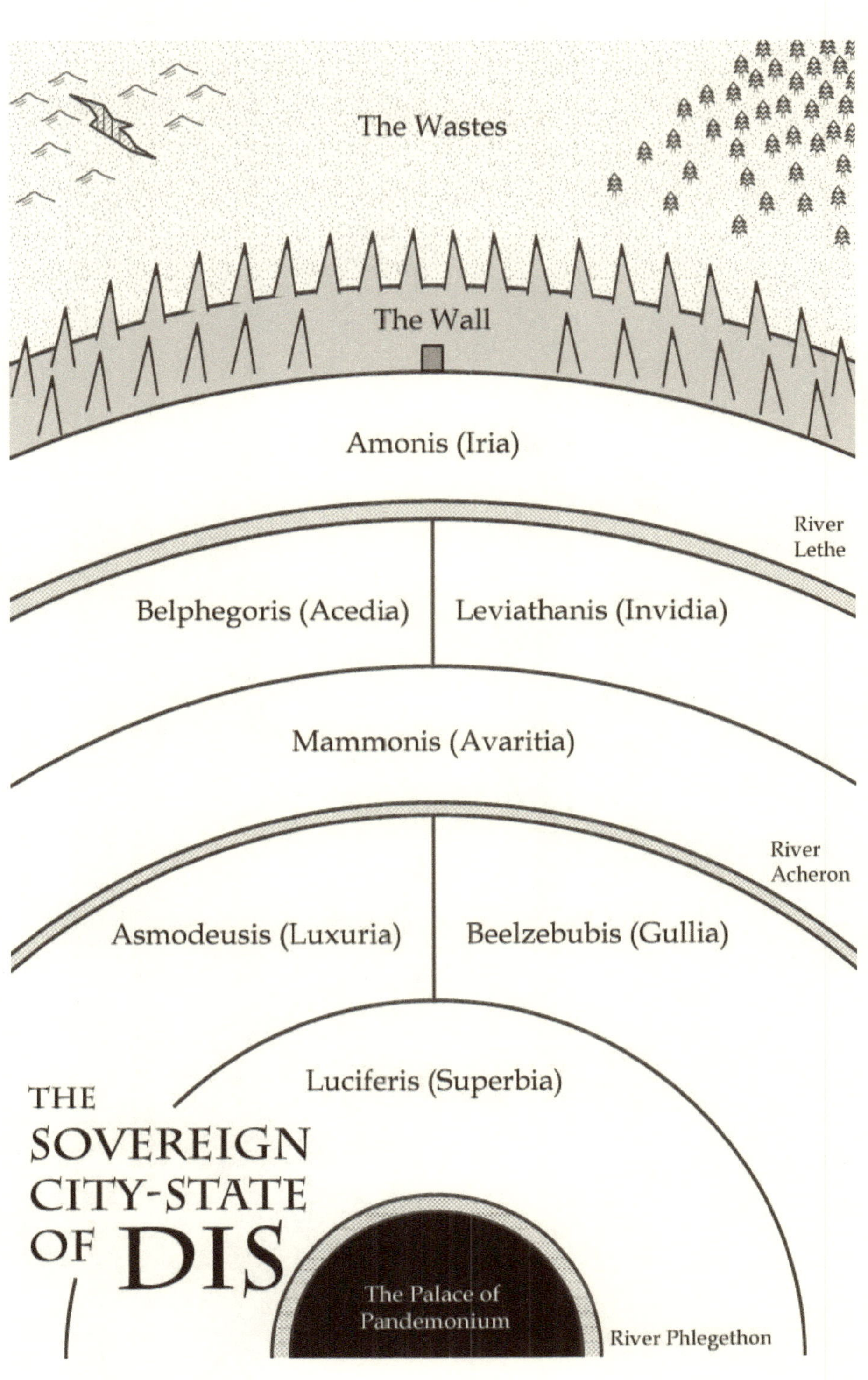

The Wastes
The Wall
Amonis (Iria)
River Lethe
Belphegoris (Acedia)
Leviathanis (Invidia)
Mammonis (Avaritia)
River Acheron
Asmodeusis (Luxuria)
Beelzebubis (Gullia)
Luciferis (Superbia)
THE SOVEREIGN CITY-STATE OF DIS
The Palace of Pandemonium
River Phlegethon

Chapter 1: Obsession

It all started with that damn book. The *Morganomicon*, she'd called it. With a name like that, I should have known to leave it alone.

I've never been a bookish type of girl. Nothing against it, but there are a dozen other things I'd rather waste my time on than reading just for the sake of the reading. So I couldn't explain, then, what caught and held my attention so much about a dusty old tome falling apart at the spine on the shelf of a hole-in-the-wall consignment shop. The shop itself was sandwiched between a Lucky Dragon Chinese restaurant and Old Sound, the music store where I worked part time. It had shown up overnight; one evening leaving work, I glanced through the window to see a dark, empty room with a handful of dusty shelves and a few loose boards of plywood, and the next evening that same window displayed antique mahogany jewelry boxes and a gleaming suit of silver armor, among other things. The lights were on, and the shelves were full, though nobody could be seen inside.

That first time, I passed it on by and didn't think much about it. The next evening was payday, so with check in hand, I decided to stop in and browse. It was one of those rare months for me when the rent on my one-room apartment wasn't overdue, so I could afford to act like I had money to burn on cheap used junk. The shopkeeper, a pale and willowy lady with dark black hair and a sharp, angular face, smiled at me as I walked in. Her eyes followed me as I wandered down the nearest aisle, passing over gauzy pastel dresses and ceramic castle miniatures. It was kind of off-putting having a stranger and the only other person in the room blatantly and unashamedly staring after me. I was about to turn around and walk out when my gaze landed on the bookshelves and I saw it. That damn book.

The cover was a faded and ratty gray-black without any words or pictures, and as I got closer, I could smell it even among the rest of the musty old books. It smelled like a moldy attic, like dust and moist wood; but when I picked it up, it was dry, though the cover did feel like some weird hybrid of leather and tree bark. It was also almost as thick as my hand, and the pages were ragged on the edges, some of them sticking out past the cover's edge without any pattern. When I opened it up, a few fell out. I stuffed them back in hurriedly before the shopkeeper lady could see, and that's when I realized that many of them were already missing, some even torn halfway down the middle. What was left looked like it was written in gibberish, in strange flowing letters that didn't resemble any font or language I had ever seen.

I put it back down and walked out before I could do any more inadvertent damage, the lady behind the counter gazing at me the entire time. That book had definitely seen better days, but even in its prime, it seemed like something I wouldn't be able to read or understand.

Which is why it surprised me so much when I went back in a second time just to see it again.

Not right away, of course. I walked to the bank first and cashed my paycheck, reviving my flat-lining account for another week. I caught the bus back to my rundown apartment and microwaved a frozen burrito for dinner. I managed to finish most of my homework before finally passing out on the futon and drooling into my statistics book. And I woke up just in time to catch another bus to the local community college only ten minutes after my first class had started. I had a very productive, very normal day. I even got to work with some time to spare.

But all day long, my mind kept drifting back to that damn book. Not longingly, like I wished I'd bought it or anything. It just kept edging its way into my thoughts. The ragged pages, the alien writing, the weird texture, even the loamy odor — it was partly curiosity and partly unbidden. I caught myself remembering it when nothing at all had happened to trigger the memory. It was confusing.

I stopped and looked in the window again that evening after work, debating whether I wanted to bother going in a second time. The lady behind the counter caught my gaze while I was window browsing and smiled at me again through the glass. I smiled back politely and didn't realize that I was walking toward the door until I was already through it.

This time, I made a point of checking out the rest of the store first before heading to the bookshelves. I passed racks of frilled and ruffled shirts and dresses mixed in with t-shirts and leather jackets. A pair of blue jeans draped over what looked like deer antlers sitting on a table wrapped in newspaper. A shelf devoted entirely to jeweled music boxes, and several shelves of snow globes depicting everything from famous monuments to a ring of naked women dancing in a circle. At the end of this aisle was a long mirror in a gilded frame with a tribal design etched around the edges. The me that stared out of it had a confused look in her dark brown eyes, like she didn't know what she was doing there. And over the faded denim shoulder of the other me's jacket, I could see the shopkeeper lady watching me and smiling.

I turned and walked over to the bookshelf, then browsed the spines of every other title on it before picking up that damn book again.

I made an earnest effort to examine it this time and maybe figure out what about it was making it stick in my mind. The flowing symbols looked like they were trying to form words and sentences, but they didn't look like an alphabet; they looked like someone had lazily drawn a pen in wispy curlicues over the pages, like they were trying to sketch smoke rather than write a book. A few of the pages had illustrations, but what they were illustrating, I couldn't tell. There were diagrams, I think, that looked like rough drafts of fractal art. About the only thing I saw in those pages that I recognized was a drawing of the phases of the moon, but even that was off — there were too many phases, and they were in the wrong order.

Someone wrote this deliberately to confuse people, I thought. Still holding it, I turned to face the lady behind the counter. Still smiling and still staring, she tilted her head at me. Probably her, then. I put the book back down and smiled back at her as I headed out the door toward the bus stop, then sat in the cigarette smoke cloud of the balding man on the bench next to me until it arrived. When the door folded open, I fished my crumpled bus pass out of my pocket and punched it before taking an empty seat near the front, where I laid my head back against the cracked leather and relaxed.

And immediately started remembering that damn book.

By the time I got home, I was pissed and didn't know why. The swirling nonsense words were floating around in my mind, bumping into other thoughts. I saw them in the scenery around me, in the darkening clouds outside, in the cracks on my ceiling, in the wrinkles of my textbook pages. I caught myself doodling the letters from memory in the margins of my notebook while I tried to read Beowulf for my world lit class, and after I threw my pencil across the room, I realized my empty fingers were still tracing the lines. I gave up on homework and put on my headphones, turned on my MP3 player, and lay on the futon listening to the Rolling Stones sing about sympathizing with the Devil. And all the while I kept trying, in my head, to match the flow of the lyrics with the contours of the strange writing in that damn book.

It was maddening. It was making me mad. If there were anything inside it that I could understand and that interested me, this unbidden obsession would make sense. If it were a nice-looking book and I secretly wanted it to display in my cheap apartment somewhere as decoration, that would also make sense. If I just got a kick out of trying to decipher coded languages, I could understand completely. But there wasn't, and it wasn't, and I didn't. So it had no right to claim so much of my attention.

The next day was a Saturday, and as I had no weekend classes, I pulled an early shift at Old Sound. I had to walk by the thrift store on my way in, and it took a real physical effort to keep my head from craning around to look in the window. Steve, the manager and only other employee in the store most days, must have seen the irritation on my face as I punched the clock. "You alright, Morgan?" he asked, looking up from a brown cardboard box of empty jewel cases with a frown. "You look… scowlier than usual."

Steve was in his late twenties, only a few years older than me, with a permanent but thin patch of curly black hairs growing out of his chin, his best attempt at growing a beard. He'd dropped out of the same college that I was currently making my way through with two years left on his business degree, and he seemed to be a permanent fixture at the shop. I always kind of assumed, back then, that I would end up right beside him in a couple years after my gen-eds were over with and I ran out of direction. I still wasn't sure what I was going to college for, other than because my parents told me I had to, and assistant manager at a used music store seemed as good a place to end up as any.

"I'm fine," I said, flinging my denim jacket over the green plastic table that served as our break room. "Just preoccupied."

"Is that the same shirt you wore in yesterday?"

I glanced down at the men's black band t-shirt I was wearing. Most of my wardrobe lately consisted of men's black band t-shirts, with only the logo on the front to differentiate them. Pants alternated between leather and blue jeans, both usually with at least one rip somewhere. Shoes were always the same pair of black combat boots. I like familiarity in my clothes, what can I say?

I grabbed the hem of my shirt and tugged it out. "Did I wear Queen yesterday?"

"You wore Queen yesterday." Steve said. "Day before that, too, come to think of it." He picked up the box of empty cases and carried them over to me. "You got more than one, or you just quit doing laundry?"

"I've been busy," I said, taking the box from him. "Or my brain has, anyway. What am I doing with these?"

"They're for that box of loose discs beneath the cash register," he said, taking a seat behind his desk. It was the only desk in this backroom and, besides our break table, also the only furniture. Everything else was boxes and milk crates. "School getting to ya?" he asked.

"Not quite," I said, and took the box to the front counter. I wished it was school distracting me; at least then it would be responsible frustration, something I could understand. I pulled out the box of loose CDs and set it next to the box of empty CD cases, then set about putting the one into the other, trying to relax with menial, repetitive labor.

I had about twenty CDs cased away when I realized that I was setting them out in patterns across the counter when I was done. Patterns that looked kind of like one of the weird geometric diagrams I had seen on one of the pages in that damn book.

Steve hurried out of the back room to see what was wrong when he heard me growl and knock about twenty CD cases off the counter to the tiled floor. I muttered something unconvincing about tripping and trying to catch my balance, then, as he shook his head and went back to whatever it is he does back there, I resolved to get to the bottom of this book business if I had to shake down that staring shopkeeper for answers.

Luckily, it didn't come to that. When I strode through the thrift store door for the third time, I marched straight to the back and yanked that damn book off the shelf, flashing a smile at the lady behind the counter along the way that I'm sure didn't match the tone of my boots stomping across the floor. I'm fairly small — only about five-three or so — so I'm sure it wasn't a very intimidating sounding stomp. But it looked impressive and purposeful to me, watching myself approach in the mirror at the end of the aisle. I wouldn't have messed with me.

Which is one reason why I was so surprised when I heard a low, sultry voice right behind me say, "This book is calling to you." I spun around in surprise to find the shopkeeper lady standing behind me, smiling down at me. She was taller up close than she looked behind the counter, her storm gray eyes more intense, her smile more… predatory. Something about her features or the light or the angle of view made it hard to tell how old she was. And something about her expression made it hard to look away.

"What do you mean?" I asked, holding the book up between us like a shield until I realized I was doing so and lowered my hands, embarrassed.

"This marks the third occasion you've come merely to examine it," she said. There was no question to her voice. She knew what I had been doing on each of these visits.

"Oh," I said. For a moment, it was all I said. Then her eyes dropped to the book, and I found mine did too. "Yeah, um. I guess it's, uh, kind of a weird book, isn't it?"

She laughed, and my first thought was that her laugh sounded like wind chimes in the rain. My second thought was, *Why did I just think that? I don't think in flowery words like that.* "It is at that, I suppose," she said. She reached down to run a finger over the cover, and I had a brief jolt of fear that she was going to touch me, though I didn't know why. "It is a unique tome, that much is certain. The only one like it in this world."

"Oh yeah?" I nodded and tried to look a polite level of interested, hoping she would go away. "It does look pretty, uh… different. I guess."

She took the book from me then, holding the spine in one splayed hand while the other leafed through the pages. "You are curious," she said in that matter-of-fact tone, "but you are hesitant to seem so. You don't understand the hold these pages have over you, so you are trying to deny it while simultaneously investigating it in secret." Her eyes caught mine over the edge of the book then. "Correct me if it is otherwise."

Who talks like that? But I couldn't deny it to her; if it was that obvious, there'd be no point. "Something like that, yeah," I said hesitantly. "I'm, uh, not usually one for old books, normally. And I don't even recognize the language, so…"

"It is lost," she said. "Popularly, anyway. The alphabet was rarely shared outside of its niche even in the days of its flourishing."

I nodded again. "That would explain it, then."

"You want me to tell you what it is, but you do not want to ask."

"Then why don't you just tell me if you know that?" I snapped. Part of me felt bad about it afterward, but she was getting on my nerves.

She only smiled again. "Because you will not believe the answer."

"Why not?" I demanded. "What's the answer?"

She turned the book around to face the pages toward me. For a moment, it almost looked like the flowing letters were drifting across the paper. "It is written in Old Elven," she said.

It took a moment for her words to sink in, and when they did, I gave her my best carefully-blank stare. "Elven? Like, elves? Like, Lord of the Rings elves?"

"Somewhat," she said. "To be perfectly accurate, it is the Queen's Tongue of the Daoine Sidhe, the fey creatures of the Seelie Court. But elves as they are imagined today can be traced back through the mortal consciousness to this same group."

"Ah. All right, gotcha," I said, inching forward and around her. "Thanks for that. Excuse me." I made it around her and headed for the front door. One of those kinds of people, then. There had been a crazy old fairy lady across the street from where I grew up, too, who kept rusted metal junk and old clothes strewn across her front lawn and had bits of leaves and twig always sticking out of her hair. Once, when I was a kid, she accused me of being a changeling because I didn't look like my parents. I tried to explain to her that the word she was looking for was "adopted," but she just got mad and told me she'd find the real baby someday. After that, I decided that I wasn't a fan of her particular brand of crazy.

I had the door halfway open when the lady behind me called out, "If you leave now, you will come back tomorrow to look at this tome for a fourth time, and you will be even angrier and more confused with yourself than you are now." I stopped with my hand on the knob and, despite myself, waited for her to finish. "If you leave with this book in hand, however," she continued, "then you will be able to be angry and confused in the comfort of your own space until you finally let it speak to you, and you will not have to suffer my presence while you do so."

I could feel her smiling at the back of my head. I could just see her reflection in the glass of the front door, holding that damn book. After a few seconds' deliberation, I sighed and turned back to her. "How much is it?" I asked.

She tilted her head. "How much can you sacrifice for it?"

I rummaged around in my jacket pocket and came back with a crumpled wad of bills and some coins, which I counted out in my hand. "I got two thirty-eight on me right now."

"Then that will suffice." She glided — and that really was the most accurate word for it — across the aisle and handed me the supposed elf book, taking my money in the same motion. "It is a grimoire without title," she said, "though a previous owner once referred to it as the *Morganomicon*. Make of that what you will."

"Sounds fancy," I grumbled, turning it over in my hands. "*Morganomicon*, huh? That's appropriate, then. My name's Morgan."

She laughed that very poetic laugh of hers again. "Is it? Perhaps that is why it likes you so much, then."

I looked from her to the book and back before nodding my head goodbye and backing out the door, then turned on my heel and headed for the bus stop, the book under my arm, my eyes on the sidewalk in front of me, trying to clear my head of the strange encounter. This book and that lady had started to creep me out a little, but at least she'd had a point when she'd said I wouldn't have to keep taking time out of my day to go into her store and get confused.

I went home that night with that damn book, intending to scrutinize the pages until I was sick of them, then drop it in a corner and forget about it once and for all. And I would have, except that was the night it started talking to me.

Chapter 2: Impatience

The book didn't literally talk to me, of course; however strange it was, it couldn't do that. At least I don't think it could. It probably would have otherwise. Anyway, it did pretty much the next best thing.

After I broke down and bought the book from the crazy thrift store lady, I caught the bus and went straight home with it. It was only about three in the afternoon, but I couldn't think of anything else to do, and I'm not a big fan of going out and meeting people. Once back in my cozy hermitage, I popped another frozen burrito from the mini-fridge into the microwave and, while it spun and nuked, plopped myself down in my leaky green beanbag chair — the only other seat I had at the moment besides my futon — with my new book. The *Morganomicon*, I guess. The title seems like a bad joke to me now, but back then, I didn't know any better.

I flipped it open to the first page and stared at the squiggles, looking for some sort of meaning in them, willing them to make sense. And suddenly, for a moment, in a flash, they did.

I had to do a double take. One second they were a series of doodles, the next there were perfectly coherent phrases and ideas being fed into my mind, and on the third, doodles again. It was like the page had reached out and slapped me, quick enough that I couldn't be sure it had even happened. I looked again, more carefully this time, concentrating on the contours of each letter. Nothing happened. But, when I sighed and made to look away, I saw it again.

It was like those 3D optical illusion pictures, the ones that look like chaotic blobs of colored static if you stare directly at them, but relax your eyes and look at the space just in front of them or past them and an image suddenly jumps out at you. The shapes on these pages looked like random, curvy lines when I looked at them as letters or words; and if I looked at them each in turn, all I saw was a series of nothing. But if I stared down the page as a whole without focusing on any one symbol and tried to coax the hidden images out with my eyes, suddenly everything just… slid into place. Suddenly messages and images were at the forefront of my mind, like seeing someone else's thoughts on an internal slideshow.

Like reading, I realized. I was reading a language I had never encountered before in my life. Or it was reading itself to me. It felt like, somewhere between the pages and my eyes, something was translating it and dropping the translation straight into my brain. I got a chill and, nervously, looked over both my shoulders to make sure I was really alone in my own apartment before turning my attention back to the book, this time trying to focus on what I was reading and not just the unbelievable fact that I was reading it.

It's hard to put into words ideas that didn't come to me as words, but the very first page of the book, which seemed newer and in better condition than most, also seemed to be a greeting, which made me double check my solitude again. There was also a sort of introductory warning — what I was seeing, it said, were not words but thoughts transcribed, the purest form of language that the author knew, written in such a way to withstand the changes of time and space so that anyone, in any era, from anywhere in any of the worlds (and it used "worlds," plural) would be able to eventually discern the contents therein.

I don't talk like this if I can help it. That's one way I knew that these messages were coming from the book and that I wasn't having a sudden onset of crazy. Crazy me wouldn't have had access to half the vocabulary I was suddenly thinking in. Hell, sane me, if I'm still in here, still doesn't know what some of what I was thinking then meant.

My microwave beeped shrilly, impotently, and was promptly ignored, my plans for dinner growing cold again as I sat in the middle of my room, amazed and with my insides gurgling in neglected hunger, flipping through thick, musty page after thick, musty page of unexpectedly legible gobbledygook. Concepts flowed to me as easily as watching leaves blow in the wind, and I found myself caught up in reading for the first time that I can remember. The sun began to set outside my window, but I only noticed when it eventually became too dark to read by and I had to flip on the shade-less lamp next to my futon. The white glare from the naked bulb washing through the room helped break the spell somewhat, and it was then that a few thoughts of my own finally edged their way in to my attention, and I made a few realizations.

First, that I had forgotten all about dinner, I was starving, and my burrito was almost certainly a cold and mushy lump of soggy refried beans slowly oozing into a puddle in my microwave. Second, that I was already fifty or sixty pages into the book, and had breezed through several illustrated parts that had looked like otherworldly nonsense the first time I'd seen them with perfect understanding. And third, I had a very strong, very creeping suspicion that I somehow knew magic now. And not the "rabbit out of a hat" kind — the "rabbit out of thin air" kind.

I had to set the book down then, get away from it for a while and rethink recent events a bit. I threw myself out of the beanbag chair, punched a few buttons on my microwave to reheat dinner, and paced a circle around the perimeter of my room while it spun to life once more, going over everything I'd just read in my head a second time. It was hard to recall at first, vague as the messages were; but when I started thinking about the swirled letters again, letting them drift through my thoughts without stopping them like they'd been trying to do since I first saw them, I began to recall the same impressions I'd been reading. There was some background information, some theories and philosophy on the mechanics of reality alteration that I'm not even going to attempt to put into real words, dense and tangled as they were. Most of what I'd been reading, though, I realized were instructions: think in this mindset, picture this, breathe like that, move just so, and little details about the world can be… changed.

I stopped pacing. *What, that's it?* It was like a room in my mind that I'd just never noticed before was suddenly being pointed out to me, the words hidden on the page saying, "There. That's where you're keeping it. Door's not even locked." I couldn't believe it was so easy to grasp. But then, I hadn't been able to believe most of what had happened to me in the past couple of days.

On a sudden whim, I ran back over to the microwave and punched the cancel button, stopping the light and humming from inside. I opened the door, pulled out my lukewarm pseudo-Mexican pile of mush sitting on its soggy little napkin, and plopped it on the table. It smelled like old bean paste and tomato sauce, and a quick touch test told me it was still cold inside, the shell around it barely warmer. With a deep breath and plenty of mental derision about how ridiculous this would look to anyone watching, I spread my hands in the air on either side of the burrito, closed my eyes, and focused.

I let the not-quite-words swirl around in my head, mumbled something incomprehensible under my breath, and imagined one of the tangled diagram-things floating just behind my eyes, mentally tracing the lines from the inside out. There was a small voice that accompanied all of this that was telling me that I was an idiot to believe in this stuff and that it was stupid to expect anything to happen, but with some convincing, I was finally able to shut her up.

That's when I felt the heat on my palms, radiating outward like I were about to grab a hot stovetop. It started faint, but as I mentally completed the pattern in my head, nearing the edges of the image, it grew hotter and hotter, until I thought I'd plunged my hands beneath a bed of hot coals. I yelped, more in surprise than actual pain, as my eyes snapped open and the strange focus of my thoughts was cut off.

The burrito exploded, splashing red-brown goo over my outstretched hands and the table, as well as my shirt, my face, and my shoulder-length black hair. Spatters of three-bean glop even managed to reach the far walls on either side of my one-room apartment. Only my hands spread above the napkin had prevented it from hitting the ceiling.

Welp. There it was — I knew magic. I was Morgan Amell, Kamikaze Burrito Witch. Let the world tremble at my name.

Slowly, mind carefully blank, I got a wet sponge and mopped the glop from the walls and table, dropping all evidence into the white plastic trash can by the door. Then I grabbed a clean t-shirt, a pair of sweat pants, and a towel and headed down the hallway to the communal bathroom, where I took the most meditative shower I can remember. My landlord, a little hunchbacked old man with suspenders and balding white hair, saw me come out of my room, looking stunned and covered in bean sludge, like I'd just been run down by a taco truck. He stopped and blinked at me as I passed, then walked on, shaking his head. I didn't have the wherewithal to think of a good excuse for him just then. Actually, I don't think I ever offered him an explanation for that moment, come to think of it.

A million thoughts must have run through my mind while I stood under the shower, head bent, hair plastered to my face, watching rivulets of water run off of me to swirl over the cracked ceramic tile and down the drain. The water reminded me of the words in that damn book. Most things did lately, it seemed.

Do I tell somebody about this? On the one hand, I couldn't imagine who would believe me — I certainly wouldn't have before today. On the other, though, making food self-destruct from across the room might convince a few people. And if it really was magic that I was doing, like real wizardy stuff and not just some elaborate and convincing prank that I still hadn't figured out, then that could very well be a ticket to bigger and better things. Having real superpowers had to be worth something, right? I could drop out of school, if nothing else — no need to learn microbiology when I could light fires with my brain. No need to learn any science, come to that, if I could change the rules with a thought. I could be rich and famous if I wanted, move out of my rinky-dink apartment loft and get a real place, a big mansion all to myself. I wasn't sure how I felt about famous yet, but rich I could definitely go for. Maybe even get my own island. That was something that most people in movies about superheroes or sudden fantastical crap never seemed to think about: just come right out with it and be an instant celebrity.

But then, I thought, I probably wouldn't like the attention that would bring. I didn't even really like what little attention I got from strangers now. And then I'd have to explain myself, and the government would probably take the book away and lock it up somewhere, deny it ever happened and start some big conspiracy. And lock me up somewhere too, maybe, and stick needles and stuff in me for the rest of my life trying to find out how I could do what I did. I'd be like E.T., only without a home planet to escape to.

I finally had to get out of the water once the heat had run out and the shower felt like ice splashing over my skin. I toyed, briefly, with the idea of using my new microwave hands to make the water warm again, but I realized I couldn't pay to replace the plumbing if it also exploded, and I didn't want to have to explain that to the rest of my neighbors. So, goose-bumped and shivering, I got out and toweled off, then slipped into my oversized PJs and went back to my room. I resolved not to make any decisions until I knew more about what I was getting into — for now, I'd keep reading the *Morganomicon* and see what happened, if it explained things any better, and if I could get a better grasp on what I was doing. If, by the end of it, I still felt like I had to demand an explanation or share my discovery with the world, I would. Until then, best not to make a big deal out of it. I mean, I was still freaking out in my head, of course, but no one else had to know.

My stomach was roaring at me when I got back to my room. I considered having the last frozen burrito for dinner and letting the microwave handle things this time, but decided against it. I'd had the same tubed slop for dinner three nights running, and even to my unrefined palate, it was getting old. If nothing else, I decided, I'd see if I could at least learn a summon pizza spell from this damn book so I wouldn't have to choke down another frozen tortilla for a while. I ended up ordering a pizza instead from the delivery place a few blocks down, then sat and ate with one hand while flipping pages with the other, careful not to get grease on the ancient parchment. It would probably drip straight through to the back cover if I did.

That was Saturday night. I managed to stay up until 5 a.m. Sunday morning, then slept through 'til one in the afternoon. When I woke up, I went straight back to the book, and had a quarter of it read by mid-evening when a thought occurred to me. Or, well, less of a thought, more of a plan. An experiment. It wasn't really well thought out at all, come to think of it.

I stripped off my PJs and threw on some clothes that I wouldn't mind being seen wearing in public — black leather pants, AC/DC t-shirt, bra — then grabbed my men's-sized denim jacket and my keys and headed out, tugging on the jacket on the stairs and juggling the book in whatever hand I wasn't shoving through a blue jean sleeve. I must have been excited to try out my idea, because I realized just as the bus was pulling up at the stop that I had my MP3 player on me, but not my phone. Ah well, I didn't bother running back to get it, just climbed the bus steps and plopped into the first available seat; this would either work or not quick enough that I'd be right back here walking home again within an hour anyway. Best laid plans and all that.

My college's campus was only a twenty-minute ride away. When I got there, I did a quick circuit of the quad, which at this late on a Sunday was very nearly empty. I needed fully empty, though, so I headed for the corner where the library butted up against the history building, leaving about fifty square feet of hidden grass between them tucked behind the library wall. My only audience here was the AC unit and a squirrel that got bored the moment I showed up and wandered off.

Satisfied that I was as alone as I could be while still having room to try this dumb stunt, I flipped the *Morganomicon* open to where the spell in question lay. After glancing through it again, I snapped the book shut, braced my feet, closed my eyes, and then took a deep breath, concentrating.

I'd always hated riding the bus. It was always either trundling off just as I ran up or else didn't arrive until I'd already been waiting at least fifteen or twenty minutes. After three years of living in this city, I still didn't quite know all of the bus routes; so if I missed my stop at school, at work, or at home, it meant either getting off several blocks out of the way and hurrying back or, if the weather or look of the area was especially bad, waiting until it made another circuit and potentially riding for hours. And every time, without fail, there was someone waiting at the bus stop with me blowing smoke in my face, and every time, without fail, the seat I finally got when the bus showed up was either sticky or else felt like its last occupant had snuggled up shirtless against the back rest and sweated for a few hours straight. It was terrible. There were a lot of things about my current living situation that I didn't care for, but the bus was somewhere near the top of the list.

So when, that Sunday evening, I realized that the last several pages of the *Morganomicon* that I'd been poring over had segued from some airy explanation on the particulars of redirecting objective observations to the basic fundamentals of interplanar transportation — and also gave a handy, albeit complicated, recipe on the new subject, complete with a handy, complicated diagrammed illustration — the part of my mind that was trying to digest what I'd been feeding it piped up with a practical application. "Interplanar transportation," my logical brain told me, sounded like a fancier way of saying "teleporting," and "teleporting" was another phrase for "no more bus rides ever again." Even taking this newfound discovery slow and skeptical like I had planned on doing, the prospect was enough to warrant an immediate field study. And since I had a class to get to the very next morning, it couldn't come too soon.

Standing alone behind the library, I tried to recall the exact process I had read about in my head, along with the images. The diagrams seemed to work like a pattern in that tracing it mentally made the magic happen physically. It had been that way for the exploding food, anyway. It didn't occur to me then that maybe I shouldn't use the same method that had destroyed my dinner for trying to relocate my body.

I pictured the pages and, under my breath, began to mumble what I thought was the closest verbal representation I could think of, at the same time redrawing the images that came along with them in my head. There were a lot of steps to this one, and the visual was intense, even more complicated than the first one I'd tried. I didn't think, at first, that I would be able to remember it all without stopping to read it again, but I suppose something about their nature helped me recall what I'd learned. If only my textbooks were written in Old Elven, I thought. I'd already put more hours into studying that damn book than I had ever put into any of my classes.

Nothing was happening. I forced my brain to shut up, then started over, putting all of the concentration that I could summon behind the task at hand.

I started to feel like I was slowly sinking, like I was underwater in a pool rather than standing on hard ground; then, just as I began to register the sensation, I felt myself bob slowly back upward. Was I floating? I didn't want to open my eyes to find out and potentially mess up the spell. Instead, I doubled my focus, ignoring my sudden possible weightlessness and hurrying through the rest of the steps. My hands kneaded the air beside me as if pulling on some intangible rope, the book tucked under my arm. My breaths came slow but shallow, my brow unable to decide if it wanted to scrunch up or relax. My mumbling had died away to just rapid, silent lip syncing around my breathing. I felt minor chills run up my spine, followed instantly by minor hot flashes, back and forth from one to the other. Whatever it looked like, it certainly felt like I was making magic happen. Concentrating on all these little steps and details, it was something like mentally driving a car, only with no windshield, no seat, and no walls. And also the car was flying, and I was solving a connect-the-dots puzzle while I drove.

My plan, near as I had one, was to zap myself from one end of the hideaway lawn to the other. The book had said, somewhere in all the reading I'd done that day, that the destination was as much a mental factor as it was proper execution. I guess I figured that if I just went through all the motions correctly and thought really hard about where I wanted to go, I'd go there. And if I were casting the spell that I thought I was casting, maybe I would have.

I looked up "interplanar transportation" later, much later. I think I see where I first went wrong. Intra- was the prefix I was looking for; inter- means something else entirely. Something I had not intended to do.

The sudden, crushing pressure was my first sign I was doing something wrong. It hit me like a concrete wall from all sides, knocking the air out of me. I would have wrenched my eyes open in shock and pain if I could, but my eyelids wouldn't move. I could see a succession of lights flash by behind them, bright bursts of blinding whites and reds followed by flickering black-green afterimages. I felt like I was spinning, tumbling, my limbs flailing on all sides of me but touching nothing. My skin was ice cold and stung all over, and I could feel the sweat running down my body. And up my body. And around my body. Despite all this, my lips wouldn't stop mouthing their alien chant. I couldn't tell if I was speaking the words aloud now or not because of the background noise, a deep, throbbing, constant hum that I felt in my bones as much as heard, overlaid with a shrill keening as of two knives being scraped across one another, unending, all of it growing louder and louder and louder. At some point I added my own terrified screams to the cacophony, though when or for how long, I can't recall. I felt like I was being ripped apart from the inside out, dissolving cell by cell while I fell through a torturous expanse of nothing.

And then it all stopped, all at once: the heat, the cold, the throbbing and screaming, the falling and flailing, the light and the dark. I was laying completely still, my back pressed against some hard surface, be it ground or wall or ceiling. There was no sound but a low, moaning breeze, and all I could see behind my eyelids was black.

I fucked up. It was all I had the power to think before my consciousness left me in a rush and, mercifully, I blacked out.

Chapter 3: Impertinence

"What is this… *creature?*"

"S'a girl."

"Yes, I can see *that* much, you *simpleton*. But a girl *what?*"

"Dunno."

My head ached, my mind stuffed full of cotton and smoke that made thinking a chore. There were voices talking nearby, though muffled at first, like someone shouting through a towel on the other side of a large room. As I slowly came to, I realized they were actually just above me. Or below me; I assumed that the flat surface pressing against my side was the ground, but after that massively botched spell, I couldn't be sure of anything just yet. Could be the ceiling. With everything that had happened lately, that wouldn't have really fazed me much.

"Of *course* you don't. You don't actually *inspect* any of the *refuse* that you bring me, *do* you? You just drag *anything* you can carry to my door and let *me* deal with sorting the junk, *don't* you?"

"Yep."

"Tch. *Typical.*"

Whatever they were talking about, at the moment, I was just happy to hear any sound other than my own screaming and the chaotic din of bad magic. It seemed like a pretty good indicator that I was still alive, if nothing else, which was more than I could have hoped for.

"Hmm. She doesn't look like any Sin *I've* ever seen. Where did you *find* her?"

"Outside."

"'*Outside?*' Outside the *city*, you mean? Beyond the *wall?*"

"Uh-huh."

I finally came to enough to try and open my eyes. It was difficult, though, like waking up after an all-nighter and only an hour of sleep. My eyelids actually hurt, like I'd pulled a muscle in them. I didn't even know eyelids had muscles. After a few moments of effort, I finally got them cracked enough to make out vague shapes and blurs of color. I realized that I was lying on my side, and someone — one of the voices, I assumed

— was standing in front of me. I could only make out the legs, and even those only barely. As I watched, they scrambled back away from me.

"You *idiot*! You don't bring creatures from the *plains* into the *city*! *Especially* when you don't know what they *are*! Who knows if this *thing* is dangerous or not? Are you *trying* to destroy my store?"

"No."

"Where am I?" I managed to mumble. My voice sounded scratchy and weak even to myself, and my throat felt like I'd just swallowed a handful of glass shards. All the screaming, probably. Slowly, I rolled to my back and pushed myself up on my elbows, shaking my head to clear the fog. The world lurched and spun, but nowhere near as bad as it had been doing.

"It… can *speak*?" one of the voices behind me asked. The one who'd just been shouting, I realized, though now the voice sounded quiet and thoughtful. "It's *intelligent*, then. Maybe it's *not* feral…"

I tried to reach up and push my hair out of my eyes, but my hands wouldn't move yet for some reason, so I settled with just shaking my head to fling the stray bangs away. They were stiff and grimy where they touched my forehead. All of me was, I realized — I could feel the patina of dirt and dried terror sweat clinging to my skin, holding my clothes to my body like failing glue. My arms were cold; I wasn't wearing my jacket anymore, I realized. More curious than miserable now, I glanced up, risking a pounding headache to see a far wall covered by shelves of cluttered objects of all shapes and sizes. In the dim light, I couldn't quite make out what any of them were, and I didn't care to. Not that damn thrift store again, I thought with a mental groan, turning to look behind me toward the voices I'd heard.

I froze. And immediately wished, as hard as I've ever wished for anything in my life, that I *was* back in that damn thrift store again.

"It looks almost… like a *human*," said the louder voice. Its confusion was understandable; the creature that spoke with it was definitely not human. It could maybe pass for one in dimmer light than this — it had a head on a torso, with two eyes, a nose, and a mouth. But its nose was wide and flat and slitted like a reptile, and its long, pointed blade of a chin jutted out from its jaw like a snow plow lined with short spikes. Between them sat a lipless mouth that stretched about twice as long as a mouth should, ending directly below long, pointed ears that curved outward from its head and dripped with rings and studs of gleaming gold. More gold lined its forehead where its eyebrows should be, and two rows of ivory-colored horns, each as long as my hand, ran down its skull in lieu of hair, all of them curving down like they'd been slicked back with hair gel. In lieu of skin, it was covered in a tight pattern of small scales of dark matte green, and the slitted pupils of its yellow-white eyes darted curiously over the length of me. It was inspecting me, I realized, though for what I didn't know.

It took a step toward me, which instinctually sent me skittering backwards across the table I was sitting on. It raised a hand, as if unsure what to do with it, and each of its fingers, though viciously clawed, sported at least one ring, often two or more, and each glittering with a different colored gem. That's when I noticed its outfit, which offset my fear somewhat; in stark contrast to its monstrous face, it wore several layers of immaculate robes in deep reds and blues and greens, with silver brocaded edges and a dark black sash tying them all together. Granted, there were spikes sticking out of its sleeves at regular intervals, but still.… They were nice. It's a demon pimp, was my first thought. And I was half right, at least.

"*Hello*?" it said. "Can you *understand* me?" Its voice was a kind of guttural hiss around its words, like it was speaking entirely with its throat. And what it lacked in lips, it made up for in teeth. But its tone sounded nervous somehow.

I didn't trust myself to open my mouth and not start screaming again, so instead I just bobbed my head rapidly up and down, not daring to take my eyes off the pimp demon thing staring at me. I wasn't sure if the fact that I hadn't pissed myself in fear yet was a sign that I was holding up better than I thought I was or that I had already done so back when the spell went awry.

The sharp-dressed monster stiffened, its eyes darting out to the side. "What is it *doing*?" it whispered loudly. "Did you *see* that? Its head just *spasmed*."

"Means 'yeah,'" drawled another voice just out of view. I recognized it as the other voice I'd been hearing, the one this demon pimp had been arguing with. With a deep breath and a steeling of my frayed and deteriorating nerves, I turned to look at this one as well, braced for another horror.

It wasn't as bad as its partner, actually. In fact, if the first one was a demon pimp, this one was a demon hobo. Its body sagged visibly all over, its skin covered in short, dense, fur-like gray hair. It looked emaciated, and it stood as if the very practice of standing was somehow offensive to it, and it was only grudgingly going along with the idea. Its arms, long and thin, hung limply at its sides; its whole body was hunched forward so much that it was almost curled in on itself; and its short, squat legs were wide-set beneath it to support the spread weight of its bad posture, its knees bent at an angle that announced that it was ready and willing to sit down at a moment's notice. Where the other monster was dressed like royalty, the only garment this one wore was a sort of half-toga, half-bath towel-looking thing of coarse brown fabric that draped over and around its waist.

I blinked finally, more stunned now than scared, as its small, drooping head slowly swiveled in my direction. Its face was hard to make out behind its bushy, tangled, gray-brown beard and beneath its bushy, tangled mop of gray-brown hair. I couldn't see its mouth, and I didn't think it even had a nose. Between its sagging brow on top and the massive bags on bottom, I wasn't sure it had eyes either. It did have a pair of horns, but these were covered in knots and notches and hairline cracks, and the tips look like they'd been broken off long ago.

Collected now, I glanced between the two monsters, both of them also now looking at me. The first one was scary-fancy. The other one was scary-ugly. Neither of them looked like they knew what to do with me, which seemed like a small comfort.

I took a closer look at my surroundings now. The two walls to either side of me looked much the same as the one behind me, all racks and shelves holding an assortment of objects: books and statues and bottles and boxes and sharp, pointy-looking metal things. Some of them looked like they were glowing faintly. The far wall behind the demon-things was missing, a half-shut curtain in its place that blocked most of the light from outside. What did filter through was tinted red, and mixed with the flame lantern hanging from the ceiling to cast everything in a warm, surreal hue of yellow-orange. I was sitting on a rectangular table of dark gray wood in the center of everything — a human centerpiece in a demon's junk shop.

The green one stepped up closer to me, apparently more emboldened now, and reached out a clawed hand toward my face. I wriggled frantically away from it on the table until the table ran out, stopping myself just shy of tumbling backward over the edge as it took my chin in its hand. I was worried what those claws might do to my skin, but it touched me like it would rather not have had to, gingerly turning my face around between its fingertips and examining it in the dull light. I swallowed audibly and held perfectly still, trying to control my panicked breathing. This close up, the creature's well-dressed aesthetics were severely overshadowed by how much it resembled a cheesy horror movie monster.

It made a thoughtful sound in the back of its throat, then started lifting and pulling on strands of my grungy hair, frowning as it went. "If it *is* a human," it said to the room in general, "then it's kind of a *gross* one. It's all… *gritty*. Reminds me of one of *you* lot," it added over its shoulder to the hobo-looking monster. "Was it like this when you *found* it, or is this just what happens to *everything* you touch?"

The hobo-looking monster blinked once, slowly. And that seemed to be the extent of its response.

"Hmph," grumped the demon pimp, then grabbed one of my ankles and dragged me back to the other end of the table. The sudden lurch tipped me onto my back, and as I landed on my hands behind me, I realized why they hadn't moved earlier; my wrists had been tied together with a thin, scratchy rope. I couldn't feel it through my boots, but the way my ankles wouldn't come apart said there was another down there too.

Now that I knew they were there, I struggled against my restraints. I still wasn't sure where I was or what I was doing there, but the fact that I'd been tied up in the process wasn't exactly encouraging. The green demon-thing back-stepped when I started squirming, then grumped again and grabbed my legs mid-thigh, pushing them back down to the table. "Awful *fidgety* too," it mumbled. "It *might* be feral after all."

"I'm not an 'it,' asshole!" I yelled, and the strain of trying to use my voice at full volume again so soon sent me into a coughing fit. Losing my temper probably wouldn't help my case any, but I was already edgy after waking up lost and disoriented, and the more this green thing inspected and manhandled me, the more my fear gave way to irritation. It let go of me in shock when I yelled at it, and I took the opportunity to throw a kick at it as best as I could with both legs stuck together, the tips of my boots clipping it in its fancily-robed arm and sending it skittering back into the corner.

The hobo-thing cracked a smile at that. The pimp-thing just stared at me in surprise until my coughing tapered off and I was able to glare back at it.

Without taking its eyes off of me, the green demon reached into one of its robes and pulled out a long, thin, black rectangular case, flipping it open to reveal a thick stack of thin white rods, each the size of a drinking straw but shiny and solid like some sort of crystal or jewel. Its eyes went to the rods then, and slowly, with an almost religious care, it counted out a handful of these, then snapped the box shut and returned it to its inside pocket. "Here," it said, holding the rods out to the hobo-thing. "I'll *take* it."

The hairy gray demon took the crystal sticks, reluctant though the green one was to let go of them, and gazed down at them for a moment before frowning at its companion. "Worth more," it grouched. This was a monetary transaction, then.

The pimp-demon's head whipped around to glare with contempt at the squat ugly hobo-thing. "Don't presume to argue with *me* on worth," it spat. "What do *you* know? You never have an *inkling* of the value of the *trash* you keep dragging to *my* stall until I *deign* to inform you of it. Now suddenly you *insult* me by telling me I don't know *my own* business?" He strode back over to me and, ignoring my glare, picked up another strand of my hair. "*Look* at it — it's *dirty*, it's *ratty* around the edges, and for all *we* know, it may be *unhealthy. And* it has violent fits. You saw so *yourself*." He ducked away before I could perpetrate another fit of violence on him with my boots, his robes swirling as he rounded on the frowning hobo. "If it were in *better* condition, I could *maybe* see my way to paying you *more* for it. As it is, you're *lucky* to get a *single* soul. I'm paying based *purely* on speculation of *potential*, you realize. This really is a *gamble* on my part."

The squat gray demon frowned down at the softly shining sticks in his hand again, then stuffed them into a pocket of his toga-towel thing. "Be back later," it said, then turned, slowly, and shuffled out through the curtain.

"Of *course* you will," the pimp-thing said to the hobo-thing's retreating back. "Pfah. *Acediates*. Lazy, leechy good-for-nothings…" It turned back to me, looking me up and down again. "Though I guess they *do* have their *occasional* use, *despite* themselves. Now… about *you*…"

It walked back over to my table, its hands floating in front of it as if it wanted to keep prodding at me but didn't want to get kicked for it again. I would have been more disgusted by the prospect had I not just learned that it was interested in me purely as something to buy or sell, and not for… well, any other reason. That said, I still wasn't going to let it manhandle me anymore without a fight. "What about me?" I snapped. "Where the hell am I? And what the hell are you supposed to be? The boogieman?"

"Ah. *Right*. I suppose you *would* be lost, wouldn't you?" It tapped its pointed chin with a pointed finger, staring down its nearly nonexistent nose at me. "I know of only *one* human accounted for in all of Dis, and *you* are obviously not *him*. This has the potential to be very… *profitable*." Its eyes glazed over on the last word, its freakishly long mouth quirking up at the far edges. That expression creeped me out more than any of its prodding so far. "I need to know who you *are*, female human."

"And I need *you* to kiss my ass, male slimeball," I said. I assumed it was a male whatever it was. "Let me go before I blow your little shop to little pieces! You are fucking with the Great Witch Morgan Amell, and I will magic you a new asshole if I have to!"

To my satisfaction, his eyes widened at that, and he rushed over to the curtain, drawing it quickly closed and blocking all light from outside before spinning back to me with a panicked look on his face. "Don't *say* that, you *fool*!" he hissed at me. "Are you *trying* to get me executed?" His eyes narrowed then. "Hmph. You probably *are*. You'd *like* that, *wouldn't* you, you feral little *beast*?"

I didn't give him the satisfaction of an answer. Truth be told, I'd forgotten until just then that I still knew a few spells that might be useful. After the last one dropped me here, I was skittish of using any kind of magic, but I figured I had the exploding burrito spell down well enough to at least abracadabra the ropes from my wrists. So while I glared at the pimp-demon from my table, I spread my hands behind my back (palms pointed carefully away from the rest of me) and tried to concentrate on the spell. It would have been easier if I could have closed my eyes and mouthed along with the swirly language as I remembered it, but nevertheless, I still felt it inching its way toward completion. Only my second attempt, but I was already getting better at it.

The green monster sighed. "Very *well*, if it will quell these little *fits* of yours." He spread his robed arms, splayed his ringed fingers, and did this little dip-bow gesture that jangled the rings in his ears. "*I* am Master *Dramoc*, of House *Avaritia*, purveyor of *rare* and *quality* merchandise. *You* are in my *shop*, in the Merchant Circle of Dis. *There*." He took up scowling at me again. "Is that *quite* sufficient, human?"

My spell faltered as I listened, my concentration swarmed. I frowned at the pimp-thing — Dramoc, I suppose. "What the hell does any of that mean?"

He paced the length of his shop once, and I heard him grumbling under his breath. "You *do* know where Dis is, *yes*?" he asked me. "Every *savage* little holdout beyond the wall at least *knows* about the city, if only because they *wish* they were permitted *within* it." He turned a look on me as if it was the most obvious thing in the world.

I shook my head. Anything to keep him talking while I worked at my ropes. And also because I really didn't know what he was on about just yet.

He blinked rapidly and said nothing for a moment. "Where did you *come* from, human?" he asked, and this time there was no condescension in his tone. He really didn't know.

I didn't answer; this thing didn't need to know my address. Instead, I took advantage of the momentary silence to concentrate on the magic in my hands. They were warm — it was getting close.

He cleared his throat after a few seconds. "Yes, well, *wherever* you appeared from," he said, "I've told you *where* you are in Hell. It's no fault of *mine* that you cannot even *recognize* its most prominent city, you waste-roaming *savage*. I suppose *I* should be grateful you even *comprehend* which world you live in, *should* I?"

It took a moment for the full meaning of his words to seep in, but when they did, the spell went cold in my hands. I stared incredulously back at him. "Wait," I said, and that was it for a second or two. "Wait," I then elaborated, "what are you.... Are you serious?" Dramoc only raised a line of golden studs where his eyebrow should have been at me. "Are you.... Wait, Hell? We're in *the* actual Hell? As in, *Hell* Hell?"

"This is some *human* custom of stating the *obvious*, is it?" he asked. "Do you have *more* than one Hell where you're from?"

I didn't answer that. I didn't say anything. I only stared at the dark wood next to my face and tried to let that sink in.

Hell. Hmm. It seemed my transportation spell had worked after all, then; just a bit too well, and completely in the one direction which I would have least cared to go.

Or maybe it really had killed me. And I'd died and gone to Hell.

Huh.

...Well, damn.

"You really are a demon," I was finally able to accuse Dramoc. I'd been thinking it as a metaphor for his looks this whole time, but part of me was holding out for a rational explanation. I don't know why; I should have known better by then. But if he was telling the truth, and this was Hell — *the* Hell, with the fire and pitchforks and death metal music — and he wasn't just demonic looking but an honest to goodness actual *demon*, well... suddenly he got a whole lot more intimidating. I closed my eyes and renewed my attempts to free myself with double effort.

"Human custom it *is*, then," I heard him say. "Very *well* — yes, I *am* a demon. An *Avaritiate*, to be exact, of House *Avaritia*; one of the *seven* governing courts that any *civilized* individual would already *know* about. Please, *stop* me once this gets to be *too* obvious for your weird little *customs*, because *I* am beginning to find it *quite* pedantic."

I said nothing, only willed my palms hotter and waited for my body to catch up.

Dramoc sighed again. "If you *really* do use magic like some lawless *savage*, then I *suppose* it could be *conceivable* that you come from somewhere *far* enough into the wasteland to have *not* heard of Dis. I'd think the *only* beacon of civilization in the known *world* would, you know, be *heard* of at least, if only in awed *rumor*. But, then, *I'm* not a clueless and uncultured *feral*, so I suppose I won't tell *you* your own business."

Listening to his voice was starting to get me angry again. That was good, I told myself. Anger seemed a more useful mindset to have at the moment than fear. I tried to put the ramifications of what I'd done out of my mind and stoke my ire instead. My fingers were hot enough to have started to blister, had the magic not kept them from doing so.

"Oh, what else, what *else*," Dramoc grumbled. I could hear him pacing again beside me. "Well, magic is *outlawed* on pain of *death*, of course. I suppose, as a half-feral *human*, that might actually *not* be obvious to you. But the law has been in effect for *centuries* now, so I *doubt* claiming ignorance would *save* you if you insist on blabbing on about it so *openly*."

The heat was spread all over my palms now, leaking down to my wrists, and growing hotter.

"Let's see.... *No one* alive today has ever seen a *human* outside the *palace*, hence your potential *value* if your brains aren't entirely *addled*. All non-Sin demons are slavering *beasts* unfit for society. Is *any* of this getting *through* to you? Stop me when I *finally* touch on something you can *comprehend*."

I ignored him and finally got that familiar burning coals sensation spreading through my arms, pressing into my back like a hot brand. The magic was ready.

"Oh, for the *love* of.... The sky is *red*. Water runs *downhill*. I'm an *immaculate* dresser. *You* are trying my patience. Anything *else*? No, that's *enough*. Now —"

I opened my eyes. Dramoc was leaning over me.

"— quit playing and *explain* yourself, *human*."

I grabbed the ropes around my wrists and yanked. They seared away to ash under my touch, my hands springing suddenly free at my sides. So I balled one up into a fist and drove it into Dramoc's hovering temple.

He yelled, crumpling sideways to the floor. I doubt a normal punch of mine would have fazed a full-grown man, much less a full-grown demon, but luckily, my fists were currently on fire. Literal fire. My knuckles felt bruised, but I'm pretty sure he got the worst of it.

I lurched up to a sitting position and grabbed the rope around my ankles, squeezing it to cinders and only slightly scorching the leather on my boots in the process. Dramoc was rolling on the floor next to me, either in pain or to extinguish the flames, I couldn't tell. Without any further hesitation, I shoved myself off the table onto legs only slightly wobbly at this point and bolted through the curtain.

And straight into a half-naked purple lady who screamed as I appeared and scurried off in the other direction. I back-stepped to get my balance and cast a quick glance around to get my bearings.

Bad idea. *Never mind, I'll think about it later! Just go!* So I ran, my still-burning hands held out to either side to keep from scorching the rest of my clothing.

The street was crowded, but I was an oddity and still partially on fire, and the stir I caused was enough to send most of the people creatures parting just before I reached them and bullied past. None of them were a recognizable human skin color — purposely unobservant as I was trying to be at the moment, I still felt like I was running through a crowd of evil Skittles. Sometimes I bumped into flesh in my mad dash, sometimes it felt more like scales, sometimes leather. At some point I jabbed my shoulder on someone's — something's — elbow horn, tearing a shallow gash through the sleeve of my t-shirt. I spun from the impact, but the pain mobilized me, as did seeing Dramoc floundering after me through the traffic not a hundred feet back. I turned and dashed.

Right into a wall of eight-foot blue demon man planted in the middle of the road.

The impact knocked me onto my ass, but before I could get up, a hand the size of my head grabbed my non-gashed shoulder and hauled me up until my toes were three feet off the ground. Pale white eyes with bright yellow irises stared at me, and two massive black horns blocked the view behind him. "What is this?" he asked, a deeper baritone than I had ever heard before, at least without the help of post-production audio tricks.

I yelled in what I hoped was a warlike fashion and shoved my palms against his face. This resulted in two ineffectual pats that jarred my wrists somewhat and made him glance down at my fingers just below his eyes. That was it. My hands had gone cold.

"You *got* her," a familiar voice panted behind me. Dramoc finally caught up, then bent his head at the blue demon holding me, either in a polite bow or to hide the fact that he was trying to catch his breath. Both, possibly. "My *earnest* thanks, Lord Ulfris. I thought I was out a *hundred* souls."

The blue demon's eyes flicked to Dramoc with the same unflustered contempt he had watched me smack him with. "This is your property, Dramoc?" he asked. "What is it?"

"Yes, *mine*," said Dramoc, standing straight. I noticed the black mark on the side of his head with some satisfaction, partly bruise but mostly burn, his matte green skin shiny with the damage. One of his golden eyebrow studs had melted partially and tried to drip down his face. Not bad for my first assault. "Just came in about an *hour* ago," Dramoc continued, glaring at me while he spoke. "She's a *human*. Possibly from *outside* Dis."

The blue demon regarded me again, and I got the impression that he was slightly impressed. "A human female? From Earth, perhaps?"

Dramoc frowned. "Hm. I *suppose* that's possible, however unlikely. We *do* see the occasional *flotsam* from there, as your Lordship is *no doubt* aware."

That sounded promising. I stored that away for future examination — Earth stuff other than me does occasionally wind up in Hell. Maybe that meant it worked the other way around, and I could get back home somehow. Looking up at the blue guy — Ulfris — I wasn't sure how likely that was to happen anytime soon.

"How much?" he asked. It took Dramoc and me both a moment to realize what he meant.

"Oh, you're *interested*?" Dramoc asked. I could hear that creepy smile in his voice somehow. "In *that* case, for *you*, m'lord, I can make a *deal*. Five hundred souls and she's *yours*."

Ulfris glared down at the smaller green demon. "You said you paid a hundred."

"Ah. Yes, *well*." Dramoc splayed his hands in front of him, showcasing his rings again. "A steal from an *Acediate* who didn't recognize the *value* involved. But as you *know*, m'lord, Earthen items *naturally* carry a markup to counterbalance the *difficulty* in acquiring them."

Ulfris added a frown to his glare. He didn't emote much, from the looks of him, but every little bit was slightly more terrifying. "You said you didn't believe she was from Earth."

"Ah. Heh, *yes*, well…" Dramoc looked nervously from him to me, visibly weighing his greed against the possibility of angering this Lord Ulfris guy.

The blue guy turned his stare back on me, and I did my best to shrink away as much as I could while being held midair with no way to move. "One hundred fifty souls," he said with finality. "And my recommendation." It sounded like a threat when he said it.

Dramoc debated the offer for only a few seconds. "*Sold*," he said with another bow. "Enjoy the *rarity*, m'lord."

Ulfris smiled a faint, barely-there smile, but I noticed. I wouldn't be going home anytime soon after all, it seemed.

Chapter 4: Anxiety

To his credit, Ulfris was a less aggravating host than Dramoc. He didn't prod me and stare at me and call me a feral savage like that greedy green merchant did. No, he didn't interact with me much at all except to drag me along to wherever he'd been heading when I plowed into him — which, while I was sure I didn't want to go there, was marginally better than being tied down in a demon junk shop waiting for something else to happen. And hey, I reasoned, truth be told, I didn't really want to go anywhere in Hell except the exit, but I had to start looking somewhere and getting a feel for my surroundings. At least this was forward motion, however reluctant I was to move forward.

That was the only upside I could find to trading Dramoc for Ulfris, because everything else about Ulfris was scary as… ahem… Hell.

I promise I'll try and stop using that comparison so much in the future.

Thankfully, Ulfris didn't have me tied up again like I thought he might. Instead, once Dramoc had disappeared into the crowd once more, counting his weird crystal stick money like he was caressing a lover and giving me that creepy vibe one last time, Ulfris set me back on my feet and spun me around, keeping one massive hand clamped firmly on my shoulder. "Walk," he commanded from three feet above my head. "And do not try to escape. You won't make it far."

I gulped and decided to take his word for it. And so, for the next half hour or so, we walked. And I got a street-level view of Hell.

The first thing I noticed, when I felt brave enough to start noticing things, was the sky. Dramoc had said it was red, but I was too busy getting ready to kick his ass and run to pay the statement any attention. But sure enough, as far as I could see, the sky overhead was a uniform deep crimson, a few gray-black clouds scudding by in long, smoky tendrils. There was no sun I could see, no source of the strange color, but what shadows there were stretched back away from the direction we were heading. I wasn't sure anymore if the things I was seeing were colored the way they were because of the red light or not. My own skin looked the same hue it always did, but my frame of reference was being seriously screwed over in this place.

The area we started out in — the plaza outside Dramoc's shop, which he'd called the Merchant Circle — was the most crowded, with stone streets and a thousand tiny alleyways threading between squat stone and wood buildings, and every other patch of empty ground taken over by tents and booths. Every one we passed that I could see into had a demon like Dramoc inside, all points and gaudy finery, surrounded by a hoard of stuff that, at least in passing, seemed to have no discernible order to it. Baubles, books, chests, furniture, weapons, food, clothes: everyone had a bit of everything, though some had more than others. One shop might have had more of a certain item than the shops next to it, but there were no specialty stores, no one that sold just rugs or just chairs or just shiny spinning things hanging from the ceiling. They were like demon magpies.

The crowd was as varied as the selection here. I didn't have to turn my gaze much to see demons of every shape and size thronging together, moving up and down the streets, ducking in and out of shops, standing around talking or staring. They all looked bizarre — some were terrifying at first glance, like Dramoc had been or Ulfris still was, and some just looked alien and strange, like the furry gray hobo demon whose name I never caught — but they were acting like any downtown mob of traffic I'd ever been stuck in back home, which was sort of comforting. Except for the way that everyone who got close to us stared at me like I was from another world. Which I was, but they didn't have to make it so obvious.

There were red-hued demons that looked like they were made entirely out of long, knotted strings of muscle. There were more half-naked men and women in varying pinks and purples whose proportions resembled characters from over-sexualized comic books. There were a few more shaggy grayish ones all standing or sitting around on the sides of the streets and looking like they needed a bath. There were gaunt, long-limbed demons in oranges and yellows with hollowed out pits where their stomachs should be, thin lips pulled back over sharp teeth making each one look like it was grimacing at its surroundings. There were smaller creatures about my own size in a myriad of brownish shades, skulking through the crowd and eyeing everyone they passed suspiciously. There were a few scant giants like Ulfris behind me, mostly blue-green with gigantic horns and white hair, glaring out over the crowds and making the throng stand aside as they passed. And, of course, there were the pointy green merchants inside their shops, blinged out and grinning suspiciously at their customers, except for the ones that were fingering their weird stick money with glazed eyes.

I stared at all of them as I passed, not bothering to hide it since they were just as openly staring back, until Ulfris's hand on my back shoved me forward. "Move more, gawk less," he rumbled behind me. "I will not be late to court."

Court? Like, with a judge, or like with a king and stuff? Hell had a government?

I froze in my tracks, despite Ulfris's urging. Of course Hell had a government. It was a dictatorship, wasn't it? I grew up on hard rock and old metal; I'd heard countless songs about the guy in charge.

We were on our way to meet *him*?

"Walk," Ulfris commanded again, shoving me with more force. So with trembling legs and a mind once more numb with impending terror, I walked. It wasn't like I had any other options.

The crowds thinned somewhat as we continued down the same road, leaving the bustling bazaar behind. I tried not to think about what was coming up, but the occasional thought floated through my head. Thoughts like, *Will he know who I am somehow? Is there a list?* and, *Does he look like his picture in old books or like his picture on album covers?* But mostly, *Oh God oh God oh God someone get me out of here please!*

The city scenery changed as we walked, but now I was too stuck in my head and my anxiety to notice anymore of the places and people around me — at least until we came to a long, stone bridge that spanned what looked like half a mile over a massive, roiling black river, alternating between straight stretches and steep staircases that led down to the next level of the city, which was apparently built in rings heading downhill. I glanced over the side of the bridge as we came up to it, earning a growl from Ulfris but no more shoving; I was allowed to be curious so long as I kept walking, it seemed. I'd thought the water was maybe just dark because of the weird light the sky had here or because it was it was a hundred feet or so down in a chasm. But no, it really was black, and bubbled like it was boiling as it flowed. Short wisps of steam were rising off of it, so it's entirely possible that it was. Not wanting to give myself any opportunity to slip in and find out, I backed away and looked up again.

That's when I saw it — a gigantic cluster of walls and spires rising up over everything else with a kind of death metal opulence. A royal palace, but bigger than any one I'd ever seen in any pictures, reaching so high that it vanished into distant sky before I could see the top. If it even had a top. Pandemonium, I would later learn it was called. It sat in the distance at the bottom of the hill, ringed on all sides by more city. Not a hill, then, but a crater, or else a valley in a perfect ring of mountains. Dis, it seemed, was layered in concentric circles that shrank and focused down onto the massive, magnificent, ominous-looking palace. This is what I'd seen before looming above the buildings we'd passed, I realized; the obsidian cluster of huge spires in the background, veined in red highlights, which I hadn't been able to place. It hadn't occurred to me that it might be a single building — it hadn't occurred to me that a single building could be so enormous.

From our vantage point on the bridge, I could make out the rest of our journey. The road we were on led straight through the next ring of the city, over another river, and right up to the door of the palace. Inside, I assumed, was this court that Ulfris was in such a hurry to get to, being held by the biggest and baddest villain in all of creation.

"Are you nervous?"

I slowed even further. The voice had come from behind me, and for a change, it sounded downright polite — the first voice since I'd woken up that wasn't barking orders or insults at me. I turned my head halfway around and glanced back behind me, wondering what I might see.

Directly behind us, in a newly forming loose queue of demons that were all apparently headed in the same direction as us, stood a young woman about my own height, but with pinkish-purple skin and dark purple hair. She wore a gauzy dress of some white fabric that looked like half of the cloth was missing, and tiny, blunted horns sprouted from her temples to curve slightly back over her hair. When she saw me looking, she offered a shy smile. "This will be my first time in the palace too," she said. "Exciting, isn't it?"

I was definitely not in the right frame of mind for casual conversation, so I made no reply. I do remember thinking that "exciting" was entirely the wrong word for it, though.

It was at this point that Ulfris apparently grew tired of my stalling and grabbed me around the waist, hoisting me over his shoulder and carrying me the rest of the way like a sack. My face hanging over his back, I saw the pink-purple girl turn her sheepish smile away as an indigo-colored man next to her, wearing a sash and a codpiece and nothing else, laid a hand on her shoulder and murmured something into her ear with a frown. The two of them melted back into the marching crowd.

For the remainder of the journey, I got a good view of the road and the rest of the city as it slowly stretched on away from me, every foot of it that passed a foot closer to what I imagined to be the worst possible fate for anyone anywhere. My vision started to swim, and I felt my heart pounding a constant staccato against Ulfris's rigid skin. Much as I would have liked to, I don't think I actually passed out. The next thing I remember, though, was hearing the rush of water from the river below us suddenly muted as we passed through the palace gate, and Ulfris dropped me to my feet again. The crowds around us had thinned, but there was still a loose line of people in front of and behind us heading into the giant building. "You will be entering the presence of our prince," my massive escort said, turning me around. "Carry yourself with dignity and show respect." And we walked on.

The inside of the palace matched the outside, walls of some black, semitransparent crystalline material veined throughout in garnet red. Golden sconces held fire that illuminated the wide entry hall, and a massive golden chandelier hanging from the ceiling above added to the light. In front of us was a grand staircase much like any I'd seen in pictures of old palaces, carpeted in red velvet, intricately banistered, and wide enough to lead a parade down. The only big difference was that this one led down to a lower floor instead of up to a higher one; everything about this place was inverted from what I would have expected.

There were guards in the hall standing post by the door and the top of the stairway, demons of the red and sinewy variety, wearing thick armor of a deep red-brown, like the color of old leather — or, as a less cheery thought, dried blood. The way it hugged their bodies and showed no chinks or gaps, it looked almost like the armor was growing out of them. I couldn't tell if the spikes on the edges were part of the uniform or poking through from the person beneath. They glared straight ahead but glanced at us as we passed and nodded at Ulfris. He came here often, I took it.

The stairs led down to a long, wide corridor, still richly carpeted and lit by sconces. A large tapestry hung on one side, a single piece of multicolored fabric stretching the length of the hallway. It started out with an empty field of gray, growing gradually more complicated as we walked the length of it — tall figures of shapely, winged people flying through the air, then diving down into a long spiral, an explosion of color, and a crowded procession of demonic beings that resembled the masses outside marching on to the end of the picture, the background behind them changing gradually from dark mountains against a red sky to squat buildings to what looked like a cityscape like the one outside, complete with the massive palace looming over everything at the end of the scene. The opposite wall held framed portraits of more demons, each one looking wickeder than the last, staring out of their canvases with expressions ranging from smugness to outright hatred.

I didn't know what was going on in the tapestry on the first wall, and I didn't care who the people on the second wall were supposed to be. I was more absorbed by the massive double doors bound in gold at the end of the corridor and my quickly growing sense of doom. The line we were in was paused for the moment, with only a few people between us and the doors — a couple of the gaunt, stomachless type of demon, one orange and one more yellow, and a pointy green one between them. Two more guards stood at attention on either side of the doors, and the faint sounds of a milling crowd could be heard from the other side.

After a minute, there was a deep clunk as the doors' latch was thrown, and they swung inward, the orange and green demons quickly striding through before they closed once more, the guards flanking them unmoving as they glared out at the rest of us. I couldn't see around the two long-limbed things in front of me before the door closed, though, so I didn't see what was beyond. All I saw was the dark wood and gold binding of the doors staring back at me, unobscured. Which meant we were next in line.

I didn't have long to dwell on it; all too soon, the clunk sounded again, and the doors opened. One guard glanced up and nodded at Ulfris behind me, who placed his massive hand on my shoulder once more. We entered.

My heart jackhammered in my chest. I really would have preferred to go anywhere else but across that threshold. But the only other direction I could go was back, where a wall of blue demon was waiting to shove me on through if I didn't go myself. So instead, I did the next best thing; I shut my eyes tight and inched my way forward into the loose mass of bodies just beyond the doors, praying fervently to any force that might be listening to make me be somewhere else. I even seriously contemplated using that horrible interplanar spell again and taking my chances with being dropped on another plane of existence at random, and I probably would have if I could have remembered all the steps involved in time. Or if I thought I could get away with standing still long enough to pull it off.

"Presenting the honorable Lord Ulfris of House Superbia," a voice rang out. The low murmur of the crowd died down, leaving an uncomfortable, rustling silence. I stopped, feeling as if all eyes were on me but not brave enough to look and see. Ulfris's hand on my shoulder guided me down the carpet. Eyes still closed, I shuffled forward until he held me back, then suddenly felt myself being pushed down to my knees. I was having trouble breathing — if he was making me kneel, I could only assume that meant that I was standing directly in front of their leader.

The literal Devil. Evil incarnate. The absolute most dangerous possible being in almost every version of cosmology.

I thought I might break down and finally piss myself then if I weren't terrified of the theological implications.

"My prince," Ulfris's deep voice intoned behind me, "as tribute to your power and for your favor, I bring you a gift unlike any before — a live, authentic human woman from Earth itself."

This was the third time I'd changed hands in one day, and I was starting to feel like one of the items on that mysterious thrift store lady's shelves. I was also severely missing that sleaze Dramoc. As much and as quickly as I'd taken to hating him, at least he was someone I could handle. And he wasn't Satan. That was a big plus.

But as I knelt and waited and thought these things, I realized no one else was talking. A long moment of silence was spreading throughout the room, broken finally by a quiet voice asking, "Where did you find her?"

From what I had heard so far of demon voices, this didn't sound like one. It had a hard undertone of authority, a bit of awe, but beyond that it just sounded like a regular man's voice. Young, even, maybe close to my own age. But it spoke from right in front of me, and the only person in front of me at that point should have been...

"An Avaritiate in the Merchant Circle, who acquired her from an Acediate scavenger," Ulfris answered. "From the story he told, she is a new arrival who washed up in our plane just outside the city limits, beyond the wall. That she seems not to know where she is and marvels at commonplace occurrences speak for her validity as an Earthling."

There was another stretch of silence, and I found my curiosity growing. Hesitantly, I opened my eyes, keeping my gaze on the carpet below me. I could almost hear the heavy thinking going on around me.

"Is it true?" the voice in front of me asked, the wonder in its question not entirely hidden. "Are you really a human... from Earth?"

He was talking to me directly, and this was not a menacing voice. Terror faltered for a moment, and before it could overwhelm me again, I made myself look up. Into the face of the Devil himself, evil incarnate, lord of Hell.

And I could not stop myself from recoiling in utter disbelief.

I wasn't actually anticipating any particular sight; just something with most of the expected elements. Horns and wings and cloven hooves, I guess. Something massive and terrifying and awe inspiring, maybe with multiple faces or arms or something, sitting on a throne of human skulls bleeding out their eye sockets. Anything from any metal album, really.

What I saw instead was... a guy. Just some guy. He didn't just sound close to my age, he also looked like he was only a few years older than me, late twenties at the oldest. And he looked human: white, kind of pale, only a few inches taller than me, with gray-green eyes and short, choppy hair almost as black as mine. The closest thing to odd about him was that he wore what looked like a Renaissance Fair knight outfit: shin-high leather boots, dark gray trousers, and a shirt of polished, silvery mail, but with a faded denim jacket overtop that threw off the whole image. No horns, no skulls, not even a crown.

This was the terrible prince of demons? He didn't look like any of those things.

Whoever he was, he was staring at me expectantly, leaning forward in his throne (a throne of boring gray stone, at that; it didn't even match the red-black walls around us) with a hand on his chin. Where the jacket sleeve slid back, I could see more armor on his wrists, silver bracers that —

Wait a minute. "That's my jacket," I blurted out. The incongruity of the observation bypassed my ability to reason through the situation and popped out of my mouth before I could think to stop it. The prince raised his eyebrows at me, and then I felt Ulfris's hand on the back of my head, shoving it down to make me look at the floor again.

"I apologize for her lack of respect, Sire," Ulfris said hastily. "As I said, she is only recently arrived, and I did not have the opportunity to instruct her on proper etiquette myself before presenting her to you. I believe, if she can be taught manners, you might find her a welcome addition to your collection."

"Collection?" I asked aloud, still staring at the floor. "You collect other humans?" I couldn't be held responsible for the wiring in my brain at the moment.

Ulfris's grip increased painfully on the back of my head. "Silence, insolent girl," he growled. "You will show the prince respect,"

"Stop, Ulfris," the prince said. Not angrily, but in a voice that sounded like it was used to not needing to give instructions a second time. Ulfris's hold disappeared, and I looked up again.

The prince was standing now at the top of the few stairs that led up the dais to his throne, still gazing down at me. He held out a hand and made a gesture, lifting it palm-up a few times. It took a moment before I realized he wanted me to stand up. With a nervous glance around me at the crowd, I did.

He kept staring at me. With no other clues about what I was supposed to be doing, I stared back. This went on for several moments, until the silence started to feel oppressive.

"Are you really from Earth?" he asked again. Right, I'd forgotten I was supposed to be answering a question. His voice was slow, even, emotionless, but his gaze bore right through me. Hell, as intense as his stare was, it probably bore through the rest of the crowd and straight out through the walls, too. This was a big thing happening, apparently.

I cleared my throat, composing myself as best as I could. "Yes," I answered. A low murmur started up in the people assembled. The prince only kept staring. It was getting kind of hard to take.

"Your name?" he asked finally, and the murmur died down again.

"Uh… Morgan," I answered. I thought I saw his eyes widen at the name, but I didn't know why, if I hadn't answered appropriately or something. The silence continued, so I tried to fill it. "Amell," I added. "Morgan Amell. Um, Morgan Samantha Amell, in full, I guess, but I don't, uh… like Samantha, so I… just use Morgan…" I petered out. The crowd began whispering again.

The prince slowly took his seat after a moment, lounging back in it like a recliner and steepling his fingers. I'd never seen anyone actually use that gesture outside of a movie before. "Morgan Samantha Amell," he repeated, and the room went silent once more. Everyone here was hanging on his every word, it seemed. "I am Prince Vambrace of Caerleon, sovereign ruler of the city-state of Dis, Lord of the Seven Houses, Archfiend of Hell. I welcome you to my world, to my palace, and to my retinue. While I am sure you have many questions, know that they will be answered shortly. Is there anything else you would care to say in my presence?"

If his appearance didn't belie his authority, his speech sure did. I think I almost bowed. I probably should have. "Uh… sorry about the jacket comment?" I glanced back at Ulfris behind me. "I, uh, wasn't trying to be rude or anything…"

He smiled slightly, which seemed like a good sign. "You are forgiven," he said, then gestured at a nearby red guard demon. "Take the Lady Morgan to a private parlor. See that she is comfortable and contained for now. She is not permitted to leave, and neither is anyone else permitted to enter." He turned back to face the crowd as the guard bowed and headed toward me. "A fine tribute indeed, Lord Ulfris. You have earned my favor."

I was a lady now? Like the capital L royalty kind? Out of the corner of my eye, I saw Ulfris bow his head slightly. Very slightly. "Sire," he said simply, and that was the end of it.

The guard demon stopped at my side. "This way," it said quietly. Its voice was female, which surprised me a little, but not as much as the apparent anger she spoke with. Was she angry at me? I couldn't see why. I looked up at the prince again, but he was looking out at the crowd now. Almost pointedly so.

When I looked back to the guard, I found her only a few inches from my face and glaring down at me like I'd just insulted her mother. "This. Way," she repeated. I glared back, an instinct I'd picked up back in high school whenever someone was looking at me too hard, but I nodded. She turned and headed toward a side door in the far wall away from the multicolored crowd, and I followed her, thinking mean words at her back.

The corridors we passed through looked much like the one I'd walked through on my way to the throne room, only this time, I was in a better frame of mind to observe them — knowing that the Satanic overlord I had been expecting to meet was just some guy wearing my jacket cut down on my fear, but really amped up my suspicion. After all, I was human, and all of my experiences so far told me that, here, that fact meant I was some sort of rare collector's item up for grabs; meanwhile this punk gets to sit on the throne and boss around a city full of demons like he owns the place. Which he did, I guess. It didn't make sense to me yet, like I was being set up for some huge and elaborate candid camera moment with a massive special effects budget.

Anyway, these halls matched the first, but without any portraits or tapestries: red velvet carpet, golden sconces keeping everything surprisingly well-lit despite the black walls. We passed doors of dark gray wood at irregular intervals, as well as the occasional open archway that showed only more hallways branching off. I briefly entertained the idea of slipping away from my escort and making a run for it, but even if I knew how to find my way out of the palace, I couldn't think of any better destination. Besides, the only other human I'd seen so far — possibly the only other one in all of Hell, from the sound of it — was inside these walls with me. Whoever else he might be, that fact alone made him seem like preferable company to any of the spectrum of demons I'd been seeing.

That got me thinking — why weren't there any more humans around? Why wasn't the place packed with them? Wasn't this where the bad ones all ended up eventually? Come to that, where were the molten lava pits and the torture chambers and the fields of broken glass and salt that you had to walk barefoot across to get to the bathroom? The one river I'd seen so far didn't look exactly like a pleasant swim, but was that it? Everything else about the city looked almost normal save for the color scheme and clientele. Was all that horrible stuff somewhere else? Did I just happen to land in the swanky part of Hell, where all the demons hung out and lived their lives in between bouts of chewing on sinners? Was everybody off work at the moment? Not a single one of them so far even carried a pitchfork, though this red woman in front of me did have a sword dangling from her hip.

The guard I followed led me down some more stairs, another batch of corridors, and then even more stairs one final time before finally stopping in front of a pair of dark wooden doors that looked much the same as any of the dozens of other doors we'd passed, save for the carving on the front — seven concentric circles all inside one another, with another one banding them in an oval around the middle like a belt. It resembled, to me, one of those cutaway pictures of Earth showing all of the inner layers, plus the Equator. But with too many layers.

Actually…

I stepped around my escort and took a closer look at it. I recognized this symbol — it was on one of the pages of the *Morganomicon*, somewhere around the section that had the long and complex spell that sent me here. It was one of the simplest looking illustrations I'd seen in the book so far, though the actual diagram I'd been focusing on when I'd used that magic had about a dozen other symbols layered on top of it.

The *Morganomicon*. That damn book. What I wouldn't have given to have had it with me right about then. I remembered holding it when I cast the spell, but with all the flailing and falling I did afterward, who knew where or in what dimension it had ended up.

The guard sidestepped between me and the door, glaring at me as she reached out and opened it. "Inside," she demanded. "Wait for the prince."

I sidled around her through the door, then spun back around with a glare of my own. "Stop growling at me, demon," I snapped. "Just cuz we're in Hell is no reason to be such a bitch."

She looked taken aback, which surprised me as much as I apparently surprised her. The last I saw of her before she closed the door on me was the confusion that sprang to her face. Interesting, I thought, and filed that observation away for later in case it came in handy. There's no way I could have intimidated her; she was bigger than me and had a sword and armor, whereas I had a dirty cotton t-shirt and thin leather pants singed at the ankles. But something about my reply was unexpected, at least.

I sat down in the nearest chair, a leather-backed lounger of the same dark wood as the doors, and waited, holding on to that annoyance I'd felt. If it worked on armed demons, maybe it would work on the prince as well. Maybe I could trick everybody here into thinking I was more threatening than I felt and get them to send me home that way. And if that didn't work, I still had a sparse bit of magic up my sleeves: the heat spell I'd used twice now, and a few other tricks I remembered reading but hadn't tried out yet.

Suddenly, I didn't feel as hopeless and defenseless as I had been feeling since I first woke up. Sure, I was stranded and alone in a strange world, surrounded by demons who apparently saw me as some rare zoo animal that could be owned and bullied around. But I was also Morgan Amell, Street-Smart Magic Newb, with an encyclopedia of classic rock knowledge and a prince of demons who owed me a jacket.

It's cool, I thought. I got this. Bring it on, Hell!

But I thought it very quietly to myself in my head, just in case Hell was listening.

Chapter 5: Uncertainty

I was about half an hour in that little office-looking room by myself before the prince showed up. I think. I didn't have a watch or anything, so timeframes were mostly guesswork.

During my wait, I investigated the study, just in case it had any secret advantages to offer me. I scooted the furniture around and looked under all of the rugs; I lifted the few tapestries and ran my hands over the wall beneath; I pulled a bunch of the heavy books off of the thickly packed bookshelves and flipped through them. No trap doors, no hidden switches, no secret passageways that I could uncover. There were no windows to look out — I was in an interior room, it seemed, and probably even underground if I had the geography right in my head. Not that there was much of Hell that I was dying to get a look at.

All of the books that I pulled out were written in strange, jagged symbols that I couldn't recognize. I tried that weird sort of unfocused concentration way of reading that worked on the *Morganomicon*, but it didn't work here — this language was going to stay foreign, and no amount of really wanting to understand it was going to make it cooperate, it seemed. There was the occasional illustration that I could make sense of, but these mostly involved woodcuts of groups of demons like I'd already seen on the tapestries, all of them thronging or fighting or sexing it up in equal measure. I got the feeling that, if I could read these books, they wouldn't be boring.

I was flipping through one of these when the door opened and the prince stepped in alone, shutting the door behind him. I was standing at the time, leaning against the massive ebony-colored desk on the far wall from the door with one of the older, heavier books in my hands. I looked up as he came in to find his eyes already on me, and we both froze as our gazes locked. Inwardly, I was wavering on whether or not I should bow or something. Part of me thought it was the respectful thing to do, since he was royalty and had been the least of a jerk to me out of everyone I'd met here so far. Another part of me told me that I didn't owe him anything, and in fact he might even owe me an apology for the way I'd been treated by his subjects. I settled on watching him expectantly and waiting for him to say something, neither outright confrontational nor subservient.

He only stood and stared back at me. Intensely. I couldn't read the expression on his face, but it looked like a few emotions were warring for the space there. I considered myself pretty good at reading faces after a lifetime of watching people while trying mostly to avoid them, but I was coming up blank here. He was definitely thinking hard, though, whatever his thoughts were. I closed the book in front of me and kept waiting, watching him watch me, neither of us taking our eyes off of the other. This would be the perfect opportunity to quizzically lift just one eyebrow, I thought to myself. If only I'd had that muscle ability.

Finally, he took a deep breath and exhaled slowly, then crooked his neck toward the door he'd been standing in front of all this time. "Come," he said, and motioned for me to join him.

I straightened up and set the book down on the desk but didn't move. "What happened to answering my questions?" I asked.

"Another time," he said in that flat, I-am-never-argued-with tone. "Soon, I think. But there are other matters I have already lined up to which I must first attend."

I frowned, but only because I couldn't do that eyebrow thing. "And why do you need me to come along for them?"

There was a brief moment of silence during which his expression, eyes, and voice changed absolutely not at all. "The correct answer to a royal order," he said slowly, "is not 'why.'"

That threw me. It was easy, just looking at the guy, to forget that he was supposed to be a prince. Hell, I'd just learned it not half an hour ago and was wondering about it not five minutes ago. It was literally the only thing that I knew about him so far, and I'd forgotten just by looking at him. "Alright," I mumbled, stepping toward him. I wondered if he got that a lot.

He stared at me some more, either curious or suspicious, I still couldn't tell. This guy hid his feelings better than most. He opened the door and stepped through it, then waited just outside the room as I followed, all the while watching me with his piercing but unreadable expression.

I was used to weird looks like this from strangers. Having Japanese heritage but without the ability to speak the language or any particular insight into the culture had required repeated explanation in the small rural town where I grew up, as did having two red-headed parents of Irish descent who look nothing like me. Adopted, unsociable, and standing out from everyone around me in both looks and interests while growing up, never quite what anyone expects me to be at first — I've always felt like an anamoly in my own life, a piece that doesn't fit right in any puzzle I've ever found myself in. I supposed being a weirdo in Hell, especially this so-far very un-torturous version of Hell, was no worse than being a weirdo on Earth. Better, maybe — at least now I had an excuse.

Once we were both in the hallway, he turned and started down it in the direction the guard had brought me. He didn't once turn back to see if I followed, just assumed that I would. I did; it seemed the smart thing to do, and arguing for the sake of asserting my independent will didn't seem like a good idea when I had maybe one card to play at most and he had the rest of the deck. Still, he didn't have to act like I was just gonna tag along without incident like a lost puppy. I definitely felt like one right now, but that was no excuse for him to go around realizing it.

We went down more corridors and more stairs, passing more doors and the occasional painting that I didn't pay attention to. My eyes were stuck, for most of the trip, on the prince's back, where there hung a long, gleaming sword without a scabbard, swaying gently with each step he took. When I first glimpsed it as he turned his back on me, I thought I'd seen it glowing, and I still had that impression as I watched it walking away from me. The blade was a pure silver color, simple and unetched, but it caught every stray particle of light in the hallway and seemed to keep some for itself, softly illuminating the back of my jacket over which it was strapped. The hilt and pommel, in contrast, were a dull brass-gold-looking metal, the actual grip wrapped in smooth but fading brown leather that bore deeply grooved finger marks. The handle looked old and long-used, but the blade itself was like a sliver of moonlight made solid.

I was never one to coo over swords and weapons like my dad, who got a catalog in the mail once a month. Some of the stuff in there looked kinda cool, admittedly, but also expensive and bulky, and I knew I didn't need any of it. This thing on the prince's back, however, woke up my inner weapons nerd and made me want to swing it around my room when no one was looking. The fact that an edged weapon might actually come in handy for a change in my current circumstances may have influenced that feeling a bit.

The spell was broken somewhat when we passed through a pair of larger double doors flanked by two more of the red, angry looking demons, both in tight, compact, dark armor and holding spears taller than any of us. They somehow glared respectfully at the prince as he passed, then glared at me with a look of irritated surprise as I followed. I made a note to myself that the red ones seemed to be super pissed all the time for no immediately obvious reason.

Then we were in what looked like a large locker room/backstage area, the firelight of the lamps brighter than the muted passageways we'd come from, the floor and walls a red-brown-gray like you'd see in normal stone instead of the red-veined onyx of the rest of the palace I'd seen so far. There were no lockers, but there were cubbies along two of the walls stuffed with balls of coarse fabrics in browns and grays, shoved into the shelves in unceremonious wads. The rest of the wall space was lined with crude wooden mannequins draped in the same red-brown armor as I'd seen on every one of the angry red demons I'd passed so far. The rest of the floor space was mostly empty, with a line of benches taking up the middle.

And more of those red demons were back here, men and women both, milling around in what would almost look like a conversational group were it not for all the scowling and glaring going on. An angry conversational group, maybe. Only one of them, one of the men, had his armor on; the rest were half-naked knots of spiky limbs and shiny, straining muscle, even the women, who didn't seem at all uncomfortable or even aware of their bare chests. Come to that, no one else but me seemed to think it odd either. They all looked up at our approach, the unarmored group bowing their heads, while the armored demon stepped forward.

The prince stopped to look up at him. "You are my opponent tonight, then?" he asked.

The red man bowed his head. "Mersio, m'lord," he said, his voice a raw grumble. "It is an honor."

"Let us not keep our jury waiting any longer, then, Mersio" the prince said, clapping a hand to the armored demon's shoulder. The demon was only a bit taller than the prince but much broader, with a barrel chest and thick, sinewy arms that hung almost to his knees. Like every other demon I'd seen so far, Mersio had horns jutting from atop his head. His were long and black and shiny, curving to razor points above a shock of wild black hair, looking like something worthy of being pointed at in admiration by mall-going weapons enthusiasts. At his hips hung two curved swords, each as wide as his arms and almost as long. As stylish as the prince's sword was, it looked like a kitchen knife compared to what Mersio was packing.

If there was to be a fight between these two as they made it seem, I worried for the prince. Or rather, I worried for myself should the one person with whom I had even the briefest and most tenuous familiarity in this place suddenly get killed and leave me the last remaining human soul in a room full of angry monsters made entirely from spikes and muscle.

But I didn't have time to dwell on my apprehension; the prince turned and marched away to the other side of the room, the armored demon following suit, the rest of the group behind him and sweeping me up in the process. The far wall held a single door of thick, heavy-looking iron, which the prince calmly kicked in. The whole door swung back with a reverberating gong as it bounced off the other side of the wall, the prince and his opponent striding out amidst a sea of cheers from the other side.

The half-naked group, though, headed down a narrow corridor along the same wall, half of them hanging back to herd me along with them. We went up a flight of stone steps, turned, went up another, and then two more before finally emerging into the cheering crowd I'd heard a minute ago. It was an indoor arena, the seats laid out in concentric rings around a wide circle of packed dirt. Like in the marketplace, demons of every shape and color congregated together, those closest to me taking a moment to stare in interest or shock as I passed with my entourage toward the center, the majority not even noticing that I was there. Almost all of them were on their feet and cheering while, down in the earthen pit over the edge of the stands, the prince and the armored demon stood on opposite sides of the circle. The barrel-chested, man-shaped pile of sinew that was Mersio had both of his curved swords in his hand, casually slicing the air in front of him as he waited, and even up here with the noise of the crowd, I could faintly hear the quiet whistle of their passing, edges sharp enough to cut the air. In contrast, the prince held his perpetually-moonlit sword in a loose grip at his side, slowly rolling his shoulders but otherwise still. The bracers on his wrists gleamed beneath the sleeves of my jacket, which he still wore.

He was gonna ruin my jacket with this fight, I just knew it. And I didn't have anything with me to patch it with. Ridiculous thought for the moment, I know, but the whole situation still seemed ludicrous to me.

Then one of the women from my escort pushed her way to the edge of the stands next to me and, in a moment, the whole theater fell silent. "Lords and ladies," she called to the crowd in a voice like tempered steel. "Mersio of House Iria will now face our revered Prince Vambrace in single combat for the first time. Bear witness." She turned toward the demon Mersio and held up a hand. "Challenger, what have you to say?"

Mersio bowed his head briefly, then crossed his swords over his chest and addressed the crowd. "I, Mersio Iria, in concord with the forces of Commander Enkida, have lent my wrath to the aid of Dis for the span of an eon, driving back the nuckelavee and mearcstapa, the harpy and gorgon, and all beasts of damnation that plague our vale beyond the wall. I have with my own hands ripped the head from a kelpie as it sought to drown me in the rushing waters of the River Acheron, and carried its limp and bleeding husk back to camp to feed my brothers and sisters in arms." He clanged the hilts of his swords together and spread them wide in a gesture of proud satisfaction as the crowd cheered their approval for his boasts.

The red woman turned to the prince and raised her other hand, bringing the blanket of silence back down on the crowd. "My liege?" she asked.

Prince Vambrace nodded across the field to Mersio. "This is acceptable," was all he said. Nowhere near as showy as Mersio's display of his own honors, but if anything, the crowd roared even louder.

"Then as always, may the worthiest combatant take his rightful victory," the demon woman said, raising a hand to the arena at large before slicing it down in front of her. "Begin!"

There's an expression I've heard before, usually on TV or in action movies, to describe the particularly badass: "He fought like a demon." As far as metaphors go, it's fairly colorful and packs a nice little punch, but I'd never given the phrase any real thought before.

I was giving it real thought now.

The woman's hand hadn't even finished dropping before Mersio launched himself across the pit with a shout of rage that shook dust from the ceiling and almost knocked me back off my feet by sheer volume. He cleared the entire space between himself and the prince in that leap, dug his heel into the dirt a few feet in front of his ruler, spun in a tight circle like a murderous top, and laid into the prince with both swords at once, hacking away like a vengeful lumberjack chopping down the tree that murdered his parents.

The mad roar that announced his attack thundered on as he put the full force of his volcanic muscles into each slash and stab. It was like watching a cannonball with arms explode again and again with every swing. It was the single most impressive display of pure violence I had ever seen up to that moment.

And in the next moment it became the second most impressive, because Prince Vambrace fought even better than a demon.

He took only one step back as Mersio landed in front of him, slipped his own sword up between his opponent's two in a two-handed grip, and simply stayed there, eyes locked on the enraged demon in front of him as he carefully blocked each and every blow. He didn't roar or scream or even open his mouth, just whipped those three feet of shiny metal around Mersio's blades and wove a midair cage between the demon's swords and himself. I couldn't even see his arms in those moments between one blow and the next, just caught fleeting glimpses of silver light flashing from his blade and wrist guards.

The staccato clash of metal on metal from one blade hammering on another grew deafening; between that and Mersio's unending battle cry, I had to raise my hands and cover my ears, each time thinking that one of those weapons had to be close to snapping in two just from the sheer force of it. With each blow, the prince shook a little in his stance, but it was like watching the wind howl at a skyscraper; it seemed fearsome, but you knew it wasn't going anywhere.

Until suddenly it did.

I didn't even see it, but Mersio must have slowed just a little bit, or swung just a little bit too widely in one of his blows, or else the prince was simply finished defending himself. Whatever the reason, one second we were all watching the red typhoon in man shape wail ineffectually at the prince, and in the next, Vambrace took a sudden step in and swung his own sword out beyond the space between them. One of Mersio's swords sped through the air, whirling blade over handle like a frisbee of death before stabbing into one of the stone walls of the pit halfway to the hilt, ringing and quivering with the leftover energy of the action as if complaining that it was out of the game. While it was still in the air, though, the Prince whipped his own sword up and battered it against the remaining blade in the red demon's clawed hand. This one Mersio managed to hold on to as he leapt backward across the packed dirt, disengaging from the prince, who stood his ground.

For several long seconds the entire crowd held its breath, myself included, as the two simply stared at one another. Mersio's face was contorted in fury, his pupils mere pinpricks that glared out from under his furrowed brow, his lips parted in a snarl to show his teeth grinding together.

Across from him, Prince Vambrace took up the same loose, relaxed pose he'd had at the fight's beginning, his own expression still blank and unreadable as ever. "You're good," he said, loud enough that everyone could hear him. "Try again."

Either that pissed the demon off, or else Mersio was just really obedient, because once more he launched himself toward the prince like an arrow loosed from a bow. This time, when he touched the ground again in front of Vambrace, he spun to the right and quickly circled around behind him, his last remaining sword drawn back. He dug his heel into the dirt, then whipped the blade toward the prince's lower back in a vicious underhand swing.

The prince didn't turn to follow his opponent, but his sword did. Without looking back at Mersio, he brought his blade around behind him and stabbed down past his own shoulder blade, catching the demon's swing with the tip of his own.

Basic physics said it should have slid off or knocked the prince's sword out of the way, the full force of that swing catching just the tiny edge of Vambrace's casual defense; but it didn't. Instead, Mersio's blade rang out like it had just smacked against a steel wall, the impact momentarily fucking up the demon's momentum.

In that same moment, the prince turned and ducked under his own arm, coming face to face with his opponent once more. A look of shock passed through the perpetual mask of rage on Mersio's face before Vambrace stepped in and stomped down hard on the demon's blade. It didn't break, but the prince drove it down into the ground under his heel, whipping his own sword up in the same moment and jabbing it toward Mersio's throat. The demon backed away, but could not get out of the blade's reach without releasing his captured sword, which he seemed unwilling to do.

There was another pregnant pause as the two stared one another down wordlessly, the audience silent and rapt around them. Then a particularly hateful grimace passed across Mersio's face, and he released the hilt of his stuck sword as if it suddenly disgusted him. "I yield," he muttered, the sound halfway between a growl and a bark.

Nevertheless, we all heard it, for the cheering and applause went up once more. The prince bowed his head slightly to his opponent, then stepped back and lifted his sword, sliding it into the holster harness thing on his back.

"All hail Prince Vambrace," the red announcer woman called over the din, making the cheer sound more like a command. All across the arena, the crowd began chanting his name — "Vambrace! Vambrace! Vambrace!" — while Mersio yanked his other sword from the wall and sheathed them both at his hips. The prince raised his arms to the crowd, bowed his head again, then strode back through the doors through which he'd first entered.

I didn't have the chance to wonder what I was supposed to do this time, as the demon lady who'd been MC-ing the fight cut through the crowd to my side. I forced my eyes away from her bare chest, which was exactly at my eye level, and made myself meet her gaze.

It wasn't pissed or hateful, which was a surprising change of pace. Merely intensely cold. "Come with me," she said in her hard steel voice, making herself heard even through the shouting crowd around us. "His majesty desires your presence."

I wasn't even gonna try and be snarky again, not after what I'd just seen. I followed close behind her as she led me back out of the arena, squeezing through the mass of bodies around us. It was easier with her in front, as she seemed to part the crowd before her like a wedge, somehow without needing to physically shove anyone out of her way.

We descended the stairs back down to the locker room-esque area, where the prince already sat alone waiting for us. I could see his chest heaving beneath his mail as he looked up, but he wasn't panting or anywhere near as out of breath as he should have been after an event like that. "Thank you, Enkida," he said, standing at our approach.

The red woman beside me pressed a fist over her chest and bowed her head. "Sire," she said simply, then stepped past him to one of the mannequins along the wall and began pulling off armor pieces.

His gaze followed her a moment, then he turned and looked at me again with that same blank, unreadable expression he'd been giving me so far. "What did you think?" he asked.

My brow furrowed, and my eyes shifted around the room as I considered. "Of?" I asked.

He jerked his chin toward the nearby doors to the arena grounds, now closed. "Of what you saw," he said.

"Oh," I replied, looking toward the doors. It was easier than looking at him looking at me and wondering what was going on between us. "Um… yeah, it was pretty cool," I said in what I hoped was a casually airy voice. "Kinda like something out of a movie, y'know?"

I risked another glance at him and saw that same curiously blank look again before his head tilted slightly. "No," he said after a moment, "I confess, I do not know. What is a movie?"

I blinked. That one caught me off guard. How old was this guy? How long had he been here? "I, uh… don't really know how to answer that," I said. "Like… a play, maybe, but with better special effects?"

"Special effects," he repeated, as if the phrase was familiar but he couldn't quite place it. I thought I saw a momentary glimpse of excitement in his eyes; but then he turned to look at the red demon woman behind him, now almost fully dressed in her armor, and his blank mask came back. "We must speak more of these things," he said as he turned back to me. "But not now. First, I will show you to your room."

"I have a room?" I asked, only realizing after the fact that I'd asked it aloud. "Uh, thanks," I added just for good measure. "Uh…"

He cocked an eyebrow at me. Damn, I wished I could do that. "You have concerns?" he asked.

"I was, uh, just wondering… am I like a prisoner now, or…?" I trailed off, but he looked at me as if expecting me to continue, so I did. "A guest? A… collectible? What?"

For another long moment, he only stared at me until it got uncomfortable again. Then, surprisingly, he smiled slightly. "That is a good question," he said, then turned toward the demon woman again. "Enkida?"

"At your command, sire," she answered, stepping up behind him. She was decked out in her full armor now, including shoulder pads with wicked-looking spikes coming off of them like some sort of demon samurai. The full ensemble fit her body snugly, but you could tell just by looking at it that it was thick and dense, and no part of her bright red skin showed through except for her fingers, neck, and face. Long, black, pointed horns curved back over her head from her temples, and her feathery white hair was caught in a tight knot at the nape of her neck, all of it pulled back out of her eyes.

I only just then realized, looking at her, that her eyes and the eyes of all of the other red demons like her were white rather than the strange colors I had seen in most other demons so far; although her irises were an angry red like her skin, her pupils smaller than normal. Or what was normal in humans, anyway.

Between the long-ish hair, the sharp angles of her face, the snug fit of her armor, and the lean muscle of the body underneath, she looked oddly feminine for one of the red demons. A strong, sharp, not-to-be-fucked with sort of femininity, granted, like an elegantly serrated dagger. But still.

I realized then that I was staring; but she was staring right back and not saying anything or making any show that it bothered her, so I rolled with it.

"I'm going to show the Lady Morgan to her room in my quarters," the prince said to her. "We will attend dinner afterwards. Let the guests and staff know that they may start without us."

Enkida's gaze flickered very calmly from him to me and back. "Sire," she said simply, then bowed her head quickly and left the room.

The prince watched her leave, then turned back to me. "Come," he said, then stepped toward the door himself.

This time, I hesitated. "You still haven't answered my question," I pointed out.

He stopped with his hand on the door, then turned and looked at me over his shoulder. "No, I haven't," he said, then opened the door and stepped through. "Come."

Once again, I had to remind myself that he was royalty, somehow, and this was just how royalty talked to people. He most likely didn't mean to speak to me like I was a dog he was training. And even if he did, I couldn't afford to get angry about it right now. With a deep breath, I swallowed what pride I had and followed him once again.

This time, as we walked the halls of the palace together, I made myself pay closer attention to where we were going. It would be an understatement to say that I'd never been good at directions before — before moving into the city for school, I'd spent most of my life in a tiny town that took about five minutes to drive through from one end to the other, and after eighteen-plus years there I'd still never been able to get anywhere in it without written directions or a map. Now, though, I hoped that greater need might be the key to unlocking that hitherto useless part of my brain that knew where I was going. And if I was going to escape from here at some point, as I got the feeling I would need to do, then it would be useful to know which direction was the right one to run in.

Unfortunately, so much of the palace that I was seeing looked the same, and it was so damned big. It felt like we had walked half a dozen city blocks before the prince turned again and we set off down a different hall. Most of the corridors had a slight curve to them, I noticed, as if we were walking part of a giant circle.

Along the way, we passed the occasional demon going about their business, including plenty of the angry red kind in their pointy armor. There were also a few of the pink and purple kind that I had noticed before, the ones with the comic book character anatomy — chiseled jaws and washboard abs on the men, narrow waists and luscious curves on the women.

Even more than them, though, I noticed a lot of smaller, squatter demons scurrying about in outfits that wouldn't have looked out of place in a medieval period movie or TV show — tunics and breeches, thick skirts, sashes, the odd robe, and things of that sort that nobody wore these days outside of a Renaissance Fair, albeit much shabbier and more weathered on average than your typical nerdy costume. These demons seemed to come mostly in shades of greens and browns, like different colors of dirt and grime, and none that we passed stood more than three feet tall. Each had a stocky body, slightly hunched, that put me in mind of a beetle, and their gangly, spindly arms and legs only further emphasized the comparison. Their heads were bulbous in comparison, with each one sporting small, squat horns on top and small fangs jutting from a slight underbite. None of them had ears, just small holes where they should have been.

But what stood out most were their eyes — each of the them had massive eyes, especially compared to the smallness of the rest of their bodies. Each eye was compounded like the tiling on a soccer ball, and each section of eye had its own pupil moving independently of the rest. The effect was like watching a bunch of small black bugs crawling around on a couple of those fancy dice that you use in tabletop games like Dungeons & Dragons, both dice stuck into the round head of a malignant-looking little imp straight out of a fairytale.

Maybe it sounds rude to say that, but I swear, every one that I remembered passing at the time was malignant looking. They all ducked their heads in quick deference to the prince, but even then, I got the sense that all of their dozen or so pupils were glaring at the both of us. By then, I'd gotten used to most demons that I passed looking at me in surprise or curiosity. Either these guys had already heard the news about me, or else they just didn't care, because the only vibe I got from them was resentment.

It was a creepy walk.

Then the prince led me down a large staircase deep into the next level of the palace, and after only half a block of walking this time, down yet another. At that point, my thoughts about the little drudgery beetle demons turned to thoughts at how deep down these palace levels went. I remembered seeing spires and towers on the palace when I was reluctantly approaching it with Ulfris, but so far, we hadn't climbed any of them, only gone down. How much of this building was underground? I imagined an upside down skyscraper, buried in the earth with just a few bits sticking up into the air, like a dart or missile that had embedded itself into the ground.

Finally, just when my legs were starting to get tired, we came to a large set of double doors made of the same shiny black rock as the walls, emblazoned in milky white crystal inlay with that same belted concentric circles diagram thing that was on the door of the first room I'd been left in. The doors were flanked by two of the angry red types of demon, each clutching a spear and with a sword hanging from their hip. They clenched their hands not holding spears into fists over their chests and bowed overtop of them to the prince, who nodded back and pushed the doors open.

After we stepped through, the demon guards closed them behind us, and the prince stopped and turned back to me. "We are now in my private, personal suite here inside of Pandemonium," he said to me. "Only myself, those servants and attendants handpicked by me, and those few to whom I have granted special access may freely come and go from these halls."

He seemed to want some kind of reaction as he stood there and looked at me. Maybe I was supposed to be flattered? I couldn't tell. "Okay," I said after a moment. It seemed the safest response.

Apparently satisfied with it, he turned back and gestured down the hallway. "Your room is just a bit further in," he explained. "Come."

Like I even had a choice. I went.

The area behind the prince's special door didn't look any different from what I could see, and it wasn't any smaller than the space we'd just left, because we kept walking and walking and walking. I've walked the blocks around school, work, and my apartment plenty before, and my college campus is big enough that I've usually got a few minutes' walk at least between my classes; and still, holy shit, this was a big house. What all did he keep here that he needed this much room and these many miles of hallways? He oughtta get a tram installed in here or something.

Finally, right when I thought I'd need to stop and rest before we went any further, we turned a corner into more open bit of corridor that looked like a hotel lobby. There was only one door in the middle of the inset wall, this one a plate of riveted metal that looked like pure silver, with a rounded top edge and an engraving in gold filigree of that familiar symbol again, seven circles inside an eighth. Another lithe red demon stood before it, this one a tall, lanky man with no sword or spear, but wearing what looked like spiked brass knuckles across his hands. He bowed to the prince as we approached, then opened the door behind him and stepped aside. The prince nodded back and the two of us entered, the demon man following close behind.

The room inside was nicer than the study from before; in fact, it was the nicest room I could remember ever being in, akin to a five-star hotel suite. A massive four-poster bed dominated the right side of the room, the mattress thick and plump and larger by far than a king-size, with shimmery satin sheets of dark purple and at least a dozen pillows of every shape and size in differing hues of red. It even had a canopy with dark blue curtains hanging all around, each drawn back and held to the posts by thin golden ropes.

In the center of the room, a plush lounge and two matching plush armchairs were arranged around a large, thick rug sporting the same concentric circle design again, all of it sitting in front of a large white marble fireplace, currently empty, on the far wall from the door. To my left, in the corner of the room, a large desk of dark red wood sat next to a tall bookshelf that was half full with the same thick, ponderous looking books that I hadn't been able to decipher back in the study, which probably meant I wouldn't have any more luck with these. Beside the bookshelf, another silvery door like the one we'd just passed through led away into what I assumed was a side room and what I hoped was a bathroom. I hadn't seen one since I'd gotten here, and if it turned out that demons didn't need them, then we were all going to be in trouble here before long.

The prince stopped in the center of the room and turned back to me, one hand held out at his side. "These will be your quarters for now," he said. "I trust they will suffice. Stay here and rest until I come for you again. In the interim, is there aught you would request to aid in your comfort?"

The more he talked, the more I got the feeling we probably didn't both come here from the same time period. Just how old was this guy? "I don't suppose you have TV or a radio, do you?" I asked, because you never know. The pause that followed and the blank look on his face answered me about like I expected. "Yeah, didn't think so," I said before he spoke again. "Then, uh, I think I'm…" I glanced around the room, then trailed off as I saw the bookshelf again. "Actually," I said, pointing at the shelves, "do you have anything to read in English?"

His eyes widened at that, and he took a small step backward, which sent the red demon behind him tensing and glaring at me.

Oh shit, what did I do wrong? "I mean, it's fine if you don't," I added hurriedly, hands raised between us. Whether I meant the gesture to soothe him or protect me, I don't know, because either possibility seemed equally dumb. "I just, uh, I figured I'd get bored, and I can't read the alphabet here, so… uh, Old Elven would work too, I guess, if you, uh… have any of that lying around…"

"No," he said slowly, eyes narrowing again. A bit too much for my taste. "But I do have a few scant tomes writ in English. Great rarities, of course, but I can see fit to loan you one or two, if you take extreme care with them."

"Yeah, of course," I said, not taking my eyes off him. "No worries. Uh, thanks." I probably looked as startled as he had a moment ago. What the hell had I said that could spook someone who bosses demons around for a living? Was asking for reading material a taboo here? Did he only have old Playboys or something?

Whatever I did, it seemed to have passed, because he only nodded and turned halfway to the guard behind him. "This is Rezavix," he said, motioning to the demon, who was still glaring at me. "He will be assigned to your guard just outside. If you have urgent need of anything else, let him know."

"Yeah, cool," I said, raising a hand at the demon. "Uh, nice to meet you?"

Rezavix snorted and kept glaring. Awesome.

"Then if there is nothing else," said the prince, turning and heading back through the door. "Do try and rest up, Lady Amell," he added over his shoulder at me. Rezavix followed him out, closing the door behind them with a soft click. I didn't hear the prince walking away back down the hall, nor did I hear any voices through the closed door. This room was likely soundproof, then, between the weird black walls and whatever that door was made from. Maybe that was a useful detail, maybe not; either way, I added it to my mental notes.

Before I did anything else, I went to the side door on the left-hand wall and opened it. Sure enough, the room beyond looked like a bathroom, albeit one the size of my entire apartment back home. A massive tub filled the center of the room, roughly the size of a kiddy pool but about four feet deep. It was inset somewhat into the floor, with a couple of marble stairs leading up to the rim, and the bowl inside looked to be either gold plated or just pure gold. (Or golden colored, anyway. Who knew if Hell had the same metals and minerals Earth did?) A small hole opened in the ceiling above the basin, a chain with an ivory handle hanging down next to it. I gave it a quick, experimental tug, and a steady stream of steaming hot water poured out of the ceiling and into the tub until I let the chain go again.

Hell had indoor plumbing and hot bathwater? So much for eternal torment. Thus far, anyway, Hell was at least way nicer than my place.

Other than the ginormous tub, the bathroom also had a shelf built into the black and red-veined wall on one side, with a golden basin sitting on top in front of a polished silver mirror. Another built-in shelf nearby held an assortment of glass bottles of varying shapes, sizes, and colors, some opaque, some transparent and filled with various shimmery liquids and creams. The other side of the room was mostly hidden behind a gossamer screen; when I looked behind it, I found what looked like a marble armchair with a sliver of cushion running across the edge where the knees would go and a hole cut into the actual seat, disappearing down into darkness.

It took me a minute to realize what I was looking at. Talk about a throne. Well… could be weirder.

No time like the present, my bladder chimed in as I regarded the, uh, special chair. Strange as it seemed, I'd seen and used way more intimidating before. Any port in a storm. There was no paper, but there were little stacks of what looked like silken handkerchiefs on a cubby shelf built into the wall next to the seat, a covered silver bucket on the floor nearby. I could put two and two together.

Afterward, I nosed around the different bottles and bowls of multicolored pastes and gels by the sink until I found one that I thought had the greatest chance of being soap, in that it was a slick, milky cream of pastel blue that smelled faintly of chemically processed flowers. At the very least, my skin didn't melt using it.

Investigation concluded, I went back into the main room.

Though the prince had said to rest, I had every intention of being more proactive than that, somehow. But then I sat down on the edge of the massive bed, and it was like the mattress was sucking me down. Before I knew it, I was lying back on the bed, staring up at the curtained canopy, willing my eyes to stay open and failing. My thoughts were still spinning in circles even as I drifted off to sleep.

Chapter 6: Apprehension

I woke to someone pounding on the door, and my first thought was that I'd forgotten to pay my rent somehow and the landlord was pissed. My next thought was to wonder what the heck I'd eaten to give myself such a weird and lifelike dream.

And my third thought, after I sat up and looked at the room, was, *Son of a bitch, I'm still here.*

Whoever was hammering on the door was still here too, unfortunately. "What?" I shouted groggily, which turned into a yawn.

"Wake up and make yourself presentable," a man's voice called out. Since it sounded even more annoyed than I felt, I assumed this was my new guard. Rexazef or whatever.

I'd slept in the clothes I'd shown up here in, which admittedly felt pretty stiff and grimy now after everything they'd been through; but since I didn't have any other options, this was about as presentable as I was gonna be. So, running a hand quickly through my hair to get the worst of the sleep tangles out of it, I went to the door and yanked it open.

My guard was standing right next to it, and he spun toward me with his spike-knuckled fists raised as the door opened. I gasped in surprise and stumbled backward, tripping over my own boots and landing on my butt on the large rug. The two of us stared at one another for the moment, and when I was sure he wasn't about to attack after all, I bridled. "What the shit, man?" I said, standing again with as much dignity as I could muster. "You trying to kill me? What'd I do?"

Uncertainty clouded the look of anger on his face, just like it had the last time I'd snapped at one of these red people. "You are not to leave this room without proper escort," he said.

"I wasn't trying to leave!" I said, stepping forward. "I was gonna ask you a question. You're the only one here, right?"

He stared at me a moment longer before finally lowering his fists. "Ask."

I held my arms out at my sides. "Do I look alright?"

His eyes narrowed, his brow furrowed, and then he finally said, "What?" as if I'd spoken a different language.

This guy was not my favorite guy so far. "Do I look okay?" I repeated. "You said to make myself presentable. I assume that means the prince is coming back, but I'm new to all this royal deference stuff. This presentable enough?"

His eyes narrowed again as he looked me up and down, from my singed boots to my hair made lank with dried sweat. "You look unclean," he said.

I sighed. "Well, I got time for a bath, then?"

He turned and craned his neck back, gazing down the corridor outside. "I cannot say," he said. "But no, most likely not."

"This is gonna hafta do, then," I said, dropping my arms to my side. "Well, it was good enough yesterday. This morning." I paused. "What time is it, anyway?"

"Nearing the dinner gathering for archdemons and other assembled courtiers," he said.

I wasn't a fan of the way he dropped "archdemons" so casually, but my worst fears had been subverted so far, so I tried not to dwell on it. "But what time specifically?" I asked. "Afternoon, evening?"

Again, I got his perplexed stare. "What?"

"Right," I said with another sigh. "Nevermind. Thanks, Rexazef."

His scowling and glaring returned instantly at that. "Rezavix," he said.

"Rezavix," I repeated, "right, sorry. I'm Morgan." I held out my hand to him.

He stared at it a moment, then pulled the door closed. Dick.

I may not have had time for a bath, but I went to the bathroom anyway. The washbasin on its shelf against the wall seemed the closest thing to a sink, and there was a small spigot coming out of the wall just above it with a short chain dangling just beside. I pulled it and watched more steaming water pour out into the basin, filling it halfway before I let go. At least the water here didn't look like that black, boiling stuff in the river I'd crossed over with Ulfris to get here. Not sure yet what I did if I wanted it colder than steaming, though.

I didn't see any towels, so I washed my face and wetted my hair with my hands, then peeled my t-shirt and bra off and rinsed as best I could. Some of these bottles next to me were probably demony cleaning things, soap or scale conditioner or horn polish or something, but I wasn't going to experiment.

Once I was at least a little bit fresher than I had been, I pulled my clothes back on, pausing to chuckle without any real humor when I realized I'd been wearing my Highway to Hell shirt. I mean, when I stopped to think about it, a lot of my music shirts had some sort of demonic reference on them, so it probably wasn't that much of a coincidence. And it probably wasn't my shirt's fault that I ended up here after that botched spell.

Probably not.

When I walked back out of the bathroom, Prince Vambrace was already standing in the center of the bedroom, gazing idly at the sheets on the massive bed I'd ruffled with my nap. I stepped back with a start as he turned to me. "Hey, whoa!" I said out of reflex. "I, uh, didn't hear you knock."

"I didn't," he said, blank as ever. "This is my palace."

"Yeah, but still," I said, hovering in the bathroom door. "What if I'd been naked or something?"

He shrugged. "I would have waited for you to dress," was his only answer, and then he looked me up and down the same as Rezavix had done earlier. "You are ready, I assume?"

"Ready for what?" I asked, deciding for the moment to ignore the creep vibes he'd just been sending.

"A feast," he said, then turned and added, "This way," before heading through the door.

My stomach answered for me, rumbling as if on cue. I hadn't eaten since that pizza I'd ordered who knows how long ago back in my apartment with the book. So once more, I followed the prince, this time a bit more eagerly. Rezavix stayed behind by the doorway as we headed back up the long and winding corridor.

I'll skip the riveting tale of the blocks and blocks of long hallway we walked down again. Seriously, I'd walked through airports that didn't take this long to cross. I will say, though, that we passed more people the further we went: the grumbling little brown bug-looking things, the way too skinny orange things, hulking blue things like Ulfris, the occasional slutted-up purple thing or a scaly green grinning thing like Dramoc, and of course, the leathery red ones that seemed to be guarding and patrolling everything. Every one of them stopped what they were doing as we approached, bowing to the passing prince and casting surprised and/or curious glances my way. The only exceptions were the dirty, scruffy gray things that we walked by two or three times, slumped against the wall or sitting in the corner of where two or more corridors intersected. These ones didn't move even to look up at our passing, much less bow. If the prince noticed or cared, he didn't show it.

Once again, we were about to the point where my legs were getting tired when we finally reached a pair of massive doors flanked by two red demons with a tall light-blue one in the middle, this one a woman in a flowing purple dress and elaborately plaited purple hair to match, but with two long, thick horns sprouting from amidst the delicate braids and curling down around her face like a ram's, the points ending next to the sparkling teardrop earrings she wore in her ears. She smiled as we approached and, most noticeably, didn't bow or curtsy or even nod. "Sire," she said to the prince, then glanced at me behind him. "You've brought your new novelty to dine with us, I see. Interesting. I'd heard you'd gotten one, but I wasn't sure until now."

Well damn, I wasn't gonna like this one either. I leveled my best glare at the giant woman and wondered if I was ever going to meet someone around here who wasn't an asshole. Where were all the nice people in Hell?

"Duchess Sidona," said the prince, stopping just before her. She had to be at least seven feet tall, and this close together, she made the human prince look almost like a twerp. Still, he didn't seem intimidated at all, and however dismissive she'd been with me, none of it showed toward Vambrace. In fact, she even dipped her head a very little bit as he said her name. "Yes," he continued, "I knew rumor would be swirling soon. Best to let everyone know at once and spread the word. One more human to get used to around Pandemonium." He turned and looked at me over his shoulder, expression unreadable as ever. "Novelty, however, is likely not the right word. I am still deciding."

Fuck you too, prince, I thought. Out loud, I said, "Am I gonna get a say in any of this stuff you're deciding? Uh, sire?" I added at the last second, just to be safe.

Sidona chuckled, bringing a long-nailed finger to her lips as she regarded me with a twinkle in her eyes. The prince just said, "Perhaps. I am still deciding that, too." Then he turned back to the seven-foot blue lady. "Shall we?"

"Of course," she said, still smiling, then turned and flung the doors open to a cacophony of voices beyond that suddenly quieted down. "All rise for his highness, Prince Vambrace," she called through the doors, then stepped inside.

The roar that followed her words nearly deafened me, and when I stepped through the doors after the prince, I saw why. To call the space beyond a room was wrong, because it was roughly the size of a football field and absolutely full of demons, even more so than the indoor coliseum where the prince had fought the red demon Mersio for reasons I still hadn't figured out. Stretching away into the distance all around us (I couldn't see any of the far walls for all the people in the way) were multicolored crowds all on their feet and cheering like a concert audience when the band finally shows up.

What space wasn't taken up by demons was filled in with massive tables draped with rich tablecloths, each one with at least one small fountain on it flowing with liquids that varied in color as much as the people around them. In the center of the room, though, leading from the doorway into the depths of the giant space, was an aisle of dark red carpet that looked more like a silk tapestry than a rug. The prince strode down this aisle and past the cheering masses without so much as a glance in either direction. I tried to mimic that detachment somewhat as I followed, Sidona right behind me. As soon as I let myself be overwhelmed by this place, I was afraid I'd never get back to whelmed again.

The roar of the crowd died down as we went but didn't quiet entirely until we reached a set of stairs on the far side of the room, which I ascended behind the prince, keeping my eyes on the sword at his back the whole while. It was a tall set of steps, and at the top was one final table, smaller than the others and without any little fountains. Seven demons stood around it, one of each of the different varieties I'd seen so far, each one looking expectantly at us.

Prince Vambrace walked around all of them to the far end of the table, and I followed out of habit to where what looked like a throne draped in soft black fur waited for him. I stopped when he did, wondering if maybe I was supposed to have gone somewhere else; but then he caught my eye and gestured at the empty chair at his left, across from a giant blue-green man and next to a half-naked purple guy who I realized was staring at my ass. Sidona had disappeared somewhere along the way. When I looked back over the stairs, I couldn't see her, but I did see the enormous crowds of the feast hall stretching away in all directions. Tall lanterns like inverted chandeliers dotted the rainbow masses at regular intervals, lighting up the cavernous room. I realized why when I looked up and couldn't see the ceiling, only smoky darkness that stretched away higher than I could see.

Then the prince sat down, and everyone else around the table also sat down. I followed a moment later into my own seat, and the massive shuffling of chairs as the hordes below us also took their seats echoed off the walls a bit before thousands of conversations picked back up once more.

There was no talk at our table yet, though, and I took the opportunity to glance around at my dining partners.

Other than the prince at my right at the head of the table, there was the giant blue-green guy across from me, nearly eight feet tall and broad enough to fill out his height. He had a clean-cut, square jaw set tight as he eyed the prince. Pure white hair swept back over his scalp from a high widow's peak and hung halfway down his neck, while giant black horns, the biggest pair I'd seen so far on any demon, curved forward out of his temples like a bull's, the points almost touching in front of his trimmed and arched eyebrows. And while I'd thought Dramoc's fancy clothes had been a bit much, this guy had him easily beat, looking more like a member of royalty than the plain prince between us — ruffled red silk shirt under a silver vest embroidered with small gemstones, sapphires and emeralds alternating in a tight diamond pattern, with a heavy cape of midnight blue overtop all of it. Basically, if I'd looked up in the throne room to see this guy sitting in front of me, I wouldn't have been so surprised.

Next to him, diagonally from me, sat another of the red sinewy demons, this one a woman with ash gray hair pulled back in a tight bun and slender black horns like oversized needles stabbing out behind her head. She had a pointed chin and a jaw that jutted out far enough for two long, thick fangs to stick up over her upper lip, almost like tusks. Her eyes with their pinprick pupils looked wide in perpetual outrage as she glanced around the table, hands folded into polite fists in front of her. Unlike the blue guy next to her, she wore much the same thing that the rest of her type wore — dark red armor that looked like either hardened leather or some sort of carapace, polished to a shine, consisting of a breastplate and armguards. Her elbows ended in spikes at her side, and the knots of her muscles strained as if she was flexing continuously where she sat.

On her other side was an orange man that looked like he was made almost entirely of arm and spine and an oversized ribcage, like someone had taken a massive barrel and hacked out the middle portion before strapping two saplings to the sides, then draped a formless white robe overtop as an afterthought. His long-fingered hands hovered in the small cavern where his stomach ought to have been, stroking the shadowed emptiness in anticipation. Large, deep-set eyes that looked like they were mostly giant pupils sat atop a bulbous nose and below a hairless forehead that sloped up to two short, sharp horns sprouting from his skull like TV antennas. He ran a long, wet tongue over his sharp, perpetually exposed teeth; but by the way that the corners of his nearly nonexistent lips seemed slightly upturned, I gathered that this was probably actually a purposeful grin he was sporting right now, rather than just the neutral rictus grin that all of his kind of demon seemed to wear by default.

Rounding out the row opposite me, at the far end of the table, sat one of the frumpy gray demons. This one I assumed to be female just by the lack of a beard like I'd seen on the hobo-looking guy in Dramoc's shop, though her whole body was covered in a short, matted, gray fuzz that might have been fur or might have been some sort of mossy mold. Either way, it was stained and matted and unkempt, like a carpet that had seen too many messes without ever being cleaned. Her mouth was closed, her eyes were shut, and she had only two vertical slits where there should have been a nose, so her whole face was just a series of lines and creases but for her thick, pursed lips. Gray-brown hair grew in tangled, snarled tufts from her head, dusty and unwashed, and a pair of bumpy, notched, off-white horns stuck up without any kind of symmetry, cracked in some places and with the tips jagged and uneven, like they'd broken off at some point. Her hands were on the table, so I could see the long, yellow, gnarly nails like claws that sprouted from each finger. As far as her outfit went, I assumed the stretch of brown hide that loosely draped down her was some sort of toga or wrap or something instead of just a giant stain, but I couldn't be sure. All in all, she looked like some kind of big animal that desperately needed grooming, like a feral old cat or one of those mangy dogs you see slumped in a cage in those sad TV commercials that want you to adopt a rescue animal.

On my own side of the table, right beside me sat the purple guy who'd gone from staring at my ass to staring at my chest. His skin was a light eggplant color, his straight, shiny hair that hung halfway down his back the same vibrant crimson as the pointed, immaculately trimmed goatee that framed his smirk. He caught me looking at him looking at me and winked one golden eye, gold all across without iris or pupil. Almost against my will, my eyes swept down his form-fitting outfit, cut from what looked like black PVC and revealing enough to show off all of his pecs, the tops of his abs, and that crease on either side below where his hips dipped toward his pelvis. He wasn't anywhere near as ripped and sculpted as all of the red people I'd seen already, but he was still lean and toned, in almost too perfect shape, with a line of light red hair trailing down the middle of his chest and disappearing into what little there was of his outfit. He looked like he belonged either in a male strip club or on a poster on the wall of some teenage girl with particularly raging hormones. And he apparently knew it, because as I took him in, he leaned back in his seat and slid his hips forward, giving me a particularly clear look at the long bulge stretching down one leg of his outfit. I cleared my throat and leaned forward until the table between us blocked my view again, looking pointedly past him while he chuckled and hoping I wasn't blushing as obviously as I felt.

Past him sat one of the green and scaly demons, draped in layers of different colored, vibrant robes much like Dramoc had been. Also like

Dramoc, it had rings hanging in long rows all up and down its tall, pointed ears, each one gold or silver and with a different marble-sized gem hanging off of it. Gold studs lined its eyes where eyebrows should have been, and two more dotted each slitted nostril above a lipless mouth that stretched from ear to ear above a long, sharp chin that pointed down half the length of her neck. I guessed it was a her by the higher cheekbones and more slender features compared to how I remembered Dramoc's. And finally, just like that greedy leering merchant prick, she had two rows of short ivory horns running from her brow over her scalp and down the back of her neck, each one curving slightly back like a short, greased mohawk in lieu of actual hair.

At last, at the far end of my own row, there sat one of the squat brown goblin-looking ones with the multifaceted eyes and spindly arms and legs, their small, round face barely reaching above the edge of the table. This one looked much like the others I'd seen, like some sort of giant bug with a scowling, fanged underbite and two squat, pointy horns on the sides of their earless head. I wouldn't have been able to tell this one apart from any of the others I'd seen scurrying around the palace except that they weren't wearing the plain, coarse clothing of the others; instead, they wore a black robe with long, baggy sleeves that covered their hands and made them look too small in their own clothes, with a green sash overtop. And they had a little bronze crown perched atop their head, like a kid's dress-up toy. The pupils in each facet of their eyes were moving independently, lazily sweeping the table and looking like flies swarming two multisided dice. A lot of their eyes were looking at me, though, which was unnerving.

I sat back in my seat, staring down at the table in front of me. I was either the only normal thing sitting here or the strangest, I wasn't sure yet.

The purple guy beside me was the first to break the silence. "Good to see you again, sire," he said, voice husky and oozing charm. His eyes were still roving over me when he spoke, though. "Who is this lovely creature you've brought among us?"

"I'm sure you've heard already of the human woman Lord Ulfris gifted to me during court, Archduke Melchius," the prince replied, raising a hand in my direction. "This is Lady Morgan of Amell, newly arrived from Earth."

"How very exotic," the purple guy, Melchius, said as he took my hand beneath the table, then lifted it to his smirking lips and kissed my fingers. I wasn't sure, but I thought I felt his tongue dart out against my knuckles as well. "Archduke Melchius of House Luxuria at your service, my lady."

"Uh, nice to meet you," I said as I tugged my hand back, wiping it against my pants. "I think." Subtly as I could manage, I slid my chair away from his. Without any subtlety at all, he slid after me.

The blue guy across the table harrumphed. "Typical of you to chase anything new without a thought, Melchius," he said, voice an even deeper baritone than Ulfris had spoken with. "You know nothing about where she is from or what she has brought with her. She may be diseased for all we know so far."

"And typical of you to think the worst of her already, Abdeles," Melchius returned with a smarmy smile. "You miss out on so much fun when everything is beneath you. Although," he added, stroking his beard as he turned his smile back on me, "having her beneath me also sounds like fun. Does it not, my lady?"

I scooted so far away from him I nearly rounded the edge of the table next to Prince Vambrace, who put his elbows on the table and rested his chin on his fists. "Melchius," said the prince, "remember that this is all new to her. Leave her be so she can get acclimated without you trying to climb into her lap."

Melchius only chuckled. "Of course, sire. My apologies, my lady." He leaned back in his seat before adding, "But my offer stands if you change your mind later."

"Yeah, thanks," I mumbled. I'd been hit on by creeps before, but not very often, so I was unused to deflecting their attention. Granted, if I was being honest with myself, except for the weird color scheme he had going on with his skin and hair and eyes, Melchius was far from hard to look at. Especially compared to everyone else seated around us.

"Perhaps proper introductions are in order," the prince said, looking at me and motioning to Melchius. "You've already been thoroughly introduced to Archduke Melchius. This is Archduke Abdeles of House Superbia," he added, gesturing to the giant blue man across from me.

Abdeles lifted his square chin and peered down his nose at me. "My lady human," he said, almost begrudgingly. I nodded back.

"Beside him is the Archduchess Pyrresa of House Iria," the prince continued, nodding to the sinewy red woman. She nodded back to me, still glaring at me as if she were considering vaulting over the table and murdering me where I sat. I started to wonder if the red ones were all actually super pissed all the time or if maybe they all just had extreme cases of resting bitch face.

"Beyond her, Archduke Grodon of House Gullia," said the prince. The grinning orange man grinned even harder and bowed in his seat, a movement that made the hollow alcove of his midsection momentarily look like it was eating his hands inside them. His chair creaked loudly with the motion, belying a heftier weight than seemed possible for his selectively emaciated frame.

"And at the end, Archduchess Bargryf of House Acedia," said the prince. The scruffy gray demon on the end turned her slumped head very slowly and very slightly in my direction. That seemed to be the extent of her greeting. I wasn't even sure her eyes were open beneath all those bags around them.

"On this side," the prince continued, "beyond Archduke Melchius, the Archduchess Cinaedemis of House Avaritia." The green lady smiled her creepy Glasgow smile and dipped her head, the jeweled rings in her ears jingling against one another.

"And finally," the prince finished, gesturing at last to the small brown demon, "on this end, Archduke Aleviathan the 43rd of House Invidia."

"Last as always," the little archduke grumbled in a raspy voice, looking at me with the same amount of eyes as before.

"Last and least, as appropriate," Abdeles grumbled more clearly. Most of Aleviathan's eyes darted to the blue archduke at that, and his scowl deepened, but he only mumbled under his breath in reply.

"Enough," barked the red archduchess, Pyrresa, as her glare swept from Abdeles to Aleviathan. "The royal table should be one place free of tired bickering, especially with an envoy of Earth in our midst." Her glare came back to me again. "Pay these fools no mind."

I could only gulp and nod under the force of that glare. Still, this was the nicest any of the red demons had been to me yet. Maybe it really was just resting bitch face.

"The royal table should also not be so empty," said the orange archduke, Grodon, as his gaze swiveled around the room. His voice sounded strangely thick, as if he were speaking through a wad of meat caught in his throat. "That's our only real problem. Where is our meal?"

At his words, the prince turned back toward me. It took me a moment to realize he was looking past me, though, and when I looked around, there stood the tall blue lady from before. Duchess Sidona, I think. There were so many names being dropped lately, it was hard to keep track of them all, especially since they were all so weird. Then again, I suppose any demons named Tim or Susan or whatever would have been a bit underwhelming.

Sidona smiled at the prince and spun on her heel, clapping her hands together. "Bring out the first course," she called to the room, as if she were announcing an awards show rather than overseeing dinner.

"Bring out all the courses!" Grodon called over the table, his tongue extending nearly a foot out of his mouth before he brought it back under control and pinned it between his teeth.

Without turning around, Sidona shrugged. "Bring out all the courses," she repeated in her red carpet hostess voice.

Several doors opened on the nearest walls as a procession of demons poured out — mostly the small brown ones holding giant steaming platters and pots and covered dishes, though interspersed among them were some pink and purple men and women in their form-hugging, highly revealing outfits, each carrying large pitchers of different colors. This small army of demons swarmed around our table, ducking in between seats to set down their burdens before us until the table itself disappeared under the sheer amount of food spreading out across it. Quick as they appeared, the brown buggy ones scampered away and disappeared through the doors once more. The oversexed ones stayed behind, circling with their pitchers and filling up the large goblets that had been placed at every seat.

I had no idea where to begin, or how. The plate set before me was empty, so I assumed I was supposed to get my own food from the spread. What was proper etiquette for a feast with demons? Come to that, what was proper etiquette for a normal feast? I'd never eaten any meal fancier than a family dinner at the local bar and grill before.

Hesitant, I waited and watched, looking around at the food and my dinner companions. The prince was waiting quietly and expressionless as always, so I probably wasn't going to get any hints there. Melchius beside me was busy sliding a hand through the wide open slit on the skirt of the pink demon woman pouring his wine, grinning as she giggled. Good, less attention for me that way. Everyone else also seemed to be waiting on their servers to finish filling their drinks, except for Grodon, who reached out before him and grabbed a roast bird twice the size of any turkey I'd ever seen, pulling the whole thing onto his plate. He also commandeered a bowl bigger than my head of steaming yellow broth, a sideboard of what looked like a whole loaf of flaky bread covered in shiny, dark purple goop, and a tray of exotic looking sliced fruits of all colors dusted with sugar. Or something white and powdery like sugar, anyway.

Wait, that was a good point. Did Hell have foods like sugar and fruit? Cows and pigs and chickens? Normal vegetables and grains and stuff? And if not, where did all this food come from, and what was it, and was it safe to eat any of it? Maybe that wasn't a giant turkey the orange archduke had — maybe it was a roast baby dragon or griffon or something. Maybe everything here was actually toxic to someone like me. Maybe I'd starve to death before I found a way out of here, surrounded by all this demon food I couldn't eat.

I hoped not. Truth be told, I was starving, and it all looked and smelled delicious.

But wait. Prince Vambrace was human, and he didn't look starved or poisoned or anything. Maybe if I just watched what he ate and copied him.

I turned toward his direction again just in time to get an eyeful of silk-clad, lilac-colored cleavage. Startled, I looked up at heart-shaped face of the demon girl who'd stepped between us.

"Uh, pardon me, ma'am," she said, holding up the silver pitcher she carried and turning her sapphire blue eyes down toward my cup. "I hate to bother you, but I don't know what drink you would prefer. I've never served a human before."

Good question. I looked at my cup, then leaned around her and nodded toward the prince. "I'll drink what he's drinking," I said. "Uh, what Prince Vambrace prefers," I added quickly. Deference still took some getting used to, but better safe than sorry. "Please."

"Yes, ma'am," said the lilac girl, dipping a quick curtsy. She turned and looked at the prince, then turned back to me, curtsied again, and said, "Um… Only, his highness's preference changes from meal to meal, I'm told. So…"

"You're new, aren't you?" Melchius chimed in from behind. I turned to find him looking at my purple server, one hand still disappeared up the skirt of his own pink waitress. "Neophyte?"

"Gift class, my lord," she answered with another curtsy. "Still learning. I was presented at the most recent court holding, and this is my first—"

"Yes, fine," the archduke interrupted, waving the hand that wasn't groping the woman next to him. "If the lady doesn't know what she wants, then just pour her whatever you have and leave already."

"Oh, right!" my waitress answered, curtsying again. "Sorry, my lord. Sorry, my lady," she added with one more curtsy, then poured something dark green and shimmering into my goblet before curtsying a final time and backing away.

The prince had apparently been served in the interim, for he held up his own cup then. The rest of the table followed suit, as did I a moment later. "To our new guest," he said, looking my way. "May our envoy from Earth find Hell to her tastes."

Everyone else made a general noise of agreement and drank, Archduke Grodon knocking his back in one massive gulp, Archduchess Bargryf drinking slowly beside him and spilling much of her goblet's contents down her sagging chin. I gingerly sipped my own drink, strangely sweet and just a bit earthy. I couldn't place the taste, but it wasn't bad. The warm burn that swept back up through my mouth after I swallowed, though, clued me in that whatever it was, it was alcoholic. I set it back down with a mental note to be careful with it.

Dinner didn't get any less awkward after that, but the brunt of everyone's attention at least moved on from the strangeness of my being there. For the most part, the archdemons were content to talk amongst themselves while the prince and I sat mostly silent at our end. I watched as subtly as I could which food he took for himself and followed suit, ending up with a roll of the flaky bread-looking stuff, a hunk of the giant turkey-looking thing, and a bowl of something dark red and thick that might have been chunky barbecue sauce back on Earth. The bread stuff tasted like bread but a bit salty. The turkey stuff tasted just a bit heavier than chicken, like it was halfway to a red meat, with some very aromatic spices I couldn't place. The red goop, I wasn't touching until I'd worked up a little more courage.

"Delectable, is it not?" Archduke Grodon asked me when I was halfway finished with my meat. It took me a minute to realize he was talking to me. When I looked up, I noticed that the mountain of food I'd seen him take at the beginning of dinner was all gone, replaced with a new mountain of completely different food. The table practically bowed in front of where he sat.

I nodded as I swallowed my current mouthful. "Yeah, it's pretty good," I said. "Definitely better than what I'm used to."

"Excellent," Archduchess Pyrresa said beside him. "I felled the beast myself not long before the meal began. As much of a fight as it put up, I worried perhaps its meat would be too tough for some of our tastes."

"Oh," I said, carefully putting the forkful of meat I'd raised back down. "Fresh, then. Nice."

"I take it they do not prepare roast harpy so well where you come from, my lady?" Archduke Abdeles asked from in front of me, swirling his goblet.

I swallowed empty air this time. "Harpies are the ones that are like big birds with a woman's face, right?" I asked.

"Face and breasts, yes," Archduke Melchius answered beside me while the rest of them gave me curious looks. "For all that, they're not as fun of company as you might think, though. Roasting much improves their agreeability."

"Then, no," I answered, clearing my throat. "No, they do not." Abandoning the meat, I dipped into the dark red stuff and came up with a thickly dripping spoonful. "And, uh, what is this, exactly?" I asked the table in general.

"The nuckelavee pudding?" the green archduchess, Cinaedemis, answered with a disturbingly wide grin. "Oh, it's to die for, dear. The best I've had anywhere in Dis, this. You must try it."

Well, if she insisted. How bad could a pudding be? I steeled myself and put the spoon in my mouth. It was warm and creamy, sweet but with a hearty tang, and it felt like pudding going down, which was heartening. "It's pretty good," I said, scooping up another mouthful. "What's in it?"

"Fresh kelpie milk, ripe caina berries, and the triple distilled ichor of a nuckelavee at the prime of its strength," Grodon answered, then opened his mouth wide and dumped a full bowl of the stuff down his throat. And as much as the green ones' big mouths weirded me out, when the orange archduke opened his mouth wide, he opened it *wide*. I probably could have climbed inside myself with room to spare, if I'd been of a mind.

So startled was I by the sight that I'd swallowed another mouthful of the stuff before I remembered to ask, "And, uh, what is nuckelavee ichor?"

Again, that got me a round of curious stares. "The lifeblood of a nuckelavee," the prince answered calmly. He was staring at me too, but with something other than curiosity. Wistfulness, maybe? "They were a rare sight on Earth, if I remember correctly," he continued, "and may be even rarer today. If you've never seen one, imagine a wild stallion with no skin, with a man-shaped beast, also skinless, growing out of its back, its arms ending in sharpened spears of muscle and bone, both mouths overflowing with jagged, flesh-rending teeth." He nodded to my bowl of pudding. "That is a nuckelavee."

I dropped my spoon back into my bowl with a plop. "Ah," I said around the pudding already in my mouth; and because I don't think spitting it out would have gone over very well in present company, I forced myself to swallow it. It was still pretty good, much to my discomfort. "And, uh... and this?" I asked nervously, picking up my bread-like roll.

He glanced briefly at the lump in my hand. "That is bread," he said.

"Ah," I said again, and took a relieved bite. "Uh, this is also good," I added a moment later.

"So our envoy knows little of harpies and nothing of the nuckelavee," said Archduke Abdeles, turning to the prince with a raised eyebrow. "Earth must have changed a great deal since your time there, Sire."

"Indeed," said the prince, not looking up from his food. "Perhaps it has grown more peaceful, as was my hope. As have we also, since travel was sealed so long ago." He did look up at the archduke then — pointedly so. "I admit, I am curious to hear how my homeland fares of late," he added after a pause, turning his unreadable gaze on me. "We must speak of it later."

I smiled politely back. "We must," I said, giving him a pointed look of my own. "I have a lot of curiosity myself."

"One wonders what new beasts have arisen to fill the gaps in the interim," Abdeles continued, then looked at me. Or at least, he looked down his own nose in my general direction. "Tell me, my lady, how does the Original Sin fare in an isolated Earth, free from our drifting castoffs?"

I risked another sip of my drink. It didn't burn as much going down this time. "I, uh…" I started, then shook my head. "No, sorry, you lost me. Original Sin?" I got no answer from him or the rest of the table. "What is that?" I clarified after a silent moment. "Like, the thing in the Bible, with the snake and the apple? Or like the Jim Steinman song?"

That got everyone's attention. Even Archduke Grodon stopped stuffing his face long enough to stare at me in confusion, and Archduchess Bargryf looked at me with the closest thing to alert attention I'd seen on her since I'd sat down. Around us, the ever-present sexy servants were giving me the same looks.

I shrank in my seat, once more hyper aware how much I stuck out and how tenuous my situation was here. "I mean," I said slowly, trying to stall, "you'll, uh… just hafta be a little more specific, I guess, is all…"

"The Arch-Sin," said Archduke Aleviathan from the end of the table, his first words in a while that weren't muttered and incoherent from this far away. Honestly, I'd nearly forgotten he was there. "The Original Sin from which the rest of us descend, of which the seven houses are mere imperfect reflections of one facet, like the divided spectrum of colors to the pure light of the master race."

Well, that didn't clear anything up, though his choice of phrasing did add a new layer of awkward to things — although, yeah, the kind of person who used the phrase "master race" in earnest was the kind of person who belonged in Hell. Everyone was still staring at me as though they couldn't comprehend that what they were saying wasn't obvious to me yet. "Ah, uh, right," I said. Dig that hole deeper, Morgan. "Master… race. I do remember learning about something like that. But, uh, that idea stopped being popular a long time ago, so…" And here I officially drew a blank. In a panic, I looked toward the prince.

Surprisingly, he looked nearly as anxious as I felt, staring back at me with wide, urgent eyes. Our gazes met for only a moment before he clamped down on his expression, hurriedly turning to the table at large with his stoic mask back in place. "My lords and ladies," he said quickly, "please remember, Lady Morgan has only newly arrived in our world. This is likely her first contact with the seven lesser races of sin. As such, the terminology involved may be confusing the idea." The curious gazes all on him now, he leaned back in his seat while I breathed a silent sigh of relief. "After all, one cannot consider themselves the progenitor of beings that they don't know exist. Modern humans have likely abandoned the qualifier and instead think of themselves as the only, the one true race. Correct me if I'm wrong," he finished, giving me a covert look that I took to mean *Don't you dare correct me.*

I nodded, probably more eagerly than was strictly necessary. "Yeah, that's about it," I said. "Something like that."

"Homogeny, huh?" said Aleviathan, still muttering. "Sounds nice. Simpler."

"Sounds dull," said Melchius. His server had disappeared, and with her, his perpetual grin. Instead, he picked at the roast harpy on his plate, dragging it through a dollop of the nuckelavee pudding. "No offense, of course," he added to me a moment later. "I personally just get bored without plenty of variety."

"Oh, yeah, well," I said, grabbing another roll. "There's definitely more of that here than back home so far…" I turned my attention back to my plate, hiding as best I could behind my hair on either side and the roll I held in front of me, like a shy child at a dinner with strangers. But not before I caught Archduke Abdeles still looking at me over the table, as if to make sure my awkward discomfort didn't dissipate completely.

After that, though, the rest of dinner progressed without any more notable issues. For what felt like a couple of hours more, the archdemons all talked amongst themselves, usually with caustic undertones. Abdeles had nothing to say to anyone that didn't sound condescending, and Pyrresa had nothing to say that wasn't testy and impatient. Bargryf simply had nothing to say; I don't remember hearing a single word out of her, just wet slurping sounds as she leisurely sucked down bowls of broth and soup-looking foods. Grodon likewise preferred to stuff his face rather than converse, though he did offer an unsolicited review, usually glowing, of everything he ate as he ate it, complaining only that the pudding ran out about an hour into the meal. And the only thing Aleviathan seemed to dislike more than being ignored was when he had to talk to anybody around him.

The actual topics of conversation turned mostly to matters of palace and city management, as near as I could follow. Cinaedemis talked at length about funds and budgets and other weighty but mundane matters. Or they would have been mundane if she didn't keep mentioning "souls" as a unit of money, but I was choosing to deliberately not think about that for now until someone sat down and started answering my questions. Pyrresa gave clipped reports of guard and soldier activity, while Grodon waxed on about food stores and production until Abdeles interrupted him to ask questions about servants and their working conditions, which Melchius and Aleviathan both answered. And Archduchess Bargryf stayed silent as ever, only nodding to something unheard that Pyrresa said quietly around Grodon.

Through it all, Prince Vambrace listened calmly, only occasionally chiming in when questioned or to interrupt an argument with a command or instructions. The pink and purple servants — including my own waitress from earlier, who had stopped asking questions or looking at anyone — hovered politely at the edges, ducking in to top up drinks or take away empty dishes. At some point, the tall blue lady, Sidona, disappeared again, and the wiry red woman he'd introduced me to earlier — Enkida, I think — showed up, standing silent and still behind the prince's chair, this time dressed in the full spiky armor like the rest of her... race, I guess? Species? The differences in the demons I'd seen so far went beyond regular ethnic traits. Aleviathan had said something about seven different houses. There were seven different types of demon I'd encountered, one of each sitting at the table with me now. And there were the classic seven deadly sins — I hadn't been to church since I was a little girl, but confused as I still was, I wasn't that slow. The prince had a lot of clarifying to do later.

I looked up to find him watching me again while Pyrresa and Cinaedemis argued about how much to pay a company of soldiers to trek out of the city and through a forest somewhere. He kept staring at me for a few seconds before suddenly looking straight down the table at the green archduchess. If he was trying to subtly check me out or something, he was doing a horrible job. But if he was studying me outright and didn't care that I knew, he also still wasn't volunteering why. Unless I really was just some new and rare bauble to him that he was continuously admiring. I still couldn't discount that, but the idea hadn't gotten any less unsettling.

So I sat and listened and fretted and tried to stay out of everyone's attention. And in the meantime, I filled up on the bread while my harpy grew cold.

Chapter 7: Disobedience

After dinner was over (or at least after everyone but Archduke Grodon was finished eating), the prince rose and bid everyone but me a very formal goodbye. I took that as my cue to stand up too, and with Enkida behind us, we walked back down the stairs and through the enormous dining hall, now drastically quieter and calmer while most of the hordes of diners sat around half-empty tables, talking quietly or rubbing their stomachs in contentment, like the afterglow of the world's largest Thanksgiving. I wasn't sure if this was some sort of special feasting holiday or just what every dinner was like around here.

The now-familiar corridors seemed eerily silent as the massive doors closed behind us, and for a moment, the three of us simply stood in the hall, the prince looking down one of the corridors at nothing, the two of us looking at him. "Enkida," he said after a minute. "Do I have any other pressing engagements left?"

"None that I know of, sire," said the red guard behind me.

"Good," he said without turning back. "Then take the Lady Morgan to my chamber. I'll be along shortly."

"Wait, what?" I asked, but he was already walking away, naked sword glinting at his back in the light of the hall sconces. "What?" I called, taking a step after him.

A hand with a grip like gentle iron landing on my shoulder stopped me, and I craned my neck to look back and up at Enkida, the gaze of her pinprick pupils freaking me out all over again at close range. "His majesty said he will be along shortly," she said. "Don't be impatient."

"Impatient isn't the word for it," I said. "Apprehensive, maybe. A chamber's like a bedroom, right? Why am I going to his chamber?"

"Because he ordered such," she said, turning me around with her powerful grasp and pointing me the other way down the corridor. "Now come with me."

"But what's he gonna do when we're in there?" I persisted as we walked. "Why does he keep putting me in these rooms and leaving?"

"I cannot attest to his majesty's every whim," she said, sounding strangely calm for one of the red demons. I would've expected her to get snappy by now. "Why? Do you fear for your safety? If he wished you harm, you would have been harmed by now."

That didn't exactly put me at ease. "It's not that," I said. "Look, I know I'm new here, and I don't know what all customs I still don't know or whatever, but where I come from, when two people go to the same bedroom to be alone, it usually leads to just one thing."

"Sex?" she asked, and her forthrightness made me stop in my tracks a moment. Rather than drag me along — which, lord knows, she could do easily enough — she stopped as well, giving me a curious look. "You think his majesty wishes to have sex with you, and you... don't wish to?"

You'd think I'd be used to these looks by now. "No, I don't wish to!" I said, giving her the same perplexed stare she was giving me. "I barely know the guy, and... just, no! For, like, so many reasons!"

We stood like that for a moment, disbelieving one another, while people trickled past us with curious glances in our direction. "You are... different than I would have expected," she said slowly at last, head tilted. "Hmm."

"Yeah, I get that a lot," I said. She pointed with her chin back the way we'd been heading, and I kept walking beside her. Again, as if I had any other choice at the moment.

"Still," she said after a few seconds, "you don't have to worry about his majesty having sex with you. If such a thing is truly worrisome."

"It truly kind of is, yeah," I said. "Shouldn't it be? I mean, this is Hell, right?"

"Yes," she said, curious expectancy in her tone again.

"Yeah. So..." My hands fluttered in front of me for a minute, looking for a gesture that meant that this stuff should be obvious, and failing to find one. "Y'know... bad stuff happens here. Doesn't it?"

"Sometimes, yes," she said. "Why? Does 'bad stuff' not happen in your world as well?"

I had no answer for her. We walked the rest of the way in silence.

The prince's room was near my own, down just a few halls and around a few bends from where we passed Rezavix still standing and glaring outside the doorway where we'd left him. He nodded brusquely at Enkida as we swept by, and she back at him. I could feel his angry gaze on me until we finally rounded the slow curve of the walls out of his sight.

"I don't think he likes me," I said once I was confident he was out of earshot.

"No, he doesn't," Enkida said. "But if it's any consolation, he doesn't like anybody."

There were two more of the red demons, a man and a woman both with sword and shield, standing before the door to the prince's room. They stood aside as Enkida approached and ushered me through. Beyond was a large sitting room with the same plush seating, fancy rug, and marble fireplace as my new room. More bookshelves lined the walls, all full, and tapestries with that now-familiar concentric circle design hung intermittently on the walls.

What jumped right out at me, though, was the enormous painting hanging above the fireplace mantle, a portrait that had to be at least fifteen feet tall and nearly as wide. In it, Prince Vambrace stood surrounded by the kneeling multicolored denizens of hell against a backdrop of fire and smoke rising into a dark red sky. Blood spattered his gleaming silver mail and the ground beneath him, one booted foot planted atop a black and fanged skull nearly twice the size of his own, with massive horns curving out of it nearly up to the prince's knee. In one hand, he held aloft his silvery sword, bloodless and gleaming; his other hand was clenched at his side around a heavy golden crown which, so far, I'd never seen him wearing.

Okay, presented like this, I could admit he struck an imposing figure. It would be hard not to, given the context. And it was a really good painting, detailed and lifelike and vibrant. He might have been standing before me himself.

Along every wall in this anteroom were more doors, all closed. Behind one was his bedroom, I assumed. Maybe another would be a study or something. The rest, I had no clue. I turned back to Enkida. "Now what?"

"Now, you wait," she said, still standing in the doorway with her arms crossed. "Make yourself comfortable. I only ask that you not wander, as I don't know to what extent his majesty has granted you freedom."

More of those uneasy feelings. I knew better than to ignore them. "So, we're just gonna sit here and look at each other until the prince shows up?"

I asked, trying to stay civil. This woman, at least, had been more or less polite with me so far.

"You are," she said. "I still have duties to see to." And she turned back to leave.

"Wait, you're leaving me alone?" I asked her retreating back.

"His majesty will be along soon," she said over her shoulder. "And the chamber guards will keep anyone unauthorized from coming to bother you. They'll also keep you from straying too far away, should you choose not to heed my advice not to wander." The closest thing to a smile that I'd seen on any of the red ones so far crossed her lips. "My lady," she said with a slight tip of her head, then closed the doors behind her as she left.

Once again, I'd been left alone to wait for someone else to decide what to do with me. This time, though, I wasn't about to stay that way.

I'd gleaned a few more things from the *Morganomicon* before I'd lost it than just how to microwave my hands and how to accidentally damn myself to the pits of Hell. Not much, admittedly, but I'd gone through a good chunk of pages before I'd reached that disaster of a spell. And on the way, I'd been introduced to an interesting idea.

Conjuring enough heat from my body to start fires was a fairly basic technique, according to the book. Not changing reality so much as amplifying an effect that already existed in much smaller doses. Even easier from a heavy lifting standpoint was not changing anything about the world, but changing others' perceptions of it, such as what they thought they saw — or, if I did this right, what they *didn't* see.

It wasn't invisibility, per se. The book had pointed that out. It was more like a heavy suggestion to any who might notice me not to notice me. And as reaching into and influencing the mind of another would be, from what I gathered, much more complicated and delicate work than my *nouveau witch* self would probably be able to do, the better course of action would be to coat myself in the idea that I wasn't really there.

It would definitely be a gamble. Unlike my hot hands trick, I'd never actually tried this one before, just read over it once. I wasn't entirely sure I'd read all the pertinent bits, either; there could be missing pieces I'd need, and if I guessed to fill them in and got it wrong, it might not work. Or worse, it might work in reverse, and magically draw every pair of eyes in the palace my way.

That idea made in and of itself me shudder. I hated standing out. The last thing I needed was my misuse of arcane forces beyond my comprehension amplifying my awkwardness.

But my other option was to sit and wait quietly like a good girl for an entitled and demonstrably violent guy who may or may not believe that he owned me to take me to his private room to do… whatever.

Nope. Wasn't taking that chance. Time to work some magic.

I found the most open spot in the room off to one side near the bookshelves, took a deep breath, closed my eyes, and tried to remember. I couldn't exactly put a mnemonic device to the swirly, wordless Old Elven, so it took a minute to get my thoughts moving in the right patterns; but once it started to come back to me, it all came back in a rush at once, like a controlled dam burst. I could practically see the non-words scrolling by on the backs of my eyelids. I saw myself in my mind's eye, standing still and slightly hunched over: dirty AC/DC shirt, black leather bike pants, boots with the slight scorch marks on the ankles from the first escape I'd orchestrated in this place, black bangs hanging over my closed eyes, breathing slowly and calmly. I reread thoughts with no words that couldn't be articulated but which somehow made perfect sense to me now so long as I didn't try to make sense of them. I saw the words flow past me, over me, around me, wrapping me in their meaning, growing tighter and denser the more I thought them, until they enwrapped me like a mummy bandaged in pure thought, their swirling ideas embedded in the fabric of my clothes, in my skin, coiling and twisting over and through me.

You can't see me, I thought, addressing no one and the world in general. *There's nothing to see. I'm not here. Look away.*

The wordless words flared at the thoughts, glowing and pulsing in time with the cadence of my inner voice. I felt their tingle on my skin as they did so, like that feeling you get when you've charged yourself with static, just before you touch a doorknob — only stronger, all over, constant. When I opened my eyes, the feeling was still there. I felt like I was glowing along the swirling lines of the spell around me, but I dared not look down at myself to see for sure, for fear that I might break the effect if I did.

It had worked. Or at least, *something* had worked; something was very definitely going on with me that hadn't been going on before. Whether it would have the effect I wanted, I was about to find out.

Right, then. Time to leave.

I walked over to the door and opened it, careful not to look at my own hand as I reached for the knob. There was nobody in the hall beyond. I closed the door behind me and, carefully and with a healthy amount of worry, made my way down the corridor, expecting with every step for someone to round the bend and see me and sound an alarm.

That didn't happen. Soon I passed the door to my own room, but thankfully, Rezavix wasn't standing outside. A minute later, I managed to find the double doors I'd passed through three times now, the ones that marked the boundary between the prince's private suite and the rest of the palace. They were still open, both guards still standing at attention at either side, facing down the hall away from me.

The moment of truth. I took a deep breath and held it against my urge to hyperventilate, approaching them slowly and quietly until I stood just behind them both. And then, swallowing my fear once more, I stepped out between them, in front of them.

The one to my right, the woman, turned her head toward me. I froze, eyes wide as I stared down at the floor in front of my feet. *You don't see me,* I thought frantically, again and again like a mantra in my head. *You don't see me, I'm not here, you don't see me, I'm not here —*

"What?" the other one, the man, grumbled under his breath.

The woman shrugged and turned back to the empty hallway. "Thought I saw something," she grumbled back.

"Been standing here too long," the man muttered. "Wish someone would try something for a change. Liven things up."

"No one will," the woman said. "No one ever does. Who's gonna risk the prince's wrath?"

"No, not his," said the man. "Ours, though. Haven't raged in days, and I ain't due to march for more days yet."

"So sign up for the pit. Maybe even fight the prince, if you're lucky."

"Did once. Ain't trying *that* again for a while. No, I want something I can *pulverize...*"

I snuck away while they chatted. Or rather, I just kept walking straight ahead in front of them until their growling voices disappeared behind me, thanking any version of God that might be listening to a place like this that the magic had worked and held.

As it turns out, though, walking unseen past two posted guards was the easy part — now I had the rest of the palace to navigate, hallways filled with more guards and servants and all manner of other demons coming and going. It was kind of like navigating the crowds in the halls of my college, except that the building was miles across and nobody paid me any attention whatsoever but for the occasional passing turn of the head as someone checked their peripheral vision for movement. *Don't see me*, I kept repeating as I picked my way around them, ducking and weaving around pairs or groups, occasionally ducking into a doorway or flattening myself against the wall when things got too congested.

At one point, I bumped against the arm of a tall blue woman, who spun in my direction with an offended glare. I sidestepped out of the way of her gaze and held my breath, my mantra on fast-forward in my head; but luckily, there had been a light purple man passing by on my other side who caught her eyes. He smirked and ran his hand down his collarbone and chest, half exposed by the deeply plunging line of his shirt. The blue woman harrumphed and strode on, head held high. The purple guy shook his head and did the same, heading in the opposite direction. Between them, I finally took another breath and followed after him, redoubling the care I took with each step. *You don't see me, none of you see me, there's no one here, just keep moving…*

There was one other difference between moving through the palace and moving through my college halls, though: here, I had no idea where the hell I was going. A lot of the walls around me curved slightly, and as long and winding as the passages were, I lost what little sense of direction I'd started with pretty early on.

After about ten minutes of near aimless wandering, I finally stopped and ducked into an alcove in a side wall at a T-junction of two different halls, away from the slow stream of people. Here, I leaned against a bronze statue recessed in the pocket of space, some skinny guy with curly horns and a pointed goatee, and rested while I tried to retrace my steps. I'd come through the front doors and straight back to the throne room, then through a side door and down a hall to a waiting room. Then the prince came and took me through two… maybe three intersections, down some stairs to that indoor coliseum. Then back out, down about a block of hallways, down some stairs, another block of hallways, down some more stairs, and around to what I thought of as my guest bedroom. Which was…

I peered out of my cubby down the hall and swore silently in my head. I had no idea which way I'd come from anymore. All I knew was I needed to go up a couple of floors. Maybe three. Shit, I couldn't remember.

As I was stepping out of the alcove I shared with the statue guy, though, I noticed there was a third party I hadn't seen at first: one of the fuzzy gray demons, this one scrawny and curled around the statue's base, most of their body hidden beneath their long snarl of hair. Their head, resting on the floor, peered out between my feet down the corridor. Though they didn't move but for the very, very slow rise of their trunk under their mane, their eyes weren't entirely closed, either. They may have been dozing, but they weren't asleep.

I'd practically been standing on them. Did they still not notice me? Was the spell that strong? Or did they just not care?

Well, they weren't raising any alarms, and I was getting tired of stopping and holding my breath for every worry. Time was limited anyway. Leaving the furry gray demon to their curious choice of napping spot, I struck off down one of the halls mostly at random.

I didn't have to walk far to confirm that I was now absolutely lost. Whatever slim inkling of direction I'd had before was gone entirely. I couldn't even be sure if this part of the palace was unfamiliar or not; every damn hall looked the same so far. And this was just one floor — There had to be dozens, maybe hundreds or more judging by the height of this place I'd seen from outside. And that wasn't counting however deep these basement levels ran. How did these people find their way around this behemoth of a building? Where the hell was the map?

I was just starting to wonder if I'd have any luck turning around and retracing my steps when the wall to my left slid open. I pressed back against the opposite wall, surprised. I hadn't noticed any doors in that spot, just a flickering sconce; this was a hidden panel or something. Three of the small brown demons stepped out of the tiny room that was exposed, the last one sliding the wall back into place before all of them headed down the corridor the way I'd just come from, grumbling all the way.

As they left, I hurried to the wall they'd just exited, feeling along the sliding panel. It had closed flush with the rest of the wall, not even a hair's breadth of a seam showing. Did it not open from this side? Frustrated, I turned my attention to the sconce instead, running my fingers along the metal stem on the underside of the bowl that held the fire. There was a small ball affixed to the bottom that looked like just an accent of the fixture but had a bit of give to it. I gave it a small twist; there was a click behind the wall somewhere, and then the panel slid open once more. Bingo.

I slipped inside the small room and looked around. The space was about the size of a broom closet, and there was nothing in it but me and a crank attached to the back wall. Pushing the panel closed once more from the inside, I felt my way to the crank in the gloom and gave it an experimental turn. It spun smoothly along whatever mechanism it was attached to, and I felt the tiny room slowly lurch upward.

I was right, then. This was a crude elevator. Just what I needed. If I couldn't navigate the halls with any sort of plan, at least I could get myself to the right floor. Or thereabouts, at least.

Somehow, hand-cranking an entire room, little though it was, up a couple of floors wasn't as strenuous as I would have thought. Some feat of engineering in its mechanics, I guess. It was hard to tell just how technologically advanced Hell was, alien as so much of it still was. Not as advanced as back home, though, I was noticing. That might have been more interesting if I hadn't had more pressing matters on my plate.

There was no number counter in here, no floor display to tell me what level I was on, but I could vaguely make out the discrepancies in the walls sliding by that marked more of those sliding panel doors. They weren't as hard to notice from this side as they'd been from the halls. I counted two floors passing by and stopped the crank, bringing the elevator to a rest just in front of the panel two levels above where I'd started. This was the floor I wanted. This or the one above it. I'd start here first. I slipped my fingers into the groove on the wall in front of me and started to haul the wall open.

I'd barely put any pressure on the panel, though, when it opened by itself and two more of the short goblin-looking demons stepped inside, pushing a big rolling basket between them. Caught off guard, I shrank back into the far corner of the room before they walked right into me. Before I could slip past and through the door, the trailing demon slid it closed. I bit down on a silent curse as the other went to the crank on the wall and started spinning it, quickly hauling us up the shaft.

"Damn tribute days," the one at the crank grumbled. "It's like the whole damn city shows up and expects to be waited on. I'm starving, but ya think those stuffed robes at the feast care? No."

"Didja see the new human?" the other asked, and I shrank further into my dark corner behind their rolling basket. "One of the Superbiate bigshots brought it in not long ago and gave it to the prince. I heard he brought it to dinner with the arches."

"Another human?" the one at the crank asked, still turning effortlessly and pulling us further and further up the palace. "Great, just what we need. One more ass to kiss. Well, we only got the one palace, so they're gonna have to share or something."

"Might not be a bigshot, this one," said the other. "I heard from one of the pink-skins that waited on the arches this new one seems lost and confused all the time. Not so intimidating as our prince."

"What, a weak human?" the cranking one asked, sounding as if he didn't quite believe his companion. "That'd be interesting. Like a pink-skin with its legs closed."

"Or a blue-brute without the stick up its ass," the other concurred. "Still, it got to feast with the arches, and it just got here. That seem fair to you?"

"Nothing's fair," the first one muttered, releasing the crank at last. The elevator slid to a smooth stop, flush with one of the wall panels, as the wheel slowed to a stop. "C'mon, I wanna be done with this in time to scrounge a meal together before they crack the whip again."

I waited until they'd slid the wall open and wheeled their giant basket out between them before I hurried back over to the crank. Unfortunately, as the first two pushed their load out of the way, I saw about a half dozen more of the goblin-y ones waiting to get on. No way I could squeeze in here with that many without bumping someone. With another silent curse, I hurried out into the hall after the rolling basket, just barely slipping by the group pressing in to replace them. The wall slid closed once more, invisibly flush from this end, and a very, very faint rumble signaled the elevator traveling on without me.

I was stranded somewhere way, way the hell above where I needed to be, and my ride had just disappeared without me. Fuck.

Rather than stand there and wait, hoping someone would bring the elevator back up to this level again, I decided to go look for another one, or maybe a straightforward staircase. What's the worst that could happen? I'd waste my time in aimless wandering? I was a damn pro at that already.

This floor was different from what I was used to, at least. The simple wall sconces were replaced by elegant, opulent chandeliers hanging from the vaulted ceiling at regular intervals, and every dozen feet or so along the walls — which curved much more severely this far up — was another column or plinth with a piece of art on top. Lifelike busts in creamy marble or that red-veined onyx stuff sported horned male and female heads with every variety of features and expressions. Intricately carved small statues, exquisitely detailed, of figures dancing or fighting or fornicating or relaxing, each one an entire scene, figures and background both, small but lifelike in three dimensions, some painted in a variety of vivid colors. Vases and bowls and elevated globes, gilded or bejeweled or gorgeously painted. It was like walking through a circular art gallery.

I stopped at the first door I came across, a heavy wooden portal of cherry red, the front carved with a scene of bowed, flowering trees growing up around a slender, horned woman in an elegant gown, a haughty smile on her lips. She looked familiar. More importantly, the door was cracked open, and I couldn't hear anybody on the other side. Pressing my eye to the opening, I peered through into a richly-carpeted room that looked otherwise empty from this angle.

This seemed like as good a place as any to look for clues as to where I'd ended up. With a deep breath, I risked pulling the door open a smidge more and slipping inside.

The room wasn't quite as empty as it had looked from the doorway, turns out. Most of the center of the floor was taken up by a large white cloth draped over the soft red carpet. At the far end of the draping, near the back wall, an artist's canvas as tall as I was stood with its back to me on a tripod easel. And across from it, on the edge of the cloth right beside the door I'd just entered through, was—

I froze, my breath catching in my throat, my heartbeat following suit. Standing beside me, arms crossed in a pose of defiance, was another human, a girl like me.

No, not like me. She *was* me, the spitting image, from her jet black bangs and bob cut to her rumpled black t-shirt to her heavy black boots. As I watched, stunned and mesmerized, the other me tossed her head and lifted her chin, smirking toward the far canvas, radiating smugness.

"No, no, no, you silly slut," said a lilting voice from the other side of the canvas. I tore my gaze from my doppelganger long enough to watch as a woman's face, blue and horned, peeked out from behind the easel, frowning. It was Sidona again. "I said defiant, not proud. No one's seen her smile once yet, what are you doing?"

The other me immediately frowned, her face tilting back down as she glared at the blue woman behind her canvas.

Sidona's eyes narrowed. "Better," she said. "But more vulnerability. A bit of confusion, too, like you don't really know what's going on but you know you don't like it."

"Defiant *and* vulnerable?" the other me asked, but not in my voice. Hers was huskier, more breathy. "How do I look defiant *and* vulnerable at the same time?"

"I don't know, but she does," Sidona said, ducking back around behind her canvas again. "You know. You saw her at dinner, waiting on the prince's table. Weren't you paying attention to her?"

"Not as much as you, my lady, clearly," said my clone, squaring her shoulders and tilting her head. "Archduke Melchius was busy distracting me. Like this?" She furrowed her brow, looking like she was still trying to hold her glare at the same time.

This was fucking weird, watching myself strike these poses, let me tell you. I drifted further into the room as I watched, drifting slowly around the front of my surprise twin, mesmerized by her uncanny existence.

"Oh, no, that's awful," I heard Sidona say. "I know you're trying, dear, but the face. It's just... all wrong. Hmm..." There was a long lull in the conversation, and somewhere in there, I distantly registered Sidona's soft gasp and the clatter of a paintbrush bouncing to the floor, but I still couldn't take my eyes off of myself. "Oh...well..." the duchess continued quietly after a while. "I suppose we can just ask the expert herself. What do you think, my lady?"

I was still studying my clone, so I didn't notice the new awkward pause until my doppelganger turned my way in frowning confusion, her gaze searching the space between us. My face likely mirrored her own for a moment before I turned around to the painter behind her canvas.

Sidona was staring directly, intently at me. As our eyes met, she smiled.

The blatant attention caught me by surprise. "Er, what?" I asked before I could stop myself. On the other side of me, my twin jumped with a small gasp, her eyes finally settling on me.

So much for stealth, then. And I'd been doing so well, too.

The blue demon noblewoman chuckled. "You're the best at looking like yourself, one assumes," she said, stepping out from behind her easel entirely. Her elegant dress from earlier had been replaced by a billowing, long-sleeved smock of creamy off-white that gathered under her breasts and hung in ruffles to her ankles, the neckline reaching near to her chin. Small splotches of paint, mostly black and dark gray, spattered the front of the outfit, and in one hand, she lightly held a long-handled brush dripping with a dollop of black paint, the way women in old-timey advertisements held those long cigarette sticks. "Care to model for my model so she can get the look right?" She tilted her head, still smiling at me. "Or, better yet, care to cut out the middlewoman and just model for me?"

I blinked, looking between her and the other me. "You're... painting me?" I asked, eloquence failing me. "How... why...?"

"Why?" the blue lady echoed. "Are you not worthy of being put to canvas, my dear? I've only had the pleasure of immortalizing one other human, you know. Not that he needs it, it seems. Still." She brought the end of her brush not covered in paint to her chin, tapping it against her bottom lip and spattering her smock still further. "Tell you what," she continued, her smile twisting into a smirk. "Help me with this, and I won't tell him you snuck away just to see me again. Sound fair?"

"Er… what?" I said again. Was that a threat?

"You do like that phrase, don't you?" Sidona answered, still tapping her chin. "I'm asking if you'd do me the courtesy of helping with my art, Lady Morgan. Or if you'd prefer, if you're too busy, I can summon someone to see you back to his majesty's suite. Which is where I assume you were before you came here."

Yeah, I think that was a threat. "No," I said with a scowl, "that, uh, won't be necessary. I can just… stand here and look like myself for a while, I guess."

The blue woman grinned widely, pointing at me with the bottom tip of her brush. "That's the look exactly," she said, then waggled the brush tip at the other me. "You're free to go, dear. Thank you for your time and effort."

The other me looked from me to the noblewoman and bowed her head, her hair obscuring her face as she did so. But when she straightened again and opened her eyes, they weren't my eyes — they were ruby red, bright and vibrant without pupils, like opaque gemstones set into her eye sockets.

I blinked hard, shocked once more; and when I opened my eyes, she wasn't me anymore. Her face, which had been my face, was rounder now, her skin suddenly hot pink. Where my straight, chin-length black hair had been a moment before were now wavy, reddish-purple locks hanging to her shoulders, with pointed pink ears sprouting through and, above those, squat bone-colored horns curving slightly back from her temples. My black t-shirt was replaced with a lacy forest green blouse, open at the top and bottom to expose her taught pink stomach and much more cleavage than I've ever had. My black leather pants had vanished, leaving her bare from her blouse down but for a lacy g-string of the same deep green. And in place of my heavy boots, she was now in a pair of stiletto heels that I would never have been able to walk in.

Wait, no. Not heels. She was barefoot — those were just three-inch bone spikes jutting out of her feet. Jeez, that poor woman.

By the time I realized I was looking at another one of the sexy pink lady demons I'd been seeing around the place, she was already sweeping past me, now nearly half a head taller than me. Her gemstone eyes cast a curious glance at me sidelong as she passed, heel bones clicking as she reached the doorway and stepped off the plush carpet. How in the shit did someone like her look like someone like me just a moment earlier?

"I'll call on you again for touch-ups," Sidona called after her. The pink lady nodded as she pulled the door closed, leaving me alone in the room with the noblewoman, who stepped back behind her canvas but craned sideways to peer around it at me. "Thank you for your help, Lady Morgan," she said, smiling again. "Shall we make some art?"

Chapter 8: Dishonesty

If you'd asked me before all this craziness started if I'd ever consider being a model, I would have laughed. But here I was, standing and posing in a palace art salon, having my portrait made by a noblewoman. Who was also a horned blue demon pushing seven feet tall, but still.

It was easy enough so far, if still bizarre. After I'd taken the pink woman's place, Sidona went to work without any instruction for me, so I just stood there glancing around the mostly empty room and listening to the tiny rustle of her brush moving across the other side of the canvas. Simple enough. So long as she didn't want me getting naked or anything, I guess I didn't mind.

"I'm not getting naked," I said. That seemed like an important sentiment to share, now that I'd thought of it.

"Of course you're not," she said without looking around her easel. "You're more interesting clothed anyway, I'm sure."

I wasn't sure how I felt about that.

Easy as this was, it was still a major detour from my original plan. I don't know how successful I'd actually expected to be, sneaking out of such an enormous palace, the layout of which I didn't know, with magic I'd never done before; but I didn't expect to fail *this* badly. Maybe I could put the spell back on when Sidona was looking away and sneak out once more, find my way back downstairs and try again. She'd be able to tell anyone who came asking that I'd been here, but maybe that could serve as a decoy, lead anybody who was looking for me up the palace in the wrong direction. Assuming I actually found my way to the ground floor this time.

And also assuming, come to think of it, that the stealth spell worked on Sidona at all. She'd seen through the first one, though it seemed to take her a minute. Was that because I'd dropped my concentration in my surprise at seeing another myself? But my pink doppelganger hadn't seen me at first until I'd spoken up. Maybe the blue lady had some sort of demon magic that saw through my own. Or maybe it was just because she'd been actively looking for me already, what with her portrait and that model mimic.

I didn't want to ask her about it; questioning aloud how she saw through my hiding and sneaking spell meant admitting that I'd been trying to hide and sneak. I still had a vague hope that I could weasel out of that accusation if I played my hand right. Instead, I asked, "How did that pink girl manage to look exactly like me just now?"

"She didn't," Sidona answered, peering around her easel. She held out a manicured thumb and squinted past it at me, then disappeared again. "If she had, I wouldn't have needed the real thing. Not for a while, anyway. The art would have demanded authenticity eventually."

"Well, she looked pretty damn close," I said. "How?"

"She's a Luxuriate," the painter said.

When no further explanation seemed forthcoming, I asked, "What's a Luxuriate?"

"His majesty still has yet to explain anything to you, hasn't he?" She glanced around the easel again, smiling her haughty smile. "You've noticed the distinct races amongst the general populace by now, I assume. Turn your face to the side a smidge, please." She waited until I'd complied, then nodded and ducked back out of sight. "If nothing else, your dining companions should have served as a basic primer. Luxuriates are the lavender-esque individuals with the vibrant eyes and lusty dispositions. Archduke Melchius is the current leader of House Luxuria, as well as one of its more incorrigible members."

Well, at least I had a name for them now. I was starting to wonder if calling them 'the pink and purple ones' was racist or not. "So, then, are you saying all Luxuriates are chameleons?"

"Are what?" Sidona asked, peering around at me again.

Right. Chameleons were probably too tame to live in a place like this. "Uh, like shape-changers," I explained. "Can they all look like different people?"

"I suppose that's an easy way of thinking of it," she said, going back to her painting as she spoke. "They're not really changing shape so much as others' perceptions of them, of course, and the range of their glamour potential depends on the individual. But yes, in a broad sense, every Luxuriate has the ability, to an extent."

"Weird…" I muttered, only realizing a moment later I'd said it aloud.

"Is it?" Sidona asked. "Perhaps to an otherworlder, it is. Interesting…"

"So, uh, what are you, then?" I asked. "What's your, uh, race called?"

She peered around her easel at me again, tapping her brush against her chin with narrowed eyes. "That is a rather strange question to be asked, I must say," she said. "I wonder, strictly speaking, if it's within proper manners."

"Isn't it?" I asked, shrugging. "Sorry. I wouldn't know."

Her brush handle stilled against her chin, eyes narrowing further. "Interesting…" she said again, mostly to herself, then ducked away once more. "Earth has no Superbiates, does it?"

"Earth has no giant blue people that I know of, no," I said. "Superbiates?"

"The superior Sin," she said, and I could hear the haughty smile she wore as she spoke even if I couldn't see it. "Greatest and most esteemed of the seven houses. Archduke Abdeles, that rather stern fellow seated across from you, currently heads Superbia."

"So, he's like your boss, and the prince is his boss?" I asked. It was nice to finally get some answers for a change. It was also weird to think that Hell had middle managers.

Sidona's unseen laugh cast doubt on the understanding I thought I was piecing together, though. "Does Abdeles command us, you ask?" she said, peeking around with a grin. "My dear, *nobody* orders a Superbiate to do anything. Might as well try to domesticate a nuckelavee." Her grin fell then into more of a wan smile. "Well, nobody but Prince Vambrace, I suppose, but the man has tact. All of Dis is beholden to the Archfiend, so long as he or she remains worthy of the station. And dear Vambrace has been Archfiend for several lifetimes, so he must be doing something right."

Her explanation raised so many new questions, but the one I found myself asking first was, "He or she? Hell has been ruled by women before?"

"Now and then throughout recorded history, yes," Sidona answered, back to work and out of sight again. "Why? Is that another oddity for an Earth human?"

"Just, uh, unexpected," I said, wondering what my parents' old preacher friend and the theology professors at my college would say if they knew. "I'd always thought Hell just had the one guy in charge forever and ever."

"Getting to be that way," she muttered, "but we used to have more turnover, back in the old days. From the history I've read, it was a more chaotic time, new Archfiends usurping old ones every couple centuries or so. Having a human in charge has been wonderfully stabilizing, it seems. Power of the Original Sin, I suppose."

I was about to ask about that next before I remembered the prince's panicked look at dinner when the topic had come up, his rushed explanation and pointed gaze. Not the safest conversation, it seemed, though I didn't know why not yet. Instead, mouth already opened as the question died on my tongue, I asked another instead. "So, Superbiates... Can you change what you look like too, or is that just a pink thing? Uh, a Luxuriate thing?"

"It's a pink Luxuriate thing," she answered. "Purple ones too, of course. Color and shade don't have any bearing, at least to currently understood science. Their glamour is their racial talent, I suppose you could say. The power of their Sin made manifest. Naturally, each house has its own distinct skill."

"And what's yours?" I pressed.

She leaned out again with a smirk. "My Lady Morgan," she said slowly, "if you haven't experienced a Superbiate's power yet, I'm certainly not going to be the one to demonstrate it. Be grateful for that."

Between her veiled threats, her general politeness otherwise, and her consistent stuck-upitude, I still didn't know if I liked this one or not. I let the conversation lapse after that.

Sidona, for her part, seemed content to paint me in silence but for her occasional "Shoulders back" or "Turn your head" or "No, the other way, please." I complied and stood and waited for her to be done with me, wondering all the while what was bound to happen next. By now, someone had to know I was missing, Enkida or the prince or both. Would there be guards looking for me to drag me back? Did this count as breaking the law? Was I on my way to a dungeon somewhere if I didn't sneak out first? The thought that I had just thrown away the only tenuous advantage that I had, the apparent goodwill of the prince, in this gamble was almost as concerning as the thought that I'd be stuck here forever as an idle curiosity if I hadn't tried to do something.

I was still lost in thought, Sidona still working quietly away, when there was a knock at the door. "What?" Sidona called testily, not taking her attention from her work.

The door opened a crack to admit a red demon who leaned through the doorway. "Apologies, Duchess," he said, not sounding at all apologetic. "But his majesty wishes to know if you've seen —" He stopped as his gaze swept the room and landed on me, standing idly in my pose with my arms crossed and my hip cocked, watching him with the same look that Sidona had bid me hold for the past ten minutes. Vulnerable defiance, she'd called it. " — the human woman," the guard finished, setting his jaw. Like he was grinding his teeth. Like finding me was irritating.

"I have, in fact," the blue duchess answered, looking around her easel at last and smiling at the guard. "Fascinating specimen, is she not? It's not every day that one gets the chance to capture a human female in image. A genuine one, at least, not those guesswork copies House Luxuria provides."

The guard turned his annoyed glare on Sidona. "You realize she's missing from his majesty's private chambers, right?" he practically snarled.

"Of course, I realize," she sneered back. "Where do you think I found her, fool?"

The guard's confusion mirrored my own. Thankfully, he wasn't looking my way to see it. "*You* stole her from his majesty's rooms, Duchess?"

"Like she's a sack of souls I snuck in and swiped?" Sidona asked back, contempt dripping from her scowl as she walked fully around her canvas, standing at her full imposing height. "Bite your disrespectful tongue, growler. I stopped by to ask her to accompany me here to my salon and model for my art. She graciously obliged. I am allowed in his majesty's suite at my discretion, last I heard, and nobody informed either of us that the Lady Morgan was to be a prisoner rather than a distinguished guest. You contest either claim?"

The red demon seemed to shrivel under Sidona's ire, his angry scowl replaced by a look very near to guilt. "Of course not, my lady," he muttered quickly, then ducked into a deep bow, attention directed at his own feet. "Apologies, my lady. I meant no disrespect, my lady."

"I should certainly hope not," Sidona said, advancing on the guard. With every step she took, his bow bent lower, until the black horns curving in front of his forehead nearly scraped the floor. "Now, if his majesty has requested her return, I shan't go against his wishes. Keep a civil tongue in your head and your snarling to yourself, and I'll allow you to escort her back to our prince. Am I understood?"

"Yes, my lady," the guard said to the ground. "Of course, my lady."

"Good." She spun on her heel to face me then, and for a brief moment, I felt the sudden urge to drop to my knees and grovel as well, contrite for some slight I hadn't known I'd given. But before I could act on the impulse, she smiled politely at me, and it passed. "I suppose you'd better get going then, my dear," she said as I blinked away the strange feeling of contrition and inferiority. "Thank you again for indulging me. I'll call on you again to continue our work when your time is not as in demand, yes?"

"Uh… yeah," I mumbled, then bowed my head slightly to her. Not because I felt compelled to this time, just because it seemed like what people did around here. And because her lie was useful to me, whether or not it was really for my benefit. "Thanks." I turned to the guard, still bent double.

Sidona turned to him too, scowl returning. "Get up, fool," she barked, and he straightened so quickly I thought I could hear his spine crack. "Take the lady where she needs to be and tell his majesty what I told you. And the next time you come to interrupt my work, leave your growling behind."

"Yes, my lady. Sorry, my lady." He turned to me with that same guilty look — a definite first for the red demons I'd seen so far, all of which looked irritated at best and pissed off at worst. "This way, please, my lady."

That last "my lady" was directed at me. I followed the guard out into the hall, tossing a parting glance at the duchess over my shoulder as I went. She was still smiling politely my way when the guard pulled the door closed behind us and started leading me down the posh, curving hallway, his eyes staring fervently ahead of him as if he was afraid to risk causing more offense unless he concentrated fully on his task.

We were standing in front of another elevator, this one not hidden like the one the little bug-eyed demons had used, when my escort finally snapped out of it, pausing with his hand on the sliding wooden door and staring blankly into the waiting room. The annoyed scowl I was used to seeing on his type returned, and he bared his fanged teeth in anger.

"Fucking blue-bitch," he growled, stepping into the elevator. He gestured me in after him, but kept his scowl averted from me while we rode it down. Whatever Sidona had done to him, either it hadn't worn off entirely or else she intimidated him enough without it that he didn't want to go back on his word.

Was that the Superbiates' power, the one she'd said I should be grateful she wasn't using on me? It was… troubling to think about, if so.

Honestly, I'd half expected crazy magic shit from the demons around me ever since I'd used crazy magic shit to land here. But I hadn't expected weird mutant powers from each one. And the best I could do was escape notice for a while if I slunk around like a rat, or start small fires if I sat and thought about it long enough. What the hell kind of hope did I have against shapeshifting and mind control and who knew what else?

Come to that, what the hell kind of hope did the prince have? Besides a weirdly long lifespan and a neat sword, however good he was with it, what did he have that thousands of magical demons didn't? Why the devil was *he* the Devil instead of one of these crazy people I kept running into?

I couldn't talk to the guard leading me back about any of this, obviously. Even if I'd thought it a good idea, he didn't seem in a mood to listen, much less join in a conversation. I thought about asking after his own race, what they were called and what they did, just to see if he'd tell me to shut me up again. But no, the fewer people I came off to as uninformed and confused, the better. I followed in silence, ignoring the glances I got on the way, well past used to them already. No chance to go invisible again now with all that scrutiny. No point wasting Sidona's lie on another fumbling escape attempt just yet, either.

I recognized where I was again only once we passed the two sentries still standing watch outside the open doors of the prince's private suite, each one glaring at me with bared teeth. Blaming me for getting past them somehow and showing up their efforts at standing watch, most likely. I glared back for a moment before pointedly looking beyond them down the hall, lifting my chin in what I hoped was a haughty, "I don't give a shit what you think" look like what the blue ones — like what the Superbiates kept putting on. They didn't say anything.

We reached the sitting room I'd snuck out of and opened the door to find Prince Vambrace pacing the floor. He spun on us as we entered, my denim jacket that he still wore swirling with the motion. No longer blank and stoic, the look on his face was equal parts panic, relief, and anger as he looked between us, taking a single step forward before stopping himself, hands lifted at his side as if he meant to grab one of us. He turned the motion into an imperious crossing of his arms a moment later, letting loose a deep breath before turning his glare on the guard. "Report," he commanded.

The red demon clapped a fist to his breast. "Sire," he said, "the lady was with Duchess Sidona in her tower salon. The duchess says it was she who escorted the lady away from your rooms, that she was unaware the human girl wasn't supposed to leave."

"Sidona," said the prince, turning to look up at the massive portrait of himself hanging over the fireplace. One of the Superbiate noblewoman's paintings most likely, I realized. Was I getting the same treatment on that unseen canvas of hers? Damn.

No one was saying anything, so I figured I'd better. "Uh," I said, always a good start. The prince turned to look at me, so I continued. "Right, so… sorry if I, uh, worried anyone. I figured it'd be alright if I helped her out. Figured you'd know. Uh…"

His eyes narrowed as he looked at me, but I couldn't tell if it was anger or suspicion or something else. A moment later, he turned to the guard. "Thank you," he said, waving dismissively at the door. "Leave us. Find

General Enkida and tell her to call off the search, put everyone back on their previous assignments."

The guard bowed, but nowhere near as severely as he'd bowed to Sidona. "Sire," he said, then turned and strode from the room, casting his glare at me as he went before pulling the door shut.

That was Vambrace's cue. "I remember saying that I would be along shortly," he said, voice clipped and curt as he spun on me. "What part of that statement made it seem like a good idea to leave and go model for a portrait in the upper reaches of the palace? Even if Sidona did not know my will, you did."

I actually backstepped under the force of that curtness. No one had talked to me like this since I was a little girl being scolded by my parents. "Well, no, not really I didn't," I said with a scowl. I was trying to still be polite, trying to remember that I was talking to the closest thing to Satan I was hopefully ever going to meet. But I was also still not used to addressing people this apparently important, or being talked to like a disobedient child, and everyone's shitty attitudes were getting to me. "And I didn't know exactly what she wanted, either, not until I got to her room. But I figured if she was allowed in here, it was alright to do what she asked, right?"

"Perhaps it would have been," he said, taking a step toward me. I resisted the urge to take another step back, standing my ground. He wasn't that much taller than me; compared to some of the other demons that had been trying to intimidate me lately, he should have been nothing but for his title. "But you knew I would be back soon and expected you to be here. Whether or not you knew fully what I wanted, you knew that much. You should have waited."

I took a deep breath, steadying my slowly fraying nerves and fighting against the fear that I was pushing my luck too far. "With all due respect, sire," I said, trying not to sound sarcastic and unsure how successful I was at it, "ordering me to your bedroom to wait for your arrival without telling me why wasn't exactly a good way to make me feel at ease. At least I had an idea what Duchess Sidona's intentions were."

"What her—" His hands rose again, then fell. I did flinch back then, worried he might make a grab for me, but he only stared with something like stunned bafflement. "You would—" He clamped his mouth shut against his stammering, whole body going so tense it practically vibrated. Then he spun again, striding to the desk against the wall. A pile of books was stacked on top, one of which he grabbed before spinning back around and holding it up. "I was procuring books writ in English," he said testily. "You had asked for as much, had you not?"

That threw me off. "You... oh," I said with a frown, deflating. "Uh, yeah. I didn't... I mean, uh, thanks."

He looked like he didn't know what to feel, which made two of us. When he walked back over to me and held out the book, I awkwardly took it. It was old, older than any other book I'd ever seen besides the *Morganomicon*, its heavy cover smelling of must and dust. "I don't think this explains your readiness to defy a clear command," he said, not sounding as angry as he had a moment before.

I kept my eyes on the cover of the book rather than look up at him. It was a dark, desaturated red, the dust having been ground into the material until it was a part of the color. Other than the strange old runes dully embossed on the front, the cover was otherwise blank. Rather than a regular spine, though, the whole thing was held together by what looked like leather thongs threaded through down the left side. I worried about opening it lest I damage it, old as it was. I was also worried that whatever was inside would hold no interest for me after the prince had gone to the trouble of bringing it to me.

It took me a second to realize he was expecting an answer from me still. "Oh," I said, looking at him finally. "Well, like I said, you sent me to your room. I thought you were making moves on me."

"Making moves?" he repeated, raising one eyebrow.

Right, he was too old for slang, wasn't he? "I thought you were propositioning me," I explained with a polite, awkward smile. "You know. For sex."

His eyebrow stayed up. "And... you were perturbed by this prospect?" he asked, sounding as if he were trying to grasp a foreign concept.

"Uh... yeah," I said after a pause. "Yeah, I was."

Another pause. "Why?" he asked.

Good lord, was he that arrogant? Yeah, probably, I realized. "Because… I don't want to have sex with you?" I said. "No offense. Uh, your highness."

In the silence that followed, his brow slowly went from lifted to furrowed, his gaze from me to the floor as if deep in contemplation, and I wondered if I'd just made him reevaluate his own self-image. That's the only way I could interpret his expression — that no one had ever rejected him before, and the very idea was alien to him.

"Thanks for the book, though," I said once the quiet grew too uncomfortable.

That brought him back from wherever he'd gone. "Yes," he said, then cleared his throat and adjusted the collar on his jacket. My jacket. "You're quite welcome." Then his authority followed him back and slipped over him once more, and he held a finger out at me. "But do not wander off on your own again," he added sternly. "That is an order."

"Yeah, sure," I said. "I mean, uh, yes, your highness," I added, standing straighter and holding the book to my chest.

"I mean it," he said, finger still up and pointed at me. "It is not just my will being obeyed at stake in the matter, my lady. For your own safety, limit your interaction with my subjects when I am not present."

"No talking to demons," I said, still making a conscious effort at good posture. "Got it."

"Good," he said, then turned away toward the pile of books on the desk again.

"Why not?" I asked his back.

He stopped midway to the desk and turned back to me. "Pardon?"

"Why not?" I repeated. "Why shouldn't I talk to the demons around here? I mean, from what I've seen so far, everyone but me and you is a demon, so… I mean, that kind of limits my options, doesn't it?"

He turned fully back to me, that thoughtful look on his face once more. "My reasons are… complicated," he said slowly. "But you are correct. The human population in Dis is only we two, and before your arrival, just myself. This is part of the issue." His eyes turned then to the closed doors as he stroked his chin, as if he could gaze through the walls at the mass of inhuman subjects filling his palace. "My people are not used to dealing with our species, but they are familiar with their prince. Your presence raises new questions and curiosities. I would decide the impact I wish this to have on them before exposing them overmuch to you."

"Oh," I said, shoulders slumping. Some familiar but uncomfortable feeling was growing inside me at his words. "So, you're saying I'm weird, then," I continued, tone flat. "I stand out, and you're trying to figure out how to make me fit in easier."

"Essentially, yes," said the prince. "I have kept the same style of order in this realm for ages. You could disrupt that if I am not careful. So, I will be careful for now. Swear to me that you will be as well."

I took a deep breath, fighting down the same reaction I've fought down since childhood. This guy wasn't even from my world, not really, I reminded myself. Whatever Earth dumped him here, however long ago that was, it wasn't the one I came from. Standing in the palace of Hell, I was about as far removed from my normal life as I could conceivably get.

But not removed enough, it turned out. And apparently some types of bullshit spanned dimensions and followed me even here.

Looking at Prince Vambrace, I put on my most polite customer service smile. "I promise," I lied. Suddenly, I felt more at home here than ever.

Chapter 9: Annoyance

It was a stupid, probably childish reaction, I know. The prince of Hell basically called me a weirdo, and I got all quietly sulky and annoyed about it. Of course he was right, given the circumstances — I was one of just two humans in this entire world, and the only girl one, so of course I was gonna stand out and invite curiosity and stares from the locals. My rational brain realized this long before he came out and said it there in his chamber.

But still. I was the only other person of his species that this guy had seen in who knows how long, this guy surrounded by giant horned people and little bug people and all manner of crazy CGI shit come to life, and yet *I* was the oddity? It made sense to the demons I'd run into, but this guy?

Fuck this guy.

Yeah, like I said. Childish and stupid. But at the moment, I didn't care. Human or not, and even if he wasn't trying to get in my pants after all, at that point in time, I didn't want anything to do with Prince Vambrace, and I didn't give a solitary shit about his orders.

So when he asked me if I had any more questions for him, I flashed a quick smile and opened the English book he'd handed me. "Not right now, thanks," I said, then turned to the first page and made a show of reading it.

And it was just a show, because I couldn't understand a thing I was looking at. This wasn't English; this wasn't even the right alphabet. This was a gibberish of weird symbols and runes that looked more like chicken scratches than letters.

Standing by the rest of the books he'd gathered atop his desk, Vambrace placed a hand on the topmost cover and said, "Look through these and take what you will. I only ask again that you treat them carefully."

"Sure thing," I said, turning my fake smile back on but not looking up from the book written in English-that-wasn't-English. "Thanks again."

He stepped away from the desk, still looking at me. "You are sure you have no further questions you would like answered?" he asked. He almost sounded disappointed.

"No, not right now," I repeated. It was a lie, obviously, but I was slowly concocting another plan. As much as I still didn't know, as much as I still wanted to understand, I had other ideas on how I was going to figure it out. Ideas that didn't involve relying entirely on what this arrogant bastard deigned to let me know. A moment later, I finally looked up at him. "I'm actually pretty tired from all that's happened," I said, and that one wasn't a lie. "Mind if I go back to my room and lie down for a while?"

For a moment, he looked like he would argue or flat-out refuse. But then he forced a smile that looked every bit as false as my own. "Of course, Lady Morgan," he said. "You must be overwhelmed. We will speak at length anon. There will be plenty of time."

Not if I can help it, I thought as I stepped up beside him and perused the books on offer. Every one of them was written in the same chicken-scratch alphabet as the first one he'd handed me, so I grabbed a couple of the smaller ones that looked least likely to fall apart at a strong breeze. Didn't want to look ungrateful, after all, even if they were pretty much useless to me.

No music, no TV, no reading material, and now I wasn't allowed to talk to people. What the hell did he expect me to do with myself while I sat and waited on his regal whims?

The prince glanced briefly at my selections and frowned as if he disapproved of my taste in reading. If only he knew what I'd *really* been reading before this. "Follow me, my lady," he said, then turned and swept from the room with me in tow, scowling at his back the whole walk back to my chambers.

Rezavix was still standing guard outside my door, still wearing those spiky glove things and scowling at the opposite wall. As we approached, he uncrossed his arms and clapped a fist over his chest, bowing his head to the prince, who stopped outside my door and turned back to me a moment after I'd put my own scowl away. "Rest as long as you need to," he said to me. "I will summon you after a while, once I have finished with other business."

"Will do," I said, then bowed my head like I'd just watched the red demon do. "Thank you, your highness."

The prince nodded to me, then turned and nodded at Rezavix, then strode off down the corridor. I watched until the faint gleam of the naked sword on his back disappeared around the slight curve of the hallway, then reached for the door.

"Where were you?" Rezavix asked, stepping between me and the door. Not enough to block me, but enough I took a surprised step back.

"Where do you think?" I asked with a scowl. I was so not in the mood for any more of this intimidation bullshit, to the point where even this spiky, muscley monster man was getting more irritating than scary.

"I think I saw you being led down this hall toward his majesty's rooms," he said, returning my scowl. "And then I think I saw you being led in the same direction later without ever having been led out first. That doesn't make sense to me." He raised his brows, his scowl turning curious. "How did you do that?"

I couldn't safely answer that even if I wanted to, so instead I lifted my chin and looked up at him along the bridge of my nose. "To be honest," I said, then leaned toward him — and to my petty satisfaction, he leaned back away from me. "That is none of your damn business." I opened the door and brushed past him into my room.

"It is my business!" he called after me, not quite a shout but pretty close. "I have been charged with watching over you, and I will not be—"

"Goodnight, Revavez," I said, spinning on my heel. With the same motion, I closed the door in his fuming face.

"Rezavix!" he shouted through the closed door, and I admit, for a moment, I worried he'd break it down and storm in after me. When he didn't — when instead I heard him growl to himself outside my room before falling silent again — I smiled. Whether this assertive act really worked that well against him and the other angry red types, or whether it was just Prince Vambrace's orders keeping him from actually acting on his anger, it seemed I was safe from his impotent rage. So far, anyway.

I dropped my old gibberish books on top of the desk here in my borrowed room, then pulled off my boots and climbed into the massive bed, this time getting underneath the shimmering satin blankets. I really was near exhausted; but for that brief, impromptu nap I'd taken here earlier, I'd been running off a mix of adrenaline, fear, and momentum since waking up in Dramoc's shop. I needed proper energy for what I had planned next, and I needed to buy some time before attempting it.

And holy shit, this bed was comfortable. I sank slightly into the incredibly soft mattress, the sheets silky smooth as I pulled them up to my chin, thin but warm. Nothing but the best for a palace, I guess. Despite everything going through my head, I was asleep in minutes.

When I awoke, the light was the same, the candles in the chandelier overhead shorter but still burning steadily. Without a watch or a clock or windows looking outside, it was hard to tell how long I'd been out. I took a deep breath, wiped the grogginess from my eyes, and swung my legs out of bed. Normally, I'm slow to wake up unless there's an alarm prodding me, and mustering the will to climb out of this awesome bed was even harder than getting off my secondhand futon back home. But I had a plan, sort of, and getting down to it and getting out of here was enough to motivate me through my morning laziness. If it was even morning.

Before I did anything else, I went to my bedroom door and wrenched it open. My ever-present guard was still standing there, though he turned with a start as the door swung in away from him, spiked fists half-lifted in reflex before he caught himself.

"Rezizaf," I said in my airiest voice.

His lips pulled back in a silent snarl, showing sharp fangs from his canines back to where his molars should have been. "Rezavix!" he growled, crossing his arms so forcefully he nearly stabbed himself through the biceps. "My name is Rezavix, woman!"

"Right, whatever." I knew what his name was by this point, but if it bothered him this much, I was prepared to keep up the habit. I needed him off his game for this bit. "That's not important. I need to see Duchess Sidona."

His snarl turned to a sneer. "You jest," he said.

"I do not," I answered, trying to conjure the arrogant outrage I'd seen the Superbiate duchess muster earlier. "And how dare you imply such!" I glared down my nose at him, crossed my own arms, and took a step forward, sending him backstepping once again. "The duchess and I have prearranged business. Would you keep us both waiting?"

"I can't let you leave, and you know it!" he argued, voice rising again. But was that doubt I heard creeping in?

I hoped so and pressed on. "Then bring her to me," I commanded. "Tell her the Lady Morgan is ready to continue with what we discussed in her salon."

He blinked at me, scowl slowly slipping away, eyes narrowing. "You lie," he said, quieter than before. "How would you know Sidona so soon after arriving?"

I bristled. "Excuse me?" I said, feigning outrage and taking another step toward him. He didn't back off this time, but he did look uncomfortable. "You dare, Rexaziz? You know so much about recent events by standing here outside my door that you're calling me and the duchess both liars?"

He didn't say anything, even to correct me on his name, just glared and stood ramrod straight.

I took that as a good sign. "Go talk to Sidona if you don't believe me, then," I said, chin still haughtily lifted. My neck was beginning to get a little sore, actually, but I kept it up. "See if she can't vouch for me, if you're so sure in your assessment of us both."

"I can't leave you unattended!" he growled, though quietly this time. "His majesty has ordered—"

"Then find someone else who can," I said slowly. "Send someone else to inform her, if you're so scared that I'll run away and embarrass you. I don't care. Just do it." And without waiting for his next reply, I stepped back into the room and slammed the door on him.

I waited just on the other side of the door, holding my breath, listening. Again, I heard his low, angry growling. There was silence for about a minute after that; and then, miraculously, I heard the sounds of his booted footsteps hurrying off down the hall.

As they faded away, I stepped back to the far wall and finally let out the breath I'd been holding. It had worked, somehow. *I should have been a drama major*, I thought. *Or an heiress.*

While I waited for my little tantrum to bear fruit, I slipped my boots back on and headed into the attached bathroom to wash my face and get my hair under control. My clothes were getting grungier by the hour — it was nearly to the point where I would have been willing to eat a whole bowl of nuckelavee pudding for a clean t-shirt or a chance to do my laundry. Since neither opportunity seemed forthcoming still, I settled for just peeling off my outfit and shaking out each piece, trying to work some of the stiffness from the fabric. The duchess hadn't seemed offended by my appearance when she was painting me, so I didn't think I'd need to worry about any social faux pas now.

Once I was finished in the bathroom, I went back to the hallway door and opened it. Rezavix was already back at his post, and the look he flashed me dripped with annoyance. "I had word sent to Sidona," he grumbled. "We'll see what comes of it."

"Good boy," I said, then shut the door again and listened to him growl to himself some more.

Considering the distance that had to be crossed from my room to the duchess's tower chamber and how long it took me to bumble my way up there, I wasn't kept waiting all that long. I was leafing through the books I'd taken from Prince Vambrace's selection, looking for pictures that might tell me what they were about since I couldn't read the words, when I heard a now-familiar voice just out in the corridor say, "You are Lady Morgan's doorman, then?"

If Rezavix made a reply beyond frustrated grumbling, I didn't catch it as the door swung open and the seven-foot artist stepped inside, her horns barely clearing the archway. She'd changed out of her painter's smock into some elaborate, gilt-edged gown of pale crimson that exposed her bellybutton through a diamond-cut window and, at the top, sported about a full foot of stiffened collar. Like some sort of sorceress out of a fantasy game.

Looking me up and down in a way that made me second guess the appropriateness of my outfit after all, she flashed a supercilious smile. "And here we are again," she said.

Rezavix was looking in at us through the open doorway. Before I said anything, I strode over and closed it on him again, then backed as far away from it as I could while still staying within polite conversational range with Sidona. "Thank you for coming, my lady," I said, then bowed low at the waist for good measure. I wanted Rezavix annoyed at me for this plan, but Sidona I needed on my side, so I wasn't gonna pull any punches.

"Well, I didn't have much choice, did I?" she said with a light chuckle. "I was *summoned*, after all. And as no one but his majesty summons me, I figured this must be a matter of utmost import."

"Please forgive me if I seem presumptuous," I said, rising. "But it's a matter important to me, yes."

"Finishing our earlier business?" she asked. "Correct me if I'm wrong, my dear, but I don't think you're available to come back to my salon anytime soon, and I'm not having that massive canvas hauled all the way down here."

"I know," I said, glancing at the doorway, then back at the duchess. With an urgent look, I nodded behind me at the far end of the room and began backing toward the wall. With an arched brow and pursed lips, the duchess followed my retreat until we stopped near the bookcase by the bathroom door. "I actually have a different favor I need to ask, my lady," I said quietly then.

"Clearly," was all she said, watching expectantly.

I took a deep breath, hoped one last time that I was choosing a decent ally, and took the plunge. "I need to go into the city," I said in as low a voice as I could while still being audible.

Her pursed lips turned down into a pursed frown. "Prince Vambrace has ordered that you remain here, has he not?"

"He did," I admitted. "That's why I need help."

She tilted her head, staring at me in that way she had back behind her canvas, looking at me more as a curious puzzle than a person. "I can't take you out of here," she said. "I drew enough suspect attention claiming responsibility for your first disappearance. Interesting though you may be, I'll not be damned on your account, dear."

Interesting choice of words, I thought. "I know," I said. "I'm not asking you to, I hope. At the least, I just need directions. I think I can manage the rest on my own after that."

"Directions out of the palace from here?"

I nodded. "And then to the merchant district. There's something I brought with me when I came here from my world. Something I lost along the way. Something I need to get back."

The more I talked, the further her air of superiority seemed to slip from her expression as she regarded me, the stuck-up quirk to her eyes and lips disappearing. "And have you tried simply asking his majesty for help in retrieving it?" she asked. "Instead, your first course of action seems to be to circumvent him entirely."

"Prince Vambrace," I said, trying to keep the disdain from my own face and voice as I spoke, "has not yet decided what he wants to do with me, he says. So I am doing for myself in the meantime."

She smiled again at that, but not haughtily. More like she was enjoying herself. "Why should I not simply take news of this plot you're forming to his majesty?" she asked. "It would clear me from whatever minor displeasure he holds against me for taking your blame."

"Or it would make you look more suspect, saying you took me away one minute and then accusing me of sneaking off the next," I said. "And then whatever help or favor I might have given otherwise, I'd be disinclined to share after that. You'd have to finish your painting with those pink girls instead of the real subject."

"Luxuriates," she chided, "not 'those pink girls.' Let's not be crass."

I wanted to point out I'd first walked in on her calling her former model a slut, which seemed ruder than 'pink girl,' but decided against it for the moment.

"But I see your point," she continued after a moment, eyes narrowing as she stroked her chin. "So, you just want direction around Pandemonium and the immediate city? I could provide that easily enough. There is no sedition in providing information, near as I know. But..." She froze, and again the smile came out. "Why would I? What do I gain from it?"

I'd figured she'd be like that. And if she had asked a half hour or so ago, I wouldn't have had an answer for her. But one nice thing about being left to wait so much lately was that I had plenty of time to think and scheme.

"You're an artist, my lady" I said. "Are you a poet, too? A songwriter?"

Both her brows rose at that. Whatever she'd been expecting from me, I don't think this was it. "Naturally," she said, quickly recomposing her expression. "I am a Superbiate, dear lady; without us, without our genius, there would be no art, no beauty or culture to be had in Hell but for the primal yawping and rutting of six inferior, barbaric races scraping at the dirt and rolling in the mud. And I am a duchess at that, with the Archfiend himself as a regular patron. I could have been Archduchess over the entirety of House Superbia if I had been of a mind, but I chose to rise above base politics and dedicate myself entirely to my art in all forms, to better all of demonkind rather than merely my own people. You ask if I am a poet as well as a painter? I am, and a singer, a writer, a lyricist, historian, playwright, designer, storyteller, and more, much more. I am the celebrated Duchess Sidona, the jewel of House Superbia, and my talents will not be confined by limits or labels."

Sweet Jesus, and she called *me* crass? Listening to her monologue about herself, I half expected to see the sun come shining out of her backside. "Are you familiar, then, with the poems and songs of Earth?" I asked once I was sure she was finished patting her own back.

She didn't answer immediately, instead looking at me as if I'd presented her with a puzzle she was solving in her head. "I am familiar," she said slowly, "with the songs and tales that Prince Vambrace has brought from his native land and shared over the generations."

I shook my head. "Prince Vambrace has not been to Earth in a long time, though, right? How many years? Decades? Art and culture have changed since then." I smiled. "But I am new here. And I come with knowledge of the latest and most successful achievements of human culture. And if you help me out, and keep my plans secret, I can share them with you." I paused for emphasis. "Maybe *exclusively* with you. What do you say, my lady?"

I could see the wheels turning, the sparkle in her eye, at the suggestion. I knew her answer even before she voiced it, in a voice dripping with honey and affection. "My dear Lady Morgan," she purred, "you are a good deal more shrewd than your gormless demeanor would first lead one to believe. I admit, this is quite the tempting morsel you dangle before me. But I would have a taste first before I commit to a full meal."

I frowned. "What?"

"A sample of the goods on offer," said the duchess. "A song, perhaps. Just one, of course, for now, so make it a good one."

I frowned deeper. "You want me to sing for you?"

"How else does one share a song, my dear?"

Right. Great. I've never sung before except to myself, in the shower or alone in my room, or to my parents, back when I was a little girl who didn't know how to be embarrassed. "Alright, but I'm no great singer," I warned her. "I'm just the messenger."

"Of course," she said with her usual haughty smile. "I shall temper my expectations accordingly."

Right. So now the question was, what would a demon of pride want to hear? What would best resonate with someone so incredibly self-absorbed? I made a show of thinking about it for a few long moments before I realized the perfect answer, then nodded and took a deep breath. "You have to stop calling me things like 'gormless,' too, by the way," I added at the last second.

She only smiled wider. "To your face, of course," she said. "Agreed."

Still a bitch, then, however helpful she was. We could probably never be friends. Ignoring that for now, I took another deep breath and began. *"Why you wanna tell me how to live my life?"* Pause for a soundless guitar riff. *"Who are you to tell me if it's black or white?"*

I'd thought I was being facetious before when I included my encyclopedic rock knowledge in my list of advantages I had over this place. Now, though, if this actually worked, it might prove just as useful as the tiny bit of actual magic I knew. Never again would I let people tell me I was wasting my time sitting in my room with the radio on all night.

I wondered if Rezavix could hear me through the door. I wondered what he thought we were doing in here that was so important and also required a singalong, or if he realized I'd thrown around weight I didn't have and he'd been duped.

When I finished with my amateur hour rendition of the song, Sidona was still looking at me with her narrowed, critical eyes, fingers resting mid-stroke on her sharp chin. I focused on getting my breath back, watching her, waiting for her judgment. I was no great singer, true, but I wasn't tone deaf; I could keep a rhythm, even if I didn't know what to do with it, and I'd put enough energy into my performance to at least suggest the shouting, belting high notes, even if I didn't get that loud myself for fear of drawing Rezavix's attention.

At last, the duchess cocked her head, a hint of a smile playing on her lips. "A bit repetitive," she said. "A bit more crude than I expected, but I suppose there's a layman's charm in that. You are sure there are no Superbiates where you come from?"

"Nope," I said, "just humans. Though some of us come pretty close, I'll admit."

"Fascinating," she said half to herself, falling silent for another few moments. "Yes," she continued, still half to herself, "there is a certain primal appeal. A certain smug satisfaction in the bluntness of the piece. At the very least, it is... different." Her attention turned from her own thoughts back to me as she resumed stroking her chin. "A couple of questions, though."

"Shoot," I said.

"Pardon?"

"Go ahead," I amended.

Another thoughtful moment. "'Gets me through the night,'" she quoted, easily the poshest I've ever heard that lyric recited. "What is this 'night?'"

And now it was my turn to offer a moment of blank silence. "What is... night?" I asked. "You don't have that here?"

"His majesty has used the term as well," continued the duchess. "And it comes up now and then in the native human art that he himself has offered. I gather it is some Earth phenomenon, but I would hear a second perspective for clarity."

What the hell, I'd shrugged off weirder from this place by now. I shrugged this off too. "It's when the sun goes down and it gets dark and colder," I said. "It lasts for about half the day. Most humans spend most of the night asleep; we do our business while the sun's up, then go home at night."

Sidona nodded. "And what is the sun?"

I've heard weirder, I reminded myself again. "It's the… giant ball of fire and light in the sky," I said slowly, not entirely convinced she wasn't messing with me. "Out in space. It's the thing all the light and heat on Earth comes from. You, uh… you don't have one of those here, either?"

"Not that anyone has noticed," she said. "It sounds terribly inconvenient. Inconsistent. How does it stay up there?"

Yeah, I couldn't do this anymore right now. "You don't have day and night around here?" I asked instead. "It's just… just that weird, dull red light all the time?"

"Unless clouds roll in," she said, then arched an immaculate eyebrow. "Weird? Is your sky a different color?"

There was another lengthy pause where the two of us just stared at one another in bemusement.

"Perhaps this is a branch of conversation best saved for later," said the duchess, breaking the silence. "Regardless of… cultural anomalies, I admit I am intrigued. You have a deal, Lady Morgan: my insight for your arts."

"Sweet," I said. "So how do I get out of here?"

She frowned. "You are, of course, planning on staying around long enough to actually continue sharing your end of the bargain now that we have struck an accord, are you not?"

Not if I could help it. "Of course," I said. "I'm not trying to escape; I just have errands to run."

"Very well," she said, stepping closer. "I'll not write this down and incriminate myself, so pay attention."

After a frankly ridiculous amount of directions, which she had to repeat twice and have me recite before I was comfortable I could remember them, Duchess Sidona took her leave once more, sweeping by Rezavix outside my door without a single glance. Eager as I was to sneak out after her, I knew better. I needed at least a small window of time between her visit and my next disappearance, or it would be too obvious that she'd had a hand in it. Whatever I thought of the Superbiate personally, I wasn't going to risk my only confidante so far. And there was my stolid guardsman to deal with.

I went back to browsing through the books I'd received, marking the time that passed in my head and trying not to think too hard on the fact that I had technically, successfully, just summoned an honest-to-God demon to bargain for forbidden knowledge. Much as I wanted to go home, at this rate, they were gonna burn me at the stake when I got back.

After approximately five minutes had passed since Sidona's leaving, I dropped the still-useless book back to the desk and went to the door, flinging it open. Rezavix didn't even flinch anymore, just grit his teeth and sighed at the idea of having to deal with me again. Good.

"Rexadex," I barked.

"You know that's not it," he groused.

"Who cares," I continued. "I'm bored. Can't you bring me some music or something?"

"Let me just summon you a personal symphony, my lady," he growled, glaring at the wall in lieu of looking at me. "It might even work. You're already summoning nobility."

"Indeed, I am," I said, stepping out into the corridor beside him. "So maybe you shouldn't be giving me such sarcasm, don't ya think?"

"How can you be bored already?" my guard asked, fists clenching repeatedly at his sides. "You came back with an armload of ancient books. You can't have read them all already."

"I have, actually," I said, hands on my hips. "Don't tell me what I can't do, doorman."

"Let me tell you what *I* can't do, then," he said through his teeth, voice rising. "I can't put a whole concert together just for you. I can't go wandering around looking for more books. *I can't leave you alone here, human.*"

I took a deep breath, loosed it in an exasperated sigh. "Useless," I muttered, then went back into my room and closed the door. But not before I noticed the tendons bulging in his neck as I passed.

Poor guy. I didn't really have anything against him, temper aside. He was just in my way.

I went back into the bathroom and tugged the ivory-handled chain hanging over the massive golden tub, watching the water pour steaming from the ceiling hole above. It filled surprisingly fast for its size. By the time I'd released the chain, the air was already steaming.

That water could probably stand to cool off a bit before it was comfortable, I figured, so I busied myself studying the various goops and powders on offer on the wall of bathroom shelves. A few of them came with little scrubby brushes or twisty sticks that looked like warped makeup applicators. Fascinating, I supposed, but just looking at them again but harder wasn't making any of their uses more discernible. Still, I made myself study each little jar or tube or vial for several dedicated seconds each, one after the other.

A safe enough amount of time had passed after I'd finished with the last little jar on the shelf, I'd decided. Anyway, this was boring and I was getting impatient.

I headed back into the bedroom, leaving the door between the rooms opened, then flung the hall door open once more. "Revalex!"

"What?" he snapped, whirling on me, pinprick eyes wide with anger. "What now?"

I admit I flinched a bit, but I managed to hold my ground. "I need a bath," I explained.

The muscles in his jaw twitched a moment before he answered. "I'm not going to give you one," he growled. "I just stand watch, human, I am not your damned servant!"

"Ew, no," I said, and I didn't have to entirely feign the disgust in my voice or on my face at the idea. "I was going to say that I need a change of clothes."

"What? No. Why?"

"Why do you think?" I said, spreading my arms and gesturing at myself. "Because these are filthy. I don't want to put these back on afterward."

"Then don't," he replied. "No one is making you."

"Then what will I wear?" I griped, rolling my eyes.

"I don't know," he griped back. "I don't care. Nothing. It doesn't matter."

I raised my brows at him. "Are you suggesting I go naked?"

"Yes."

Well, I hadn't planned for that response. He didn't seem to be suggesting it sarcastically, but I couldn't imagine he was being suggestive, either. If Rezavix had any sexual inclinations at all, I was by now clearly not part of them. And I remembered a number of his kind of demons in the locker room-esque space beneath the prince's indoor coliseum standing around half or fully naked with no apparent shame or concern. Must be a cultural thing, I decided.

Doesn't mean I shared the sentiment, though. "I'm not going naked," I said flatly after a few seconds. "I need fresh clothes."

His arms crossed over his chest. "I don't have any," he said just as flatly.

"So go get me some," I said slowly. "Surely this is an easier task than summoning Duchess Sidona for me. Am I a guest here, or a prisoner?"

"I don't know," the demon growled. "I'm not convinced you do, either."

He had me there, but I wasn't gonna let him call me out on it. "Trust me, demon, I know which I am," I said, crossing my own arms over my own chest. Not as intimidating a gesture as when he did it, with his spiked gauntlets and thick leathery breastplate, but still. "Now, for the last time, hurry up and fetch me some fresh clothes. Or do I need to talk to his majesty about how my so-called guardian treats even my simplest requests?"

Again, I watched as the tendons bulged in his neck, all of him slowly bristling around the glare he pinned me with. If looks could kill, I probably would have been eviscerated by now. "Back in your room, then," he growled at last. "I'll be quick."

"Finally," I sighed, heading back through the door. He pulled it closed behind me this time, but I quickly pulled it back open, stopping him midstep as he prepared to leave. When he reached impatiently for the latch again, I pulled it wider out of his way. "Leave it alone, Rev," I said, returning his glare. "I don't want the whole room getting steamy."

"So close the bathroom door!" he said, not quite shouting but damn close.

"Then I'll be too hot," I explained patiently. "What, you're worried I'll escape or something while you're gone? I can work the door without you, y'know. And how would I slip by you unnoticed anyway if you're doing your job?"

In lieu of answering me, Rezavix simply growled through his teeth as he spun and stormed off down the corridor.

"Leave my clothes on the bed when you get them!" I shouted after him. "I'll be bathing for a while and I expect to be left in peace!"

He didn't look back, but I knew he heard me, because his low growling began to steadily grow in volume after that. I half thought he'd start yelling outright once he was around the corner, but apparently he still had enough control of his rage to keep from that much.

And at last, I had my window. Time to work quick.

Ducking out of view of the open door, over by the desk, I closed my eyes and concentrated. The not-quite-invisibility spell was easier the second time, but still harder than the heat spell by virtue of my not having studied it as closely. I had to work against my own apprehension, my worry that Rezavix would return before I was done, so despite being easier to remember, actually casting it took longer than it had before. When I finally opened my eyes, feeling myself wrapped in the magic, glowing words of Old Elvish that warned any eyes turned my way to look elsewhere, I went back to the doorway and peeked out. Still no guard.

With a sigh of relief, then another deep breath to steady my nerves, I struck out.

Chapter 10: Stubbornness

I found Rezavix arguing with the two guards posted before the open doors that separated Vambrace's private rooms with the rest of the palace, trying to talk one of them into leaving their post again to fulfill the errand I'd given him so that he wouldn't have to. Just as I'd feared, I would need to get past my erstwhile watchdog to continue on.

I wasn't sure I'd be able to; if what I'd surmised from Sidona was right, then this spell only worked to keep me from the notice of people who were otherwise occupied. Against anyone actively looking for me, it apparently did little to nothing. And Rezavix's entire job, after all, was to keep an eye on me. How to avoid that?

My plan, and the reason for my bitchiness, was to make him so irritated with me that he didn't even want to look at me — to make myself, at least momentarily, someone who even the mere thought of was unpleasant, so that hopefully he'd be consciously trying not to watch or think of me.

Would the magic understand my arguably semantic logic? Hell if I knew, but it was the best I had.

Just to be safe, I gave the three red demons a wide berth as I passed, keeping to Rezavix's back as much as I could, once more chanting silently in my head and willing them not to notice me. Whether my plan worked because of my reasoning and pestering, or whether it worked just because he wouldn't have had a great view of me anyway, I couldn't say.

But it did work. And as soon as I was past their little group, I took off running, just in case it stopped working.

I kept Sidona's directions forefront in my mind as I went, reciting them over and over, my recitation shortening as I passed each checkpoint that led to my goal. Whenever I came upon anyone else in the halls, I slowed to a walk and turned my thoughts instead to commanding them not to see me. Whether this actually helped to strengthen the spell or was just for my own edification, I don't know, but I wasn't taking chances.

The crowds thickened the further I wandered away from the prince's suite and toward the front of the palace. Or at least, I assumed that was the way I was going. It was possible, I reflected briefly, that Sidona had lied to me and was sending me directly to a guard room or the dungeon or something. The thought was worrying, but I didn't linger on it for long; the duchess didn't strike me as disloyal to her ruler, but she *did* seem like the sort more interested in a chance to be exceptional than a chance to be obedient. If I didn't trust her, I at least trusted in her self-absorption.

I turned down a corridor and followed it to the end, where it spilled out into the massive front hall where I'd first entered the palace with Ulfris. I paused a moment, sticking to the wall and looking around. Golden sconces on the walls, golden chandeliers on the ceiling, thick red carpet leading off to the right and down a massive, banistered staircase. It was a familiar sight despite my having only walked past it once before, and that under extreme duress. I'd been too preoccupied to notice this side passage and the matching one across the floor from me, I guess. To my left, the carpeting ended shortly before the enormous double doors that led out of the palace, both of them standing wide open, the dull red sky beyond beckoning me like a distant, muted flare. A handful of demons of all shapes and colors drifted slowly in and out, a few milling about in the doorway.

I threaded my way through them and took off running, through the opening and out onto the wide bridge road. Far below me, threading through distant and shadowed crags of the same red-veined onyx that made up the palace, snaked a roiling river of steaming black water that churned and turned over itself more than it seemed like it should, even given the rocky course and apparent boiling. Once again, I spared it only a short, nervous glance before turning my gaze toward the sprawling, bustling, glittering city in the near distance. Finally, I was free of that gargantuan labyrinth called Pandemonium.

Now I only had the even more enormous maze of Dis to navigate. But at least no one was looking to corral me into some room out of the way out here.

Just to be safe, I left my unnoticeability spell on. Hunted or not, I'd learned from my first time here just how much I stood out. Better to get as far away from the palace as I could first before I had to risk that, if I had to at all. Sidona had broken my first spell by finding me; without intervention like that, how long could I keep it up? What kind of toll would it take on me to do so, if any? Only one way to find out.

The crowds on this main road were thinner now than they'd been the first time I walked it. Less going on at the palace today? Or had everyone who needed to be there just arrived all at once? Without knowing more about how this place ran, if it had a schedule or something, I couldn't be sure. How could anyone keep to any schedule, though, without days and nights to mark time?

It was questions like this that occupied my thoughts as I made my way unseen into the city. According to Sidona's directions, I pretty much just followed this road straight through three massive districts and over another river until I reached the bazaar. This jelled with what few details I could recall about my walk here, so I no longer needed to pay too close attention to where I was going — though I still did, this being the first time I had the luxury or forethought to actually look more closely at my surroundings.

From what the duchess told me, and from what I remembered walking downhill to the palace the first time, Dis was built in massive, concentric ring districts surrounding the palace. Sidona said there were seven, called Circles, one for each House of Sin.

I kept my tongue bit on hearing that. We'd only skimmed Dante in my world lit class, but I remembered the broad details. His count was off a bit, but still, a lot of this stuff was starting to sound eerily familiar. Really lucky guess on his part? Or had he actually been here, walked down this street I was on now? And would that have been before or after Vambrace took over things?

I should have been a better student. Or better yet, someone with a better grasp of this stuff should have landed here instead of me. Some of my classmates or professors would probably love to be on this little adventure I found myself on. Me, I'd never missed my crappy one-room apartment so much.

The ring of city nearest the palace was one of the thickest to make up for being dead center, and according to the duchess, it surrounded Pandemonium entirely. Walking through it, I craned my neck to look at towering, opulent manors that stretched for entire blocks before they finally ended, only for another to begin on the other side of a wide lane. Architecture was another subject that I had next to no grasp of, but still, even I found the disconnected variety of shapes and styles strangely disparate. I'd walk for five minutes or more past the front of some Gothic-looking manor, all pointed arches and high towers and ornately detailed wrought iron on the fencing and window frames, and when I finally reached the far corner of the last outbuilding and crossed the street to its neighbor, I'd find myself strolling by massive walls of what looked like pale blue marble carved with sweeping murals, set with thin windows of stained glass and topped with bulbous domes of silver and gold. More often than not, each complex held sprawling and beautiful gardens visible through its high fencing or the crenellations of the surrounding walls. These were just as varied as the architecture, with one holding a neatly trimmed lawn dotted with neatly trimmed trees and shrubbery like you might find at a country club, while another showed wild beds of flowers and grass overflowing beneath sprawling canopies so thick they blocked out the light from above.

I paused by one yard, curiosity getting the better of me, and looked in through a slit in the high wall of greenish metal that enclosed it. The open courtyard beyond was taken up mostly by terraced pools of water flowing into one another. Thin stone bridges led over the waters between what few patches of dry land there was, with vine-laden trees twisting up out of the surprisingly clear waters — not the bubbly black stuff from the rivers I'd passed, but normal-looking water, and not nearly as swampy as it should have been, I thought. A single Superbiate, nearly eight-foot tall and with curling goat horns, lounged on a divan beneath one of the trees on one of the landmasses. A Luxuriate man, thin and lithe, lay across the blue demon's massive chest, idly feeding him small orange fruits he held cupped in his hand in a shimmering green handkerchief. Another Luxuriate, this one a woman, sat perched on a stool nearby, strumming what looked like some kind of harp and humming along with the melody, her song so soft it didn't carry beyond the enclosing walls

If they weren't all pink and blue and horned, it would have been an idyllic scene worthy of a Renaissance painting. To be honest, it still looked pretty fancy and peaceful. This was a strangely un-torturous Hell I'd landed in, but I wasn't going to complain. At least, not about that particular aspect.

It took a while to get through this first ring of the city, but eventually, the wide road turned into a wide ramp leading up at about a thirty-degree angle, flanked on either side by steep stairs. These I climbed until I was above the enormous manors I'd passed, with only the tallest towers and spires rising up out of the crater behind me. I turned at the top of the stairs and looked out over the sea of opulence now sunk beneath me, most of the open garden and courtyard areas still coyly obscured even from this height by crowding walls and overhanging ceilings and the occasional mass of thick foliage. In the distance, beyond all of the intricately designed mansion compounds, Pandemonium towered in stark contrast — a jet black, rough cut, unadorned monolith budding with simple, spiky towers like a ginormous stalagmite stabbing straight up from the pit of the city to stab at the bleeding red sky above.

I felt like it was watching me through the distance and my obscuring spell, like it knew I was free of it and trying to escape. With a shudder, I turned and marched on.

The next ring of the city, according to Sidona, was actually two different districts; the main road I traveled dissected them, one on the left, the other on the right. She hadn't offered names for them, and I hadn't asked, more concerned as I was with just getting past them. The buildings on either side were less distinct and ostentatious than those I'd already passed. Large, yes, and they probably would have been more impressive if I'd been coming from the other direction, before I'd seen that first whole neighborhood of little palaces. From a glance, the designs seemed more uniform here: mostly stone walls and tiled roofs, still impressively designed as far as such things went, but without excessive detail or ornamentation. Built more for function than form here, I guessed. Since I was passing between both of them, I couldn't get a closer look or impression without deviating from my path, and my curiosity wasn't strong enough for that to happen. Instead, I just fell in behind a crowd of red demons I couldn't easily squeeze past and kept pace with them, another massive Superbiate at my side a safe distance away, still safely ignoring me.

I'd been walking beside the guy for about five minutes before I realized I recognized him. There weren't a lot of faces I'd seen so far that I could say that of, but I'd sat across from his withering stare long enough at dinner that it stuck with me. Looking over and up at him now, he was still wearing it.

Archduke Abdeles of House Superbia, one of the prince's dinner guests and the one who'd seemed most offended at my being there, for some reason. Not a lot of people out here in the city proper would know that I was supposed to still be tucked inside the palace, I assumed. Him, though, he would definitely know.

Shit. Shit shit shit. If my spell faltered, if he noticed me, it was over. The magic was still holding up so far, or he would have seen me beside him, but it had been Sidona who'd broken it before. What if it wasn't because she had me on her mind already? What if it was something to do with Superbiates instead?

I slowed, letting him pull ahead of me. I wasn't gonna duck down a side street to avoid him in case I somehow lost my way, so my best bet seemed to be to just give him some space. It wasn't until he was a good hundred feet or so in front of me that I picked up my pace once more, keeping stride with him in the distance, far enough back that if he stopped to turn, I could hopefully scamper off in time. I didn't want to be found out, but I also didn't have the time to stop and wait for whatever pursuit I'd invited to catch up to me.

We must have had the same general destination in mind, though, because once I'd spotted him, I didn't lose sight of him for the entire rest of my walk. When the contingent of armed red demons broke off to head down opposite side streets, Abdeles sped up as if in a hurry, unintentionally leading me through the remainder of these two bisected districts and over another massive bridge spanning another boiling black river. I remembered this one from my walk with Ulfris as well; and sure enough, once I was over it, the crowded and bustling bazaar stretched out in front of me, squat and simple stone buildings interspersed with large tents or open-air stalls. The ambient noise of the city increased dramatically as I stepped off the bridge, as if I was walking into a wall of sound. It seemed like most of Dis congregated either in the palace itself or in this district right here.

This was where my directions ended. I'd told the duchess I needed to get to the merchant district, but not where exactly I was headed within it. Even if she knew how to find the exact shop I had in mind, I wasn't comfortable with her knowing that much of my plan. So now it was up to me to find my way.

Unfortunately, this is also where my vague memories of my first march through the city broke down, which meant I would likely need to wander for a bit in the thick crowds and crowded lanes. Getting through without bumping anybody would have been impossible even were I visible, which meant my hiding spell was likely about to outlive its usefulness.

Except...

I looked ahead through the thickening crowds. I'd caught up halfway to Archduke Abdeles, who was leaving a wide wake through the crowds as other demons parted before him. With a title like his, I guess it would make sense the citizens recognized him; and as massive and imposing as he was, it made equal sense they would go out of their way not to be in his.

I didn't have to think too long before I came to a decision. Hurrying through the reconvening masses between us, I caught up to the Superbiate giant and tagged along in his wake only a dozen or so feet behind. I still didn't want him to see me, but I was slightly more concerned about losing my spell altogether. So long as he cleared the way first, I could put it off a while longer. Besides, with these crowds, it would be easier to get lost in the press of bodies at a moment's notice if need be.

And it's not like I knew where I was going anyway. Maybe I'd luck out and he'd lead me somewhere that looked more familiar.

Once again, I passed stall after stand after store full of so much different stuff that I grew dizzy just browsing past it all: racks of clothing of every cut and color, shelves of books of every size and age, chairs and tables and other pieces of furniture of every shape and material. Each space was overseen by a scaly green demon dressed in layers of colorful clothing and dripping with golden and gem-studded jewelry. One of them, standing beneath a dark blue tent speckled with silver embroidered starbursts, displayed a wide table covered in different sized bottles of different colored creams and gels and liquids that resembled the selection in my bathroom back at the palace. If this venture fell through, I thought, I should remember this particular booth and maybe ask what all that stuff was. And also how they knew what a star pattern looked like if they didn't have nighttime or stars.

I got a little worried once Abdeles broke off the straight path we'd both been following until now to weave down the narrow lanes in between shops. He took the pocket of space he created with him, so I kept tailing him, but now I was heading off the main way. If I needed to head back to Pandemonium after all, I'd need to do a bit of searching for the way first. Then again, even this far out, I could still see it towering over the surrounding buildings if I looked up and toward the city's center. If I couldn't find the exact same road leading to the exact same exit I'd used, I could at least head in the right general direction.

I wasn't keeping too close an eye on Abdeles — I didn't really need to, large as he was and as clearly as he made his presence known — so I was taken by surprise a moment when I glanced up and he was suddenly gone, leaving me alone in the pocket he'd made in the crowd. Quickly, I pressed back against the side of a nearby tent as the space he'd left began to fill in with milling pedestrians. I scanned the crowds in every direction but couldn't see so much as his horned head peeking up from the other shoppers. How the heck does someone like that sneak away so quickly?

I was still asking myself that and casting about looking for him when I realized where I was. My surroundings weren't particularly ringing any bells, but as I turned to look at the deep yellow-orange fabric of the tent I'd been pressed against, hints of firelight flickering out from underneath the cloth walls, I got the inkling that I'd seen it before. But from the inside. Carefully, so as not to bow the fabric and reveal my presence, I placed my ear against the wall and listened.

"…know how those *scavengers* are, my lord," came a muffled but familiar voice from inside. "Grabbing up every bit of *refuse* they come across, pawning it off on the first *convenient* taker without a thought to real *value*. So no, sir, I'm *afraid* I never…"

I pulled away, irritated again already. Dramoc's shop. This was the place; somehow, by blind luck, Abdeles had taken me straight to it before vanishing. I breathed a sigh of relief as I ducked quickly around to the front of the tent and hurried inside.

And then skidded to an immediate stop, my breath and heart both caught in my throat, as I suddenly found myself standing not an inch away from Archduke Abdeles's broad back waiting just through the entrance. Pulse pounding, fearing that I'd already given myself away, I scrambled backward and sideways to duck down in between a display table and the wall of the tent, wedging myself into the small space as deeply as I could. Gripping the edge of the table, I peeked over it and around the gilt-edged boxes atop it at the two demons standing in the shop's center.

"Is your clairvoyance busted?" the archduke was saying. "I've never met an Avaritiate before who couldn't locate their own possessions, no matter how long ago they may have parted with them." He made no sign that he knew I was there with him, so I allowed myself a very quiet sigh of relief.

Dramoc also didn't seem to have seen me, focused as his attention was on the Superbiate in front of him. "Of *course*, my lord, and I *would*, if I could, I assure you," he said with his too-wide smile and his ringed hands held up plaintively. Much the same subservient show he'd made to Ulfris when he'd sold me. "But I *cannot* locate any item which I have never even laid *eyes* on, my lord — which, again, I *must* reiterate, includes this *particular* item you are after. *Apologies, sir."*

Abdeles sighed dramatically. "You are quite sure you have no leads at all, then?" he asked. "Because if I find out later that you were holding out on me, merchant..."

"I *assure* you," said Dramoc, "the *last* thing I wish is to deceive an *archdemon*, my lord. There is *nothing* I would stand to gain by lying to one such as *you*, sir. All I can do is point you to the band of *reprobates* that Grumbelge has been known to associate with. Perhaps one of *their* number can —"

"No, no need," answered the archduke, turning from the merchant toward the open doorway. "My sources will no doubt prove more competent than yours in this matter." He turned his head halfway back to the green demon but stopped short of actually looking at him. "You have been even less useful than expected in this matter," was the last thing he said before striding through the open entryway and out of Dramoc's shop. Whether that was in lieu of a goodbye or just how Superbiates usually parted with people, I couldn't tell.

"Of course, my lord," Dramoc simpered at the blue demon's retreating back. Only once Abdeles was safely gone did the merchant's double-wide grin turn into an equally overlarge grimace. "As if I could keep up with *every* transaction in all of Dis," he muttered then. "You want *that*, then make *me* archduke, you stuck-up giant."

I waited until he was turned away, hunched over one of the shelves against the shop's back wall, before I unfolded myself and squeezed out from behind the table. I was nervous about what I had to do next, but there was nothing for it anymore. My only other option was to keep bumbling blindly around this massive demonic city and hope I got impossibly lucky somehow. Still, just to be extra careful, I first untied the cord holding the entryway curtain open and let it fall shut, muffling the noise outside and hiding us from passing eyes.

Dramoc turned around slowly at the change in lighting, frowning at the errant fabric. I let him look through me for a moment before I took a deep, steadying breath and willed the spell away. "Hello, Dramoc," I said at the same moment.

To my petty satisfaction, he started and reached behind him to grip the edge of the back shelf, upsetting a yellowish marble statue of some long-armed troll-looking thing as he did. It fell sideways into a clutter of loose rings and necklaces, scattering them and sending a couple rolling off onto the floor. "You!" said the merchant, ignoring the mess. "Where did… *how* did you…?" His wide, yellow eyes cast about his shop for a few seconds before he quickly swept up beside me, drawing the curtain closed even tighter. "What are *you* doing here, human?" he demanded in a hushed whisper as he spun back to face me.

Just as cagey as last time. That worked for me. "I'm looking for something," I said, careful to keep my face and tone as blank as possible for now. "Something I misplaced when I came here. I was hoping you could tell me where it ended up."

His eyes narrowed. "Does Lord Ulfris know you're here?" he asked, still hushed. "If I sold a something to a customer that *escaped* and came back to my shop, do you *know* what that will do to my reputation? To my *profits?*"

"Lord Ulfris won't care," I told him. "He passed me off himself. Nobody owns me to get mad at you, Dramoc." *You creepy fucker*, I added in my head. He was a lot less intimidating by this point, after all I'd been through already, but I was still uncomfortable around him. Being sold like an antique rug will do that to a girl, I guess. "I just need some information and I'll be on my way, don't worry."

He sniffed. "You too, huh?" he grumbled, then steepled his fingers beneath his chin. "Nothing comes *free*, human, not even information. And *something* tells me you don't have a *single* soul to your name."

I frowned. "What the hell is that supposed to mean?"

"Ah, right," he said, cocking one of the lines of gold studs he had instead of eyebrows — the one I'd partially melted during my short-lived escape, I noticed. It was still misshapen from the heat, the scaly skin around his temple on that side still darker than the rest of him. "This whole *stupid questions* thing you do," he continued. "I had *forgotten*." He reached into one of his layers of robes and pulled out the same long, thin box as before, snapping it open. From this he reverently lifted one of the thin, crystallized white rods he'd used to pay the gray demon. "Souls," he said slowly, as if talking to an infant, as he held the rod up to his face. His gaze went instantly from me to the crystal stick as he spoke, his eyes adopting that same glazed and rapt look, like a starving man spying a steak dinner. "*Currency*. You use it to *buy* things. Or at least, we *civilized* demons do." He returned the rod to its case, snapped it closed, and turned his usual condescending gaze back to me again. "Maybe *your* kind just trades clods of *dirt* or something like that. I'm sure *I* don't know."

I resolved to ignore his smarminess. I'd be here all day otherwise. Or at least, all of what passed for a day here. "No, I don't have any demon stick money," I said. "But I don't remember seeing Abdeles paying for any information either."

He bristled at that, though in offense or fear or what, I couldn't tell. "Archduke Abdeles," he said slowly, "is the *ruler* of House Superbia, heir to the legacy of Lucifer *himself*. No sane businessman withholds *any* information from someone of *his* stature." His gaze dipped briefly down at my outfit — the same one he'd disparaged the first time around, now even dirtier — and he sniffed. "I *highly* doubt, however, that *you* can make any similar claim of influence, rare or not."

"You'd be surprised, Dramoc," I bluffed, tucking away the offhand mention of Lucifer in the back of my mind. Something to chew on later, maybe, when more pressing matters were taken care of. "I'm still new here, you're right, but as you said, I'm a rarity. And unlike you or Abdeles or anyone else in Dis, I'm also the same species as Prince Vambrace. And trust me, we've met." I saw his eyes widen a bit at that and allowed myself a small smile. "So no, I don't have any money. I won't be paying for any info, but you're gonna give it to me anyway. Because you're a smart businessman who knows how to network, right?"

He frowned. "How to *what*?" he asked.

"How to get in good with important useful people," I amended impatiently. Stupid vocabulary barrier. How come these demons knew what I was talking about sometimes and not others? Come to that, how were they all speaking perfect English? Did Vambrace teach all of Hell his language? Did they just know it already? And why did they speak it to one another instead of whatever demony language was the native tongue around here? I'd taken sociology last semester; I knew what ethnocentrism was, and I knew better than to assume that American English was so universal that everyone in a whole other dimension had mastered it while still knowing nothing about Earth itself.

Dramoc stroked his chin with one clawed hand, eyes narrowed. "Perhaps you're as important as you *think* you are, human," he said slowly after a moment. "Or perhaps not. But *I've* no reason to believe you, so no. You will pay like *everyone* else, or you will *leave* my shop without any further outbursts like the *last* time I had the displeasure of your company."

I crossed my arms and glared at him down the length of my nose. It worked with Rezavix after a while; maybe it would work here too. "No," I said slowly, "*you* will answer my questions for free, or I will leave your shop without any further outbursts, go find Archduke Abdeles, and let him know just what you had to say about him as soon as his back was turned. Think his goodwill will hold up then, demon?"

He bared his teeth at that, both extra-long rows of yellowing fangs. I thought it was a threat for a moment, but then I heard them grinding together. "You are *not* worth your sale price anymore, woman," he muttered darkly, then turned with a dramatic swish of his robes and stalked away from the closed entranceway back over to the center table — the same one I'd woken up on with my wrists and ankles tied, now covered with a fringed red sheet but otherwise still empty. I followed him until he spun back to face me. "Fine," he grumbled. "*Ask.* But I cannot guarantee that I will know the *answer*."

I nodded. "I had a book with me," I said quietly, glancing around at the surrounding shelves. "A big, very old book. I notice you don't have it. I want to know where it went."

Dramoc took a deep breath and let it out through his overlong nose. "You *clearly* weren't listening as closely to my conversation with the archduke as you *insinuated* you were, then," he said. "I'll tell *you* what I told *him*. The Acediates who bring me their flotsam do not just bring it to *me*. Anything they pick up beyond the wall, they *scatter* it across every merchant in Dis, like disorganized *harpies*." He crossed his arms, his overlarge sleeves hanging down his torso. "*Grumbelge*, the lazy layabout who brought me *you*, brought me *only* you. Likely some other *furball* in his association picked up your book. I can't tell you *where* they took it; at *best*, I can only tell you where to find Grum, and maybe *he* can elucidate things for you." He sniffed again. "Likely do it for *free*, too," he added, lipless mouth curling in distaste.

"Alright," I said with a nod, "where is this Grumbelge?"

"Leave my shop," he answers with a toss of his head toward the closed tent flap. "Take the road *away* from Pandemonium until you reach *Belphegoris*." He paused, searching my face, probably looking for some sign of recognition at the word. When he found none, he sighed. "Until you reach the *edge* of Mammonis — the merchant circle — and find yourself in a dingy, dirty, run-down *slum* of a neighborhood unfit for anyone with any kind of *standards*. Grumbelge lives just inside somewhere. Ask around."

"That's it?" I asked. "Just head straight down this road until I find him?"

Dramoc sniffed. "If the route to my shop were *complicated*," he said, "the useless oaf wouldn't *take* it. He'd sell his refuse to some *other* shop instead." He sniffed again. "More's the pity."

"If you dislike this guy and the stuff he brings you so much, why do you keep buying things from him?" I asked.

The green demon's golden brows rose at that. "*Why?*" he repeated. "Because he sells it for *cheap*, obviously."

Seven races of demon. Seven deadly sins. If it weren't obvious which sin the green ones corresponded to before, it was clear to me now. "Thanks for the help," I said as I pulled back the tent flap and made to leave. "For both our sakes, I hope I don't ever have to come back here again."

"Nothing would make me *happier*, human," Dramoc muttered with a big fake smile as I stepped out of his shop. "Nothing *you* could afford to give me, anyway," I heard him add as the tent flap swung closed again.

Putting the scaly merchant behind me for what I hoped was the last time, I turned and made my way through the crowd in the direction he'd given me, now clearly visible once more. Thankfully, Abdeles was nowhere in sight, and the thick crowds parted easily enough once they'd caught sight of me, though no one tried to stop me or ask any questions. So, I still stood out enough to merit stares and cautious curiosity, but not enough for people to quit whatever it was they were doing. Right now, I could live with that.

Densely packed as the bazaar was — Mammonis, he'd called it — it didn't take as long to walk through as the other districts had. Maybe that was because, by the rough map Sidona had drawn for me in my head, it was in the middle of the city and circled all around the inner districts, so it made up in circumference what it lacked in thickness. I hadn't had any real call to use geometry since high school, but the reasoning sounded right in my head. Despite what the ethnic stereotypes said, I was only just okay at math.

After a few more minutes of walking, I reached another staircase leading up a slope to a higher level of the city. This hill wasn't as high or as steep as the one leading out of the fancy mansion district; the crater that the city nestled in was starting to level out. It became more apparent once I reached the top of the stairs and looked out away from the palace. In the distance, on what I guessed was the edge of Dis, a massive wall rose up to tower over even those buildings nearest to me, blocking out the lower half of the sky in every direction.

I turned and looked back toward the palace, the ground floor of which was now far away and far below me, obscured by the cluster of manor homes in the ring immediately around it. Still, the crest of Pandemonium loomed high enough up even here that I had to crane my neck to make out the tip of the single tallest tower that sprouted from the middle. The city sprawl beyond the palace was hazy, obscured by distance, but I could barely make out the vague outline of the border wall as it circled around the far side. Dis was huge, no doubt, especially when you were traversing the whole thing on foot. Still, when it came to sheer area, it was still smaller than most modern cities back on Earth. That thought gave me a bit more hope. If I could manage my city back home, I could manage this one.

Scouting finished, I turned back to the new circle before me. Belphegoris. As much as I hated to give Dramoc credit for anything or validate his shitty attitude, he was right. From what I could see spread out before me, this was a dingy, dirty, run-down slum of a neighborhood.

Walking through it didn't improve my estimation of it any. The buildings were all squat, simple, deteriorating piles of gray, crumbling stone and gray, rotting wood — where they were still buildings at all, anyway. More often than not, a plot of land where a building should have been would instead sport one, maybe two half-demolished walls leaning over piles of refuse that I assumed used to be more of the construction that had collapsed in on itself. Tarps of rough-spun cloth hung from doorways or holes in the walls here and there or were stretched over the remaining architecture, either for privacy or to replace a missing section of wall. I saw more of these hanging limp, gently swaying in the light breeze, than actually fastened down to anything.

In the streets and open spaces between buildings and bare foundations, I kicked through loose refuse and piles of dirt, stepped over potholes and loose spaces in the stonework that held stagnant water and debris. Gutters on either side of the road were clogged with mud and trash, bits of rotting wood and the discarded remains of food, as well as the occasional pile of what looked like clumped, dried dung. As of yet, I hadn't seen any animals anywhere in Hell except for what was fed to me at dinner. So where were these piles coming from? The demons who lived here? Ew.

I'd made it a block into the neighborhood by this point and still hadn't seen another soul, which was a first in my wandering so far and especially jarring after navigating the heavily crowded bazaar. I paused at a crossroad, looking around. There were no lights on anywhere I could see in any direction, either on the street or inside any of the ramshackle structures, leaving only the dull red light of the sky above to illuminate the district. Shadows ran rampant, which was a bit unsettling. It didn't look like the kind of place where anybody worth mugging or anything worth stealing was likely to be found, but I didn't trust that meant nobody would try. I'd walked back through the ghetto in my hometown once when I'd missed my stop riding the bus. Just once. Since then, I'd decided I'd rather pay the extra fare and hour or so of my time to ride it back around rather than risk that again.

The more I looked about now, though, the smaller my worry grew. Belphegoris was a ghost town without a soul in sight. Unless...

Carefully, I headed back down the street to a collapsing stone wall. There was a pile of moldy trash beneath that I thought I had seen move slightly. Or so I thought. It wasn't until I was standing over it that I realized what I thought was mold was really short, matted, gray fur threaded with tangles and dirt. What I'd assumed was the discarded remnants of a sacking were some sort of tattered garment that enwrapped the body beneath without any discernible eye to comfort or fit. And what had looked at first glance like bits of broken timbers I saw now were two gnarled, cracked horns, like broken branches from an old tree, poking up from the wrinkled, sleeping face of one of the gray demons. Acediates, Dramoc had called them.

I turned and looked around myself again. Now that I knew what to look for, I realized I wasn't as alone as I'd thought I was. Just within sight on this block, about half a dozen Acediates lay or sat slumped against walls and in the nooks of buildings, blending in with the general mess of their surroundings. It was unsettling, but it probably would have been more so if any of them looked alert at all.

When I turned back to the demon at my feet, it had its eyes open, though just barely, and was looking up at me. "Oh, uh… hello," I said quietly. The streets were near silent, and with everyone just lying around, I felt like I was intruding in some kind of giant communal bedroom where everyone had been sleeping peacefully before I barged in. "I'm looking for Grumbelge. Do you, uh, know where I could find him?"

The Acediate didn't even lift its head, just rolled it to one side and pointed with its horns. I followed the gesture to two stone half-walls that formed a right angle rising no taller than myself, a stained beige cloth pinned to the tops of the remnants with loose stones to make a sort of tent. Judging by the lumpy shape the cloth was draped over, someone was under there.

"Thanks," I said, turning back to the demon before me. Its eyes were already closed again, ignoring me. These were the lazy sins, then, I decided. If it didn't show in their demeanor, it definitely showed in their housekeeping.

Whoever was under the cloth didn't poke out and didn't stir as I approached. I cleared my throat, but that didn't accomplish anything either. "Excuse me," I said. "Grumbelge?"

Still nothing. With a sigh, I bent down and took the edge of the dirty cloth in hand, lifting it over my head and peering down at its occupant. I felt rude doing it, but I needed to get this business over with.

Grumbelge lay curled beneath it in the dirt like a big, slovenly stray cat. He cracked his eyes at the intrusion, looking up at me through heavy, baggy lids. "What?" he asked.

Good, he was a talker. "Hey," I said, "I've been looking for you. It's me. The human you sold to Dramoc?"

He blinked. I got the feeling that was all the recognition I was gonna get from him.

"Right," I said. "I need to ask you something. I should have had a book with me when you found me. Do you remember it?"

He took a deep, slow breath, his torso slowly rising. It was the most activity I'd seen out of any of them since I got here. "Yup," he said at last.

I waited for more to follow, though I should have known better by this point. "Do you have it?" I asked after a few more moments.

Then I waited a few more while he just as slowly breathed out again. "No," he grumbled.

"Do you know who does?" I asked, trying to stay patient.

Again, the deep inhale. "Breg found it," he said. "Sold it." Again, the deep exhale.

"Do you know who this Breg sold it to?" I asked. "I need to find it."
Breath. "No."

I tried not to grumble. "Do you know where I can find Breg, then?"
Breath. "Near river." Breath. "By Amonis."

I waited a few moments before I spoke again. Slow as this conversation was progressing, I still felt like I was rushing him, which was strange. "And where is Amonis?"

He actually craned his neck at that, looking toward the street behind me and down the road the way I'd been heading. "Beneath wall," he said.

Even further away from the palace, then. Well what the hell, I'd already gone this far. I might as well walk the whole radius of this weird city. "Thanks," I said. "You've been very helpful. And much more, uh, interactive than the other folks around here."

Grumbelge made some deep murmuring noise in his throat as he lay his head back down. "Deal with merchants," he said. "Need to be energetic for that."

By this point, I was actually a bit startled that he'd volunteered any words on his own volition. "I see," I said, nodding. "Thanks again." I went to lower the cloth back over him, but stopped at the last moment and lifted it again. "Out of curiosity," I said, "do you, uh, scavenge and sell people very often, then?"

Deep breath. "No," he said, and closed his eyes. "Just you."

"Ah," I said. Suppose I should feel special, then. "Well... be seeing you, then." And I dropped the cloth back over him like a blanket, then set off through Belphegoris toward the distant wall.

This was the most uneventful leg of my walk so far. This circle wasn't as thick as some of those before it, but that didn't mean it was a small neighborhood. Still, unlike the merchant circle or the one with all the opulent manor houses, nothing seemed to be going on here. There was no traffic, just the regular glimpse of a still and silent Acediate propped against something or, once or twice, lying in the middle of the street so I had to step around it. At one point, I passed one on its feet, hunched over until its knuckles were nearly dragging the ground, shuffling toward me through the dirt at a pace that would see it reach Grumbelge's house that I'd left about fifteen minutes ago in maybe a couple of hours. That was as hectic as these streets got, apparently.

I stopped at a cluster of mostly intact buildings on a corner as the next bridge came into sight. There wasn't much else in the way of landmarks around here, and unlike Grumbelge, I'd never seen this Breg person before. I had no real idea who or what I was looking for, only that he'd be gray and furry and I should have been in roughly the right place by now, so I found the nearest group of Acediates lounging together in the same ruined half-building and asked after my target. After a couple minutes of passing the question to each of them, waiting for replies, and moving to the next, someone was finally able to tell me that Breg had left over the bridge into Amonis about an hour ago, heading toward the wall to make another scavenging run beyond it.

I sighed at this new information, though I figured I couldn't actually complain too much. My luck had been better than expected so far, after all; if I now found myself hunting down an unusually enterprising Acediate, well, it could be worse. At least these guys were still fairly stationary, even when they were on the move. Thanking the group of demons, I hurried onward toward Amonis.

By the time I reached the bridge, the change of scenery and the sound of roaring water far below were almost overstimulating. I peeked down at the river as I crossed this bridge, expecting the same distant, roiling black water as I'd seen at my other two river crossings. True to expectation, the river itself ran through a gulley far below, though not as deep or rocky of a canyon as encircled Pandemonium; and while the water was still black and roiling, it wasn't as dark and didn't bubble and churn as violently as the other rivers either. Whatever messed with the water around here, it apparently calmed down somewhat this far out. The water I'd been using in my bathroom at the palace seemed just like regular water, so I had no idea what made it act up like this in the riverways. Unless black and boiling *was* the normal here and my bathing water was the strange stuff.

The quietness of Belphegoris faded into the sounds of the rushing river, which only grew louder the further I went across the bridge. By the time I reached the far side, I realized that it wasn't just the water I was hearing — more than half the din was coming from in front of me. Over the rooftops of tile and beaten metal came the sounds of distant shouting and the regular clang and scrape of steel, like I'd just wandered into a busy foundry or factory. Nobody was headed my way toward the bridge to Belphegoris, but the traffic picked up again on the cross streets that I could see. At a glance, I saw a mix of demons like there had been in the market, but the armored red ones heavily outnumbered the odd blue or green or pink demon that passed by.

This was where the angry people lived then, probably. That was gonna be fun. I briefly thought about trying to put my unnoticeable spell back on before I entered the district proper, but decided against it. Hopefully, I'd catch up to Breg in a block or two and could turn around and leave afterward.

There were no wooden structures here in Amonis, only heavy stone and heavier metal. Not the gold and silver of that first manor district, though; about half of this neighborhood looked like it had been beaten out of thick, blackened steel, the walls and rooftops more armored than adorned. I didn't have to walk too far into this ring of the city to find the problem with this design choice; after just a couple of blocks away from the bridge, the air grew uncomfortably warm, like standing in a kitchen where the oven had been left running and half-open. There was no sun, so I wasn't sure where the heat came from yet here in Hell, but whatever the source, the closely crowded metal construction here was trapping it and radiating it back down the streets.

No wonder the red ones went casually topless sometimes, if this was the climate they were used to. I was almost entertaining the possibility myself by now. But even if my modesty would have allowed it, I was still drawing enough eyes as a clothed human. I didn't know what kind of attention a half-naked one would draw, and I wasn't interested in finding out. As I fanned myself as best I could with the hem of my stiff black

AC/DC T-shirt, though, a new change of clothes jumped up my list of goals from a nicety to a necessity, second only to finding Breg and my book. Maybe something light and airy, like what Sidona had been wearing. Mom *had* always tried to get me to wear more dresses. Though I could do without the belly window.

I soon found out what those scraping, clanging metal sounds I was hearing were when I wandered past the open stone front of an otherwise gunmetal gray building and peered in to see a sprawling blacksmith layout, fires blazing in three different kilns against the far wall, the heat wafting out through the roofless space in a shimmering plume of air. Half a dozen red, sinewy demons, men and women both, milled about inside, pounding pieces of red-hot metal against anvils or dunking them into vats of water with sharp hisses and clouds of sudden steam. In the middle of all the red ones, though, stood a broad, thickly muscled Superbiate man in a heavy apron, bent over an anvil and raining blows down on one side of a massive double-bladed axe, pausing occasionally to bark an order at the workers around him. Weird that one of the haughty blue ones should be in charge here in the red ones' home turf, I thought. Unless he wasn't really, just acting like he was. I didn't know. I'd only slowed a bit as I passed on my way to, hopefully, catching Breg.

After passing the one smithy, though, I noticed it wasn't the only one. Every second or third building seemed to house a blacksmith's workshop, a few of them with a single Superbiate lording over everything within. Now that I was in their midst, the clanging din intensified all around me, nearly deafening. I quickened my pace to be through it sooner.

But smithing wasn't the only source of the noise, just one of the most prominent. I found the other major source of the chaos a block later.

I had nearly reached the street corner when something made me pause — a change in the noise, maybe, though it would have been hard to pick out in the general clamor. Whatever it was, I stopped just before reaching the intersection, so I was spared a sudden trampling when a couple of armed and armored red demons came half-sprinting, half-tumbling down the road from my right, right in front of me. One skidded on the cobbles and spun; the other fell, rolled to the middle of the intersection, and found her feet a second later, so that the both of them were diving back the way they came, swords swinging, when three more screaming red demons rushed out to meet them. The whole group clashed together not six feet in front of me, which sent me scurrying backward in sudden fear for my safety.

I couldn't quite follow the action of the five-person brawl, only saw red limbs and gray steel flailing wildly in a knot of angry confusion. One of the first two demons who'd appeared before me, the man who'd thrown himself into the fray first, loosed a piercing scream that choked off as suddenly as it began as he crumpled to the ground in the midst of the fight, a sword through his throat and a hatchet-sized axe embedded halfway through his stomach. His accomplice, the woman who'd rolled further away from their pursuit, managed to break away and took off at a dead sprint down the street once more. Two of the three they'd been fighting gave chase, one brandishing a heavy mace, the other unarmed, presumably the owner of one of the weapons sticking out of the fallen demon. The third one stayed behind, falling to his knees atop his fallen opponent, gritting his teeth and growling as he pinned the dead demon's twice-impaled body to the street.

On second glance, this was because the skewered demon wasn't dead after all. Not yet, at least. Blood flowed freely from his pierced throat and his half-chopped stomach, but his muscles still strained against the hold of his captor, clawed hands grasping at nothing as he bucked and struggled and gurgled angrily through the bloody foam on his lips.

It was the single goriest thing I had ever seen in person up to that point in my life. So I don't really feel ashamed to say that, after the stunned surprise of what I'd just witnessed wore off, the first thing I did was turn around, double over, and vomit into the gutter behind me. As if I wasn't already in bad enough need of cleaning up.

When I looked up, I realized I had an audience: two Avaritiates, a Luxuriate, and one of the little brown ones that I didn't know what to call yet. And despite the carnage just a few feet away, they were all looking at me as if *I* was the most surprising thing on the street at the moment.

"Sorry," I muttered, supremely embarrassed that a group of strangers had just watched me barf in public. "Bad harpy. I'll just, uh…" I pointed to the nearest wall, then shuffled over to it and leaned against the warm stone, which somehow felt even warmer than my own red face.

After a few more moments of staring — during which only the light purple man looked concerned, and the other three just looked disgusted — the group moved on, stepping around my sick with much more care than they showed stepping around the two struggling red demons, one of which was still bleeding profusely. Violent bloodshed was common enough around here not to warrant concern, it seemed. I'd thankfully been spared that until now.

I kept my eyes averted from what was left of the fight until I'd fought my own revulsion down far enough and caught my breath. When I looked up again, the twice-stabbed demon had stopped struggling and instead lay bleeding and twitching on the ground in a pool of his own blood. The fight finally over, the other demon stood and grabbed his opponent by one ankle. Still snarling, he turned and headed back the way he'd come, dragging the fallen one by the leg across the stone street, leaving a long smear of dark blood as they disappeared around the corner.

I had to take another few deep breaths at that, but finally, I passed by the scene of carnage and headed forward, keeping a much more watchful eye on my surroundings as I went.

It was another several blocks and about twenty minutes of walking before I spotted the gray, shambling shape on the street in front of me, parting an impatient trickle of traffic that had to flow around its slow pace. Excited, I hurried toward it. It was the first Acediate I'd seen so far in Amonis; it had to be Breg.

As I came up beside it, I slowed to match its steady, plodding pace. "Excuse me," I said. "Are you Breg?"

It was eye-level with me, which made it short for its kind, though it might have stood half a foot taller if it stood up straight. It was the first Acediate I'd seen standing upright since I'd seen Grumbelge in Dramoc's shop as he was selling me. Like him, Breg stood on squat, bent, splayed legs that it dragged more than lifted with each step, as if merely walking was a considerable labor. When it slowly turned to me and nodded, I guessed this one was a woman, if only because she had no beard beyond the fuzz that covered her everywhere else. Again, it was hard to tell with these gray ones beneath all the grunge and fur and folds of sagging skin.

"Oh, good," I said, stepping in front of her and stopping. She stopped as well rather than try and shuffle past me. "I've been looking for you. My name is Morgan. Your friend Grumbelge found me not long ago. I'm told you were with him?" I clasped my hands together in front of me, imploring. "I had a book. A big, old book. He said you found it? Do you know where it is now? I really need it back."

"Hmm." She took a deep breath as she slowly stood up straighter. Not straight, nowhere near it, but straighter. "Sold it."

"Yes, I assumed as much," I said, once more trying to stay patient and civil. It was getting harder the closer I got to the *Morganomicon* and the more I had to deal with Acediate conversation. "But can you tell me where you sold it, or who you sold it to?"

Breg blinked. It took longer than it sounds. "Gilderos," she finally sighed.

I tried not to sigh myself. "And this Gilderos is a merchant, then? Back in Mammonis?" She started to nod. "Can you tell me where, exactly?" I asked before she was midway through with the gesture. "Give me directions or something?"

Slowly, she turned and lifted one long, thick arm, pointing back down the street from which we'd both come. "That way," she said.

I bit back the groan that rose in my throat. "Yes, thank you," I said slowly, "but can you be a little more specific? There are lots of shops and merchants that way. How am I supposed to find this Gilderos?"

Breg just as slowly turned back around to face me, then leaned in toward me. I leaned away from her slowly encroaching face, holding my breath against the smell of must that accompanied it. "Ask," she said with a sour breath.

I stepped back, exhaling deeply both in frustration and just to clear the smell from my nose before I had to breathe in again. "Right," I said, and flashed her only the briefest, most perfunctory of smiles. "Well. Thanks then. Carry on." And before she could take five minutes to respond, I swept by her and headed back down the road toward the merchant district at a swift stride. The backtracking was annoying, but I'd been about to run out of city going this way anyway judging by how close the wall loomed overhead.

So intent was I on finishing this errand, and so annoyed with the runaround it had required so far, that I paid no attention to the people I swept past. Most of them were the armed red demons, striding alone or with a partner up and down the streets as if on patrol. Their kind seemed to be the police force around here, which meant I could only assume that fight I'd seen earlier was some sort of criminal apprehension. If you could call a sword to the throat "apprehension."

Anyway, most human police I'd met didn't care to be stopped and bothered by passing citizenry without reason. I couldn't imagine the perpetually angry demon kind would appreciate it any more, so I safely ignored every one that came close and kept my gaze fixed straight ahead, resolving to draw no attention to myself by paying none to anyone else.

That tactic worked well enough for about ten minutes or so. Unfortunately, it was also the reason I didn't notice who I was advancing toward until I was attempting to brush past them, only to be stopped by a hand coming down on my shoulder with a grip like gentle iron, stilling me mid-step.

"Lady Morgan," a calm, cold, female voice said about a foot and a half above my head. "Do you remember what I said about wandering?"

I froze, breath stopping in my throat. It didn't change anything; the grip on my shoulder didn't loosen, and she didn't say anything else. With a gulp, I turned and looked up into her pinprick gaze. "Um," I said. "No."

Enkida actually smiled at me. "No," she said, "apparently not. That's alright. I do." And sweeping around behind me, she draped her full arm over my back, holding me in something like half a hug, companionable and inescapable. "Come, then," she said, sweeping me down the street with her. "Allow me to remind you."

Chapter 11: Indignation

I couldn't really be surprised that I had been caught. To be honest, I knew, whether or not I wanted to admit it, that this was the more likely outcome — that the chances of my actually finding the *Morganomicon* and using it to get home on only my first attempt (or my second, if you counted my getting pitifully lost in the palace as a full-fledged attempt) were slim to none.

Still, I had been so close! I think. I had the name of its current owner, anyway. Unless this Gilderos had also already passed it on, which may have been likely, them being another merchant. *I'd* sold fast, after all. Still, I had gotten through three links in this annoying chain of events and made it almost the entire way across the city on the way. I felt like I'd accomplished something, and to be stopped now rankled.

"Uh, excuse me," I said to my chaperone as we crossed the bridge from hot, noisy Amonis back to dark, quiet Belphegoris. "Miss Enkida?"

"General Enkida," she said beside me. "If we're using titles." She still had her arm draped companionably over me, but her grip had loosened — probably because she knew that, this close to her, I couldn't really make any kind of evasive move she couldn't immediately deal with. I hadn't seen her in action, not yet, but I'd seen others of her kind, most recently much closer up than I'd liked. I would have been hard pressed to get free of any of them if it came to a struggle. Against their general, I knew I would stand less than a chance.

"General Enkida," I repeated. "Right. Would you mind if we made a quick stop on our way back to the palace?"

"Yes," she said, glancing sidelong and down at me, "I would."

I nodded. "Thought you might," I said, then turned on my most polite "asking Mom and Dad to cover my rent this month" smile. "But it's on the way. We're gonna walk right past it in the shopping district."

"Right you are," she said with a nod of her own. "Right past it."

My smile dropped. Couldn't be saved. "It's just, I lost something when I got here from Earth," I continued doggedly. "Something really important. That's what I was looking for. I've been all over the city already tracking it down, and I've got a lead now with a merchant named Gilderos. Do you know them?"

"No, I don't," she said, looking down at me fully then. "Do you?"

"Uh… no," I said.

"Then how do you know they're on our route rather than the other side of Dis?"

"Because whoever they are, they bought the *Mor* – my item from an Acediate scavenger," I said, proud that I actually had an answer for this. "And I don't know much about demonkind, I'll admit, but I know an Acediate wouldn't trek all the way across the city to sell loot that they could instead sell to the first available buyer to cross their path."

"A sound point," she said. I'd expected more to follow. We'd gone another full block before I realized it wouldn't.

"So…" I said. "Does that mean we can make that stop?"

"No," she said, "it doesn't."

I sighed. "Why not?" I asked.

"Because," she said, "his majesty told you to stay put in the palace. When you didn't, he told me to find you and bring you back as soon as possible. One of us is going to follow orders." She glanced down at me, her pinprick eyes half-lidded. "If you've got an issue with that, if this errand of yours is that important, you can take it up with Prince Vambrace. In this instance, though, the decision is not mine to make."

I suppose I couldn't much argue with that. I mean, I could, and I was, but I saw her point. "You're, uh… strangely calm right now," I said instead. "Aren't you?"

She actually smiled a bit at that. "Strangely?"

"Oh, I didn't… I mean, we were arguing just now. Weren't we? Rezavix would've been trying not to rip my head off by now."

"So you *do* know his name," she said. We were nearing the stairs down to the bazaar again, and she very deliberately draped her arm over my back again, hand resting gently on my shoulder. "Yes, most Iriates would be boiling by now, I'll admit. Consider it a uniqueness of mine that I never boil."

"What, you never get angry?" I asked her, brow raised. I found that hard to believe.

"That's not what I said," she said, fingers tightening on my shoulder to just shy of painful. "I said I never boil. I am very nearly always angry." She was still smiling as she looked sidelong at me. "It's an important distinction. Don't forget it, Lady Morgan."

She'd made her point; I was suddenly more nervous with her now than I'd ever been so far under Rezavix's fiery glare. "Are you, uh… are you mad at *me* right now?"

She laughed lightly, her grip relaxing. "You've proven somewhat irritating," she said. "But you haven't earned my ire — leastways, not yet. That I grant only to the most privileged and deserving. No offense, of course, lady."

I tried to echo her unconcerned laugh, but it came out less convincing. "Oh yeah," I said, looking over at her powerful fingers on my shoulder. "None taken."

An Iriate, she'd called herself. Sounded appropriate. Just two types of demon still to figure out, then. I could probably ask Enkida about it, but… well, intentional or not, she'd just done a good job of intimidating me. Right now, I was gonna cut my losses and shut up before she changed her mind on how undeserving I was of her anger.

We made our way briskly through Mammonis, her arm around me a gentle but ever-present threat about what would happen if I tried to break loose again. Tempting as it was, I didn't try. I'd already lost my book and my jacket. Much as I'd like them both back, neither of them were worth losing an arm.

People had gotten out of Archduke Abdeles's way when I'd shadowed him through this district, but they nearly tripped over themselves to scatter before the calm, measured pace of General Enkida. It was interesting to note, I thought. Did generals outrank archdukes here? Was it because she was an Iriate and therefore more likely to walk through someone rather than around them? Or was there more and worse to her reputation than her patient treatment of me so far belied? She didn't so much as glare sideways at anyone we passed, near as I could tell. She didn't need to. In fact, she even nodded politely to a few of the more finely dressed shoppers and merchants that crossed our path.

A friendly Iriate, huh? Well, it was nice to know I wasn't the only oddity around here, even if it did throw me off my game somewhat. "The red ones are easily riled up" was one of the few facts I'd thought I'd figured out for definite so far.

We passed fairly quickly through Mammonis this time, then over the river and into one of the two half-ring districts I'd passed between when I'd left straight from the front gate of the palace. It didn't take long to figure out which Sin this neighborhood belonged to. The crowded streets of the merchant circle were replaced by wide avenues between buildings that were mostly open arches and fluttery awnings over shaded patios. The smell in the air was so distinct I could nearly taste it as much as smell it: fruity and floral, like a lush garden in full bloom, but with a distinct, pervasive undercurrent of sweat and salt. Like the garden was on a hot beach somewhere, maybe. But there shouldn't have been any beaches here in the middle of the city.

And then we turned the first corner, and I saw my first glimpse of the pedestrians here at the same moment that I heard the first of what would turn out to be many loud, uninhibited moans ring out down the open streets. Down the road from us, a group of about seven or eight of the pink- and purple-skinned demons — sorry, Luxuriates, as Sidona insisted — lay or stood or knelt in various combinations with one another in the middle of a square of blue-green grass at the nearest intersection, like a wriggly game of Twister going on in a roundabout.

No, wait... no. Not Twister. Not at all.

Despite Enkida's arm still around my shoulders guiding me on, I stopped in a dead shock, forcing her to push me about a foot down the road on the heels of my boots before she stopped as well to cast a curious glance my way. I couldn't look at her, though. I couldn't look away from the giggling, lavender-hued orgy happening maybe half a block away from us.

I wasn't smelling a warm beach. Oh, good lord, it was in the *air*! It was in my *lungs*!

"Something wrong, Lady Morgan?" Enkida asked at my side.

I looked up at her, but it took another few moments to rehinge my slack jaw enough to speak. "What... did we...?" was about all I could manage. I gestured awkwardly at the group in front of us as I turned wide-eyed back to the spectacle. "What are they…?"

"Fucking," said the general with a shrug. "Isn't it obvious?"

"In the middle of the street?" I demanded.

The look she gave me said she was concerned for my mental prowess. "Yes, clearly," she said, then tilted her head. "Are you well, m'lady?"

"But… but why?" I couldn't look at her again as I spoke. The writhing mass of lilac limbs was downright hypnotic.

"Why?" she repeated, sounding a bit confused herself now. "You mean… why do people have sex?"

"Why the middle of the street?" I demanded again, louder this time. Too loud, probably. This was upsetting. Still, not like they could hear me over the sounds of themselves.

"Convenience, most likely," she answered. "Does it matter?"

"I…" It took me a short while to answer. In that span of time, I watched as two women climbed off the same man and onto each other, two new men stepping up in front of and behind them. "I guess not," I said, quickly turning my gaze away and swallowing against the rising heat in my face. "I just, uh… wasn't expecting to see… all of this." I waved in the general direction of the action, my eyes on my boots, hoping that my chin-length hair hid my red face.

"You weren't expecting to see sex in Asmodeusis," Enkida said in a dry voice.

That one was a mouthful. I was gonna need a notebook or something soon to keep track of all these weird new words. "I didn't know what this place was," I said. "I didn't come through here the first time. And it's —" I was cut off by a loud, guttural groan from down the road, followed quickly by two tinkling, feminine giggles. "It's the choice of location that surprises me more than anything," I added, reaching up to tug a lock of black hair closer to my burning cheeks.

Enkida was silent for long enough that I knew she had to be staring at me and my sudden awkwardness. "You are not quite what any of us expected, Lady Morgan," she said, and then her arm was on my shoulder again. "Come along," she said, taking me further down the street toward the group. "We're going around it anyway, so it's a moot point. Neither of us has the time right now to join in."

I had nothing to say to that. Nothing coherent, anyway.

We gave the orgy a wide berth as we passed, and I kept my gaze pointedly turned in the other direction. Still, it was a palpable thing. The moaning and grunting and panting were louder, and this close, I could hear all the smaller noises as well: the slap of skin on skin, the sighs and whispers of the revelers, the *squishing*. I held my breath against the pungent smell. You probably couldn't inhale an STD, but I didn't want to take that chance. If demons could even get those kinds of diseases.

It took less than a minute to reach, walk around, and walk away from the mound of sexing. If any of the sexers even noticed us, they were too absorbed in their fun to interact, thankfully. Still, as we walked away from the open-air banging, the sounds didn't fade, not entirely; instead, I heard them coming from all around us, men and women both, unabashedly making their enjoyment of each other known from the open windows of the buildings we passed, from underneath the awnings of patios, from the depths of nearby alleyways. More than once, we passed people on the street walking with their hands around or, just as often, inside of one another. At one point, we turned a corner where a pink man with short, feathered blue hair and no shirt had another man, this one a short Superbiate with horns that curled forward like a bull, pinned against the stone wall, their mouths frantically locked. I watched despite myself as their kiss finally broke off, both of them taking a quick breath before their mouths found one another again. In that blink of time, though, the blue man had turned a light emerald green, his shock of white hair vanishing, black bull horns morphing to a double row of short, yellowed spikes sweeping back from his temples. I blinked in surprise, staring until we'd passed, then turned and looked behind me. He was red this time as we walked away, pinprick eyes half-lidded, the elbow spines of his new, sinewy arms locked together behind the pink man's back.

I hadn't seen one do that since Sidona's model had stopped being me before my eyes. At least the spectacle helped detract from the sexual tension. This place was inundated in it, a constant, humid warmth overtop the distant moaning and the scents of delicate flowers and bodily fluids. It was getting to me even through my mortified awkwardness. I'm pretty sure my flush never went away until we finally reached the stairs and descended the crater back into the fancy mansion district.

The air cooled as we went down, like walking out of a lusty haze. I breathed deeply the smell of regular, unsweaty air, clearing my lungs and my head. As my face cooled, I chanced a glance at Enkida beside me to find her smiling slightly. "What?" I asked.

"You seem oddly concerned with sexuality," she said. "In yourself and others."

I frowned. "Maybe," I said. "I'm, uh… not used to it, I guess. Not like everyone around here, anyway."

"Not like his majesty, either," she continued. "I'm wondering now which of you is more representative of your species."

"I dunno," I said with a sigh. "Can we drop it?"

She shrugged. "As you wish, m'lady."

We walked side by side past all the fancy houses, the general not bothering to keep her hand on me here. This close to the palace looming hugely overhead, it didn't matter anymore. Gilderos, whoever and wherever they were, they were halfway across the city now. My quest was temporarily postponed. I hoped. I had to keep telling myself it was temporary, because the thought that I wouldn't be given another chance to get the hell out of here was too unpleasant to dwell on.

"So what's this place called, then?" I asked my escort.

"Luciferis," she answered without turning her head. "Home of House Superbia."

"Lucifer," I said. "Like the devil."

"Like one of them, yes," she said. "The circles of Dis are named for the ancestral founders of the seven Houses. Lucifer is the founder of Superbia."

"Is?" I asked. "Not was? He's still around somewhere?"

Enkida shrugged. "The deaths of the original seven archdemons were never recorded. They lived during the era of the Original Sin, so it might not be impossible that they still exist somewhere outside our knowledge. There is no evidence one way or another."

All these parallels between what I'd heard on Earth and what I was hearing here were getting confusing. "So who founded Hell originally?" I asked.

Again, the general shrugged. "Who founded Earth?"

I sighed. "Yeah, people argue about that. Alright, then. Who founded Dis?" I waved a hand up at the monolithic palace drawing nearer before us. "Who built this?"

"Dis is the first and only place of civilization in all the world," said Enkida. "Founded, and then apparently abandoned, by the Original Sin. Their names, their leaders, their deeds, even what their race was called, all of it is lost to unrecorded antiquity. Our history, what we know of our past, begins with the seven founders. Further back than that, all we have is speculation. But that," she added, also gesturing at the towering onyx palace, "does not look like something built by the hands of any race. The palace inside, perhaps, the excavated spaces. But Pandemonium itself? It is as ancient and unknowable as those primordial days, I think."

I could believe it. As much as I could believe anything that was happening to me, anyway. I'd just thought demons would have a more impressive grasp on history than humans, given their longevity. Although from what I'd seen and heard so far, they weren't unaging and undying like a lot of media portrayed. "How long do demons live?" I asked Enkida, suddenly curious.

"Until they die," was her answer.

I frowned. "And when is that?"

"Depends on what kills them." She raised a thin, white eyebrow at me. "Do humans do it differently?"

"I meant, what's the average lifespan?" I asked. "I'd kind of thought demons were ageless before I got here, but now I'm learning otherwise. Humans usually can make it to 80 or 90 years old before they die of old age. How many years do demons get?"

She shrugged. "What is a year?"

I should have expected that. I guess I half did, because I wasn't surprised at the answer, not after Sidona's confusion over day and night earlier. "Is there *any* concept of time in Hell?" I asked. "Days, years, months, weeks, centuries? Hours? Minutes? Seconds? There must be *something*."

"We understand time," said Enkida, starting to finally sound as if she were growing impatient. "We understand events or tasks taking longer or shorter times than others. You speak of measuring it objectively? Do I understand correctly?" She frowned at me, but the slight irritation I heard in her voice wasn't in her eyes. All I saw there was the same bemused curiosity I'd seen on Sidona and Rezavix and nearly every other demon who'd spent any length of time near me so far. "It sounds like rather weighty philosophy, this topic. You want to debate the nature of time with an Iriate soldier?"

"I wasn't really looking for an intellectual debate, no," I said. "I'm just trying to figure out how anything gets organized enough to work around here without days or hours or anything like that to work by. Like, how do you know when to eat? When to sleep?"

"When you're hungry," said the general. "When you're tired."

"How do you know when it's time to gather for something?" I argued. "Like that big dinner the prince put on? Or when he holds court?"

"His majesty tells you," she said. "Or someone brings the word to you. If it applies to you, anyway."

"Everything is either based on a whim or word of mouth, huh?" I asked. "Doesn't sound efficient. Is that the same way you know your shift is up? Wait for someone to come tell you?"

"Your shift?" she asked, turning her curious glance on me again.

"When you're done doing your job," I clarified.

"Ah." She nodded, eyes forward again. "When you finish it or die," she said. "I can't help but feel you're overthinking things, Lady Morgan."

I dropped the issue with a sigh.

We'd walked as we talked, and we continued walking after the conversation lapsed. So long as I kept pace with her, Enkida seemed willing to entertain my questions and confusions without any obvious resentment, unlike Rezavix. More of that uniqueness she'd mentioned, I guess.

I wasn't looking at the ornate buildings around us this time as we passed through Luciferis, impressive and beautiful though they still were.

Knowing that this was where the Superbiates lived made the architecture seem even more pretentious than it had the first time, as if every structure were demanding my attention and expecting my admiration; and with that idea in mind, I ignored them all out of spite. Hell was demanding enough of me already. No, it didn't make any sense, but I was feeling defeated and powerless and petty right about then, and the looming prospect of being shut away in the bowels of this palace looming before us wasn't helping matters.

By the time we reentered Pandemonium, my brooding had made me angry again. I didn't feel like talking, not even to someone as patient as Enkida, not even to ask questions. She escorted me in silence down the winding halls, past staring demons of every color. The armed and hurrying Iriates we passed slowed when they saw us and bowed their heads in deference to their general, their haste gone in our wake. Another search, I realized — the guards had been tasked with finding me again, and now that they could see I'd been found, they were going back to their usual business.

Prince Vambrace hadn't been happy the first time I'd disappeared, and I'd only gone upstairs then. What would be his reaction when he heard I'd made it nearly to the city wall this time? I'd managed to put off thinking about it until now, but now the thought was in my head, apprehension seized me. Whatever he thought about me, he likely wasn't my biggest fan after that first disobedience. The feeling was mutual, but I was still dependent on his good graces here, much as the admission galled me. Would I still have that now? And if I didn't, what then?

My gut roiled with anxiety and frustration as we entered the halls leading to his suite of rooms once more. As we passed the door to my own room, I noticed Rezavix wasn't there this time. I didn't have time to be curious about it, though, as I was marched up to the prince's private room once more.

We stopped before the closed door, then Enkida had her hands on my shoulders, spinning me around to face her. Her pinprick eyes searched my face for a moment, the tiny pupils and lack of any iris giving her gaze more intensity than I think she was actually regarding me with. "You're angry," she said quietly, sounding slightly surprised by the idea. "Interesting. I would ask why if there was time." She held up a finger between us, looking into my eyes around it. "A word of advice, though," she said. "Nobody in all of Dis dares insult his majesty with open disobedience. Nobody has for a long, long time. You've done so twice now." She lowered her finger, her other hand moving from my shoulder to the door latch. "I don't know all of his thoughts toward you, but some respectful contrition would not go amiss, lady."

She opened the door before I could reply. I took a deep breath as she ushered me in.

Prince Vambrace sat on the floor beneath the massive battlefield portrait of himself, his back half to the door, still wearing my denim jacket over his silvery mail and those long steel gauntlets he wore. His head was bent over his lap, his strangely luminescent sword held across his knees in one hand, a fist-sized gray stone in the other, scraping repeatedly over the edge of the blade. Sharpening it, I would have thought, except that he was going through the motion too quickly, practically bashing the whetstone against the sword with each swipe and ripping it down the length of the weapon, one side and then the other, with such agitated force that his whole frame rocked with the motion, filling the entire room with a loud, piercing, scraping clang of metal on stone that set my ears ringing instantly. No way that was good for the blade, I thought; he'd be dulling it more than sharpening it, and he'd be lucky if he didn't break it outright.

The raucous sound stopped as Enkida and I stepped into the room. I would have been grateful for that, only it stopped because his head jerked up from the task, his glare piercing straight through me with all of the intense wrath that Enkida lacked. If looks could kill, I think I would have been disemboweled just then. Respectful contrition suddenly didn't seem like such a bad idea after all.

After a frozen moment of glaring, he shot to his feet, spinning to face us and flinging the rock across the room with the same motion. It crashed into one of the bookshelves lining the far wall to the accompaniment of the loud crack of breaking wood and a tumble of books, ricocheting hard enough that it rolled halfway back across the floor and stopped at my feet. I flinched back at the violent outburst, but it wasn't over yet. Sword raised, he stomped toward the both of us, his face a storm cloud, his mouth opening in a snarling shout. "Where—!"

"Sire," said Enkida calmly beside me, raising a hand in front of her and draping the other casually, protectively, over my shoulder again.

I hadn't expected her, loyal as she apparently was, to challenge him even this much, especially on my behalf. And I definitely didn't expect such a subdued appeal to have any effect. But she had, and it did; Prince Vambrace froze in his tracks, clenched fingers trembling on the handle of his sword, his furious glare turning from me to his general.

In that tense, still moment of frozen reckoning, I noticed that there wasn't so much as a nick or a scratch on his raised blade, the gleaming metal as perfect and flawless as it had ever looked. I glanced down at the whetstone at my feet. Deep, fine grooves were sliced through it all along one side, the surface notched where small wedges of the dense rock had been sliced out.

"Are you certain?" Enkida asked the prince. There was no threat in it, no warning, no pleading. Just simple clarification.

It worked, though, miraculously. I could see him thinking as he turned his glare back on me. And a moment later, he swung his sword. I flinched again, but I wasn't his target — instead, he drove the thing point first into the ground, stabbing through the black marble-onyx floor as easily as if it were warm butter. The blade bit about a foot into the rock, practically vibrating under his white-knuckle grip on the handle. The prince closed his eyes and took a deep, quick breath, forcing it out in a harsh, angry sigh as he let go the sword. It actually seemed to sink another inch or two down into the floor of its own accord before settling to a stop, the unsheathed length of it wobbling slightly.

When he opened his eyes again, he still looked pissed off, but he looked less like he wanted to murder me, which was a definite plus. "Where were you?" he demanded in a tone as flat and sharp as his sword.

I took a deep, steadying breath of my own. "I went into the city," I said. "Looking for something I lost."

He turned his eyes on Enkida. "She was in Amonis when I found her," said the general. "Halfway to the wall."

"I was on my way back," I argued, trying and failing not to sound petulant.

Prince Vambrace blinked once, slowly, and looked back to me. "And did you find it?" he asked.

I shook my head. "I might know where it is now," I said. "I hadn't made it that far before I was, uh… collected."

He nodded. "And why," he continued, the heat returning to his voice, "did you think it would be a good idea to defy me *again* — in the exact same manner, I might add — after I had very specifically demanded otherwise the first time we met like this?"

Respectful contrition. "I, uh…" I clasped my hands in front of me, looking down at my boots. It wasn't entirely an act; this guy legit scared me. "I really wanted to find the thing I lost," I said to my feet. "Sorry. Uh, sire."

"Why did you not bring the matter to me before taking it into your own hands?" he asked, taking another step forward.

I made myself meet his angry gaze. "I didn't think you'd help," I said. "And I was impatient, and… well, frankly, I was mad at you at the time." I don't know what possessed me to admit that, but I felt Enkida's fingers tighten on my shoulder in warning. "Your majesty," I added.

He straightened slowly to his full height — which wasn't too impressive, but was still taller than mine — and regarded me without blinking for several seconds. The anger was still there, but so was that curious unreadability I'd seen on him so much already. "Enkida," he said without looking at the general. "Thank you for bringing the Lady Morgan back. Leave us, please."

"As you wish, sire," said the general, releasing me and stepping back. "Will you do something you'll regret later if I do, though?"

"No," said Vambrace, pinching the bridge of his nose. "No, we are past that now. Thank you, General."

She clapped a fist to her breast and bowed her head over it. It wasn't as smart of a salute as I'd seen other Iriates do, more of a casual gesture. "Highness," she said, flashing me one last, pointed look before she turned and walked from the room. For all her warning about defying the prince, she seemed to second guess him a lot herself, especially for the loyal servant she'd made herself out to be.

As soon as the door closed behind her, the prince was on me again. "I don't think I have to tell you how unhappy I am with you right now, do I, Lady Morgan?" he asked, taking another step toward me.

I resolved to hold my ground. "No," I said in as neutral a voice as I could manage. "I don't think so."

Again, he shut his eyes and took a deep breath. Shit, just how angry had I made this guy? I knew he was royalty and I hadn't listened to him, but with the effort he was apparently putting into reigning in his anger, it seemed a bit much for just going on a long walk after being told not to. "What is it you were looking for that is so important it merits this much disobedience?"

"A… book," I said, caught between telling enough truth to sound believable and too much to get me in further trouble.

"A book," he repeated, flat. "I supplied you with multiple books already, did I not?"

"A specific book," I said. "One I brought with me from Earth. It got lost during the trip."

"What manner of book is it?" he asked.

I looked back at my boots. "I… would rather not say."

"And I would rather you did," he said slowly.

I took a deep breath and looked up at him. "It's personal," I argued.

He turned away from me, staring at the far wall. One hand came up to rub his eyes again, the other clenched at his side. "Lady Morgan," he said, audibly strained. "Who is king where you come from?"

"Uh… No one? We don't, uh, have any kings back home."

"Truly?" he asked, looking sidelong at me, hand still on his face. "Odd, but I can believe that given your demeanor. Who rules your village, then? Who is your local authority?"

I wasn't expecting a quiz on civil government. "I, uh… don't know," I said. "The city's got a mayor, I guess, but I don't know who it is. I don't really interact with the government at all."

"Well," he said, turning back to face me again. "You've got an excuse, at least. Because so far, you are deplorable at obeying authority. Surely you see a problem with this."

I clenched my own fists at that. Respectful contrition. It was hard to get into that kind of mindset with his patronizing me like that. "I suppose," I said. "Sorry."

"Are you?" he asked, taking another step toward me. He was close enough now he could have reached out and grabbed me. Instead, he held his arm out at his side, hand open, gesturing to the room behind him, or perhaps the palace as a whole. "Since my reign began, my lady, I have not been disobeyed. Defied, yes. There are always lawbreakers to deal with, few and inconsequential as they have grown under my rulership. But you?" He dropped his arm, shaking his head. "No one has so flagrantly, so repeatedly, ignored my direct orders since... well. Suffice it to say that I find myself out of practice for how best to deal with something like you."

The intensity of his words slowly instilled a growing worry in me as he spoke — right up until the end, when it all suddenly vanished. "Some*thing?*" I asked, eyes narrowing. "So, I'm a something now, your highness?"

"What?" he said, momentum derailed. "No, that's not —" He stopped and took another deep breath. "Just... tell me why you are so dead set against doing what you're told."

"I'm not," I argued, trying to reign in my own annoyance. Both of us being angry was a recipe for making my situation here worse than I'd already made it. "It's just... I don't..." I sighed, shaking my head. "Everything is so overwhelming here! I didn't even believe in demons until I got here. I didn't know other worlds existed. I've never met royalty before. And the way you talk to me..." My hands fluttered at my side. I stuffed them impatiently into my pockets. "You're a prince," I said. "I get it. You're the most powerful person I've ever come in contact with. And I'm still trying to figure things out, and you're here dragging me back and forth around the palace without giving me any answers, and I don't know what's gonna happen to me, and then you send me to your bedroom of all places, and I panicked and —" I stopped, took a breath, held it. The more I explained myself, the more the weight of everything reared up and threatened to overwhelm me, all the absurdity and incomprehension and distress I'd been shoving to the back of my mind to deal with later. If I kept going, I thought, I would break into tears. And maybe the sight of that would soften his demeanor toward me a bit, but I absolutely hated crying, even to save myself from demon princes.

Tears or not, my growing distress may have been working in my favor regardless. He said nothing for a moment, and though he didn't look like he was softening, he'd stopped vibrating in anger. "You keep coming back to that point," he said after a second, brow furrowing. "What, pray tell, is so frightening about my room it incites fear and fleeing?" He held both arms out to the room in question, gesturing at the comfortable splendor. "I'd have thought it an honor in your shoes. Would you prefer we meet in a dungeon instead?"

I took another steadying breath. "At least in a dungeon, I'd know where we stood," I muttered. "I'd prefer, your highness, to not have to question your motives. I have no idea how safe I really am around here."

There were a number of things he could have said here, I thought. But what he went with was, "Is this about sex again?"

It was my turn to be derailed. "What?" I asked.

"You said you fled the first time because you worried I had sexual intentions toward you," he said. "I thought we had passed that misunderstanding, but the first thing you did afterward was run away again."

"Oh. No, we're done with that," I said. At least, I'd thought we were. "I really did leave to find my book."

"A book you refuse to speak about still," he said, "and which you never saw fit to mention to me."

"Well… yeah, I guess. I didn't exactly trust you. Maybe the bedroom/sex misunderstanding was part of that."

"I see," he said, then sighed. "Frankly, Lady Morgan, if I wanted you like that, I would have you like that. I wouldn't need to hide my intentions."

There was a beat between us as I processed that. "Pardon?" I asked, while my blood went ice cold inside me.

He shrugged. "I am Prince Vambrace, Archfiend of Hell," he said casually. "If that's what I wanted from you, that's what I'd get. You don't —"

He didn't get any further, because before I knew I was doing it, I reached out and smacked him.

I'd thought my blood had frozen in fear, but nope. Turns out I was just pissed again, more angry in that moment than I'd felt since I got here, than I'd felt in years. And Vambrace had a nice pink palmprint on his cheek now, head still turned sideways where I'd put it, staring wide-eyed at the far wall. It was a good slap — I don't remember ever having struck someone so hard before, other than my heat-infused punch to Dramoc's face after I'd first woken up here. Myself, I was fuming, glaring daggers at the man.

I'd opened my mouth to tell him off before it occurred to me what I'd just done. That I had just bitchslapped Satan.

I froze all over again. Well, at least I was about to die in the most metal way possible. That was something.

His head came slowly, very slowly, back around to face me, eyes still wide with shock and something else I couldn't quite place. He didn't blink as he stared down at me, my palmprint growing slowly more noticeable on his cheek.

I swallowed, trying to hold my indignant look of outrage against the panic rising through. I took a deep, trembling breath, set my glare, and opened my mouth. "Um?" I angrily squeaked.

The prince grabbed me by the wrist before I could react, snatching up his sword with the other, and hauled me after him as he nearly ran to one of the side doors in his sitting room. I stumbled along behind as he quickly threw the door opened and pulled me through into a massive, fancy bedroom. He released me then, turning to pull the door shut and throw a heavy sliding lock. I stumbled nearly to the foot of the canopied bed, massive enough to sleep a dozen people, then snatched up an errant throw pillow from the coverlet before spinning back to face him. It was a nice pillow, soft and fluffy, and it would absolutely not stop that sword of his. Maybe he'd be hesitant to damage it, though. Maybe I could set it on fire and throw it at him.

When he turned back to face me, he still held that same half-crazed, wide-eyed look. He didn't lose it, didn't even blink, as he slowly advanced. I hoisted the pillow higher, backing to the edge of the bed and nearly falling back on top of it, hoping I looked more angry and intimidating than my mounting panic belied. He walked right up to me, the space of only a few inches between us. Right before I could swing my fluffy cudgel at his freaky royal face, he dropped to one knee, kneeling before me like a knight greeting royalty.

And just when I thought I was done being surprised. I stalled my swing at the last moment, turning my panicked gaze down at the prince where he knelt. His expression as he gazed up at me was nearly feverish. "Do that again," he said.

The pillow nearly slipped out of my fingers gone slack in surprise. "What?" I breathed, trying to find my voice again. "You're not...?"

He quickly shook his head. "I dare not, my lady," he said, an inexplicable grin slowly splitting his face.

I snapped. This was too fucking much. Dropping the pillow to the mattress behind me, I hauled off and slapped him again across the same cheek as before. "What the shit?!" I squeaked in breathless hysteria. "You drag me in here and... and what the actual fuck, prince?! What sick fucking game are you playing at?!" Stumbling sideways, I extricated myself from between him and the bed, backing halfway across the room, my eyes trained on him at all times.

Vambrace lifted a hand to his stricken cheek, closed his eyes, and laughed. Actually laughed aloud, joy and disbelief mingling in that sound as it echoed through the bedroom. Myself, I only felt the latter, along with a healthy dose of leftover fear and rekindling anger at whatever the hell kind of weirdness was going on here now.

The prince's laughter finally began to subside, and when he opened his eyes to look at me again, they damn near sparkled. Were those tears? Was he gonna cry? Shit, I hadn't hit him that hard, had I? "I... oh, I do apologize, my Lady Morgan," he said, still grinning wide. "Hell has no need of chivalry, and in all my years, all my dealings, I..." He took a deep breath, steadying his mirth and forcing a somber mien as he turned in place, still kneeling, to face me. Once he did, he ducked his head, black hair hanging to cover his face. "I have forgotten much. Forgotten myself. Forgotten the ways of man. You remind me, a breath of fresh air in my long sequester, a breeze blown in from a life long lost and forgotten. You are right, my actions have been unbecoming of a knight to a maiden. I apologize for the offense."

This was a far cry from the guy I'd slapped the first time, and it wasn't exactly putting me at my ease. "The hell are you talking about?" I asked, anger and fear both being replaced by a familiar confusion. "Just who the hell *are* you?"

He lifted his face to look at me once more, expression burning with a fierce pride. "I am Victor of Caerleon, known as Prince Vambrace, sovereign ruler of the city-state of Dis, Lord of the Seven Houses, Archfiend of Hell, former squire to Sir Mordred of Orkney, and last remaining knight of Camelot and the court of the great Arthur, the Once and Future King of all Britons."

I said nothing as he beamed at me, pride and joy and relief dancing across his face. I said nothing as I slowly sank to my knees on the soft carpeting, staring through him, until my head fell and I stared through the ground. I said nothing, because I thought nothing, because I had no idea where to begin.

"My lady?" the prince said after a moment, still on his knees as well.

I cradled my head in my hands and loosed a heavy groan at all the weirdness upon weirdness I was drowning in, wondering if I'd ever come up for normal air again. "Fuck me," I muttered.

The prince rose to his feet then and took a step forward.

I held out a finger between us that near sizzled with heat. "Don't you dare," I said without looking up.

He stopped, then fell back to his knee a moment later.

Man, I just wanted to go home.

Chapter 12: Connivance

Prince Vambrace, Sir Victor, King Whoeverthehell, he sat on the edge of his massive bed and stared across the room at me, hands clasped under his chin, trying and failing to suppress a giddy grin, like a kid sat in front of a Christmas present he had to wait to open. It wasn't a look that was winning him any points from me.

I sat in a plush chair opposite him on the far side of the room, another throw pillow propped up in my lap like a shield between us in case he got weird again. Actively weird, I mean, beyond the uncomfortable staring. "Okay," I said, taking a deep breath. "So... I've got about a million questions by this point, and I'm not sure where to start anymore."

"As do I, milady," said the prince. "It has been ages uncountable since last I had chance to converse with a fellow human. I dared not seize the opportunity until we were alone, but each attempt I made to that effect was thwarted by your vanishing. How must the world have changed in my absence, I wonder?"

That seemed as good as any a place to start. "Ages uncountable, huh?" I said. "Are you really one of the Knights of the Round Table? I don't remember ever hearing your name in the stories. Er." Shit, make things even more awkward and tell the guy he was forgotten by history, Morgan, good idea. "Sorry."

"The Round Table?" he repeated, a wistful smile on his face as he did. "Centuries later, and the shape of the table is a detail historians have chosen to emphasize. Interesting. But yes, I am of that order, of a fashion." His glance slid down to the floor and back to a far-gone past, and when he spoke again, I thought I detected a hint of embarrassment. "To be honest, my official knighthood could be contested. I was still a squire for most of my service to Camelot, sworn to my master Sir Mordred of Orkney. He knighted me himself just before the Battle of Camlann, but by that point, King Arthur was obviously in no position to officially recognize the appointment."

"Mordred I know I've heard of," I said. If my memory of World Lit II served, Mordred was the bad guy, but maybe that was another point best left alone for now. "So then, you're… from the Middle Ages? Like, the 1200s or something?" Holy shit, he was even older than I thought.

He frowned at that. "I do not know this term, 'Middle Ages,'" he said. "And I never had great cause to mark the exact year on the Roman calendar. But if I were to guess, I believe the year was somewhere in the mid 530s anno domini when I left Britain behind. Perhaps… 537? The number feels familiar. Mayhap I heard a priest mention it in passing once."

I blinked over my pillow at him, doing the math in my head. It took longer than it should have. "So… that would be nearly fifteen hundred years ago," I said slowly. "It's 2016 on Earth right now." Last I checked, anyway. I wouldn't know if time worked the same here until I got back.

Prince Vambrace raised his eyebrows at the news. "Not uncountable after all, then," he said. "That is… quite a long time indeed, isn't it?"

"How the shit?" was my next natural question.

He frowned. "Pardon?"

Right, let's do this more eloquently. "How are you so old and still alive?" I clarified. "Fifteen hundred years in Hell and you don't look much older than me. Are you immortal or something? Are you dead?"

His frown turned thoughtful again. "I have wondered this as well," he said. "Dis has no calendar to speak of, no day or night, no seasons. I can mark the time here even less accurately than I did on Earth. But I feel the years sliding by, the long ages. Not acutely, but after so long…" He shrugged. "And yet I grow no older, you are right, though everyone around me does. The longevity of demons is astounding, but I have seen generations come and go, and I do not change. Will you? I cannot be sure, but I think not. But why?" He shook his head, stroking his chin as his gaze went unfocused in thought. "Something in the magic that put us here? Something in the water, in the very air, that preserves humankind but not demonkind? It seems farfetched. Perhaps the native beings have somehow become immune to whatever unaging effects are present here, if such a thing is even possible. Perhaps I too shall begin to succumb to time once more once I have spent enough of it here. I cannot say — I am ill-versed in both magic and natural philosophy, and in all my years here, I've not met anyone who had the answer."

It was starting to scare me how easily I was just rolling with all of this by this point. Maybe once I got home, I could take a few days off and have a proper breakdown, get it all out of my system. "Wouldn't all your, uh, subjects get suspicious?" I asked. "Wonder how come their human king wasn't getting any older? Come to that, how in the hell do a bunch of demons let a human be their ruler anyway?"

He smiled and waved a hand in an airy, dismissive gesture. "Eminence of the Original Sin," he said. "On both counts."

"And what is that?" I asked. "They brought that Original Sin thing up at dinner, and you kinda freaked out. Enkida mentioned it on the way back. What the heck is it?"

"A very useful explanation for a lot of things, for starters," he said before a more serious look settled on his face. "You know of the seven cardinal sins espoused by the Christ church, I take it?"

"Yeah, kinda," I said. "My religion's a bit rusty, but they come up on TV and stuff now and then." I ignored the eyebrow he raised at my mention of TV and began counting off on my fingers. "There's, uh, pride, greed, gluttony… lust, uh, rage, jealousy… and laziness?"

"Superbia, luxuria, gullia, avaritia, invidia, iria, acedia," he said solemnly. "Pride, lust, gluttony, greed, envy, wrath, and sloth. The seven sentient races of demon who comprise civilized Hell are divided among these categories. You've noticed, I'm sure."

"Yeah," I said. "And Sidona told me a bit. I've heard most of those words by now, I think."

"But there was an eighth," Vambrace continued. "Or more accurately, a first. Where now there are seven, there used to be just one. The Original Sin, unknown and forgotten, the primordial ancestor from which the seven modern races all descended. Great Dis was founded by this first master race long ago, a small settlement that sprung up around Pandemonium here, where the first Archfiend resided and ruled before the entire race vanished into the shadows of history."

"Huh. Ominous." I frowned. "But what's that got to do with you?"

"Not just me," he said. "You too, Lady Morgan. This great ancestral race is the human race; humans *are* the Original Sin, and Earth is where they vanished to all those many eons past."

"What?" I said, deadpan, and clamped down on whatever feelings I was about to feel. An origin story for the source of all human life was a bit more than I was still willing to roll with. "No way. You're shitting me."

"Of course I am," he said as if it were obvious. "Humans are just humans. We didn't come from here, and I don't think we're supposed to be here at all."

"Oh," I said, releasing a breath. "Okay. Good."

"But it's not just you, milady," he continued, dead serious again. "To borrow your phrase, I'm shitting *everybody*. And if you value your life and any of the favor shown to you, so will you." He stood from his seat on the bed finally, gaze intent on me as he stepped forward. "Humanity is the Original Sin," he repeated. "It is what I've told the people for as long as any of them remember. It is what they believe. It is what you will affirm if ever it is brought up. Understood?"

Shit, and here I thought he was done with the macho posturing now that I knew his secrets. I held the pillow up between us and nodded.

"Swear it," he pressed.

"Fine, I swear it," I said. "I'm not gonna run shouting down the halls that the prince is lying to everybody or anything."

He took a deep breath and let it out slowly, nodding. "Good."

"You think they'd kick you off your throne if they knew?" I asked once he'd backed off again.

"Of course not," he said, sitting again. "But someone might try to, and I would not relish showing them the error of their ways. I've not had any dissension or even outright impertinence in, apparently, well over a thousand years. I do not wish to have any now."

Cocky bastard, this guy. But then, I'd seen him fight, for whatever reason he showed me that; it wasn't too much of a stretch to believe him, that he could easily handle any threat one of his demons might come at him with. "No impertinence, huh?" I asked. "Seriously? In a thousand years, you've never been in a real fight outside that coliseum thing you got?"

"Not with any of my subjects," he said. "The beasts of the wastes beyond Dis now and then, of course, but no Sins, no civilized demons.

Beyond regular combat exhibitions, nobody has so much as raised a hand to me in centuries."

"So is that why you got so weird and excited when I slapped you?" I asked.

He cleared his throat and looked away. "That is a fair assumption, I suppose, yes," he said in the closest thing to a mutter I'd heard from him so far.

I wish I could've done that raising one eyebrow thing. Instead, I furrowed my brow and narrowed my eyes, giving him my best look of suspicious caution. "This isn't some kind of weird masochistic sex thing, is it?" I asked. "You're not gonna want me to step on you and call you names or anything, are you?"

"You're quite hung-up on this suspicion of my sexual intentions, aren't you, milady?" he asked with an annoyed frown. "I told you I had none where you're concerned, did I not? And what is 'masochistic?'"

Right, he was probably older than that word, wasn't he? "You know," I said, "like … when you get off on being hurt and stuff. Like —"

"Oh," he said, cutting me off. "That. No, we have Luxuriates for that sort of thing. Giving or receiving."

Of course. I don't know why I'd thought I needed to explain S&M to the ruler of Hell.

Thankfully, when I didn't respond right away, the prince changed the subject. "Now I have a question, Lady Morgan," he said, leaning forward. "A great deal, of course, but first among them, I must know: How did you come to be here?"

"Me? I — uh…" I stopped myself before I answered, a little alarm going off in my head. I'd mentioned magic to Sidona, and she'd seemed to think the idea dangerous. Dramoc had been downright scared of it, accusing me of trying to get him arrested. Whatever was at play here, one thing I could infer fairly safely: magic was a no-no. "Accident," I said with a shrug.

Vambrace cocked an eyebrow at me, the jerk. "I gathered as much," he said. "But in all my years here, you are the only other human I have ever encountered. It must have been quite the singular accident."

Shit, I had to elaborate. "Yeah, uh… there was a witch. Not a very good one. Showed up in my apartment — uh, in my home one day. She cast this weird spell on me, and when I woke up, I was in some demon's store. An Avaritiate named Dramoc."

"From whom Lord Ulfris bought you," said the prince with a nod. "But what did a witch want with you? And why send you here?"

"I don't think she meant to," I said. "Pretty sure she was trying to do something else and screwed up. Like I said, she wasn't very good at what she was doing."

He stroke his chin a moment longer, looking at the ground between us. "This witch," he said slowly. "What did she look like?"

Son of a bitch, really? "I didn't get a very close look at her face," I said. "It was nighttime, and everything happened so fast." I was still waiting for the point where I had to break into outright lies.

"Did she have raven black hair, by chance?" the prince persisted. "Long, probably? Tall for a woman, with high cheekbones and gray eyes?"

Well, she had one of those things. "Maybe," I said. "That sounds vaguely familiar. Why, you got a particular witch in mind?"

"I do," he said, frowning intently at the ground. "The one who sent me here. And if she sent you as well…" He rose suddenly, then set to quickly pacing the floor between us. "But why?" he asked, but not to me. "We have no connection, you and I. Impossible you could be any distantly descended relation. I left none. Sent to bring me back? To kill me?" He stopped, eyeing me sidelong with a good amount of open suspicion. I shook my head and tried to look as nonthreatening as possible, which didn't feel like too much of a challenge. "Doubtful," he concluded after several long seconds of scrutiny. "She would be foolish to have forgotten the advantages I hold or to assume I had lost them, and she was never foolish. It would take more than one confused woman to do the job."

I scowled. But I was inclined to agree with him, and anyway, arguing that I could kick his ass just out of pride was a bad move and a dumb one, on top of being obviously wrong.

"Unless you were meant to subdue me through more subtle arts," he continued thinking aloud. "It would fit her pattern. But if you are bait sent to seduce me into a trap, you are taking an interesting approach."

I smacked the pillow down on my legs in annoyance. "Dammit, dude, I've told you already —"

"I know," he said. "I'm inclined to believe the veracity of your lack of interest by now, Lady Morgan, don't worry." He turned fully toward me then, studying me with the same air Sidona had back in her salon. "Perhaps this is a foolish risk on my part, but I'm also inclined to believe that this air of being harmlessly out of your depth is no act either."

"Anyone ever tell you you're kind of a jerk?" I asked. His veneer of intimidating authority was wearing thinner the longer I spent with him alone.

He smiled. "Not in a very long time, no," he said. "Apologies, my lady. If you are not secretly her agent, I can think of no other reason for you to be here. At least, none that have to do with me. And if you did not ask to be sent here…"

"I'm pretty sure there's no real reason," I assured him. "Pretty sure it was just a big fluke."

"Hmm…" Again, I got his thoughtful study. "What is your heritage, Lady Morgan?"

"My huh?"

"I grant that it has been a while since I saw any of my former kinsmen," continued the prince. "Still, I do not remember any Briton women with features like your own. I am curious."

"Probably because I'm not British," I said. This was going to be a complicated conversation coming on, I could feel it.

He cocked his eyebrow again. "Yet you speak the king's tongue eloquently, if with strange dialect. From the continent, are you?"

"From America," I said. "You wouldn't have heard of it back in 500 AD or whenever. It's a whole other continent across the ocean to the west."

"Near the edge of the world?" he asked, that look of hungry interest coming back to his face. "And they speak the king's British?"

"It's not —" I started, then abandoned the thought before I could get to it. I really didn't feel like explaining to him about the roundness of the Earth. "Britain sent people over a few centuries back," I settled on saying. "Most people there can speak English now."

"English?" he said, as if the word left a sour taste in his mouth. "The Angles have had a presence as well? Not at the same time as the Britons, I would imagine."

For the first time since sophomore finals, I wished I'd retained more of what I'd learned about European history. "Yeah, Angles," I said. "Anglo-Saxons and Britons. That whole general area. There aren't a lot there now, though. Mostly just the native Americans." I paused. "Well, not a lot of *Native* Americans these days, actually. It's, uh, a bit complicated to explain, I guess."

"Your heritage is American, then?" he asked. "You are sure?"

The easiest, simplest answer would have been "Yes," but damned if I would realize that in time. "Well, my birth mother was Japanese," I said, falling back into the rote explanation I'd practically memorized word-for-word by now. "She came to the U.S. for college and had me while she was there. Surrendered me as a newborn. I was in foster care until I was three and my mom and dad adopted me. They're both white. That's why we don't look alike." I hadn't realized just how fully I'd slipped into my usual, automatic story until I reached that final point and remembered he hadn't asked because of my parents. And had probably never heard of Japan either, or knew what "the U.S." meant.

But he didn't ask about any of those things. Instead, he just nodded and said, "I see."

Something about the way he said it bugged me, though. "What do you see?" I asked.

"I was thinking that you have a bit of a fae look to you," he said as if his suspicion had just been confirmed. "Are you certain that you're not a changeling?"

Oh, what the hell? This shit again? "Yeah, I'm pretty certain," I snapped, rising from my seat and glaring at him. "I'm pretty damn sure I'm a human and not a damn fairy or some other mystical bullshit. It's really not that big a fucking mystery, especially after I just finished explaining it!"

I reined in my temper after I'd already crossed about half the space between us without thinking, watching his smug face change to confusion and then concern as I advanced. He didn't back away from me, though, and I had to remind myself he probably wasn't being an asshole on purpose. Especially considering we were both surrounded by plenty of actual mystical bullshit, this might have been the first time that the question was actually somewhat warranted.

Still. Here I was on an entirely different plane of existence, in a different world or dimension or whatever, and I was still fielding these stupid questions. The universe had a crappy sense of humor.

"My apologies again," he said when I'd finished yelling at him. "I meant no offense, my lady, I assure you."

With an effort, I calmed down. "Yeah," I said with a sigh. "Yeah, I know. It's fine." I ran the heels of my hands over my eyes, suddenly very tired. Physically from all the walking, mentally from absolutely everything else. When I opened them again, he was still staring at me, a weird smile on his lips. "What?" I asked.

"Such venom!" he said, shaking his head. "T'was unexpected."

"T'was it?" I asked, smiling despite myself. "Sorry. People get nosy with me about that subject a lot back home, without your excuse."

"No, don't apologize," he said, shaking his head again. "Embrace it. It will be one of your advantages in this place."

I frowned. "Being adopted?"

"No," he said, "being unpredictable. Showcasing the full range of what a human can feel, who we can be."

My frown deepened. "I don't follow."

"Let me ask you this," he said, sitting down on his bed again. "You've had enough dealings with demonkind by now, for better or worse, in spite of my attempts to prevent them. Have you had similar outbursts with any of them?"

"Uh… yeah, I suppose," I said. "Once or twice. I'm not usually that snappy, I promise, but my nerves have been frayed since I got here."

"And what was the reaction?" he asked.

I thought of butting heads with Rezavix, his confused arguments against doing what I demanded of him before ultimately complying. I thought of Dramoc and the suspicious caution that he'd greeted me with at both of our meetings, the way his eyes had lingered on me as if looking away might be dangerous.

"Bewilderment?" the prince continued before I could answer. "Surprise? Fear, maybe?"

"Dunno if I'd go that far," I said. "But yeah, something like that. I figured it was because I was human and that made me strange."

"Because you're human, yes," he said, nodding. "More accurately, because you're not an Iriate. Violent outbursts and smoldering anger are their purview alone, and to see that aspect in another race is jarring."

I started to nod out of habit, but stopped. "Wait," I said, "no. That doesn't sound right. I saw Dramoc get angry with the Acediate who brought me to him when they were discussing my price. I saw Sidona snap at the Iriate guard who took me from her salon because she thought he was disrespecting her."

"Frustration, yes," said Vambrace. "You saw an Acediate's indignation at being haggled with, and you saw a Superbiate get defensive of her pride when she suspected insult. But you didn't see wrath from either, did you?"

"I guess not," I said with a shrug. "But I haven't exactly gotten violently angry with anyone yet myself." I paused, finger to my lip. "Oh," I amended, "well, I did punch Dramoc in the head, I guess, but I was scared at the time."

Prince Vambrace laughed at that. "A demon was menacing you, so you punched him?" he said as his chuckling petered out. "Is that how young maidens are brought up back home now?"

"It's how *I* was brought up, anyway," I said. "First time I've ever actually needed to hit a guy, though, near as I can remember."

"And I'm willing to bet that with that single assault, you've committed more violence in your young life already than nearly every demon in my realm besides the Iriates." He paused a thoughtful moment. "Well, and besides the Luxuriates I mentioned before, the ones they train to use those whips." He trailed off for a few seconds after that, gaze turned inward at some image I didn't care to peek at. "Anyway," he continued a moment later, "the point is, a demon's personality skews very heavily in a single direction. They feel and think and experience, very intensely and with great nuance, according to whichever aspect they align with by species. Very much in that one vein, and very little outside of it. You and I may never know rage, may never fully understand hatred or the thrill of revenge, as intensely and intimately as even the calmest, nicest Iriate in my kingdom. But we *do* know it within the scope of human ability and may act accordingly, which is more than all but one-seventh of the demon population can say." He grinned, tapping his temple with a finger. "At all times, you have seven times as many options open to you, seven times as many ways to behave or react to the world, than any demon you meet. One realm in which you are outmatched, six more in which you hold an advantage. It keeps everyone guessing, hesitant and unsure as to what you think, what you will do, how to deal with you to get what they want from you. Remember that. Use it."

"Huh." I sat back in my chair, gazing up at the vaulted ceiling and letting that sink in. What would that be like, I wondered, having your personality cordoned off like that just because of what race you were? I would have thought it sounded like stereotyping if I hadn't seen pretty convincing truth of what he was talking about myself. Still, sounded like a shitty draw to me; like, maybe if you were lucky enough to be born a Superbiate, you'd love yourself and everyone would respect you, but what if you got stuck as one of those grumpy brown ones no one seemed to pay any attention to? Or you were an Iriate, and you were pissed at the world all day every day, even when nothing was wrong? Or, hell, what if you were one of the other ones and you could never get properly angry, even when you needed to, even when it was deserved? Having whole spectrums of emotions locked off and unavailable sounded almost as bad as being stuck feeling just the one at full throttle forever.

Then again...

I picked idly at the seam of the pillow in my arms as I frowned at the ceiling. How often did I really use my emotions? They'd been running rampant since I got here, fear and confusion and anxiety ramping them up until I felt like a mess in my own head. But back home, back in my normal world in my normal life, how often did I really feel... anything? Anything substantial? Not in the broody goth girl sense — I'd flirted briefly with that idea in high school, but I couldn't even make myself care enough to not care about anything that flagrantly. No, aside from streaks of irritation at schoolwork or my transit system or other people, I'd always lived a fairly subdued inner life. No great peaks or troughs, no flares of happiness or depression or anything, no great desires other than to keep my head down and get through life, do well enough at school and see what came next when it got there.

And then that damn book happened, and now I was here. If this whole thing ended up being some orchestrated journey to find myself and learn some life lesson, like some reverse Narnia-style bullshit, I was gonna punch that shop owner lady in her stupid smiling face when I got home.

And there it was again, that flare of anger sharper than I was used to feeling before meeting her and the *Morganomicon*. Crap, it was working! All this demony-ness was rubbing off on me; I was becoming one of *them*!

"M'lady?" said Prince Vambrace, snapping me back to the present. "Did I lose you in reverie?"

"Yeah," I muttered, sitting up straight in my seat again. "Sorry. Digesting."

He nodded. "It's a lot to take in at first. You're doing better so far than I did, though, when I ended up here."

"Yeah?" I pulled my legs up in my seat, hugging the pillow to my chest. "And how did that happen, exactly?"

He flashed a wry smile. "Same way you did," he said. "A witch did it."

"A witch you're still worried about fifteen hundred years later, if I caught that right," I said. "You think she's even still alive?"

He shrugged. "I am," he said. "And to be frank, I was nothing special back on Earth. I'd be thoroughly surprised if I managed to keep alive this long and Morgana hadn't."

I frowned. "Morgana? The witch's name was Morgana?" There was another stupid, unbelievable puzzle piece coming my way, I could feel it.

"They apparently still tell tales of Arthur in your present time," the prince said with a knit brow. "They even mention the table. Do they not speak of the fae sorceress Morgana in any of these tales?"

That feeling like the bottom dropping out of my stomach was getting annoyingly familiar. "Morgan le Faye," I said flatly. "She was really a person too."

He nodded. "So, you can understand my hesitance when another Lady Morgan appears in *my* court all of a sudden all these years later. You even bear similar features, which is why I wondered, perhaps rudely, if you were also of the fae." He quirked an eyebrow at me. "We've already established that you can't share blood with me, though, so don't try and play the lost half-sibling card."

Morgan le Faye. The *Morganomicon*. And here we both were in Hell together. Motherfucker.

"Why don't..." I began slowly, but had to stop and take a deep breath before I could continue. "Why don't you tell me what happened? What's *your* story with this witch?"

Vambrace frowned. "She kept a regular presence at court. I spent years bumping into her during my squirehood. You want the full story?"

Something in his demeanor made it sound like the full story was something he'd rather not share, or at least not with me, not yet. "I'm mostly curious how you ended up here," I said.

"Ah. Well..." He ran a hand through his short black locks, taking a deep breath himself and letting it out slowly. "It is not a proud story, nor a flattering one, and none alive today know it. But..." His eyes locked with mine, and that steel of regal authority he'd largely set aside up til now came back to them. "Advisable or not, we needs must trust one another if we are both to continue surviving this place. Very well. I will tell you." He squared his shoulders and shut his eyes. "My last shame, and the second biggest mistake I ever made."

Chapter 13: Dishonor

Vambrace crouched in the overgrowth behind a wide tree and watched as Sir Bedivere struggled to climb the rise in front of him, their king draped awkwardly over his back. Neither man had their full armor on anymore. There was no need; their enemies were dead or scattered, and time was precious, bleeding as it was down the knight's back.

He managed to top the rise before stumbling and falling to one knee, jarring the king hanging over his shoulders, who mumbled something inaudible into Bedivere's ear. The knight grit his teeth against his heavy breathing, nodded in acknowledgement, and slowly eased the king backward against a nearby tree trunk, carefully propping him up before collapsing himself to catch his breath. His copper hair was plastered to his face with sweat and dirt and other men's blood.

Perhaps it would be best to rush the both of them now. Bedivere was wounded, that much was obvious — crusted blood peeked through a gash in his trousers at his thigh. He would survive, but at the moment, pain and blood loss weakened him. And Arthur…

Vambrace shuddered as a fresh pang of guilt lanced through him. Great Arthur, beloved sovereign of the Britons, the Once and Future King, looked like shit. Blood leaked in rivulets from his lips and bloomed a dark crimson through his tunic, visible even under his rent mail. One of his eyes was swollen shut, and blood caked his mat of red-gold hair. Sir Mordred was as fine a swordsman as any at Camelot's court, but with a mace he was a terror, able to crush a man's life out through his armor. That Arthur was merely broken and bloody instead of outright pulverized, that Mordred now lay headless in a field, was testament to the king's prowess in battle, though that served him little now.

"Bedivere," the king rasped, "here. Take my sword." Despite his weakness, his hand reached unerringly for the weapon at his waist and closed firm about the hilt, and the dying king unsheathed it in a single fluid stroke. The overcast sunlight, weakened still further through the treetops and forest haze, nevertheless gleamed from the polished silver blade like torchlight at midnight as he proffered the sword to his last remaining knight.

Bedivere reached for it in awe, his gauntleted hands pausing in hesitation over the mighty weapon, then turned his face away. "I cannot, Sire," he said quietly. "I am not worthy."

"Bullshit." Arthur smiled through the blood on his lips as his knight looked back at him with widened eyes. Vambrace stifled a contrite groan at the sight of it; that their king could find any shred of cheer left in him after what had befallen them cut like an unwanted benediction, and he felt more the Judas than ever. "As worthy as any," said Arthur, the deep timbre of regal decree still audible in his voice beneath his labored breathing, "and more worthy than most. Please, Bedivere. I ask not as a king to his knight, but as a man to his dearest friend. Take Excalibur..."

Sir Bedivere reached again for the sword in Arthur's hand, hesitating once more before finally closing his gauntlets firmly around hilt and blade and lifting it from the king's grip.

Arthur nodded in gratitude, still faintly smiling. "...and throw it into the lake," he finished.

Vambrace was lucky that Bedivere's surprise mirrored his own; the rustle of the knight's armor as his head snapped up and his gasped "What?!" drowned out the strangled protestation that died in Vambrace's throat. He bit down hard on his naked finger in agitation as well as to stifle any more noise he might unexpectedly blurt out.

The king shook his head, waving his hand in a dismissive gesture. Now that it no longer held his sword, it trembled in the air as he did so. Arthur was draining quickly. "Oh, do not look so stricken, Bedivere," he rasped. "I ask only what is proper."

"But m'lord," Bedivere protested regardless, "surely this is the fever of injury speaking. To throw it away as though it were but used rags seems unseemly."

"I am not disposing of it, Bedivere," Arthur reassured him. "It was never mine to begin with, so I hold no claim over its fate. I merely seek to return it to its rightful owner. As I am not long for this world, the task now falls to you. Take my sword, and throw it into Lake Evienne, and return to me with what you see." With that, the king lay his head back against the trunk he sat propped against, while Bedivere, looking the picture of reluctance but nodding his understanding, slowly walked off into the trees, leaving his king behind to carry out his final order.

Vambrace bit down hard enough on his own finger to break the skin, his other hand gripping the bark of the tree he hid behind with enough force to gouge the bark and drive it under his nails. He paid neither injury any heed, but instead stared frantically after the retreating Bedivere, bouncing on the balls of his feet as he crouched with nervous energy but unsure as to the wisest way to spend it, knowing only that he must either act soon or resign himself to doom.

They were going to throw away Excalibur! The idea seemed monumental in its folly, yet their king had ordered it done with nary a pause. What good would it do anyone sitting at the bottom of a lake? And without it, what would Vambrace tell the witch? Their contract would be broken, and then he would have her wrath to deal with as well as the combined total wrath of the entire country. He wasn't sure which he feared more: Britain or Morgana.

He risked another glance at Arthur and found the dying king resting where he'd been left, eyes shut, a faint smile still playing on his bloody lips, his chest rising and falling only faintly. Only when he was sure that his former lord wouldn't spot him did Vambrace dare rise from his position in the brush and creep, quickly and quietly as he could, across the trail after Bedivere. There was no way that Arthur could give chase or stop him even if he were spotted, the shamed squire knew, but he still hated the thought of anyone witnessing his final act of betrayal, least of all the king. Best to finish his crime quickly and spare any God-fearing Briton the sight of him ever again.

If it were still possible. If Arthur's delirium and Bedivere's damnable obedience hadn't doomed him already.

Trailing the knight through the darkening forest proved no challenge. Bedivere was slowed by his injury and the exhaustion of a desperate battle that had ended barely over an hour ago, and he crashed clumsily through the trees and underbrush with no thought to quiet or hiding his path. Why should he? Their enemies had been crushed utterly, and what few stragglers might have survived would be in even worse shape than the last remaining of Arthur's loyal knights, in no shape to even follow Bedivere, much less catch him unawares and overpower him.

Except for Vambrace, who had fled the field the moment that chaos broke out amongst their ranks, abandoning his master and his king both to their long-coming clash. He couldn't have saved Mordred even had he stayed, and he couldn't have stood against Arthur, so he didn't regret his choice. He regretted only that it had come to making it.

Vambrace gave Bedivere a wide berth as he trailed the knight, sticking to the shadows and the thickest patches of growth on their way to Lake Evienne. There was no easy path through the choking forest, not even so much as a deer track to follow; the lake was disconnected from civilization, small and isolated, its location unknown even to most of the Round Table. But Arthur knew where it was, which meant so did Bedivere. And if Arthur's right hand was willing to leave the king propped and bleeding behind him to carry out this task, then it couldn't be too far away.

He tracked the knight for maybe half an hour through the mist-laden woods, slowing when Bedivere stumbled and stopping when he paused to catch his breath. Twice Vambrace lost sight of his quarry over a rolling hill or in the steadily gathering mist ahead, but even then, the knight's labored breathing and heavy footfalls never dimmed from his hearing, and his heavy, shuffling gait left a clear enough trail regardless in the damp leaves covering much of the forest floor. The chill of mid-autumn grew the further they went, until Vambrace's fogged breaths were lost in the thickening mist — until he followed Bedivere into an unexpected clearing that appeared suddenly before them. Here the air grew temperate, and the mists parted as if an unseen boundary had been crossed.

Vambrace stopped on the edge of the clearing, still behind the tree line, straddling that strange border of chill mist and warm, calm air. In front of him, Bedivere had stopped and stood with his back to his unseen pursuer. Before the knight stretched Lake Evienne, clear and placid and completely still, looking more like a massive silver mirror set into the forest floor than any natural lake. Though it had been early evening when they both set off from where Arthur lay, and they had been walking not even a full hour, here in the clearing about the lake, it seemed like night had fallen. Soft light that more resembled moonlight than the sun's rays filtered through the thick treetops to reflect off the surface of the water.

Still facing the lake, Bedivere lifted the sword in his hand, its gleaming blade matching the lake's strange silver radiance, both of them near glowing in the gloom. With Excalibur held out reverently before him, the knight took a slow step toward the water's edge.

Vambrace knew panic once more. This fool was really going to do it! Not that he should have expected aught else — Bedivere would likely cleave off his own sword arm if only Arthur asked him to. A fault in the knight brought on by blind devotion, or one more sign of the Pendragon's unnatural perfection? He couldn't say, and at the moment, it didn't matter. All that mattered was getting that sword.

He could jump the knight, take him by surprise while he was absorbed in his task. With Bedivere injured and tired, he might even be able to best Camelot's most seasoned veteran. But if he left the knight alive and fled with the sword, he would be pursued, first by Bedivere himself, and then by the full might of what was left of Arthur's loyal forces. Supposing the witch kept her word and worked quick, it wouldn't be a problem, but if she didn't…

He could kill Bedivere. Doing so would never be easier than right now, especially if he got a hold of the sword. But with all of the sins he'd committed already and the one he still had yet to finish, was he willing to add the knight's murder in cold blood to that list? Likely it would be but a drop in the bucket by this point, but then who would be left to tend to Arthur? The Once and Future King would bleed out on the side of the road with none to mark his passing. The thought of being the cause of such an ignoble end was too much a blasphemy to bear, even now.

Perhaps he should let Bedivere toss the blade and leave unmolested. He could always dive in after it once the coast was clear, save it from rusting in obscurity beneath a forgotten pond in the middle of nowhere. The lake had an unmistakable awe about it, true, but it wasn't that big. He could find it again easily enough. Unless the whispers about this place were true, of course, in which case Excalibur would be lost to him forever the moment it touched that water's surface, and with it, any hope he had left of escaping the retribution he was soon due.

Vambrace ground his teeth against the frustrated expletives rising in his throat. None of his options were ideal, but he'd abandoned ideals long ago. No need to rediscover them here at the end. Whatever he did, the important thing was he do it now. Bedivere pulled his sword arm back, readying to throw. With a deep breath, Vambrace darted out from his place in the tree line.

And skidded to a halt only a few feet away, the damp grass masking the sound of his movement. Bedivere had paused, arm still cocked behind him, his breath expelled in a wordless huff. Slowly, the knight brought the sword around before him once more, gazing down at the simple blade of gleaming silver. Vambrace kept his eyes on both knight and sword as he slowly crept backward to his hiding place once more. He'd only just crouched down again in the mist and shadow when Bedivere turned, striding with new purpose not toward the lake's edge but toward the scrubby bushes nearby. The squire watched with anxious curiosity as the knight crouched amidst the low foliage, obscured for the moment from Vambrace's view. When he rose again, he was no longer holding the sword, but gazed down at a spot just before his feet, hands clenching and unclenching at his sides. A moment later, he turned and strode back the way they'd both come, back and shoulders stiff, injury apparently forgotten for the moment as he marched almost angrily away from the enchanted lake. Vambrace hunkered down further in the shadowed roots of the tree he hugged and willed the knight not to see him, but Bedivere strode by without a backward glance not three feet from where he hid, shivering when he hit the chill mist but not slowing, as if he could not be away from this place fast enough.

Vambrace willed his breathing to slow as he listened to the knight's departure, and only once he could no longer discern the tromp of Bedivere's heavily booted feet in the distance did he risk standing. The knight had no longer held the sword as he passed. Surely he hadn't...

The squire almost tripped as he rushed over to the brush where Bedivere had knelt, falling to his knees and frantically parting the brush all around him. He stopped, his breath catching in his throat, as he caught sight of the silver gleaming back up at him from the ground, wedged deep in the tangled roots at the base of the thickest patch of growth.

Vambrace swallowed, unsure whether he wanted to laugh or cry, and unable to believe his luck. Sir Bedivere — loyal, obedient Bedivere, the right hand of the king in polite company, Arthur's lapdog according to Mordred and those who had been loyal to him — had disobeyed his king at the eleventh hour, deliberately failing to fulfill what may well be Arthur's final wish.

A perverse smile spread unbidden across his lips at that. Just more proof to validate what his master had said all along. Arthur's charm and perfection inspired blind devotion, but only to a point. In the end, nobody could live unblemished before such an unattainable example. Arthur's light cast all of Camelot in shadow by comparison, even the most righteous of his knights. If even Bedivere forsook his vows, even now, then none of them had really ever had any hope. Arthur's dream had been doomed from the start. King and dream alike were too good for this world.

Like Bedivere before him, Vambrace hesitated as he reached for the sword, wondering briefly if he could even touch the thing. Pure and perfect Arthur wielded it like God's own wrath, and Bedivere seemed to have no problems carrying it, but himself? The only mortal more tainted than he in all of Britain was his master, and Excalibur's bite had been like poison to Mordred, cleaving man and armor alike with unnatural ease. Maybe Vambrace couldn't take it after all. Maybe its mere touch would sear him like the hellfire that awaited him if he was found and fell now.

But it was Morgana to whom he was to deliver the blade, who had coveted it long before Camelot began to fall apart. Even with whatever terrible magic she possessed, if the likes of she could hold it, then he had no excuse.

He grabbed the handle and rose from the brush in one quick motion, holding the blade breathlessly out in front of him. Once more it gleamed in the scant moonlight, polished silver not of this world, but strikingly plain otherwise — a far cry from the gaudy, gilded, gem-encrusted thing that some of the more farfetched tales of it mentioned. No, Excalibur was the perfect complement to its perfect wielder: simple, unassuming, but flawless and with an unnatural power far more practical and terrible than mere wealth and pomp.

But it didn't burn him at his touch like he'd feared, nor did it turn on him to strike him down for his crimes. It merely sat in his grip, light and comfortable and perfectly balanced, as if designed specifically for his hand.

The thought unnerved him, for some reason.

Vambrace pulled his own sword from its scabbard, and holding the two at once, he couldn't help but compare. His blade was a heavy iron bastard that really had been designed specifically for him, wieldable with one or both hands as his need saw fit. Now, though, it felt clumsy and unwieldy in his grip next to Arthur's discarded sword — an ugly metal club for an uncivilized brute with which to beat his fellow savages to death. Scowling, the squire slipped his personal sword naked into his sword belt on the right side, sliding Excalibur home in the vacated scabbard on his left. The two blades were about the same size, and it seemed smarter than carrying the king's sword unsheathed for all the world to see.

Until he turned to leave and heard a sharp hiss, followed by a thud on the ground to his left. He pulled his foot back reflexively as Excalibur's blade came to rest right where his toes had been, and when he felt for his scabbard, he found it gaping open on the side. The blade had parted the leather like parchment on its way to the ground.

With a muffled curse, Vambrace picked the sword up once more and fled the clearing, his iron blade bouncing unrestrained against his right leg, the useless remains of its scabbard flapping open on his left, Excalibur held carefully out before him as if to part any obstacle in his path. Just before he crossed the unseen barrier back into the mists, he felt the unmistakable pinprick at his back of someone unseen watching him, but when he spun around again, Excalibur raised before him, all he saw was the placid and gleaming waters of Lake Evienne. There was no doubt he stood alone in the clearing, but regardless, the feeling didn't abate. Swallowing his nervousness, he turned and ran, ignoring the sensation of phantom eyes staring after him.

It was about a three-hour trek from the trail by Lake Evienne to the rolling, untamed hills in the northeast that the witch had designated for their meeting place. Vambrace made the journey in just over an hour, sweating so fiercely even in the chill evening air that he feared he'd rust his shirt of mail, and wondering if he'd ever fully get his breath back.

His own sword had slipped and fallen out of his sword belt long ago in his flight; unwilling to go back and look for it, he instead opted to drop the whole belt and ruined scabbard as well, shedding all the weight he dared. He arrived at the hillside ring of crumbling stones — one of many that dotted the landscape beyond Camelot's civilizing reach — with only his mail shirt, breeches, tunic, boots, and the steel vambraces he wore on either wrist, an unsheathed Excalibur in one hand, the other braced against his knee as he leaned forward and tried to catch his breath.

"You're early, pup."

The voice sent him straightening to his feet again, brandishing his stolen blade in front of him out of reflex. He'd recognized the voice before his stance was finished, though, and so knew the gesture to be worthless bluster. Even if he did have Excalibur now, someone like him would need more than that to threaten someone like her.

She laughed softly like wind chimes in the rain as she stepped out from the shadow of the tallest stone, raven black hair hanging straight and gleaming but speckled throughout with bits of leaf and twig. The same natural debris clung to the red velvet and gold brocade of her form-hugging gown, and when she smiled, he saw hints of the same moonlight gleam that seemed to perpetually glimmer from the sword in his hands. "How was it done?" she asked, striding — stalking — toward him, heedless of the blade still leveled at her. "Did the wolf pup truly best the wounded dragon and take his claw? Or did he just pry it away and run while the injured beast slept?"

She stopped with the tip of the sword less than an inch from her chest but didn't move to take it or even look at it. Instead, she smiled levelly at him, tall for a woman, her storm gray eyes unwavering as they gazed into his own with the same color. Near as he could tell, this fact that they shared the same irises was the first and strongest thing that drew the witch to him in the beginning. That he'd willingly served Sir Mordred, whom some said was her son, as squire even after his treasonous talk began seemed more a nice side note to her than the basis of their mutual alliance.

With another deep breath, Vambrace lowered the blade. "Neither," he said. "I took it from Sir Bedivere, who tried and failed to throw it into the lake at the king's command."

She threw her head back and laughed aloud then, wild and unrestrained mirth carrying across the empty hillside. He flinched and turned, scanning the horizon for approaching enemies cued to their location by her voice, but of course there were none. She'd promised they'd be alone in this place. Whatever else he might say about her, her confidence was always well-founded, at least.

"From dragon to lion to wolf!" she said as her laughter died down. "Such an appropriate decline to usher in the dark days ahead. Well and so, here we stand. Are you ready, pup?"

He'd asked her once to stop calling him that. She'd ignored him then, and he knew not to ask again. Still, he made no show to hide his annoyance as he laid the sword across both of his hands, gazing down at its mythical edge one last time before holding it out to her. "Take it," he said.

Instead, she turned and strode back to the shadow she'd occupied earlier, returning this time with an empty, unadorned scabbard of dull gray metal. Unpolished silver? he wondered. It couldn't be iron or steel or else she wouldn't have been able to hold it so closely with no signs of pain — at least, if the stories about her were true. Many were, but just as many were not, and it was nigh impossible to separate fact from fiction.

Holding the scabbard in both hands, she held out the empty top to him. "Place it," she said.

He hesitated. "It won't stay," he said. "I lost my own in the same manner. The one you hold seems sturdier than mine, I grant you, but you especially ought to know the power of this blade."

"Smart fool," she cooed, stepping closer. "You would be right, were I as ill prepared as you assume." One of her hands found the crook of his elbow, and she gently guided his arm in its movement, hefting the sword and lining up its point with the open scabbard. "But tell me, pup. What happens when an unstoppable force meets an immovable object?"

Before he could answer, she quickly slipped the scabbard up and over the blade until it connected with a ringing click with the hilt. Vambrace was surprised enough that his grip on the weapon loosened, and with a tug and a turn of her body, she pulled Excalibur from his hand and away from him, cradling sword and scabbard alike to her bosom like a doll. The blade held inside its new housing, gleaming edge contained at last, and the scabbard showed no sign of damage from its presence.

As if it were made for the blade, the squire realized.

"You had it," he said, accusation and realization mixing in equal measure in his voice. "Excalibur's original scabbard, the king's aegis. The one that was lost. You've had it all along."

"Of course I have, stupid boy," she said, still smiling sweetly, her ivory cheek resting against the sword's pommel like a lover's caress. "It was never lost. I merely took it back. Your king didn't tell you?"

"It could have saved him!" Vambrace said with a menacing step forward. "It could have saved everything! If the stories about it are true —"

"Such stock you put in stories all of a sudden!" she returned, smile dropping. It wasn't a threat, not quite, but it was enough to send him stepping backward again. "Was that not why you joined with your master, because you both spit in the face of Arthur's many wondrous stories? Stories that stoked your own inadequacy? If the king had this scabbard and it had saved him, as you say, would that not have ensured your own destruction, little pup?" Her lip twitched. Not a smile this time, but more a thoughtful smirk. "A bit late for your allegiance to be so unstable, is it not? Tell me true, what is it you actually want? Do you even know?"

He grit his teeth against fear and anger. The time for either was long gone and fading fast. "What I want," he said slowly, "is to be quit of this place and far away. Somewhere Arthur and Mordred and these delusions of chivalry cannot follow seeking revenge." He forced himself to meet her eyes once more. "The dream of Camelot is over. I want to go somewhere I can wake up."

With another light, tinkling chuckle, her grin returned. Whether he'd impressed her with his conviction or amused her with his cowardice, he couldn't say. But she pulled her face from the otherworldly sword and nodded all the same. "I know just the place."

With a crook of her finger, she ushered Vambrace to the center of the stone ring, stepping carefully as she did over lines of loose, raised dirt.

Runes, he realized; the dirt had been poured evenly in looping, geometric shapes that made a circle concentric with the stones surrounding them. If he looked too long at the pattern, the loose earth seemed to writhe and shift as though it were a thing living, so he kept his eyes on her and the sheathed blade she carried.

She spun with a flourish, halting his steps, one of her arms outstretched to her side, the other holding the scabbard before her. "It will be a one-way journey," she said. "One that very few have taken throughout the vastness of time. You are quite sure that all of your affairs in Britain are well and truly complete?"

"There remains but one left," he said, patience thinning, "and I am here because I would keep it from being completed. No more reassurances, witch — I have made what peace I can, I am done with my country, and I would not lament it if I never return. Do your spell, send me on my way, and let's be done with it." A beat later, he added, "Please," remembering to whom he spoke.

Her expression didn't change in the slightest. "As you wish, wolf pup," she said, then shut her eyes and, with a deep inhale, began to murmur something incomprehensible under her breath.

Vambrace stood and waited, trying not to fidget or look around and scan the hills for enemies again. He distrusted magic like he distrusted everything else about Camelot, and if he'd had any better options, he wouldn't be here. One last compromise, he told himself, just to be free and make a new start. Once he got wherever he was going, he'd be quit of magic and legends and impossible ideals for good.

He didn't notice at first when the spell began to kick in; he only noticed when he tried to shift the weight on his legs and found that he had no weight, that he was in fact floating slightly off the ground. He sucked in a quick, surprised breath at the realization and held it, muscles tensing and freezing in place. Despite the constant familiarity of magic that Arthur's court had allowed through persons like Merlin or this witch, Vambrace had never been the target of such unnatural powers before. If he didn't relax, would he botch the incantation? Or was his input irrelevant now that she had him in her mystical net?

The thought suddenly bothered him, as any sense of powerlessness always had. He could feel her power surging around him, growing, holding him aloft like a bauble in her hand. Chills ran down his spine, replaced by flashes of heat before he could even shiver. Magic — her magic — coursed around him, through him, her very will suffusing him. He took a deep breath and reminded himself that she was only doing as he had asked.

Wasn't she?

As soon as it crept in, the paranoia gripped him as surely as her magic and grew steadily. She'd promised to send him away, yes, but she hadn't been any more specific, and he hadn't cared enough to press for details. Who could say that where he landed would be any safer than where he was now? He had no sword; he'd lost his in his flight, handed Arthur's to the witch. He'd never had a shield, never gotten the hang of wielding one effectively in a fight. He had only his mail and vambraces for protection. If she betrayed him now and sent him somewhere hostile, either as her own idea of justice or through some mercurial whim, he'd make for an easy target.

No. No more. He'd been swept along by the wills of others for long enough, king or master or wizard or witch. He no longer knew what it was like to be free of others' influence, to be beholden only to his own strength and direction. But he would find out.

He could feel the spell reaching its climax, felt the sensation of being buffeted by swirling winds of fire and ice even as the tall grass on the hill around them stayed perfectly still. She stood before him with her eyes serenely shut, raven hair rustling gently as if in a soft breeze, lips still silently mouthing along to words he could neither hear nor comprehend. Her free arm floated at her side, fingers upraised and curled as if she held her power in her hand. Her other arm still hung in front of her, hand wrapped tight around the scabbard of Excalibur, the grip and pommel of the sword angled up and pointing away from her.

Pointing toward him.

For a moment, the whirlwind of magical power paused, and the whole world seemed to hold its breath. That's when he felt reality about to rip and fall away beneath him. That's when the witch finally opened her eyes once more as a mischievous grin crossed her lips. That's when the stars in the sky suddenly flared to impossible brilliance, swallowing up the night sky around them.

And that's when Vambrace reached out and grabbed Excalibur with both hands, ripping the blade up and out of its scabbard just as he was ripped up and out of the world.

"No!" she screamed, and he felt it more than heard it, felt her sudden rage streaking after him like lightning, bright and searing, as he tumbled away from her, from the hill, from everything he'd ever known. Sudden, intense pressure crushed down on him like a battering ram from all sides, forcing the air from his lungs. His eyes shut tight and refused to open as a series of blinding lights burst around him, just outside his eyelids or just beneath them, he couldn't say. He opened his mouth to scream but could not hear his own voice if it came out, only a deafening roar like a hundred waterfalls crashing all around him. He felt himself dissolving, felt as if he was being shredded bit by tiny bit from the inside out. And then, just as suddenly as it had begun, he felt nothing, heard nothing, saw nothing. Everything was stillness and blackness and silence, and whether he was dead or alive, he no longer cared.

But even as his last shred of consciousness faded and all sensation melted away, he held Excalibur clutched tight against his body like a frightened child clutching a doll, the pommel pressed firm against his cheek like a lover's caress.

Chapter 14: Admission

His sword was sitting propped against the bed beside him. I tried not to stare at it and failed, then tried to pry my eyes from it and failed at that too. The silence stretched on into long minutes after his story finished, the light rustle of his clothes and mail as he shifted in his seat on the bed the only noises in the room.

"M'lady?" he said eventually, voice hesitant. "Reverie again?"

"That," I said, pointing at the simple, faintly shining blade. "Your sword. You're saying… you're telling me that *that*… is Excalibur?" I jabbed a finger at the weapon again. "That's the *really real* Excalibur you got?"

"The very same." He reached for the blade, lifting and laying it across his knees. "Unfair, isn't it? Such an ignoble end for such a noble weapon, consigned to Hell with the man who stole it. Whatever fate Arthur imagined for it, whatever plans Morgana had in mind, I wrecked them both. I wonder, when the king returns, will he need to find a new weapon? Will he call this blade to his side once more across worlds? Or have I played a hand in dooming his second coming as well as his first with my treachery?"

"You seem broken up about it," I said, prying my eyes from the blade at last. It was easier now that staring at the sword also meant staring at his lap. "You didn't seem like you liked what you were doing in your story, either."

"So why did I do it?" he asked, looking up at me. I nodded. He smirked and went back to staring ruefully at the weapon. "What do you know of Arthur Pendragon? What do they say on Earth today of the Once and Future King?"

I stared down at the pillow still in my hands. I'd just had a test on this last semester, but we'd moved on since then. I was halfway through Beowulf now and didn't think I'd need Camelot anymore. "I know a lot of different people have written about him and Camelot and that whole period," I said. "The general consensus is he was a pretty great guy. United the country, stopped a lot of fighting, invented chivalry. Went on quests, saved damsels, fought bad guys. Generally a big hero who got a bunch of other heroes together and did great things, until…" I stopped. Would it be rude to bring up the adultery stuff in front of this guy?

"Until those closest to him, who had sworn their loyalty to him, began to betray him," Vambrace finished for me. "My master, Sir Mordred, plotting against him. Sir Lancelot and the queen cuckolding him. Even Merlin, abandoning him just as things grew most dire. Slowly, bit by bit, Arthur's great kingdom began to collapse, all his grand plans eroding and failing." He looked up at me again. "Do you know why?"

So much for sparing his feelings, then. "Because he wasn't as perfect as the stories say?" I guessed. "I assume he did at least a few unpopular things. I mean, he was only human, after all, right?"

"No," the prince said, eyes suddenly and uncomfortably intense as they bore into me. "No, my lady, not right at all. If Arthur had been only human, he may have succeeded. But he was not." He took a deep breath, exhaled raggedly, stared morosely down at Excalibur again. "He was the perfect king, the perfect *man*. An angel come to lead us weak mortals. In all he did, he made us love him. He made us want to better ourselves in his image."

The fanaticism in his voice was putting me on edge again. "And that's… bad?" I asked. "Why?"

"Because we could not!" he growled with such sudden vehemence that I swung the pillow up in front of me like a shield. He wasn't angry with me, though, just clutching the handle of his sword so tightly his knuckles blanched. "Because he gave us an ideal that we desperately wanted but could not attain, and the light of his unnatural perfection cast otherwise great men in shadow. Many of us, our love turned to resentment, and from there, for some of us, it turned to a perverse hatred. In the world before, full of strife and chaos, we may have been heroic; but under Arthur's leadership, we were merely flawed children playing at goodness and continually falling short." He stood then, holding Excalibur up before his face and staring into the point like a mirror. "Lancelot, who had the strongest sense of justice amongst all the knights, gave in to lust and temptation, lied to his liege lord, even tempted a civil war. Gawain, ever daring, ever willing to help those in need, grew more and more reckless attempting to prove himself worthy of the king's favor, until he finally disappeared on some unbidden fool's errand that served no one but his own guttering glory. Even our Queen Guinevere, who loved the king more than any of us, could not help but turn from him by the end, seek solace in the bed of another mere mortal rather than stay by the side of her godly husband. Camelot, Arthur's dream, was doomed from the start, but not because of Arthur — because of the rest of us who could not be worthy of his dream, who rendered the pursuit of his Earthly paradise into vain exercises in futility."

His rant done, he stood ramrod straight in place, his sword hand quivering under the force of his grip as he glared into the blade, lost in his brooding. I'd never met anyone this legitimately self-tormented, this poetically tragic, outside of something I was reading for a literature class. Must come with being a character from romantic legend because I hadn't seen angst like this in anyone else yet in Hell.

I didn't know anymore which was scarier to think about — that I was meeting ageless figures from mythical history, or that I was meeting literal demons.

"That sounds pretty heavy," I said after another few moments of awkward silence. "Sorry. I wouldn't know anything about how that feels." He turned slowly back to me then as if just remembering I was there, his posture slowly relaxing as he did. "If it makes you feel any better, though," I continued, "the world's not a total nightmare mess these days, even without Arthur or Camelot. Or at least…" I paused and frowned. "Well, it depends on who you ask, really, but we get by. We got laws and order, even if a lot of the laws are kinda… hateful to a lot of people. And I mean, there's always wars and hunger and disease and stuff, but not *everywhere*. And the Earth overall, it's… well, there's climate stuff, but…" I shrugged. "Look, it's not all bad all the time; and the stuff that really needs work, I don't think one guy with a sword was ever going to be the solution, no matter how good a king he was. The world you left is way far from a paradise, and it probably never will be, but I'm happy enough to be alive, if that helps."

He sighed slowly through his nose and let Excalibur drop in his hand, the tip pointed at the floor again. "That is… heartening, I suppose," he said, then tilted his head back and closed his eyes. "Apologies, m'lady. I have not had cause to think on my crimes for a long, long time, and I have no desire to relive them further now. Have you other questions?"

I was tired, I felt gross, and I had a lot to process and think about again. At that moment, flush with revelations and explanations though I'd just become, all I wanted was a bath and a nap. But I also wasn't sure when I'd get another shot at this guy behind his royal veneer, and I'll admit I was still curious about a whole lot of stuff. "What happened after you got here?" I asked, slipping my pillow behind my head and reclining against it. "They sat you on a throne for being human? The archfiend before you bought you and tucked you away in the palace somewhere while he figured out what to do with you?"

"Neither," he said with a slight, amused smile. "Dis was a very different place back then — more chaotic, less regulated, more dangerous for everyone. I did not make quite the same... splash as you have." He turned and sat back on the bed once more, carefully laying Excalibur aside atop the coverlet. "I was considered a curiosity, an outsider, but the demons of those days had more contact with humanity than they do today. Humans coming here almost never happened, but demons visiting Earth was not unusual. I was largely left alone to fend for myself as I could, to carve out a place for myself in the discord and defend myself as necessary. It was an easier task than it would have been otherwise with Excalibur at my side, of course. After a while, perhaps a year or two, word had gotten out fairly far and wide about the errant human living in the city, still alive and doing relatively alright for himself, and able to cut down any who tried to harm him. I was unusual, and I was competent. By then, fewer of Hell's denizens approached me with open malevolence, and more came seeking to make a deal." He steepled his hands and leaned over them, his elbows on his knees as he gazed into the middle distance between us. "For quite a while there, I made a fairly decent living doing mercenary work. I belonged to none of the seven Houses, so I had no vested political interests, no authorities to answer to for my actions. And I was willing to venture past the wall and into the wastes beyond if necessary. Or at least, I was more willing than any of the city's denizens. There were a great many people who brought me their problems, their jobs, that few other demons would want to touch."

"Jobs like what?" I asked.

He shrugged. "A good deal of killing," he said, then smiled when my eyes widened at the admission. "You have to remember," he continued, "I had just played a part in tearing down the great Arthur. I had a measure of the guilt surrounding his death, I'd stolen his sword, and I'd run from the consequences of those actions only to end up in Hell, which at the time seemed like terribly poetic justice. Indiscriminately killing demons sounded like as noble a calling as I was like to find by that point, even if other demons were paying for it. After all, if human worth had lost its luster for me after Camelot, what chance did demonkind have? Here, at least, there were no innocents, nobody to protect from the horrors and darkness of the world. We were all evil in some way, I thought, and nobody in those days cared who murdered who unless it directly affected themselves somehow. Justice was a foreign concept, and I assumed my work was the closest thing to it that Hell would get."

He shook his head. "Of course, it wasn't all murder. I stole, I threatened, I maimed to send a message. Destruction of property was a popular request, arson and vandalism and the like. I earned my biggest payments when I ventured out of the city to collect something someone needed from the forests or swamps or lakesides in the wastes, some rare specimen of flora or fauna needed for an Avaritiate's buyer or a Superbiate's art or a Gulliate's experiment. Before long, I had a standing residence in Ammonis, on the edge of Leviathanis. I had few expenses beyond food and shelter and upkeep of my armor, so I began amassing wealth and favors, growing in the esteem of my new neighbors, until I was no longer a dirty back-alley secret shared amongst my clients but a long-established and prominent merchant peddling a special, quality service."

"So, you just kept getting rich and famous until they elected you king or prince or whatever?" I asked. "Or, what, you bought the throne from the last guy or something?"

"Not quite," he said with a smirk. "I killed the last guy."

"You what?" I asked, frowning. "You killed the guy in charge, so they put *you* in charge? How does that work?"

"Usurping a throne? As it turned out, that was the longstanding rule of succession. You only get to hold the throne until you can't anymore, and whoever is enterprising enough to take it from you gets to try their hand at it next. That way, only the most ruthless and personally capable individuals are at the top of authority. All the better to keep Dis a formidable target and repel any dangers that may encroach from the wastes." He shrugged. "I didn't know any of that at the time, though. All I knew was I'd just finished a perilous and particularly unpleasant job for a client who'd insisted on keeping our meetings and his identity secret. When he tried to renege on payment, things turned violent. I had to cut down three expertly trained Iriate bodyguards before I could lay my hands on him, and even with Excalibur, I barely survived the fight. I would have had no chance with any other blade, I'm sure. It wasn't until I was dragging the bodies through the streets to display in front of my business that I learned who my former client was." Again, he shrugged. "Archfiend Ilxarvethel, a Superbiate who'd held the throne for all of a year, by my reckoning. He'd been on a campaign to preemptively eliminate anyone he thought might threaten his new reign, a task for which he'd hired my services. But apparently, he thought dealing with a mercenary was beneath him there at the end and didn't want to risk word getting out that he'd bought help from the city's resident human."

He stopped for a moment and looked to me, like he was waiting for a reaction. "Huh," was all I could think to say at the time.

That was apparently enough, because he continued after that. "His corpse and those of his bodyguards ignominiously paraded through the streets had the opposite effect, of course. Suddenly I was someone that even archfiends called on for help, someone to whom they fell if they displeased me. Ilxarvethel's bodyguards were also highly feared killers, but I had taken out all three of them, if barely and with luck. Not only was his throne mine now by virtue of my killing him, but I came to it with a bigger reputation of awe and respect than he'd ever managed to garner without his minions or using the cowing power of his innate magic."

"I'm surprised you took the position if you were so disillusioned with kings and stuff," I said. "Or was it just Arthur that was the problem?" This all sounded like storybook stuff to me still, something I'd find in a paperback on one of my parents' shelves. If I kept thinking of it in those terms, I could keep suspending my disbelief for now and roll with it.

Vambrace sighed, fidgeting with his sword as he spoke. "I had no respect for kings and crowns, it's true," he said. "The problem with Arthur had been the loftiness of his dream. There were no idyllic dreams to craft here in Hell, though, and I had no respect for anyone I met. I cared nothing for anyone's livelihood but my own. If taking the throne painted a target on my back, it also gave me a measure of control over my situation that I had never once had before in either world. I meant to revel in it until my inevitable assassination freed me of my concerns and the guilt of my sins."

"Sounds pretty emo," I said before I could think better.

He paused with a frown. "What?" he asked. Obviously.

"Sounds pretty gothic," I amended.

"…What?" he asked again.

Right. Damn, he was old. "Sounds very dark and broody and defeatist," I tried again.

Whether that clicked or he was just tired of being sidetracked, he smiled and nodded. "Perhaps. Very little changes here without being forced. Maybe it's something magical in nature, maybe it's just a product of the culture. Whatever the reason, I had very little in the way of character growth. Plenty of time to reflect on my life, but I always came back to the same conclusions."

"Alright," I said with a tilt of my head, "but you obviously care more about the job now if you've got rules and devoted fans and you eat dinner with everyone, right? So, what changed?"

"A fair point," he said, tapping his lips with his steepled fingers and staring at me for a long moment. "A great deal of time, I suppose," he said at last. "Whatever I thought of my new position, I did what duties were expected of me. A familiar routine was welcome after so long without one. It reminded me of better days, squiring in Camelot before it all fell apart, when I had clear tasks to perform and a reason to wake up every day. I fell into familiar patterns, I defended myself from the odd attack when they happened, and Dis more or less ran on fine with my minimal involvement."

He paused again with another frown. "In fact, I realized, the city ran itself almost entirely without me but for the odd judgment I was called to give. But it ran itself the same way it had always run, a mire of discord and in-fighting, most of the citizens scheming or defending against constant enemies. The only reason it worked as a society was because no one cared about anyone beyond their own spheres of influence and grudges. If the house next to yours burned down, that had no bearing on your life. It was a city of deadlocked self-interest, not a real community." His gaze turned then to the sword in his lap, as if he could see his own past in the blade. "And maybe some of Arthur's influence had still stuck with me, or maybe it was more useless atonement, or maybe I was just bored and wanted a challenge. Whatever the case, slowly but eventually, I decided that I could do better. Not good, I thought, nothing so idealistic as Camelot's future or even its ruinous end. But if I had absolute authority, and if the city could sustain itself without me but for my occasional act of guidance, then I may as well guide it somewhere that better suited myself. What did I have to lose? At worst, I would accidentally pull Dis down around my head. As I had no great love for Dis or my wellbeing, I had no reasons not to do as I pleased.

"So I set about tyrannizing my subjects, taming the city and forcing it to a different shape. I'd make no end of enemies doing so, I knew; but if I wasn't particularly concerned with losing, I still didn't intend to work with any disadvantage I didn't need to. So one of my first major decrees was to seal travel between worlds, cut Hell off from Earth entirely. Eventually, I knew, if I could enforce such an edict, a new generation of demons would rise who knew nothing of humans except that there was only one here, and he ruled them all. With no other examples of humanity existing, I could build my own image as I saw fit without fear of contradiction. But stopping travel between worlds meant stopping any form of magic that wasn't an inborn ability. Luckily, that was a task I relished completing."

"Not a fan magic, huh?" I asked, hopefully not too lightly, and suddenly became very interested in the hem of my shirt.

"It would not be an understatement to say that I despise it and any who pursue its practice, no," he said in a low voice that did nothing for comfort level. "Camelot was plagued with magic and magicians, none of it healthy. The magic that helped build Arthur's rule only reinforced the impossibility of anyone else living beneath that rule with any dignity. The magic that threatened it was treacherous and corrupting. Even Merlin, who supposedly had nothing but Arthur's prosperity in mind, did nothing to help the rest of Camelot once he was safely ensconced in his own power and authority — and when we needed him most, where was he? Embroiled with some grasping sorceress, abandoning us all to a fate he'd helped bring and did nothing to avert, the demon-spawned lech! And *Morgana*!" He stopped himself as he made to rise indignantly to his feet, calming as quickly as he'd angered and slowly shaking his head. "So no," he continued more quietly, "after all I've seen of it, all I've dealt with it, suffice it to say that I am not a fan of magic. Which is one reason why, even beyond my leadership goals, I made its practice or even its first fumbling attempt punishable by expedient death."

Well fuck, so much for finally feeling safe around this guy. "You, uh… you don't think that's a bit hypocritical?" I asked, fascinated by the hem of my shirt once more. "Your sword's magic after all, ain't it? And you got where you are now because of Excalibur."

"No," he said, leaning forward and raising a finger as he stared intently past it at me. "I got where I am today because of human exceptionalism and the superiority of the Original Sin, of which I am one of the more powerful specimens. My rule was inevitable, my authority beyond reproach or question. That's common knowledge that nobody living will comfortably gainsay." His point made, he put his finger away and turned his gaze to the carpet. "That aside, I can't say for certain that Excalibur *is* magical. It seems to be, yes, but I don't know where it comes from. I don't know what it really is beyond a powerful weapon. It is not of Earth, though, of this I am sure; and it cannot be of Hell either, or I would not have held the advantage I have for so long. But yes, I realize I'm something of a hypocrite, among other unflattering things. No matter. I have not been a good person in a long, long time, and I feel no compulsion anymore to change that. I am an effective ruler, feared and respected and unchallenged. And however you measure goodness, I have done good for Dis. The citizenry are productive now, with purpose in an inclusive system that works. Unrest is nearly nonexistent beyond the small scale. Hell is stable and largely content. Despite my initial intentions, I am proud of my work, no longer willing to see it fall apart around me. I am fifteen hundred years old, and death has long forfeited its opportunity to claim me. Any sin is permissible if it serves my reign, any character flaw — because Hell is *mine* now, and I will hold it until time itself unravels around us, whatever the cost."

His eyes had that angry fire in them again the more he spoke, until by the end of his latest spiel, I had the pillow back in my hands again between us without realizing I'd done so. "Uh… yeah, cool," I muttered when he was done. "Sounds fair."

He blinked, the fire going out of his gaze, and for a moment seemed like he wasn't sure where he was. "Apologies, my lady," he said then, whole body visibly relaxing. "I have not… I have never been able to speak of these matters so openly before. It is oddly refreshing. Perhaps I became overexcited."

"No one at all?" I asked, lowering the pillow again. "You and Enkida seem pretty close. Or Sidona."

"Sidona makes herself pleasant and useful, yes, but I'm under no illusion as to her motives or measure of self-interest," the prince said with a wave of his hand. "If she ever thought she had any leverage over me at all, she would be sure to make use of it. The Duchess is as loyal as any of her House, but I would not jeopardize that by tempting it unduly. Enkida…" He paused, then smiled. "Enkida is my right hand, my Bedivere. There is little I would not trust her with, I admit. If any of my subjects would hear such a confession unweathered, it would be her. But it would also serve her no purpose but as a weight upon her shoulders to know her infallible prince is something of a charlatan. I only admit what I have to you because I need you complicit in the story, you understand, because another human might undermine my long con otherwise, advertently or no."

"Well, I'm…" I began, then interrupted myself with a long, unbidden yawn, bringing the pillow up to cover my face. "… flattered," I finished afterward.

"And tired, evidently," said Vambrace with a smirk. "You've been taxing yourself rather heavily while undermining my authority, it seems. I trust, after our time here, you'll refrain from such acts in the future."

"I'll try," I said, mostly truthfully. "Hard to do when you're under house arrest and no one tells you anything. Will I still be treated like something of a prisoner?"

"I'll try not to," he said, rising from the bed and hefting Excalibur over his shoulder.

"Hey, careful with that," I said as I stood as well. "Don't cut my jacket. Sire."

"Trust me, my lady, I am always well aware of where my sword is and what it may be endangering," he said with a smile, tapping the flat of the blade against his shoulder covered in my denim. "It would be a tragic anticlimax to make it as far as I have only to inadvertently cut off my own head. Now, if you please," he added, sweeping beside me and raising his free arm behind my back, "allow me to escort you back to your room where you can rest for a while."

I had no objection to that, so I tossed his pillow back onto his massive bed and let him escort me out of his rooms and back to mine. Rezavix wasn't at his usual spot fuming just outside my door, but at the moment, I was too tired to wonder where he was or whether or not I should care.

Vambrace pushed my door open, then stood back as I stepped through. "I trust you have everything you need for now, my lady?" he asked.

"Yes," I said, turning back to him in the doorway. "No. I'd like a pen and paper, please. And I need some new clothes to change into. These are disgusting."

"Of course," said the prince. "I'll have them brought up shortly. In the meantime…" He raised his hands, palms out and down in supplication. "…*please* just stay put for a little while."

I sighed. "Right."

"At least limit yourself to my private suite," he continued. "If all else fails, just stay in the palace. On this floor."

"Okay, I get it," I said, rubbing a hand over my heavy eyes. "I'm just gonna stay here and chill for now, promise."

"Good. Thank you, my lady." He smiled, and then, after a moment of hesitation, actually bowed to me, extra formally. It surprised me, I admit, and I wondered if he'd have done it if anybody could have been watching us. When he was finished, I tried to return a curtsy as best I could in a grungy T-shirt and leather pants. It failed horribly, but he was smiling when he pulled my door closed.

So. I'd bitchslapped Satan and managed to score brownie points. If I'd stayed home, maybe I could have won the lottery instead. That would have been so much nicer.

With the prince gone and my privacy assured for a while longer, I immediately shucked all of my clothes and tossed them into a pile by the bed. Whatever demony outfit showed up, however weird or inscrutable it may be, anything would be preferable by this point. Maybe if I got lucky, I'd discover Hell had a washer and dryer somewhere in the palace — if I hadn't already used up all of my luck. I had to be getting close to that limit if I wasn't already overdrawn.

Tired as I was, I wasn't lying down again until I'd had a bath. Those were nice sheets and blankets, nicer than anything I'd ever owned. Crawling into them in my current state seemed almost sacrilegious. Instead, I headed into the attached bathroom and shut the door. The water I had left running when I snuck out was gone now, drained away, though whether of its own accord or because someone came in here and turned it off, who knew.

It took some tinkering to figure out how to work the tub drain, but after a few minutes, I had the massive basin full of hot, steaming water, the haze of which was already fogging up the room. Carefully, gingerly, I dipped my feet into the water, which was just shy of burning. Inch by slow inch I adjusted, until at last I was submerged up to my chin, my head leaning back over the rim, my eyes slipping shut.

It was blissful, the heat easing aches in my body I hadn't realized I had until then. I meant to simply sit and bask for a few long minutes before I got on with my washing. Instead, I ended up drifting off right there in the tub, with the warm water as my blanket and the steam for a pillow.

I don't know how long I was out, only that when I finally stirred and opened my eyes again, the steamy haze had dissipated, and the water had cooled to just above room temperature. I sat up in the tub and stretched, then set to actually rinsing off. Since I hadn't thought to grab soap and wouldn't have recognized it if I had, I settled for just scrubbing with my hands under the water and dunking my hair a few times. At last, when I was satisfactorily clean and the water was nearing too cool for comfort, I rose pruny and dripping, then set to drying off with a nearby towel while the basin drained. Afterward, with a sigh of refreshed relief, I dropped the towel in a corner and stepped naked back into my bedroom.

"Greetings, mistress."

I nearly slipped on the damp floor backpedaling into the bathroom, then nearly crushed my toes slamming the door closed on myself. It took most of a minute of deep breathing to calm down enough until I was ready to try again. Slowly, I cracked the bathroom door and peeked out.

On the desk against the wall was a sheaf of off-white paper with a quill pen and inkwell sitting on top. Across the room, a pile of colorful fabric sat folded on top of my fancy bed. And between them, kneeling on the rug and drumming her long fingers on her knees, was a Luxuriate girl with lavender skin and violet hair, eyes the color of vibrant sapphires throughout looking my way. She tilted her head when she caught me peeking, delicate brow furrowing. "Mistress?" she asked in a light, buttery voice. "Are you well?"

"I, uh… j-just a moment!" I squeaked, then yanked the door closed again and leaned my head against the ornate wood, feeling as though I might burn a hole in it with the heat coming from my face.

"If you require assistance bathing or dressing," she called to me brightly, "please let me know. I am at your service, mistress."

So much for privacy.

Chapter 15: Ungratefulness

Her name was Kriseia, and the prince had seen fit to send her up along with the paper and clothing I'd requested. She'd been kneeling patiently in the middle of the room, waiting for me to appear, nearly the entire time I'd been napping in my bath.

"But… why?" I asked, sitting on the edge of my bed and holding the massive, fluffy towel wrapped tight around me. A quick glance at the outfits assembled for me made me wonder if I could get into them without assistance after all, and that was not a topic I was willing to broach right now. Not until I had some answers, at least.

Still kneeling where I'd found her, Kriseia shrugged her bare shoulders. "I was not sure if you would permit me into your bed or not, so without knowing, I simply thought —"

"No," I interrupted, "I meant why send me a… you?"

Her heart-shaped face fell into a full-lipped pout. "Do you… wish me gone, mistress?" she asked, her voice so hurt I felt like I'd just kicked a puppy. "If I have displeased you, I am deeply sorry, but —"

"Oh, no!" I interrupted again, free hand fluttering awkwardly in what I hoped was reassurance. "I didn't mean, I just… I wasn't expecting… um." I stopped, sighed. "I mean, why did he send me anybody? What are you supposed to do for me?"

Her head tilted again. "What would you like me to do for you, mistress?"

I blinked. "Wait," I said. "You… oh. I'm sorry, are you like a…?" There was no way to say this without it being awkward, was there? "Did he send you here to be my servant?"

Her smile nearly lit up the room. "Of course, mistress. I am your gift."

This is Hell, I reminded myself. *This is a palace in Hell. Of course they'd have stuff like this. It's probably not weird at all.*

Logic didn't make me any less uncomfortable, though. It also didn't make my throat any less dry. I owned a person now.

"I, uh… I don't think I need anything right now," I said slowly. "No offense."

She nodded. "As you say, mistress. Then, is there anything you *want*?"

She was one of the pink ones. It didn't take much thinking to figure out what she meant. "Uh, no," I said, turning my reddening face to the wall. "Not, uh, not right now. Thanks for offering."

She nodded again. "Of course, mistress."

We sat there for a silent minute longer, me turning from my examination of the wall to pick at the folded outfits beside me, Kriseia kneeling in front of me with her hands on her knees and a smile on her face. "I, uh, should probably get dressed now," I said eventually, pulling the pile of clothes into my towel-covered lap. "Would you mind, uh...?"

She rose, her long, bare legs unfolding gracefully beneath her. "Of course, mistress," she said, stepping toward me and reaching for my towel.

I fell onto my back pulling away to avoid her. "No, no, uh, no thanks," I stammered hurriedly. She yanked her hands back as if she'd burned them, frowning down at me with wide, pure blue eyes. "I meant, uh, could I have some privacy, please?" I continued, pushing myself back up on one arm.

Kriseia blinked and turned to the room, looking at the closed front door. "We do have privacy, mistress," she announced, looking back at me with confusion.

I suppressed the urge to sigh aloud. "I mean, can you look away for a minute, please?" I said. "While I'm dressing."

"Oh," she said, though the confusion remained on her face. Still, she bowed her head to me. "As you wish, mistress," she said, then turned daintily and stood staring at the bathroom door.

I slid off the side of the bed and backed up to the wall by the headboard, bringing the pile of clothes with me and eyeing her bare back. The outfit she wore was some gauzy, translucent violet thing with more fabric on her shoulders and around her neck than on the rest of her torso, leaving her back exposed down to her tailbone, from which sprouted a long, slender lavender tail ending in a flat, blunt spade tip, like the head of a snake. Below that, the bottom part of her outfit, if it could be called that, was just a pair of snug panties made from the same sheer material, leaving her naked from her thighs down to the stilleto heel spikes of her bare feet on which she somehow balanced.

Would she put on something more substantial if I asked her to? Probably. She seemed eager enough for me to boss her around. Would that be rude of me, asking a lust demon to cover up? I didn't know. Maybe I could just learn to ignore her. At least she didn't seem inclined to turn around and peek.

Acutely aware of her presence, I dropped my towel and pulled a handful of leathery black straps from the pile of clothing, then looked for the outfit they went with for a few moments before I realized they *were* the outfit. A Luxuriate option, most like, because they resembled about three and a half belts more than actual clothes. I dropped those to the side too without bothering to try and figure them out.

Below that was what looked like a loose, slinky dress in light green. I held it for a moment and was about to slip into it when I realized I could see my hands clearly through both layers of the thing; and, holding it up before me, I realized it was wide open right about crotch level. Another Luxuriate outfit.

Who the hell picked these out? Vambrace? Was he trying to be cute, or did he really not realize how these all failed as clothes?

Eventually, I settled on a deep red evening gown type of thing with an intricate diamond mandala-like pattern stitched into it in golden thread. This ostentation combined with the shimmering ribbon around the neck that held it up and the corset lacing that closed it up in back reminded me of what I'd last seen Sidona in, like a cross between a fantasy sorceress and a prom dress. Appropriate enough for a novice witch, I guess. Now I just needed a pointy hat and a raven to sit on my shoulder, and I'd be set for my first LARP.

I dug through the clothing pile a second time just to be sure, but there didn't appear to be anything resembling underwear in my available options. Not even as part of the luxuriate lingerie clothes. I could do without for now, I supposed, but I didn't have to like it.

Unfortunately, what I couldn't do was tighten and tie all the necessary bits of lace and ribbon and stays to keep the dress up once I'd gotten into it. It was the only thing that fit, though, even if it did trail the ground by half a foot or so. More importantly, it was the only thing that actually hid all the bits I wanted hidden. No choice for it, then.

"Uh, Kriseia?" I asked, still facing the bedroom wall. "Can you give me a hand with this, please?"

"Of course, mistress," she said, already right behind me and making me jump a bit. How she moved that quietly on those unfortunate heels, I didn't know. Then her fingers were on my back, gently and quickly tugging everything into place.

"Sorry if I'm sending mixed messages," I said while she worked. It seemed the less awkward option than ignoring her while she helped dress me.

"Oh, it's no problem, mistress," she said brightly just behind my ear as she gradually tied me into my new outfit.

"Thanks," I said, ducking my head so my hair fell off my neck, freeing it for her to tie the ribbon. "It's just I'm used to doing all this personal routine stuff by myself. I've, uh, never had a... servant before."

"Really?" she asked, fingers pausing on my shoulders a moment. "But you are from Earth, yes? I would have thought all humans had their own servants in the land of Original Sin."

"Yeah, well... some do," I said, inwardly swearing. "A lot. Not me, though." I wasn't sure what details would be safe to give beyond that and which might screw up Vambrace's carefully cultivated lies. So I opted to give none.

"I see," said Kriseia, fingers moving once more. "Well, I am honored to be your first, mistress, truly."

"Yeah, uh... thanks," I said, hoping my blush stayed on my face and wasn't spreading down my neck.

"If I am permitted to say, mistress," she continued slowly, hesitantly, "when I was presented before the Archfiend, I had thought to find myself placed in his collection and forgotten about. To instead be gifted to a dignitary from Earth is humbling indeed. I swear that I will try and prove worthy of the position, mistress."

"Oh, you're... yeah, you're fine," I said. "Don't worry about it."

"Mm. Mistress is kind to say so."

I was pretty sure by now that the dress was on as snug as it was gonna go, but her hands were still running lightly over my bare shoulders as if searching for something else to do.

"So, uh, Kriseia," I said, perhaps louder than I needed to, as I stepped forward out of her touch and turned around with my best customer service smile. "How, uh, how long have you been at the palace, then?"

Her hands hovered for a moment where my shoulders had been before she clasped them beneath her breasts, the bottoms of which peeked out from the gauzy purple top that draped loosely over them — and through which I could still see everything. I tried not to dwell on it. "Do you not remember, mistress?" she asked, tilting her head again. "I was presented to his majesty directly after you yourself were. We stood in line on the bridge before Pandemonium together. I spoke to you briefly of my nervousness before Lord Ulfris ushered you in at his side."

Now that she brought it up, I did vaguely remember a hopeful purple face trying to talk to me as I hung over Ulfris' shoulder and contemplated my impending damnation. Of course, I was a bit preoccupied at the time. "That was you?" I asked, bringing my hand up to scratch at my cheek. "Sorry, I didn't recognize you at first. I'm terrible with faces with people I've only met the one time."

She frowned in that pouty way she had. "I was your attendant at dinner as well, mistress," she said. "I poured your drinks. Until Lord Melchius ordered me away, at least," she added, eyes turned downcast.

I swallowed down the social awkwardness. "I'm *really* bad at faces," I lied. "Sorry."

Her bright smile snapped back into place. "No, there is no need to apologize, mistress," she said. "In fact, it is… well, almost refreshing, if I may say so."

"Really?" I asked. "Why?"

"Because, I am not…" She stopped and sighed, her hands rising to gently rub at the short, rounded nubs of ivory horns she had sprouting from just above and behind her temples. "No one who has met me has ever not recognized me on seeing me again. It is nice to be able to blend in for a change, is all, mistress."

"Oh," I said. "Yeah. I know what you mean, believe me."

Her fingers paused in stroking her horns, and she looked up at me again with those radiant gems of eyes. "You do?" she asked.

"Feeling like you stand out too much in a crowd? Yeah. I know what it's like to get those looks." *For completely different reasons, though, probably,* I added to myself.

Kriseia's face lit up so much it almost hurt to look at. "Thank you, mistress," she breathed, ducking into a deep bow and showing me the top of her head. "Your understanding flatters me."

"Does it?" I asked, backstepping from the profuse gratitude. "You're, uh, welcome, I guess." All this servility hadn't gotten any less weird. With her head still ducked, I cast a glance at the desk across the room where paper, pen, and ink had been left for me. "I'm just gonna… I got something I gotta do now," I said as I sidled around her. She straightened again, smiling at me, and I pointed to the desk. "If you don't mind."

"Oh, of course not, mistress," she said, hands clasped before her once more. "I shall await further orders quietly, then."

She did. As I sat down at the desk, she once again sank to her knees on the rug and set her gaze to the far wall, her attention turned inward. Or at least I hoped it was, that she had her own thoughts to occupy her and wasn't just staring blankly into space until further notice. It was hard to tell with her pupil-less eyes.

Still very aware of her silent, nearly naked presence doing nothing at all behind me, I pulled paper and ink toward me and got to work. It took a little while to figure out how to write with a quill; I went through half a page of scribbly lines before I started to get the hang of it. Once I had it, though, I got a fresh sheet and started making my cheat sheet:

7 types of demon
Superbiate: blue ones. Prideful. Sidona, Abdeles, Ulfris. Mind control?
Iriates: red ones. Angry. Rezavix, Enkida. Very very strong and fighty.
Luxuriates: pink ones. Sexy. Kriseia, Melchius. Shapeshifty. Think Mystique.

And so on. I wrote down what I remembered of the city, the different districts, Sidona's directions to the bazaar. I wrote down what I knew so far about Vambrace, his story as he told it and how that held up to what I remembered of Arthurian myth from my classes. I wrote down all the names I'd heard so far, then went back and made notes on who they were so I wouldn't forget anyone who seemed important, either to the city society as a whole or to my own personal quest to get the hell out of here. Most importantly, I wrote down what scant leads I'd gathered on the Morganomicon before I was caught, ending with "FIND GILDEROS" underlined twice and then circled repeatedly for good measure.

As I wrote, I started to calm down finally. It helped to have a project to focus on, especially something as banal and normal as taking notes. I tried not to think about what I was missing in class back home, what homework I was behind on or what tests I wasn't going to be there to take. It wasn't too hard; my grades took a distant backseat to my new concerns, and when I got back (I made myself think in terms of "when" and not "if," because that was a hole I couldn't afford to fall into just yet), whatever I did about all these new discoveries, keep them to myself or try and reveal them to the world, I doubted if I would be able to focus on school for a long time to come.

Kriseia seemed content enough to just keep waiting on her knees behind me, still and silent. I noticed her again about a half hour later out of the corner of my eye when I stopped writing to rub out a hand cramp. Near as I could tell, she hadn't moved at all.

"Do you want to sit down or something?" I asked her, awkwardness rising in me again in the face of that servility.

She turned her head to me and smiled. "If my mistress wishes."

"That's not —" I stopped and had to bite back a sigh. "No, I don't care one way or the other. What do *you* want?"

Her head tilted. "I do not care either, mistress. I'm here to do as you please."

I couldn't stop the sigh that time. "It just seems uncomfortable, is all," I said. "Staying like that this whole time."

She shrugged her naked lavender shoulders. "I feel fine, mistress. I am trained to serve. Patience was a large part of that training, and I have learned to be content with a variety of situations."

"If you say so," I muttered. "I mean, you can sit on the bed if you'd rather."

She bowed her head but made no move to stand up. "Thank you, mistress."

"And you can just call me Morgan," I added. "Please."

She bowed her head again. "Yes, Mistress Morgan."

Right. I gave up then and turned back to my notes. By this point I had a few pages (parchments?) worth of them and nothing else to add. If I wanted to navigate this place well enough to find my way out of it, though, then I couldn't afford to be as lost and confused as I had been. Every little bit of info helped, if only to familiarize and orient myself with everything going on around me; because if Vambrace was to be believed, then any lack of confidence shown on my part to the wrong person could be disastrous for both of us.

No pressure.

Gathering my notes, I left the desk and stretched out on the bed to go over them. *Superbia, Luxuria, Iria, Avaritia, Gullia, Acedia, Invidia. Pride, lust, wrath, greed, gluttony, sloth, envy. Blue, pink, red, green, orange, gray, brown.* Like a science vocabulary list, or a character sheet from some ancient literary epic. There were still plenty of gaps I'd left to fill in as I figured more out, but my best-case scenario was to get home before they were all filled in.

When I'd gone through all my pages once, I reshuffled them to start over. While I was doing that, though, I glanced up to find Kriseia, still kneeling in her spot on the floor, now looking at me with those unreadable sapphire eyes.

I paused. She didn't look away when I caught her staring. "What's up?" I asked.

She looked confused for a second, but then frowned. "Mistress Morgan," she began, then trailed off, looked away at the floor, and continued. "Are you quite sure that you desire nothing from me still?"

I raised myself up on my elbows. "I'm fine, yeah. Sorry if you're bored."

"Oh, no, Mistress Morgan," she said, ducking her head again. "As I said, I am well trained for patience. It's just..." When she looked up, she still wasn't looking at me, and her hands fidgeted in her lap, clasping and unclasping. "Well, I have never known of a patron receiving one of us as a gift and not wishing to do... anything. Do you... are you certain, mistress, that you do not find me displeasing in some way?" She glanced up at me very quickly then before bowing once more. "Not that I mean to bother my mistress with my insecurities," she continued hurriedly, "only that if she would be better pleased by another, I would not want to importune her with my presence or—"

"Whoa, Kriseia," I said, sitting up and setting my notes aside. "It's fine. Take a breath. You're fine, honest."

She glanced up at me through her lashes. "Honest?" she repeated.

"I promise," I said. "I just don't need anything right now. I don't want anything." I stopped, paused. "Actually…"

Her head perked up. "Yes, Mistress Morgan?"

I gazed down at my notes. *FIND GILDEROS* glared out at me in bold on the page. "Say I wanted to find a specific merchant," I said slowly, "but I didn't know where they were. How would I find out?"

"You desire… information, mistress?" she asked, brow furrowing. I don't think it was the request she'd been hoping for. "I suppose it would depend. Does this merchant have an established shop location, or are they suppliers for other enterprises?"

"I don't know," I said. "All I have is a name."

She stroked her delicate chin. "Then I suppose mistress would want to inquire with someone who keeps records in House Avaritia. Perhaps they could point you to the merchant's location, or set up a private meeting if you desired."

"Cool," I said. "And how do I talk to House Avaritia if I'm stuck in the palace?"

"Well…" She glanced ceilingward. "Mistress might ask Archduchess Cinaedemis, if she is willing to meet with you. She dined with you and his majesty, so she is likely still in the palace. She could point you in the right direction. Barring that, mistress may also bring the matter to Prince Vambrace himself. Such a thing would be impertinent of one of lower stature, but as mistress is a human and seems to have his favor, it might be allowed. No information or request is denied the archfiend unless it is truly unknowable or impossible."

I had Cinaedemis in my notes, though I'd only heard the name once and wrote it down as *?Cinnamonis?* until I could remember what it really was. She was in charge of the scaly, greedy ones, I remembered. We were less than acquainted, but she'd seemed polite enough at dinner; and while I probably had a better shot of talking with the prince again than an archduchess I'd barely met, I didn't relish his reaction if he thought I was still trying to skulk about and undermine his orders.

"Alright," I said. "If I wanted to talk to the archduchess about something, how would I go about that? Do I just go find her, or do I gotta send someone to ask someone to ask someone else?"

"Forgive me, mistress," said Kriseia. "If I had a clearer grasp of your social status, I could tell you more certainly. You may be able to approach the archdemons directly without rebuke. But without being certain, perhaps it would be best to send a messenger on your behalf first."

"Cool, I can do that," I said, sliding off the mattress. "Thanks, Kriseia." As she bowed again, I strode to the door and flung it open. "Rolladex!" I called into the hall.

My stalwart guard had returned to his post at some point and now stood leaning against the far wall, arms crossed, glaring at my doorway. "No," he said flatly.

"Come on, this is important," I said. "I need to get a message to Archduchess Cinaedemis."

"You need no such thing!" he snarled, his fingers tightening where they rested on his exposed biceps. If his claws were just a bit sharper, I thought, or his skin a bit less tough, he would be drawing blood right about now. "What you need, human, is to turn around and go back into your room, because if you try and slip away *again*, then so help me Amon, I will—"

"Do nothing," an icy voice cut in, and the both of us turned to find General Enkida striding down the corridor toward us. "Rezavix, you are dismissed," she said as she drew up, and my guard clapped a fist over his chest in salute. "Lady Morgan, you are to come with me."

"General," said Rezavix, "when you say 'dismissed,' do you mean—"

"Return to the barracks," she replied without looking at him. "Find a way to make yourself useful until told otherwise. Dismissed."

He gaped at the back of her head a moment. "But General—"

He stopped when her head snapped sideways, wide pinprick eyes staring over her shoulder at the cowed guard. "Dis. Missed."

I could swear I almost heard his teeth grinding as he saluted her once more, then stormed away down the corridor without another word. Given how much shit he'd given me, I admit it was gratifying — but only for a moment, until I remembered that I'd intentionally started almost every argument I'd had with my long-suffering guard.

"He's not in trouble, is he?" I asked the general once Rezavix was safely out of sight and earshot. "Because it's not really his fault I kept slipping away."

"It was his job to prevent it, and he didn't," Enkida said, gazing down at me. "And no offense, Lady Morgan, but you have next to no idea where you are or what you're doing yet. Stopping you should not have been as difficult as he made it seem."

"Yeah, but I—" I started, then stopped. Clearing Rezavix's reputation wasn't worth giving away my unnoticeability spell; it was the most useful tool I had in my incredibly limited arsenal, and if I never got free reign of this place, I'd be using it until my luck finally ran out. "I didn't make it easy for him," I said instead.

"Regardless," said the general, reaching past me to close my door just as Kriseia leaned forward into view to peer out at us. "Don't concern yourself over Iriate matters, Lady Morgan. His highness has requested your presence in the throne room. This way, please."

"He has?" I asked as I fell into step behind her. "What's up?"

"A formal audience to clear some confusion and answer some questions," she said as we walked.

"Oh, really? Great," I said, "I've got plenty of both."

"And you may still, afterward," she said, glancing back at me. "Yours is not the confusion this gathering is intended to address."

I frowned. "Then whose?"

"You'll find out shortly," she said.

"Some sort of secret meeting, then?" I asked.

"No," she answered, "I'm just finished talking to you. No offense, lady. Only, Rezavix's impertinence has fouled my mood, and now I feel conversation disagrees with me. You'll find the silence preferable to what I might say otherwise, I assure you."

I had nothing I could think to say to that, so we made the rest of our way in a politely tense silence. And though the walk was as long as it ever had been, I once again paid careful attention to the directions, trying to etch them even deeper into memory. This was a more direct route than the one Sidona had given me, the one I'd taken earlier when I'd finally made it out of the palace, alone and invisible. From the throne room, though, I remembered it was a straight shot down the entrance hall to the front doors. Depending on what this meeting was, if I had to, I might be able to make a break for the entrance. I might even make it out onto the bridge, I thought, before Enkida ran me down.

Not a great plan, admittedly, but I wasn't as worried this time that it might come to that. Not after my tête-à-tête with an openly fascinated Vambrace.

Just as she said, I found out who the meeting was for as soon as we entered the throne room. The prince lounged in his throne, as expected, looking much the same as the last time I'd seen him here: incongruous, especially still wearing my jacket, and not particularly intimidating compared to the demons around him, at least not to another human. Still, he had the air of someone long used to authority and comfortable wielding it, and Excalibur still peeked up from over his shoulder, only the barest sliver of metal visible but gleaming as purely as ever.

Unlike the last time I was here, though, the throne room was largely empty. Besides the prince, Enkida, and myself, there were only six other people here, one of each sin except the blue pride ones, all of them standing in a loose group before the throne. Every head turned my way when I entered behind the general, and it was then I recognized them — six of the seven archdemons I had dined with earlier.

I took a deep breath. Was it too late to go back and get my flashcards?

Enkida didn't break stride as she led me right up to the dais and turned to the assembled archdukes and archduchesses. "Presenting the Lady Morgan Amell," she said to the group, then stepped behind and to the right of Vambrace's throne and simply stood looking attentive.

I hesitated on the edge of the dais, unsure whether I should bow or kneel or curtsy or what. Everyone was watching me expectantly, but no one had told me what was going on yet. What the hell did they expect me to know about court formalities with demons?

Probably quite a lot, I realized, thanks to whatever stories the prince had made up for them. Thanks for cluing me in on the plan, Vambrace, you jerk.

They were still looking at me. "Hello," I said, staring at the ground halfway between the dais and the group. "Again." And then I waved a little, because I'm a social idiot who chokes under scrutiny.

One of the archdemons chuckled, and I risked looking up. Probably the purple perv I'd sat next to at dinner. Melchior? No, Melchius.

Beside and behind me, Vambrace sighed on his throne. "Still no word of Abdeles?" he asked the room at large. The other archdemons shuffled but didn't answer, and I knew he wasn't asking me, so I simply stood in the scrutiny and played with my fingers. A moment later, he slowly rose from his seat. "Well, I tire of waiting, so someone can relay my words to him later. My lords and ladies—"

The sound of a large door opening from down the front corridor made him pause, and a few seconds later, Archduke Abdeles came striding into the throne room with his heavy cloak of midnight blue billowing behind him. The other six parted to let him pass up to the foot of the dais, where he bowed his head only slightly. "My liege," he said, then stepped back. From where I stood, I could see his chest working for breath, as if he'd run part of the way here, though his face was schooled to show no signs of fatigue.

His eyes were on me as well — not the glare I was used to from the Iriates around me, but also not the condescending amusement I'd seen in Duchess Sidona. I had no idea what he was thinking, but he wasn't even trying to be circumspect. I turned away and took a step back toward the prince, partly on impulse, partly for good measure.

"Lord Abdeles," Vambrace said coolly. "You took your time arriving."

"Not at all, Sire," said the archduke, looking back to Vambrace again. "I came as soon as I received the summons. I was simply out in the city on personal business when it came, and your order took longer reaching me than it otherwise would have. I assure you, though, Sire, I finished my business and hurried straight here once I had word."

"Personal business in the city?" asked the prince. "Of what sort?"

Again, the massive archduke lightly dipped his great horned head. "A trifling fancy, highness, nothing more," he said. "I'd heard tell through my sources that a vintner in Beelzebubis had opened his stores of caina berry wine infused with crushed jeza bells, and I'd thought to sample—"

"Yes, enough," the prince interrupted, raising his hand. Abdeles fell immediately silent. "You've made your point. Very well. My lords and ladies," he continued, voice raised to the group, "as I was saying, I've gathered you here now to set clear a matter that many have no doubt been questioning recently. As the heads of your respective houses, I expect each of you to make sure my message carries through to the rest of your subjects. My lady."

This last bit was addressed at me as the prince turned my way and held out an expectant hand. Hoping I looked more sure and less confused than I felt, I stepped toward him and took it.

He lifted it between us and turned back to the assembled archdemons. "With the sudden arrival of another human in our midst, many of you have been wondering what this means and where she stands," he continued. "I want to make circumstances perfectly clear. The Lady Morgan shall not be a prisoner here in Pandemonium, nor is she gift nor servant." He glanced sidelong at me then, that same faintly urgent look he'd given me at dinner when he'd been explaining Earth to the rest of them. "I hereby dub her royal consort, official mistress to the archfiend."

"What?" I blurted before I could stop it. "I—"

The sudden warning crush of his hand on mine probably wasn't visible to anyone looking, but I felt it nonetheless.

"— would be delighted," I finished with a wince. "It's an honor, *Sire*."

He smiled at that, all haughty self-satisfaction, while I glared sidelong at him. Not subtle, I know, but it was the best I could manage on such short notice.

And I made a mental note to slap him again once we were alone.

Chapter 16: Presumption

It was the Invidiate archduke, the one with the number in his name, who broke the silence first.

"What?" he demanded, shouldering forward to the front of the group and glaring at me. "This one just got here and she automatically gets such a high title? She has done nothing to earn it! I have served the throne faithfully with my every breath for a time uncountable, scraping for every scrap of respect, but she—"

"Archduke Aleviathan," the prince interrupted, and the squat demon immediately bit his lip. "Such protest was unexpected. Were *you* hoping to be named my consort instead?"

"Of course not!" Aleviathan said while someone behind him snickered. Melchius again, probably. "It's merely the principle of the thing. Sire. I know she's human, but surely—"

"Your majesty," Archduke Melchius cut in, stepping up beside his goblin-like peer and ignoring Aleviathan's scowling, "perhaps if you were to enlighten us all as to what the lady's new position entails, exactly, we could circumvent things like… this," he finished, looking pointedly down at Aleviathan with a disdainful curl to his lips.

"'Things like this?'" the Invidiate repeated, rounding on the Luxuriate. "Look, you sweat-stinking piece of—"

"Enough!" shouted Vambrace, and the room went silent again at the outburst, Aleviathan still fuming, Melchius looking smug. "None of your statures are changing or in jeopardy by this decree unless you continue to annoy me with your pointless outrage. This is just clarification. What this means," he added, turning to look at me as he spoke, "is that the Lady Morgan has the archfiend's favor as his sanctioned companion. She shall be given free reign of the palace, the same as any other duchess — though since her house has no representation here in Dis beyond herself, she will not officially be taking that title. So you can relax, Aleviathan."

With a last muted grumble, the Invidiate archduke stepped back from the dais and rejoined the group.

"Furthermore," the prince continued, "as my consort, I expect her to be treated with the same deference and respect as shown to the nobles of your houses, even if she holds no direct political power. Think of her as an ambassador to the city from Earth."

"An ambassador who's in bed with rulership," Melchius added with a sleazy smile. "Saucy."

"Hey," I said, "that's not—"

"—any of your concern," Vambrace finished for me, matching me glare for glare for a moment. "What happens in my quarters, or between the Lady Morgan and me elsewhere, is the business of those involved and no one else. Whatever rumors you lot decide to spread, keep them unobtrusive, because I will not have the patience to entertain them one way or another. Now." He took a step back and sat down on the throne again, hands draped across the armrests. "Are there questions?"

"Is the lady off limits then?" Melchius asked immediately, his gaze traveling slowly over me. "Or is this new pact an unexclusive one?"

I think I might have jumped down off the dais and strangled him if I thought I could manage the feat in this trailing dress. Or if I didn't think he'd probably enjoy it.

"Take that matter up with the lady," the prince said. "I'll not stand in the way of her desires in that regard, if they even exist. But in your case specifically, Lord Melchius, I wouldn't get your hopes up."

I'd have something to say to that too, but he wasn't wrong. Instead, I just crossed my arms and turned what I decided was a withering stare on the smarmy Luxuriate noble. Not that it seemed to deter him at all, but it was the principle of the thing.

"Will she be requiring a personal guard as well?" the Iriate archduchess asked. Seeing her now, standing with her peers rather than seated down a table from me, I realized she was surprisingly more petite than most of the other Iriates I'd seen so far, though no less sinewy. I also realized I had completely forgotten what her name was.

Vambrace steepled his fingers and looked over them for a silent moment. "We will confer and come to that decision ourselves," he said. "If so, General Enkida can assign one of her command to the task."

"Of course," the red archduchess said, her eyes darting up to Enkida beside the throne, her jaw visibly clenching. Enkida returned the gaze without flinching. Whether there was animosity there or that was just a normal acknowledgment amongst Iriates, I had no idea.

Archduke Abdeles stepped forward then. "If we are accepting a representative of Earth as a diplomatic ambassador," he said slowly, "then should we not also appoint an ambassador of our own to send to Earth, Sire?"

Vambraces brows rose at that. "Are you saying, Lord Abdeles, that you favor reopening the gateway between our worlds?" he asked, his voice stoic. "That after all these ages, the work I painstakingly fought to see realized so long ago should be undone?"

Again, Abdeles dipped his head in the faintest of bows. "I would of course not presume to dictate anything to my liege concerning such weighty matters," he said. "And I was not speaking of hypothetically allowing a blanket allowance of the practice. I merely suggest, Sire, that if the lady does indeed represent a wish for better relations with the humans of Earth, then perhaps it follows that we should in turn reciprocate by —"

"We should not," said Vambrace, leaning closer in his throne. "You all know by now how the Lady Morgan arrived in the palace, so I'll not pretend her appearance is part of some opening treatise with Earth. She came to our world by accident — by incredibly rare accident, I should add, the first occurrence in eons. We are under no political obligation to reach out to Earth itself now, to open the means of travel and reach across that long dormant border, so I will not needlessly endanger our sovereignty for the sake of moot appearances."

"But with her here, would Earth not be a potential ally?" asked the archduke. "I understand that your edict against interference with the world was for the benefit of all Hell at the time, your highness, but as you say, that was long ages ago. Would the danger still be so great now? Perhaps if we reexamined the issue —"

He stopped again at Vambrace's raised hand. The prince took a deep, slow breath before continuing. "You were not there, Lord Abdeles," he said quietly. "You did not exist yet. So perhaps you do not fully grasp the gravity of what you are suggesting. Allow me to try and impress it upon you now." His gaze swept from the Superbiate to the rest of the nobles in turn before he continued, gazing out above all their heads. "You all know how well Dis runs now, because you all help to run it. It does not run perfectly by any means, but it *does* run. It functions as a city. It benefits all of us who have a hand in its oversight, as it benefits most of those who live within the system. And do you know why?"

His fist came down on the arm of his throne before anyone could answer, his metal bracelet things clanging against the stone seat hard enough that I started a bit.

"Focus and discipline. Order and obedience to the laws I set. Before contact with other worlds was sealed, back when magic ran rampant, there was none of that. Even after I ascended the throne, even after I began to wrangle Dis into someplace worth living, chaos and anarchy were widespread. Not a day went by that I wasn't executing someone, that demons weren't losing their lives and their livelihoods to every opportunistic neighbor or passerby who thought to steal or maim or kill with impunity. Magic was to blame for that mindset, that if one could just muster the right power in the right amount, there was no reason the law should apply to them; there was no reason to respect the will or boundary of anyone else. And Earth was a source of fuel to feed that chaotic flame. Stray humans, with less discipline or respect for demonkind than I, came or were brought to our city and ran wild, doing as they pleased to the populace and flitting back to their own world to avoid the consequences."

Wait, but didn't he say earlier that no humans ever came here but himself and then me? How much of this was bullshit to keep everyone else in check? How much of this did I need to know so I could lie for him? I was gonna need extra flashcards just to keep all of his stories straight.

"The worst demons emulated the practice," Vambrace continued, "seeking an edge over one another from Earth, importuning my own kind with their visits, seeking powers they should not have or running from the punishments due them for crimes they committed here. Other demons returned from Earth with tales of being enslaved by the humans that drew them across the border against their will, forcing them into service with stronger magics and turning their powers, their very natures, against them. Still others never returned at all, meeting more gruesome fates in my native world than could ever have befallen them here.

"*That* is the past you are suggesting we return to, Abdeles; *that* is the risk we put ourselves in by loosening even a little the sweeping ban that has kept us safe for so long and allowed us to finally stabilize and grow our culture, to improve our lives rather than merely struggle to keep them. Finally sealing off the last contact between our worlds, stamping out every means of any renegade criminal gaining access to that contact, is how I saved Dis and drug it out of its darker ages. I will take no step back toward that chaotic past that is not absolutely, unequivocally necessary for the safety and security of the realm as a whole."

"Then forgive my confusion, sire," Abdeles continued, "but what purpose then is her ambassadorial status if we are to remain isolated from our closest neighboring world? Will the lady not be returning to her own world after a time?"

"Not likely, no," the prince said. "We all know how arrivals from Earth work by now, if not why, and all evidence points to a one-way leak. Objects or artifacts — or in rare cases such as this, people — at times slip from that world to ours, for whatever reason. Unrestrained magic on Earth's end, most like, or perhaps some strange magnetism of our own. But there are no known instances of anything of Hell slipping the other way across the divide, and no Earth artifacts that have ended up here have ever gone back or been reclaimed." He turned to face me in his throne. "Like myself, I imagine Lady Morgan shall remain indefinitely as a resident of Dis."

I wasn't looking at him, though, not directly. I was gazing off into the corner of the room, my hands behind my back and clenched so tightly that my nails dug into my palms, focusing on breathing normally and trying not to let my panic rise or show.

It had been a possibility, of course, that I would never leave this place; it had always been a possibility, and probably the most likely one at that. I was toying with forces I didn't understand when I sent myself here, and I was trapped among more now. It was likely I would never find the means to recreate the complex magic I'd caught myself in and go back, to perfectly and conveniently reverse the mistake I'd made. I didn't want to admit it, and I wasn't giving up yet, but statistically speaking, realistically speaking, that was the most probable outcome.

Still, hearing it said aloud like that, with such finality and no room for argument … it cut deep. It threatened to drag up a resignation I'd been trying to keep tamped down, and with it, a whole host of fear and sadness and whatever else might bubble up in me if I stared too long at that possibility. Vambrace had managed to carve out a decent life for himself, but he had advantages I didn't, and from the story he'd told, he'd had nothing to lose once here. I still had everything to lose. I had a life back home that I *wanted* to return to.

But, I reminded myself, I couldn't know how much of what he was saying was for the sake of the image he'd built and the not-entirely-true narrative he'd woven for these demons. And more importantly, he still didn't know about the book; he didn't know that I'd put myself here, rather than some ancient enemy witch or whatever who was now beyond my reach. If I could just find the *Morganomicon*, I might be able to figure out what I was doing and do it again. And so long as that book was out there somewhere, I still had hope.

I glanced back toward the group of archdemons, picking out the Avaritiate duchess, Cinaedemis. She was standing in the back of the group, inspecting the gilded edges of her sharp, pointed nails and looking as if she were only here for formality's sake. She looked up and caught my gaze a moment as I watched, then turned it back to the prince without any apparent emotion beyond bored attention.

I need to talk to her, I reminded myself, and I latched onto that thought with enough focus and urgency to ignore the panic I'd been threatening to feel and tamp it back down just a bit longer. The prince had just officially granted me some amount of clout with these people. How far did that extend? How much could I get away with now?

Might as well find out.

"… much knowledge the Lady Morgan might impart to us all from a more modern Earth," the prince was saying when I finally gave my attention back to the proceedings. "View it that way, if you like. Regardless, you have all heard the decree, you have all had your answer. If there are no further concerns, then that is all I have to say at the moment. Dismissed." With a wave of his hand, he rose slowly from his throne, while the archdemons all bowed in their own fashions and turned to leave.

"Wait," I called, louder than I'd meant to, and everybody in the room paused in their leaving to turn back to me. "I mean, hold a moment," I amended, trying to don the same haughty tone I'd affected when talking to Rezavix. It was harder to find standing up here and staring down at a group of half a dozen aristocrats than it had been arguing with a single door guard. I turned to Vambrace. "I thank you for the honor, Sire. But if I'm going to be staying here as long as it seems now, then there's some business I'd like to get in order. Archduchess Cinaedemis?" I turned to the green scaled demoness and watched her gem-studded brows rise ever so slightly at the address. "May I borrow a few moments of your time?"

Now all eyes were on the Avaritiate, all with varying degrees of curiosity. She glanced between the rest of the room before looking back to me and shrugging. "You have them now, I suppose," she said. "What is it, lady?"

All eyes shifted back to me again. I took as deep a breath as I could without being obvious about it, trying to hold my composure. "I meant privately," I said. "For a private matter I'd like to ask about."

The multicolored jewels above her eyes rose ever so slightly yet again. "If you wish," she said, and raised a golden nail to tap at her chin. "I've no pressing business at the moment. You may walk with me back to my chambers, I suppose, if his majesty will allow it."

All eyes turned to the prince then, who was himself looking at me with that unreadable way he had. The longer I hung around him, though, the better I felt I was getting at reading it. And in the brief instant before he turned his attention to the archduchess, I thought I detected a mote of nervousness in his look, like maybe he was wondering if he'd just messed up by granting me some measure of token authority.

Nevertheless, when he looked to Cinaedemis, it was gone. "Of course," he said. "If I've need of the lady, I shall call upon her. In the interim, she is of course free to see to her own agendas."

"Thank you, your highness," I said, bowing my head, then stepped off the dais.

As the rest of the archdemons broke up once more and headed away, with plenty of curious backward glances, I followed along beside

Archduchess Cinaedemis as we exited the throne room down a connecting side corridor — with Archduke Melchius on our heels, for some reason.

I looked back to find him still grinning to himself and staring at my ass as we went. He looked up and caught my glance for a moment before looking right back down at it again. "M'lady?" he asked my backside.

"I don't remember asking for you to join us," I said, and briefly considered covering my butt with my hands to block his view. But no, best not to give him the satisfaction, probably. It wasn't even particularly emphasized in this gown; he was just staring out of perverted obligation, most likely.

"I don't remember saying I intended to," he said with a shrug. "My quarters just happen to lie in this direction as well. There aren't that many exits to the throne room, you realize."

"His quarters are more quickly reached by going the other way, though," Cinaedemis said beside me, still facing forward and not breaking stride. "I believe the Luxuriate is simply trying to ogle you, Lady Morgan."

"So I gathered," I replied, narrowing my eyes at the purple duke.

He looked up from my butt again then, guilty but unashamed. "What can I say? You are new and interesting, my lady, so I am interested. And the human female glamours of House Luxuria have all been guesswork up until now, no matter how accurate our guesses may have been. When an opportunity to study the real thing comes along, I am professionally bound to take it, am I not?"

"Melchius," I sighed, "I'm not—"

I interrupted myself by tripping over the front hem of my too-long gown then, and I would have gone sprawling face first into the floor had the archduke not darted forward and grabbed me, steadying me on my feet again. That his hands ended up on my breasts in the process might have been attributed to simple accident, if one were being incredibly forgiving — and if he hadn't followed up by immediately squeezing them. "Dress need hemming, m'lady?" he asked as I grabbed his arms and forced my way out of them. "I have an excellent tailor that I can let you borrow, if you wish."

"Melchius!" I snapped, rounding on him with a seething glare. "Back the fuck off! I don't care what your title is, I am *not* interested!" And to his credit, he stopped, then backpedaled a couple steps when I raised a finger at him. "And you touch me again like that, I'm asking the prince to cut your hands off. See if I don't. See if he doesn't."

And there it was again. Melchius stood warily, blinking down at me, and behind the smirk he was still fighting to keep on, I saw it flash across his face: the shock, the confusion, the hint of worry, the second guessing. Not because of my threat itself, I knew now, but because I had made it, because of the anger it had been made with. I was a human, and for the moment, I was acting like an Iriate, and Vambrace was right: it threw them off, maybe even scared them a little, made them wonder what I might be capable of, what I might do next.

It was heartening. If the prince could coast this long on bluff and bluster, perhaps I could too, at that. Not for a thousand years, but long enough to get out of here.

"Apologies, Lady Morgan," the Luxuriate archduke said when he'd recovered a moment later, bowing at the waist. "Next time, I shall simply let you plummet."

"It would be preferable, thanks," I said, then turned and strode away from him again. Archduchess Cinaedemis fell into step beside me, glancing sidelong at me with the same wariness I'd seen in Melchius, though without the defensive worry. Behind us, Archduke Melchius followed at a greater distance. I didn't look back to see if he was still ogling my ass, but something told me he wasn't.

He left us before we reached the first staircase, slipping away without another word or leer. I wouldn't have even noticed if I hadn't been staying acutely aware of his presence. I didn't think he'd still be mollified by the next time I saw him, but hopefully he'd at least be wary enough to remember my threat and keep his hands to himself.

At the top of the staircase, Cinaedemis turned us left down a corridor that sported a pair of armed guards posted halfway down on either end of an open archway. They glared straight ahead as we passed by. The hall ended in another left turn, which led us past what I recognized as an elevator door, one of the unhidden ones that I'd ridden on my way back down from Sidona's salon. The hidden ones like the one I'd accidentally ridden up must be service elevators. I supposed if I was gonna be a lady here, I'd need to get a handle on whatever weird caste system Hell was operating on.

The archduchess stopped in front of the elevator door and turned to face me, her gaze as cool and level as ever. "I'm headed up to my private tower suite now," she informed me. "You're welcome to come as well, Lady Morgan, if whatever business you wish to discuss is private enough to warrant it. But if it's not, we should be sufficiently alone here."

"Nah, this is probably fine," I said, glancing around us. She was right, we were alone in these corridors past the guarded archway. Another private section of the palace, I gathered, like what the prince had. There hadn't been much of anybody wandering around Sidona's room either, come to think of it. How many cordoned chunks of palace were in this palace? Massive as it looked from the outside, I supposed there could be a ton of private sections with room to spare leftover. And it was taller than probably the tallest office buildings in downtown back home. How high could I ride one of these elevators? And what was at the top of each of these spires?

"Lady Morgan?" Cinaedemis said, impatient, snapping me from my wandering musing.

"Sorry," I said, "lost in thought. Does every noble person get their own private set of rooms here?"

"Everyone of import," she answered, inspecting her gilded nails again as she did. "Pandemonium sports seven spires around the central column, one for each House, and anyone favored with extended business in the palace is granted rooms in the tower of their own Sin. The upper levels of each are reserved for the current archdemon leading their House."

"But Prince Vambrace's rooms are downstairs, not up," I realized aloud. "Shouldn't the archfiend be at the very top in the center?"

"Of course not," said the archduchess, as if it were obvious. "The archfiend abodes below Pandemonium, in the center of the palace crater, to be nearer to the Throne."

I frowned. "But we just came from the throne room," I said. "It's on this floor. And not in the center."

Her gem-studded brows knit together as she looked at me over her nails, frowning like a professor unsure how best to let a student know that the point she just made is moronic. "No, not *that* throne," she said. "That's just a fancy chair. *The* Throne."

I heard the capital "T" that time, but self-consciousness prevented me from questioning further. "Ah, right," I said, as if the obvious had momentarily slipped my mind. "Of course. Sorry."

Cinaedemis picked at a golden cuticle. "Was that the private matter you wished to speak of, then?" she asked. "Pandemonium's architecture?"

"No, no it wasn't," I said, stepping closer and glancing around us again. Still, nobody had walked up on us. Good. "I actually wanted to ask you about something a bit … closer to home. My home, specifically."

Her lips pursed. I think. On a mouth that inhumanly wide, it was hard to tell and kind of hard to look at. "Meaning?" she asked.

"Do you know about a merchant named Gilderos?" I asked. "I've heard he or she may have items from Earth available for sale, and if I'm going to be stu — I mean, living here for as long as it sounds like, I'd be interested in shopping for some. To help me feel more at ease, I mean."

Again the bejeweled eyebrow quirk. "And how have you heard what a merchant you've never encountered may or may not be selling when you've only just gotten here and have yet to leave the palace?" she asked.

So news of my more successful excursion hadn't gotten out, huh? Because it was still too soon, or because Vambrace didn't want anybody to know who didn't already? Either way, that might be good to know. "Even if I'm new here, I have my sources," I said, waving away the question. "That's not important anyway. Do you know how or where I can get in contact with Gilderos or not?"

Cinaedemis frowned the same too-long frown that Dramoc had worn every time I'd dealt with him. "If you're asking if I know of them and their wares off the top of my head," she said, "then no. If you're asking if the Archduchess of Avaritia can get in touch with a merchant somewhere in the city, then obviously. But why would I?"

I frowned. Admittedly, it wasn't as impressive as hers. "Because I asked nicely?"

"Not especially nicely, you didn't," she said. "But what I meant was, what's in it for me if I point you to this person?"

Shit. Of course. Why did I think a demon of greed would do anything for anyone for free? "Well, you'll earn my favor, for starters," I offered.

"Ha!" she laughed. "And what is that worth, pray tell?"

No idea yet, I thought. Out loud, I said, "A lot, depending on how you use it. Duchess Sidona has it, and it's helping her artistic pursuits. The prince has it, of course. And I have his. I like to think I could be a pretty influential friend to have."

"I would like to think so, too," she replied, folding her hands into the several flowing sleeves of her many expensive robes. "But until I see definitive proof of this, I'm not betting on it as sufficient payment. What else are you offering?"

My frown deepened. "Alright," I said, "what about information for information, then? I can tell you the sources I used to get this lead in the first place."

The archduchess sniffed. "Why would I need an outsider's source for information about the House I control?" she said. "No. What else?"

I sighed, trying to keep the irritation out of the sound. "C'mon," I said, "I'm basically just asking directions to the store here. Is it really worth the arguing? Finding one merchant can't be *that* valuable of information."

"And yet it was you who came to me to bargain for it," she pointed out, "so clearly you think it holds worth. If so, then I will get at least an equal exchange of worth for it. Therefore, until you offer me something that *I* would deem worthy of seeking *you* out to obtain, the information will stay with me, my lady."

Geez, no wonder this woman was in charge of the greedy ones. But she had a point; however banal the knowledge might be to anyone else, it was the single most vital question I needed answered at the moment, so I was willing to pay a good deal for it. Or I would have been, if I'd had any money or anything worth trading for it at all. All I had were my dirty Earth clothes, the fancy demon clothes Vambrace had gotten me, and, I supposed, a mostly naked new servant. And I had a feeling that this archduchess wouldn't really be interested in any of those things, so —

No. Wait.

I had more than that. I had my fabricated lineage. I was an inscrutable Original Sin, wasn't I? My whims and moods could be mercurial. There was no telling which direction my interest might take.

I took a deep breath as if to sigh again or keep arguing, then shrugged instead. "Alright," I said. "Whatever. Too much hassle anyway. Thanks for nothing, m'lady." I flashed a quick customer service smile and raised a hand in farewell as I turned to leave. "Maybe I'll try asking someone else later," I added as I walked away.

I'd made it down the hallway to the turn, wondering as I went whether or not this was as clever a move as I thought it was, and was just rounding the corner when Cinaedemis called, "Lady Morgan?" I paused, then turned slowly back her way to find her stroking her chin and staring after me. "Perhaps you make a fair point," she said. "Likely nobody else would particularly care one way or another about this Gilderos's goods, and I suppose your favor would only become more valuable as you grow into your new position. And you *did* seek me out specifically in good faith, in front of all of our peers."

I walked slowly back toward her as she spoke, suppressing a grin all the way. Dramoc had prepared me for this kind of demon better than I'd realized. There was no way I could match her greed, true — but I could deny her a sale. However small it was, it was apparently better than nothing. "I did, didn't I?" I said as we came within companionable speaking distance again. "Thank you, archduchess."

Cinaedemis was all smile now — and I mean her face was almost literally all smile, with that toothy Cheshire grin. The Avaritiates were a bit dragony. "I suppose you're welcome, my lady," she cooed. "Gilderos, was it?"

"Gilderos it was, yes," I said with a nod. "I don't know if it's a man or a woman, if they're a retailer or distributor or what. I've just got a name and an idea of the type of goods. If you could point me to them — or maybe point them to me, even — that would be great."

"Of course," said the archduchess. "I'll have my people see what we have on record and call on you once I've found out more, shall I?"

"It would be most appreciated," I said, customer service smiling again, the both of us flashing clearly fake grins at one another. "Thank you, my lady."

"Of course," she said again, then reached out and slid the nearby elevator open. "Now, was there any further business? Because before I can see to that, I still have several books that need balancing, and there's a matter of a mining delay that I've been setting aside for far too long, so I really must be going."

"Of course," I echoed, taking a step back as she stepped through the door. "That was all I had for the moment, thank you."

"Of course," she said, and then the door slid closed and I heard the muffled trundling of the elevator as it rose up through the palace.

I took another deep breath and let it all out in a relieved "Whew!" as I surreptitiously pumped my fist a little. Bargaining with demons. I was quickly becoming a pro at that, I realized. If they *didn't* burn me at the stake when I got home, I had a good shot at employee of the month with these new skills.

Banal thoughts like that would help keep me sane, I think.

At any rate, with my only lead set to be followed, all I could do now with my escape plan was hang out and wait for whatever Cinaedemis found out to make its way to me. I had some breathing room at last, time to get my bearings and maybe even relax a little.

Time to think about what I'd done, what the future might hold. Time to really let it sink in finally.

I imagine Lady Morgan shall remain indefinitely, he'd said.

No! None of that! Stay positive, Morgan. I had plenty to dwell on besides that. I had plenty to distract myself with if I wanted. Just had to stay busy.

Well, I had the run of the palace now, for starters, so that was a plus. Besides the general area around my room in the prince's quarters, though, I had no real idea where anything was beyond the abstract. I could wander around blindly, I supposed, learn the place that way; but it probably wouldn't look good if the newly appointed Lady Morgan, delegate to Earth and, ugh, consort to the prince, was seen stumbling around lost in the hallways. I'd need a guide for that sort of thing. A chauffeur of sorts.

I made my way back to the throne room as I mulled all of this over. By the time I got there, though, I was the only one left. Prince Vambrace, Enkida, all of the archdemons, they'd all cleared out on their own business, it seemed.

Like it or not, the prince was probably still my best bet for learning my way around this place. At least I remembered the directions back to his suite from here. Was that where he'd be? If not, probably better to wait for him there than go searching for him. At least it didn't seem like he'd be taking this consort thing seriously if he was just gonna wander off without me like that. Not that I'd thought he would, not after that display of manic chivalry I'd been witness to in private. Whatever else I thought of him, I'd decided I wasn't worried about that particular issue anymore.

With no better plan, I made my way in that direction, planning to wait for him in my own room for now, maybe send for a snack or something. It felt like ages ago since I'd eaten dinner with everyone. As I walked, I consciously stood straighter and held my chin up higher whenever I passed a guard or servant or whoever else these people were wandering Pandemonium. I was a lady now, and I was banking more and more on a mix of honorary and imaginary clout to get by. Best to look like I knew I was important, just in case.

Rezavix was still gone when I finally made it back, but in his place, Enkida was leaning against the wall beside the door. "How long have you been here?" I asked as I drew up. "Is the prince in there?" I added, nodding at my own door.

"His majesty is testing his soldiers in the arena," she said with a shake of her head. "Perhaps seeking a suitable replacement to stand sentry over your quarters now that Rezavix has been reassigned. In the interim, I shall fulfill the task myself."

Where did she find the time? Wasn't she a general as well as being Vambrace's personal guard? Shouldn't that make her too important to stand here in an empty hallway and stare at the walls? Or was this supposed to be a show of just how high I'd suddenly risen on Hell's social ladder, that I had its general guarding my door against ... whatever it was it needed guarding against?

I was curious about all of this, but I was tired and hungry too, and the questions didn't really seem worth the asking at the moment. Instead, I just smiled and said, "Well, thank you for that. Can you let me know when he gets back?"

She nodded in acknowledgment. "Of course, Lady Morgan," she said, her lips quirking up just a bit; on an Iriate, that was practically a beaming grin. I suppose she liked me well enough, then. Hopefully I wouldn't need to make myself as much of a nuisance for her as I had for my last door guard. Getting on Rezavix's bad side had been uncomfortable enough; pissing off Hell's general would be an infinitely stupider move, and I doubted I could get away with anything useful under her watch anyway. Which had been her point when she'd dismissed Rezavix, I guess, but I still felt kind of bad about getting him in trouble with his boss. At least I was unlikely to need to use the unnoticeability spell to sneak off again now that I'd been given the run of the place, so there was that.

With these quiet, partly guilty mullings in my head, I stepped past her and opened my door. Kriseia was waiting right where I'd left her, on her knees on the rug in the middle of the room; only now she had her hand between her lavender thighs under her outfit, her head tilted back, her eyes closed, her lips parted in breathless panting as she went to town on herself.

I slammed the door. Then I just stood and stared at it for a moment.

"Something wrong, my lady?" Enkida asked beside me. "You've gone nearly as red as I am."

Oh yeah, I had a lust demon now. One who'd been very eager to please, whom I'd shot down a few times and then left all alone. No one to blame but myself, I guess. Should've knocked first.

From the other side of the door, a breathy and concerned voice called, "Mistress Morgan?"

I took a deep breath, let it out, took another, held it, and being careful not to even glance in Enkida's direction, I opened the door again and stepped quickly through, then immediately shut it behind me. "Hello," I said to the floor. "I, uh, I'm back."

"Welcome back, mistress," Kriseia said, rising and walking over to me. I kept my eyes on the floor still, which meant staring down her bare legs as she stepped into view. Her thighs glistened, still damp. "Are you well?" she asked. "You look upset." Gently, as if worried it might get her in trouble, she reached out and laid a tender hand on my cheek.

Her fingers were wet.

"I'm fine!" I squeaked, recoiling from her touch and striding brusquely past her toward the bathroom, flinging the door shut behind me and leaning against it.

"If… if you're sure, mistress…" I heard her mumble.

Crap, I was doing it again, wasn't I? Hurting her feelings with my uncomfortableness. *This is Hell, Morgan,* I reminded myself. *These people are demons. Manners work different here. Shame is probably a foreign concept. Don't be such a prude.*

Right. Demons thought humans were hot stuff because we could act just like any of them on a whim. Being angry at the angry ones gave them pause and made them wary of me. Freaking out whenever the sexy ones did something sexy was just going to send the opposite signals. I had to be unfazeable, like Vambrace.

First, though, I had to wipe my face off. Once that was done, I opened the door and stepped back into the bedroom, where Kriseia was still standing in contrition by the front door. "Sorry," I said, "just couldn't hold it in anymore. How've you been?"

She looked confused for a moment, then bowed her head. "I am fine, Mistress Morgan, thank you," she said, smiling politely as her head came back up. "I was just masturbating while I waited for your return."

I choked on nothing, turned away and coughed. "Oh yeah?" I said to my desk. "I, uh, I noticed. I…" Deep breath. I cleared my throat and forced myself to look at her again. "So, what do you do for fun around here, anyway?" I asked.

"Me, mistress?" She tilted her head.

"Yeah," I said. "You've been asking me what I want you to do, but if nobody's got any orders for you, what do you like to do to keep yourself entertained?"

She shrugged. "Mostly I pleasure myself, as I've said," she said. "Why do you ask? Are you bored, Mistress Morgan?"

Not *that* bored. I really don't know what other answer I expected.

"Alright," I tried again, "say I wasn't here for you to wait on, and you were finished with… doing that. What would you do?"

She looked confused again. "If I wasn't waiting on you, Mistress Morgan?" she asked. "You mean if I was serving someone else?"

"No," I said, "I mean if you weren't serving anybody."

"I…" She trailed off, staring down at the floor between us. She seemed uncomfortable. "I don't know, mistress," she said slowly after a moment. "I have never not served somebody. I am gift caste; my whole life, I have been waiting on someone."

I stared at her in silence for a second while that sank in, then slowly pulled out my desk chair and sat down facing her. "Kriseia," I asked, "are you saying you've never done anything for yourself before?"

"Besides masturbate, you mean, Mistress Morgan?" she asked.

"Besides that, yeah," I said with a wave. "From what you're saying, this gift caste thing doesn't sound any different than slavery."

She shrugged again. "I do not know, mistress," she said. "What is slavery?"

"What is—?" I started, but I couldn't finish. "Are you—?" I shook my head. "You don't know what slavery is?"

"I'm sorry, Mistress Morgan," she said with a pout. "I've never heard the word before. Is it an Earth custom?"

Was this girl serious? They didn't have that here? We had slavery on Earth, but it was a foreign concept in Hell? What the hell? How was that fair?

"Slavery is like forced servitude," I explained, marveling as I did so that I needed to teach this concept to a demon. "Like being made to do whatever someone says all the time without getting paid or getting a break or anything. A slave is a person who's treated like a piece of property instead of a person."

Kriseia raised a slender finger to her delicate chin and appeared to think about it for a minute. "I suppose that does sound similar to a gift caste Luxuriate," she said. "But… may I ask a question, Mistress Morgan?"

"Of course," I said. "You don't need to ask permission for that kinda thing."

"Thank you, mistress," she said, quickly ducking her head. "Then in the terms you've just described, how is this slavery different from the positions of any ignoble?"

"Ignoble?" I parroted.

"We individuals who are not members of our House's aristocracy, mistress," she explained. "I am no duchess to guide House Luxuria, so I serve it as a gift to patrons. Perhaps I am a slave, as you say, in this regard." She tilted her head at me, still stroking her chin. "But an Iriate who does not give orders as a duke or duchess follows those orders as a soldier or a guard. An ignoble Gulliate serves as a cook or a farmer or a disposer. An ignoble Invidiate spends its life cleaning or keeping records. Are these ways of life not also slavery?"

Well, this little talk was getting deeper than I'd expected. "I'm gonna be honest with you," I said, "I'm still learning how your society works here in Hell. But those all sound like jobs or occupations. Y'know? They're different because those are positions you choose to be in instead of being forced into them. Don't you?" I added, frowning at the end. "I mean… like, I've seen the merchants in the bazaar being paid for stuff, for example. They're not being forced to live as merchants… are they? They made a choice. Right?"

"You mean choosing one's caste, mistress?" Kriseia looked about as confused as I was. I was getting used to that look on her face, as I'm sure she was getting used to it on me. But then she smiled brightly. "Oh, wait," she said, "but I forget. Apologies, Mistress Morgan. You are human, from Earth. I imagine there must be a greater degree of fluidity for the society of the Original Sin, mustn't there? We must all seem so provincial to you here in Dis." She giggled, then continued, still smiling. "The seven derived Houses of Sin are not as innately gifted or accomplished as your own race, mistress. I was placed in the gift caste because I did not have the skills or inclination to serve as a dancer or a singer or such. Perhaps it seems stifling to one with your talents, mistress. But if given the choice, I would not choose to be a soldier or a merchant or anything like that instead, nor would I be very good at any of them, I imagine. If that is this slavery, I am not unhappy with it, if such is your concern."

"Such was my concern, yeah," I responded, making a mental note to write some of this down on my flashcards when I could do so without it being rude to her. "You don't feel, I dunno... objectified by that?"

Again, the furrowing of her brow and the slight frown. "Of course I do," she argued. "That is the point. I am your gift, mistress, to do with as you please." This declaration was punctuated by her running her hands up from her own still-glistering thighs over her bare stomach to her breasts, which she cupped and lifted as if presenting them to me, smiling proudly. "But as I said, I am not unhappy with this situation," she added as her hands slipped up over her chest and shoulders to cup behind her neck, her head bowed slightly as she looked at me through her lashes, her body on prominent display. "And I don't just say that because you are an important woman whom I wish not to insult. I am genuinely honored to be given to you, Mistress Morgan, and I will dutifully act either as your object or your companion. However you wish to have me."

She stood in silence like that for a minute before I realized it was my turn to say something. I'd forgotten because I was too busy staring at her and feeling my face slowly heat up. At last, I gulped down my nervousness as best I could and turned to address the top of my desk, because if I kept looking at her, I would never get my words back. "Well, I mean, I guess if you don't mind..." I mumbled at the wood, my hands in my lap as my thumbs fidgeted together. "I... thanks? Yeah, thanks."

That was all I could say for the moment. When it stretched into silence again, I risked another glance at her, my composure mostly back again by that point. She was still standing, but not as brazenly; now she was staring down at her own feet, her shoulders slumped, her hands hanging clasped in much the same fidgety gesture as my own. And she was pouting.

Aw fuck, I was doing it again.

"No, I mean..." I stammered, rising from my seat. She didn't look up, and I felt like I'd just kicked a... well, not a puppy, clearly, she was entirely too sultry and naked for that analogy to be comfortable. Like I'd just kicked a cute naked girl, I guess. "I mean, I'm flattered, really, I've just never... I don't..." My hands fluttered in front of me for a second before I sighed and dropped them.

Alright, screw all this. I set my jaw and walked over to her, putting both hands on her lavender shoulders. She blinked and looked up in surprise. "Mistress?" she asked, her solid sapphire eyes gazing into mine. She was actually a couple inches taller than me, which made this mistress–servant thing between us just that much weirder; but then, she was wearing permanent stiletto heels, I reminded myself, so that was kind of like cheating.

"Okay, look," I said as frankly as I could, given the circumstances. "I'm bad at this, and I feel like I keep screwing it up. I'm sorry. I think I'm hurting your feelings. But I lived a pretty solitary life before I came here. I don't really even know how to have friends, much less servants. So." I squeezed her shoulders and smiled. "Let's start over, eh? Get to actually know each other a little. And I'm starving, so let's start by getting some food together."

Her slowly growing smile was interrupted only briefly by that familiar look of confusion. "Would you like me to fetch you something, Mistress Morgan?" she asked.

"No, I'm tired of sitting here waiting and being waited on," I said. "I mean, let's go to the dining hall or a restaurant or whatever kinda thing you've got in this place. You can show me around the palace, we can talk about something other than how great I am. We'll make it a girl date. It'll be great."

Kriseia beamed then and stepped forward, suddenly wrapping me in a soft purple hug. "Yes ma'am, mistress!" she said, one of her hands coming to rest on the back of my neck.

That reminded me. "Cool," I said. "But before we go, would you mind, uh, washing your hands first?"

She released me and stepped back. "My hands, Mistress Morgan?" she asked, holding them up for inspection and looking at them quizzically.

"It's just, they were a bit… slick earlier," I said, trying to be tactful.

"Oh, yes," she said, smiling again. "Not to worry, that was just my sex juices. Because I had been pleasuring myself, you remember, mistress."

I don't know why I tried. "Yeah, I know," I said, and reached reflexively to rub the back of my neck before I remembered what had just been back there and stopped the gesture. "It's just… let's call it another Earth thing for now."

"As you say, mistress," she said, then strode past me toward the bathroom.

I followed her. She could show me which of those goop bottles was the soap, I reasoned. At this rate, we couldn't have too much of the stuff.

Chapter 17: Obstinance

Between what Archduchess Cinaedemis had said earlier and what Kriseia explained to me as we made our way through the palace together, the inscrutable labyrinth that was Pandemonium started to solidify into a clearer picture in my head.

What had looked like a mass of jagged, patternless obsidian spikes from the distance in the city was actually eight different spires: seven comparably shorter, thinner ones wrapped around one thicker, massive center tower. The seven Sin-centric levels were laid out however the House in charge of them wanted, and for the most part, nobody who wasn't part of that House knew or cared about the fine details of the floor plans, because it was this massive center spire where all the communal activity took place. It housed the throne room and entrance hall, every door out into the city, the massive dining hall, the coliseum, the prince's and my own quarters, and probably hundreds of other spaces that I hadn't seen yet, plus the miles and miles of hallways that connected them all, spiraling around and up and down throughout the enormous column as it tapered up impossibly far into the distance.

Did the floor plan extend all the way up to the tip of that center spire? Kriseia didn't know — she was just as new to the palace as I was, though she'd studied it as part of her lessons at whatever demonic finishing school she'd apparently just graduated from — but it seemed unlikely. Even if every single resident of Dis piled into the castle, I still didn't think they'd need that much room to house everybody. But did that mean the cap of the center tower was still solid obsidian or whatever weird material this stuff was? Or were there hundreds or thousands of empty, unused rooms up there? Or were the floors just really vertically spaced out to make up the difference?

I supposed this was just my curiosity being cautious again, trying to figure out everything I could about this place in case I needed the info later. It didn't really matter in the long run, though. Or I hoped it wouldn't. Mine and the prince's rooms, the throne room, the kitchens and dining rooms, the libraries and theaters and music halls and all the other myriad entertainment areas, they were all here in the central tower within a few floors of one another. Anyplace I might reasonably need to go within the palace was no more than half a dozen staircases or so above or below me. Exactly how high it all went could comfortably remain a mystery to me for now. So could how deep the palace ran.

That was apparently the bigger question, to hear Kriseia give the locals' take on it. The general height of Pandemonium could be seen by anyone out in the city, even if the tippy top of it was obscured by distance; but the depth was an idle curiosity to the particularly curious, or at least those who weren't authorized to go down and find out. Only the archfiend and those few he granted the privilege to were allowed to venture further than five floors below the palace's ground level, and even then, nobody did, to anyone's knowledge. Whatever was down there must not be too vital to the day-to-day running of the place, I guessed. Cinaedemis had mentioned a capital-T Throne, though, which sounded like a big deal.

"You mean the Abandoned Throne, mistress?" Kriseia said when I asked about it, and this time I heard the capital letters right away. We were sitting together in a dining hall; not the massive one I'd been in before with the raised table for the prince and archdemons, but another, smaller one somewhere a bit more out of the way. The huge one must've been reserved for special functions or something; this one was about the size of my college cafeteria back home and similarly laid out, with smaller tables scattered around the floor space and a bar with seats stretching along one wall, behind which a few Gulliates and Invidiates mingled — the former to take food orders, the latter to do the serving and cleaning. An opening in the wall behind them led to what I was told was just one of many sub-kitchens. Pandemonium never stopped cooking, because there were always plenty of people in it willing to eat.

"I guess so," I said, smearing jam on my third piece of toast. Hungry as I was, jam and toast was all I'd eaten during this meal, because the mundane bread here was the one thing I'd found so far that I knew was safe for human consumption and not ground from some demonic hell-wheat. The jam was made from caina berries — which, granted, didn't sound familiar, but I figured exotic berries had less chance of doing something weird and unpleasant to my digestive tract than esoteric demon beast meats. Unless I got desperate, I was probably gonna stay vegetarian here in Dis. "All I've heard is that it's some sort of big deal buried in the center of the palace, and that's why Prince Vambrace's rooms are downstairs or something."

Kriseia nodded. "I don't know very many details, of course," she said. "I suppose nobody but the archfiend and some of the historians would. All I know is that it's supposedly the throne of the very first archfiend, whose name has long since been lost to time, back in the earliest days of the Original Sin at the dawn of Hell itself and the splitting of the seven Houses. If that's true, that would make it one of the only known artifacts left from that legendary era, one of the only sure pieces of evidence to still exist of the Original Sin's reign and supremacy."

That would probably explain why Vambrace wouldn't let anybody else go take a look, then, I thought. If the Throne didn't look like something he could comfortably sit in, it would raise too many questions.

We sat there for a while, Kriseia and I, just hanging out and snacking. Unfortunately, my new resolution to get better acquainted with this woman I would apparently be living with for the foreseeable future didn't magically grant me better social skills, so I mostly just listened while she talked and picked daintily at a glass goblet of some wobbly, flesh-colored substance that looked like whipped pudding sprinkled with shimmery white chips like shaved crystal. It was a lot fancier looking than my toasted rolls with red-brown jelly; if I weren't being cautious, it would be a lot more tempting.

"What is that?" I finally asked during a lull in the conversation, pointing a bread crust at her fancy pudding.

"This, mistress?" she asked, tapping it with her long-handled silver spoon. "This is a jeza bell creme. Would you like some?"

"No, no thanks," I said. "I'm just curious. It's pretty. What's in it?"

"It's made of ground jeza bell petals whipped with honey and kelpie cream, then sprinkled with crushed soul." She smiled as she scooped up another small spoonful. "I haven't had it since I was an acolyte, but it's just as good here as in my old madame's kitchens," she added, her eyes slipping closed as she took another bite.

So Hell had honey too, did it? That sounded promis— "Wait, crushed souls?" I asked, watching the little chunks of white glitter.

"Yes, mistress," she said, spooning up another bite and holding it out to me. "Do you wish to try it?"

"Wait," I said again, pulling my flashcards from a hidden pocket on the front of the dress and flipping through them. I felt silly bringing them along, but hey, they worked. "Oh, right," I said to myself as I found the note I was looking for. "Soul is that crystal money stuff. Wait, you're eating money?"

"Um, no, Mistress Morgan," she said with a patient smile. "This soul was not fashioned into money first. The palace kitchens have their own separate stores." She held the spoon up before her, studying the soul-studded creme. "Though it may have been toasted," she added, popping the bite into her mouth. "Yes, I think so," she said around the pudding, and I heard the quiet crunch of the crystals as she chewed them.

"So the money here is … edible?" I asked. By this point, I had no idea how stupid my questions were sounding. And around Kriseia, at least, I decided I wouldn't care. I'd never get anything figured out otherwise.

"Yes, mistress," she answered after quickly swallowing. "Strictly speaking. Even processed into currency, soul retains enough nutritional value that one could survive off of it alone. A lot of Acediates do just that, since it's simpler. But it's not a good value conversion — you could buy more food that's better for you and more satisfying for the worth of the money than you'd get from just eating it. And it also doesn't taste like much unless you're a skilled chef who knows what you're doing with it. That's why you only ever see soul being eaten in gourmet dishes like this, or by scavengers and the like who can't be bothered to use it to buy other food."

"Huh," I replied, wishing I had a pencil to add that to my notecards. "Well, that's… different. All the money back home is paper or metal or electronic. Can't eat any of it." I dipped my fourth piece of toast into my jam bowl. "Sounds convenient, though, I gotta say. There've been days where I probably would've just eaten my paycheck if it would've worked, if it meant not having to go to the store and stock up on more frozen dinners."

Kriseia smiled. "Your homeworld sounds so exotic, mistress," she said, licking traces of fleshy pudding from her lips. "Whole meals, frozen?

Paper used as currency? Like something from a fantastic dream. And what is electronic?"

I couldn't help but smile back at her attitude. "It's not so fantastical, really," I said. "Though I guess it'd seem that way if you went there. It's real different from here in a lot of ways, for sure." I picked up my little silver knife and started evening out the jam on my bread again. "And I'm not sure I know how to explain electronics to a world without electricity. It's like really complicated machines powered by… well, by lightning, I suppose would be the closest point of comparison." I paused with the food halfway to my mouth. "You do have lightning here in Hell, right?"

She nodded, eyes wide. "You use *lightning* as currency on Earth?" she asked with uncontained awe. "Amazing…. The Original Sin is powerful indeed. No wonder Prince Vambrace has ruled so well for so long."

I stuffed toast in my mouth in lieu of correcting her or laughing at her misconception. But hell, she was technically sort of right, I supposed. In a world ruled by a guy from medieval times, which hadn't seemed to advance much past them scientifically, modern technology would be indistinguishable from magic. Hopefully just not too indistinguishable to get me in trouble with the anti-magic law.

Kriseia was still looking at me in wonder, smiling again. "Mistress Morgan," she said, a bit quieter this time, "may I ask a question?"

She'd been asking plenty of questions already without seeking permission first, I noticed, like she was forgetting to lapse back into that unbridled deference of hers. Good; her reverence made me feel weird. I liked this informality better. Since there was too much food in my mouth to politely say anything, I settled on nodding instead.

"Are you to rule beside the archfiend now that you are here?" she asked, leaning across the table and her goblet. "Such a thing would be unprecedented, but I had heard that Prince Vambrace has named you his consort. And if you are anywhere near as powerful as he is…"

I stuffed another bite into my face and chewed slowly, like I was mulling the idea over, while I hurriedly tried to think of what to say. Any sort of guidance at all from the prince before he made that announcement would have been helpful, but no, no such luck. If he didn't want me accidentally screwing up his cover, why didn't he explain more of this crap before he pulled it?

Maybe he didn't have the answers yet either. I wasn't about to make them for him, though, not with something this big. But I was pretty sure he wasn't about to give me half of his throne, whatever happened next.

"I don't think so, no," I said slowly after I'd finally swallowed my food. "Like you said, it would be a weird arrangement, and I'm not really interested in being a queen or a princess or whatever I'd be in that scenario. A co-archfiend. I think I'm going to be more like a… like a counsel, maybe. Someone he can talk with about things special to humans. Maybe to offer an Original Sin's perspective besides his own. Maybe just to share stories of Earth with. He's been away a lot longer than I have, after all."

"I see," she said, gazing down into her by now empty pudding cup. "You are to be his companion similar to how I am yours, then." She flushed lightly then, her lilac cheeks pinkening, as she glanced up at me through her long lashes. "Well, not entirely similar, I suppose," she added, "since he is male."

"Yeah, not… entirely," I said slowly as my brow furrowed. "What's his being a guy got to do with anything?"

"Oh?" she said, fingers rising to her chin. "Because mistress is not sexually interested in men. Is she not?"

My turn to flush. "Am I not?" I asked. "Who says?"

"His majesty says," she informed me, head tilting. "That was of course one of the reasons I was given to you, mistress. Because you…" Her hands went into her lap, fidgeting nervously, as if she wasn't sure she was supposed to be saying what she was saying. "Because it is said… very discreetly, understand… that you preemptively rebuked any advances Prince Vambrace may have made on you, as well as Archduke Melchius. And it was decided that, if you emphatically did not prefer men in your bed, then you would be given a woman instead to keep you satisfied." She glanced up again when she was finished, smiling shyly.

I stared at her with my mouth hanging open for several long seconds, then grabbed another roll and shoved it in, dry and unjellied.

That busybody son of a bitch! I thought we were over this. Why did he have to keep shoving his nose into my sex life or lack thereof?

Because you kept bringing it up first, my brain reminded me, *when you kept looping all of your earlier conversations back to how much you didn't want to bang him, even though he'd never broached the topic himself.*

Okay, yeah, but that was different! He kept trying to get me alone in his room, what was I supposed to think? That didn't mean he needed to make any decisions for me himself on that front. Who the hell thinks, "Hey, maybe that girl likes screwing other girls, I should get her one"?

Probably the ruler of Hell, my brain chimed in, *who has an army of sex demons at his command specifically for that kind of purpose.*

Well, shit. Good point, brain. He was probably just trying to make me more comfortable while I was stuck here and still confused by everything. He probably thought it was a totally sensible idea that wouldn't weird me out or make me uncomfortable at all. I had my own super hot sex buddy now. Who wouldn't be grateful?

Good lord, and this man used to be a chivalrous knight once upon a time. How long does a literal knight in shining armor like that have to live with demons before he forgets that giving people to other people for sex stuff isn't odd?

I glanced down at my notecards on the table. *About 1,500 years,* they read. Yeah, I supposed that'd do it.

"Mistress Morgan?" Kriseia chimed in, still glancing shyly at me while I sat there with my face stuffed with unchewed bread. "*Are* you satisfied with me? I mean, I don't mean to sound needy again, mistress, only whenever the subject comes up, you don't seem like you want—"

"Nn, mm fnn," I mumbled around my bread. I bit off what was actually in my mouth and set the rest down, then chewed and swallowed as quickly as I could. "I'm fine," I repeated more coherently, "really. I'm just... Look, I don't know what the prince is like, but I'm not what you'd call... active, I guess. Sexually speaking. For men or women. It's not you, it's me, I promise." I couldn't believe I'd just said that.

She swirled her spoon around inside her now-empty goblet, making it ring quietly. "If mistress says so," she pouted.

I reached over the table and grabbed her other hand, startling her. "Mistress says so," I reassured her. "And please, just call me Morgan."

She nodded. "Yes, Mistress Morgan."

"No, *just* Morgan," I said. "None of that 'mistress' stuff, please. I don't want to be your owner, Kriseia, I want to be your friend."

I guess I expected her to be grateful for the sentiment, but I saw panic flash across her face as her hand tightened on mine. "You... don't wish to own me?" she asked, voice going quiet. "Is it... I'm sorry, did I...?"

"No, *stop being sorry*," I insisted, squeezing her hand back. "Look. Listen to me. I like you, alright? You're real friendly, a lot more than everyone else I've met here so far, and I appreciate that. I'm not kicking you out or telling you off or having you sent away or anything. It's nice to have someone to talk to. A friend." I leaned in further, putting my other hand on hers. "But that's what I want most, alright? Not a servant or a... a sex toy, or anything. Just a friend. Someone who can think for herself and will treat me like an equal companion, not a mistress to obey or an oddity to wonder over. Can you do that for me, please?"

The room went quiet after my declaration, and I froze, feeling the familiar prick of eyes staring at me. I'd forgotten we weren't exactly alone in here; this cafeteria space wasn't anywhere near as crowded as that first big dining hall, true, but there were the cooks and servers behind their bar I'd forgotten about, as well as a handful of other diners scattered throughout the room: half a dozen more Gulliates, a Superbiate sitting with an Avaritiate, and a few Acediates slumped against the walls or squatted in corners. All of them were watching us after that little display.

Shit. I probably shouldn't have said all of that out loud, not right here. How weird did it look, one of the only two Original Sins declaring that she didn't want too much respect or to be considered a big deal? Would that screw up Vambrace's long con? Or would it just make us seem more mysterious and unpredictable?

While I was worrying about that, Kriseia let out a long sigh and laid her other hand on both of mine, completing the pile. "I will try to, mistre — Morgan," she said with a smile. "It will be new and strange to me, willfully being undeferential. I have never not been a servant of some kind before; it is the role I was raised and trained for. But for you, I will try to be less of one." She giggled then, her hands clasping mine tighter. "Not because you are my mistress and you ordered such, I suppose," she added. "But because I like you as well, as a friend. As you say, it is an uncommon thing to find in another person here."

I flushed again, though this time not because of any innuendo or her mostly nudity. That was probably one of the most heartfelt things anyone who wasn't my family had ever said to me. More than that, I realized, more than her being the closest thing I had to a friend among the demons here — she was probably the closest thing I had to a friend at all. Back home, I had classmates and acquaintances, and a few old friends from childhood or high school whom I'd grown apart from and hadn't seen since graduation. I had my parents and a couple of professors I got along with and my manager Steve back at Old Sound, who was nice enough. But I had no real friends, no social life to speak of, no particular desire to make any, and no real idea how to go about doing so if I'd wanted to. I just went to work, went to school, and went home to study or listen to music and hermit it up.

And now here I was on a girls' night out in a palace in Hell, holding hands and bonding with a succubus. It only took being indefinitely damned to make me sociable.

And we were still holding hands, I realized. Very much so. And her lavender skin was soft and warm, her slender fingers squeezing mine in reassurance, and her shy smile was still beaming as she gazed tenderly into my eyes with those deep blue —

"Right, yes," I blurted out, extricating my hands from hers as delicately as I could and sitting back again, intently studying the remaining crusts of my meal. "Thank you. I, uh, I appreciate it, really." I cleared my throat, reached up and brushed my hair behind one of my ears. "And I mean, I don't want to impose too much, though, if it's weird for you. I mean, I don't know what it's like being you, but it's weird for me to be called mistress and stuff, but if it's too weird for you *not* to, y'know, I suppose you could a little, sometimes, or something, if it… helped, or…" And here I finally reined in my babbling enough to cut it off, for better or worse.

Kriseia just giggled again. I decided to interpret that as a good sign.

We left the cafeteria then before I could do any more accidental damage to my new image I was supposed to be maintaining.

"It occurs to me I don't actually know much about you," I said as Kriseia and I wandered the halls. I had no particular destination in mind — I was clean and relatively rested and full of carbs, so now I was just wandering for the sake of it, getting more familiar with the place and getting a change of pace now that I was no longer under house arrest in the prince's quarters.

"What would you like to know, mist— Morgan?" Kriseia asked beside and slightly behind me. Since I didn't have a destination in mind, she didn't either. Baby steps, though.

"I dunno," I said. "I just feel like if we're gonna be living together for a while, we should know more about each other, y'know?"

"'For a while,' mi— Morgan?" she asked. "You mean to be rid of me after a time?"

"Dammit, no," I said with a sigh, "it's just a saying. Sorry. Slip of the tongue." I glanced sidelong and back at her. "I'm assuming, since you're my gift, you're with me until I say otherwise, right?"

"Yes, m— Morgan," she said with a smile and a nod. "Yours for life, if you wish it."

I gulped and looked ahead again. No sense worrying how to cross that bridge until I got the *Morganomicon* back, I decided. "Thanks," I said. "For the sake of argument, though, what if *you* wished otherwise? Like, what if I was a total bitch, and you couldn't stand me? Do gift caste people get to ungift themselves? Can you lodge a complaint somewhere, or what?"

She didn't answer for a moment, and when I looked back again, I saw her fingering her chin and staring blankly ahead in thought. "I suppose if you were the sort of person that I would be miserable being around, then I wouldn't have been given to you in the first place," she said slowly. "The madames and messires of the House are very observant and precise when it comes to assignations. If you were indeed, as you said, a total... bad-tempered person, and I tested poorly with that sort of personality, then another gift would have been given to you who got along better with your temperament."

"But what if there was a mistake?" I persisted. "Like, I'm still new here, nobody really knows for definite what kind of person I am yet. But I was still given you. What if whoever assigned you to me guessed wrong? Could you ask to be switched out or something?"

"I… do not really know, I'm afraid," she said after another thoughtful moment. "Such an assignment would likely be just as undesirous to the recipient as to the gift. I imagine the other party would demand someone different before the gift did. If not…" She paused to rub at her chin some more and frown in consideration. "Well, any matter that cannot be handled within House infrastructure goes to the archdemon for their deliberation. If they cannot resolve the matter, or if they think the issue extends beyond the province of their House alone, then it goes before the archfiend in court whenever he has the time and inclination."

Hell had local and federal governments, then. I supposed I already knew that, given I'd met archduchesses and archdukes and then Vambrace above all of them, but it was weird to hear that it worked so mundanely. I couldn't tell whether I should have really been surprised or not, though; depending on which version I'd read about or watched or whatever in church or movies or something for school, Hell was either a chaotic pit of suffering and anarchy or a precisely regimented system of personalized attention and punishment. So far, the reality was somewhere between the two, minus all the torture. And let me reiterate again how grateful I was for that little anomaly.

"You said something about testing with personalities," I said after a moment. "What's that about? You have exams at Luxuriate school?"

"Examinations, you mean?" said Kriseia. "Yes, of course. We are always being tested and examined throughout our training, encouraged in areas we are found to excel in and polished to adequacy in those where we fall short. We are not permitted to take on our full ranks, not even in gift or entertainer castes, until we are deemed sufficiently skilled in the pertinent areas by our messire or madame."

"And what kind of training do you have, then?" I asked. "What were your best classes?"

"I… um…" She glanced down so that her hair fell around her face somewhat, hiding in it like a small curtain. I knew the trick all too well.

"Well, with patron personalities, it was determined I served best for someone with a firm hand and strong sense of decisiveness. My madame always said I was too scatterbrained if left to my own devices, given more to passivity than assertion. Beyond that, I always tested well at attentiveness and agreeability. And self-stimulation, but nobody falls short in that area. I'm told I'm perfectly acceptable at sensual responsiveness. And oral stimulation, though I performed better in manual. Physically, I'm… acceptable, I suppose, except…" And here she lapsed off.

I'd been trying my best to take in what she was saying purely scientifically, which was taking a mental effort, so I didn't notice her hesitating at first. "Wait, except what?" I asked, pausing in my walk and turning to her, incredulous. "Just acceptable? That's bullshit. Look at you," I said, waving a hand up and down the general direction of her body. "I've known girls who would kill to look as good as you. Literally kill. You're like the hottest person I know, hands down. How's anyone say you look just okay?"

"You… really think so, mistress?" she asked, flushing slightly, and I could tell by her tone she was genuinely surprised to hear the compliment. "Oh, I mean Morgan," she amended hastily. "Sorry."

"It's fine," I said. "But seriously, what crazy standard are they holding you to if you barely pass in looks?"

"Well…" She was staring at the ground, and her hands lifted to lightly touch her short ivory horns poking out from her purple hair. "I've never been good at glamour," she said. "I mean, I can do it, but it's not… It's never convincing. My madame always said my range was limited at best, and my horns…" She took a deep breath, then closed her eyes and sighed. "I can't change them," she said flatly. "At all. I can't hide them. I can't even recolor them. No matter what I try, they're always there." Her eyes were sullen when she opened them, her lips set in less of a pout and more of a curdled frown for a change. "I hate them."

"What? No," I said. "They're fine. Cute, even, compared to some of the others I've seen here." As cute as horns could be, anyway, I added silently to myself.

She went wide eyed at that. "You… really think so?" she asked, smile slowly growing. "You don't mind? Oh," she added, smile dropping again, "but you've never seen me try my glamour yet. When I change races and they're still there, it's…" She stopped, shook her head, and smiled again. "But I'm sorry, I shouldn't talk so much of my own problems. What about yourself, m — Morgan?"

"What about me?" I asked as we walked on, reaching a staircase and descending on an aimless whim.

"I am sure you're much more interesting than a lowly gift like me," she said. "What must your life have been like on Earth amongst other such lofty beings? What does the Original Sin do for enjoyment and fulfillment in their native world? I must confess, I've been wondering a great deal since the day I first saw you in court."

Ooh boy, we were in dangerous waters again. Still, I wasn't as concerned with Kriseia as I would have been if any other demon had asked me to regale them with Earth stories; besides the fact that she was apparently one of my biggest fans here (which was weird to think about, but I was coming to terms with it), from all I'd heard, she was at the bottom of the demonic totem pole, for better or worse. If I slipped and gave away some detail that undermined the prince, she one, wouldn't go gossiping to everyone, or two, even if she did, I doubt anybody would believe her hearsay over Vambrace or myself.

"Don't get too excited," I said as we reached the bottom of the stairs and kept going. "I was actually one of the lower ranked humans back home. One reason I'm not used to having servants, like I said."

"I understand," she said, walking more at my side than behind me now. The halls were curving more sharply here, which I think meant we were getting nearer to the center of the main spire. "Still, I imagine even a lowly ranked human must impress more than even some of our highest ranked nobility here. What was your title? What was your life like?"

She was practically bouncing on the balls of her feet in excitement. Given those heel spikes of hers, that didn't seem too safe. "My title, eh?" I replied. "I suppose… uh…" Screw it, an embellished truth was easier than making up something more impressive. "To be honest, I was still in training myself before I landed here. I hadn't graduated from my own classes yet."

"I see," said Kriseia, sounding way too impressed already. "What were you training to become, may I ask?"

Good question. My academic advisor had been on my case for the same issue lately; I could only take gen-eds and electives for so long before I had to decide on a degree track, but try as I might, none of my options really sang to me. Growing up, I'd wanted to be everything from a ballerina to a firefighter to an archeologist, but each of those fleeting dreams had been thrown away when I'd realized that I had no real sense of grace or balance for dancing, or that I'd never be strong or disciplined enough for rescue services, or that real archeology didn't look anything like Lara Croft's adventures. My only real lasting passion had been music, but just as a fan. I couldn't play any instruments; I'd gotten bored and frustrated with guitar lessons after about a month, and I vehemently shunned any suggestion of piano lessons after we read that short story from *The Joy Luck Club* in sixth-grade English and all the other kids started wondering out loud how well their own local Asian's piano skills compared to the protagonist's. But professional music-liker wasn't a career, so…

"I was… still deciding on my options," I answered eventually. "Education on Earth covers a wide range of subjects and skills. Even with my lower ranking, I've been trained in math and the sciences, in art, history, literature, philosophy, social and government studies, physical education, you name it. Humans are exhaustively educated to excel in almost any field."

"Wow…" Kriseia breathed, open-mouthed, eyes twinkling. They twinkled really good, those unbroken sapphire-like eyes of hers.

"Yeah, it's no big deal," I said, immediately feeling awkward with even the small amount of bullshitting I was doing. It was different than posturing for other self-important demons who were in my way, like Dramoc or Cinaedemis. Kriseia was just naive and star struck. "I mean, I was only ever alright at best in my classes," I added. "Plenty of other kids — of other humans were better than me in different fields. I was always more a jack-of-all-trades than a specialist. And outside of school, I just worked as a music store clerk to pay for rent and food."

"As a what?" she asked. "A music… clerk? At a store? Like an accountant for music?"

"Sort of?" I said. "It's more like… Well, let's say, I was a cataloguer of famous bards. It was my job to keep records of songs and musicians, to collect them in one spot and sell them to others based on what they most liked to listen to."

"Selling music," she repeated in her awed voice. "What a strange idea. Oh, not to say that you're strange, of course," she added hastily, "it's just… I can't imagine. Artistic experiences catalogued and traded as commodities — it's incredible."

"Is it really?" I asked. "I mean, I'm biased, granted, but even when you put it that way, it doesn't sound like that fantastical of an idea."

"No, perhaps not the actual practice," she said. "I'm not sure how to describe it exactly, but… well, maybe it's a cultural thing. I forget how much of this must be new to you."

I shook my head. "Still lost me."

"I will try and explain," she said, then held out a finger and counted off on it. "Artistry is the work of House Superbia; any music worth listening to was invariably created by a Superbiate. Something in the nature of pride and exceptionalism makes them better suited to the creation of great works, it's said — usually by Superbiates themselves, granted, but still."

She stuck out another finger. "For the actual performing of art, though, the translation and presentation of those ideas, House Luxuria is far and away the most talented. We have the passion and grace that most creators prefer when interpreting their works, so we are almost always the ones called to do the singing or dancing or acting, to bring the art to life."

A third finger extended. "But cataloguing, record keeping, historical documentation; that sort of work is normally the purview of House Invidia. Some of my instructors say it is because they have so few personal skills as a House that they've no better uses to be put to, but the kinder reasoning is that Invidiates are much more observant and detail oriented than the other Sins, which leads to more accurate and higher quality accounts of people and events. Most of the palace seneschals and historians throughout Prince Vambrace's endless reign have been pulled from House Invidia, I've heard.

"And then any financial or mercantile endeavor is obviously going to be governed by House Avaritia, as I'm sure you know by now," she finished with a fourth finger, then held all four up between us. "So, the creation, production, recording, and sale of a musical piece would require the work of four of the seven Houses here in Dis. Yet on Earth, a single race, a single House, does all of that work itself, and all of it just as good or better than we lesser Houses here in Hell." She ended with a beaming smile. "Perhaps it's just me, but I find that incredibly fascinating."

"When you put it like that," I muttered, mulling it over. It seemed like a weirdly restrictive system to me, which I guess just lent credence to the comparison she was drawing. "But I mean, I don't write and sing the songs myself or anything. I just keep them in order and sell them to people. And not just me, I work with other people doing the same job."

"But the implications for humans in general are still the same," Kriseia argued. "And even just with yourself, you're doing the work of an Invidiate and an Avaritiate both, at once. And if you've studied art and government and physical disciplines and all that you've said, then you've touched on every single other House in your training and taken strengths from each."

"Alright," I conceded, "but it can't be that amazing, can it? It's just a difference in who learns what. I mean, you're a Luxuriate, but you know some history, don't you? You can do math, I assume."

"I know some stories from history, yes," she said, "but only the few that interest me to remember. I wouldn't know how to begin recording it. And I understand mathematics, yes, but not how it applies to economics or value or whatever else it is that makes money work. I know how much someone of my skills would be expected to charge for cunnilingus in a brothel, and I could add up my personal profit and subtract my madame's share. And if you're curious, I can tell you the story of how Dalariasa, one of the prior Archduchesses of Luxuria, once oversaw an expedition to Passion's Rift far beyond the wall to stage a mid-air orgy of one hundred-plus people in the moaning winds. Beyond things like that, though, I don't have much knowledge, and I don't really care about gaining it, and I'm not sure I'd be able to retain and understand most of it if I tried to."

"Ah. I guess I understand. Passion's Rift?" I asked, because I wanted to change the subject, but I wasn't gonna ask about her hypothetical whoring prices.

"It's a great gorge out in the wastes," Kriseia explained, "home to an eternal maelstrom of blowing winds that supposedly sound like the continual, drawn-out moans and sighs of some unseen orgiastic revel. Dalariasa was interested in exploring the truth of that impression, though most of the participants that went with were probably more interested in the novelty of what sex was like while suspended on the winds."

"Holy shit," I said. "Are you for real? How did nobody die trying that?"

"Oh, about half the expedition did," she said, far too casually. "They say the winds pick up gradually as you approach, but once inside the whirlwind, they get very powerful very quickly. And I imagine it's hard to steer yourself when flying through the air, tangled up in other people's limbs. They say if you visit the rift today, you can still see the remains of some of the participants being bandied about, unable to dissipate because they can't land anywhere. There's a memorial monument in a park in Asmodeusis with the names of those lost in the winds. It's all very impressive."

Dammit, I should have asked about the cunnilingus instead. "Impressive's one word for it," I said, fighting the mental images that were trying to come to mind. "Insane's another. Why would anyone risk their lives just to try dangerous tornado sex?"

"Because… they wanted to?" Kriseia answered, frowning. "Because sex is enjoyable in any situation, and anyone can have it on the ground, but doing it on the wind would be an entirely unique and potentially incredible experience. What other reason would there be?"

I turned and looked at her a moment. No, she was too nice to be sarcastic; that was genuine confusion again. "They were so interested in the novelty that they killed themselves for it, though? That's idiotic. No matter how much you want to try something, if you die doing it, what's the point?"

"Well," she said, stroking her chin, "I suppose the point is that you've done it. If they didn't do it, then their desires would have gone unfulfilled."

There was a pause. That was the end of her rebuttal, then. "Yeah," I said, "but they wouldn't be dead."

"Correct," she said. Another pause. "I'm sorry, Morgan," she added after a moment, "I don't think I understand the argument anymore."

"I don't think I do either," I replied, then stopped walking, Kriseia coming up beside me. "Also, where the heck are we?"

We stood at an intersection of three corridors: the relatively straight one we'd just reached the end of and two more curving more tightly off to the left and right. All three of them were completely empty except for us two; I'd been more focused on our conversation than our direction or surroundings, and I hadn't noticed when we'd stopped passing other people.

But what this part of the palace lacked in traffic, it made up for in decoration. The lights along the walls burned brighter in more ornate sconces of some polished red metal, and between each of them along the curving wall was a painting, portraits of fancily dressed demons of every House interspersed with wildly disparate scenes of everything from violent battles between Iriates, to Superbiates shaking hands and looking important, to Avaritiates surrounded by piles of treasures and trinkets and stacks of milky white crystals, all just within eyeshot of the intersection we stood in.

Kriseia took a moment to gaze at the paintings alongside me, then perked up. "Wait, I know this place," she said, taking the lead and heading off to the left. I followed behind, watching new scenes and portraits crawl into view along the curving wall. "I mean, I've never been here myself, but this hall matches what I've heard of the royal theater." She paused in front of a portrait of an Acediate lying prone in a pile of vividly multicolored pillows, its gray hair plaited into a long braid, its antler-like horns unbroken and uncracked, generally looking cleaner and nicer than any of them I'd seen so far in person "Listen," she said. "Do you hear that?"

I strained my ears while I stared at a scene of two Gulliates sat behind a banquet table, so heavily laden with food that it bowed in the middle, while two Luxuriates draped in pastel robes poured pitchers of red wine directly into their open mouths. "I hear… shouting?" I said. It was faint and muffled, but if I was listening for it, I could just make out wordless shouts and what may have been the distant clang of metal. "Sounds like a fight."

"A fight scene." Kriseia smiled. "I don't think I've seen any plays with a fight scene before. I scored low at acting potential fairly early in my studies, so I never spent much time in the theaters."

"You wanna go check it out, then?" I asked.

She blinked at me. "If you wish to, Morgan," she said.

"No, that wasn't the question," I said, putting my hands on her shoulders. "Do *you* want to, Kriseia? Because I told you, I don't have any plans, I'm just wandering for something to do right now."

She hesitated for a moment, pursed her lips, turned and looked at the curved painting wall and whatever was going on behind it. If making even minor decisions like this for herself was this difficult, she was gonna have a tough time ahead with me, because I'd decided I was going to try and wean my servant off of that heavily servile attitude of hers — for her own good, maybe, but also to make it less awkward being around her, if I was being perfectly honest.

Then there was a particularly loud cry of fabricated anger from wherever the action was happening, and she smiled. "Well," she said, "seeing a play would certainly be something to do. And it would be your first one in Dis, no less." She turned her smile on me then. "Shall we, Morgan?"

It was a bit wishy-washy, but I'd accept it for now. "Lead the way," I said, smiling. "Because I still don't know where I am."

Chapter 18: Intrusion

I followed Kriseia around the curving hallway with the painting wall on our right. The only thing they all shared in common — besides the pattern of scene, portrait, scene, portrait — was a realistic style; pop art and cubism and the like hadn't found their way to Hell yet, evidently. Beyond that, each new one had a different subject and tone, from a somber rain-soaked field strewn with corpses to a warmly lit kitchen with baked goods covering nearly every surface to—

I froze momentarily in front of one of them, just long enough for Kriseia to notice and stop beside me. She smiled up at the painting. "Oh, there's Archduchess Dalariasa's expedition," she said helpfully. "See the woman with the braid, in the foreground up in the corner? I think that's her."

Sure enough, this newest artwork showed a rocky cliffside with a massive whirlwind just beyond taking up most of the frame. And scattered across the ground and throughout the air were dozens and dozens of multicolored demons, most of them unglamoured Luxuriates, locked together and twisting around one another in the howling winds. The one Kriseia guessed was the archduchess was a particular focal point, suspended naked and upside down above all the other revelers, her head and neck thrown back in ecstasy (or possibly broken) while a lean Iriate man clung desperately to her flailing legs with one hand and her long green braid with the other, his face buried between her thighs, thick droplets of… something streaming by his head.

Dear lord, I couldn't look away, much as I wanted to. It was like staring at a train wreck. A train that had been carrying nothing but horny naked people.

"Morgan?" Kriseia said after a moment, ducking in front of my view and breaking the spell of my morbid fascination. "Are we still going to the theater?"

"Yeah, yeah," I said, shaking my head. "Right. Sorry. Where is it?"

"The entrance should be just around here somewhere," she said as we started walking again. Sure enough, a minute later we finally rounded the long-curving wall to another intersection of halls where it flattened out, the paintings replaced with a long line of wide double doors, all of them currently closed. "Here we are," said Kriseia, hurrying to the nearest set. "If we slip in quietly, we should be fine."

I followed her into a vast, dark room, standing just beside the door while my eyes adjusted to the gloom. The theater was laid out in concentric circles again, like the fighting arena or the city as a whole; they really liked that layout around here. All around us, I could barely make out a sea of people, all of them seated except for a few standing at the top of the audience rim like ourselves, and all of them facing inward and down to a distant stage that I couldn't quite see through the immediate crowd but which was the only source of light in the room. Here and there, both close by and in the distance, I could hear the quiet, muted mutterings of occasional audience chatter, but besides that, the huge theater was mostly silent. What had happened to the muffled fighting we'd heard earlier? Were we too late and the play was over? But nobody looked like they were getting ready to leave, so —

The sudden drums hit so hard and loud that I reeled back a step, feeling as much as hearing the bass as it pounded through the floor and the air around us. It was a rapid, angry rhythm, tribal and warlike, like some blockbuster army charging into battle. After a few bars came the strings, something like a guitar or mandolin weaving around the drums, then sharp, shrill violin notes punctuating the melody, stabbing through in rhythm like daggers, over and over again.

It was the first music I'd heard since I got to this world, and it was loud and raucous and hellish, like proto-metal being covered by a symphony orchestra.

It was awesome.

I stood and let it wash over me for a moment, so lost in the surprise concert that I forgot about the stage for a moment until Kriseia took me by the hand and pulled me closer to the crowds at the edge of our upper level. She said something at me with a smile that I couldn't hear through the music, then pointed over the heads of those seated in front of us at the stage below.

I looked down. The stage platform was wide and circular, lit by a ring of lanterns set into the sides of the raised floor. There were no backdrops, no props or scenery, just the actors — two at the moment. One was the largest Iriate I'd seen so far, a man standing at least six feet tall and over half as wide, with muscles like slabs of red granite and a body covered in gleaming plates of red-brown armor. His head was exposed, thick black horns sweeping back on either side of a mohawk of short white braids, and his lips pulled back in a wide snarl as he bellowed and shouted and threw himself across the stage, swinging wildly with a huge mace of black, spiked metal in either hand.

The other actor was Prince Vambrace, dressed just in his slacks and a shirt of dull silver mail, holding a plain sword that didn't gleam enough to be Excalibur, and smiling smugly as he skipped past every missed swing.

Wait, no. It wasn't the prince; it was an incredibly faithful copy, but even from up here, I could make out the delicate ivory horns curling back along his short-cropped black hair. A glamoured Luxuriate, then. But why leave the horns on? To hear Kriseia talk of it, unglamoured horns were a no-no.

As I watched, the faux-Vambrace ducked and twisted through the flurry of mace swings, dozens of certainly crushing blows just barely brushing past him again and again, until the massive Iriate screamed and brought both weapons down in an overhead smash. His opponent twisted out of the way at the last second, and they hit the stage with a crack as the wood beneath splintered. Before he could heft them again, the faux-Vambrace planted a booted foot across the heads of both maces and stepped up to the Iriate's level, then loosed a single laugh of triumph as he swung his ordinary sword and caught the red demon across the face with the flat of the blade. The Iriate released his weapons as he grunted and threw himself sideways, tumbling over and over again until he fell off the edge of the stage and the music came to an abrupt halt. Horned Vambrace turned and bowed to the audience, and a smattering of mild applause answered him.

"Choreography's a bit shit, isn't it?" I heard a woman's voice say quietly somewhere nearby. "Not very believable."

"Believable as it gets in theater," someone else answered. I followed the sound to a slender Luxuriate man seated in front of me to my left, beside a small Invidiate woman staring down at the stage with most of the pupils in her half-lidded, multifaceted eyes. "If the scene were two regular soldiers fighting, you could maybe get away with actual trained Iriates," the man continued, "but for a believable archfiend, you need glamour, and then you need another of us to play opposite to even things out. Putting a Luxuriate in a fight with the real thing, even a staged fight, is just a bloody accident waiting to happen."

"Maybe, but I'd still watch that," the Invidiate said with a sniff. "It'd probably be more entertaining than this, at any rate."

"Coming here was your idea, you remember," answered the Luxuriate. "And anyway, I think this is one of Duchess Sidona's best productions, don't you?"

"Because it's about the prince. Again." She scoffed. "*All* of her more decent work is about the prince."

"Artists have their muses," the man said. "Can you blame her for being fascinated by the guy?"

"Fascinated." The Invidiate woman scoffed again. "She's a sycophant, is what she is. If I were the prince, I'd —"

"Quiet," the purple man interrupted, nudging her with his elbow and sending her scowling. "This is the best scene."

I turned my attention back to the stage as well, where a slender, sinewy Iriate woman had stepped up opposite the prince, her jaw set as she gazed placidly at him, her hair hanging in a long white braid down the back of her red-brown armor, which seemed lighter than the last guy's. A glamoured Enkida, I realized, right down to the perpetual calm stare that contrasted so weirdly with the angry glaring of the rest of the guards and soldiers I'd seen. She had a spear at her side, loosely held in one hand, and stood with the same relaxed stance as the fake prince opposite her.

For a moment, they simply waited like that in the quiet theater, regarding one another across the stage. Then the music kicked in again — slower this time, the drums quieter, more of a backing thump than a driving pounding. The guitar or mandolin or whatever it was began a slow, fluid flutter, like a softer instrumental spot in an Yngwie Malmsteen track. The stage Vambrace hefted his sword in one hand, holding it out before him in challenge. The stage Enkida, though, simply started walking toward him in slow, even steps, her spear hanging at her side. The prince held his ground, and when she came to just beyond the range of his blade, she paused, and the music quieted, and they stood silently looking at one another again.

Then there was a violin sting, and Enkida poked forward half-heartedly with her spear. Metal rang on metal as Vambrace swatted the spade-shaped blade tip aside with his own sword and hopped back a step. Enkida didn't follow. Instead, there was another pause, and then she gently thrust again. Again, the sudden note from the violin; again, the prince parried; and again, there was a moment's pause afterward. The spear swung up from underneath, and the prince retreated again to avoid a lazy swipe to the crotch. Enkida smirked, taking a step back, and —

The music suddenly swept up into a rapid, frenzied tempo as the Iriate spun back on her heel, whipping her spear around her in a tight circle and stabbing forward. The prince blocked again with his blade. But the spade tip danced up and around it toward his face, narrowly missing as he ducked aside. It swept downward. The blow glanced off the sword's crossguard, then caught on Vambrace's metal gauntlets as he hurriedly crossed his arms in front of his chest. The spear tip hovered level with the hollow of his throat. With a quick step inward, Enkida shoved the blade forward along his guard. She only narrowly avoided impaling him through the neck as he swung both arms up and out, redirecting the stab, at the same time as he flung himself backwards with a grunt.

Enkida didn't let up. She rushed forward with her spear pulled back for another thrust. The prince skidded on his feet, trying to catch his balance and barely remaining upright. He righted himself just in time to swing at the thrust that never came — his opponent whipped her feinted stab out and down as fluidly as an artist with a paintbrush, sweeping toward his legs. He narrowly hopped up over the blade, saving his shins from being sliced, but the spear haft caught him under the thigh and swept his feet from under him. He landed with a dull thud on his lower back as his sword went skidding across the stage.

There was a collective gasp from most of the crowd at that, coinciding with a musically cacophonous crash from the unseen orchestra, then silence. Even the stage Enkida seemed surprised, pulling her follow-up stab and instead skipping back a step, spear twirling in her hand as she watched her prone prince with widened eyes.

The moment of surprise was immediately broken as the glamoured Vambrace rolled back, then sprung forward to his feet, landing on them in perfect sync with the returning upswell of the soundtrack. He made a lunge toward where his fallen blade lay, but so did Enkida. Her whipping spear cut him off as she swung for his stomach. He spun back away from the slash, then darted around to her other side in time to meet her return swing. His armored arms flew up in front of him, and the spear glanced off the gauntlets again. His hand shot out, grabbing the haft of the weapon just below the blade. Enkida yanked him toward her, then shoved the spear forward again, catching him in the side of the gut. His mail shirt saved him from a disemboweling, but the force of the blow staggered him just enough that he didn't react in time to her upsweep toward his face.

The music died out again except for a quiet, sad violin as both her spear tip and Vambrace's head whipped upward in unison, a light splash of red accompanying the blade. The stage Vambrace spun toward the audience, clutching at his cheek with one hand, and even from back here behind everyone else, I could see the blood leaking between his fingers.

The audience gasped again, louder this time, and I could dimly make out a few people rising from their seats in my peripheral vision. Stage Enkida's spear held its position as she stared toward her opponent in open surprise; the small gasp that escaped her lips in the theater's hush was the first sound I'd heard her make so far during her fight.

Then the horned Vambrace looked up, glaring out at the audience, and smirked. The orchestra came back to life with a triumphant riff as he turned and smacked the spear out of his way with one of his gauntlets. Enkida, presumably still in shock, did nothing as he drove his other fist into the side of her head, sending her staggering sideways as he again rushed for his sword. She recovered in time to make a wide, desperate swing at him — but he leapt over the sweeping spear and hit the stage rolling, gaining his feet just in front of his sword. As the Iriate bore in toward him, he snatched the blade up and spun around. Both of them swung in unison at one another. The prince's sword met her spear midway down the shaft and sliced through, the top half spinning off across the stage and taking the blade with it. He whipped the sword around again, this time catching her across the breastplate and cleaving it. She grunted and stumbled backward, and he followed with a full-force kick to the stomach, driving her to the stage and sending her sprawling. Before she could move, his blade was stabbing down toward her face.

As the audience gasped for a third time and the music cut out once more, Vambrace pulled his stab at the last moment, the tip of his sword hovering just in front of her nose. The two held that pose for several long moments, Enkida sprawled and clutching her breastplate with one hand, Vambrace poised overtop of her and slowly bleeding from the gash in his cheek. Then the sword pulled back, and in its place, the prince extended a gauntleted arm, offering her his hand slick with his own blood. The Iriate gazed at it a moment, then reached up with the hand that had been holding her sliced chest, also covered in blood. The two clasped hands wetly, the slick smack of blood on blood audible even up here in the quiet, and the prince hauled the Iriate to her feet, where she stood staring intently at him for a moment, still holding his hand, before releasing it and dropping to one knee in front of him, clapping her fist over her bleeding chest and bowing her head over it.

Vambrace smiled benevolently and laid his sword over her shoulder like a king knighting a knight. There was a brief, triumphant fanfare of horns out of nowhere, and then the stage lights went out, and most of the audience rose to their feet to applaud and cheer.

It was certainly another impressive display of violence, I had to give it that. The prince was fond of letting everyone see how proficient he was at kicking their asses. Given what I knew now, this play and that gladiatorial exhibition he'd drug me along to earlier made more sense, though he seemed to me to be laying the message on a bit strongly. Still, it seemed to be working for him so far, I guess.

When the cheering continued unabated and the lights didn't rise again, I assumed the show was over. I turned to Kriseia to ask, but she didn't hear me; she was also caught up in the excitement, fists raised to her chest as she cheered at the stage and hopped up and down in place. Bouncing and jiggling.

I turned away again, back toward the theater's entrance.

And found myself face-to-stomach with a giant standing directly behind me.

With a gasp, I backstepped and looked up the massive, silver-vested torso into the square-cut blue-green face of a Superbiate. Specifically, Archduke Abdeles.

He gazed down at me with level, golden eyes, then lifted a hand and crooked a finger. It took me a second to realize he was motioning me to follow him, and another few panicked seconds to decide if that was a good idea. But I was an honorary capital-L Lady now, and he was still an archduke, so it probably wouldn't look good to ignore him. I touched Kriseia's arm to get her attention, then motioned to the Superbiate with my head. She dropped into a quick bow, but she rose to watch as I followed him toward the theater door. So if something weird happened, well, at least one person would know where I'd gone.

He exited into the hallway just ahead of me, then stopped and turned as I closed the door behind us, blocking out most of the crowd's cheering. "My Lady Morgan," he said in that dry baritone of his. "Enjoy the performance?"

"Yeah, it was pretty good," I said, leaning back against the wall behind me, then immediately standing straight again when I remembered that was probably bad manners when talking to nobility. "Though I only really caught the end of it, the prince fighting Enkida and that other guy."

"And what did you think of it, may I ask?" he asked.

"It was… pretty good," I repeated, not sure what he was getting at but unconvinced he just wanted small talk. "Why did the Vambrace actor have horns, though? Can't Luxuriates' talents cover those up?"

"It's a bit inauthentic, yes," the Archduke replied. "But necessary for legal purposes. Nobody is allowed to flawlessly replicate the archfiend in glamour, whether or not they have the range to. Such a thing would make treason and usurpation entirely too easy, if one were to put one's mind to it. But dramas depicting him will of course always be in demand; therefore, glamours of the prince are allowed only so long as one can see through them at a glance."

"Ah. Makes sense, then," I said, nodding.

"But to be more specific, I was asking you what you thought of the fight scenes in particular," he continued.

"Oh. Uh. Real impressive, yeah," I said, feeling as though we were back in dangerous conversational territory. Vambrace wasn't here to flash me subtle cues on what not to say this time; best to keep it short and vague, then. "His highness is certainly very good with a sword. I think the actor did a good job showing that part."

"I agree," said the archduke, looking over my head and beyond me, as if he could still see the stage through the wall. "Remarkably true to life for theatrical standards of combat. Our Duchess Sidona has an eye for detail in her fighting choreography. I can attest that the performance came impressively close to life in showing his majesty's capabilities with his sword."

"Cool," I said, nodding. Not sure what else he wanted me to say here, really.

"He compares favorably to others of your kind, then?" Abdeles asked, looking down at me once more. "I admit to curiosity on that front, disrespectful though some may think it. Our prince is certainly a consummate warrior when pitted against Hell's best, but how does he rank amongst other humans, I wonder?"

Shit, which was the better path here: talking up Vambrace even more, or implying that our whole species was just as impressive? In the heat of the moment, I opted for wishy-washiness. "It's hard to say, really," I replied. "I admit, I don't have a lot to do with the warriors back on Earth. I spent more of my time with the scholars and tradespeople. But I've seen a few fights in my time, here and there, at the theaters or some combat arenas. I've seen skills like his before, no doubt, but he's definitely at the upper tier just of what I've seen of our kind."

"You say so?" said the Superbiate, stroking his chin. "I can't really say as I'm surprised, though. I suppose I should have expected no other answer."

"I suppose so," I said. *Now go away*, I added silently.

"I do find it interesting how his tactics switch when he is disarmed, though," he continued in spite of my mental command. "His offense and defense are both unerring with his blade in his hand, but without it, his movements turn a bit erratic. Did you notice?"

"Well, like I said, I'm no expert on fighting," I replied. "But if you want me to guess, perhaps it's to keep his opponent guessing."

"Perhaps," he said. "He does lean heavily on his vambraces for defense. Is that a common tactic, do you know, with your limited experience, my lady?"

"His who?" I asked. "Vambrace's vambraces?"

"Yes," the archduke said flatly, raising one arm and pointing at it with his other hand. "The long metal bracers on his forearms, like gauntlets without the gloves." His finger traced a line from his wrist to just before the bend of his elbow.

"Oh," I said, understanding dawning. "Those are called vambraces too? Huh."

"Peculiar Earth idea for an armor piece. They are named after himself, says our prince, thanks to his famous proficiency with them in his native place and time." He raised an eyebrow at me as he gazed down his nose. "You didn't know, Earthling?"

"I don't wear armor," I said flatly, wary again and tired of being it. "So… no, no I didn't. Like I keep saying —"

"You are no warrior," Abdeles finished for me with a nod. "Not like our archfiend. Of course, Lady Morgan. From what I've gathered, you yourself are more interested in books, yes?"

That sent the alarm bells ringing in my head. I immediately tamped them down, hoping my moment of panic wasn't noticeable. *Nobody else knows about the* Morganomicon *but you,* I reminded myself. *He's probably talking about the requests you made to the prince earlier. You were in more dangerous waters talking about Vambrace's fighting than you are about your own fake hobbies.*

"Yes, actually, I am," I said with a smile that I hoped masked whatever else I was just feeling. "Mainly, I've just been bored since I got here while my official position in the palace was still up in the air. Not a lot of the amenities I'm used to around here, so I wanted something to do."

"Of course," he said, returning my empty smile. "It only makes sense. You were specifically asking after books written in one of your Earth alphabets, did I hear correctly?"

"You did," I said, pouring the fake smile on harder. "It's a bit embarrassing to admit, but I can't read the Hell books I found, so I was looking for a more familiar language. But I'm more interested in how you heard about that at all, archduke."

"No great mystery, my lady," he said. "I simply asked. It's a singular event to receive another human in our midst, after all, so I was curious if there was anything she wanted or needed from us. It behooves us all to help make such an important guest more comfortable in her new surroundings, after all."

"I see," I said. "How kind of you, sir."

This guy had been snooping around about me? As early as right after my first appearance in court? And he'd gotten wind of something as inconspicuous as that request I'd made?

I wasn't sure how concerned that ought to make me, if at all. Crap, did I fuck up somewhere? Was I not being as sneaky as I thought up 'til now?

Whatever else he was about to say, the door opening behind me interrupted him, and Kriseia slipped out. "Is everything alright, Morgan?" she asked, then ducked into another quick bow when she saw the archduke was still here.

Abdeles lifted both an eyebrow and his chin as he turned his attention to her. "Just 'Morgan?'" he asked, tone dry. "Awful informal for a servant, isn't it, gift girl?"

Kriseia's head had been raising, but she tucked it back down at that. "Oh, I didn't..." she stammered. "I meant no disrespect for my mistress, my lord, of course, but..."

"I prefer it," I answered for her, lifting my own chin as I gazed coolly up at the nobleman. "She has my permission to be that familiar, sir, don't worry. That won't be a problem, will it? I'm still learning the customs here, after all."

The archduke's ensuing smile was downright creamy. "I see," he said. "No, then, there is no issue if you've allowed it. I was merely making sure that your due respect wasn't being impugned."

"It wasn't," I said, crossing my arms. "Don't worry about it."

"As you say, Morgan," he said, still smiling.

"Ah, no," I said, shaking my head. "I meant I gave *Kriseia* permission to call me simply by name. Sorry, maybe I didn't make myself clear."

His smile faltered just the tiniest bit, while beside me, I heard Kriseia's breath very quietly catch. Heck, even I was surprised by my sudden backbone in front of this archdemon. But while years of being a student and a part-timer had made me long since used to snide superiority and backhanded smuggery, I wasn't letting any of that fly against my royally assigned new friend, apparently.

Abdeles recovered admirably, though, his smile never dropping fully. "Apologies, then, my lady," he said. "I shall —"

He was interrupted again as a door further down the wall flung wide open and Duchess Sidona strode out. She caught sight of us immediately and checked her pace, but it was clear she'd been in a hurry only a moment ago. "Good," she said, sweeping toward the three of us, her short golden cape fluttering with the movement, her silver gown beneath trailing behind her by several feet. "You're still here. I thought I saw you in the audience, and I didn't relish the idea of hunting you down again." She drew up directly in front of me, then turned to Abdeles as if only just then noticing him. "Archduke?" she asked, raising her pencil-thin brows.

"Duchess," said the archduke, nodding to her before looking back to me. "I see your attention is much in demand, Lady Morgan, and I have taken up enough of it. Excuse me." He nodded to me, then pointedly didn't nod to Kriseia, before he turned and strode away down the corridor. Even with his own velvet blue cape trailing behind him, his exit was nowhere near as flamboyant as Sidona's entrance.

With him gone, the duchess turned her attention back to me. "Did I miss anything interesting just now?" she asked.

I took a deep breath before I answered. Dealing with Sidona could be taxing in its own way, but if she was gonna save me from more of Abdeles's scrutiny, I'd take it. "Nothing too much," I said. "The archduke was just playing twenty questions with me, for some reason. Apparently, he's been snooping on me, and he really wanted to know what I thought about your play."

"My dear, half the palace is snooping on you by this point," she said, lifting one pointed, manicured nail to her chin. "Just remember that I was doing so before it became popular. What *did* you think of my play?"

"Oh, I thought it was impressive," I answered again. "The choreography was—"

"Yes, never mind," the duchess interrupted, hand fluttering impatiently. "I'm getting distracted. It's an already finished work, it's not important. What matters is the work to come. You are free now with the archduke gone, I take it?"

"I… am, sure," I said. "Didn't really have any plans after this."

"Good, then I have plans for you," she said, then frowned as her eyes jumped quickly up and down me. "What is this you're wearing? This is boring. Where are your Earth clothes?"

I tugged at the waist of my demon gown, instinctually self-conscious. "Still in a pile in my bedroom, probably," I said. "They were getting disgusting."

"Have them washed, they're vital to my art. But no matter, I can make this work," the duchess said, waving a hand at my current outfit. "We'll just focus on your face this session. Now come along, if you please," she added, spinning on her heel and striding away, her outfit swishing around her. "We've more culture to create together."

"Sure, whatever," I said, falling in behind her.

"Um, Morgan?" Kriseia said. Sidona and I both paused, turning back. The Luxuriate stood with her hands clasped at her waist, smiling politely. "Shall I wait for you back in your quarters, then?"

"Yeah, if you want," I said with a shrug. "Or you can come with us, whatever you wanna do."

Disappointment I hadn't noticed before fled her face. "Can I?" she asked.

"Can she?" Sidona echoed, and I turned to see her frowning. "I wasn't really extending the invitation beyond yourself, my lady. I don't really need another Luxuriate right now."

"*I'm* inviting her," I said airily. What the hell, if I wasn't letting an archduke get away with it, might as well throw my weight at a duchess too, while I'm at it. "I enjoy her company, and there's enough room she won't be in the way. What's the harm?"

The duchess tapped her chin for a short moment. "I confess there isn't any," she said, then shrugged herself. "Very well, if you must. I've really no mind either way. Just do hurry," she added, turning and striding away again, "I'm a busy woman, and this floor will be swarming with bodies once the audience disperses."

I followed, while Kriseia hurried forward and fell into step beside me. I noticed her smiling in my peripheral vision, then noticed that I was, too.

Chapter 19: Ethnocentrism

The rich carpet of Sidona's apartments was mostly covered by a wrinkled cloth stained all over with multicolored swaths and splotches and tiny dribblings of paint. The huge canvas from before was still set up on its easel on one side of the room, the small staging area across from it sporting a platform flanked by wall sconces for better lighting. Even the other me was still here, perched on the edge of the platform with her elbows on her knees, tapping her heavy boots against the wood of the platform with a light clicking noise that belied the illusion and her spiked, bare feet beneath it.

As the three of us filed into the room, my doppelganger looked up at us with her ruby red eyes, sweeping each of us but lingering on me. I caught her gaze and smiled. She blinked, and when she opened her eyes again, they were the same dark brown as my own. She didn't return my smile, only kept gazing at me with something like nervousness.

It was still really freaking weird looking at her and seeing myself, but I managed not to ogle this time, at least.

"You remember the pose, yes?" Sidona asked as she crossed the room, unfastening her golden cape as she did so and letting it fall to the stained tarp behind her. "The rough estimate, anyway. Of course, I'll polish it from there. Yes, hello," she added as she turned at her easel and noticed the other me for the first time. "Why are you here?"

Other me frowned. "You called for me, didn't you?" she asked, not in my voice but her own deeper, huskier tone. "I've been waiting."

"Yes, well, never mind," said the duchess, bending over a corner cabinet behind the easel and sliding open the top drawer. "I found the real one on my way up, so I'll be using her again for now. You are dismissed, my dear."

Other me sniffed and rose from her seat, and by the time she was standing fully, she wasn't me anymore, but the same hot pink Luxuriate I'd walked in on last time. She turned to leave, then paused, casting a backward glance at the duchess.

Sidona, meanwhile, had pulled some small glass vial from her cabinet and unstoppered it, dipping a long nail into the mouth and scooping up a tiny pinch of what looked like azure blue powder. With the rest of us watching, she held her nail up to one delicate nostril and sniffed, inhaling it, which sent her head reeling back with her eyes fluttering.

What the hell was I watching now? She'd struck me as the yuppie bohemian type, sure, but was she really snorting demon cocaine?

"Hey, duchess," the hot pink Luxuriate said. It took a moment for Sidona's eyes to calm down and focus on the girl. When they did, the pink model nodded at the vial in the Superbiate's hand. "Mind if I get a hit of that?"

Sidona stared at her glassily a moment, then sniffed again, but in a disdainful way this time. "Why?" she asked. "Your type don't have to worry about solitusia. I'm not wasting it on you, dear, no."

The model frowned, then glanced back at me again. "If you say so," she muttered, unease passing over her face once more. It stayed there, and her gaze stayed on me, a moment longer before she abruptly brushed past Kriseia and me and strode through the salon door, her heels clacking on the onyx floors as she disappeared down the outside corridor.

I looked back at the duchess, who was snorting another pinch of the blue powder up her other nostril. "What was that about?" I asked.

Sidona's eyelids fluttered rapidly some more as she looked up at nothing for several long seconds. When her frenzied blinking stopped, she stared straight ahead as she slowly re-stoppered the vial, then shook her head and turned to replace it in the cabinet. "What was what about?" she asked.

"She didn't exactly look happy to see me," I said, nodding toward the door after the model. I hadn't gotten her name, I realized, but that just meant one less note for my flashcards, so I was okay with that. "And now you're here snorting blue coke. Did I miss something?"

"Blue who?" The duchess stared at me a second, then turned to stare at the cabinet a second, then turned and stared at me again. Slowly, I watched the daze lift from her face to be replaced with her usual smug amusement. "My medicine, you mean?" she asked, then turned and crossed to a thin wardrobe in the opposite corner. "Not to worry, my lady," she said as she opened the door and pulled out a billowy white smock. From the look of it, billowy white smocks were all that were in there. "Simply a precaution. It doesn't alter the senses, if that's what you're wondering. It won't affect the art."

I looked away as she shrugged out of her silver gown. "What's solitusia?" I asked.

All I heard was the rustling of her changing clothes for a moment. "Nothing for you to worry about, my lady," she said. "To your position, please."

I stepped up onto the small platform and turned toward the easel, but looked down at Kriseia leaning idly against the wall by the doorway. "Do you know what it is?" I asked her.

"Solitusia?" Kriseia repeated. "I've heard of it somewhere before. It's a mental condition that some Superbiates can develop. It makes them unable to notice other people around them or even acknowledge their existence. Right?" She frowned and looked to Sidona for confirmation.

The duchess, now in her painter's smock, frowned even deeper and disappeared behind the canvas. "Like you're the only being left in the world, so I'm told," she said dryly. "Still perfectly seeing and hearing and feeling your surroundings, but not the other people in them. According to your own mind, you're absolutely alone in an empty universe." She snorted. "Yes, something like that. But it's only a problem for House Superbia, and even then, only for the very young or the very old; and I am neither of those things, and so it won't affect *me*."

I frowned along with the rest of them. "Then why take medicine for —"

"Shut up," the duchess snapped, her face darting out from behind the easel to scowl at me. "My lady," she added. "Merely a precaution. It's never too soon to get a jump on potential symptoms. Lean on your other hip and tilt your head up a smidge."

I shut up and posed in silence like she demanded, feeling a little bad for pressing the issue and apparently touching a nerve. A few minutes later, I felt even guiltier when I realized where the other model's tension had come from and why Sidona was suddenly snorting medicinal cocaine for what sounded like demon Alzheimer's.

My unnoticeability spell. It had broken right here in this room when Sidona spotted me, but it had taken her a minute, and the Luxuriate woman hadn't seen me at all until I spoke up. Nobody here knew that I knew some rudimentary magic, which meant to those two, they probably just assumed that they were starting to lose their minds.

But I couldn't tell them they were wrong without also telling them I was a kinda-sorta witch, so I had to just let them both keep wondering if they were maybe going crazy. So that was kind of shitty of me.

With both Sidona's and my mood dampened for the moment, the painting session drug on slowly, mostly in silence but for her occasional directing. After what felt like an hour and some change of standing quietly in a quiet room, I was thoroughly bored. I risked the duchess's rebuke to turn and look at Kriseia and found her sitting against the wall, head and arms resting on her drawn up knees. I thought she was asleep at first until she glanced up at me and flashed a small smile, eyes half-lidded. She looked even more bored than I was, but of course she'd never say anything if she was.

I cleared my throat. "So, how's it going?" I asked the back of the canvas.

"Mm," was the only response I got from Sidona at first. A minute later, she leaned out from behind the painting and squinted at me. "I don't know how long it takes a human who's so inclined to finish a masterpiece," she said, her brush hand still moving against the canvas as she peered at whatever detail on me was concerning her for the moment. "But for me, at least, it's going to be a long while still before we're finished. Though it helps that I had your imperfect glamour to start with as a base. She got your proportions and physical structure correct, even if she couldn't find your personality."

"Can I see it?" I asked.

She ducked out of sight again. "Of course not," she said. "I can't have your opinion muddying my vision, and I don't want you purposefully or otherwise trying to mimic an incomplete work with your stance and expression."

"May *I* see it, ma'am?" Kriseia asked from her spot on the floor.

"No, not you either," said the duchess. "I don't need *your* opinion on anything, and I don't trust you not to then give it to your mistress and present me with the same problem."

"That's not fair," I said, frowning. "You don't even know her."

"Exactly," Sidona said. "And I don't need to. I already know far too many people who don't inspire me." A few seconds later, as if in afterthought, she added, "No offense, of course, dear, you're in good company."

I let a few more quiet minutes tick by for decorum's sake. "So," I said then, "any idea how much longer it's going to be? Just outta curiosity."

"Longer than you're willing or probably able to stand there for the remainder of this sitting, I'm sure," said the duchess. "I'll be needing to come borrow you again for a few more sessions like this one before I run out of use for you, lady."

"I figured," I said. "Any idea of an overall timeframe, though? Like how many total hours?"

She leaned out again and held up a thumb, gazing unblinking over it at my face for a few seconds before lowering it. "My dear, I don't know what those are," she said, then disappeared again.

I sighed. "Right, forgot," I said, half to myself. "No concept of hours or days or nights here. No changes in the sky, no mornings or sunsets. How does anyone possibly stay on any kind of schedule around here?"

"Do most humans need to know where a floating ball of fire is in the sky relative to themselves to keep their lives in order, Lady Morgan?" the duchess asked.

It didn't sound like sarcasm — at least no more than anything she said sounded like sarcasm — so I answered her. "Not exactly, but it moves in a regular pattern, and we can get measurements from that to know what time it is. And when it's the same time everywhere, it makes planning things easier."

"Hm." There was a small flurry of soft brush strokes, and the plop of a gob of paint landing somewhere in the room. "Perhaps I merely lack your race's prestigious faculties," Sidona said, not sounding like she meant it, "but I still fail to see how that makes anything easier or why its absence should make things more difficult."

I raised a hand to rub my eyes, careful to put it back in as close to the same position afterward as I could. "I mean, like, how do you know when it's dinner time?" I asked. "Or how do you know when it's time to go to sleep?"

The duchess leaned out again to show me a quizzically raised eyebrow. "How do you know… when to sleep?" she asked slowly. "Is that really a problem that humans have?"

"Really, yeah," I said. "Especially for students like me. I can wreck my whole day if I don't get to sleep at the right time the night before."

Even Kriseia was giving me the baffled look now, I noticed. "We sleep when we are tired," Sidona said slowly in her talking-to-a-moron voice. "And when we're hungry, we eat. We bathe when dirty, and we rut when aroused, and when the ideas strike, we make art. Whenever a desire or an urge comes, we act on it. That is the only schedule anyone here understands, I'm afraid. I would have thought it perfectly natural and obvious before you came along, dear lady."

"Well when you put it like that, yeah," I said. "But you can't always act on *every* desire right when it hits."

Sidona and Kriseia actually shared a look. "You can't?" Kriseia asked, and I could see the question was for both of them. "Why not?"

"Because… lots of reasons?" I replied. I'd lost my pose entirely by this point, but it was fine, because Sidona had stopped painting for the moment to stare at me like she'd discovered a new species. Which she kind of had, I suppose, if you looked at it a certain way. "I mean, like, what if you're a guard or a soldier, right, and you get sleepy while you're doing your job? You gotta ignore it, right? What happens if you try and take a nap in the middle of a fight?"

"You die, clearly," said the duchess, stepping around from her easel to face me directly. Her smock was splotched and streaked with fresh paint, most of it the same jet black as my hair. A dollop of the same color clung to the tip of the brush she was still holding in her crossed arms, leaking paint over her sleeves. "But one assumes that at that point, in the middle of danger, the desire to prevail and continue living would be more pressing than the desire to sleep, wouldn't it? Attend to them in order of preference and there's no issue."

I turned to Kriseia. "But then what about people who get themselves killed acting on dangerous desires, like humping in a tornado?"

"Dalariasa's expedition?" Sidona answered for her. "Obviously the participants wanted to try fornicating in the moaning winds of Passion's Rift more than they wanted to risk living without the experience. My lady, I'm sorry, but are these scenarios you're posing us really so hard as that to understand?"

"I… no, I guess not," I said, still wearing the same stymied frown as both of them. "When you put it like that. It's just the lack of restraint that seems weird. And crazy and dangerous. Maybe it's just a cultural thing."

"Maybe," Sidona said, then sighed. "Lady Morgan, you are clearly bored if you're delving philosophically into such basic ideas, and now you've lost your posturing entirely and completely derailed the portrait's progress."

"Yeah, maybe a bit," I said, half-heartedly trying to find the pose I'd been holding again. "Sorry. Maybe if we had some music or something."

"Humans also need orchestral backing to their daily routines to stay focused, do they?" the duchess asked with a sardonic smile.

"This human does," I answered. "Or it helps, anyway. And I hadn't heard any music at all here until your play, and now afterward, I'm realizing how much I miss it."

Sidona's lips pursed as she regarded me a moment. "Unexpectedly lavish of you, I admit," she said half to herself, then turned her head and pointed at Kriseia with her chin. "You there. Gift girl. Can you sing?"

Kriseia's head bowed slightly. "I'm not really trained, ma'am. I took a few of the classes, but—"

"So no," said the duchess. "Instruments?"

Kriseia shook her head. "None past the basic scales, no, and even those were early in my—"

The duchess cut her off with a sigh. "Well I've no troupe on hand to call upon, and no patience for them to gather if I did, so." She turned back to me, tapping her pointed chin with the handle tip of her brush. "Seems if you want music, my lady, you'll have to provide it yourself. You remember the arrangement we made in your quarters?" She smiled again, slyly this time. "Care to honor it?"

Yeah, I remembered the deal we made. "You want me to sing for you again?" I asked, suddenly uncomfortable.

"You're the one who wanted music, aren't you?" she answered. "But yes, I've decided that I do. I've lost the thread of this painting for now, and there wouldn't have been much more I could have done anyway with you dressed incorrectly. This has been a somewhat half-hearted sitting, but we can salvage it with another cultural exchange, don't you think?"

Shit, I had really been hoping to find the book and disappear before she called in that favor. I hate karaoke. "But you don't have any instruments or anything," I said. "And I'm even less trained in singing than she is, I'm sure," I added, nodding at Kriseia. "You've heard me try before. Wouldn't you rather —"

"Your skill is irrelevant," said Sidona, waving her brush dismissively and sending droplets of black paint raining. "I merely need the lyrics and the general idea of the melody; I can polish it up and give it to a more skilled performer later. And I do, in fact, have instruments." She dropped the whole brush then as she turned and strode back to her wardrobe of smocks, shucking her current splattered garment over her head as she did. I barely had time to turn away before she was pulling a clean white smock over her horned head, then striding back across the room toward the door. "Let's take a walk to my music room, shall we?"

As if I really had a choice in the matter. She had, after all, kept her end of that bargain; like it or not, if she was asking, I ought to keep mine. I followed Sidona's exit, with Kriseia close behind.

We were the only ones in the halls as she led us down them, past the odd statue or painting displayed along the way. Several of them were of Sidona's likeness. Most were not. All of them, though, had the same general style to them, each subject seeming larger than life in its frame or on its plinth. There were no scenes of tragedy or mundanity here, only heroic portraits and proud busts, every chin held high. All of it accompanied by the sparkling light of ornate chandeliers hanging from the ceiling that, anywhere else, would have been the focal points of the decor. Here, I realized, the fancy lighting was just there to better showcase the hallway art galleries, each piece subtly highlighted by its own mini spotlight.

As it turns out, it was all Sidona's art; the entirety of this tower floor belonged to the duchess. It seemed excessive at first until I realized how tightly the halls curved and remembered how high up the spire we'd traveled to reach them. This floor couldn't be that big, comparatively, and there had to be hundreds of them at least, all stacked on top of each other. And Sidona definitely maintained a big enough presence here in the palace from what I'd seen, so a small story all to herself somewhere up and out of the way made sense.

Hell, if anything, maybe I ought to be asking for a slice of a tower myself instead of the one room I had in Vambrace's suite. Then I'd have more room and privacy to practice dark and forbidden arts and plot my escape.

I wondered suddenly if the archduchess had gotten my message to Gilderos yet. How soon was too soon to ask after it? It was impossible to tell without any sort of clock. Probably best to let them get back to me, then, even if the waiting made me antsy.

We reached the music room while I was absorbed in these thoughts, Sidona flinging open a couple of wide doors with such a flourish that I expected us to walk in and find an audience. Instead, the space stretched out over twice the size of her small painting studio, the walls and floor all bare red-veined onyx with a single bright, simple light hanging from the center of the room. Scattered across the bare floor were a selection of instruments of every size and type, some of them exotic, some of them surprisingly familiar. In one corner sat what looked like a small piano next to what looked like a big, round, hollow rock half as tall as me with a wooden club sticking out of it. One wall sported a row of stringed things all hanging on a rack, all of them different shapes, from what was clearly a violin to some mostly guitar-ish things to something that looked like a giant fork folded over itself and strung. A line of what I guessed were weird dancing clogs made a circle around some sort of thick wooden pole full of holes and grooves, with what looked like two long-handled metal ladles hanging off of it. Next to that was a big harp with a stool beside it, strangely plain among such other esoteric oddities.

The duchess threaded her way through the crowd of instruments to sit at the stool beside the harp, then turned in her seat back to me. "You're the cultural envoy here," she said, "so if you've any inkling which of your songs would be best to start with, I'm open to suggestion. Any particular instrument here seem most appropriate for what you've in mind?"

"I don't know what most of these things are," I admitted, turning in a small circle and looking at each option in kind. "Can you play all of these things?"

"I'm passable with all of them, yes," Sidona said, and I didn't miss her chin lifting just a bit as she answered. "Through no small amount of effort on my part, I admit. Of course, I bring in actual musicians from House Luxuria when it comes time to perform my pieces, to enthuse them with the passion they deserve. I'm merely the composer. The ideas woman."

I crossed the room and took a seat beside the corner piano. Kriseia followed, perching on the edge of the hollowed out rock thing. "I'm honestly not sure how a lot of these would work with my musical repertoire," I said. "Most of the songs I know are heavy on electric and bass guitar, with drum backing and some keyboard."

Sidona frowned, a hand rising to her chin. "I have drums, though you may need to be more specific," she said. "I have a guitar, and I have a bass. Electric, though?"

"Yeah," I said, "like a guitar with lightning running through it."

Her eyes narrowed. "Be serious, please," she said after a moment.

"Yeah, I figured you wouldn't have those here," I said. "That's a bummer. And I *am* being serious."

"Surely you're not," Sidona continued. "Capturing a thunderstorm and playing it like an instrument? A fanciful jest against one who admits to unfamiliarity with your culture, surely."

"When you put it like that, yeah, it sounds badass," I admitted. "But no, I promise, I'm not joking. And don't call me Shirley," I added.

She frowned again. "Don't call you what?" she asked.

"Shirley? Because — see, *that* part was a... y'know what, never mind." I should've known not to bother. "The point is, yes, lightning-powered guitars are a real thing we have, and most of the music I know uses them. I guess you could do good enough acoustic versions of most of them; it's a case-by-case basis which songs would work well that way and which would lose a lot of their soul. Though I suppose almost all of them could work with any sort of orchestral translation, if it were done well." I frowned. "But, I mean, I'm no composer or anything, so I dunno how well anyone could make a useful music set out of what I can give you."

"Leave that to the artist, dear," the duchess said, leaning toward me in her seat. I'd noticed her skepticism changing slowly into legitimate interest as I spoke, so I supposed I'd sounded enough like I knew what I was talking about to convince her I wasn't lying after all. "You give me the kernel of the piece; I'll find a way to make it my own. Probably improve on it, from the sound of things; I can't imagine a thunderstorm can be made truly melodious, controlled or not." She tapped her chin some more in silence. "What must it sound like, though?" she asked, half to herself. "Strings infused with lightning?"

"It sounds… well, it's kinda hard to explain if you've never heard it," I said, leaning back in my chair and staring up in thought at the vaulted ceiling. "It sounds like you'd expect lightning to sound if you stretched it tight and strummed it, I guess. The electric signal goes from the strings to the pickups and into the speaker, and it distorts the twang and the tone and amplifies it, making it louder and more powerful and… kinda sizzly and crackly. A bit fuzzy, I guess. Depending on the kind of instrument and who's playing it, though, you can distort it to sound like almost anything."

"Fascinating," Sidona said, and for a change, she sounded like she actually meant it. "It's sometimes easy, looking at you, to forget the stories you hear about human exceptionalism. I suppose I should remember to stop discounting such tales."

"Yeah," I said, frowning at the ceiling. "Yeah, suppose you should." *Bitch*, I added in my mind. But I was getting used to her casual displays of assholery, and I doubted she even realized she was doing it, so it didn't make me too bitter.

"There was something else you mentioned," the duchess continued. "A… keyboard, was it? I take it this is some sort of piano, yes?"

"Yeah," I said, sitting up again. "Like a little electric piano."

She blinked at me slowly, and I could almost see the cogs spinning as she tried to decide if I was making stuff up this time. "There is a good deal of lightning involved in your Earth music, to hear you describe it," she said slowly.

I shrugged. "Not in all Earth music," I said. "There's a lot of different types and styles and genres of Earth music. But the music I like best, yeah, it's pretty electric."

"This sounds suspiciously like magic," she said. "Capturing and transmogrifying lightning so. Are these Earth musicians who play these electrified instruments some sort of mages, then?"

Electricity had been my weakest science unit in high school. We'd gone over it right after I'd gotten my first MP3 player and right after I'd discovered Meat Loaf, so I'd spent those couple of weeks surreptitiously listening to all three Bats Out of Hell albums instead of paying attention in class. Second hour science was the only class I'd had where I sat far enough in the back of the room to get away with something like that. I'd gotten a D- on the unit wrap-up test and never covered it again in college, so I barely knew the basics of how electricity worked, much less how it powered things like guitars and keyboards and amps. I absolutely wasn't able to explain it in detail to Sidona, and I wasn't sure she'd comprehend it even if I could.

But I was pretty sure I needed to take and keep charge of this narrative if I was going to keep the duchess on my side and amenable to any more favors I may need in the future. This expertise on musical culture that I'd claimed was the only card I had to play with her, and I doubted she'd accept "I don't know" as an answer to any of her questions on this subject — especially given how we humans were supposed to be all-knowing and all-competent beings, as the prince had painted us. And what was that they said about technology you didn't understand looking like magic?

"Yeah, some sort," I answered hesitantly. "Magic isn't illegal on Earth like it is here, so it's not such a big deal. Some humans use it to harness lightning for a variety of purposes, and some make music with electrified instruments. Why not? Not me, though," I added, just in case. "I don't really know anything like that. I just know about the songs."

"Interesting…" the duchess said slowly, drawing out each syllable while she stroked her chin and stared at me. "So then, you are not a mage yourself, Lady Morgan?"

"Nope," I said, hands clasped in my lap so they couldn't fidget. "I'm not."

"And yet you say magic is both freely allowed and commonplace in your world," she continued. "Why, then, would anyone not take up its study?"

Shit. I thought we were supposed to be talking about music. "Well, it's not exactly *freely* allowed," I ad libbed. "There are regulations and stuff, y'know. It'd be crazy otherwise. And I haven't studied it because I… don't want to."

Both her eyebrows raised at that, but her eyelids narrowed. "You don't want the power to command reality when it is available to you?"

"… No?" I said. "No, not really. I get by without it. I mean…" My hands had started to fidget after all, I then realized, but hopefully it would look like I was searching for a good argument instead of grasping at straws. "I mean, soldiers and stuff learn how to fight, right? You could probably go down to that arena they got and learn to fight too if you wanted, right? But you don't."

"No, I don't," Sidona said, lips curling in distaste. "That idea is preposterous. My time and talents are put to far better use elsewhere."

"Well, there ya go," I said. "I've got better things to do than try and learn magic."

"Such as?" she asked.

"Such as finish college and earn my bachelor's, for starters," I said. "I'm overdue to commit to a major. And I got a job, and I gotta pay rent. And I've also got this duchess who keeps asking me to sing for her, so there's that whole project."

Sidona smiled wryly. "A project which, if I recall, you were none too anxious to work on only a short time ago," she said. "Yet now it seems you would find that preferable to discussing the magical practices of Earth. I find that curious."

"Well, don't," I said. "Magic's not easy to learn or use, and it's not as incredible back home as it seems here. But apparently it's illegal here, and I don't know if just talking about it like this is also against the rules, but I don't wanna get in trouble. Honestly, it's just a topic that I find boring and uninteresting."

"And I find *that* most curious of all," the duchess said with a smile. "But if you insist, I'll drop it. Where were we? Ah, yes." She rose from her seat and threaded her way through the instruments to the wall of stringed things, grabbing what looked like a long oval guitar made of dark gray wood. "I've nothing electrified, obviously," she said as she made her way back to me and sat down again. "But I believe I can make do. Now, care to serenade us, milady?"

Chapter 20: Finicality

From what I'd seen so far, life in Hell wasn't entirely different from life on Earth. Once you got past the obvious physical variations, the people here were like people anywhere else, mostly, except that their personalities all tended to skew heavily in specific directions. But far as I could tell, everyone had their own jobs and goals and schedules (minus any real precision since time was more abstract), and they mostly dealt with the same emotions and experiences as any human.

Still, as many similarities as there were between my world and theirs, demon society was still very clearly alien enough to stand out. No electric technology, for starters, as I'd ascertained with both Kriseia and Duchess Sidona. A social hierarchy fairly close to one that we'd thrown out back on Earth a couple hundred or so years ago. Everyone lived almost in a caste system, it seemed, so social interactions were all a bit different. Even a few basic experiences on Earth, like night and day cycles, weren't applicable here. The broad strokes of life might match up between demons and humans, but the details were where things clashed.

I didn't realize just how much they clashed until I tried singing for Duchess Sidona.

With no real direction in mind from either of us as to which songs I should share, the duchess asked me to simply sing some of my favorites for her. I eventually muddled my way through a sort of Morgan's Greatest Hits collection of half a dozen tunes, but selecting them was harder than I'd anticipated — so many of the lyrics in my personal playlist assumed the listener understood the intricacies of high school, or had an idea what it was like living in a modern American city, or knew what a radio or a motorcycle or space aliens were. A good number of them referred to Hell in terms that I now knew were inaccurate, so those would definitely have raised some more confusing and potentially dangerous conversations.

Because of stuff like that, I ended up shying away from a lot of classic narrative rock and focused more on those with vaguer subjects. There were plenty of love/lust choices to choose from in that regard; Sidona wasn't the biggest fan of those herself, but Kriseia's attention perked up noticeably when we started working one of those, and the duchess conceded that was useful for Luxuriate audiences. Sidona, it turns out, was more of a Bon Jovi fan herself, which didn't surprise me. I sang a bit of Dio that I figured any Iriate listeners would appreciate. And we both agreed that "The Unforgiven" would be a huge hit with the Invidiates in her hypothetical audience.

Throughout our jam session, the duchess listened intently, took a few notes, and sometimes spitballed a series of musical chords she thought would best match my lyrics, strumming or plucking experimentally on her long, gray guitar or crossing the room to tap at her piano or bang on her big stone drum, all while I offered what creative direction I could with my untrained voice and off-key lala's and nana's. Whatever instrumentation she was devising from all of this, it was happening mostly inside her head. I doubted how effective a creative method this kind of approach really was, but she assured me that the wheels of her genius were in motion, and an orchestra was coming together in her mind.

So much of this music lived and died on the actual *music*, though, with the vocals there more as a backbone or another instrument. It was hard to impress upon her how much this applied to a lot of these songs. Still, even if she did seem somewhat skeptical at times of the musical prowess of Earthlings, expressed entirely through my warbling the words out of context, the novelty of music from another dimension was strong enough to keep her requesting more.

The only reason I didn't lose track of how long we were there was because I never had a way to keep track in the first place. Still, it felt like hours, singing and re-singing AC/DC and Metallica, pausing and enunciating while Sidona experimented with her arsenal of instruments, and explaining the occasional unavoidable Earth term that cropped up in the lyrics. We only stopped when my growing hunger and drying throat converged to make my growling stomach louder than my hoarse singing. When it became apparent my amateur hour performance was only going to get more amateurish unless I had a break, the duchess thankfully shooed both me and Kriseia from her music room, impatient to be alone with her tools and her ideas to hammer out the musical accompaniment in earnest.

The dismissal suited me just fine by that point. I'd been carb-loading out of fear for my last few meals, and being grown in Hell didn't seem to change how grains worked on human digestion, so now I was both starving again and ready for a nap. Maybe this time I'd work up the nerve to add some of the native fruits and vegetables to my diet. Maybe I'd eventually work my way up to the dairy, depending on where this kelpie milk I kept hearing about came from.

I'd probably never be brave enough for Hell meat, though. But that was an easy enough truth to come to terms with when all the meat I'd heard of so far came from man/horse hybrids or things with human faces. What I'd give for some spicy demon chicken strips or something.

On our way back to our room, Kriseia and I swung by the same small cafeteria we'd visited earlier. We got more rolls and jam, and then, with a bit of direction from Kriseia and the Gulliate behind the counter, I added a few of the least suspect-seeming plants to my order: some round, orange things the Gulliate called *mearcalum* but said were known colloquially as marsh apples, which were plump and weirdly squishy; a handful of *dhari*, or thornfruit, which looked more like thick, meaty, brown thorns than actual fruit; a bowl of dark red caina berries, since I'd already eaten them in jelly form without dying; and a couple of pomegranates, because somehow Hell also just had regular, perfectly normal pomegranates along with all the other evil foods. And some jeza bell tea to share between the two of us, which came cloudy and warm in a big glass jar and looked a lot like any other tea, except that it was pink. All of this got packed up in a big cloth sack which we carried back to our shared room.

We hadn't paid for any of it, this time or the last time. Was all the food in the palace complementary if you lived here? Did Pandemonium have some sort of meal plan I'd been unknowingly signed up for? Or was this something to do with my reluctantly growing celebrity? I wasn't sure. I didn't have any money anyway, though, so I guess it didn't matter.

Enkida was outside my door again when we got back, leaning against the wall with her eyes closed. I might have thought she'd drifted off, but no sooner did we step into view than her eyelids snapped open, her gaze pinning us. I stumbled a moment under the force of that stare until she smiled and shut her eyes again. "Didn't mean to startle you, my lady," she said as we reached the door.

"It's fine," I said, pausing with my hand on the knob. "You're just… intense, is all."

"We saw your fight earlier, General," Kriseia said brightly. "Or rather, we saw the stage performance. Of your legendary bout with Prince Vambrace."

"That Superbiate woman's dramaticized version of it, anyway," said the Iriate. "I've seen it too. The real thing was a bit more brutish and bloody, I assure you."

"No doubt," said Kriseia, as casually as if they were talking about the weather.

I held up our big bag of food. "Hungry?" I asked the general. "We just got back from one of the cafeterias."

"I know," Enkida said, eyes still closed. "Thank you for the offer, Lady Morgan, but I ate while you were away."

"Wait, you knew where we were?" I asked. "And you knew when we were coming back?"

"Of course," she answered, and her eyes cracked just enough to gaze at me as she smirked ever so slightly. "I have been assigned to look after you for the time being, after all."

"Yeah, but… how, though?" I asked. "*We* didn't even know where we were going or when we'd be back. How did you?"

She made a quick sniffing noise that I think may have been a laugh, if I could believe it. "I control the palace guard, the city guard, and the army," she said. "There is nothing that happens in this palace that is beyond my knowledge, if I decide to know it. Please remember that, my lady."

I sighed. "Alright, be mysterious," I said. "But yeah, I'll remember. Thanks." That was going to make it harder if not impossible to use my unnoticeability spell again, I thought as we passed by her and into our room. Hopefully that would be a moot point now that I had free run of the palace. If I needed to head back into town again, though, and couldn't get permission or an escort or something, well… I'd worry about testing that bridge if or when it came time to cross it.

Back in the room, we spread our to-go orders out on the desk and picked through them. The bread was still fine, but I was getting tired of it, so I left it for a last resort along with the pomegranates and instead gave the weird hell fruits my best college try.

The caina berry jam was also still fine, and the berries themselves even moreso, like kind of earthy cherries that were all slightly colder than they ought to have been at room temperature. Kriseia, who split the bowl with me, told me that they were grown underground in frigid subterranean gardens kept by House Gullia beneath their district out in the city or in the basement levels of their tower here in the palace. That didn't quite explain why the berries themselves were still cold by this point, I thought; but I was trying to worry less about the food here, so I didn't think about it too hard.

After we'd eaten all of those, I flipped a mental coin and decided to give the thornfruits a try, careful not to stab myself with the points as I bit into one inch-wide triangular spike. It was a pretty short experiment; the thing had the consistency of thick coconut meat beneath a coarse skin that was like biting through construction paper, and once it was in my mouth, it was dry and bitter, like pure ginger but without even a hint of sweetness. I forced myself to finish the one thornfruit I'd started, then set the rest aside with a grimace. Kriseia wasn't a fan of them either, she said, so they remained untouched.

Next came the marsh apples, which I'd had higher hopes for until I took my first bite. They were already weirdly soft and squishy on the outside; inside, the fruit itself was dirt brown and sat like mud in my mouth. My revulsion showed immediately, but Kriseia assured me that no, they weren't incredibly rotten, they were supposed to be like that. If I could ignore the texture, though, difficult as it was, the taste was surprisingly rich and sweet and slightly nutty, almost like honey. It also went down weirdly warm, but after the naturally cold caina berries, I didn't think anything of it.

It wasn't until I'd eaten three of the things and the room started to sway around me slightly that I realized marsh apples were alcoholic. Which maybe helped explain why they seemed to ripen directly into spoiling, if they were also fermented. It wasn't an unpleasant way to get drunk, I had to admit; but I didn't want to be drunk right now, so I set these aside as well and finished with the pomegranates, which were thankfully mundane in every way I could discern.

All of this I had been washing down with plenty of the jeza bell tea we had, which was lightly sweet and vaguely floral, like drinking roses. "This stuff, now," I said, holding my glass out to Kriseia. "I think this is my favorite Hell food so far. The caina berry stuff's good, but this delicious." I was a bit more forthcoming with the chatter by this point, I realized, now that I was slightly tipsy.

Kriseia smiled as she poured me a refill. "Honestly, I'm a little surprised at that," she said, with a pause at the end where I thought I could hear her wanting to add a "mistress" before stopping herself and continuing. "You seemed hesitant to try my creme earlier, though perhaps that had more to do with the confusion about the soul sprinkles. And you've said several times by now how you are sexually uninterested in… well, in general."

I paused with the glass halfway to my lips. "Wait, what's sex stuff got to do with flower tea?" I asked, eyeing my glass with new wariness and dreading what her answer might be.

"Oh, it's just that jeza bells are considered to be mildly aphrodisiacal," she explained as she poured herself another glass as well. "They're very popular in House Luxuria, in the brothel gardens and dancing halls and the like. There is some doubt about whether there is anything in the flower's properties that actually induces arousal or if it's all just the long-running mental association with the taste and image, but that is what they're popularly used for, anyway, to add a sensuous element to decoration or cuisine."

"Ah," I said. "Gotcha. That's… that's alright, then, I guess. I was worried you were gonna tell me there were, I dunno, sex fluids in the tea or something." I took another drink, albeit a more modest one, before setting my glass aside with everything else. Tasty as it was, I didn't need to be horny any more than I needed to be drunk right now.

"Oh, no, don't worry," said Kriseia, then paused to lick pomegranate juice from her fingers. "Not in this tea," she continued. "You usually have to ask for that sort of thing, and then it's usually mixed with milk and the like to make it creamier and blend the flavors better."

"Oh. Okay," I said, still too buzzed and, by this point, growing too jaded to be as aghast as I should have been. "So you do have that here. That wasn't just me jumping to conclusions. That's a real thing you do."

"Of course," she said brightly. "Though it's a niche market, as you might guess, and the chefs who would be preparing the drink would likely insist on only fresh ingredients of high quality and with specific properties. There are probably only a handful of Luxuriates in the city producing the fluids for those sorts of beverages, and even then, that wouldn't be their primary work."

"Well, so long as there are industry standards," I said, then took another drink of my tea anyway, because aphrodisiac or no, it seemed pretty tame again by this point in the conversation. "Honestly, I think I would have been more surprised if that idea had seemed as weird to you as it did to me."

After dinner, or breakfast, or whatever meal this was, we got Enkida to summon one of the Invidiate servants, who showed up surprisingly quickly to collect our bowls and glasses and the handfuls of foods that neither of us ate. I also gave him my dirty Earth clothes to be taken to wherever the laundry was done around here. The servant scowled at the extra request, but he'd been scowling when he walked in as well, and he said nothing else as he bundled up the clothes with the dishes. I was a bit reluctant to part with them, and I hoped that I'd actually see them again; they were more comfortable than the opulent gown I was wearing now, and I needed them to finish modeling for Sidona's portrait, *and* they were the last touchstone of familiarity that I had in this place other than the jacket I'd lost to the prince.

Once the dishes and washing were sent away and we were alone again, Kriseia and I went together into the bathroom to wash the various fruit juices from our hands, and so she could teach me what all of the different multicolored jars and vials of liquids and creams on the shelves actually were. A lot of them were thankfully familiar: lotions, skin creams, cosmetics, things I could identify even if I hadn't used them much myself. Other concoctions, like horn lacquer or scale polish or fur oil, I had less use for, but it was nice to at least have them identified. I grabbed a bottle each of soap, shampoo, and what passed for tooth paste and set them apart from the rest of the jumble, just so I didn't accidentally end up brushing my teeth with Acediate antler grout or whatever.

It was when we walked back into the bedroom, clean and full and with nothing else to do, that I realized how tired I was. I had no idea how long it had been since my bathtub nap, which was the closest I'd gotten to a full sleep in… all day? Days? How long had I been here by now? My grasp of time was already shot to hell. But it didn't matter; there was no night here, and I was sleepy now, so by demon standards, that meant it was bedtime.

That's also when a couple of problems that I hadn't considered before suddenly became much more immediate.

First, there was only the one bed in here. Which meant unless we took turns, the only place for Kriseia and I to sleep was right next to each other. That wouldn't be so bad, except that, second, I had sent my only clothes — or, at least, my only clothes that would work acceptably as pajamas — away to be washed. This meant that all I had to sleep in was the ornate gown I was wearing, and while it was passably comfortable to walk around in, it didn't make for a good sleeping outfit with its long train and stiff collar and tight midsection.

But my only remaining option was sleeping naked. In the same bed as a half-naked-at-best succubus. Who kept politely trying to get into my figurative pants.

"Is something wrong, Morgan?" that same half-naked sex demon asked beside me, stifling a yawn. "You look pensive all of a sudden."

Right. So. How to go about this without being rude, but also without spooning nude with another woman?

"Yeah, no," I said. "I'm fine, just… trying to figure out sleeping arrangements."

She gave the bed a confused look, then turned it on me. "Arrangements?"

"Cuz we've only got the one bed, and I've got no clothes to sleep in," I said. Might as well be honest; I'd been open with most other things already with her. "And I like you, but I don't really wanna sleep naked with you."

"Oh," she said. "Why not, may I ask?"

I sighed. This was difficult enough, and she wasn't making it any easier. "Because I'm not really into the sex stuff like you are, like I said."

"Yes, I know you said," she said, and her confusion melted into a frown. "Have I not been respecting your wishes on that front since you told me?"

"No, you have," I said, "it's just..."

"You do not trust me to continue?" Her frown turned hurt, and she looked away from me as she spoke. "You worry that I may go back on my word as soon as the chance arises."

"No, I..." My hands fluttered in front of me until I made them stop. "I mean... kind of, yeah," I said more quietly. "A little, I guess. It's not *you*, though, it's not that I don't trust you specifically, but... I'm new to demons, and with Luxuriates, it seems like..."

"It is our nature," Kriseia said sadly. "No, I understand. I forget at times how barbaric we must seem to the Original Sin. And I have not yet been in your service long enough to have earned your full trust just yet. Forgive me, I did not realize I had been causing you worry."

"What? No! You're not..." Shit, were we fighting? I hadn't had a roommate fight since freshman year of college, and that one was waged mostly with passive aggressive sticky notes. But no, I didn't think this counted as a fight. I think I'd just accidentally stomped on her feelings, is all. I sighed. "I never said you were barbaric, it was just... an uncomfortable thought, I guess."

She looked at me again, finally, then nodded. "My apologies," she said. "I shouldn't have assumed. If it pleases you, I can sleep on the floor instead, so that way—"

"No, it doesn't please me," I interrupted. "Get in the bed, Kriseia."

Her confused look came back. "I'm sorry?"

"No, don't be," I said. "Just get in the bed." I pointed for emphasis. "You're tired, I'm tired, we'll figure it out."

"Are you sure?" she asked. "If you would not be comfortable, though—"

"I'd be less comfortable with you on the floor," I said, then turned and strode toward the bed myself. "And I'm not arguing anymore, because I'm too exhausted." I reached behind myself for the lacing that held me into my gown, but I could barely reach it, much less untie it. "Can you help me out of this dress, though, please?" I asked.

"Of course, mist— Morgan," said Kriseia, stepping up behind me as she did so.

"Thanks," I said as she began working at the laces on my back. "And… I'm sorry if I hurt your feelings just now. I'm still learning how to behave in this place."

"Don't be," she said with a quiet chuckle. "I am too."

Once my dress was sufficiently loosened, Kriseia helpfully turned away while I shrugged out of it and climbed into bed. The pile of blankets and sheets was half a dozen layers deep, with the thick comforter on top and each layer beneath it growing thinner and more satin-y. I commandeered one from the middle and wrapped it entirely around myself in lieu of pajamas, then laid back on one far edge of the mattress. "Thanks," I said once I was situated. "Would you mind getting the lights?"

"Of course," said Kriseia. If she tried to suppress the chuckle that came when she turned to find me burrito wrapped and curled on my side, she failed. I couldn't blame her, though. I was being ridiculous from her point of view, and starting to feel that way from my own as well by now. Nevertheless, she said nothing more about it as she made a quick circuit of the room, fiddling with some mechanism on the wall sconces and snuffing each light in turn.

When they were all out, the room was left pitch black, with not even a crack in the door to let the hall light in. Enkida was as silent as ever at her post out there, so the only sound was the soft clack of Kriseia's heels as she walked across the marbled floor — and then the quiet ruffle of blankets as she climbed into bed beside me, the mattress sinking with her weight and rolling me slightly back toward her.

I really *was* exhausted, like I'd said. But I was also still slightly tipsy from the marsh apples, and possibly mildly aphrodisiacked from the tea, unless that was just placebo effect and anxiety working on that front, which admittedly was pretty likely. Nonetheless, whatever the chemical state of my brain right now, I was hyper aware of the body laying only a foot or so away from my own, with only a sheet separating us. I didn't know if she was still in her clothes or if she had slipped out of them in the dark without me knowing, but it hardly mattered with her outfit.

For all the sexual hang-ups I'd been having recently, and as justified as they may have been in a world with lust demons and public orgies and sex juice beverages, I was no pure, prude innocent on the matter. As socially averse as I tended to be, I'd been a teenager in public school once upon a time. I'd even had a boyfriend-of-sorts before in the first half of high school; or at least, I'd had a guy friend I'd had a crush on, one who'd come over to visit a few times. Granted, the furthest we'd ever gotten was some heavy petting, mostly above the clothes but a little below, and some awkward making out in the family den before my parents came home; a couple of fumbling hormonal encounters we both pretended hadn't happened as soon as we weren't alone anymore. We never made it past second base or to either of our bedrooms. Hell, we never even really made it to officially dating — a week or so after the second such encounter, he found a girlfriend in someone else. I had been taking things too vague and slow for him, I'd reasoned later. And for better or worse, that had been my entire sexual history.

And now here I was naked and in bed with a woman who was both a real-life succubus and, from the sounds of it, a literal whore. Or who had at least had whore training. Suddenly I was an awkward and confused teenager again, wading inexperienced through new hormonal waters.

It didn't help that, partially thanks to all these thoughts keeping me up, Kriseia fell asleep first. I don't know how long I laid in my blanket cocoon, staring up through the darkness toward the ceiling, while I listened to her deep breathing beside me and subconsciously tensed every time she shifted position, waiting for her to roll over and try to cuddle in her sleep. I tried my damnedest to think of this as just a sleepover with a friend; but if I'd ever actually had one of those as a kid, I didn't remember it, so it wasn't much help.

Eventually, though, sleep won out. And I'll say this in Hell's favor: one nice thing I would never have expected before coming here was the lack of any alarm clocks. When I finally conked out, I slept like a log; and when I did wake up again, it was a comfortably slow process with much rolling over and dozing off again. Right up until I finally opened my eyes enough to notice that my blanket shell had come unwrapped at some point and I was lying naked and coverless in the middle of the bed, with my face buried in the pillows and my ass in the air.

That woke me the rest of the way up in a hurry. I snatched one of the many pillows in one hand and the nearest blanket in the other and scrambled to a sitting position, yanking them both up over me as I looked out across the room. Kriseia was already up, though; I could hear her splashing in the tub through the closed door to the bathroom. How long she'd been awake, and whether she'd seen anything in that time, I didn't know, but she wasn't here now, so I was safe. With a sigh, I dropped the pillow and blanket and turned to swing my legs off the bed.

In the process, I almost kicked Prince Vambrace, who was lounging in a chair in the corner of the room by the door. Our eyes met, and he smiled. "Hello again, m'lady," he said. "Sleep well?"

My scream was echoed by a loud splash from the bathroom, and Kriseia came hurrying out, naked and dripping water from the horns down, as I fell back into bed and yanked the blanket up over me again. Vambrace merely looked surprised and didn't even rise from his seat.

"What is the matter, Morgan?" Kriseia asked as she slid to a halt, her heels scraping the rug across the floor. "I heard — oh." She stopped as she caught sight of the prince, then ducked her head. "Greetings, your majesty."

"Yes, hello," said Vambrace, waving her off and turning back to me. "My lady, are you well? I didn't mean to startle you."

"What the fuck are you doing here, you creep?!" I demanded. The only reason it wasn't a shout was because my voice had pitched too high from first fear, then embarrassment, and now anger. "Were you watching me *sleep?* The hell is wrong with you?"

Kriseia gasped, both of her hands flying up over her mouth. That was my first clue that I might have screwed up. She of course didn't seem bothered at all that the prince was seeing her naked and soaking wet; it was my reaction, the tone I'd just taken with the archfiend, that horrified her. At that moment, though, I really couldn't care.

Vambrace did, though. For a moment, at least. He stiffened in his seat, his eyes darting first to Kriseia's horrified face, then back to my livid one.

"In point of fact, I was not," he began in his lowest, most imperious voice as he rose slowly from his seat. "I am here to call upon my royal consort, and rather than wake her, I had taken it upon myself to let her awaken naturally. However, if this is the welcome I get, then I don't—"

He stopped as his eyes fell down from my face over the hidden lump of my body behind the blanket. I pulled it tighter around me and scowled harder.

"Oh," he added more quietly. His eyes widened. "Oh!" he said again, louder. And to all of our surprises, perhaps even his, his cheeks reddened slightly. "Oh, I had forgotten… I didn't realize…" He stopped, closed his eyes and cleared his throat. When he turned back to Kriseia, his composure was back. "If you wouldn't mind," he said to her in his calm, authoritative public tone, "I would like a few moments alone with your mistress. Please remove yourself to the hallway for the time being."

Kriseia's horror melted to confusion as she looked between the two of us. A moment later, she bowed quickly again and scurried toward and then out of the door, still glistening with bathwater. I heard her clicking as she walked a short ways down the corridor.

The prince watched her leave and, once we were alone again, took a slow, deep breath. Then he fell to one knee beside the bed, his head bent, staring down at the ground. "Please forgive me, lady," he said quietly, sounding as if he had to choke out the words. "It had not occurred to me that… well, my knightly honor is rather rusted here, as I've said. At no point until you awoke did I realize and remember how untoward it must seem to you for me to accost a maiden while she lay disrobed in her own bed. My apologies."

"You didn't—" I stopped, my mouth gawping like a fish for a few moments. "How?" I demanded finally. "How do you forget something like that?"

"You are literally the only person in this world who cares about such a thing, my lady," he answered, head still bowed.

I sighed. I was still angry, but it was wearing off. "Yeah, I guess I can buy that," I said. "But how did *you* forget? And so soon? We've been over this already. We *just* did this yesterday. Or whenever. However long ago it was now. It wasn't that long."

He raised his head a bit then, but not his eyes. "You remind me of my old ways, lady, but I am still set in my newer ones," he said. "It will take a concerted effort on my part, I think, to recall them whenever I am around you and it is safe enough to do so. As we spend more time together, alone but for one another's company, I believe the specter of my gentlemanliness shall return and become more familiar once again. That is, in fact, why I have come here seeking you."

"What, to help teach you knight stuff again?" I asked.

"To enjoy your companionship in private," he said, looking up at me again with a slight smile. I tightened the cover around myself, and he dropped his gaze again in a hurry. "I have heard that you are interested in items and artifacts that find their way here from Earth. If you like, I would show you my personal collection."

My eyes narrowed. "I asked Archduchess Cinaedemis about hooking me up with someone who sells Earth stuff, yeah," I said. "But that was a private conversation. Did she tell you about it?"

"She did not, but I am the archfiend," said Vambrace. "I hear a good many things that go on in my domain, private or otherwise. Why, did you mean to keep your interest a secret?"

"No, not really," I lied. "I'm just surprised you knew already. Enkida's been having an eye kept on me too, from the sound of it. Do you guys have spies following me around or something?"

"Of course," said the prince with a shrug. "Or rather, not following you, no, but I do have my spies and sentries, hidden or otherwise. I *am* the reigning power in this land. Did you think I would not?"

"I... didn't really think about it at all, I guess," I said. It made sense, though, when he put it like that. And I guess it wasn't as disconcerting if I was being watched as a matter of course along with everyone else, instead of being singled out and stalked for whatever reason.

I mean, it was still really inconvenient either way for my purposes of trying to sneak contraband magic and get the hell out of here. But I wasn't as creeped out as I was prepared to be.

"Alright, then," I said, then yawned into the bunched-up blanket that I still held up to cover myself. "I'll come look at your Earth collection, sure. Just let me get dressed first." My gaze slid over to my desk and the bundle of mostly unusable outfits he'd sent up for me earlier, and I frowned. "You wouldn't happen to have any more human clothes in this collection of yours, would you?" I asked.

He turned toward my clothes pile as well. "Some, yes," he said, "though I cannot promise you will find them suitable. Are the clothes I sent already not to your liking?"

"Not most of them, no," I admitted. "Too revealing, or didn't fit, or both. That dress from yesterday was fine, but probably a bit fancy for everyday wear."

"It is a Superbiate design, yes," said the prince. "There is no such thing as too fancy where they are concerned. However, it is also hard to find a Superbiate garment in your size. You may have noticed that most of them are almost twice your height."

I sighed. "Yeah," I said, "I'm petite, I know."

"Are you?" he asked, looking at me a moment and then quickly looking away again. "You do not seem to me to be especially diminutive for a human woman; but then, I have not seen another in literal ages, so mayhap my judgment on that matter has grown hazy with time. Regardless, most of the outfits I had brought to you were in the Luxuriate style, I admit. I… see now where I may have erred there. Unfortunately, the only other demon species with members of your approximate size are the Iriates and Acediates. Iriates mostly wear either armor or nothing, and Acediates… well, your station here has been made too high and prominent to be seen in Acediate rags. And Gulliate clothing would be too large for you, while Invidiate clothing would be too small."

Fashion headaches like this were one reason why my wardrobe never varied much beyond t-shirts and jeans, if I could help it. "What about the…" I snapped my fingers, running through the list of houses he'd just rattled off and trying to remember the one that was missing. "The greedy ones? The Avaritiates?" I managed at last. "They're about our size, and they've got those layered robe things. Those could work."

Vambrace frowned. "Technically, yes, but you are not an Avaritiate," he said. "The layering and coloring of Avaritiate robes is a complicated symbol of status, denoting the wealth and social standing of the individual wearing them. You *could* wear them, in theory, if you knew the rules behind them and dressed accordingly; but all the realm would know that you would not really understand them, so House Avaritia would likely take it as an insult if you adopted their garb."

I groaned. "Are you sure I can't just wear one of the lazy guys' togas?" I asked. "Or would that be offensive to the Acediates?"

"Oh, no," he said with a scoff, "House Acedia wouldn't care at all. House Acedia doesn't care about *anything*. They can barely function as a proper House. I meant that no other House would take you seriously or think you respectable at all if you went around dressed like one of them. As an emissary of humanity, I cannot allow that."

"Jeez," I said, "why's everyone hate them so much? They don't seem like they get up to much."

"Which is precisely the reason for the hate," he answered. "Or perhaps 'hate' is too strong of a term. Still, the fact remains that Acedia is simply no other House's favorite neighbor. Complacency and idleness do not easily lend themselves to anyone else's benefit. As such, Acediates are often overlooked by the rest of society, with most other demons considering them beneath their notice. A sentiment I rather depend on, actually."

"Oh?" I said. "Why's that?"

"Who do you think I have spying on everyone?" the prince replied. He rose to his feet again finally, though he still kept his eyes averted. "My lady," he continued, "I will happily continue this discussion with you, if you wish. But perhaps it is best we do so in the more comfortable privacy of my vault, after you have clothed yourself and permitted your servant back into her room."

"Oh, right," I said, then scooted off the bed and stood up, still draped in my blanket. It put me closer to him, which I still wasn't entirely comfortable with while naked. But if he was going to try something, he would have by now. "Can you send Kriseia back in?" I asked. "I need help getting into my gown."

"As you wish," said the prince. "It seems we shall have to have some clothing made especially for you, in the near future. Remind me and I will summon my tailors for the task later. Perhaps they can replicate the style of the garments you arrived in." He turned slightly in my direction without actually looking, then smirked. "You may even set new fashion trends among the nobility, if you are not careful."

"Probably," I said. "I think I'm already starting new musical trends soon."

Vambrace's brow rose. "Indeed?" he said. "This I haven't yet heard of."

"It's, uh… it's nothing," I said, remembering belatedly that I had promised Sidona I would keep that a secret. "A surprise for later, maybe."

"If you say so," he said, then turned toward the door. "I shall be waiting outside, whenever you are ready."

When he'd closed the door behind him, I took a deep breath and let it out slowly. Maybe I could get a lock put on this door if I asked. Then again, I already had Hell's general standing guard outside; no doubt she was an even greater deterrent. And neither option would keep the archfiend from barging in again if he wanted.

I stepped out of my sheet and had the gown in my hands, my back to the door, when it opened and Kriseia stepped back in. Oh well, I decided, let her look at my ass if she wanted. She had to help me get dressed anyway, and I was getting tired of defending my modesty. Hell seemed intent to shove me into provocative situations. Might as well start picking my battles.

"Mistress?" she asked nervously as she hurried up behind me. "I mean, Morgan? Did you… are you alright?"

I pulled the gown over my head and shimmied my way up and out the top. "Yeah, I'm fine," I said as I tugged and adjusted. "We were just talking, is all. I think he's going to get me some new clothes."

"He is?" she asked, shocked. "But you… you insulted him. Very loudly. I have never heard of anyone shouting at the archfiend like that before. I was afraid that he would… that you'd be…"

"Oh. Yeah, no, it's alright. We just had a, uh, a kind of misunderstanding, is all," I said, waving a hand. "Don't worry."

"Oh, thank sin," she said with a sigh of relief, then grabbed my gown laces and started cinching me up. "I must say, I am surprised, though. Human or not, his majesty must think a very great deal of you already to allow that kind of talk to go unpunished."

"I guess so," I said. "Lucky me. Don't tell anyone else this," I added more quietly, "but I think he kind of likes it when I challenge him a little. Something about us both being human. I think he finds it nostalgic." *Or he's afraid I'll screw up his long con if he's too mean to me,* I added to myself.

"I suppose I can understand that," said Kriseia. "As much as I can understand human complexity at all, anyway. It still surprises me somewhat, though, if I'm honest. I have heard it rumored that his majesty does not allow even his sexual participants to exert any sort of real challenge or dominion over him, playful or otherwise."

"I really wouldn't know about that," I said carefully. "He has a lot of those, does he?"

"Of course," she said as she reached the top of my gown and tied off my laces. "It is a great honor to be selected by the archfiend, though I imagine it must also be very intimidating. We have no way in our training to practice pleasing a human patron, after all, and he has been around for so much longer than any of us. I can't imagine the craft and ingenuity that pleasuring him must require. Only the very uppermost tier of Luxuriate are even permitted to try, and succeeding is a badge of honor that you carry for life."

"Huh," I said. "Is that why Archduke Melchius kept pestering me, then? So he could get the 'banged a human' merit badge?"

"One reason, perhaps," said Kriseia. "But I imagine he also just wants to. You're very attractive, after all."

I sighed. "Am I really? Or am I just 'exotic?'" I asked, with big, throbbing quotes around the word.

"You're both," my naked, glistening sex demon said with a frown. "You do not sound happy with it, though. I'm sorry, did I offend?"

"Nah, not you," I said, then turned and smiled at her. It was hard to keep my eyes on her face, but I managed somehow. "Anyway, I'm heading out with the prince for a bit, I guess. You don't gotta sit here waiting for me if you don't want to; you can go wander around, see another play or something."

"Thank you, Morgan," she said, bowing her head slightly. "In truth, I do not know what I want to do lately, but I will figure something out, do not worry."

"Really?" I asked. "I thought demons always knew what they wanted, at all times"

"Yes, well..." She glanced away, one arm reaching across to hold the other and, possibly inadvertently, lifting her breasts so they were staring at my face. "I cannot have what I *really* want, so I will have to find something else to want instead for now."

Cryptic. I probably would have asked what she meant, but I'd been keeping Vambrace waiting long enough, and anyway, all her rampant nudity was starting to make me uncomfortable again. So I simply smiled and said goodbye.

Enkida was gone from her post when I stepped out into the hallway. In her place, the prince lounged against the wall. He straightened up as I came through the door. "Ready at last, m'lady?" he asked.

"Yeah, ready," I said. "Lead on."

Chapter 21: Materialism

It occurred to me, as I followed Prince Vambrace down the corridor toward his private rooms, that I was going to have to lean harder into the offhand lie I'd made about wanting a bunch of Earth stuff to remind me of home, and also that I was almost certainly wasting my time right now. But I couldn't tell him I was looking for one thing in particular without telling him what it was, and I couldn't just say I was looking for books without giving away that I hadn't and couldn't read the ones he'd already given me.

Hopefully, I thought, Archduchess Cinaedemis wouldn't hear that the archfiend had beaten her to the punch in supplying me with a source of Earth stuff. Or if she did, she wouldn't decide that meant she didn't need to find this Gilderos person for me after all. The deal we'd made was still the best and only thread I had to the *Morganomicon*. It certainly wasn't going to be in Vambrace's private vault.

Unless it is, I thought suddenly. It wouldn't be outside the realm of possibility, after all, that the book had already been passed along and that it had eventually found its way to the prince since he was a known collector of Earth stuff. After all, that's exactly what had happened to me.

Except… was the *Morganomicon* really an Earth thing? If it was really written in Elvish like the shop lady had said — a claim which sounded less ridiculous the more time I spent hanging out with demons and knights with magic swords — then it wasn't a human thing. Were elves Earth things? If they were, would Vambrace know that? He'd fallen right out of Arthurian legend. Did they have elves back in his day? Or would that have been too fantastical even for Camelot's standards?

Come to that, would Gilderos or anyone else who picked the book up think it was from Earth without the Earthling who'd brought it with her still nearby to back it up? If the prince saw it on its own, would he recognize it as an Earth book?

Oh shit. Would he recognize it as a *magic* book?

"Lady Morgan?" the prince asked beside me, slowing in his walk. "You've been rather silent. Is all well with you?"

"Oh, yeah, I'm fine," I said with a smile and a wave of my hand. "Sorry, just lost in thought."

Vambrace smiled back politely. "As you say, then," he said, turning back ahead.

He knew magic people in his day. He'd talked about Merlin and Morgan le Faye with open disdain; according to him, they had been real, and he'd known them. He had been familiar with magic, and he'd hated the stuff. If the *Morganomicon* did fall into his hands first, he probably wouldn't know or care where it had been recently. But he'd know it was magical, and that made it dangerous in his mind. Hell, with a name like *Morganomicon*, it was probably Morgan le Faye's book to begin with. He may have even seen it before himself.

Would he have it locked away somewhere if that were the case? Or would he just destroy it?

I definitely had to find that damn book first. And soon.

These were the thoughts that plagued me as Prince Vambrace took me back to his private rooms and through a door opposite his bedroom. This one led to another short corridor with another door at the end, which opened onto a small, empty room like a closet. I saw the crank handle on the wall after we stepped in. Another elevator, then. Still quietly worrying to myself, I said nothing as he shut the door behind us and began quickly turning the handle, dropping us down to even lower levels.

At least, I said nothing at first. After what felt like five or so minutes of constant descent, though, I was compelled back to the present. "Are we still not there yet?" I asked. "How far down are we going?"

"Only to the first sublevel, don't worry," the prince replied, his arm still pumping tirelessly at the crank. "There's quite a gap of unusable space to traverse to get there, I'll grant you. We are mostly just bypassing nothing but stairs and solid stone right now."

"Well, thanks for that," I said, watching the faint rumble of the walls around us. "I'd hate to have to climb this far down. How deep does this palace run, anyway?"

"The first sublevel, where I keep my personal vault, is only a couple of leagues beneath Pandemonium proper," he said. "There are several more leagues beyond that, at least, but you need not concern yourself with them.

Even I rarely have cause to descend so deep into the crater, and then usually just to check up on things."

"A couple leagues?" I repeated. What was that in miles? I'd always sucked at measurements. Were leagues metric? Did the metric system even exist yet back when he did?

"A couple of leagues, yes," said Vambrace. "I would hazard to guess that Pandemonium is about as deep as it is tall, though it is hard to say. Its true depths are up for debate. Or they would be, if I allowed the scholars interested in such come down that far. Most people are not allowed even to the first sublevel, so count yourself fortunate to be made an exception."

How fortunate I was to be here was also still up for debate, but he didn't need to know that. Instead, I asked, "Why have all that wasted space, then? Leagues of nothing but stairs? Why not build floors in that space and put it to use instead? Or move whatever's down this far up to a more convenient spot?"

"Because neither I nor any archfiend before me had the sunken portions of Pandemonium built," he said, still cranking away. "I merely found a pocket of space in which to store my private treasures. If I had to guess, the sublevel architecture was likely in place when Pandemonium was first discovered, unchanged since time immemorial. Altering it in any meaningful way would be difficult at best and ultimately impractical." He turned to me with a slight, wry smile. "And the contents of those depths are not something you could simply haul up to a more convenient floor, even if I were of a mind to do so."

"Mysterious," I said, crossing my arms. "You gonna leave it cryptic like that, or you gonna tell me what's down there now that you brought it up? Do I wanna know?"

"I am going to leave it cryptic," he said, still smiling. "Apologies, my lady, but it is not something you need to concern yourself with, and it is easier if the general public stays in the dark as well. Demons are impulsive creatures, as you yourself have seen. I do not think many would be foolish enough to try and sneak down this far without permission, but I would still like to avoid the possibility as much as is feasible, regardless."

His cranking arm was finally slowing, the elevator following suit as we slid toward our stop. I stared at the door in front of us, tapping my foot. "Is it that Throne thing?" I asked. "I heard rumors about it while I was wandering around earlier. Something about the legendary throne of the original archfiend sitting deep underground."

"Something like that, yes," he said, still faintly smiling, as our elevator finally crawled to a full stop. "Do you know any details about this rumored Throne beyond those, Lady Morgan?"

I searched my memories. There weren't many, so it didn't take long. "Not really," I admitted. "Just that it's kind of a big deal."

"It kind of is," said the prince. "And like I said, it also is no concern of yours or anyone else's, so there is no point in allowing further details to escape into rumor. Now, this way, please," he added as the door slid open and he stepped out.

The draft was the first thing I noticed, as the temperate air we had carried down with us spilled out into the subterranean chill. I wrapped my arms around my bare, now-goosebumped shoulders. Suddenly this gown didn't cover as much as I would have liked after all. *Maybe the prince will lend me his jacket*, I thought as I stepped out after him. It was technically *my* jacket, after all.

I forgot to ask in the next moment, though, as I followed him down the gloomy tunnel before us, gawping at the scenery. The walls and floor here were the same red-veined onyx-looking stuff as the upper floors, but rougher hewn, the edges less uniform and squared. The red veining was more pronounced as well, not the spidery lines of upstairs but wide, crimson rivers thicker than my arms, crowding out the sleek black around it like hellish zebra stripes and glowing with a faint red light that, if my eyes weren't weirding out on me, I *think* was pulsing very slowly and faintly. There were no sconces or torches on these walls, no paintings or hangings adorning them; the glowing red was the only decoration and illumination. It would have made the corridor look like a setting in a particularly surreal haunted house if it weren't for all the crystals.

They were mostly small clusters, fist-sized chunks or smaller, sitting just beneath the surface of the walls and ceiling and floor, or jutting out like little stalactites. Near as I could tell beyond the faint red glow of the walls, they also appeared to be the same milky, iridescent white as the crystal soul I'd seen used both as money and as pudding sprinkles. If that's what they were, though, then it seemed weird to me that Pandemonium's basement had what amounted to loose change embedded in the walls. Maybe it just would have been too inconvenient to go chopping into the architecture to dig them out. If nobody was allowed down this far, then —

I yelped and hopped back as something fell from the ceiling only a foot or so in front of my face, clattering over the floor at my feet with a semi-musical tinkling. It was a chunk of soul, only about as big as my thumb. I looked up and, in the faint red glow near the ceiling, could only just make out a small divot in the red-black stone where it had presumably fallen from like a loose baby tooth.

"Ah, yes, watch out for those," said the prince, about ten feet ahead of me and looking back with an amused smile. "Falling soul's not likely to hurt much, but it can be startling nonetheless."

"So I've gathered," I said, then squatted down to pick up the little crystal that had dive bombed me.

It didn't budge. I tugged, but it stayed where it had fallen, as if it were attached to the floor. A cursory probing with my fingers told me this was because that's exactly what it was — embedded about half a centimeter or so into the hard stone, and sinking slowly further.

I rose up with a frown and looked around me again, at the chunks of soul pockmarking the walls. They were *moving*, I realized, all of them drifting very slowly, very steadily downward through the solid rock around us. The bits jutting from the ceiling were gradually growing more exposed; the lumps in the floor, including the one that had almost fallen on me, were slowly disappearing. I watched, slightly fascinated and fairly confused, as a long hunk of soul in the wall beside me drifted down through the black into a thick vein of glowing red. As it reached it, its trajectory changed, following the flow of the crimson light rather than sliding straight down as it had been.

"Soul is a mostly subterranean substance," Vambrace said, breaking the long silence of me staring at the slowly shifting walls. "You find deposits now and again in the beds of rivers and lakes, or strains of it in trees. Generally speaking, though, the deeper underground you go, the richer the veins you find. Partially this is due to basic geology, and partially this is due to it being a migratory substance." He glanced up and reached out a hand, just in time for a piece of soul the size of a tennis ball to fall into his palm. "The floors of the mints and treasuries of House Avaritia are plated with a handspan of bronze to keep the money from sinking into the ground if it's set down or dropped," he continued, dropping the soul in his hand. "Novice merchants, those just starting their businesses and without much that they can afford to lose, tend to be anxious or uncomfortable around bare dirt and rock. One reason for all the thick carpeting you see vendors employing in the bazaar." He swung a booted foot idly at the soul he'd dropped. It barely budged, already embedded.

It really *was* loose change, then. We were underneath the couch cushions of Hell.

"It just… tunnels its way down on its own?" I asked. "Wait, this stuff's alive?"

"No," said the prince. "Well, probably not. It's a crystalline mineral. But yes, it sinks through the earth on its own power, or by whatever power draws it down. Think of it as a sort of lodestone, if that helps."

I didn't know what a lodestone was, so it didn't. "It's not even leaving any holes, though," I said, prodding the last visible nub of the thumb-sized soul that had fallen in front of me with my toe. The floor had mostly swallowed it up by now, and true to my observation, there was no indentation in the shining onyx around where it had been laying pre-sinking. The floor around it was as solid as if that bit of crystal had always been there.

"Not in Pandemonium, no," the prince said slowly. "It leaves holes in normal rock and dirt. In fact, House Gullia employs a somewhat ingenious technique with soul placement and patterns to till and aerate the soil in their gardens. But the guilt walls of the palace swallow soul readily and fill up the space behind it."

I watched the long piece of soul drifting through the glowing red vein in the wall, pondering how many questions I'd already had, how many I was still accumulating, and if I should even keep bothering at this point. "Wait, the what walls?" I finally asked. A clarification seemed safe enough, at least.

"Guilt," he repeated, drawing his sword. "The substance that comprises the palace." He waved an arm generally around us, at the glowing red-veined walls of shining black in every direction, then stuck his sword in the ground at his feet and scooped with it like a shovel. "Soul can be found, somewhere, everywhere in Hell, but guilt is unique to Pandemonium." He tossed the unearthed chunk of floor up into the air and caught it, then held it out to me.

I took it, almost cutting my fingers on its sharp edges. It felt hard and cold like any other rock, but way denser and heavier than I was expecting. This chunk was only about the size of my fist, but it must have weight something like ten pounds. The single tendril of red threading through this piece pulsed balefully as I ran my finger over it, like an angry nerve in a rotten tooth.

"You guys have some pretty intense naming conventions here, you know that?" I asked as I handed him back the fistful of guilt.

Vambrace chuckled and took the rock from me. "They predate my arrival here, so I cannot help that," he said. His eyes flicked toward the ceiling, and he reached out just in time to catch a thin finger length of falling soul. "Soul sinks through guilt and leaves no trace," he said, kneeling to replace the excavated chunk into its spot on the floor. "And guilt guides stray soul on its way downward. But soul can also erase or define the edges of guilt."

He slowly dragged the stick of soul along the perimeter of the misplaced guilt chunk, and I watched as the gap in the floor disappeared behind it, like it was being soldered back together. When he was finished drawing the floor back together, he set the soul sideways overtop of the now hidden wound, where it was quickly (by stone's standards, anyway) swallowed up, leaving the spot where it had been looking as uniform as it had before the prince had taken his sword to it.

"In fact," he continued, standing back up, "soul is the only thing besides Excalibur that seems able to put any kind of dent in the stuff, even if transitory. The spaces upstairs, the ones that seem more sculpted for actual living and use, were probably excavated with great difficulty using massive implements of soul to carve away guilt bit by bit without sinking fully into it."

I took a deep, slow breath as I stared at the floor and wondered why I thought any of my questions, even the seemingly small ones, would have simple answers. "So at the pit of Hell is a black tower of guilt that swallows all souls," I said. "That is some thick ass symbolism in the naming there, don't you think?"

Prince Vambrace shrugged. "Again, I didn't name any of this. Blame my predecessors if you think it overwrought, but I would hazard a guess that this place and these laws predate even humankind's understanding of the symbols they seem to harken to."

"So why does this guilt stuff only show up here at the palace, though?" I asked. Fuck it, in for a penny. "Why's this place so singularly weird? What's down there that's sucking up all the soul, and what happens to it when it gets there?"

Prince Vambrace shrugged again. "I cannot say," he said.

I narrowed my eyes. "Does that mean you don't know, though?"

He smiled ever so slightly. "I cannot say," he said again. "If you have finished marveling at it, though, shall we continue?"

"I thought you wanted me to be in on all your lies and schemes and stuff," I said as I followed him further into the trippy hell cave. "We're already conspiracy buddies about what humans really are and what Earth's really like. Why keep secrets about Hell from me, then?"

"You don't need to be informed of *all* of my lies and schemes, my lady," he said. "There are still some things you are better off not knowing, for both of our safeties. My apologies."

"Eh, whatever," I said. "I was only curious anyway." Let him keep his secrets if he wanted, if he still didn't trust me that much. Not like I could really be offended by that; I didn't trust him that much either, and I was keeping secrets of my own.

We walked through the creepy glowy Halloween cave for probably ten minutes or so as the path twisted and snaked seemingly arbitrarily, with the distant tinkling of falling soul echoing in front of and behind us like wind chimes in a soft breeze. It was an unexpectedly relaxing sound for the bowels of Hell. Finally, the tunnel we were in ended in what I thought at first was a dead end until the prince kept walking forward and disappeared between two disconnected veins of glowing red. There was a crack in the wall, a dark crevasse that blended in with the shiny black bits. On closer inspection, it was tall and wide enough to easily admit someone about exactly the prince's size, the edges smoothly rippled as if they'd been hand-scooped away by either soul tools or Excalibur. The prince squeezed his way through the rocky crevasse without difficulty, and I followed close behind.

We emerged into a massive cavern, roughly the size of my high school gymnasium but with the edges rounded out. The ceiling seemed so high up at first that I thought it had vanished into the shadows, until I realized I was looking at a huge stretch of white cloth suspended high above us like the roof of a tent, faintly reflecting light of the hanging lanterns and some of the red glow from the walls back down into the room. A faint thump and roll high above us, followed by a light tinkling somewhere on the edge of the room, showed that it worked as a kind of soul gutter as well, keeping stray crystals from the ceiling from dropping unchecked into the center of the space and onto the warehouse of stuff that was proudly displayed there.

Prince Vambrace stepped to one side, gesturing with that same pride to the room at large. "What do you think, my lady?" he asked with a smile.

The massive room, the prince's treasure vault, was set up like a fine arts museum dedicated to random junk, like a flea market that was putting on airs despite being lodged in a dim cave underground. From where we stood by the entrance, on the edge of this homage to hoarding, I looked out on aisles of plinths and short pillars, each lovingly supporting a single item: a cracked vase here, an old boot there, a dented bronze helmet, a dirt-stained cloth doll, most of a straw broom. Interspersed with them were hanging racks and mannequin-esque contraptions on poles showcasing single pieces of clothing in various states of cleanliness or repair, as well as easels or short walls holding chunks of cloth or rug like they were tapestries, or the occasional framed painting or metal sign. No rhyme or reason to any of it, no distinction made for quality between what looked like it was still useable and what looked like it had been pulled from the bottom of a trash heap.

Except that it was all from the same planet, or dimension, or whatever. All of it something you could have, at one point, found on Earth. For a guy who'd been away from home for the better part of two millennia, that was enough.

"It's… very expansive," I said, smiling back. "You've got a whole lot of stuff squirreled away in here. Lots of very different stuff."

"Indeed," he said, turning and striding forward toward his carefully displayed hoard. I followed. "This collection is the work of a lifetime — an incredibly long lifetime, as you have informed me. I daresay I have by now amassed the most extensive and concentrated pocket of humanity to be found in this entire realm."

"Definitely looks like it," I said, glancing as we passed from a gleaming and nearly immaculate katana on one plinth to the yellowed, half-rotten clump of rags that I think was the remains of a hat on the pillar beside it. Attached to the front of some of the displays were framed pieces of paper or parchment which, I assumed, functioned as title cards or explanations of what we were looking at, like the note cards that art museums had beside all the paintings and statues. I couldn't read any of them, though; each was scribbled with what looked like the same handwriting in two different systems of gibberish symbols, one above the other. The top translation looked frustratingly similar to the regular alphabet I was used to, but still different and foreign enough — or maybe just old enough — that I had no idea what they were spelling out. The bottom translation, written in chunkier, sharper, more alien scribbles, also looked vaguely familiar for a minute before I realized it was the same demon letters I'd seen in the native books here, before Vambrace had found me a stack of older human books that were still no more readable.

"If you were looking for any particular Earth item or amenity," the prince continued, "then that information did not make it into the report I received. If you were simply curious of your options for the sake of comfort or homesickness, that also is fine. Either way, my lady, let me know if there is anything you wish for or if anything catches your eye that you would like to borrow. Most of the items I have here I am not averse to lending to you, provided you treat them well, of course."

"Of course," I said, glancing at the rusted and somehow partially charred remains of what looked like a farming plow and wondering how the hell I could possibly mistreat something like that. As far as specifics went, I'd wanted some different clothes, but the idea of slipping into a pair of half-rotten pants from over a millennium ago sounded even less appealing than settling on the various pieces of fetish lingerie that passed for what he'd brought me already. Besides that…

Was it worth the risk to ask to see his book collection again, in case the *Morganomicon* was in it already? In case he'd found it, didn't realize what it was, and hadn't destroyed it? If all of those ifs somehow miraculously came together, did I want to draw his attention to it by admitting I wanted it, and potentially show my halfway magical hand? And if I did end up revealing too much, to Vambrace's mind, would my being the only other human in the world trump my also being a witch who had been keeping secrets?

"Lady Morgan?"

His voice cut into my worrying and made me realize I hadn't been paying attention. "Sorry," I said, waving a hand. "Just browsing and lost in thought. I don't really…"

I trailed off as we passed another short plinth, stopping and doing a double take as I realized what was sitting on it. Vambrace stopped as well, one eyebrow cocked. "Yes?" he asked.

Lying like a crown jewel on a small velvet pillow atop the display was a cell phone. A silver flip phone, specifically, the same brand but a slightly different model from the one I had in middle school. I grabbed it without thinking and flipped it open with a jolt of unexpected nostalgia. The screen was cracked, the 7 button had fallen off somewhere, and the edges were scuffed and scratched up, but the hinge was still functioning good as new, and it even still had its antenna. I held my breath as I held down the power button, but of course the battery was long dead. For good, or just empty?

For a brief moment, I fantasized about finding a way to power it back up and calling home. Let my parents know I was okay and still alive, let my professors know I'd be missing class for a little while, maybe call the police just in case they could patch me through to some secret MIB-type government agency that knew how to fight supernatural shit and could come rescue me. But, no, that plan was dead in the water as soon as it formed. Even if I could find a way to juice it up and turn it on, even if it still functioned, there's no way I'd get any cell service here in another dimension — I barely got any in my own apartment.

Also, while I was fantasizing, I wouldn't have felt good turning secret government demon hunters loose on people like Kriseia or Enkida, even if it got me out of here. Maybe Dramoc, though.

I looked up from the dead phone to see Prince Vambrace standing maybe a foot away on the other side, wide-eyed and frowning, his hands up and hovering in between us, fingers twitching, as if he wanted to snatch his treasure back from me and was only barely stopping himself. "What are you—" he started, eyes glued to the phone in my hands. Slowly, with effort, he brought his hands down and took half a step back. "Do you know what you're doing with that?" he asked in the tone of someone who strongly suspects that I don't.

"Sorry," I said, but I was still too potentially excited about the discovery to really feel too bad about grabbing and fiddling with what he probably assumed was a priceless Earth artifact. "But do you know what this is?" I asked, turning the phone to show him the battered insides.

The gesture didn't bring him any clarity, of course. "It is… some sort of small puzzle box, maybe?" he said. "There are numerals on the depressible ridges, so perhaps a sort of abacus, or—" He stopped, then frowned and cleared his throat. "No, that question was rhetorical, wasn't it?" he asked. "You already know what it is, I take it."

"It's an old phone," I said. "Or a new phone, for your time. A remote communication device. We use these to talk to one another or send messages over long distances." Despite my immediate skepticism, I still held my breath as I held down the power button; but just as I thought, nothing happened. No life in it at all.

"Indeed? Fascinating," said the prince as he stroked his chin, still eyeing the phone. "Such a power in such a small device? It sounds sorcerous. How does it work?"

"I don't really know the details," I said, "but it's technology, not sorcery." I glanced up at him from the phone. "Would that be a problem if it was?" I asked, careful to try and sound only marginally curious.

"It would be a moot point, I suppose," he said with a shrug, "since there are no sorcerers here to use it if that were the case. Unless the device itself had been ensorcelled." There was a definite suspicion that creeped onto his face as he considered his own words. Luckily, he was still looking at the phone in my hand and not me, so if I looked any more nervous in that moment, he didn't see it. "But you say that this is a common mechanism among present day humans?" he continued a moment later. "I suppose that it cannot then be magical in nature, if it is really so ubiquitous with the common folk."

"Incredibly common, yeah," I said. "It's really complicated science that I don't entirely understand, but it's electronic, not magic. You talk to it, and it turns your voice into an invisible signal that it sends to someone else's phone, and they can hear you speaking, and you can hear them speaking back. More or less."

He frowned. "Electronic?" he repeated, with the same unfamiliarity Kriseia had also expressed.

"Electrically mechanical," I said. "Intricate little machinery powered by very little electric signals. Like… tiny lightning moving through tiny mazes, making things happen." Like I'd said, I didn't really understand the science, so I had no idea how close to accurate I was being; but it wasn't like he could check my work and correct me on it, so hey, I was technically the leading expert on computer technology in the world at the moment.

"Fascinating," he said again, sounding even more fascinated this time. "Humanity can harness and command lightning on such a level without the use of magic? Such wonders as I've missed." His fingers paused on his chin, and he looked up at me with sudden urgency. "Does it still function?" he asked. "Could we use it to communicate with Earth?"

"I had the same thought, but no," I said. "I've been trying, but this one's dead. At the very least, the battery's empty. Can't tell if anything else is wrong with it if I can't power it on."

Vambrace frowned again. "The battery?" he asked. "Does the tiny lightning maze inside have tiny fortifications?"

"Huh? Oh, no," I said. "The battery, that's like… the internal energy source that powers the device. It's like a little container for all of the lightning. This one's all outta juice. Er, energy." I shook the phone for emphasis, for some reason. As if the fact that you couldn't hear little lightning bolts rattling around inside proved my point. For all he knew, it did.

"I see," said the prince. "One moment." I waited while he turned and strode to the edge of his junk museum, stooping to pick up something near the wall in the corner. "I do not believe you will find lightning juice anywhere in the palace," he said as he returned. "I do, however, have plenty of these, if they will work."

He held out his hand. I held out mine as well, and he dropped a couple of soul crystals into my open palm, each about the size and shape of a pink school eraser.

I stared at them a moment, wondering if I was missing the obvious, before I gave up. "A couple of soul rocks?" I asked. "How do these help?"

Prince Vambrace shrugged. "I do not know that they will," he said. "I confess, I cannot quite grasp the idea of these 'electronics' as you explain them. But soul is, at its most basic, energy in a crystalline form. I do not know if it is a comparable form of energy, but short of capturing more lightning yourself somehow, it is the closest that I think we have to offer."

I rolled the crystal chunks around in my hand. "But isn't this stuff edible?" I asked.

"Yes," he said, "if prepared correctly. Is lightning juice not?"

"That's not quite—" I started, but then decided not to. "I don't think this will work. There's cords and plugs and stuff we're still missing. Maybe if I replaced the battery with one of these, but I've never taken a phone apart before, so that's probably beyond me. I could play around with it a bit later, though, I suppose, but I wouldn't get your hopes up."

He nodded. "Very well," he said. "I will allow you to take the phone with you for now, then, and experiment with at your leisure. I only ask that, if you cannot restore it, you return it intact, please. If it cannot function, it can remain an artifact."

"Yeah, no problem," I said. "If this thing survived a trip here, it's probably indestructible anyway." I tucked the phone and the two soul crystals away in a pocket of my gown. The technology in Hell may have been hundreds, maybe a thousand years behind Earth, but they'd still beaten us to the idea that women might like pockets on their clothes too. Whatever other complaints I had about the fashion in this place, I had to at least give them that victory. "Still," I said, "even if this thing doesn't work anymore, you know what this means, finding it here?"

"I have an idea, yes," said the prince. "Though I suspect you have a more complete idea, given your familiarity with the object. What does this mean, Lady Morgan?"

"This thing can't be more than, like, twenty years old at the oldest," I said, gazing out over his assortment of Earth items with a more critical eye. "That means stuff is still somehow finding its way from Earth to Hell even today, probably, or at least as recently as the last couple of decades. It means there are little holes between these two worlds in some places, for some reason. Somebody lost their phone in their couch cushions, or it fell out of their pocket on a bus, or they left it in a bathroom somewhere, and instead of just falling to the floor and sitting forgotten in a corner or something, it slipped dimensions and landed here." I turned back to the prince. "How? Why? How does that happen, and does it happen in reverse? How long have the two been connected, sharing bits of random flotsam and lost junk?"

Vambrace shrugged. "I cannot give you an exact account of when or how the connection began," he said. "How long? That is a question for a historian, and the earliest histories of both worlds are by now cloudy and uncertain. Why do they persist? All I can say is that it is far easier to close a door than to plug every tiny hole in a wall."

I frowned. "I don't think I follow."

"I told you that I sealed off travel between Hell and Earth, did I not?" said the prince. "The banning of non-innate magic was a part of that, yes, and that goal was in turn a large part of why I outlawed sorcery overall. Beyond that, though, sealing travel meant sealing actual doorways between our worlds. Or, well, not *actual* doorways in the literal sense, but ensorcelled sites dedicated to crossing worlds. Obelisks with the magic carved into them had to be defaced. Monument sites with the spell woven into their architecture had to be torn down and destroyed. Where possible, I had the offending components ground to dust and scattered, desecrated far beyond repair. But I am no sorcerer, and at the time, there were no native sorcerers whom I would have trusted to advise my efforts even had I offered their lives in exchange. So I annihilated the sites and relics, burned and destroyed all records of magical knowledge or practice, and had all known magic practitioners of any skill or talent executed. That seems to have done the job well enough. If I were to hazard a guess, perhaps there is some ambient sorcery in the remaining stone and dust that occasionally pulls some small item through the veil. I cannot discern or control it, but so far, I am not threatened by it — though I will of course gather and secure as many such objects as I can locate, just in case. One reason for the collection you see here, besides my own curiosity and nostalgic fascination."

I nodded, turning to look again over his collection, so that he couldn't see any of the nervousness or fear that may or may not have been threatening to show on my face. "Burned all the books and killed all the mages, huh?" I said. "You don't... I dunno... think maybe that was a bit excessive? In retrospect? I mean, it sounds pretty harsh, but maybe that's just me..."

"Oh, it was incredibly harsh, yes, and massively unpopular," said Vambrace in the same tired tone as someone talking about a bad day at the office. "One of the bloodiest periods of my reign, in fact, even including the direct aftermath of my ascension as the first human and foreign archfiend. The entirety of Dis was in near constant chaos for what was probably a decade or more. Blood running in the streets, whole city blocks on fire. I had a lot of people killed whose only crime was knowing too much of a study that had been perfectly legal mere years beforehand. I lost a quarter of my army to dissension, and a third of what remained just in the course of all the fighting that followed. I will admit with no sense of pride that I was the most brutal of tyrants."

I heard him sigh, and it didn't sound particularly heavy or guilty. "But Dis then was not the comparable bastion of order and peace that it is now," he continued. "Chaos and terror were never strangers even before my controversial rise to power. I decided that more of the same would be an acceptable price to pay for the eventual long-term peace of separating our worlds for good. And when the dust finally settled and no trace of illegal magic remained, I spent decades rebuilding what was wrecked in the collateral damage, then decades beyond that improving and bettering my city. By the time the last demon to live through that age of turmoil died, there was no sign that any war had ever happened within the city walls, no stone out of place to suggest that we had ever been anything other than the only functioning example of peaceful civilization in the known world."

I took a deep breath and let it out slowly. "So, no regrets, then?" I asked. "No price too high to kill any trace of magic?"

"No," he said. "None."

I swallowed. "Even today?" I asked. "All this time later?"

"Even today," he said. "If anything, magic now would be a worse crime and a bigger danger. It has been forbidden for long enough that there is no plausible excuse for it. Anyone caught practicing it would knowingly and deliberately be committing sedition of the highest order."

I nodded. "Yeah, makes sense," I said.

"Lady Morgan," said the Prince, "look at me. Please," he added as an afterthought.

I didn't want to. With the weird conspiratorial understanding we had, I probably could have refused without incident beyond raising suspicion.

But suspicion was the absolute last thing I needed now. He'd made his stance clear enough; friendly or no, chivalrous knight or not, Prince Vambrace was the single biggest threat to my plans and my life if I wasn't careful.

So I sighed, and I turned to him without looking at him, and I hoped that he misread whatever it was he saw on me.

He did. "I've upset you with all this talk of bloodshed and tyranny," he said with a frown. "My apologies. Whatever your life was like on Earth, it must have been infinitely more peaceful and pleasant than the history I have described. I apologize for distressing you with the details." He sighed, then reached out and placed his hands on my bare shoulders. I flinched a bit, and he noticed, but he misinterpreted that too. "But in a way, I must say, your reaction is heartening," he added with a smile. "If such a tale offends you so, if you are a stranger to the horrors I have recounted, then my actions, however reprehensible, were not in vain. If an Earth severed from demonic interference can find peace and stability and produce a maiden like yourself, then the chaos and death here in Hell was worth it. You are the proof of the fruits of my many terrible labors."

I think he wanted me to thank him for that, but at the moment, I didn't think I could sound convincingly grateful. Instead, I took another deep breath and tried to compose myself. "Sorry," I said, looking up at him at last. "Didn't mean to freak out on ya, but—"

I stopped. There was a shine to his eyes as he looked at me, reminiscent of that same strange look he'd had after I'd slapped him, when he'd dragged me to his room and knelt in private. Like tears threatening to form, but behind that, something more intense, some manic triumph.

"What?" I asked, trying to backstep and failing with his hands on me.

He pulled me forward, and there was a moment of panic as he squeezed me against him before I realized what was happening. "Thank you, my lady," he said, his voice barely above a whisper. "For so long, I have had only the assumption that what I have done here has helped my — our — home world, but you… you are the proof. It is as if your arrival were a sign from Arthur himself. Your very existence is evidence that my attempts at penance have not been entirely in vain."

I stood trapped in his hug, my face smooshed against the cold mail of his chest, the denim of my stolen jacket pressed against my bare back by arms so toned with corded muscle that it felt like being hugged by an oak tree in jeans. The leather strap that reached across his torso was digging softly into my collarbone — the strap that held the harness on his back through which Excalibur was tenuously slotted.

The moment he learns the real reason for my arrival here, that sword is going straight through me like a hot knife through warm butter.

So I didn't say anything, or try to escape the embrace, or even voice my discomfort at having a face full of metal chains squished against my cheek. Let him come to his own conclusions and revere me if he wants. Maybe it would make him more hesitant to order my execution later on. Maybe it would buy me just a bit more time to find that damn book and get the hell out of here.

I was finally rescued from the awkward display of affection by the sound of footsteps walking up and stopping behind us, then someone clearing their throat. "Am I interrupting a substantial moment, Sire?"

"Enkida?" the prince asked in surprise. He cleared his throat as he released me and stepped back, and when he opened his eyes again, that desperate teary shine was gone. "A private moment, yes, but not… I was merely expressing my gratitude to the Lady Morgan for…. Do you have something to report, General?"

I turned to find the Iriate general smirking at us, her two bottom fangs peeking through her lips like little tusks. "I'm glad to find your demeanor improved, then, sire," she said. "Last time I was alone with you two, you were ready to throttle her, if I remember correctly." The reminder wasn't particularly welcome at the moment, and probably would have worsened my anxiety, if she hadn't continued. "Yes, I have a report from Archduchess Cinaedemis on that merchant she was investigating?"

"Gilderos?" I asked, heart leaping before I could think. One more step on the road to going home. It couldn't have come at a more welcome time.

"Gilderos?" Vambrace echoed, looking between us. "I remember ordering no merchant investigated. Is this news for the Lady Morgan?"

"For the both of you now, if I judge correctly," said Enkida, smirk vanishing. "Otherwise, I would not interrupt. The merchant in question was purportedly known to trade in esoteric goods presumed to be Earthen in origin. That fact, the archduchess was able to confirm."

"Awesome," I said, smiling. "Can I arrange a meeting with him?"

"Wait," said the prince with a frown. "*Was* known?"

Enkida nodded. "Yes, sire," she said. "Seems he's been murdered."

Chapter 22: Guilt

"I want to talk to him," I said. "Please."

"What? No," said the prince. "Why?"

"Because, I… have questions," I said, mentally flailing.

Vambrace raised an eyebrow. "What questions could you possibly have for this one man in particular that would make your meeting him a good idea?"

That was a fair point, actually. What good reason could I give for demanding an audience with the alleged murderer of the merchant that I had also demanded an audience with, besides the truth: that I desperately needed a highly illegal spell book, and the guy who killed the guy who'd supposedly had it was my last chance at following its trail?

"I just… I want to know why he did it," I said, staring at the floor of the elevator as General Enkida cranked us back up from the depths of Pandemonium. I was hoping I came off more as the righteous and naive maiden that Vambrace was convincing himself I was instead of the bad-at-lying liar I really am. "I want to know his side of the story. I'd been really looking forward to seeing what this Gilderos person had to offer, so I feel like I need to know."

Vambrace sighed. Honestly, I couldn't really blame him for not buying it. "My lady," he said patiently, "I can understand your eagerness for familiar human comforts all too well. But this Gilderos was not the only Avaritiate in Dis who would sell you such things if you were looking, and whatever stock he had would not have simply evaporated with his death. Whatever his wares, they will be subsumed by House Avaritia and reintroduced into the market somewhere else. You can find them then. You don't need to interrogate a murderer for some misguided sense of closure."

"It's not…" I started, then stopped. This wasn't going to get me anywhere.

I considered dropping the argument and just following the both of them with my unnoticeability spell; but no, Enkida at least would probably half-expect me to sneak out after them after this failed persuasion and my record of having already disappeared twice against Vambrace's orders. And worse than losing the trail of the *Morganomicon* would be getting caught wearing its magic by the prince.

But losing all traces of the book would still be a nightmare. And I was getting so close! *Alright, let's see if we can do this carefully.*

I took a deep breath. "The truth is," I said slowly, "I'm not just looking for any general Earth stuff to browse through. I'm looking for something in particular. I think Gilderos might've had it, and I'm worried about losing it."

"Oh?" asked the prince. "What would that be?"

Shit. "It's a… book," I said.

Vambrace raised his eyebrow again. "You are a rather voracious reader, my lady," he said. "Or are the tomes I have already gathered for you not to your liking?"

Shit, shit, shit. "It's a specific book," I said. "One I had with me when I came here. It's, uh, got sentimental value. My grandmother gave it to me. Been in the family for ages."

Vambrace frowned. "Is that why you've been asking me for so many books?" he asked.

No, that had just been for something to do while I was stuck in a room by myself. But if the notion might work in my favor, I wasn't going to correct him. "I was hoping it would turn up," I said. "I mean, I didn't have my jacket when I woke up either, but that turned up," I added, waving a hand at him and his appropriated fashion. "When it didn't, I started trying to find where it went."

"Ah yes, I remember you laying claim to this garment when you were presented to me," he said, holding out an arm and running his hand over one of the denim sleeves. "It is a surcoat of a most interestingly rugged cloth, I must say. I confess I still find it strange to think this is the sort of attire in which modern young Earth maidens clothe themselves."

"Well, that one's a men's size," I said, then shook my head. "Besides the point. But hey, make you a deal? Let me come with you, check out this Gilderos's shop, talk to the guy who killed him, and I'll let you keep the jacket."

I heard a snort from Enkida at that. She was facing away, still cranking the elevator, so I couldn't see if it was in derision or amusement. Vambrace just reached up and started stroking his chin. "You'll *let* me keep it?" he said. With him, I could tell it was amusement, but that wasn't necessarily a good thing for me. "That's rather bold, my lady. I do already have it, and I *am* the Archfiend, you know."

Yeah, I thought, *I know, you keep on saying that.* Out loud, I said, "That's why I haven't made a fuss about it. That, and the book is more important to me. I like my jacket, but I wouldn't go on a treasure hunt like this for it, and it doesn't upset me too much to give it up as a gift. But I mean, it *was* technically stolen from me, so..."

The Prince kept stroking his chin for a moment, then frowned. "If this family book is so important to you, my lady, then why did you not simply say so earlier?" he asked. "Why keep your concern a secret? Why go so far as to steal into the city against my orders, especially before you knew what my disposition toward you may be?"

This part, at least, I didn't need to tweak or embellish. "Like you said, I didn't know the first thing about you, or anyone here," I said. "I was new, I was scared, I didn't know what was gonna happen to me, and I didn't trust anyone around me. I still don't trust most of the people I've met, if I'm honest."

"Fair point," Vambrace said with a nod. "And a smart one. I don't know what exchange you made with Cinaedemis to get the investigation you got, but if she knew you were in the market for one specific item of high personal value, no doubt her price would have risen dramatically." He paused, his face thoughtful.

That boded well for me. Time to press the issue. "Besides," I said, "you and General Enkida are both gonna be there, right? It's not like I'll be in any real danger. I've seen you fight, and I've... well, I've seen someone pretending to be Enkida fight. I've heard the hearsay and stories. If this guy could get past the both of you, then we're pretty much all screwed anyway, right?"

Vambrace pursed his lips while he looked at me. "I think I detect some flaws with that logic," he said, then sighed. "But you do have a point in that, and you are clearly adamant in this, folly or not. It would be the height of foolishness to disobey me a third time and seek out a murderer on your own, but I don't trust that means you won't still take that action.

And I do rather appreciate this surcoat," he added more quietly as he tugged at the hem of my jacket, rubbing the denim in his fingers. "Very well, Lady Morgan. Against my better judgment, I will allow you to accompany the general and I while we look into this matter."

"Yes!" I said under my breath, pumping my fist a little. "Thanks. Sire. I appreciate it."

"Don't be too optimistic," Enkida said to the wall while the crank spun in her hand. "This interrogation is merely something of a formality given a few of the details involved, such as the Earthly nature of the victim's goods and the fact that he was the subject of an archdemon's interest at the behest of a human dignitary. Archfiends and generals naturally do not concern themselves overmuch with the details of petty crimes, so neither His Majesty nor myself will be handling this case beyond passing inquiry, nor is there likely much in the way of investigating to be done into a simple murder in the bazaar." She turned to look at me over her shoulder as the elevator began to slow. "And just from the preliminary report I've heard so far, it sounds as though there will not be much left of the dead merchant's shop for you to peruse," she added. "The killer was an Iriate who went on an apparent rampage before he was apprehended. The body was found because the shop drew attention when it caught fire. Most of the inventory was either smashed, burned, or both."

"…Oh," I said, deflating. A mental image of the *Morganomicon* burning to ash filled my mind, and I shuddered. Would a spell book burn like that, or would the magic protect it somehow? I wasn't sure if the book itself was magical at all or if it was just an instruction manual to magic, but I *did* know it was old and dry and the pages felt brittle as autumn leaves when I turned them, none of which were points in its favor.

No, Morgan! You've been grasping at optimism this long, don't stop yet! Maybe the book wasn't in his shop when it burned. Maybe it had already been sold on. That would be one more hurdle to jump, sure, but I'd take a hurdle over a bottomless pit.

The elevator finally stopped and spit us out back in the prince's quarters. I wanted to let Kriseia know my plans had updated, but the door to my room was closed as we passed by it in a quick stride, Vambrace and Enkida both in an official-looking hurry. Ah well, she'd figure it out when

I didn't come back for a while. Truth be told, I was in the biggest hurry of the three of us to see this done.

I might have thought the ruler of Hell would travel in style when he left the palace — astride a giant flaming horse, say, or riding in a palanquin made from the bones of his enemies and carried by a retinue of ripped, oiled-up Iriate bearers. But no, when we left Pandemonium by a now-familiar route toward the city, we were still on foot. It was a quicker walk, at least, since now instead of having to invisibly dodge through the crowds, they simply stopped and parted for us, bowing to their archfiend.

We passed through the opulent Superbiate district of Luciferis, climbed the steep steps up out of the crater's epicenter, and set off between Beelzebubis and Asmodeusis (Asmodesius? Asmodeosusis? Orgytown) all at the same determined stride, though I was panting and falling behind the other two after getting halfway up the street stairs. Living in this place for any length of time was great cardio, I had to give it that. I thought I'd been in decent shape just with all the walking around my college campus, but Dis was kicking my ass. On the bright side, my calves were going to be rock solid by the time I got out of here. *If* I got out of —

No. None of that, Morgan. Stay positive.

That attempt at positivity took another hit, though, when we finally reached the bridge leading to the Avaritiate market district of Mammonis. Even before we started across it, I could see the smoke rising in the distance. And if it was still rising, that meant the fire was still burning.

"That where we're going?" I panted, drawing up behind the other two and nodding toward the smoke.

"That's the place," Enkida said without turning. "I'm finally taking you where you asked me to, m'lady."

"Thanks," I grumped, falling behind again. "Can't wait."

Despite the fire nearby (relatively nearby, anyway, for a city this big), the ever-bustling crowds of the bazaar didn't seem too thin or concerned. It wasn't until we were on the same street as the burning shop in question that we noticed any difference, with the bulk of the crowds clustered around metal barriers sectioning off a block of street on either side of a squat, stone-and-canvas building that was the source of the smoke. A medley of armored Iriates mixed with Avaritiates in fluttering robes rushed back and forth between the smoldering shop and a massive metal column that stood about ten feet tall in the center of the road, a spout in the front pouring water into the buckets and bowls carried by the apparent fire brigade. Two more giant metal water basins lay on their side against a wall further down the street, their spouts open but only dripping. They'd been at this for a while, then. How the heck did they get those massive water containers out here without a truck or a cart in sight?

"This seems to be in hand, at least," said Enkida as she shoved her way into the gawking crowd, this one slower to part for her and the prince owing to the spectacle in front of them. "The report I heard mentioned a wall of fire here. All the flammable goods must have been used up already."

"General," said one of the firefighting Iriates, breaking away from the water brigade and walking over to us. He stopped before Enkida and clapped a hand to his chest. "And… your highness?" he added when he spied Vambrace, his head dropping in an impromptu bow.

"His highness and his guest were curious about the contents of this shop," the general explained. "Though that may be a moot point now, it seems. Report, soldier."

The Iriate rose from his bow, his eyes sweeping me briefly with the same curiosity everyone else had when they saw me for the first time. I'd grown used to it by now. "Fire singed the neighboring structures, but no major damage there," he said to Enkida. "Replace some of the outer stonework and it should be fine. The site of the blaze itself, though, I would reckon beyond repair. The fire's contained now, mostly just smoldering and putting off smoke. We should have it drowned entirely here shortly. I'd estimate the building will need to just be torn down after that, knock in the walls and start over from foundation."

"Anyone been inside yet?" Enkida asked. "Anything likely to be salvageable?"

The Iriate turned to look over his shoulder at the water chain, then stepped in closer to the general and lowered his voice. "One of ours checked inside as far as was possible with the smoke and the heat," he said, his voice a low grumble. "And no, almost certainly not. Everything looks like ashes and glass shards and a few bits of snapped and twisted metal. Perhaps a few very small, sturdy trinkets may have survived, but you'd have to go digging in the rubble for them. Don't tell the Avaritiates that yet, though, please," he added with another glance backward. "Some of them jumped in to help to save their own spaces, but I gather most of them are thinking to pick over the remains once it's safe enough. I'll let them learn there's no spoils to be had once the job is done."

Enkida nodded. "Good to hear," she said. "As you were." The other Iriate clapped a hand over his chest again and turned back to overseeing the firefighting.

Good to hear? Not for me. If the book was in there, well, not anymore it wasn't. Which meant the most I could hope for now was that someone else had already bought my book of highly illegal magic. As far as best-case scenarios went, I'd had better.

Stay positive, Morgan, I kept telling myself, chanting it over and over in my head like a mantra while I dug my nails into my elbows and watched the thick clouds of black smoke rise into the blood red sky. *Stay fucking positive.*

We slipped back through the crowd of onlookers to a less crowded market street, then Enkida turned to Vambrace. "Well, Sire?" she asked.

"Well," said the prince, looking at me. "The merchant is dead, his shop is gone. I still don't see the point, but the Lady Morgan wishes to speak with the man who caused all of this. So." He turned to Enkida with a shrug. "Take us to the wall, General, if you please."

"If I please, Sire?" Enkida said, smiling slightly. "That is rather a polite order for a public appearance. The Lady Morgan seems to be having an interesting effect on our archfiend."

The prince raised an eyebrow. "Do you object, General?" he asked.

Enkida shook her head. "I am merely making an observation, sir," she said. "I have no opinion one way or the other. Just so long as you realize yourself, Sire," she added, voice lowered slightly.

Vambrace pursed his lips. "I do now," he said, glancing around. "I will keep it in mind, but I see no issue with the matter. The wall, General."

Enkida nodded. "My Prince," she said, then turned and led us down the street toward the city's outer rings.

I fell in close beside Vambrace. "That seems a bit paranoid, doesn't it?" I asked quietly. "You can't be nice in public?"

"To a degree," he said as quietly. "Don't worry, my lady, I have been reading this city for ages. I know what image to present to it."

I made no reply. His public image wasn't what I was worried about.

I followed the both of them out of the merchant circle, up the next staircase, and through Belphegoris, stepping around the Acediate residents shuffling down the street or slumped against the crumbling walls. As we made our way deeper into the sloth district, Enkida also slowed from the purposeful stride she'd kept up since leaving the palace to a more casual walking pace. The prince followed suit, looking ahead but with a slightly unfocused gaze, like he was staring through his immediate surroundings to some further point. Was the lazy atmosphere of the place catching? I hadn't had that problem when I'd come through here last time. I was probably just reading too much into it, but—

A memory sprung up suddenly, arresting my attention. Three Iriate soldiers stomping down this same dirty, peaceful road toward the city's outer rim, each one dragging a length of thick chain behind them. Each chain ended in a thick, wide metal band clamped around the chest or hips or legs of a fourth Iriate being dragged down the street behind the other three, thrashing impotently in his full-body shackles and screaming angrily, wordlessly. The roar of his voice and the rattling of his chains were the only sounds to be heard for miles, his shouts echoing throughout the district as his captors drug him away and out of sight.

I stopped in the street and frowned at the thought. Out of sight? But I had been heading in this same direction last time I had come through here. Wouldn't I have been following them? No, I thought, probing the memory again; I had been lying on a pile of soft cloth in my den, watching the procession through a gap in the curtains. I'd been curious, but following to find out what was going on would have meant getting up, and I had just rolled over and gotten comfortable—

My head snapped up, back to the present. Vambrace and Enkida had both stopped and were looking back at me. "My lady?" the prince asked.

I had never seen those Iriates before in my life, I realized. My walk through Belphegoris earlier had been completely uneventful but for a couple attempts at conversation with some Acediates while I was tracking my book. More importantly, my walk earlier had been a *walk*. At no point did I find a soft spot of ground out of the way and lie down to rest.

So then… why the hell was I remembering something I didn't remember? And if it wasn't my own memory, whose was it, and what was it doing in my head?

The bafflement must have shown on my face. Vambrace smiled at it, while Enkida frowned with a grunt. "Alright," she called, casting her gaze over our surroundings. "Which one of you projected at the human woman?"

An Acediate sitting on a bench under an awning about ten feet away slowly looked up at us. "Sorry," it croaked. "Missed."

Enkida's frown deepened to a scowl. "Were you aiming at me or his majesty?" she asked.

The Acediate shrugged at about a third of the speed of a normal shrug.

The general sighed. "Then pick a target next time," she ordered. "The lady is new here. We don't need your type confusing her unnecessarily."

The Acediate only nodded and slumped further into its seat.

None of it explained anything. "What just—?" I began, but the prince swept up beside me and linked his arm with mine, pulling me forward as we continued our now-leisurely stroll with the general.

When we were about half a block away and out of sight of the Acediate Enkida had scolded, Vambrace leaned in closer. "I told you I had an Acediate spy network reporting events around my domain to me, yes?" he asked under his voice. "It seems as though you just received such a report yourself."

"I just remembered something that I know I wasn't there for," I said. "As clearly as if I was watching it happen again, for the first time."

Vambrace nodded. "An Acediate talent," he said. "They can extend their awareness beyond their immediate surroundings to anywhere within their range of sight or hearing, and project that awareness into others within their range. That includes their own thoughts and feelings as well as whatever actual events they observe."

My eyes widened, and I felt like I about had a heart attack. "They're mind readers?" I squeaked. If the Prince had spies that could read all of my secret treasonous thoughts, I was fucked.

Vambrace just chuckled at my surprise. "No, nothing like that," he said. "More the opposite of that. They can put their thoughts into others' minds to be read, but it only works in one direction. Unless you are an Acediate yourself, if you want to share your own thoughts with them, you have to do it the old fashioned way."

"Oh," I said, sighing in relief. "Good."

"Indeed," said the prince. "Your modesty is safe, my lady. As safe as it can be amongst demon society, at any rate."

"Is that why this place is so quiet?" I asked, gesturing to the silent slums around us. "Everyone just talks to each other in their heads?"

"That, and Acediates are never exactly raucous even at their worst," said Vambrace. "When you don't need to move your body to move your perceptions, or even open your mouth to hold whole conversations, you can afford to be more sedentary than other races. And when you can receive the thoughts of someone up the street from you and then share them with someone further down the street from you without ever moving a muscle, you're a perfect candidate for sentry duty or quiet surveillance. No faster way to relay information than at the speed of pure thought."

Holy shit. And I had thought trying to explain mobile phones to this guy would be difficult, but he was already linking demon minds together like living cell towers. "Is that why there are sloth demons just lying around the palace halls tucked into corners and behind stuff?" I asked.

"You noticed, did you?" he said with a smile. "Congratulations. Most of my subjects don't, or if they do, they forget about it later on; or if they don't, they don't care in the first place. Demonic nature tends toward obsession — everyone is too wrapped up in their own pursuits and desires to devote any attention to those sitting quietly and uneventfully on the fringes, seemingly useless and with nothing to offer anyone. You likely paid attention only because everything is still new and strange to you, and I'm willing to bet they've slipped even your mind lately as you acclimate and find your own business to go about."

He had me there. I *had* stopped noticing the furry gray squatters in the halls ever since my first meandering excursion through the palace. I'd absolutely be paying more attention now, though. "So nobody knows about them?" I asked. "That doesn't sound likely. If it's a talent the whole bunch of them has, it can't be a secret. Whether or not you care, the first time you see a bunch of telepathic demons sitting around watching you, you've gotta know what's going on."

"Oh, they know," said Vambrace. "They know the Acediate sentries are part of palace security, same as the Iriates patrolling the halls and stationed at entranceways. And they know that our soldiers and guards relay orders and alerts between posts through Acediate awareness channels. That's how our dear general can command her forces while also serving at my side as my right hand, or at yours as a personal guard."

"I'm your dear now, Sire?" Enkida asked from in front of us without looking back.

Vambrace ignored her. "But nobody besides myself and the general knows just how wide our surveillance network extends, or who all is in it, or the full scope of what they're looking out for, or who exactly has access to it. And like I said, most don't pay attention, or they lose interest. Or if they are aware they're being watched, they behave themselves better while they're in public, which I am fine with."

Government surveillance, huh? Good to know. I'd be sure to do all my plotting and shady deals with archdemons in privacy from now on. "So that mental image the guy back there shoved into my brain?" I asked.

"That guy back there was female," said the prince. "Which is harder to tell with Acediates, admittedly, and doesn't really matter either way unless you're a Luxuriate. And the projection she showed you was our murder suspect being hauled off by the city guard down this same street. There is a standing order in Belphegoris to report crimes and arrests to passing soldiery like our general or myself. Seems she looped you in as well out of laziness." He nodded down the street in front of us. "We keep a lot of prison space within the Wall, which can make locating specific prisoners time consuming. But if we find and keep to the route his arresting officers took, we can find his cell more quickly."

That was an arrest I'd been shown? Good lord, the guy had been dragged through the dirt by three other people. It seemed a tad excessive, until I remembered the raw savagery of the Iriate warrior that had thrown himself screaming at Vambrace in the palace coliseum. Maybe all the shackles and chains involved were police brutality gone overboard, or maybe they really were necessary. I wasn't sure which idea was more concerning.

Still, judging by all the screaming he'd been doing, at least this guy still had his throat intact after the cops grabbed him, unlike the arrest I had actually witnessed last time I came this way. I shuddered at the real memory. Lucky I hadn't eaten in a while.

After that, whatever errant psychic directions were being tossed our way all went to Vambrace or Enkida, and I followed behind without another intrusion on my senses. Our suspected murderer's path was straightforward enough, and before long, we reached the bridge that connected Belphegoris with Amonis over the river. Like last time, the silence slowly gave way to the rushing of water below, then to the general hammering din of the town ahead, clanging metal and crackling fire and a wide variety of unseen shouting. Why were so many people always constantly screaming in this part of the city? I didn't get it.

The heat couldn't be helping their moods, though. I'd half forgotten about it until we stepped off the bridge and into a wall of baking air that smelled faintly of burning coal and sweat. On the plus side, I was in a dress this time, and one that was lighter and airier than a black t-shirt. On the downside, the massive train around my legs and dragging behind me gave me the feeling of being swaddled in blankets from the waist down, which was suddenly less than ideal. I was going to need another bath and another change of laundry when we got back to the palace.

Enkida didn't seem affected at all, of course. If Vambrace felt it in his mail shirt, my jacket, and who knew how many other layers, he didn't show it. I tried my best not to either, breathing deeply through my nose in lieu of panting out loud, occasionally wiping sweat that threatened to run into my eyes otherwise while my legs quietly roasted inside my gown.

There were no sudden random stabbings or dismemberments I had to witness this time, thankfully. Whether that was down to the archfiend and his general's presence or just dumb luck, I didn't know, but I appreciated the difference. With all the clanging and shouting carrying through the streets in every direction around us, it sounded as though we were only ever one turn in the road away from walking into a full-blown war zone. Neither Vambrace nor Enkida seemed concerned, though, so I put that down as just part of the cultural ambience.

As we walked, the cluster of buildings gradually thinned out, from cramped, rambling jumbles of stone and metal shacks to larger single structured with actual space between the buildings — until, at some point, the process reversed itself, with buildings squished and clustered together more and more as the wall loomed closer and closer, like they were all fighting to huddle in its shadow.

The sheer size of the wall would have been a lot more impressive if I hadn't already gotten familiar with Pandemonium's impossible bulk towering ever-present in the Dis skyline behind us. Still, that wasn't a fair comparison, and the wall was still daunting in its own right, especially how it kept growing in the distance when I thought we were almost there. We stepped over the edge of its shadow at last and into darker, blessedly cooler streets, and I still couldn't see the base of the thing in the distance. That took another couple of blocks of walking. With the bottom and the top both finally discernible, I estimated the wall to be about ten stories or so tall.

It was still hard to accurately judge, though, with the mess of structures shoved up against it and climbing up the side, growing taller nearer the wall itself and shrinking as they sprawled out away from it. It looked like someone had come through with a giant broom and swept all the buildings of this part of town into the corner. I couldn't tell where one ended and the next began, or even if they were separate buildings in the first place or just the world's biggest, most slapdash strip mall.

And then I realized that what I thought was the base of the wall we were approaching was actually the shallow edge of this sloping mess of construction. Two massive doors of black metal came into view at our end, set in a thick, relatively short wall of stone roofed with beaten metal shingles like armored scales. The roof sloped up into the distance past the door to join the rest of the sprawl, the whole top of it sporting hundreds of what looked like tall, scattered chimneys, each tapering to —

Wait. No, not chimneys. *Spikes*. The roof of the sprawl beneath this side of the wall was covered in massive metal spikes like a giant mecha hedgehog, the tips slowly smoking into the shadow —

Wait. Okay, so the spikes *were* still chimneys. A short sea of giant, jagged, smoking, spikey chimneys.

What in the hell, Hell?

I would have asked Vambrace or Enkida about it, but by the time my brain had finished processing and trying to make sense of everything it was seeing, we were at the big black gate at the end of our street. A pair of Iriate soldiers stood guard at either side, with two more on the roof above, looking out over the street from a crow's nest-looking watch post attached halfway up one of the chimney spikes. All of them watched our approach, but the doors themselves split and began slowly grinding open before we'd reached them, the soldiers on the ground clapping hands to chest and bowing their heads when we got close. The archfiend and the general both just nodded and strode by. I did the same, under the curious glances of the rising soldiers. One of them actually dipped his head back down, to the surprise of the soldier beside him who fumbled and tried to follow suit.

They still didn't know what to make of me, then. Whether or not they'd heard of my new token ambassadorial title yet, here I was, human, keeping company with their boss and their boss's boss. I was unexpected and confusing, standing out but acting like I blended in.

It was the kind of attention that bothered me back home. Here, though, I was still trying to think how I could use it to my advantage. Maybe Gilderos's murderer would also stumble under my questionably novel power. Maybe I could bluff my way into working out a deal.

Past the black iron doors, the air turned humid and stifling again. Not as hot as the inner ring of the district, walking the baking streets between smithies and their furnaces, but also not as cool as the open jumble in the shadow of the wall. We walked a straight stone corridor into the inner building, past crude torches lighting unadorned walls and the gradual upward slope of the ceiling overhead. A short ways in, the hall opened to what looked like the lobby of a medieval police station. Two more corridors led off from the right and left sides of the room, while the back wall sported a dozen more single doors of the same thick, black metal as the front gate. In the middle of the space, under the light of a hanging iron brazier, sat a massive wooden desk with a length of paper stretching across it, both ends scrolled up thickly around spindles set into the wood. At the moment, nobody was visible behind it.

That didn't stop Enkida from striding up to it and smacking the top with an open palm, sending the whole desk shuddering. "We need the location of a recent prisoner," she announced to the empty air.

"What?" a shrill voice grumped from somewhere behind the desk. Out from underneath it scrambled a short, lanky Invidiate with another thick, loosely wrapped scroll cradled in her arms. "Oh. General." With a scowl and a distinct lack of any deference to Enkida, the Invidiate clambered up to its feet on top of the desk. She dumped the scroll she held into one corner before turning to the open one attached to the desk. "Who?" she asked.

"Don't know the name yet," said Enkida, "but they were apprehended not long back in Mammonis, on charges of murdering a merchant and burning down his shop."

"Hrm," the Invidiate desk clerk mumbled, tracing a thin finger over the exposed ream of parchment. "House?"

"Iria," said the general.

"Iria?" the clerk repeated, looking up with a frown, all the pupils in its faceted eyes focused on Enkida. "One of your own? Apprehended? Huh." She reached over to one of the rolled ends of the paper and began spinning it with one hand, the other tracing the writing that scrolled by on the open middle. "How many limbs missing?"

"According to reports, none," said Enkida.

"Eh?" The Invidiate stopped and looked up again. "What, they wait til he raged himself out and jump him from behind or something?"

"I don't know the details yet," Enkida answered, tapping her finger against the wood of the desk. "But an Iriate male, apprehended recently, fully intact, and he was brought this way. Shouldn't be hard to narrow down, should it?"

"Yeah, no, not when you put it like that. Why's our General wanna see him anyway?" She looked up again, appeared to notice Vambrace and myself for the first time, and frowned harder. "And what do His Majesty and his new human pet want with him?" she asked.

"Pet?" I repeated, crossing my arms and glaring at the Invidiate clerk. I didn't have to fake the offense in my tone too much. I did have to ignore the sidelong look Vambrace gave me, though, if only for appearances.

The desk clerk cowed a little at that, which was good to note. She cowed a lot more, though, when Enkida leaned over into her attention again. "Are any of these questions required to find our suspect's name and location?" she asked, her voice calm but clipped, her finger still tapping on the wood. Tapping a lot faster and harder now, though.

The Invidiate cleared her throat. "No, not as such," she said. "Just curious. It's not—"

"I suggest curiosity be saved for later, then," the general interrupted. "After you've done your job, for instance." Her voice was still calm, but there was a new noise accompanying it, a sort of quiet, rhythmic scritching. I leaned around her to see her finger still tapping, and slowly carving a divot in the wood with each tap, little bits of splinters and sawdust jumping up around her clawed nail. Her face, meanwhile, just looked blank and bored.

The clerk wasn't watching her face, though, just the little hole she was digging in the mahogany. "Yeah," the Invidiate said after a moment. "Good idea. Okay, let's see…" A few seconds of frantic scrolling through names later, she tapped the parchment and cleared her throat. "Looks like your best bet is this guy Dorgagovek. Iriate, newest one on my record, no notes about any mutilations to speak of. Over in center marsh block. Probably ground level, if he's still got all his arms and legs. Less likely to tear out the walls that way."

Enkida said nothing, only turned and headed toward one of the side passages with Vambrace at her heels. The Invidiate clerk snorted, her glare passing over them both then lingering a moment on me. She also made no other reply, just snatched up the scroll she'd been carrying before and hopped back down off the desk with it, out of sight. It looked identical to the scroll of suspect arrest records attached to the desktop. Was she just under there reading a phonebook of prisoner names? Is that what Invidiates did for fun around here?

I didn't bother asking, just followed the prince and Enkida into the side corridor. Though I did bother leaning toward Vambrace and asking, "Center marsh block?"

"This complex encircles the entire inner perimeter of the wall," he said. "There are a lot of blocks to keep track of, most of them named after the most prominent scenery from atop their section of wall. It's easier to delineate that way than a bunch of numbers in a circle."

"So, there's a big marsh out past the city near here?" I asked. "I thought I heard everything past the wall was dangerous wasteland."

"Oh, it is," said the prince. "But that danger comes in a variety of flavors, one of which is marshy. There's also a gorge, some woods, a molten plain, volcanic mountains, rocky desert, stuff like that."

"Ah," I said. Just needed an ice world and an underwater level and we'd have the whole roster here. "The Acediate who found me when I first got here said he found me out past the wall," I said after we'd walked in silence for a moment. "Wonder where in the wasteland I landed?"

"Not in the marsh," said Enkida. "Otherwise you'd have drowned first, or been eaten. Likely both, in either order."

"That bad, huh?" I replied with a shudder. "Maybe the woods, then."

"Doubt it," said the general. "You seem like you've still got all your organs and internal fluids. And you haven't been eaten."

I gulped. "The mountains?" I asked.

Enkida shook her head. "Flayed, then eaten."

I winced, then rubbed at my bare arms, suddenly very conscious of my own skin. "The desert."

"Poisoned and/or crushed," said Enkida. We walked in silence for another few seconds. "Oh, and eaten."

The Prince sighed. "You probably washed up not far from the wall itself," he said. "Many Acediates turn to scavenging, yes, and their perception projection helps them stay safer by scouting ahead of and around themselves, but anything set on finding and killing them will still likely succeed. The man who found you would know better than to stray too far from Dis without a protective envoy. And, as our general is so helpfully pointing out, process of elimination means there are few other places you may have been found alive and intact."

"Cool," I said. "Hey, so, just throwing this out there, I don't think I'll need to go on any field trips while I'm here. I'm fine just staying in city limits, thanks."

"Good," said Vambrace with a chuckle. "Because I was beginning to worry you would be uncontainable. It's nice to know you have some sense of boundaries after all."

I decided to let that slide.

The hall we walked now curved slightly, though not as much as the perimeter halls of Pandemonium. On the walls, lit sconces alternated with more heavy metal doors, all of them closed except for the brief moments when someone, usually an Iriate or Invidiate, passed through one on their way to another. At those times, it was a crapshoot what noises issued from the few seconds of open door — whether it was normal everyday shouting, the extra large bellowing of a pissed off Iriate, or, a few times, the loud, out of place moaning of someone having a notedly better experience than the people around them. Did they allow conjugal visits here? Or did they just have some extra kinky Luxuriates locked away back there getting off on the prison vibe?

Probably both, come to think of it.

The hall ended in another set of doors flanked by two posted Iriate guards, who opened them at our approach and did that fist-to-chest salute thing as we drew even. "I'm looking for a prisoner," Enkida said, pausing in the doorway. "Dorgagovek, Iriate male, new addition, no major injuries."

"Oh, *that* guy," one of the guards replied with a snort. "Third door on the right, General, then in one of the center cells. You'll know him immediately, unfortunately." His hand tightened on the haft of the mace in his hand. "If it were anyone else but you, ma'am, I'd wish them good luck keeping patient."

Enkida smiled. "We'll see if we can get him to behave for you," she said, then kept walking. We followed her to the third door on the right, which she swung open, and we stepped through to—

"—RIP YOUR STUPID HEADS OFF AND BURY THEM IN YOUR ASSES IF YOU'RE NOT GOING TO USE THEM, YOU SHIT-STAINED MEARC SPAWN! YOU FUCKING HEAR ME?! SET ME FREE, DAMN YOU!"

—to a head-splitting voice that ricocheted off the walls and slammed into both my ears hard enough that it nearly knocked me off my feet.

"I think we've found our man," Vambrace said in the pause that followed the impossibly loud voice's threat, right before it started wordlessly screaming in blind rage. I clamped my hands over my ears, half expecting to feel blood dribbling out of them. The gesture did nothing to help.

Thankfully, Enkida did. I stood where I was by the door, as far from the voice as I could be without leaving, and watched as the general strode quickly down the corridor to a cell about halfway down. Her arm whipped out and slammed into the prison bars hard enough to dent them, the clang reverberating off the walls and even shaking the floor slightly. The screaming voice instantly shut off — not, I suspect, because the clanging had startled him, relatively quiet as it had been compared to his outburst, but because Enkida now stood stock still and glaring through the dented bars, frowning slightly and with her bottom fangs peeking through her lips.

The quiet that immediately followed was nearly as deafening as the shouting had been. I pulled my hands from my ears, hearing only the quiet rattling of metal chains and some muted moaning from the other cells around us as the prince and I walked past them toward Enkida. For a moment, I worried that maybe this was a sign my hearing had been noticeably damaged, until we passed a cell with a thin Superbiate man lying stretched out on a cot in the back, his fingers digging at his temples. He looked sidelong at us as we passed and scowled. "By Lucifer's balls, can we get that one a muzzle?" he grumbled, then winced and returned to rubbing his head. I heard him well enough, at least, so I wasn't deaf yet, just deafened.

Two more Iriate guards were in the cell block with us, both of them coming to stand with the general, who stepped back from the bars as we drew up. Behind them, the Iriate man who'd been dragged through the street in the memory I'd been shown hung suspended in midair, lengths of thick chain stretched taut between him and about a dozen points in the ceiling, walls, and floor. He was still in the full-body shackles he'd been wearing in the memory, now with an iron band around his forehead and a chain attaching it to the ceiling, holding even his head and neck immobile. He glared out at all of us from his cocoon of steel restraints, his lips curled back over bared fangs grinding together so hard I think I could hear them, every vein of his neck bulging and throbbing.

Again, my first thought was that this was inhumane overkill for one prisoner. But if his body was even half as powerful as his lungs were and he was this pissed off, then I could see the point. So long as he didn't bring the walls down on top of us, attached as he was to every available surface.

"Dorgagovek," said Vambrace, stepping up to the bars. "You've been detained in connection with the murder of the merchant Gilderos and the destruction of—"

"I didn't do it!" he shouted, and my hands reached for my ears in reflex. Luckily, it was just a regular-grade shout, which was downright conversational after his last tirade. "That's what I keep trying to say to these morons! Whatever it looks like, I'm innocent! You can't damn me for something I didn't do—"

"No one is damning you yet, you sniveling moron!" one of the other guards standing with us snapped, stomping her foot so hard I think I heard the stone floor crack. "You see anyone dragging out a chopping block? *We* keep telling *you*, you're just the prime suspect, not—"

"That's *garm shit!*" Dorgagovek shouted, growing louder again now as he tried impotently to thrash in his bonds and barely managed a slight wiggle. "*I didn't do it!* I'M FUCKING INNOCENT, YOU—"

Quick as a whip, Enkida's hands shot out again, and in one smooth motion, she grabbed the bars she'd dented a minute ago and yanked them back into place with a screech and a clang. Dorgagovek and the other guard both fell silent again as the general took a long, slow breath through her nose. "Your guilt or innocence will be decided soon enough in the course of our investigation," she said quietly, releasing the bars, which were now perfectly straight once again except for the imprint of her fingers left in the metal. "In the meantime, the Lady Morgan would like to ask you some questions of her own relating to more personal matters. You will answer them calmly and civilly, or else I will have you gagged and muzzled for the duration of your stay here after we leave."

"*Thank* you," the Superbiate prisoner from a couple cells back called out tiredly.

"Now," the general continued, turning to the other guards beside us. "You two, leave us for the moment. We don't need his animosity distracting him anymore than it already is. Lady Morgan, ask your questions. Prisoner," she added, narrowing her eyes at Dorgagovek, "behave." Then she stepped back, and the other guards grumbled and left, leaving me at the forefront with a pissed off murder suspect glaring daggers down at me through the much-abused bars of his cell.

I stepped forward, trying not to seem intimidated — and found, to my slight surprise, that I wasn't. Between his layers of imprisonment and General Enkida and the Prince backing me up, I knew I was safe enough. But beyond that, I'd seen enough scary and violent shit by now that I think I was getting inured to it. Interrogating an enraged murder suspect and a literal demon in a max security prison didn't have the same thrill it would have a month ago. It was gonna take something bigger to rattle me at this point.

So with more composure and authority than I thought I would be able to muster, I crossed my arms and met the snarling prisoner's gaze. "If you didn't kill the merchant Gilderos," I said, "does that mean you never met him after all?"

Dorgagovek gave another angry wiggle. "I met the fucker," he growled. "I just didn't kill him. I bought a wasp nest from him a while back, but it was a dud. Whole swarm died almost as soon as I got 'em home. I went back to complain — raged and threatened the guy, sure, but that's it. He was still breathing when I left him."

"Wait, you bought a wasp nest?" I asked. "Why would… why?"

"Wanted the venom for a personal project," he said. "What's it to you?"

"Personal…?" No, on second thought, best not to get dragged down that rabbit hole. I shook my head, then turned to the prince. "Hell has wasps too?"

"Hell is their natural habitat," said Vambrace. "They originated here, but they bled over. Earth just made room for them after a while."

I blinked, my gaze slipping to the floor. "Fuckin' knew it," I muttered. And of course I'd left my emergency epinephrine at home. If I survived demons and hellbeast-infested wastelands just to die to a wasp sting while I was here, I was gonna be pissed.

"My lady?" said Vambrace, gesturing to the cell. "If you would."

"Oh, sorry," I said, turning back to the prisoner, who now looked confused as well as impatient. "Right. So, you were at Gilderos's shop a couple of times. I'd heard he had stuff from Earth for sale there. Is that right?"

Dorgagovek frowned. "I don't know," he said. "I wasn't looking for Earth stuff, and he didn't point any out to me. If any of that shit he was peddling was Earthish, I couldn't tell."

"Do you know if he had any books?" I asked. "Really old ones. One in particular. It's a kind of brownish gray, and the pages—"

"I don't know," he snarled again, with another angry wiggle. "I wasn't looking for books the first time, and I wasn't looking for anything the second time, except to get my swindled souls back. How does any of this help me get free?"

"It doesn't," the prince answered for me. "That's not why we're here right now."

Dorgagovek wiggled harder. "Then what does it matter what I say?" he growled. "I answer your garm shit questions and then those garm shit guards come back just to—"

"Focus," I said, stepping forward and gripping the bars between us. "Please. Listen, I don't know if you killed the guy or not, but if you didn't, then helping us out shows you're willing to play nice, which only makes you look less guilty, right?"

He stopped his wiggling and glared at me. "What, you believe me, human?" he asked. "Someone finally gonna listen to me?"

"I don't know if I believe you or not," I said. "I don't know enough of the details to form an opinion, and I'm not here to prosecute or defend you anyway. But throwing a fit instead of answering questions about the event in question looks suspicious, don't you think?"

Dorgagovek said nothing to that, just grit his teeth and kept glaring. But he was glaring sidelong at the wall now instead of at me, which I took for a good sign.

"Please," I said again. "Try to remember. The most recent time you were at his shop, when you say you just yelled and left without killing him or destroying the place. Can you recall any details of the shop itself?"

He growled wordlessly, then fell silent for a second. "I didn't kill the cheating scaleskin," he grumbled after a moment. "But… I never said I didn't wreck the place."

I frowned. "Wait, then," I said. "You mean you *are* the one that burned his shop down?"

"What? No!" he shouted, thrashing again. "I smashed some of his shit, but no one told me it caught fire! That wasn't me either, I didn't—"

"Focus!" I shouted, and pounded on the bars myself. They didn't budge or even wiggle under my fists, of course — if anything, I think I bruised my hands — but the effect was somehow similar to Enkida's outburst. Dorgagovek immediately stopped his shouting and thrashing to stare quietly down at me.

Surely, he didn't think I had the general's clout. Did he? Did I? No way. Maybe I'd just convinced him I was his ally here, the good cop to everyone else's bad cop.

Whatever the case, it worked. Acutely aware of Vambrace and Enkida watching intently behind me, I continued. "Tell me what happened, then," I said slowly. "If you wrecked the place, you had to get a good look at it while you were doing it. Try and remember the details. And if you didn't kill him or start any fires, then you shouldn't have anything to try and hide."

Dorgagovek growled under his breath again, then took a deep breath and released it in an angry huff. "The merchant was in the back when I kicked his door in," he said. "I shouted for him, but he didn't come out. There was something in the middle of the shop floor, between the front door and the back. I think it was a statue of someone, I don't know. The memories are all red and hazy. I knocked it over on my way to the back door, stomped over it, shattered it pretty good. Then the merchant came out, and he starts yelling back at me about whatever it is I just smashed."

The Iriate paused to take another deep, angry breath. "Wanted to rip his scaley head off right there, but I knew better, even pissed. I told him he ripped me off, I wasn't going to stand for it, I wanted my damned souls back. He told me he wasn't giving 'em back, not his fault the wasps he sold me died, tried to say it was my fault. Then he says I owe him *more* cuz of whatever it was I just smashed to get him out there." He thrash-wiggled again, but at this point, I think it was just instinct. "Everything got hotter and hazier after that. I grabbed him and started ripping at his robes, trying to find his soul case, just take my money off of him; but I couldn't find it, and I started to think if I had the guy in my hands much longer, I really would start tearing pieces off of him. So I threw him across the room before the urge overtook. He hit a shelf of… stuff, I'm not sure what. Lot of glass and porcelain stuff, I think, cuz I remember it smashing with this really satisfying, tinkling crunch, lots of shiny shards of shit raining down while the wood crumpled and the shelf collapsed."

Good lord, and he's *this* sure he didn't kill the guy? His story wasn't doing him any favors so far. It also wasn't helping me yet, though, so I stayed quiet and tried to listen with a straight face.

"Then I think, maybe he's stashed his money somewhere in his shop," Dorgagovek continued, fangs bared at the memory. "So I grabbed the first countertop my hands landed on and ripped. I remember… lots of cloth flying then, a lot of fabric fluttering over me and getting in my way, pissing me off more. I think that was all just clothing. Ripped some of that to shreds, then kicked a trunk across the room. It hit a wall and burst open, and a bunch of… parchment?" His grimace turned down into a frown. "Paper and shit like that, I think. A lot of fluttering. Maybe there were books in there? I didn't notice any, but I wasn't looking. Nothing out of the ordinary caught my eye, though, cuz next thing I know, I've got a spade in my hands, and I'm just swinging wildly. Smashed a mirror, I remember, some glass cases, lots of really good shattering and crunching. Took some chunks of stone out of the floor; I remember tripping over one of the divots. Punched through a wooden support beam at one point, but the ceiling didn't come down like I'd hoped for.

"Then I heard screaming and shouting, I think from the merchant. I remember seeing him scurry away like a pisaca in torchlight. Into the back room, and he slams the door. I threw myself at it for a long time, but it was sturdy, even for as angry as I was. After a while, I started to feel bruising, so I knew my rage was coming down and I was tiring out. I gave up then and left, ripped the door off the hinges on my way out and hurled it down the street. Figured I'd make a formal complaint and let the Houses sort it out for me." He paused at last to sigh. "I was on my way to Avaritia's offices when a bunch of mearc spawn guard cowards ambushed me and chained me up, told me I was wanted for murder. I assume you know the rest."

It took me a moment to find my words again after his story. "So, you didn't kill him," I said at last. "But… holy shit, you really did all that other stuff? And you're still offended that you were arrested?"

Dorgagovek snarled, but gently. "I'll pay the fine for my wrath," he said through grit fangs, "or sit in one of these cells until they decide I've wasted enough of my time to learn a lesson or whatever. But I'm not getting the ax for murdering the cheating fucker, not if I never got the satisfaction of actually splitting his skull in two like I wanted."

I suppose he had a point, but he wasn't helping his case. But I wasn't here for his case. "A trunk full of papers or parchment," I said, half to myself. "It might have been in there, but…" But if it was, then it would have still been in the shop when the fire started. Which meant that it was a pile of ash now.

Which meant I was screwed. Which meant that wasn't an option. There *had* to be another possibility.

"Did you notice anyone else in the shop before you?" I asked the prisoner. "Anyone else there when you first arrived? Anyone looking like they were leaving when you were storming in?"

"There was no one else in there with me, or I would have said so," he growled, growing impatient again. "And how would I know who else might have been there before I was?"

I turned to the prince. "Would anyone know that?" I asked. "Would there be a, a record of customers or something?"

"There would have been," Vambrace answered with a frown. "Though it would have been Gilderos keeping it, which means it's likely gone along with him and his shop."

I spun back to Dorgagovek, grabbing his cell bars to steady the shaking that was starting in my hands. "Okay, then... then can you remember anything about his shop the first time you were there?" I asked. "When you were buying wasps, before you were too angry to pay attention. Do you remember any books in his shop that first time?"

"My lady," said the prince, stepping up behind me and putting a hand on my shoulder. "I don't wish to discourage you, but it seems —"

I shook his hand off and leaned forward until my face was pressed against the bars. "Please, sir," I said, fighting to keep a level voice. "Dorgagovek. You're my last hope here."

Whatever scene I was making, however it looked, I didn't think about it until the chained up Iriate was staring at me as if I were some unpredictable new creature he'd never seen before and wasn't sure yet how dangerous it might be. It had been a while since I'd gotten a look like that from anyone.

A moment later, he sighed, seemingly calm for the first time since I'd met him. "My first visit, huh?" he said. "I remember... yeah, okay. I think there was a shelf of books. I barely glanced at them, but..." He shut his eyes tight and grunted. "Let me see... what did I —?"

He was interrupted by the loud, shrill clanging of bells echoing down the hall outside, followed by a sudden clamor of shouting and the scramble of dozens of booted feet running by. Dorgagovek's eyes shot open wide, and in the cells all around us, the other prisoners began to murmur and stir.

"What?" I asked, looking around us then back at Dorgagovek. "What? What did you remember?"

The prince's hand landed on my shoulder again, this time with a grip that wouldn't be ignored. "Lady Morgan," he said, "your other questions will have to wait for now."

"Why?" I demanded, spinning to face him. "What's happening?"

"Good question," he said, then turned to the guard that came running toward us from the top of the cell block corridor. "What's happening?"

The guard skidded to a stop, then bent forward with her hands on her knees and tried to catch her breath. "Attack," she panted. "On the wall."

"Enkida?" said Vambrace, turning to his general. Truth be told, I'd started to forget she was still here.

"I'll rally the garrison command," she answered, slipping past the panting guard and striding away. "You take the vantage point. Meet you up top, Sire."

"Attack?" I parroted. "Attack by what?" Things were happening too fast for me to offer anything more intelligent at the moment.

Her breath returning, the guard rose back up, looking more worried than I'd ever seen an Iriate look so far. "Garm," she said.

The Prince sighed angrily, his grip on my shoulder tightening. "Shit," he muttered.

Chapter 23: Bloodlust

The whole prison atmosphere had changed. The calm, orderly perimeter halls that had brought us to the cell block were now full of Iriate soldiers rushing past and shouting at each other, the occasional Invidiate or Superbiate or other type of demon just running in quiet panic. The only ones not freaking out were the few Acediates we passed, huddled up in corners out of the way and lost in the shuffle. I wasn't sure if they were calmer or just more resigned to whatever was happening, but evidently even a garm attack couldn't motivate them to be in a hurry.

Speaking of which.

"What's a garm?" I asked the prince as we hurried through the chaos at a brisk stride, his arm around my shoulders urging me on and keeping us from being separated in the traffic.

"Dogs," he said. "Vicious, feral dogs." We turned a corner into a cramped stairwell that wound up in a tight spiral, barely wide enough for two people at a time. The prince stepped in front of me as we mounted it, his grip tight on my wrist as he pulled me along behind him.

"Wild dogs?" I asked, tripping along in his wake while a steady stream of armed soldiers sprinted past us up the stairs. "That's what's attacking? Everyone's freaking out over dogs?"

"Big dogs," Vambrace said.

I gave him a moment to elaborate. "And they're attacking *the* wall?" I asked when he didn't. "This wall we're in right now? Isn't this thing, like, hundreds of feet high?"

"*Very* big dogs," he clarified. "You'll see."

"I will?" I asked. "Wait, why?"

He didn't answer, just kept climbing. I was getting winded trying to keep up. By the time we reached the top of the stairs, I was dizzy as well from all the spiraling.

And then we stepped out through the open portal just in front of the stairs' top landing, and a warm wind hit my face, and I got even dizzier from the view.

It was breezy at the top of the wall, which stretched open out before us, gently curving to my left. In the far distance, near the horizon, it circled back around enough that I could barely see the inner curve of it again, plunging steeply down into the nest of spikey chimneys that had towered over us on our initial walk in.

The wall itself was about the width of a four-lane highway, maybe seventy feet or so, and currently about as busy as one. The Iriates that had been streaming past us on the stairs fanned out up here, most of them scrambling to the long racks of weapons that stretched along the middle of the lane up here before taking up positions along the outer and inner perimeters. Their choice of armament had always seemed random to me before, down on the streets or inside the palace or prison — personal choice, I'd assumed, rather than some standard uniform requirement. Here, though, every Iriate who stopped and stationed themselves on one of the crenellated edges sported the same weapons alongside whatever they'd brought with them: in one hand, a great big fuck-off bow that was nearly as tall as they were (or taller in some cases), barrels full of three-foot arrows beside them, and long, jagged spears propped nearby.

Impossible sizes aside, it made sense, I thought, for the soldiers defending the wall from the outside. But why did the ones facing into the city need that much firepower?

As the prince ushered me onward, I turned to look back into the city itself. Here on the outer rim, Dis sloped down behind and below us in a big bowl of concentric rings, like a Devo hat turned upside down. I could barely make out the cliffs and the circular rivers if I stared at it for a minute, which gave me a rough idea of which district's buildings I was looking at, but otherwise it all ran together from this high up. Luciferis, the Superbiate ring, was especially tiny, sunk down deep in the shadow of the palace like a snow globe village of mini mansions. Pandemonium itself was a crooked obsidian splinter stabbing up through the whole thing, spikey towers sprouting off of it like a bolt of black lightning frozen in place. Even as far out and as high up off the ground as we were now, it still towered over us, hazy red clouds obscuring the summit. If it even had one. It was easy, looking at it from here, to imagine that it just kept climbing forever.

Truth be told, compared to the strange urban sprawl of Dis below us, the land on the other side of the wall was underwhelming. They called it a wasteland for a reason; miles of flat, bare, red-brown dirt spread into the far distance, broken only by the occasional dry scrub or patch of rocks. The terrain only began to vary out near the horizon, where, directly in front of where we'd emerged from the stairwell, the ground sunk into long patches of dark green water, with some shapes that looked like bushy, struggling trees just visible through a soft, white haze of what I assumed was fog. Marsh block, they'd said we were at. That would be their marsh, then, where I would have been drowned and/or eaten, in either order, according to Enkida.

I turned and peered over to the distance behind us, on the right of the marshy horizon. In that direction, the blurry line of fog lightened to more struggling trees, which steadily grew into the thicker, darker tree line of what I took to be a forest. Or whatever passed for a forest in Hell.

I was still looking back that way when we reached another set of steps, and I probably would have tripped right over them if the prince hadn't grabbed me by the wrist again and hurriedly pulled me up behind him once more. These new stairs atop the wall led up a relatively short incline that stretched only halfway along the outside edge of the wall's thoroughfare, the top ending maybe ten more feet off the ground at an elevated platform just wide enough to hold maybe half a dozen people, with more stairs on the far side leading back down. Up here, we could see even more of the activity stretching out on either side of the battlements, including other platforms like this one in the distance, each topped with an Iriate commander shouting orders to the men and women below them and directing the soldiers' movements.

Vambrace wasn't joining in the directing, though. Instead, he stood stock still with his hand still tight around my wrist, staring out away from the city into the land beyond. I turned to follow his gaze to the left of the distant marsh, where —

"Uh, Prince?" I gasped, taking a panicked step back before his grip on my arm caught and stopped me. "The fuck is that?! What the fuck *is that*?!"

I thought I heard him chuckle, but I couldn't be sure, because I couldn't take my eyes off the sight far out ahead of us. Maybe five miles or so away given how high up we were. Not far away enough for my liking.

"Garm," he said. "Big dog."

It was the understatement of the year, but he wasn't wrong. Way out on the rocky plains but galloping closer, tearing furrows in the earth with its claws as it ran, stomping the scrub flat under its paws and uprooting whole scraggly trees as it knocked them out of its way, there came running what looked like a mangy, underfed, *two-story tall* dog, its brown fur matted and streaked with dark red that looked like dried blood, its eyes pitch black but for the glowing points of orange visible even from this distance, its lips pulled back in a wet snarl that showed a mouthful of yellowed fangs, each one at least as long as I was tall. I could hear it growling, I realized, a low rumble I hadn't noticed at first as background noise to the bustle of the soldiers around us. I could feel its approach in the faint tremor under my feet every time one of those Volkswagen-sized paws slapped the ground.

"Does it…" I paused to swallow down some of my panic. "Does it see us?" I asked. "Can it reach us up here?"

"Not if we don't let it," said the prince. "Is that the only one sighted so far?"

I thought he was asking me at first, until a voice behind us said, "So far, yes, your highness." I turned for a moment to look up at the biggest Iriate I'd seen yet, about eight foot tall and nearly half as broad, just a slab of bulging red muscle peering over our heads at the massive beast closing in on us. "We're not yet sure if the rest of the pack is nearby, trying to flank us, or if this one is just a stray that wondered in too close."

"One way to find out," said the prince. "Is the general up here yet?"

"No sign of her as yet, Sire," the boulder of a soldier behind us answered.

"She'll just have to catch up then," said Vambrace. "Better to keep whatever happens off the wall as long as possible." He walked forward, right up to the edge of the battlements, and rested his hands on the crenellating stone before nodding at the giant dog. "Take it out."

"*Archers!*" the massive soldier bellowed, which sent me cringing away with my hands over my ears. He wasn't as loud as the fully pissed Dorgagovek had been down in his cell, but he was still right behind me. My poor ears were going to need a whole day of silence to recover after all this.

All around us, the soldiers facing out toward the wastes and the dog monster planted their massive bows. There was a short group din of metal scraping metal as a dozen or more Iriates pulled arrows the size of walking sticks from their barrel quivers and nocked them, muscles and sinews bulging in every arm as the bowstrings creaked and the great bows slowly bent until they looked like they were all about to snap in two. Every arrowhead was aimed at the approaching garm, every soldier's limbs so stock still and unwavering that they looked carved from stone despite the strain of the weaponry they were holding.

The massive Iriate on our platform looked one more time to the Prince, who nodded without looking back. "*Loose!*" the soldier bellowed again, veins bulging in his neck at the command.

The sound of dozens of gigantic bows firing at once was like a small thunderclap. Despite their size and the distance they were traveling, the hail of javelin-length arrows all hit their target surprisingly quickly; the instant the twang and snap of the bowstrings faded, the giant dog out in front of us yelped, high pitched but cut off partway through as a dozen spears rained down on it, peppering its head and back with a forest of feathered shafts and sending it tumbling over its own front paws. The ground shook as its legs ragdolled out from under it and it crashed into the dirt, digging a furrow and kicking up a cloud of dust as it slid to a halt.

I would have been a lot more upset at watching a dog get shot in the face in front of me had it not been, y'know, about twenty feet tall and coming to eat us all. Still, when it slowly lifted its massive head and loosed a last, short, rumbling howl before finally dropping down dead, I felt a twinge of sadness for it.

Until I realized what that final cry signified.

"There they are, the mongrels," the massive commander grumbled behind me, stepping up beside the prince along the wall's edge. I did likewise, standing on my toes and straining to see what he was talking about.

I didn't have to look long. Behind the body of the dead garm, rising up from a massive gouge in the earth that I hadn't noticed at first, climbed another gigantic dog — then another, and another, and another, a whole pack of monster dogs emerging from the earth and gathering around the corpse of their packmate, sniffing and nudging at the body. One of them snarled and bit into the dead garm's haunch, another sinking its teeth into its belly, and together they tugged and ripped and split it open, shoving their muzzles into the bloody meat as they began devouring the fallen beast.

The rest of the pack turned toward the wall, snarling and slavering. The garm in front threw its head back and the rest followed, the monstrous howl picked up by the group and carrying clear across the sky in all directions — an eerie, bestial battle cry that they could probably hear even in the deepest center of Pandemonium.

And then, as one, the beasts charged the city, fanning out as they approached.

"Suppose we'll need to send a team into that fissure when we're done here," Vambrace grumbled beside me. "Clear out a potential den, if they're not just moving through it on the prowl." He raised a hand and gestured loosely at the attacking pack. "Fire at will, and start dropping soldiers from the furthest edges of our defense, moving inward. I want them corralled before they start flanking the city. We'll fight the group here in front of us rather than risk smaller skirmishes all around the wall. Keep a line of spears up top, though, in case any of the beasts are particularly daring. If we're lucky, we can keep the ovens off."

"Understood, sire," said the massive soldier, then turned and strode away while relaying the prince's orders in his ear-splitting bellow. Further down the wall in both directions, other commander types picked up the message and shouted it onward. Those soldiers who weren't stationed on one of the wall's edges with a bow and a spear all hurried back to the myriad staircases leading back down into the floors below us, the crowds rushing and shoving as they left like a pack of school kids after the last bell had rung for the day. All around us, those still up on the edges began nocking their massive bows again and firing as soon as they had their strings pulled back, in a more sustained volley that made up in volume what it lacked in synchronization. The garm down below, now apparently wise to this tactic, dodged around the sporadic rain of arrows while they ran, zigzagging out of their pack formation as they rapidly approached.

Just to be that little bit safer, I took a step back behind the prince. "This kind of thing happen often around here?" I asked.

"Quiet!" he hissed under his breath, sharp enough to surprise me. "Need to focus. No distractions." Slowly, without taking his eyes from the half dozen monsters in front of us, he reached up and yanked at the strap on his shoulder. The sword harness he wore over my jacket came loose and slipped down, Excalibur's naked blade glinting unnaturally as it fell sideways. He reached behind himself with one hand and caught the hilt as it fell, swinging the whole contraption out in front of him before unfastening the straps around the sword's cross-guard and tossing the harness off to the ground beside him. He then stood with the freed sword held at his side in what probably looked, to the passing observer, like casual grip and a relaxed stance. Only I was close enough to see how tightly he held the weapon, his knuckles going white even if his hand showed no signs of trembling.

Alright, well, suddenly I didn't feel quite so safe hiding behind him as I thought I would. Still, I stayed back and beside him, out of his sight, and nervously watched the dog fight unfold.

The archers were still firing, the garm still weaving through the drizzle of arrows. Here and there, an arrow or two found a target, grazing fur or flesh or sticking haphazardly in a back or leg. A couple of the beasts slowed to a limping gait with arrows sprouting from one of their legs. Another yelped as a shaft pierced its snout, skidding to a stop just long enough to toss its massive head and shake the arrow loose before it rejoined the back of the pack, blood dripping from its nose. The archers were slowing them, hurting a few, but not killing any of them. At this rate, they'd be on us in just a minute or so.

Or so I thought, but "at this rate" didn't last but a moment longer. Then another war cry went up from our side to match the growling of the dogs, a hundred or more voices suddenly roaring beneath our feet. I risked stepping up to the edge of the wall and peering over, where, a dizzying distance far below us, streams of Iriate soldiers came pouring out of several small doors in the base of the wall, all of them charging out to meet the pack of massive monsters.

The two sides clashed uncomfortably close to the wall, the garm covering more ground faster than the comparatively tiny demons. The soldiers had spilled out onto the field in a wide line, the outside members outpacing the inside ones to close in around the beasts — at least, as best as they could, given the monsters' size. The first garm to meet the first Iriate threw itself mouth-first at the man, its paws sliding and its whole body spinning around as its attention shifted from the wall to the soldiers in front of it. I thought I'd just distantly witnessed another killing until the beast threw its head back, snarling, the soldier in question crouched in its mouth with his feet and back braced against the dog's lower fangs, his arms locked straight and struggling against its top jaw, somehow keeping it forced open while the garm thrashed its head. Other Iriates swarmed around it, flailing at it with all manner of weaponry, some throwing themselves bodily at the dog's legs and attempting to climb them while the monstrous mongrel reared and pranced carefully back from the enemies at its feet.

Similar scenes were playing out all across the field before us. Off to one side, a trio of Iriates had all succeeded in stabbing their swords into the same leg of one garm, which limped around trying to shake them off for a few seconds before collapsing over its now-lame front leg. That close to the ground, another soldier managed to shove her spear through the creature's nose, fighting to hold its head steady while another Iriate climbed the bloody fur of its muzzle and the garm itself yelped and growled.

Beyond that scene, a lone soldier who'd managed to slip through the closer chaos sprinted toward a beast at the back of the pack, waving a double-bearded axe in each hand and screaming her rage in one long, impressive breath. She'd nearly reached her target when another garm bounded up beside her and swatted her with a giant paw, sending her tumbling through the air and then the dirt for a good hundred feet or so, straight into the path of another enormous dog. Before she could gain her feet again, the garm pinned her beneath its paw, then leaned down and snapped its teeth shut around the soldier's torso. This time, I actually did watch another person's death, as the beast thrashed its head with the Iriate's lower body still hanging halfway out of its jaws, her legs flailing limply for a moment before the creature bit down harder and her bottom half went flying across the field once again, blood spraying briefly from where her waist used to be.

I gasped and spun away at that, disturbed to my core, but at least I managed not to vomit this time. A few moments of deep breathing later, when I'd worked up the nerve to look back at the fighting, I was relieved to find that at least she was the only visible casualty so far. Unless any more of our soldiers had gotten themselves eaten when I wasn't watching.

Still, only the garm I had watched brought to heel and have its face climbed was dead so far, half a dozen soldiers stabbing and butchering the still body just to be sure. More were wounded, and no more were emerging from the crevasse in the ground, but there had to be nearly a dozen of them out there now, harried by a little over a hundred soldiers at a glance, two hundred at most. It was hard to say which side was winning.

"Meaner than usual, this bunch of mutts," one of the Iriate commanders called out with a laugh as he strode up the steps of our platform. "Don't feel like wading in there yourself, Sire?"

"And deprive you and yours of your chance for fun and glory?" the prince asked with a grin, turning toward the soldier as he passed by us. "No, Captain, I think I'll leave the groundwork to the troops who are spoiling harder for something to kill. Me, I'll stick to management for now. *Someone's* gotta be up here watching things, making sure you all do your damn jobs right."

The Iriate captain laughed. "You do us all too kindly, your highness," he said as he descended the stairs on the other side, then strode away on whatever business he was about.

I waited until he was out of sight and hearing before sidling up beside Vambrace again. "And *that* wasn't an unnecessary distraction?" I asked under my breath.

"Of course it was," he muttered through gritted teeth, still faintly grinning. "But I have to make all of this look effortless to them. Unconcerned and unimpressed human commander. *You* know the truth, for better or worse. Now, let me concentrate," he added, his grin slipping as he turned back to the wall's edge, "because if one of those things comes this way and I'm not absolutely ready —"

He was interrupted by a loud crash, and the wall shuddered beneath our feet. I lost my balance in surprise and fell backward onto my ass, which only made the garm look even more massive when it suddenly popped its head up over the wall directly in front of us, not ten feet from where I sat. It must have leaped the line of soldiers and bounded away before they could rein it back in, though how it managed to climb up this far, I couldn't tell you.

I *could* tell you that I had never, ever been so scared in my life as when it slapped a paw over the edge of the wall and found purchase, its claws hooking into the crenelated stone, then opened its maw wider than I was tall and huffed a hot, wet breath over us, its other paw rising up above us like the hammer of death itself.

My mind blanked. My body froze. *This is how it ends. My family is never going to know what happened to me. And they wouldn't believe it if they did.*

The garm slammed its paw down—

—at the same moment that Vambrace swung his sword up.

The monster's ensuing yelp was deafening at close range, the rush of its breath knocking me to my back. Even still, I remember the sound just before even more clearly: the soft, silky whisper of Excalibur passing effortlessly through more than a full yard of flesh and muscle and sinew and bone. Not carving or hacking or cleaving, just elegantly separating the beast from its paw in one fluid arc.

Hot, black blood splashed down over us in a gory wave, soaking my dress and exposed skin, painting the ground beneath me. Flat on my back, I watched the severed paw sail overhead, past our lookout platform and, to judge from the shouting that erupted, past the wall beneath us. The garm, still shrieking in pain, smacked its bloody stump against the wall as it fought to keep its purchase with only one good foreleg left.

Another swipe of Excalibur lopped off all four of its front toes. They stayed upright, embedded by their claws in the stonework, as the rest of the garm slid down the wall and out of sight, yelping as it went, until it hit the ground below with a distant crash and fell silent.

A moment later, Vambrace was standing over me, awash in garm blood, his eyes wide. He said something I didn't hear or couldn't understand as he held out his free hand to me, blood dripping from his fingers. His other hand still had a trembling death grip on Excalibur, the hilt of which also dripped with blood. The blade itself was spotless, still gleaming an unnatural silver.

I stared up at his hand for a while until he finally pulled it away and crouched down beside me. "Lady Morgan?" I heard him say, his voice a million miles away. "Are you okay? Are you hurt?"

I tried to reply. It took my mouth a moment to move again, and another moment to remember how to form words. "I…" was all I managed to get out.

It seemed to be enough. Vambrace exhaled a deep breath and reached a hand beneath me. "Stunned and rattled, but otherwise fine, I think," he said as he lifted my back off the ground, pulling me up to a sitting position beside him. "If any blood got in your mouth, try not to swallow it. Bad for the digestion."

I collapsed sideways into his arm, letting him prop me up for the moment. "…I thought I was gonna die," I managed to say, my voice tight and warbly.

"Your first hellbeast is always the most frightening," said the prince, rubbing my bare, bloody back with his bare, bloody hand. His palm squished and slipped against my skin with a sound like someone messily fingerpainting. "Just breathe," he said. "Deep, steadying breaths."

I tried. Everything smelled like dog and copper and rot. I tried breathing through my mouth instead, but I could still kind of taste it. The air was heavier now that it had been soaked in garm blood. I needed to get… somewhere else. Away from all the gore I was lying in.

I reached up and laid a shaking hand on his shoulder. The denim squelched beneath my hand, and I frowned as I gripped it. "My jacket…" I groaned, slowly getting my feet beneath me.

"It will wash out," Vambrace assured me as he helped me unsteadily to my feet. "And that probably sounds like empty reassurance, but no. I don't know why garm blood specifically doesn't stain, but—"

I doubled over and retched onto the blood-soaked floor in front of my feet. Dammit, I'd been holding it together so good, too. Relatively.

"Yes, I suppose that's to be expected," the prince continued, still rubbing my back. "Get it all out if you need to, that's fine. Take your time, my lady."

"I thought—" I croaked, then paused to fight back the last gagging revulsion that shuddered up through me. When it passed, I spit the last dregs of blood and bile from my mouth before continuing. "Thought you couldn't… have distractions. Gotta keep us alive."

"Yes, true," said Vambrace. "But we've been relieved somewhat on that front. Enkida is here."

"Just in time to utterly fail as a bodyguard, it seems," the general's familiar voice chimed in from somewhere nearby. "Apologies for the delay, Sire. The entirety of wall forces has been roused; any extraneous troops not needed for prison security or border sentry have been directed to aid in the defensive assault. A couple attempts by inmates to stage riots during the commotion tried to break out in nearby blocks, but they have since both been crushed. The enemy should be contained and culled shortly."

"Very good, General," said the prince. "No need to worry about the lady or myself. She's shaken, but we're still standing." To emphasize, he slipped his arm under mine and once again tried to help me to my feet. This time, I actually managed to stand without collapsing or vomiting again, though I wasn't standing particularly steady. "How has the battle gone while I've been looking away?"

Enkida stood beside us dressed in her full armor, that dark red-brown leathery carapace material hugging her body and covering her from neck to foot, including a kind of half-helmet that covered her brow and the top and back of her head but opened at the sides to allow her long, wickedly sharp black horns protrude. "Five of the beasts dead, and at a glance, fifteen of our own," she answered, leaning on a spear as long as she was tall, the top tipped with a spade-shaped blade. "Six garm remain, including the apparent leader of this pack. We have an estimated two hundred soldiers on the field and counting, most dedicated to containing the fight within the bounds of this wall block. Archers have ceased firing now that our own are mixing so thickly with their targets."

"Just mopping up now, with those numbers," Vambrace said, glancing from Enkida to the fighting beyond the ramparts. "How quickly can we finish this, do you think?"

The general smiled. "How quickly would you like it finished, my liege?"

"The sooner, the better," he said. "The soldiers have had their fun and diversion, but fifteen confirmed dead is enough casualties for now, and I'm always leery of an understaffed wall. There's also the matter of cleanup thanks to that particularly enterprising dog that came at us, and tending to a gore-sickened maiden has dampened any thirst for battle I myself may have been holding."

"Understood," she said, turning toward the wall's edge. "Then if you will excuse me, sire." She spun the spear in her hands and casually hucked it over the side of the wall, walking after it before it had even vanished over the drop.

"Wait, where is she going?" I asked. Were there ladders on the ramparts I didn't know about, or something?

"Where does any general go?" she answered herself, pausing on the lip of the drop. "To battle." She turned to look over the full length of the field below, and I caught a glimpse of her scowl as she did, her bottom fangs bared. "These simple beasts think to threaten *our* city?" she snarled quietly, in a voice like poisoned ice. "No."

She stepped off.

I gasped and rushed forward out of Vambrace's steadying hold, catching myself on one of the crenulations and leaning over as far as I dared to watch the general plummet. Curt and occasionally meddling as she was, I liked Enkida well enough, and I didn't particularly relish the idea of her splattering on the rocky ground far below.

She didn't, of course. I knew by now that Iriates were tougher than most, especially when they were riled, but I hadn't reckoned just *how* tough they could be. Not until those next few minutes.

Enkida hit the ground feet first, superhero-style, and even up here I could hear the impact and see the cracks that spread out from her landing, kicking up a cloud of dust. Her knees buckled for a moment, but in the next she rose gracefully from her crouch and strode forward. Her spear had embedded itself in the broken body of the garm that had come at us, which now lay crumpled and dead at the base of the wall nearby, its neck snapped and twisted. Enkida yanked the weapon free as she passed, heading calmly out toward the shouting and chaos of the battle before us.

There were six dead garm now, and six still living, each harried by clusters of Iriate soldiers all rushing around the beasts, screaming and flailing their weapons and lunging at whatever openings they got. Still, they were *big* dogs, stomping and swatting and kicking at any demon who got too close, sending bodies flying across the field, though most of them stood back up again and rushed back to the fight — or another, closer fight. A double line of soldiers stood inactive but ready in a wide ring around the carnage, shouting and waving their weapons, daring the garm to try and break through their fence of bodies. Our side was winning, but it was a slow victory, carved out gradually as the monsters weakened and succumbed to hundreds of small wounds.

Until Enkida arrived.

The first garm to notice her was the closest, standing over a couple of dead and broken soldiers with two more ducking and weaving in front of it, a third clinging to its scruff but not getting any further up it. When it saw the new threat calmly approaching, it snarled and planted its feet, shaking violently like a dog drying off. The soldier on its neck went flying, crashing into one of the two below. A quick swipe knocked the last soldier aside, and then it was bounding toward the general, who stopped and planted herself to meet it. In two massive strides, the monster was on her, fangs bared and dripping as its head whipped down to bite her in two.

She stepped in and to the side of the beast's maw at the last second, its teeth clacking shut on air with a sound like two cars colliding. Before it could rear back again, Enkida's spear shot forward and up, burying in the garm's neck. The beast tried to pull away, but the general pulled down, driving the garm's face into the dirt with the new handle she had made in its flesh. I heard her shout just once, quickly, something between a roar and a grunt, as she ripped her spear down and away.

It didn't cut as cleanly as Excalibur, but it still tore through the garm's neck, carving a ragged gash through its throat in a spray of blood. The beast tried to howl but only gurgled, its head lolling back as it collapsed, twitching and bleeding out into the dirt. Enkida was already striding away without a backward glance.

Cheers went up from the containing ring of soldiers watching her approach, but those Iriates involved in the fighting who saw her coming sounded… less happy to see their general. Angry, even, though what else was new? They'd already been screaming in anger ever since the fight started. I couldn't tell if they were legitimately mad to see her or if this was just the only noise they could make at the moment.

Whatever the case, two more garm stood equidistant before her now, each snapping at the small group of soldiers around them. The Iriates backed off their targets when they saw Enkida approaching, every one of them seeming reluctant to do so, as far as I could tell from this distance. The dogs took the opportunity to break away, both charging the lone figure still approaching them, their packmate's blood dripping from her spear and armor.

She didn't let these get as close as the last. No sooner had they started charging her than she lunged forward, her spear swinging up as she reversed her grip, whipped her arm around, and let it fly. It shot from her hand quick as any of the arrows the soldiers on the wall had fired, only a slight glint and a blur in the air for a fraction of a second. The garm in front yelped and tumbled ass-over-head into the dirt, Enkida's spear lodged so deep in its eye socket that it nearly disappeared.

The garm in back leapt over its carcass and kept charging, Enkida now sprinting to meet it. The beast reared up as they met, then swung its massive paw, which collided with the general — and stopped mid-swing, braced against her upheld arm, while Enkida stood firm and unmoved before the beast. The garm growled, momentarily thrown off balance, then bared its fangs and lunged down at her. Enkida knocked its paw aside and leapt *up*, into its descending maw, stopping its jaws from snapping shut as she stood straight and tall in its mouth.

The dog thrashed and struggled against the obstruction, then stretched its mouth wider and tried to bite down again. Enkida crouched, folding against its tongue, and let it.

Those slavering jaws snapped shut at last with a crunch of finality, the beast going still. I'd gone still myself, eyes wide and fingers digging into the stonework as I watched, unwilling for the moment to believe that I'd just watched the mighty general get eaten. But I could see the blood running thick and fast from the creature's lips, pooling on the ground below, so there was no denying that—

The beast slumped quietly sideways, crashing sprawled to the dirt, its previously glowing, furious eyes now glazed and lifeless. Despite already being dead, it still stretched its mouth open after it fell — or rather, its jaws were pried apart from inside, I realized, as Enkida stretched them wide and climbed out, slick from top to bottom in black blood and bits of gore that didn't bear thinking about too hard. Blood still pooled from the dead monster's open mouth, the top jaw of which now sported a deep hole from where the general had punched her way through into its skull.

I confess my own jaw hung open somewhat after watching all of that unfold, and as I now watched Enkida shrug off being eaten. She wrung the blood from her braid and wiped idly at what dripped from her armor as she calmly walked back toward the other dead garm, then climbed up its muzzle and grabbed the barely visible butt of her spear. I turned away so I didn't have to watch her yank the thing free of the dog monster's eye jelly.

When I turned back, the fighting was over. Of the three remaining monsters, one had been felled by a group of half a dozen soldiers while I'd been watching Enkida plow through three single-handedly. The remaining two had turned and fled, leaping the far side of the ring of Iriates, some of whom flung their weapons after the retreating beasts. As the giant dogs loped away, one of them limping, the ring of soldiers cheered. The soldiers on the wall around us cheered. The soldiers who'd been fighting down in the bloody mosh pit yelled and screamed some more, which may have been the blood rage equivalent of cheering, I wasn't sure.

"Bring down the straggler," I heard Vambrace order behind me. There was another group scraping noise all along the wall around us, then another cloud of arrows passed high overhead, converging in the distance and raining down beyond the soldier ring. The limping garm in the back yelped and toppled as it got caught in the deadly rain; the last remaining beast kept running, then suddenly disappeared, diving back into whatever distant gulley it had crawled out of on the horizon.

I looked from the vanished dog back to the killing fields just in time to see the first of the surviving soldiers scream and throw himself bodily at Enkida, who stepped in and brought a knee up hard into his gut. As he doubled over, two more dropped their weapons and lunged at her from behind, both bellowing at the top of their lungs. She spun and thrust with the butt of her spear, catching one under the ribs, then turned and smashed him into the other as he landed. The cry was picked up by still more of the Iriates who'd fought the garm, as all across the field, handfuls of scattered soldiers suddenly turned their wrath on their own commander, each one dropping their weapons before they took off sprinting toward the embattled Enkida.

What the fuck was happening? Had all the garm blood covering the battlefield driven everyone crazy or something? But I was covered in the stuff, and I felt fine. I mean, I was nauseated down to my very soul, but I was still sensible.

I turned back toward the prince, who was in turn talking with the boulder-sized Iriate commander again, both of them facing away from the madness below. "Get a team of volunteers together to hunt down the survivor and do a thorough sweep of that ravine," Vambrace was commanding. "However many soldiers want to go that you can spare. Prioritize present wall sentries and members of the perimeter ring first, anyone whose blood may be up from watching the fight but not joining."

"You wouldn't rather General Enkida put this team together, sire?" the gigantic Iriate asked.

"Not necessary, but get her to sign off on it once it's assembled," said the prince. "I want any garm remains that breached the perimeter cleared away before the scouts are sent out, then light the ovens and keep the wall hot until they return, in case any more of the beasts are waiting to try something."

"Understood, Sire," the giant Iriate answered, then clapped a fist to his chest and walked away, shouting orders. The archers on the ramparts slotted their arrows back into the nearby barrels and set their bows aside, but most of them still stood at their posts and watched the infighting below, either scowling or grinning. Everyone saw it but the prince, evidently.

He saw the concern on my face as I stared at him, though. "Something still bothering you, m'lady?" he asked.

"Your army's gonna kill your general!" I cried. "Don't you care?"

He snickered. "Who?" he asked, nodding over the edge. "Them?"

I turned back to look. Enkida was still on her feet, standing in the center of a growing carpet of prone Iriate bodies, many of which were groaning. A few pushed themselves wearily to their feet as I watched and stumbled away, even as more rushed past to attack her. The converging horde had mostly spent itself, though, so that now the general was just ducking and sidestepping a crowd of only ten or so angry soldiers, throwing the occasional fist or knee or elbow to send one sprawling. None of them were armed, even with Enkida's spear planted in the dirt nearby for any of them to grab, and each one who stayed down for more than a few seconds simply staggered up and limped off once they were on their feet again. The Iriate ring had already followed suit, the fence of soldiers broken and dispersed as those who weren't brawling with Enkida made their leisurely way back to the wall, gathering up discarded weaponry as they went.

"What the hell?" I wondered again, this time aloud. "Are they mad at her, or is this just how Iriates celebrate?"

"A bit of both," said Vambrace. "She cut their bloodshed short, so they're taking out their thwarted rage on her. Or attempting to, at the least. Once an Iriate gets to fighting properly, it's hard for them to turn it off again without someone forcing it off for them. This isn't the first time she's had to calm the army after a battle."

"Isn't that dangerous?" I asked.

"Not as much as it might look," said the prince. "Enkida knows her own strength, don't worry. She's going easy on them."

I was going to correct him, but then I watched as the general laid out another soldier by simply grabbing his face and throwing him straight down to the ground. Point taken. "Isn't that treasonous, then?" I asked instead.

"I thought as much myself, when she first proposed allowing such a practice," he said as he stepped up beside me. "I spent centuries molding the flailing destruction of House Iria into an obedient force with a controlled direction, and I didn't relish the risk of letting that devolve back into a murderous quagmire by giving the rank and file any sanctioned excuse to attack the leadership. But I concede, she made a point, and we've had fewer problems with soldiers with leftover bloodlust since she implemented the allowance. If it were anyone other than Enkida…"

He trailed off, resting his elbows on the stone crenulation and leaning on his arms as he gazed down at the fighting, a distant and wistful look in his eyes. We were alone atop our lookout now, I noticed, the soldiers on the wall dispersing all around us as the group brawl below wound down. The mountainous commander had disappeared, as had his booming voice, and even the archers on the edge were filing back toward the stairway entrances leading down into the prison proper.

Still, the prince lowered his voice before he spoke, so quietly that I could barely hear him. "Without Excalibur at my side, I am still just a human," he said, his voice only slightly more than a whisper. "A human with more than a millennium of experience fighting and surviving, yes, but otherwise wholly mortal. The weakest of Iriates, without so much as a minute's martial training under their belt, could still overpower me with brute force alone and rip me in half, if I'm not careful. But so long as I hold Arthur's sword, I am more than a match for any man, woman, or creature in the entirety of Hell." He nodded downward. "Except for Enkida."

I followed his line of sight. The general had only three opponents left now, all of them calmer than the mob had been at first. Two hovered on either side of her, waiting their turn while the third swung his fists wildly at her. She effortlessly sidestepped each wide blow until she finally didn't; the fist collided with her face and stopped there, all momentum lost, which threw her attacker off his balance. He was thrown clear off his feet when she took the moment to step in and slam her open palm up under his chin, knocking him sprawling into the air, then onto his back. One of the waiting two took that as her cue to rush in for her turn.

"You have seen Sidona's dramatization of our fight, I hear," the prince continued beside me. "I have as well, of course. It is an impressive spectacle, the way the duchess interprets it on the stage, painting both the general and I in a rather flattering light. I commissioned that play, and that crowning scene in particular, for just such a reason. The more times that production is performed, the more strongly my subjects remember her safer, idealized version of events, the further we bury the messy truth of the real fight."

Alright, I'll bite. "Why?" I asked, also quietly. "What happened in the real fight?"

Vambrace laughed, his eyes still on his distant general. "I very nearly died," he said, "and General Enkida was very nearly Archfiend Enkida, accidentally or otherwise. It was only dumb luck that I survived her onslaught, even with Excalibur, and forced her to yielding. Luck… or she allowed me to live. Pulled her wrath and suddenly started going easier on me mid-battle." He shrugged. "She has never admitted as much, and I have never asked. Getting to the truth of that question seemed imprudent, for obvious reasons. Even still today, I'm not sure I want to know. But I elevated her to my personal guard after that fight, and soon my right hand as well. Outwardly, it was a reward for the exceptional prowess she had shown against me. Privately, I wanted to make sure that someone who could still pose such a threat to me was absolutely on my side — and close enough to deal with quickly and quietly if she ever decided that she wasn't."

I looked at the fight again, but it was over. The woman who'd been second-to-last was on the ground with the general's boot on her throat, while the last guy was struggling in the air, Enkida's hand around *his* throat. Both were weakly kicking their legs, their hands gripping whichever of the general's appendages was currently cutting off their air. The woman on the ground eventually gave up and tapped out, rolling away to her knees and visibly gasping for air once Enkida stepped off of her. The man in her grip was more tenacious, pounding on her outstretched arm until his own went limp and fell slack at his side. The general held his unmoving body a few seconds longer before tossing it aside. Her last distraction dealt with, she pulled her spear from the ground and began the long walk back to the base of the wall.

I nodded down at her this time. "So all this superhero one-woman-army stuff's not typical for most Iriates, I take it," I said. "You're saying she's something special and different."

"There are other Iriates like her from time to time, though rare," said the prince. "Those with a calm, cold anger rather than the explosive norm. They tend to be less impressive in a fight than their hot-tempered brethren; most don't take up military service, or if they do, they serve in more passive roles most Iriates would abhor, like equipment maintenance or duty management. Enkida, somehow, found the trick to focusing and adapting her abnormal brand of rage for combat — more of a surgically placed knife than a sweeping broadsword. That coupled with a head that can keep level enough for strategy, it's no wonder she eventually clawed her way up the ranks as she did. Her exhibition duel with me was the last boost she needed to reach the top."

Well shit, no wonder I kind of liked her. Minus the military career and the constant quiet fury, I wanted to *be* her. "Think you could still take her these days if you had to?" I asked.

Vambrace didn't answer for a bit. "If I took a swing without warning when her back was turned," he said at last. "In a fair fight, one-on-one again, both of us knowing our lives were on the line? I don't know."

"Fair except for Excalibur, you mean," I said.

He chuckled quietly. "Except for that, yes."

I turned to face him directly. "You admit a lot of stuff to me, you know that?"

"I remember that the Christ Church of the Romans had a ritual whereby the soul is cleansed through admission," he answered. "Perhaps this is my first attempt at spiritual maintenance in my unnaturally long life. Or perhaps I have been lonely, and you are nostalgic. I want you to trust me, and I want to trust you. And we both know that you cannot betray my trust without also seriously endangering yourself as well." He smiled at me and shrugged again. "And if you try to betray me anyway, I can always kill you, or have you killed by someone else. I have no reason not to follow this whim so long as I am careful about it."

I snorted. "Beautiful philosophy you got, Prince," I said, deadpan.

"It is the only philosophy that makes sense in Hell if you want to live bearably, and for longer than the moment." He pushed back from the wall's edge and headed for the nearby staircase, beckoning me after him. "Come, we'll finish your business with the merchant's murderer and be on our way. You won't wish to be here when the ovens are lit."

I followed him as we retraced our steps down the many, many levels of the wall, back to the ground floor of the center marsh block. The door to the cell corridor where they were keeping Dorgagovek was open when we got there, and yet I couldn't hear any ear-splitting screams of rage this time as we approached, which I took for a good sign that he'd finally calmed down a bit after our talks. And thanks to the absolute mess that the bleeding garm had made of us up on the wall, I also couldn't notice the new odor as we stepped into that same hallway. I'd just thought it was me I was smelling.

But I did notice all the open cell doors, and the sprays and pools of blood behind every set of bars, each complete with the slumped and lifeless body of whoever had been occupying the space beforehand. The only other living person in the corridor besides us was the Invidiate in the back hunched over a short-handled scrub brush, grumbling as he scoured the floor.

"Son of a mearc," Vambrace sighed in front of me. "She said there'd been riots, but I didn't expect *this* bad. As if we don't have enough—"

He stopped as I shoved past him and hurried down the hall toward the back cell. The Invidiate cleaner saw me running toward him and scurried up to meet me, planting himself in my way with a scowl, brandishing his brush as Enkida had her spear. "Hey, do you see me cleaning here or what, lady?" he demanded. "You're tracking through the blood where I just—"

"Dorgagovek!" I called, skirting the small and protesting demon and catching myself on the bars of the Iriate's cell. "Is he...?"

He was. The cell door was open, same as the rest of them. The cocoon of chains all hung limply from the ceiling and walls. And on his back in a pool of black blood, with his mouth open and about a dozen gaping stab wounds in his chest and stomach, my last possible lead on the *Morganomicon* lay very still and very, very dead.

G.D. Burkhead

381

Chapter 24: Despondency

The official story was that Dorgagovek had had the same thought as a dozen other prisoners when the commotion with the garm broke out: that now was their best chance to escape, while the majority of the guards and soldiers were busier with more important matters. It was a common problem, they said, whenever monsters assailed the wall. The fact that almost nobody ever actually successfully escaped for long evidently didn't deter the next batch from trying anyway.

Perhaps Dorgagovek hadn't trusted that I could actually do anything to help him out. Perhaps he figured he wouldn't be believed anyway and had nothing to lose in trying. Or maybe his impulse control was just as garbage as most any other demon I'd met so far. Whatever the case, the Iriate guard who'd been left in charge of that corridor reported that one of the impacts caused by the garm who'd assailed the wall and nearly killed me had also shaken something loose in Dorgagovek's many, many bindings — just loose enough for his thrashing to find a foothold. The guard had been paying him no mind until he heard the rattle of chains that shouldn't have been rattling, and had hurried over just in time to watch the prisoner claw free of his cocoon of shackles and jump him.

By the time he'd got back to his feet and the room had stopped spinning, Dorgagovek had kicked in the doors of all his cellmates and torn them to pieces in a blood rage. It took half a dozen reinforcements to beat him back and contain him, a process which unfortunately involved running him through about thirteen times until he finally stopped moving. Nobody was surprised it had happened, just disappointed.

Nobody but me, at least. I was shocked. More than that, I was stricken. The merchant Gilderos had been my last link to wherever the *Morganomicon* might be now. With him dead and everything he'd owned burned to the ground, the last person to see him and his shop in one piece had been my last tenuous hope. Now, I didn't even have that much. Now, finding that book blind would be like finding a highly illegal needle in an aggressive and occasionally murderous haystack.

If the book hadn't been destroyed entirely. Which it probably had, if I was being realistic.

Realistically, I was never, ever going home ever again.

This was the thought stuck on repeat in my head as we made our way back through the city toward the palace, Vambrace and Enkida and myself, all of us crusted in dried blood, none of us saying much. I think the prince realized how upset I was and was holding his tongue out of sympathy, and Enkida wasn't exactly chatty even in the best of moods. We got stares from those we passed but no comments.

It all suited me just fine. More silence to stew in made the brooding easier. I didn't even pay much attention to our surroundings this time, the people or the places we passed, the alien architecture, the route we were taking through the circuitous bowl of districts. Why bother? There was no rush to learn the city now. I had the rest of my life to familiarize myself with it. The rest of eternity, maybe, if I was careful, if Vambrace was anything to go by.

Possible immortality. There was a silver lining. Didn't really wanna spend it here, though.

We split up when we finally got back inside the palace, the prince saying something about calling on me again once we'd all rested and I felt better. Or maybe I was supposed to call on him. I wasn't sure, wasn't listening, didn't care, just muttered an agreement and let Enkida lead me back to my room. She kept looking back at me during the walk but still didn't say anything. I just nodded and mumbled a thanks when we reached my door, then stepped inside and shut it behind me with a deep sigh.

Kriseia wasn't here for a change, which was nice; it meant she was probably out enjoying herself like I'd suggested, rather than waiting here to wait on me some more. It also meant I didn't have to explain why I was covered head to toe in dried dog blood.

Speaking of which…

My dress was still damp and tacky, and it made a sound vaguely like scotch tape as I peeled it off of me, bits of garm gore flaking off as I did so like the world's grossest sunburn. I tossed it aside with a grimace, and it hit the floor with a muffled tinkling that fabric shouldn't have made. It confused me for a second before I picked it back up, whereupon the soul crystals that Vambrace had given me in his secret vault dropped out of the pocket and rolled across the floor. Right, I'd forgotten all about them. I scooped them both up and pulled the broken flip phone from the dress pocket as well, dropping all three items on my desk next to my dead MP3 player before dropping the probably-ruined garment in a corner and heading to the bathroom.

I was slightly less disgusting where the dress had shielded me, but only slightly. The blood had dribbled in from the neckline and sleeves, and where the rivulets of it hadn't been able to reach, it could only slowly get at my skin as it soaked into the dress first and sat against me like a bloody sponge. The result was that I was dyed a splotchy pinkish red from the chest down, streaked with stripes of darker red-brown that ran halfway down my torso like some kind of hellish zebra. Or like a gross Luxuriate slowly turning head-first into a gross Iriate. I didn't know what my face might've looked like, and I didn't want to know.

I did my best to scrub my arms and face in the sink while I waited for the tub to fill, then grabbed every bottle of soap and soap-like liquid I could carry before climbing in, thankful that I'd had Kriseia point them all out to me earlier. There wasn't enough disinfectant in the world right now, as far as I was concerned.

I went through four whole bottles of stuff and emptied and refilled the tub twice before I'd finally stopped shedding garm blood and turning the water pink. Then I gave myself another wash all over, just to be safe, and wondered if it was more the shock or the despair that was keeping me from being more thoroughly disgusted with the whole process.

Then, when I was satisfied that I was fully, completely clean, I filled the tub again and just... sat there, soaking. Thinking and not thinking. Trying to grasp the enormity of it all, of everything that had happened so far, everything that wasn't going to happen now. It had been easier to deal with when I'd been able to think of it all as temporary, when going back to normal had been a possibility and a goal to work toward. But now, if that was no longer an option, if I had essentially and accidentally thrown away my entire life up 'til now, everyone I'd ever known or —

The room lurched and spun, my heart pounding in my chest like a war drum. I took a deep breath — surprisingly difficult to do, shallow as my lungs suddenly felt — and grabbed the edges of the tub, holding on for dear life, until my vision stopped swaying. No, I had to stop thinking about — about anything. Everything. I couldn't have a panic attack here. I couldn't pass out all alone in a bathtub. I couldn't drown in a guest room in Hell. I couldn't let that be how it all ended, not after everything I'd been through, not after all I'd done, all I hadn't done yet.

…Could I?

The thought wasn't *entirely* without merit. And it would be so *easy*. If I'd already lost everything else, then why —

I rose from the water with a splash and practically fell over myself scrambling out of the bathtub, my breathing quick and shallow as I crawled across the floor to the towels and yanked one down off the shelf, then wrapped it tight around myself as I huddled in the corner of the room, my face buried in the fluffy fabric, trying hard to concentrate on the solid feeling of the hard floor beneath me. Familiar feelings. If I closed my eyes, I could have been anywhere. I could have been home.

Jesus Christ. What was this now? Anxiety had never hit me this bad before. A lifetime of always feeling like I never quite belonged anywhere I was, like I was never in my right place in the world, and now all I wanted was to go back. The grass was always greener, I guess.

Was that the moral I was supposed to learn from all this? Fine, there, I'd learned it. Character arc complete, journey over, please let me end this adventure now. I don't have heels to click together, but there's no place like home…

It was too much, too heavy, all of it hitting too quickly. I couldn't think about it. I couldn't deal with it on my own. I needed to stop dwelling on it for now. I needed a therapist, or some medication, or hard liquor, or maybe just a plate of cookies and a hug.

I shivered. If none of that was forthcoming, then for now, I needed to get up off the floor and dry off and put my big girl panties back on. I wasn't helping anyone by lying around in the bathroom, least of all myself.

Where *were* my panties these days, anyway? I hadn't checked when I got back to see if my laundry had been done yet. If it wasn't, I was gonna be moping around in the buff for a while, I guess. Whatever hanging out the prince had in mind, it was gonna have to wait.

I managed to get my breathing mostly back under control as I toweled off. Still a long way from feeling alright, but at least I could make it through the next few minutes without considering ending it all, and hopefully without collapsing again. It was a start, at least.

I wrapped myself in a dry towel and stepped out to face whatever happened next — which, in this case, turned out to be finding a strange new woman sitting on my bed, draped in an open robe of dark blue satin, my aforementioned panties in her hands. I started, and she looked up, and we locked eyes.

They were brown, I noticed. Brown, human eyes, framed by black, human hair, set on a face with a very human shade of light brown skin.

It threw me for a moment, and I stood there gaping in disbelief before I noticed her horns and realized what I was seeing. The only other Luxuriate I'd witnessed in human glamour before now was trying to look like me, so seeing a human countenance that wasn't mine or Vambrace's was the last thing I expected. "Hel… hello," I finally stammered out as my brain caught up.

"Hello," the girl answered with a concerned frown. "Is something wrong?"

"No, I just… Sorry," I said. "I was confused for a second. Who are you?"

It was the other girl's turn to look startled. "Who… am I?" she repeated, eyes widening.

"Yeah," I said. "Sorry. Not to be rude. I was expecting Kriseia, if anyone." I sighed, my shoulders drooping. "You're not replacing her, are you? I liked her. Not sure if I was putting her to work like she wanted, but we were getting along. She's sweet."

The girl slowly dropped my underwear and brought her empty hand up to her chest. "I… I'm not sure what to say," she said.

"Oh. I mean, no offense," I said. "I'm sure you're nice too, Miss… uh…"

Her hands slid up her face into her hair, where she rubbed her short, squat horns. "I don't believe it," she said, eyes sparkling, lips slowly spreading into a happy grin. "Do you honestly not recognize me, Morgan?"

I blinked. I squinted. "…Kriseia?" I asked.

She squealed and shot to her feet on the bed, bouncing on her toes. "You didn't!" she said, beaming. "I did it! I finally tricked someone! A human, even! I wasn't even trying, and I did it!" She hopped down off the bed then, suddenly lavender and purple again, and rushed me, nearly knocking me back as she wrapped her arms around me. Behind her, the fabric of her robe shifted back and forth as her tail slithered and coiled beneath it. Like she was wagging it.

I tentatively returned the hug. "Why did you look like a human?" I asked.

"I thought you might like it," she said, her head still next to mine. "Seeing a more familiar face. Someone who looks more like you. General Enkida told me you've been having a bad time since you left, so I wanted to do what I could to cheer you up." She pulled away just enough to look at me. "Would you really have been sad if I had been replaced?"

"Of course," I said, frowning. "Why wouldn't I be?"

She shrugged and looked away. "Sorry," she said. "I didn't mean to sound mopey. You said you don't have any need for a servant, and you weren't interested in any of the services I know how to offer, so I wasn't sure how much you actually liked having me around."

"Of course I like having you around," I said. "You're the closest thing I've got to a friend here." I pulled her closer, hugging her tight again. It surprised me as much as her. "No, that's not fair," I said. "You *are* my friend. Not just for here. Not just for a demon. You're a good person, Kriseia."

"Morgan?" she asked, her chin on my shoulder, her hands on my bare back.

"Why are you so nice?" I asked, burying my face in her shoulder. "Everything's so dangerous and confusing, and everyone else is so selfish and cold and wants something out of me, and you're here just, just acting so damn *nice* all the time. Is it just cuz that's your job? Is it just cuz I'm a human?"

She didn't reply for a minute, just started slowly rubbing my back. "It's my job to help you with whatever you desire, yes, human or not," she said softly. "But you haven't desired anything yet, so I still haven't actually done the job I was given. If I'm 'nice,' I don't know. I just am the way I am. But I *do* like you, Morgan, and not just because I was assigned to."

I felt a lump growing in my throat. "Really?" I croaked against her skin.

She chuckled. "I don't know how humans work, not entirely," she said. "But servant or no, gift caste or not, I am still a Luxuriate and a Sin. I cannot go against my own nature, even for the sake of any outside duty, no matter who gave it to me. If I like you, it's because I like you. If I want to stay with you, it's because that is what *I* desire." She gave me a quick squeeze and chuckled again. "You make it easy though, you know? You're rather nice to me yourself, especially for someone who doesn't want to have sex with me."

I laughed, which helped dispel the prickling, about-to-cry sensation that had been growing behind my eyes. "Yeah, sorry about that," I said, pulling away at last. "It's not you, it's me, really."

"It's fine," she said with a smile as we finally let go of one another. "I'm used to taking such matters into my own hands when need be. I'm, uh, not actually as experienced as most of my peers yet outside of my initial education," she added.

"Yeah, that makes two of us," I said as I walked over to my desk. My t-shirt was sitting folded next to my stack of notecards, my boots set next to my chair. Kriseia had been halfway through folding my laundry when I'd interrupted her, it looked like. That would explain why she was playing with my underwear when I'd stepped out, then. I dropped my towel, modesty be damned, and pulled on my underwear, then grabbed the shirt and yanked it over my head, reveling in the familiar, baggy comfort. One of my most prized possessions now, I guess.

The thought sent another stab of depression through me, but I was just gonna have to get used to those, I figured. In a moment of emotional masochism, I decided to take stock of what little else I owned now. The rest of the outfit I'd shown up in, plus an elaborate, blood-drenched gown and a pile of ridiculous fetish wear. Half a dozen books on loan from the prince sitting stacked on one side of the desk, supposedly written in English but still too old and unreadable for me. My notecards on Hell and the people I was meeting on the other side of the desk next to an old-timey quill and inkwell I was still figuring out. Between them, the small collection of miscellaneous, now-useless electronic crap I'd had in my pockets: my MP3 player and Vambrace's dead and banged up cell phone, which sat blinking at me next to the soul crystals he'd handed me down in—

Wait. No way.

I rubbed my eyes hard and leaned over the desk, staring at the little flip phone. It had been dead, I swear it had been, I'd checked myself when I'd first grabbed it. This was an illusion, a trick of my desperate mind. It had to be.

It wasn't. The flip phone was closed, but the little digital display screen on the outside was blinking at me, dimly flashing 1:24 am and warning me that the battery needed charging.

I grabbed it and flipped it open. The screen was dirty beneath the crack, the display barely visible, but it *was* visible. The damn thing had come back to life. It could barely hold a charge, and it had absolutely no bars, but for the moment at least, it was on.

"How in the hell?" I mumbled, frantically hitting buttons. Most of them had no effect, broken or disconnected or whatever they were, but I could open the menus. The contacts list was empty, lost or corrupted after whatever it had gone through over the years to land it here in Hell with me, and I couldn't scroll through the settings menu with the broken arrow keys; but the fact remained that, in some very limited capacity, I had a working cell phone.

"What's that?" Kriseia asked behind me as I punched the number keys. Half of them were dead as well, but I managed to force out a random phone number of mostly sixes and eights. I didn't know who it belonged to, and I had absolutely no faith it would go through, but I had to try.

"Old Earth machine," I said as I hit "send" and held the thing up to my ear. "One sec."

She watched curiously but said nothing else, both of us waiting in complete silence, me holding my breath. Not for long, though. It didn't even attempt to ring, just sat quietly for a few seconds before the earpiece issued a strained string of garbled beeps. I pulled it away and looked at the screen, which blinked "No Signal" at me while it flickered and malfunctioned. A few seconds later, the display died entirely once more.

I sighed. "Yeah, didn't think so," I muttered, dropping it back to the desk.

"It isn't functioning correctly?" asked Kriseia.

"It tried to, but no," I said. "But it was completely dead when the prince gave it to me. I don't know how, but somewhere between then and now, it got a little power back in it."

"I don't know what it is or what it does," said Kriseia with a tilt of her head, "but it was sitting next to the souls on the desk when I got back. Maybe it absorbed some of the energy in them?"

"You think?" I asked, picking up one of the little crystals. "That's not how the thing is supposed to charge, but we don't have these soul things on Earth, so who knows." I dropped it and grabbed my MP3 player, holding down the button that turned it on. It had also been dead, but it had also been sitting next to a soul crystal, so might as well try it out. I couldn't call home from it, but hey, maybe I'd get my music back. It'd be a nice consolation prize, at least, I thought.

A moment later, the screen flashed to life. *Awesome*, I thought as my library opened up. The trip across worlds hadn't damaged the battery as badly as the cell phone's now was, because it showed me a full charge bar up next to the clock and date. Great, now I also had a way to keep the time, for what little good that did in a place like—

I did a double take on the date. Everything else on the device seemed to be functioning fine, so I had no reason to think the clock wasn't. But that would mean…

"Morgan?" Kriseia asked with a frown as I sank slowly into the desk chair, still staring blankly at the screen. "Is something wrong?"

"I've been here a whole week already?" I asked no one in particular. "It doesn't feel like a week. How has it been a whole week?"

Kriseia kept frowning. "Whose hole is weak?" she asked.

"Shit," I mumbled. "I'm missing so much class right now. And I'm days late for work, so Steve is probably pissed." I looked down at the date again. "And it's less than two weeks until Family Day. I'm gonna miss it this year. Shit…"

Kriseia's brow was well and truly furrowed as she leaned down into my peripheral vision. "These are obligations you had on Earth, then?" she asked. "What is Family Day?"

"It's the anniversary of the day I moved in with my parents," I said, staring at the little MP3 player in my hand. "The same day my adoption was finalized a year later — the day we became a family, they call it. Every year, they let me pick a place for us to go, and we spend the whole day there together. Playing games at an arcade, or watching four movies in a row at the theater, or just walking around the mall and eating at the food court. It's my favorite holiday. It's better than Christmas. It's better than my own birthday."

The screen had since timed out and gone dark again. I squeezed the device tighter and didn't look away. "I was embarrassed by it for a few years back in high school. Nobody else celebrated it, of course. It was an Amell family tradition. Nobody else I knew had a family like mine. I tried not to celebrate it in public anymore, asked to go camping or hiking or something out away from people so nobody would see us all together. They wouldn't let me not celebrate it with them; I asked one year, and it just made them sad. I don't even like camping. But I liked that trip more than I thought. It's shameful to think about now, how embarrassed I felt."

I felt Kriseia wordlessly squeeze my shoulder, which made the lump in my throat return. I tried to take a deep breath, but it ended up being more of a prolonged sniff. "I've never missed Family Day before," I continued, voice tightening. "I moved away for college three years ago, but we've always managed to get together somewhere, even with my classes and their jobs and the distance. I haven't missed a one. But I'm going to miss it this year." My vision blurred, and warm tears dripped over my hand and my MP3 player screen. I dropped the gadget and shut my eyes tight. "What are my parents gonna think?" I asked, voice cracking. "When they can't get hold of me, when I don't show up this year, when they find out I'm, I'm just *gone*, vanished off the face of the Earth? How am I gonna explain this? I'm not. I can't. I'm stuck here, and I can't go home, and I'm going to miss Family Day every year forever and, and I'm never going to see them again and—"

I crumpled. Shattered. It was too much. I threw myself forward, expecting to meet the desk, but instead ended up suspended in Kriseia's arms as she bent over me from behind. Blindly, I turned and buried my face in her stomach. She kept holding me tight, her hand running slowly through my hair.

I bawled.

It wasn't pretty.

I don't know how long it lasted. I had a clock now, but I didn't check it. With someone else there with me — a friend, someone who cared about me — it was safer to let go and drown in the darkness for a while. Harder not to. I lost track of time and place and the world, clung to the soft, warm body that held me, and I cried my eyes out for the life I had taken for granted, the people I couldn't live without but now had to.

I cried for the family that had owed me nothing but chose to love me. I cried for all the friends I'd made and lost track of over the years. I cried for all the music I'd heard and would never hear again, the movies and TV I'd never watch, the books I'd never read, everything new that I would never get to experience. I cried for the nebulous degree I still hadn't decided on but was already halfway through earning and would never complete. I cried for my teachers and classmates and my part-time manager, for Old Sound and my cheap, shitty apartment and frozen microwave dinners and that fucking city bus I hated riding every damn day.

I cried, and I cried, and I cried. And when the tears finally ran out and the darkness receded and I came up for air, spent and tired and empty, I found myself lying in bed, still half naked in just my t-shirt and underwear, Kriseia still holding me. I raised my face from the sticky mess I'd cried over her chest and blinked my sore eyes. "Sorry," I croaked.

She pulled my head back down, gently but insistent. "Don't be," she said. "I couldn't understand half of what you were saying, but I think I get it. I can't imagine what you must be going through. But I'm here, for whatever good I can try and do, for whatever you need, if it helps."

"It helps," I said, sniffing. "You're awesome."

She giggled. "If you say so," she said. "You would be the first to think so, but I'll try not to argue it anymore."

"No, but you are, though," I insisted, lifting my head again. "Who says you're not?"

"Well, my glamour…" She paused, her fingers fidgeting with my hair. It felt nice. "But I shouldn't complain," she continued. "As poorly as you're feeling now, any problem I may have felt seems paltry in comparison."

"No, screw that," I said. "I'm tired of hearing myself whine. I'm done for now. I want a palate cleanser." I laid my head on her again and closed my eyes. "I always talk about myself. I want to hear more about you." And I didn't want her to stop playing with my hair yet, but I kept that part a secret.

"If you wish," she said, sounding hesitant. A moment later, though, her fingers started moving again, and she continued. "I don't quite understand this 'family' idea you mention, but it sounds like people who have been important to you for most of your life. I don't think I have anything really comparable to that. There were my instructors during my training, and the madame who watched over our brood, I guess. They helped to guide and shape us, but there was no special amount of affection there, at least not in my case. And there were my peers and broodmates, but none of them cared for me overmuch either once it became clear I was less useful than most."

"Sorry, your brood?" I asked.

"Yes, other Luxuriates who spawned around the same time as myself," she said. "It's easier and more efficient for the House as a whole to bring up and train us in groups of a decent size rather than stagger instruction for the individual, at least in the beginning. My brood was the group that I lived with and apprenticed alongside."

Her class, then. Interesting that demons also had grade schools — though thinking back to my own elementary and middle school experiences, maybe it wasn't that surprising. Spawned, though? Like a fish? Did demons lay eggs or something? Is that why they didn't understand the concept of parents? Should I ask her any of this, or would that be weird and intrusive?

"I, um, was actually part of two broods, though," she continued. "My first group, by the time they were all moving on, the madame decided I wasn't suitable yet. Stunted abilities, she said. I was placed back in training with a brood that had spawned after mine. When most of them also began to finish their training before me, it was decided I was as competent as I was going to be, for better or worse. I was assigned to gift caste to await presentation to an interested patron."

She sighed, her fingers twisting around a lock of hair by my neck. "But that never really happened either. Eventually, they decided to simply bring me to the palace and present me to the archfiend. He's known to have unexpected, sometimes unknowable preferences, so maybe he'd find some use for me, they thought. If nothing else, I'd make a more attractive servant than an Invidiate, so at least I could be a maid or waitress or something like that. I was no great talent to squander in such a role."

She chuckled. "I got lucky, though. The first task I was given was waiting at the archdemons' table at that feast you attended with them, and that I think I only got because I was on hand at the moment, over near the kitchens looking for something to eat. I just wanted to make myself useful somehow. Shortly after that, Prince Vambrace decided to gift a female Luxuriate to the new human woman who had recently appeared, and I got the summons to come here and serve you. You could have knocked me down with a harpy feather, I was so surprised."

She paused and frowned. "I'm still not sure if I was chosen because you spoke briefly to me at dinner, or because I was the only new, unassigned gift caste in the palace, or because of an error and he meant to pick someone more highly regarded. I only knew I was terrified, but I didn't want to argue."

"Terrified?" I asked. "What, of me?"

"Of trying to please you, and failing," she said. "The only other member of the Original Sin in the known world besides the archfiend himself. Serving you would be an honor I hadn't earned and a challenge I was in no way adequate enough to meet. I only hoped your desires would be as mysterious and unknown as the archfiend's were said to be, so maybe I stood a chance purely at random. Or, if not that, that the punishment for failure would not be too steep." She smiled, her fingers sliding out of my hair to brush my neck. "A little bit of both, it turned out.

I still cannot say I fully understand my duties now, but I enjoy them nonetheless."

"Not what you were hoping for," I murmured as she traced patterns on my skin.

"Not what I expected," she amended. "Not what I thought I would want. I'm happy to have been pleasantly surprised."

I took a deep breath and nuzzled closer against her skin. "What *do* you want?" I asked quietly. "Honestly?"

"Honestly? I want you, Morgan" she said. "Whatever that means, however you'll have me. As you've said, I really do like you. And I like knowing that you like me too."

I rose up on my elbows and looked down at her, looking up at me. Our eyes locked… and a notion I would have thought crazy and impossible before came to me, surprising but also not. "What would…" I started, stopped, cleared my throat and looked down at the bed between us. "What do you want to… do?" I asked quietly. "With… me?"

"With you?" she asked. "Oh, nothing you've no interest in. You've made your point clear, don't worry. I understand. Whatever you want—"

"No," I said, cutting her off. "I'm saying… I mean… I don't know how to…" I took another deep breath. Whatever sudden, crazy feeling had put the notion in my head, if I waited too long, it would probably disappear. Which might have been for the best, but…

But here, now, in this moment, I didn't want it to disappear. I wanted distraction, to get out of my own head for a while. I wanted to *act*.

I reached out and took her face in my hand, feeling it heat up under the touch. "I'm asking, what do *you* want?" I said slowly. "Not what you're allowed to want. You can't help desires, you told me. So what are yours? I… I want to know," I said, swallowing again. "Please."

"Morgan…" she breathed. Her breath warm on my face. Hot and sweet. "Are you sure?"

"I'm not," I admitted. "Not of anything. But I want to be. And I think you are. Show me." And before I could think it through or stop myself, I lowered my mouth against hers, my arms trembling and my eyes shut tight as our lips pressed together.

Not my first kiss, not exactly, but the first one I really felt. The first that mattered.

I pulled away a moment later, my face hot. "Show me how," I said, voice trembling as I looked into the solid sapphire blue of her eyes. "It's alright. Please…"

She stared up at me a moment longer, eyes wide and lips parted. Then she nodded, and without another word, she held me close and slowly rolled us both, lying atop me on the bed as she leaned in and kissed me back, but with a lot more skill than I had shown — or thought possible.

She was gentle with me. Slow and patient. Warm. *So warm.* Her lips traced a tender, tingling fire down my neck and over my collarbone, searing me in the best way.

Still, it was hard to let go of my modesty and inhibitions and just let things happen, even if I wanted those things to happen. When her hand slid under my shirt, I tensed, and she felt it. She paused with her fingers on my stomach, lifting her face from my neck to gaze down into my eyes again. "Is it still alright?" she asked softly.

I gulped and nodded. "Just nervous," I said. "I've never, uh… done *this* before."

She smiled. "With a demon?"

"Or a girl," I added. "Or… um, anyone," I muttered.

Her eyes widened. "Anyone?" she repeated. "Ever? Even other humans?"

I flushed and turned my head. "I got about this far with a boy I knew once, when I was younger," I said. "Just the once. No further. Nothing major. He turned out to be kind of a jackass."

She cocked her head. "And nothing since?"

"I haven't known or liked anyone enough since, no," I said. "Sorry if that's, uh—"

"Oh, no," she said, leaning in closer. "I'm just surprised, is all. And honored."

"Honored?" I asked with a snort. "To be my first?"

She slipped her hand under my cheek and turned my face to hers. "To be with you at all," she said. "Thank you. I promise to be worthy of your trust."

I flushed again. "That's not what I was—"

Too late. Her lips were on mine again, my tongue in her mouth, tasting her sweetness and raw lust. This time, when her hands moved up my abdomen and took my shirt with them, I didn't flinch; my body arched to follow her touch, and then her body slid down on top of mine, her robe falling open, her warm, bare lavender skin pressed against me…

Holy shit, I thought. And *this* girl was a remedial student at sex school? Good lord, how high were their standards?

It wasn't a thought that stuck around long. None of them did. Whatever flaws she thought her skills had, I wasn't enough of a carnal connoisseur to notice them, I guess.

Real or not, though, she made up for them with gusto, tracing patterns of arousal over my squirming body with her lips, her tongue, her fingers, her breasts, the trailing ends of her hair, even her tail (which I had forgotten about for a minute there, and which made for an unexpected but not unpleasant surprise when it reintroduced itself). For my part, inexperienced and uneducated as I was, I mostly just lay there and let her work while I focused on trying to breathe.

And look, my modesty aside, I'm not actually a prude, normally. Maybe by demon standards, since I'd never taken part in a public gang bang before, but I had been a teenager once. I was a twenty-something now. I'd had internet access most of my life. I'd had my share of lonely nights, and the means and know-how with which to ease them. None of these sensations or places she was touching and kissing were exactly new to me.

But the intensity was. Maybe it was just because someone else was doing it besides myself for a change, sure, but I think the fact that that someone else was a literal succubus was playing a part in it.

My point being, I can't be held fully responsible for how I behaved that night.

"Is it good like this?" she asked, her face dipping between my thighs, which I had wrapped around the back of her neck.

"Nghyes!" I panted into the sheet I had been biting on. "Just like tha — *aaaaahh…*"

She laughed aloud, the sound muffled, and caught my hips as they left the bed.

At some point I ended up on top of her, possibly upside down. I don't know, I was losing track of our relative positions to one another, which part of her it was that was touching me where. All I knew was I'd left the last scrap of my inhibition far behind by then, so I started kissing whatever was in front of me.

She gasped and giggled somewhere beneath and behind me. "You don't have to worry about me, you know," she said in a voice like warm satin. "This is my gift to you right now."

"I want to," I breathed, kissing again, my hands sliding along her curves. "Show my gratitude… Don't know what I'm doing, though…"

"Do whatever you want," she purred, squirming. "Mmm, or do more of that…"

Was she humoring me? I was fumbling at best. Whatever the case, in the heat of those moments, there was no wrong move. I ran my tongue along the quivering skin in front of me — and felt her reciprocate. All the motivation I needed to learn as I went.

She was a patient and thorough teacher.

We must have spent at least a couple of hours in that bed together. I think Kriseia could have spent hours more. Things only finally slowed down once it became clear I was too exhausted even to squirm anymore. I lay there, lightheaded from all the heavy breathing and unabashed moaning, pleasantly sore all over and still tingling in a myriad of hard-to-reach places, my whole body glistening with sweat and… other things, mine and hers alike. My warm skin slowly cooled as I lay with my arms and legs splayed, gazing unfocused at the ceiling. Kriseia lay curled beside me, her body still pressing tight to mine, her leg draping one of my thighs and her arm laying across my collarbone. Her fingers were softly running through my hair, her tail slowly stroking my calf, her lips gently nuzzling the curve of my neck.

After a few moments, when I didn't respond like I had been responding all night, she raised her head and smiled down at me. "Well sated, Morgan?"

I nodded. It was about all I was good for at the moment.

"I'm glad," she said, leaning closer. "And… thank you. For being willing to try this, and for trusting me to try it with. I know it's not an easy thing to want for you. I hope it helps with… well, in whatever way it can."

It did. I would have told her as much, but she leaned in further and kissed me again — not the urgent, passionate making out we'd been at for most of the night, but slow and soft and gentle, like our first. She tasted sweet, and a bit salty, and by now, achingly familiar.

I kissed her back with warmth in my heart and no hesitation, my eyes slipping slowly shut, and drifted off to sleep almost before she pulled her lips away.

Chapter 25: Haughtiness

My lungs were on fire, every breath agony. My legs felt like jelly as they pumped frantically beneath me, hurtling me forward across the stonework atop the wall. There was no city in the distance, no wasteland horizon, only empty red sky on all sides. And behind me, its every thunderous step sending the stones beneath me trembling, galloped an enormous, slavering garm.

I hadn't actually turned to see it. I knew better. If I dared to look, I knew I'd see it was directly on my heels, or I'd trip on a loose stone and go sprawling.

But I knew it was back there, and that it was coming for me, and that it was gaining on me no matter how hard I ran.

It's going to get me. It's going to catch me and eat me and eat the book. I have to hurry and cast the spell. I have to go home now before I die.

Struggling to breathe, my legs screaming, I opened the *Morganomicon* and cradled it to my chest. It was hard to run with an open book in front of me; I was slowing down, which meant the dog was going to get me sooner, but it was the only choice I had to survive. Loose pages tore out and fluttered away in my wake as I flipped through them, frantically trying to find the right spell, my eyes racing along the flowing elvish lines, speed-reading a language I've never actually learned. Heat generation, perception blocking, kinetic nullification, emotional transmutation, interplanar telepor — yes! That was the one, that was the —

Thunder. Not the slam of garm paws, but real thunder, as the sky opened up and began pouring. Warm raindrops spattered the pages of the book, obscuring the writing and melting through the parchment. No, not rain — blood. Thick, hot, black blood, pouring from the sky, pouring over the wall, dripping from my hair and soaking my clothes, running down my skin, into my eyes. I couldn't see. I dropped the book — then slipped in the blood pooling on the ground beneath me.

I went sprawling, screaming, as a hot wall of foul breath washed over me from behind and massive jaws snapped closed and the last thing I saw was teeth ripping into my—

I woke with a gasp, my sheet thrown off and my pillow on the floor, my hands still flailing unconsciously. My heart felt like it was trying to kick its way out of my chest, and breathing was still a chore, but I was safe. Drenched in sweat, yes, and naked, but safe.

Kriseia was still asleep next to me, her own pillow cradled in her arms. Somehow my nightmare flailing hadn't woken her. Good.

I sat up and swung my legs out of bed, surprised at first to find that, just like in my nightmare, they were sore and a bit unsteady as I stood. And then I remembered why.

In the calm of morning (or the middle of the night, or whatever the hell time it was), without last night's torrent of emotions clouding my brain, I thought I'd be more embarrassed at the memory of what I'd — we'd — done. More regretful, maybe. But no, it turned out, not really. I was surprised at myself, sure, but I couldn't think of a reason to be upset it had happened. And as first times went, well, shit, it could have been a hell of a lot worse. Couldn't complain there.

So it took some adjusting, but I hobbled my pleasantly sore self across the room without incident. The lamps were still burning at about half their usual brightness; guess Kriseia had passed out not long after I had without turning them off. There was still enough light to find my way to the bathroom, where I toweled off, washed my face, and finally got my heartbeat back under control.

I couldn't remember the last time I'd had a nightmare, especially one that vivid. Granted, I'd also never been this stressed and terrified in my life before, so it made sense. I shuddered as I replayed it in my head: the running, the garm, the terror, that damn book, and all the blood. If I closed my eyes, I could still feel the hot blood rain spattering my skin, still feel the tremble of the dog monster's steps, still see the shredded pages of the *Morganom* —

I froze with a wet rag still pressed to my face.

… No… Surely not…

I dropped the rag and leaned against the sink, shutting my eyes tighter, as if maybe that would help. I remembered… concepts. Flipping through the dream pages, looking for the spell I needed, and knowing the ones I was reading weren't it. But I knew that because I could recognize what they were instead.

So what were they? Dammit, Morgan, think!

The ones I'd already memorized were in there, I remembered that. The one that made my hands burn things, the… burning, hot, heat… heat generation! And the other, the invisibility, unnoticeability one that just kept people from seeing and hearing … from hearing? No, not the way I'd done it, talking to people was how I'd broken it both times. But I'd barely remembered that one when I cast it, and I was grasping at the instructions. If I'd done it completely right, step by step, I could have blocked all perception of me, according to —

I remembered. I remembered! Not just the gist of what I was reading in my dreams, but the page itself, the shape of the language written there, the swirls and symbols! They were faint, fuzzy, but they were there!

… But were they accurate? It was a dream, after all; I was reading my subconscious, not the book itself.

Then again… the very first time I'd ever laid eyes on the *Morganomicon*, skimming its pages in that weird lady's store, the swirly spell language had stuck with me. Just at a first few glances, I guess I'd understood enough that my brain was trying to recall and decipher the rest. Once I'd finally sat down to read it for real and began to legit take it in, those intrusive thoughts had stopped — but they'd been damn intrusive until then. The sticking power of Old Elvish in the back of my mind was no joke. Whose to say any page I'd ever so much as laid eyes on for a second wasn't still kicking around in there, waiting to be recalled and understood? Including the bastard of a spell that dropped me here?

I didn't know. But, maybe, I could find out.

I strode out of the bathroom and picked up my t-shirt, underwear, and pants from where they were scattered across the floor, impatiently pulling them on before sitting down at my desk and scrabbling for fresh paper and ink. I dipped my quill, but then hesitated over the blank page. How to go about this? I thought of the first page I'd seen in my dream, the one about heat generation. That was the first spell I'd learned, and the one I had the most experience with. I tried to recall the pattern of the language on the dream page, the length and width of the swirly lines, and started slowly tracing them from memory.

It was slow going, getting slower the longer I went. The dream images were fading as I sat there, awake and alert. Still, I kept at it. And after half an hour or so of straining my recollection and carefully tracing every curve as best as I could recall, at last I had… a page covered in useless swirls.

Was this right? I thought I'd reproduced my dream image, but it was getting harder to tell. I set my quill down and read over my progress so far, only to realize that I couldn't. This wasn't writing, magic or otherwise. This was just doodles.

I tried reading it again, focusing on every rise and fall of the lines. When that didn't work, I pulled the page back and unfocused my eyes, trying to see it like one of those magic eye puzzles. Nothing. I set the page down and looked to the side, so that the lines were only barely visible in my peripheral vision. Still nothing. With a grunt of frustration, I pushed myself away from my desk and stood, turning to glare at the opposite wall, waiting for the intrusive thoughts to start.

They didn't. Of course.

What the hell? This had been so easy before as to be unbidden, but now it was just gone? That didn't make any sense! Why couldn't I get it? What was I doing wrong?

Okay. Calm down. Think. Maybe I was going about this wrong. Just because I associated the patterns I'd read in my dream with spells that I knew were in the real book didn't necessarily mean I'd gotten them right. Maybe I was misremembering the details, somehow. If so, then even if I perfectly recreated what I remembered, it wouldn't read right.

But I knew this spell. I *knew* it. I could cast it without reading it, it was so simple. I could cast it right now if I wanted.

So why didn't I?

A quick glance at the bed told me Kriseia was still sleeping. Good. I eased back down into my seat and crumpled the page of failed scribbles into a ball as quietly as I could, then held that ball tight in both my hands. I took a deep breath and closed my eyes, remembering — not the dream, but the knowledge. My thoughts groped for the familiar pattern for a moment, but found it quickly and slid through the flow even quicker. My fingers twitched, my lips fluttered through the voiceless, unknown words of the incantation. I felt the air waving at the same time as I heard the faint crackling, smelled the slight whiff of smoke.

I opened my eyes and my hands. The paper ball was smoldering in my palm, blackened edges disappearing ahead of bright orange cinders. In a few seconds, I held only a pinch of warm ash, the glow already fading.

Right, that was heat generation on lock. My mind knew the pattern. It was getting my hands to recreate it that was the problem.

I went back into the bathroom to rinse the paper ash from my hands, then sat down again in front of a new page. Set the dream aside for now; focus on what I know I know. There was magic in my brain still. The writing in a book had put it there. There had to be a way to put it back in writing again. Stood to reason.

I closed my eyes and thought about the spell pattern. It came to me instantly this time, having just cast it only a minute ago. I kept my grip loose on my quill as I willed my hand to move, to follow along with my thoughts. Maybe if I went about this less literally, tried something more abstract rather than one-to-one image recreation from my dreams, then I could—

My quill caught fire. Right, that was gonna complicate things. Hadn't thought of that.

After rushing back to the bathroom to douse the flames, I flopped back into my chair with the singed remains of my feather pen to try again. Third time's the charm. Just don't get carried away this time.

To my credit, what I'd scribbled down this time before the fire interrupted me looked … better, somehow. Closer to the swirly nonsense I remembered. How, exactly, I couldn't tell, but I felt like I was making progress. Maybe. Hopefully.

What if…

I held out my free hand, palm up, and ran through the spell a third time. I wasn't trying to actually cast it this time, just remember what casting it was like, the feeling as the magic took shape and poured out: the tingling in my hands that gathered and then died down, the sense of something intangible streaming across my fingers, the faraway haze of growing heat, like phantom water flowing just beyond my reach.

It was hard to put into words, the sensation of a familiar spell revving up. But even if I couldn't describe it exactly, I could make a rough sketch of it. I *could*. I was sure of it.

Even trying to be mentally careful, invoking the real spell to transcribe it also meant casting it. When I felt the heat building, I focused on my empty hand, trying to will the magic into that palm and not my writing hand.

It… worked? Kind of? My writing hand still grew unnaturally warm, but my empty hand was the one that started to sizzle like a stove coil, so the bulk of the spell was definitely going where I was telling it to. But the mental steps as I knew them always ignited both hands equally, and willing a change this time had also… changed the spell somehow. The mental pattern felt a bit different. I could only tell because I'd cast it the regular way so often so recently; it was kind of like singing the wrong lyrics to a song you ought to have known by heart, where you knew you'd gotten it wrong but couldn't immediately tell what the right words were.

My writing hand had still been moving through it all, thankfully — I was crushing it with the concentration since I'd started this magic shit. Sophomore Morgan would have been jealous. My quill hovered over this most recent squiggle pattern as my eyes traced along it. Careful not to mar the spell line itself, I jotted a little dash next to where I'd felt the difference in the invocation. Not sure how I was going to dictate the two-handed version, then, unless I could find a flame-proof pen somewhere. Or maybe really thick oven mitts.

It took me a minute to realize the significance of what I'd just done. I was still staring at it maybe a full minute later when it finally clicked.

That dash I'd made. I knew where the flow of magic had differed mid-spell. And I could read this most recent attempt well enough to demarcate the change.

I just wrote, and then diagrammed, a magic sentence.

"Yes!" I whisper-shouted, pumping my fist. Stray paper on my desk fluttered away at the movement, and I realized my fist-pumping hand was still red-hot, close to being on actual fire, from the feel of it. I quickly dropped the magic before I accidentally burned my desk down. Lucky that turning a spell off was infinitely simpler than trying to turn one on.

I turned my attention back to my recent triumph. So much potential in such a meaningless-looking swirly pen scratch. So much riding on these innocuous napkin doodles. I read through my transcription again, reveling in the recognition, the familiar feeling of my brain contorting in strange and unnatural ways. The magic didn't trigger this time just reading the spell, but the potential of it was there, on the paper, speaking to me in a language plainer than language. It was the same impossibly easy feeling I had gotten reading the *Morganomicon* that first time, that breakthrough sense of suddenly solving the unsolvable. It was positively heady.

If I could tell where the change in spell focus from two hands to one had occurred, could I pick out other details as well? The answer, I quickly discovered, was yes: here was where the flowing sensation quickened, here was where I started to notice the heat growing, here was where the feeling in my skin changed from hot to humming before the burn grew painful, here was where the air wavered and sizzled. I marked off each delineation point in the spell as near as I could tell and made notes about the feeling of each, what step and sensation went where. When I was finished, pyrokinesis lay pinned and dissected like a metaphysical frog on the paper before me.

I grinned ear to ear, practically bouncing in my seat. I felt like a witchy goddess. Like that one from *Macbeth*, whatever her name had been. I hadn't read that one since 11th grade. Heckintonkery or something.

Then someone laid their hand on my shoulder from behind, and I felt less goddess-like as I jumped with a squeak of surprise, turning in my seat and half-falling over my desk in the process.

Kriseia yanked her hand away and held them both up before her, equally startled. "Are you alright?" she asked.

"Yeah, sorry," I said, righting myself in my seat. "I didn't hear you get up."

"You haven't heard me trying to talk to you either, I gather," she said. "I woke up to find you hunched over the desk in the dark, muttering to yourself. I was starting to get worried."

I looked up. Sure enough, the lamps on the walls, which had already been dim when I'd woken up, had burned down to nightlight levels of brightness, casting the whole room in a dark gloom. "Sorry," I said again. "Guess I've been too busy to notice."

"It's alright," she said, then ran a hand through her sweat-matted hair, brushing it back over one short, stubby horn. "It's weird how stuffy it is in here, though, with the fires so low," she added with a deep breath, fanning herself with a hand.

"Is it?" I asked. "I hadn't noticed that either." Which was true; even now, despite having cast that heat spell over and over again, I didn't feel any discomfort.

"It's only hot on this side of the room, though," said Kriseia, brow furrowing, as she brought up her other hand and fanned with that one too. "Maybe there's something blocking the ventilation flue?"

Oh. "Yeah, maybe," I said, only just realizing that it was hotter because I'd been using heat magic over and over. I hadn't noticed because the spell kept the heat off of me somehow, I had to assume. Otherwise, I'd have burned my own hands off by now.

Which raised a new thought.

I turned back to my diagrammed spell doodle. I'd marked where in the pattern I began to feel the heat and where the feeling in my skin stopped. Somewhere in the squiggle in between was some sort of heat protection measure. A spell within a spell?

I marked the section with a curly bracket and wrote "flame shield?" underneath. If this bit of the magic was the bit keeping me from melting my skin off, it was probably important to pay attention to it. Maybe if that part of the spell could be isolated from the heating parts, I could use it to —

"Morgan?"

"Eh?" I looked up to find Kriseia still at my side, frowning in concern again. "Sorry, sorry," I said, dropping my quill and rubbing my eyes. "My focus is all over the place today."

"Did you not sleep well?" she asked.

"Mm. Yes and no," I said. "I was out like a light when I was finally out, but I got woke up by a nightmare."

"Aww." She stepped behind me and slipped her arms around my neck, then rested her chin on the top of my head. "I'm sorry. I had hoped I'd exhausted you enough that wouldn't be a problem."

I chuckled. "You definitely wore me out, don't worry," I said, patting her arm. "I got no complaints."

"I'm happy to hear that," she said with a giggle. "But you know, if you couldn't fall back asleep, you could have woken me up. I wouldn't have minded going again, if it's what you needed."

I gulped and flushed. This girl was crazy. And as surprisingly comfortable as I found myself with what we'd just done, this level of casual solicitation was still going to take some getting used to.

Oh shit. Speaking of potential problems I wasn't used to having…

"Hey, Kriseia," I said, then cleared my throat. How to ask this nicely? "You're, uh… you're clean, right?"

"At the moment?" she asked. "I could use a bath." Her head settled more cozily onto my own. "Though, if I'm being honest, I'm not particularly in a hurry to wash the smell of your body from mine."

Wow. Okay. There's a — compliment? — that I never expected to ever receive. "No, I mean, like, uh… like, diseases. Sexual ones. Do you, y'know… have any?" I muttered.

"Oh," she said, rising off of me but keeping her hands on my shoulders. "No, of course not. A diseased Luxuriate would never be allowed to be given as a new gift. That would be a terrible insult, especially to a human dignitary. Don't worry, I'm still young and healthy."

"Right," I said. "Sorry. I wasn't even sure if demons had to worry about STDs, but you know." I frowned. "Wait, what's being young got to do with it?"

"Well, the older you get and the more people you're with, the higher the chance you catch something eventually, right?" she said, squeezing my shoulders. "I'm sure I'll get contaminated someday, in the far future. At least, I hope so."

I turned in my chair and gave her my best worried face. "You hope so?" I repeated. "Why is that a life goal?"

She shrugged. "Unless someone kills me or I'm involved in an accident of some sort, a fatal sex disease is most likely to be my eventual end. I'm a Luxuriate. That's just statistics. And dying because I had dirty sex sounds like a better end than dying to violence or falling off a ledge or something like that, don't you think?"

I tilted my head. "When you put it like that, I guess. You think about this kinda thing often?"

"Almost never, actually," she said, her fingers tracing the tendons in my shoulders. "Too many better things to think about."

"Like dirty sex?"

She smiled. "Well, not the eventually fatal kind, but otherwise, yes. Obviously, a lot of those thoughts."

"You wouldn't rather die doing it in a tornado over a cliff?" I asked, smiling back. I think all the terror and trauma of the past few days had inured me to the morbidity of the topic.

"Oh, definitely not," she said. "I respect that level of dedication to kink, but it wouldn't be for me. I don't like that dangling, high-up feeling. I can't even do suspension bondage without getting nervous."

I was thankfully spared from having to comment on that by a knock on the door. A moment later, it cracked open, and Enkida poked her head in. "There's a messenger for you, Lady Morgan," she said. "If you're not too busy."

"Too busy?" a wheedling voice sneered from beyond the door. "How dare you! Nobody is too busy for a message from Duch—effffmm!" The voice muffled, as if trying to shout through a hand clamped over their mouth. General Enkida didn't bat an eye or move a muscle, only looked at me expectantly.

I looked from her to Kriseia to my notes. "I am kind of in the middle of something," I said, "but I've got time to at least hear a message."

Enkida said nothing, only opened the door wider. A thick-set Invidiate in an embroidered doublet stomped past her into the room, half his pupils glaring at the general, the other half glaring at me. His drooping mustache twitched and bristled as Enkida closed the door behind him, and he drew himself up to his full three-foot-ish height before he spoke. "I come bearing a summons for the Lady Morgan from the eminent Duchess Sidona, who graciously requests your presence in her tower salon, post-haste."

Whether that was his own pompousness or he was just passing on Sidona's, it didn't exactly engender any compliance in me. Luckily, like I'd said, I was busy. "Thanks," I said, "but I'm kind of wrapped up with my own thing right now. Tell Sidona I said sorry, I'll stop by later."

"Tell Sid—" He sputtered, his gangly hands scrabbling at the fabric of his doublet. "One does not simply dismiss the attention of *Duchess* Sidona! Who do you think you are, the archfiend himself? I am her ladyship's *personal* messenger, and I cannot brook such—"

"Yeah, alright, thank you," I said, probably louder than necessary. "I'd love to, but like I said, pretty busy right now, sorry, maybe next time." I turned back to my desk and grabbed my quill, waggling it in the air for a second while I pointedly shuffled my papers.

I could hear his scrabbling intensify. "You—!" he choked. "I will not— ! Listen, you—!"

The door swung open again. "Message delivered," said Enkida, framed in the doorway. "Time to go."

"This is outrageous!" the messenger shouted. "I'm not leaving until—"

There was a soft crack, and he stopped. I glanced up. Enkida was gazing stoically at the little demon while ever-so-slightly stretching her neck.

"—until right now," the Invidiate finished at a more polite volume. "But I am not happy with it, and neither, I assure you, will her ladyship be."

Enkida's head tilted the other way, and her neck cracked again. "Duly noted," she said. "Now, on your way."

The messenger harshly wiggled his mustache one more time before stomping from the room, all of his many pupils fixed on me as the general closed the door behind him. I guess I still hadn't met too many Invidiates yet, because those multi-faceted tabletop dice eyes still kind of creeped me out.

Kriseia's gaze lingered on the door, her finger on her chin. "Something on your mind?" I asked.

"No, just… wondering. They never covered human dignitaries in my court etiquette classes, unsurprisingly. I'm still trying to puzzle out where that title lands alongside duchesses and archdukes and such."

"I don't know either," I said. "You worried I'll get in trouble for turning down Sidona?"

"Someone like me would," she said. "I'm sure you won't. It must be strange, though, for the aristocracy to get used to."

I remembered the looks of the assembled archdemons when the prince had made his pronouncement. "Yeah, I don't think they know what to do with me," I said. "And I honestly don't know what to do with myself. But it was Vambrace's idea, so Sidona and her like can take it up with him if they've got a problem with me. I got my own issues to deal with, and if I stop to jump at everyone who snaps their fingers at me, they'll never get done."

I turned back to my notes, but I could feel Kriseia still staring at me. "You're not at all worried of the noble demons' scorn?" she asked.

"A bit," I said, "but not as much as I was. I was almost eaten by a giant dog yesterday; what's the worst a grumpy duchess can do after that?"

She was on me then, her arms around my shoulders, her mouth on mine. My seat tilted under our combined weight, nearly toppling, but she righted me a moment later as she broke off and rose up, smiling. "Pride is my weakness," she said, her lavender cheeks flushing purple. "Not very original, I know, but... sorry." She bit her lip. "You just turned me on a little."

I gulped. "I, uh... I'm not really ready to, uh..."

"I know," she said, still grinning, one finger rising up to curl in her hair. "Whenever you want to have me again is fine. I'm going to take a bath now, if you've no objection."

"Yeah, no." I waved vaguely at the bathroom. "Go for it."

She grinned and sashayed away. I'll admit, my eyes lingered after she shut the door.

This girl was crazy. *I* was crazy. What the hell was I doing?

I was gonna miss her when I finally left, I realized. *If* I ever left.

No. I was leaving. *Morganomicon* be damned, I had another way out now, long and complicated though it was likely to be. All the hot demon sex in the world wasn't going to keep me from going home — just as soon as I figured out how.

To that end, I focused my attention back on my magic notes. I'd gotten heat projection more or less sorted for the moment; I had one more trick memorized, though not as fully, and it was admittedly a much more complicated spell than the first. Might as well get started cracking it now, then, and hope I learned something in the process.

I'd run through the mental steps and was halfway through my first fumbled, definitely flawed, sure to fail attempt at sketching it out when the door to my room opened again and Enkida stuck her head back in. "You've got another visitor, Lady," she said.

"Another of Sidona's grumpy messengers?" I asked, trying and failing to hold on to my fragile train of impossible thought.

"Not this time," said Enkida.

Another head slid through the opening above the general's and beamed at me. "Permission to interrupt, my dear?" asked Duchess Sidona, while Enkida glowered sidelong at her with her bottom fangs bared.

"Oh. Uh, hi, yeah, alright," I said. Wasn't expecting this, but she was already here, and she'd already broken my concentration. Also, Enkida looked like she was about to shove one of her horns through the duchess' throat if she didn't give her some space.

"Marvelous," said Sidona, brushing past the general and into the room. Enkida nearly closed the door on the train of the Superbiate's trailing gown, but Sidona yanked the fabric out of the way at the last second and turned it into a flourish. "My apologies for the intrusion, but when my messenger returned saying that you were too engrossed with your own labors to accept my invitation, my curiosity simply got the better of me. You managed to quite incense the little guy."

"Yeah, sorry about that," I said. "I wasn't trying to be rude, but I guess he holds you in pretty high regard."

"Him?" She sniffed. "He hates me. Every Invidiate hates everyone, or haven't you noticed?"

"What, every one of them?" I asked. "I've noticed all the servants seem miserable, but I mean, I probably would be too in their situation."

"Of course you would," said Sidona with another sniff. "Anyone would; that's why his majesty fills the ranks of palace servantry almost exclusively with the little whingers. Nobody *enjoys* drudgery, but if it must be done, then it might as well be done by those who were never going to be happy with their lot in the first place, don't you agree?" I opened my mouth to reply, but she kept going. "And of course, the more important and impressive you are, the greater the hatred you engender. Naturally, I myself am particularly despised by the entirety of House Invidia, my own personal servants included. Pitiful, yes, but I try not to let it bother me."

It's probably not just House Invidia, I thought. Out loud, I said, "So, what brings you here?"

"My lady," she said.

I was waiting for her to say more. "…Yes?" I asked when she didn't.

"No, you say it," she said. "'So, what brings you here, my lady?' Manners, dear."

I was quiet for a moment, weighing my options. I'd already been fairly surly with her messenger — didn't want to be seen as *too* bitchy. Then again, if I kept up the stuffed shirt haughtiness, Kriseia would probably want to kiss me again.

But she was in the bath now anyway. And despite all of her… self, Sidona was alright. "What brings you here, my lady, then," I repeated.

Her chin rose a little higher. Of course. "At first, I merely thought to persuade you myself to come sit for your portrait once again," she said. "But then I figured, you've graced me in my salon often enough, I suppose it's only fair that I grace you in yours. And I admit, I am fascinated to know what you're working on in here."

"What I'm working on?" My hand spread instinctively to cover my highly-illegal notes.

"Indeed," she said. "His majesty has never to my knowledge undertaken any serious artistry, so I myself have never beheld human inspiration firsthand." She stepped closer, placing one hand on the back of my chair and one on my shoulder. "Come, show me your work. You simply must."

Son of a bitch, why didn't it occur to me to hide my magic first? "I don't know, I'm still working on it," I said, gathering my assorted scribble papers together. "You know how it is, when something's not finished, and you're not ready for anyone to—"

"Nonsense," said the duchess. She reached out and snatched the top paper, the one with my fumbling perception blocking attempt, before I could stop her. "You've seen my unfinished painting often enough, so what's the difference?"

"What?! No I haven't!" I reached for the paper, but she spun away from me as her eyes scanned it. I rose from my seat, but she simply lifted her arm. She was taller than me by a good couple of feet; should I risk jumping for it, or would that be too suspicious? Would it even work?

My heart sped up — but before I could panic properly, I noticed her brow scrunching and her eyes drifting unfocused over the paper. "Fascinating," she murmured. "Or I assume so, anyway." She flashed the page at me and frowned. "A preliminary sketch of some sort? It's rather… esoteric." She squinted again at the page. "Floral, perhaps, in an abstract way."

She… couldn't read the spell?

I loosed the breath I'd been holding. She couldn't read the spell! What was stopping her, I didn't know; maybe she hadn't stared at it long enough yet. Maybe it just took a few days of quietly obsessing over before the swirly shit made sense. Regardless, I was safe, at least for the moment.

"Something like that," I said, snatching the papers back while she held them low enough to reach. Best to err on the side of caution, before she got too good of an eyeful. "It's, uh … another song."

"This is musical notation of a sort, is it?" Her eyes stayed locked to the back of the papers I now held, making me nervous. "I thought you had said you were unversed in the instrumentation aspect of musicianship."

Had I? That was true, anyway. Probably best not to lie about that sort of thing with her. "I am," I said. "This is just the lyrics."

"Lyrics? That?" She reached for a papers again, but I scrunched them in my hand and spun out of her way. "That mass of freeform looping is what your Earth alphabet looks like these days?"

"Yeah, well, language evolves," I argued. "Earth's got lots of alphabets. This one's a bit obscure, admittedly, but that just makes my ideas harder to steal, if I write them in something fewer people can read."

"Your ideas?" Both of her eyebrows slowly rose, all the way up. "So this song you're transcribing is a Lady Morgan original composition? My, my!"

Sure, why not? "Yeah, well, you know how it is," I said. "I woke up with an idea, I thought I might as well write it down, in case it was any good."

"Even if it isn't, it will be singularly novel, at the very least," said Sidona, her eyes still locked on the papers in my fist, like a dog who'd caught a glimpse of a treat. "The first new human-originating music to grace Dis since his majesty's arrival in ancient days…"

There was a soft gasp behind her, and we both turned to see Kriseia stepping naked and still damp from the bathroom, a small towel draped over her horns, her hand on her lips, her eyes wide. "Is that what you've been so busy with since waking up?" she breathed. "I had no idea. That's incredible!" She only then seemed to notice Sidona standing between us and dipped an impromptu bow.

The duchess wasn't looking at her anymore by that point. "You've been at this for some while now, have you?" she asked me. "No throwaway musing, this, then, I take it. The plot thickens!"

"I, uh…" I glanced between her and Kriseia as I felt the hole deepen beneath me. "Well, I was having a pretty bad day yesterday. Gave me some pretty bad dreams. I thought doing something like this might help, maybe. Music therapy."

"Therapy?" Kriseia repeated. "What is that?"

"Unimportant," Sidona barked, raising a dismissive hand so quickly that it startled Kriseia behind her. "You must perform the fruits of your labors for us, my lady," she said, advancing on me as she spoke. "My curiosity cannot stand to pique any further."

I backed away from her until my butt hit the desk. "It's not finished yet," I argued, slipping sideways away from the advancing demon. "I still gotta proofread, and—"

"Unnecessary," she said, then spun my desk chair around and elegantly folded down to sit in it. "The first draft of any project will doubtless have its flaws, unless it's one of mine. The potential still shines through, if it is there." She laced her fingers and settled her chin on them, leaning forward. Her posture made it look as if she were only a few impatient moments from lunging across the room at me if I didn't give her what she wanted. "Perform what you have," she commanded. "I must hear it."

Short of calling for Enkida to wrestle the duchess bodily out of the room, I could tell there was no other way out of this. I took a deep breath and uncrumpled the papers in my hands. "Say please."

Sidona frowned. "Excuse you?"

"I'll consent to sharing my lyrics," I said. "If you ask nicely."

Her frown deepened. "Have I not already?"

"No, you've only demanded," I said. "And I get it. Superbiates, it probably feels unnatural. But I must insist."

Her frown morphed to a full-blown scowl. "These are your terms, are they?"

I smoothed my papers. "Yup."

The duchess pinched the bridge of her nose and closed her eyes for a moment. "Very well," she sighed. "*Please* share your work with us, Lady Morgan."

Watching her lips curdle around the word almost made this farce worth it. "Thank you," I said, then took a deep breath and focused on the page in my hand.

Right then. What's another song that a demon of pride would like? What could I plagiarize that would sound like something I might write myself after an evening of anxiety attacks and a night of bad dreams? And most important of all, what's something that might still sound halfway decent coming from my amateur throat without any music to back it up?

I rifled through my mental playlist for several long seconds before I found the perfect candidate.

"Okay," I breathed, then cleared my throat and pitched my voice as somber as I could make it. "*Hello darkness, my old friend... I've come to talk with you again...*"

I dragged my eyes slowly over the papers, occasionally flipping through them, to simulate reading lyrics. Most of the papers were blank, and I'd flipped back around to the first one before I'd finished, but hopefully the duchess wouldn't notice.

The sound of silence in the room after my "reading" was stretching out longer than I'd thought it would. I looked between my two audience members. Kriseia had her eyes shut, a slow smile spreading on her face, which I took to mean she was pleased by the performance. And Sidona...

The duchess was staring at the floor, wide-eyed and tight-lipped, her hands clenched hard in her lap. She didn't move a muscle, didn't blink. I wasn't sure she was even breathing. Shit, was she that big a Simon & Garfunkel fan and didn't know it until now?

Kriseia was the first to speak. "That was beautiful," she said as she opened her eyes. "No wonder you've been so focused and busy. I don't quite understand all of it, but it was haunting. Don't you think so, my lady?" she asked Sidona.

The duchess didn't react at all.

"Lady Sidona?" Kriseia repeated, stepping up beside where the Superbiate sat. She frowned at the lack of reply and lifted a hand, then dropped it again, apparently thinking better of touching someone of such higher station than her.

I didn't have that same caution anymore. "Duchess?" I asked, stepping forward, careful to keep a tight grip on my note papers just in case. "Hey, Earth to Sidona? You awake or what?" I reached out and laid a hand on her shoulder.

Her arm shot out and smacked mine away, and she shot up out of her seat so quickly the chair skittered back and fell over, almost crashing into Kriseia as she sidestepped out of the way. Sidona's eyes were still wide and unblinking as she stared down at me, then around the room, her head jerking like a squirrel that had suddenly found itself in busy traffic.

"What?" she asked, breathless, her gaze darting back down to mine. "You?" She was noticeably breathing again now, her chest rising and falling rapidly beneath her decolletage. A moment of staring later and she got her breath under control, then slowly narrowed her eyes. "You wrote this?" she said like an accusation. "For yourself? Or for me? Did you know I was coming to see you? Who have you been talking to about me?" She took a menacing step forward.

I took a step back. "What? No one!" I said, raising my paperless hand between us. "I just wrote it cuz I felt like it. What's it got to do with you?"

"Nothing!" She suddenly raised her arms, then just as suddenly wrapped them around herself, hugging her elbows and blinking hard over and over again. "Nothing," she said, more quietly this time, then took a deep breath and looked away. "It is… a good song, Lady Morgan. Moving.

You should be proud." She scowled, hard, at nothing in particular. "I should be going."

The duchess strode — nearly stormed — past me to the door, her hand resting on the handle. I thought maybe she'd frozen again as she stood staring at the wood.

Then her shoulders lifted and squared. "I shall send word when I require your presence for your portrait again," she said without looking back. "Perhaps. If I do not scrap the project altogether. But…" She did look back then, peering at me over her shoulder as if she could only barely see me. "No. Maybe? If I knew how quickly…" We stood staring at one another like that for a few more seconds before her head whipped around and she yanked the door open. "At any rate, be ready for my summons at a moment's notice. Move."

This last command was barked at Enkida, whom she shoved past as she pulled the door closed behind her. The general didn't move a muscle, even as Sidona attempted to walk through her; their shoulders checked, a sleeve of the duchess's gown catching momentarily on Enkida's armor with a quiet rip, turning Sidona's purposeful stride into an awkward flail as she bounced off the stalwart Iriate. The duchess either didn't notice or didn't care as she hurried off. I could see a piece of the expensive fabric still clinging to Enkida's pauldron before the door inched shut.

I turned to Kriseia, who looked just as stunned as I felt. "Did I do something wrong?" I asked.

Her brow furrowed. "I don't know. I don't think so." She bent and grabbed the upturned desk chair, setting it back on its legs in its place. "I have heard that even among other Superbiates and nobility, Duchess Sidona is considered a bit eccentric. Too much attention dedicated too vehemently to too many arts, perhaps. Other palace Luxuriates say she's never accepted the services of anyone she didn't first sketch or sculpt or write a poem about. I could not begin to tell you how her mind works, I'm afraid."

"Ah well," I said, shrugging. "I'm getting used to weird reactions by now. If it's something I did, I'm sure I'll hear about it before long." I walked back to my desk and set my spell notes down, smoothing out the crumpled papers. "Until then, I've got more important stuff to do." I pulled back my chair, then paused as my stomach suddenly let loose with a gurgle loud enough to fill the room.

Kriseia brought a hand up to her lips to stifle a giggle. "Important stuff like having another meal first?" she asked. "When was the last time you ate anything, Morgan?"

I held my protesting stomach as I counted backward in my mind. "Before that business on the wall with the dog attack," I said. "You were there. We tried out all those weird hellfruits."

"*That* long ago?" she said, then shook her head. "That's not healthy, especially if you want to keep fucking me. We should get you fed, please."

I cleared my throat, the sound lost beneath another hungry belly growl. "Alright, no arguments here," I said. "Grub first, then back to work."

Chapter 26: Collusion

We were on our way to the usual cafeteria when we turned a corner to find Prince Vambrace headed our way. Kriseia immediately skidded to a stop and bowed deeply. I hesitated a second, still unsure where exactly I fell on the status ladder; but wherever it was, it was still somewhere below archfiend, and anyway, there were other people watching. So I bowed too, mimicking Kriseia as best I could.

Vambrace looked amused as he approached and waved us up. "Lady Morgan," he said with a nod. "Kriseia."

"You remember my name, Sire?" Kriseia breathed, still starstruck. She lived down the hall from the guy now, but I suppose he was still a big deal.

"You are handmaid to my consort," said the prince. "Of course I do. Where are you ladies off to?"

"Hitting up the kitchen to snag some food," I said.

"Then you're in luck," he said, stepping up beside us and turning us around. "I am on my way to dinner with the archdemons. Join me."

"Uh… sure, thanks," I said, cursing inwardly. I really would have rather just gotten something quick and gotten back to work decoding the spells I knew. The last thing I wanted was another formal dinner with the stuffed shirts who mostly seemed to dislike me. Not that I could admit that.

Vambrace linked his arm through mine as we walked, proper gentleman-like, while Kriseia followed close behind us. Hell's two humans together like this, of course every set of eyes we passed turned to us, every head dipped. This soon after my highly illegal studies, all the attention was making me extra uncomfortable.

"How are you feeling, my lady?" the prince asked under his breath, concern in his voice.

Shit, was my nervousness showing? Was he suspicious? No, I realized after a panicked second; the last time he'd seen me, I was despondent and covered in garm blood. I'd almost forgotten.

"I'm fine now, thanks," I said with a polite smile. "Took a long bath, had a panic attack and a nightmare, thought about some stuff and calmed down. Kriseia really helped with that."

"Did she now?" he asked with a smirk and a glance over his shoulder.

Kriseia smiled proudly. "I'm honored to have been of service," she said. "Lady Morgan is an exceedingly gracious lover."

"Is she now?" His smirk grew.

I elbowed him in the ribs as subtly as I could manage. "None of your business, your highness."

"I'm merely pleased to know that my assumption was correct," he said.

"It really wasn't," I replied. "Kriseia's just a great person. You got lucky when you picked her for me."

"*You* got lucky when I picked her for you, is what I'm hearing," he continued. "Jesting aside, I'm glad to hear that you're indulging yourself, whoever it's with."

"Which one of us is overly concerned with the other's sex life now, Prince?" I asked.

He shrugged. "No such thing here," he said. "I merely remember the murmurs and disapprovals in Arthur's court that often surrounded women who openly preferred the company of other women. If you were feeling such misgivings, I wanted to ease them."

"Wait, you remember?" I asked. "They had that kind of thing way back then?"

He smiled, a special blend of patient and patronizing. "They have had that kind of thing, as you say, since time immemorial, I imagine. Even in Camelot. *Especially* in Camelot; Arthur never saw reason to disallow any practice that did not harm anybody, much to the consternation of his neighbors. And the consternation of many of his allies and subjects, too, to be honest."

"Really?" I asked.

Vambrace looked confused. "You led me to believe that the stories and histories of Camelot were still widely known in the present, my lady," he said. "Is such a detail really mentioned nowhere among the records? Lady Nimue was incorrigible and immodest enough to stand as an example all on her own, if nothing else, and I cannot imagine any comprehensive study of our efforts could leave *her* unmentioned."

"Huh," I said. "What do ya know." I didn't have the heart to tell him I didn't know who that was.

The grand dining hall was much the same as I remembered it from the first time, a sea of every size and shape and color of demon clustered around tables piled with every size and shape and color of food, and a maelstrom of smells ranging from sizzling meat to sugary baked goods to fermenting fruit that all swirled together into a general fragrance of hunger. The sudden, insistent growling of my stomach as the doors opened and the smells hit me was lost in the sea of loud chatter that filled the arena-sized eatery, but I felt the pang keenly enough, and I suddenly was glad I'd let him drag me here after all. Another several course meal sounded more satisfying than a handful of snacks. At this point, I could eat a horse — and since I still didn't know where most of this food came from, I just might, if I wasn't careful.

I followed the prince, and Kriseia followed me, up the stairs to his private table. Once again, all of the archdemons were already assembled and waiting in the same seats they'd been in last time, with the exception of Archduke Abdeles, who appeared to be absent. Duchess Sidona was also missing this time, though that didn't surprise me. Whatever the hell was suddenly up with her when she'd left my room, I got the feeling she was going to need some space for a while.

The archdemons all rose from their seats as Vambrace crested the stairs, bowing their heads until he'd walked around to his spot at the head of the table and taken his seat. The chair at his left was empty, so I assumed that was my spot again and took it. Kriseia had disappeared, but reappeared a few moments after we all sat down along with half a dozen other Luxuriate servants, a pitcher in her hands.

"Oh, you don't have to…" I started as she came up behind me.

"I do, though," she said with a smile, leaning over me and taking the empty crystal goblet beside my empty plate. "It's my job, my lady, and I'm happy to do it, don't worry." The drink she set back down in front of me was pinkish orange, like a sunset in a cup, with a wafting scent of earth and flowers and sharp sweetness. "Marsh wine cut with jeza nectar," she said brightly. "I took the liberty of guessing your drink preference myself this time, but I based it on what you said you liked from our last meal together, so I think you'll enjoy it, my lady."

"Oh yeah? Thanks, Kriseia." Her waiting on me was weirder this time around, now that I knew her and... well, *knew* her. But I'd eaten at restaurants where people I knew from high school were waiting tables, so this wasn't any more awkward than that, I told myself. I had the drink nearly to my lips before I paused. "Uh, you said jeza belle stuff in this, right?" I asked her. "It doesn't have any... It's not the kind with, uh...?"

"Sexual fluids?" she asked, still smiling. "No, my lady, don't worry. I remembered."

"Thanks," I said, and took a sip. Sure enough, it tasted like the marsh apples and jeza belle tea from earlier: earth and honey and flowers and sweetness, and the burning afterkick of more alcohol than I was used to.

"I'll have some too, while you're here, sweet thing," said Archduke Melchius, who was unfortunately seated right next to me again. He held out his goblet to Kriseia, his arm reaching behind my seat in a way that made me think he was trying to get an arm around my shoulders. I leaned forward out of its way while Kriseia filled his cup, which he brought around over my head before putting it to his lips with a smile. "Hello again, by the way, Lady Morgan," he added before taking a drink.

Was he trying to be a pest again, or was he naturally just this smarmy? I couldn't be sure. So I smiled politely and said, "Hello, Lord Melchius. I'm surprised you don't ask for the kind with the sex mixed in."

"Why, because I'm a Luxuriate?" he asked. "Please. I'm the archduke. I don't swallow." He took another sip. "I have people to do that for me."

I nearly choked on my wine, which made him grin, and I resolved not to talk to him anymore.

Unlike the last stately dinner I'd been a part of, this one passed without incident or screwup on mine or Vambrace's part, unless you counted my continuing concern and horrified fascination with the food. I was ready for most of it this time, semi-practiced as I was; I piled up the bread again, and the creams and jellies from the fruits and berries I knew and liked. There were marsh apple tarts I nibbled on, careful not to get too tipsy on the baked goods if I was also getting buzzed on the wine. And there were thorn fruits that were roasted and then pickled in honey, which made the bitter grittiness more palatable. I didn't want to carb load exclusively, though, so I bit the proverbial bullet and grabbed myself a smoked harpy leg, figuring that if the human parts were all in the front of the thing, then the bird parts in the back should be the safest, least pseudo-cannibalistic parts to eat.

It really did taste just like chicken, which was… comforting, I guess. Compared to the alternative.

Just when I started to think I was going to make it through the local flavor without making a thing out of it, another course was brought out, this one a big pot of what looked like a creamy vegetable soup. Whatever the cream came from, it smelled amazing, and I would have scooped up a bowl of it without hesitation if it weren't for the pot that it came in, which was brown and shiny and leathery and, oh yeah, no big deal, lined with razor sharp teeth all around the lip.

I stared at the teeth for a minute and debated how concerned I wanted to be while the rest of the dinner guests all took their fill, ending with the Gulliate Archduke Grodon pulling the entire remainder of the pot over into his sprawling collection of personal dishes. Now or never, then. "Hey, uh, what's… what's up with that there?" I asked, waving a finger at the steaming, toothy little cauldron.

Grodon's orange face widened with an indulgent smile. "Cave chowder," he said proudly. "A medley of fresh subterranean vegetables, diced and spiced and boiled in a blend of nidhogg cream and truffle broth, and marinated around a soul core in a pisaca pot from start to finish." He licked his lips with an extra long tongue and looked for a second like he was about to dive in mouth first, before he instead picked up the fanged bowl and held it out to me. "Would you like some, Lady Morgan, before it disappears into my maw?"

I grabbed my empty bowl but didn't offer it yet. "I don't know," I said. "I recognized most of that, but what's a nidhogg?"

"The Northmen of Earth would tell stories of one, massive and ravenous like a terrible dragon, that lives beneath the roots of the world tree and feasts on the souls of the dead," answered the prince, smiling beside me. "The ones we have here in this world are much easier to deal with, more like a cross between moles and pigs, only about as long as an adolescent human is tall, and completely eyeless. They live underground and burrow through the earth, hunting and feeding on truffles and soul crystal."

I nodded. Alright, weird, but maybe not a deal breaker. Pig moles didn't sound so bad for a hell beast. Any pork in a storm. "And a… pisaca pot, you said?" I asked. "What's pisaca? Some kind of bowl crafting technique?"

I got a round of indulgent chuckles from across the table at that. "Not the technique, but the material," the prince answered again. "A subterranean parasite, like a leech, but with a hide of abrasive chitin, and roughly the size and shape of a grown human man, though their dimensions are incredibly malleable. They travel through fissures of any size in the ground, able to squeeze and stretch themselves through cracks even a hair wide, and feed on corpses — or live victims, if they can find someone who will hold still for long enough to be enveloped and digested." He paused to eat a spoonful of the cave chowder, as if what he'd just said wasn't absolutely revolting. "Ridding the various cavern systems and basement levels beneath Dis of these beasts' colonies was one of my earliest projects as archfiend."

"Earliest and most commendable, in my opinion," Archduke Grodon chimed in, nodding sagely. "So much of that space is required for farming and soul harvesting just to keep the city fed and the economy flowing. I can't imagine going without it, and I shudder to envision trying to utilize it while infested with those vermin." He reached out and stroked the pisaca pot in front of him with his long, spindly fingers. "Though since the beasts can fit themselves around most any shape while still alive, their hides make for exceptionally useful crafting. The trick is getting a live pisaca to try and eat a mold that isn't person shaped."

The Iriate Archduchess Pyressa scoffed beside him. "The *real* trick is firing the mold while it's wrapped in a live pisaca," she said. "You can't cook the beasts from the outside or you ruin the finish and integrity of the hide, so you have to sear them to death from inside by heating the mold to red-hot while they're still engulfing it. The timing required so they die only as they reach the appropriate shape varies by the size and shape of the project. Uncommon as the creatures are these days, only master craftsmen are allowed to work pisaca hide."

"I'm wearing pisaca right now, actually," Archduchess Cinaedemis chimed in, rising from her seat. She smiled a double-wide smile as she peeled back the many multicolored layers of her Avaritiate robes to expose what I thought at first was her naked body beneath. But no, I realized a second later, what I was looking at was instead a super tight, form fitting body stocking of the same brown, leathery, bug-looking material as the soup pot. It hugged her every curve and slope as if painted on, and what I thought at first was a zipper turned out to be, on closer inspection, a vertical row of tightly locked fangs running from her neck to her crotch. "Exorbitantly expensive for a full-body garment, of course, but worth every soul," the archduchess continued, running a long-clawed nail along the teeth over her stomach. "There's just no substitute for real quality, after all."

Archduke Melchius's eyes lit up at the display of fashion. "I've seldom seen one so expertly shaped, Cina dear," he crooned, leaning over his plate. "How is the fit? It looks rather… restrictive."

"Remarkably comfortable, actually," Cinaedemis answered, shifting her weight to display first one hip, then the other. "I often forget I'm wearing it."

"Oh," said Melchius, grin melting away. "Darn."

"But back to my initial concern," said Grodon, pot sloshing in his hands as he held it out to me again. "Would you like some, Lady Morgan? Boiling it in the pot adds a pleasantly sharp undertone to the savoriness of the soup's other ingredients that is just *exquisite* on the tongue."

I couldn't answer fast enough. "No, nope, no thank you, I will pass on the man-sized flesh-eating cockroach monster soup, thank you very much," I said, pulling my empty bowl back so hard I was hugging it to my chest.

That got me weird looks from most of the rest of the table, but Grodon laughed. "Squeamish as ever, I see," he said cheerily. "I can't say I blame you, my lady, given your newness. True epicureanism takes time and resolve. I'm sure you'll reach it someday." Then his jaw opened and distended, and he slowly poured the entire remaining contents of the pisaca soup pot down his throat.

I really hoped he was wrong. As I watched the prince eat another spoonful of cave chowder, I had to wonder: Was he doing it for show, to prove his tastes could match a Gulliate's? Would culinary squeamishness be seen as a sign of weakness in an archfiend? Or had he really been here so long and gotten so bored and jaded that it didn't bother him anymore to eat something that had been cooked in a giant man-eating bug?

Or did he just like the taste? I shuddered. That might have been the most upsetting possibility.

After the cave chowder came platters of small meat pies stuffed to bursting with more minced vegetables and generous helpings of what looked like juicy strips of fatty steak. The smell of sizzling meat and flaky crust was mouthwatering, and after narrowly avoiding the pisaca soup, I figured that whatever it was, I could probably handle it, conceptually.

Until I was told that the meat inside was garm — specifically, the same pack of garm that almost got me on the wall, that I had watched Enkida and her army slaughter just beyond the city. With most of the fauna in Hell so far being less of the safe, domesticated kind and more of the murderous monster variety, and most of that living wild out in the wastes beyond the city because of that same threat of murdery danger, there was a sort of waste-not-want-not mentality toward food in Dis.

In fact, all of the meat in these particular pies in front of us, the prince proudly informed us, was carved from the giant severed paw that Vambrace had chopped off mere feet in front of me; it had skewered on the spiked chimneys of the wall as it fell, where it chargrilled when the fires inside the wall were lit and the entire brick-and-metal ring structure was turned into a giant oven — a protective measure to make extra sure that nothing outside got in while the soldiers were cleaning up the mess from the garm attack. Somehow the wall's construction was such that the security method didn't bake every prisoner inside the wall alive, though whether or not they were comfortable was no great concern to anybody.

All of this security trivia the prince told to me in between his bites of dog pie, while the rest of our dining companions murmured their admiration and approval. I nodded dutifully, nibbling my harpy leg and stuffing more pomegranate seeds in my mouth, resolved to give a more vegan diet another college try.

I was finishing my marsh apple wine and wondering how they were going to make dessert horrifying when Kriseia tapped me on the shoulder from behind and bent her lips down to my ear. "There's someone asking for a minute of your time, Lady Morgan," she whispered uncertainly. "He says it's important, but to keep the details private."

I turned to look at her more clearly. "Does he know I'm in the middle of dinner with the prince and all the archdemons?" I asked.

She nodded. "He says you'll want to step away to meet him anyway."

I frowned. "Who is 'he'?"

She frowned back. "I'm, uh, not sure it's my place to say. He made it clear it's to be a private matter."

Someone important, then, probably. More important than Kriseia, anyway, which admittedly wasn't that high of a bar. Still, this was a new curiosity. And after the last two courses, it's not like I had much of an appetite to infringe upon anyway.

I slid my chair back and stood up with a polite smile to the table at large. "Excuse me for a sec," I said, then turned and followed Kriseia from the room through a side door that the servers had been using. Nobody said anything or stopped me, so this couldn't have been too impolite a move on my part, I figured. Or I was just that important now.

The room beyond was a small and bustling staging room between dining room and kitchen, crowded with tables laden with pitchers and platters. Luxuriate and Invidiate servants hurried between tables and another door on the opposite wall, taking away empty dishes and returning with full bowls and jugs and plates.

Standing in the center of the activity was the only person not contributing to it: a gnarled, green-brown Invidiate leaning on a bronze staff, dressed in a tattered, overlarge gray robe pinned closed with a seven-pointed star clasp. He was the tallest of his kind that I'd seen yet, at just a few inches shorter than myself, and he was missing a few pupils on his left compound eye where a patch of gauzy white scar tissue ran over the middle.

The rest of his eyes were all focused on me, though, as Kriseia led me up to him. "Lady Morgan," he croaked in a voice so dry it made me kind of thirsty. "Honored to make your acquaintance at last. I am Alastaroth the 72nd." He spread his spindly arms and bowed his head — not the deepest bow I'd seen so far here, but definitely the deepest I'd seen from an envy demon.

"Nice to meet you too," I said. Should I bow too? He didn't list a title or anything, so maybe not, though he did seem like a bigger deal than the servants around him. "Just Alastaroth?" I asked. "Not Duke Alastaroth or anything?"

He laughed a single dry chuckle that sounded more like a cough. "Ah, no, my lady," he said, "Alastaroth was a distant progenitor of House Invidia. I am Alastaroth the 72nd. And no, I am not nobility as such, though I move in many the same spheres."

"Oh? Cool. So, uh, what can I do for you?" I asked.

"Not for me," he said. "For us. Yourself included." He turned and motioned toward the door to the kitchens. "My benefactor can better explain the situation, if you'll care to follow me, please."

A secret servants' room meeting leading to a second, secreter kitchen meeting? What convoluted conspiracy had I stepped into all of a sudden? "Sure, alright," I answered with a shrug. "Lead on." After all, I thought, it was too crowded here and I was too important now for this to be an assassination attempt. Probably.

Kriseia stayed behind with the rest of the servers as I followed the scarred Invidiate through the back door, where we were hit with a sudden wall of heat. The kitchens beyond were about the same size as the massive dining hall I'd left, a cacophonous field of ovens and stoves and countertops dotted with bubbling story-sized cauldrons so massive, they had staircases leading up to them and platforms overlooking them. Gulliate chefs of various shades of orange commanded every station, chopping and stirring and flipping and frying, the air ringing with shouting and sizzling as cooks and servers alike hurried through the crowded din with all manner of foodstuffs and cooking implements. It was like every reality cooking show was happening at once all in this one room.

I followed Alastaroth the 72nd as we threaded through the chaos as best we could, heading deeper into the kitchen jungle. I got more stares back here than I had been getting lately in the palace main halls, with the occasional clatter of dropped dishes as I passed marking someone especially surprised to see a human in their workspace. Can't say I blamed them, really; I didn't know what I was doing back here either.

Then my Invidiate guide turned between a wall-length rack of dried herbs and an open-air fire pit the size of a small storefront, and I followed him through the searing heat and the sharp smell of exotic spices to another small door and out of the cooking dimension. Beyond was another catering staging room, though this one was empty but for a tray of meat pies sitting on one of the tables. We didn't stop here either, instead heading straight through and out another opposite door to what looked like a cross between a small cafe and one of those Arabian harem rooms you see in old TV shows and comics, all pillows and cushioned loungers and exotic flowers framing fancy art pieces, the whole room dimly lit in dark blue, the ceiling obscured with a cloud of some sweet smoke. There were no sultans or concubines waiting for us, though; as far as I could tell, there wasn't *anybody* in here besides the two of us.

Or so I thought, until Alastaroth the 72nd led me behind an intricately carved screen of dark wood and, through the smoke and the dim blue shadows, I could finally make out another giant, dim blue figure lounging on one of the couches. Even looking right at him, I almost still didn't see him until he stirred and sat up, his tall black horns reaching into the haze above us.

"Lady Morgan," Archduke Abdeles said in his low, deep voice, his head tilting in the slightest of nods. "Well met."

"Well met, Archduke," I repeated, confused and not bothering to hide it. "Why aren't you at dinner with the rest of us?"

He smiled slightly, leaning forward to plant his elbows on his knees. I took a step back as he did — he was a giant blue man with horns, I couldn't blame my instincts. "I've a healthy respect for my peers and his highness, of course, but I'll confess that I don't always prefer their company over my own, scandalous though that may seem to some," he said. "And besides, I was hoping to have a private conversation with you. Private conversations are best had in private locations."

"So this secret meeting was your idea, then, not his," I said, jerking a thumb at my gnarled Invidiate guide beside me.

"It was both of our ideas," said the archduke. "Alastaroth the 72nd is my personal chronicler, and we share many similar interests. Interests which, we believe, you may share as well, my lady."

I had the sudden and distinct impression that I had stepped into a demonic mafia movie. Time to be extra careful. I crossed my arms and tilted my head. "What interests would those be, my lord?" I asked.

He regarded me in silence over his clasped hands for several long seconds, until I almost thought he wasn't going to answer. "How to be delicate about this?" he muttered, then closed his eyes and drummed his fingers on his fist. "The latest gossip says that you've been searching for something important lately, and speculation has it that this most recent attack on the wall during your trip there has had some detrimental effect on that search. Perhaps I can help restore your spirits by sharing the fruits of a fascinating project of my own."

He turned his gaze past me and nodded. Beside me, Alastaroth the 72nd reached into a pocket of his robe. I took a nervous step sideways, still in my demon Godfather mentality and half expecting him to pull out the Hellish equivalent of a gun. Instead, he slipped a thick, clothlike piece of paper from his pocket and held it out to me.

I took it and looked it over. It was sturdier than my note paper, kinda grimy feeling, and blank on one side. The other had a smear of what looked like charcoal over it with a rumpled blank in the middle. Some kind of impression, I guessed, like the leaf rubbings we made in kindergar—

Wait. No… not just a meaningless blank squiggle. I stretched the paper taught and peered down at the fractured shape, took the whole thing in my vision and let my mind trace along the swirls.

This was… yeah, this was one of *my* squiggles, the Old Elven kind! An incomplete one, but… I turned the paper over, crossing my wrists to look at it upside down. Somehow, that didn't matter; I got the same impression from it I'd just had, a kind of… covering? A shell, unshaped, then cinched tight — a veil, draped, gathered — a *skin*, then a projection of… something.

The symbol ended too early, leaving my thoughts grasping and unsatisfied, like a train of thought suddenly hitting a distraction and —

"Lady Morgan?"

I don't know which of them had spoken. I was too blown away by what I was holding to care. Instead, I turned to Abdeles and held the paper in front of his face. "What is this?" I asked.

The corners of his lips rose ever so slightly. "We were hoping that you might tell us," he said. "It was transcribed from a ruined obelisk that we found walled off in Luciferis, near the River Phlegethon bordering Asmodeusis. An ancient relic of a bygone era of Dis, destroyed and forgotten before most of us were even spawned."

This had just gone from a mafia movie to an RPG side quest. "And why would you hope I would know anything about something like that?" I asked.

"Because it is my theory that this ruined monument is somehow linked to the Original Sin," Alastaroth the 72nd answered for him. "As all record of the Original Sin's initial presence in Hell has passed into legend, and most of that legend has been forgotten, I can neither prove nor disprove this. But I believe it; and if my theory is correct, then if anyone could decipher the meaning of the symbols etched into the monument, it would be a member of the same race that constructed it."

"You need a human," I summarized. "Alright, but why wait to show this to me? Why not take it to the archfiend and ask him about it? He'd know more about the history of this place than I would."

"Because it is *my* theory that the archfiend himself was the one who destroyed the relic site in the first place," Archduke Abdeles said. He leaned back in his seat slowly, hands still clasped, finger tapping his chin as he frowned at me. "There is no way to fully explain without broaching a potentially dangerous subject, I'm afraid. How open is your mind, Lady Morgan, and how amenable are you to discussing topics which may, theoretically, touch on ideas that are, potentially… less than lawful, let's say, should they be put into practice?"

My lips pursed as I parsed what he was saying. How open minded was I? After all the shit I'd been through these past few days or week or whatever, I wasn't sure my mind could open much wider without falling apart at the seams. As for the unlawful talk, well… I had the prince's favor now, that much was certain, and obviously it behooved me to keep it that way. That said, I hadn't hesitated to quietly undermine him before when it seemed like the only way toward getting back home. Whatever was going on with this elven magic written on demon ruins, this seemed like my best remaining shot if the *Morganomicon* was really, truly toast.

Besides, I hadn't committed to anything yet. It was still just discussion, right? And I was *Lady* Morgan now, retraining the knightly Vambrace in the ways of chivalry. The archfiend himself had knelt before me at least a few times now already. If there was anyone he would forgive for simply thinking about theoretical treason, it would be me, wouldn't it?

I shrugged. "Whatever you have to say, I'll hear it out," I told the archduke. "And so long as we're talking ideas and what-ifs, I promise not to go snitching to the prince."

Abdeles looked from me to his Invidiate chronicler and back, still slowly tapping his chin. Then he took a deep breath. "Alastaroth the 72nd and I both have an academic interest in the story of the Original Sin, such as it is. Their artifacts and history. This small site, and a few others like it, are our only few sources of this knowledge. Unfortunately, the one thing that they all have in common aside from their possible creators is that every one we have uncovered so far also once housed a nexus of now-forbidden magic."

He paused a moment to stare pointedly at me, and I put all my focus into not looking hopeful or excited in the slightest.

"His majesty spoke at the first archdemon meal you attended of sealing travel between our realms long ago," the archduke continued. "I assume he or some other member of his retinue has related to you by now the specifics of the deed: acquired magic, all knowledge and skills not directly tied to a Sin's innate extranormal abilities, was stamped out in all forms across Dis, all sources and examples of such learning destroyed, all practice banned on pain of death. Detrimental as such a heavy-handed approach may have been to the recording and understanding of our often nebulous history, I don't dispute that the acts were necessary for our archfiend's goals. Travel between worlds was an inborn ability to none even back then, yet nearly everyone had knowledge of the magic required, or at the least, access to it via the dedicated gate sites that existed in places around the city, where the details of the spell were carved or painted or otherwise incorporated into the very architecture. Nothing less than total destruction and erasure would suffice to suppress such widespread information."

I held up the charcoal relief again. "And you think the ruin you pulled this from is one of those interdimensional travel sites?" I asked.

"Most likely," said Abdeles. "It might have served a different purpose, of course; world-shifting was not the only magic useful enough to be given public availability in such a fashion. But from what we have gathered, it was one of the more common spells, as well as one of the more complicated. There is a higher likelihood that any such ruin site with spell marking would be a dimensional gate rather than any other purpose it may have served."

My heart was racing. I crossed my arms so they couldn't see my hands starting to tremble. "But if removing any chance of anyone knowing that magic ever again was the prince's goal, why would there be even tiny remnants like this left? Why wouldn't he have made sure all traces were ground to dust first?" I asked. I wasn't sure at this point if I was trying to rationalize the archduke's story or temper my own skyrocketing hopes more.

"A fair point," Alastaroth answered beside me. "And again, all we have is speculation. But what records we still retain and my own research have indicated that these sites were prolific in their zenith, perhaps to the extent of one on every street in Dis. Certainly multiple in every district. Perhaps some, like this one we have found, stood out less so than others and were partially overlooked. Perhaps there were simply too many to completely account for every last stone of every last site." He shrugged his thin shoulders. "Or perhaps his majesty simply grew weary with the exercise over time and eradication efforts grew less thorough as a result. It would have been the work of several generations, after all. Even to one as long-lived as our archfiend, I can imagine the task becoming tedious."

I nodded, looking down at the parchment in my hands again. "Makes sense why you'd keep this a secret, then, sure," I said. "Now you're asking me if I can read forbidden ancient magic, and if so, if I'll read it to you?"

The archduke held up his broad hands. "What I am asking," he said slowly, "is if this is indeed the language of the Original Sin, if you would be willing to translate the script for our historical recording. We've no reason nor desire to try and dredge up any arcane knowledge which our archfiend has deemed unsuitable for existence in our modern society. We merely wish to know more about where that society has been, to understand and honor the culture which brought us to now, but which was lost in the process. Understandably, to study the latter requires carefully skirting the former, but it is a risk we think worth taking. A risk which would be diminished with your help, my lady."

I didn't buy it. Not entirely. If they were keeping it a secret anyway, why not go all in and learn secret magic while they were at it? It seemed an unusual limit to impose on themselves at that point, especially for a couple of demons.

And I'd heard the fervent disdain in the prince's voice when he talked about his anti-magic stance before. I'd seen the contempt on his face. Given what had happened to and around him thanks to magic, I couldn't say I didn't understand where he was coming from. Just knowing what little magic I did put me on edge when he was nearby; actively seeking out more magic was probably suicide if he found out. At least when it was the *Morganomicon* I was looking for, I had the excuse that I was hunting an heirloom possession (which was only half a lie), and if I'd found it, I'd already have the full spell I'd need to get the hell out of Dodge if he realized what it really was. No such safety nets down this path. The safest bet would be to walk away now, forget what they'd told me, maybe turn them in to Vambrace for good measure.

That would mean accepting that I was trapped in this world forever. That would mean giving up on ever going home again.

Of course, there was absolutely no guarantee that helping these guys would actually help me learn the spell myself. If they were right — if this wasn't all some weird, complicated lie for whatever reason — then Vambrace didn't leave enough evidence intact for anyone to put that spell together again.

But he didn't know magic. These two didn't know it. I was probably the only one in this whole city who did, which meant I was probably the only one who would know exactly what I was looking at when I saw it. And if the spell couldn't be entirely pieced back together, if there were gaps left in the magic code once I had all the bits of it I could find, well, maybe I could use my context clues and puzzle it out the rest of the way. I was already way more literate in the stuff today than I had been yesterday. If there was one skill I possessed besides musical retention, it was studying.

And besides, I was pretty sure I'd already tipped my hand to Abdeles and Alastaroth here that I could read their relief rubbing, or at least recognized it. If I ratted them out that they were studying an illegal language, they would probably rat me out for being able to read it already. Sidona had seen me writing in it, after all. It wouldn't be hard to put two and two together, but it would be hard for me to pretend otherwise.

I took a deep breath, then looked Archduke Abdeles square in the eyes. "Alright, I'm in," I said. "Take me to these ruin sites, and I'll see if I can't provide some insight, from an Original Sin's perspective."

His brows slowly rose. "Take you to them, my lady?" he asked. "If it's easier for you, we can simply bring you sketches and transcriptions of what we find there, such as that which you hold now. You need not slog to each of them yourself."

"I want to, though," I argued. "There might be details you'd miss that I wouldn't, or the transcriptions might not be accurate. If I'm gonna do this, I'm gonna do it thoroughly. Besides, the trips shouldn't be slogs," I added. "I haven't actually been out to see the city that much while I've been here so far, just the one or two business trips. I wouldn't mind playing the tourist a bit and seeing more of it."

"The tourist?" Alastaroth asked beside me. "Is that some sort of instrument?"

"If you're sure," the archduke said to me, ignoring his partner. "Although not every site location we think we've pinpointed is within city limits. There may be one or two out beyond the walls of Dis. Those, naturally, will be more challenging to study."

I remembered the view from the top of the wall, the dusty field of mangled bodies and scattered entrails, and shuddered. "Yeah, I might skip those," I said. "Still. It's a deal."

Abdeles rose from his seat, unfolding slowly and towering over me as he leaned forward and extended one massive blue hand. I reached out and slipped my comparatively tiny hand into his grip, and we both squeezed, one of us much more firmly than the other. "A deal, then," he said with a smile. "I look forward to working with you, Lady Morgan."

Chapter 27: Fixation

Making pacts with demons. Hunting for arcane relics. Studying forbidden knowledge. Practicing black magic. Living in sin with a succubus.

I'd never been particularly religious — less so after coming here — but even I would start to worry for my soul by now, if I stopped to think about it.

I didn't stop to think about it.

Instead, after meeting with Abdeles and Alastaroth, I went back to dinner, where the archfiend looked at me quizzically but nobody mentioned my momentary disappearance. When dinner was over, Vambrace asked if I wanted to accompany him to… somewhere. I wasn't paying attention. I turned him down, then excused myself and headed back to my room, charcoal relief clenched tight in my palm in the pocket of my pants. Kriseia followed beside me, but we didn't talk. I was thinking too hard for conversation.

When we got back to our quarters, Enkida was already posted up in the hall outside. She nodded to us as we entered but said nothing. I nodded back, also silent, and shut the door on her.

I felt like we were really starting to bond, she and I.

As soon as we were alone, I dropped the relief parchment on my desk, climbing cross-legged into the chair for another study session.

"Are you going to be busy with your project for a while again?" Kriseia asked.

"Planning on it, yeah," I said, turning to her. "Is that alright?"

"It's fine with me, Mis — uh, Morgan," she said. She had pulled all of her clothes off as soon as we got back and was sitting naked on the edge of the bed, looking at me. As I watched, she laid back and stretched out, as if waiting for me to draw her like one of my French girls. "I'll just be here, then, if you need anything from me."

There were a few things I could think of I wouldn't mind having from her, now that she mentioned it, posing like that. But no, not now. Time to focus. "Sounds good," I said, peeling my eyes away, then shook my head and got to work.

Step one was replicating the symbol on Alastaroth's parchment. With this particular squiggle sitting plain as day in front of me, it was easier work than trying to draft out the heat projection spell by memory — which was fortunate, because this rune was more complicated, with more fine details branching off from the main lines, a more subtle curvature and balance ratio. I wasn't sure which side of it was up, but it didn't seem to matter; I wasn't reading it from one end to the other so much as from the inside out, and back in again.

Near as I could tell, anyway. To get the full impression of it, I mostly had to just let my eyes wash over it and zone partway out. I did so with my secondhand sketch, once I was sure I'd copied everything there was to copy from the relief parchment, willing the same understanding from my version as I'd had from Alastaroth's.

I got it. My version of the squiggle read the same as the original squiggle. *Holy crap, it shouldn't have been that easy. What's the catch?*

No catch so far. What I thought I was reading now was the same thing I thought I was reading then: the sensation of a kind of shell or bubble, expanding outward from a point within, then contracting again. Tight, like a seal, or a skin, or a shroud. Wrapping, compressing, protecting… from what?

The ragged edges of the thought tickled at my mind again. My transcription was complete, but the original relief was not. There was more to this symbol that I wasn't seeing, that I didn't have. A gap in the complexity of the swirling, somehow. Or… a blank?

I turned the paper over in my hands, rotating the sketch and eyeing it from every degree. Incomplete. Or… maybe modular? If I could pinpoint where in the shape the grasping end of the thought lay, then maybe I could slot something else in to complete it. But if so, what? And how?

With my thoughts trailing off, a sound from nearby caught my attention. I shook my head, clearing it. Coming back from being deep in the magic zone felt like coming up for air. My concentration was never tapped this hard before outside of all-night cram sessions before big tests. I didn't know how long I'd been sitting there, but I knew it couldn't have been *that* long.

I heard the sound again, like a slow gasp, and turned. Kriseia was still lying on the bed, still naked. One hand was at her face, her finger in her mouth. The other hand was between her squirming legs, along with her tail, which slithered rhythmically back and forth across one bare lavender thigh. And her eyes, half open, were gazing right at me.

I gulped. "You, uh… you alright over there?" I asked, concentration now shot to hell.

She bit down on her finger and nodded as her hips twitched and bucked. "I'm alright," she breathed. "I'm sorry, did I disturb you?"

Disturb wasn't the right word, exactly. "Uh, no, you're fine," I said, glancing quickly away. Then I glanced back. "Are you… have you been watching me while you do that?" I asked.

"Mmm." She closed her eyes for a moment as the tip of her tail flicked suddenly upward from between her legs, glinting wetly in the light for a second before diving back down out of sight. "I have," she moaned. "Do you want me not to?"

"I, uh…" I turned in my seat to face her, more confused than embarrassed by now. "I don't know yet. This is a new one for me." I tilted my head. "I'm just sitting here, though. That's enough to… do it for you?"

She nodded again and shut her eyes. I wasn't sure if it was a gesture of politeness or if that was just where the mood took her. "You're very attractive, Morgan," she breathed, finger tracing her lips as she spoke. "There's something so alluring about watching you work, the intense look in your eyes when you're focused and driven. And your Earth attire is very flattering."

I looked down at my AC/DC t-shirt, tugging at the hem. It wasn't even remotely form-fitting. "It is?" I asked.

"I confess, I'm fantasizing as well," she continued, eyes still shut, legs spreading wider. "Imagining you studying me with that same intense look. Pinned and exposed on your desk while you inspect and memorize my body." Her hand on her face slid down to her breasts. "Wearing your shirt."

My gaze also slipped to her breasts. "I don't think it would fit you."

Her skin shifted then as I watched, the lavender flashing pale white, deepening to olive, lightening again to a kind of light peach. I blinked, surprised and kind of fascinated to watch Luxuriate glamour happen in real time, like someone adjusting the saturation on real life. Her skin tone finally settled one that mimicked my own, her purple hair darkening to black to match. She squeezed the breast beneath her hand, and it shrank slightly, from about a D cup to maybe a C+. If she really was trying to imitate me, though, she still needed to let a lot more air out of them, and also lose about half a foot of leg, somehow.

She didn't take it that far. Instead, she opened eyes that had gone from all-blue to all-black and looked down the length of her changed body, frowning. Her hands and tail stopped their constant movement as she sat up in bed, her short ivory horns poking out of her now-black hair. "Shape is harder than coloration," she said glumly, looking back at me with a pout. "I think I can go a little smaller if I try really hard, but my size range is limited. My apologies."

"Apologies for what?" I asked, staring at the black void of her eyes. "You're still missing a bit right here," I added, pointing to my own eyes.

"Oh, right," she said, then scrunched her eyes tight. When they opened again, they looked human, though her irises were still slowly expanding and contracting like camera lenses until they finally settled on the right size, the black lightening to dark brown. No pupils that I could see, but close enough. "Apologies because there are so few appearances that I can adopt for you," she continued. "I cannot be much more petite, or much larger. I cannot lengthen or shorten my hair much without physically altering it. I cannot alter my horns at all." She sighed and stared down at her thighs. "I can only ever really look like the species that I am."

"So what?" I said. "That's all I can do too. That's all anyone besides a Luxuriate can do, right? You're still better at it than most of us."

"But every other Luxuriate I have met is much better at it than me," she said. "I just… wish I could do more."

I left my desk and went over to her, sitting next to her on the edge of the bed. "I'm pretty sure everybody, no matter their species, wishes that they were better at stuff than they are," I said, and put an arm around her shoulders, though I was careful where my hand rested. It seemed like a hugging moment now, nudity or not. "And there's always someone better than you somewhere, so why dwell on it?"

She smiled and reached up to rest her hand on mine. Thankfully, it was her mouth hand, not her other one. Her finger was still a bit wet, though. "You are kind to say so," she said. "Though I imagine that if I looked like the Original Sin, I would not need nor want to change my appearance."

"Please," I scoffed. "You think I never wished I could look different? When I was a kid, I would have loved to have half the talent you have to look like someone else."

"You?" she asked, frowning at me. "Surely not. You are beautiful. Why would you not want to look like yourself?"

The compliment made me blush more than watching her go to town on herself had. "Oh, I'm fine now," I said. "I'm not ashamed of what I look like or anything, don't get me wrong. But when I was younger, well…" I sighed and got more comfortable on the bed. "I grew up in this little town in the Midwest. Real little, on the rural edge of the suburbs. There was only one grocery store, only one middle school, and only one high school. I could count the number of other Asian kids in that town on one hand, and none of them were in the same grade as me. So I stood out a lot. All the other kids noticed. It was kind of like being the only Luxuriate in a room full of Superbiates, everywhere I went, except that none of us had any magic."

"But all of you were human, yes?" she asked. "How different can humans look from one another?"

"Not as different as you demons can, I'll give you that," I said. "But you're a little different from other Luxuriates, right? And you say you still get shit for that. Seems when people all look mostly the same, they focus harder on the smaller differences."

"Oh." She reached up to touch her horns. "Yes, I can understand that. I had not considered it before, though." She smiled. "You're very wise, Morgan."

I snorted. "I'm really not. Mostly I was just angry. And lonely. Enough people see you mostly as 'that girl who's different from the rest of us,' and you kinda give up on people altogether. I didn't have many friends; I learned to deal with it by ignoring it and keeping to myself, which ended up setting me apart more. Then I grew up and moved somewhere more urban, where there were more people who looked more different from the people in my hometown and from one another, where no one knew me or cared, and I wasn't 'the different kid' anymore, but I also didn't know how to deal with people besides keeping away from them, so I just kept doing that." I squeezed her shoulder. "You're honestly probably my best friend at this point, Kriseia, demon or human, and we practically just met. Besides my family, I think I feel less awkward around you than anyone else I know — and you stare at me while you schlick it, so I hope you realize how big a deal that is."

"Aww," she cooed, then tilted her head. "Schlick it?" she repeated.

Of course she would. "It's slang," I said. "Because the sound it makes when…" I trailed off. She was still staring at me with those earnest, pupilless brown eyes. "You know," I sighed, and made the motion in the air in front of us, because apparently I am a child.

"Oh," she said, smiling again as realization dawned. "I get it now. Schlick it." She pursed her lips. "Schlick," she repeated slowly, as if tasting the word.

I wished she'd stop. I immediately regretted introducing it to her.

Then she scrunched up her nose. "It's not a very pretty word, is it?" she asked.

"It really isn't, please don't use it," I said.

"But I think I understand," she continued. "And maybe it's presumptuous of me, but I think I can relate, when you put it like that. Standing apart, and being lonely, and giving up on people. And I'm flattered." She leaned in closer, smiling shyly. "You are my favorite person now too, Morgan, and I'm not just saying that because I was gifted to you."

I blushed hard at that. She was awfully close. "Oh yeah?" I said quietly. "Thanks."

She leaned even further in, until our noses were nearly touching, and rested her fingers on my chin. I'm not sure which fingers they were. "May I?" she breathed.

Her breath smelled like heat and flowers. I swallowed. "Yeah, sure," I breathed back, trembling slightly.

Her eyes slipped shut as she pressed her lips to mine. Her tongue shouldn't have surprised me at this point, but I still gasped when I felt it against my own. She stopped, started to pull away, but I surprised us both by taking her neck in my hand and holding her there as I closed the gap again.

That lasted for… a while, let's say. By the end, I was well beyond distracted, and I had managed to lose my shirt, though I kept my pants on this time. I left Kriseia lying languidly on the bed, sighing to herself with my t-shirt draped across her midriff, and I sat back down at my desk, topless and disheveled.

Luxuriate therapy. *Not bad*, I thought. I felt like I'd got some stuff off my chest. I'd got some stuff *on* my chest, too, but it wiped right off.

I shook my head, rolled my shoulders, and took a deep breath. Alright, no more interruptions. I had more work to do.

The gap in Alastaroth's shell rune. I didn't know what went there, but I knew something had to. Most likely, I'd have to wait until they'd showed me one of these magic ruins of theirs and hope the answer was scrawled across one of them, some more complete version of the partial thing I had now. Like reassembling spell fossils.

But I didn't know when the first of those excursions would happen. Abdeles and Alastaroth hadn't given me a specific time — how could they when they didn't measure the stuff? So until the call came, all I had was what I had: this salvaged piece of spell, my own heat generation transcription, a fuzzy memory of bits and pieces of the *Morganomicon*, and my context clues. Could I make anything happen if I rubbed all of those together?

I opened the desk drawer and pulled out my sketch of the heat spell, setting it next to the incomplete shell spell. The *Morganomicon* had been stuffed to bursting with hundreds and hundreds of cramped, powerful pages. So far, my own *Morganomicon Jr.* had two. But it was two more than I'd expected.

Maybe if I tried diagramming the shell rune like I'd done with the heat one? I wasn't as familiar with it, so I didn't know if I could, but it couldn't hurt. Worst case scenario, I'd have to redraw it, but it had gone smoothly enough the first time. I redipped my quill and held it ready while I read through the new spell again, letting my eyes drift unsupervised through the lines. Focused and unfocused. It was a weird balance to find, but it got a little easier every time.

My quill dried, was redipped, and dried again before I started to get a feel for the distinction between the different parts of the spell. They were still uncertain, but they were there. I didn't bother at first with trying to decipher the differences, just marked where the feel of the thing shifted and moved on. I could always fine tune it later; I had nothing but time.

Once I was fairly confident I'd caught all the transitions, I reviewed my handiwork to see if the different bits I'd sectioned off were coherent on their own. The overall impression of the rune as a whole had been of a growing, shrinking barrier of a sort. Here at the beginning of the thought, the first bit I'd marked, the sensation was mostly one of… readiness? Potential, maybe. A gathering of… something. The swell of possibility, pulled from deep inside, focused inward. The idea of something about to happen.

Vague, but it was something. I scribbled down as coherent of a label as I could express and kept going before my hot streak ended.

Past that bit, further toward the outer edges of the swirling scribble, the focus shifted from gathering to a sort of expansion. An outward push, a growth of sorts, like stoking a fire, or the idea of a fire — no, that wasn't right, that wouldn't work. Fire was too fine of a point, too restrictive an image. There was no room for metaphor here, no imagery, not yet. The vaguery I felt with this portion of the spell wasn't just my mind grasping beyond its means, I realized; vaguery was built into the essence of the thing at this early stage of the idea. This was empty possibility still, a building anticipation without name or word or definition, like in the first section, but growing, building.

Reading and rereading this portion of the rune, that same feeling grew and grew, until I noticed my legs bouncing frantically in my seat, my quill tapping a quick staccato against the wood of the desk, flakes of dried ink falling with each anxious stab. I had to pull my concentration away from the spell for a minute, breathing deeply through my nose while the feeling subsided. My heart was pounding against my chest, my free hand fidgeting aimlessly at my side. I felt like I'd just chugged an energy drink and then sat very still while the caffeine barreled unused through my veins.

"Are you alright?" Kriseia asked. She was sitting up on the bed, still naked; this time her skin was the same cherry red, her hair the same dark brown, her eyes the same unbroken black as the devil girl on my t-shirt, which she was holding up in front of her. Still practicing, I guessed.

"I'm fine," I said, getting out of my seat. "Just been sitting too long. 'Scuse me." I went into the bathroom and shut the door so she couldn't see me walking circles around the tub until my body finally calmed down.

Right, lesson learned. That particular configuration of elf squiggles was dangerous. The remainder of whatever the shell spell was must expend that energy somehow, but without knowing how or finishing the sequence, I'd just been doing the magical equivalent of revving the engine.

I'd only meant to read the damn thing, not invoke it. This had happened when I'd written out the heat spell, too. That was going to limit how crazy my wizardly experiments could get, then, if I had to be my own magical guinea pig each time.

Once the worst of the fidgety feeling had passed, I went back to my desk. Kriseia was on her elbows and knees on the bed, studying my shirt like I'd been studying my magic notes. Her skin had gone shiny black from her elbows to her fingers and from her knees to her toes, a mimickry of black leather gloves and boots. Given the spikes naturally jutting from her heels, it was a pretty convincing glamour, I had to give her that. I silently wished her luck with whatever she was doing and sat back down.

The third bit of the spell I'd marked off gave me nothing at first, not until I went back over from the beginning again. I needed that gathered, kindled potential held in my mind to trigger step three, I guessed. This spell was a cascading series of steps.

After that accidental overcharging of nervous magical energy, though, I didn't run into any more ill effects. The next section took that potential and stretched it, pulled and shaped it, finally gave it definition. Not a specific shape yet, exactly, but boundaries, a pattern, like weaving it into an amorphous shape. A gauzy veil, the edges of which were hard to grasp. The swirls after that reached for those edges and tugged, sculpted, smoothed, drew them back in. This was near the middle of the rune, I realized, where the expanding sensation began to contract. The ideation seemed so smooth and fluid when I'd first been looking at the charcoal marking, but the closer I looked now, the more granular it got, the more steps it took to get from one spot of the thought to the next. It was like zooming in on a beach and finding more beach, trying to trace a shoreline only to end up counting every grain of sand. At some point, the mind had to gloss over the finest details and move on, but go too macro and it lost definition altogether.

This was another way I knew it was working. Loner that I'd been for most of my life, I was well acquainted with what my inner voice sounded like, and this wasn't it. The magic changed my thoughts when it was flowing, altered the world around me from my own mind outward. Should I be more concerned about that? Maybe, and maybe I would be, later. For now, for the moment, I only wanted understanding. I'd chased it this far; I would catch it if it was the last thing I did.

Gathering, expanding, projecting, weaving, sculpting, reining in, shaping, cinching, smoothing — it was all coming together, slowly, methodically, but undeniably. My shoulders ached, my throat was growing dry, but I barely noticed. I had a building block of the world in front of me, a piece of raw reality, and I was determined to measure it from every angle. One more tool in my belt; the more I found and made, the closer I came to building a bridge back home.

It was almost galling to reach the end of the sequence and run into that empty space once again. For all the steps I'd taken and deciphered to get to this point, the overall idea still remained generic. I had all the individual, isolated steps to build a second skin, but a skin of what? The subject had never been defined; the best I could describe it, the spell was working with nothing but the potential for something from start to what passed as a finish. There was definitely a lot of utility in this spell sequence, but how and with what to utilize it, I still had no idea.

Kriseia heard me sighing as I pushed the notes across the desk and leaned back in my seat. "Still alright?" she asked. Her hair was longer and wavier now, her waist smaller, the spade tip of her tail spikier. If I hadn't looked up to see her changing herself step by step, I might not have recognized her, even knowing it couldn't be anyone else.

"Still alright," I said, rolling my shoulders and stretching my arms. "Bit fatigued, maybe. How long has it been since I started?"

She shrugged. "A while now."

That was as detailed an answer as I should have expected, I guess. I grabbed my MP3 player and turned the screen on. The internal clock read 6:42. I didn't know if that was a.m. or p.m., but it was probably incorrect whichever it was. I also hadn't checked when I started, so it wasn't especially helpful either way, but it felt like I'd been sitting here for hours.

"Time for a break, I think," I said, standing and walking to the bed. I took my t-shirt back and pulled it on. It smelled like her, faintly.

"What would you like to do now?" she asked, reaching for her own clothing.

"I dunno," I said once my head was free. "What do *you* usually do for fun? Besides the obvious sex stuff, I mean."

She drew her legs up and put a finger to her chin. It took her longer than it probably should have to think of an answer. "Well, I don't often get the time for it," she said at last, "but I've always loved music and plays, those kinds of artistic experiences. House Luxuria trains us to take part in them, but I've never been especially good at acting or any instruments myself. I always liked it better in the audience."

"I hear ya," I said. "I took guitar lessons for a bit in high school, but I sucked at it, too." I turned to look back at my poor MP3 player lying on the desk, now reduced to little more than a useless clock. "I could go for a concert or something, yeah. Where do they have those around here?"

"Oh, all over," she said. "Pretty much anywhere Superbiates and Luxuriates mingle. There's probably at least one performance going on at any given time somewhere here in the palace."

"Cool," I said, pulling on my boots. "How do we get tickets?"

She cocked her head. "Tickets?"

"Even better," I said, then took her hands and pulled her to her feet. "C'mon, let's go find a concert to crash."

Chapter 28: Callousness

"We're gonna go find a concert somewhere," I told Enkida as we left the room. "Wanna come?"

The Iriate rolled her shoulders and pushed off her usual leaning spot on the wall. "No, thank you," she said. "But if you're heading out, I'm heading to the arena. It's been too long since I've hurt something."

"You just killed, like, half a dozen giant dog monsters," I said. "Like, yesterday."

She frowned. "And I haven't been in a fight or gotten any decent exercise since then," she said, stretching her neck. Her joints popped like ominous bubble wrap. Could she do that on command? What a neat power move.

"I thought you said your kind of wrath was different from other Iriates," I said. "You don't fly off the handle like they do."

"No, but that doesn't mean I enjoy destruction and bloodshed any less," she said, eyeing me with a faint smile. "It just means I'm very deliberate when I hurt something."

Creepy. "Sorry the prince has you stuck here doing nothing so often, then," I said.

"Don't be," she replied, cracking her knuckles. I retreated a step on instinct. "I haven't been on guard duty for a long time until now. It's a good exercise in discipline. And I'm not doing nothing while I'm posted here. I'm still in communication with the rank and file, and his highness. And I perform mental exercises, image training, that sort of thing."

"Thinking about how to hurt things?" I guessed.

She smiled more openly. "A lot of that, yes. Foreplanned is forearmed, after all."

"Right," I said, and then the conversation fell into a lull while she continued to slowly pop and crack and flex in front of us. "Well… see ya later, then," I muttered, turning to Kriseia and walking away.

"She kind of scares me," Kriseia said under her breath once we were around the corner.

"Yeah, me too," I said quietly. We walked in silence a moment. "Kinda cool, though, right?" I asked.

"Oh, absolutely," Kriseia breathed, a light blush rising to her currently red cheeks. "And her figure, like coiled iron. Imagine that cold smolder looming over you. How strong her hands must be."

I didn't mean to, but I did imagine it, just a little bit. "Hey, so, what kind of music you like?" I blurted, maybe a bit too loud.

She shrugged. "I think I like all music," she said. "I can't think of a specific kind that I hate, anyway."

"Got any favorites?" I asked.

She tapped her chin. "Luxuria music?" she said. "That's a bit obvious, though, and it might not appeal to you the same way. Gullia music is interesting, but I know some don't care for it."

I could imagine what songs for horny demons might sound like, but songs for hungry ones? "What's Gullia music?" I asked. "Like songs about food and stuff?"

"Some of that, sure, but…" She frowned. "How to explain? It's very… indulgent, maybe? A lot of simple, catchy melodies. A lot of instrumental flourishes in quick succession. Very long performances, usually. Some people say every Gullia song sounds like every other one because eventually they all include the same elements, just arranged a bit differently. There's some truth in that, I suppose; but if it sounds good, I don't mind hearing a lot of it over and over, personally."

I would have whistled here, if I had the ability. "Sounds like you really know your shit," I said. "I wouldn't have taken you for a music buff."

"Oh, no, it's nothing special," she said, smiling and waving me off. "I just have more time to appreciate artistry since I'm so useless at helping create any of it."

I clapped a hand on her shoulder, and she jumped slightly. "Stop talking about yourself like that," I commanded. "Not while I'm around. Appreciation can be a talent too. You'd be surprised how many humans back home make careers out of telling people how much they like things and why other people should too."

"Apologies, Morgan," she said, flushing again. "Your world sounds very interesting. I wish I could see it someday." She reached up and put a hand over mine on her shoulder. "What kind of music do you wish to hear?" she asked. "I've always been fascinated by the culture of the Original Sin, I must admit. We have so little of it here."

I thought about Archduke Abdeles and Alastaroth the Seventy-somethingth and their plot to skirt the law just to uncover more of that "Original Sin" culture. Did Vambrace realize just how obsessed his subjects were with the concept? And how much of that obsession, I wondered, was for actual humanity versus the aggrandized super version of it that their archfiend had tricked them into believing?

I wasn't sure, but it also wasn't my problem. "I'm not sure if any of our genres will match up," I answered. "Your Gullia music sounds kinda like our pop, but it also sounds kinda prog-rocky, I dunno. As for my stuff, I like a lot of classic rock, some alt and indy stuff, early metal, but I'll listen to most things. Except stadium country," I added with a grimace. "Old western is mostly fine, but most of the new stuff is trite, pandering self-indulgence, if you ask me."

Kriseia made the same appreciative whistle that I would have made earlier, if I could have. "You seem rather musically learned yourself," she said. "Were you also one who made their living by professionally liking things, back in your world?"

The past tense in that question kind of bummed me out, but I shrugged it off. "Nah, I've never been deep enough in the craft and the specifics to be a critic," I said. "I just collected and sold the stuff."

"I admit that I did not understand much of what you were talking about, though," she added. "Much of your Earth music is geological in nature, it sounds like?"

"Not really," I said. We'd reached the first major intersection in this level's halls and paused, a wide staircase to our right, more corridor curving away in front of us, an alcove with a gilded statue of some important Superbiate or other to our left. By now, I'd moved around the palace enough to kind of recognize where we were, though I still didn't know where we were going. "So, where do they keep these concerts, then?" I asked, hands on my hips.

Kriseia tapped her lips. "Mostly in the Spire of Pride, probably," she said. "Though there are performance halls in the central section of the palace as well, like where we saw part of that play with Enkida and the prince."

"Spire of Pride sounds fancy," I said. "And ominous. Like a final dungeon or something."

"It's the tower of the palace where Superbiate nobility keep their private quarters," Kriseia explained. "We've been there when we visit Duchess Sidona in her salon. Any performances going on there are likely to be more private, or more like practice sessions than full concerts." She tilted her head in thought. "I don't know about dungeons, however. You're more likely to find those in the Spire of Lust, though I hear there are long wait lists. Oh, but you know Archduke Melchius, so I'm sure you could reserve some time in one if you wanted."

"I really don't," I said, glancing around our surroundings and trying to walk the palace in my head. Without physically going anywhere, though, my mental map was vague and fuzzy. This place was enormous, and even the tiny fraction of it I'd seen already was labyrinthine. "Do we gotta just go wandering and hope we stumble into something then?" I asked aloud. "Or…"

Something caught my eye. I walked over to the statue, peered around the base, and saw what looked like a dusty mop sitting on the floor behind it. It shifted as I approached, peering up at me with one sunken, disinterested eye, and an idea formed.

"Morgan?" Kriseia asked, stepping up behind me.

I squatted down and smiled at the reposed Acediate. "You're part of that palace surveillance network, right?" I asked him or her or them. "Any idea what kind of music's going on now and where to find it?"

The furry gray demon made a deep, slow sound halfway between a groan and a sigh, and closed their eyes. I was worried for a second I'd offended them somehow, but I also remembered how long it took to get any kind of answer out of one of these guys, so for the moment, I just stood there saying nothing.

Right when I figured no answer would be forthcoming after all, my mind flashed with a sudden swell of music, all blaring horns and booming drums. I was looking at a heavy door bound with iron, somewhere in a dark, firelit room. The music was blasting from behind the closed door, muffled but still loud as hell, cacophonous and violent. I could feel it as much as I could hear it, thrumming through my bones.

The horns cut away suddenly, and now I heard slow, groaning strings, like a violin or cello or whatever equivalent instrument they had here. I was in the room with this music, lying on a large pillow, staring up at a curtained ceiling that slowly pulsed with dim blue light, like being underwater. The long string note faded slowly away into a moment of silence, then another single note played, deeper but just as slow and prolonged, this one also fading into silence for a few seconds before the next note followed. It sounded vaguely sad, but it was hard to tell, piecemeal and simple as the melody was.

The third silent moment was suddenly broken by a quick, upbeat chord progression on something that sounded like a distorted guitar, and the scene changed to a brightly lit, colorfully tiled, outdoor patio. The scent of meat and sweets filled the air, along with muffled laughing and moaning as, in front of me, Gulliates and Luxuriates of myriad sizes and shapes draped themselves across blankets and couches in droves, platters of food and drink spread out between them, broken here and there by what looked like smoking urns of incense. Somewhere behind me, the fast-tempoed music played on, dueling guitar-esque instruments joined by rapid drums and whooping voices in looping melodies that repeated every few seconds, different instruments swapping in and out with one another every verse. Was this the Gullia music Kriseia was talking about? I could understand why she called it indulgent now, if so.

The scene and sound changed again. Now I was in the back corner of the top row of some sort of auditorium, rows of mostly empty benches stretching down to a lit stage where an orchestra was arranged around an esoteric mix of instruments, some somewhat familiar and others totally alien. Deep, brassy horns blew two quick, loud notes, then a half-circle of kneeling Gulliates near the front of the stage opened their mouths wide in a deep, throaty chant, "A-how how how *hooowww...*" Two more bass notes, this time from stringed things that looked like bathtubs but sounded like cellos, and the chant again, "A-how how how *hooowww...*" Bass. Notes. "A-how how how *hooowww...*"

No fucking way.

"That one," I said, my own voice startling me. The auditorium and the music vanished, and I found myself back at the intersection, eyes locked with the Acediate behind the statue. "That last place," I repeated. "That's going on right now? How do I get there? Please."

The Acediate sighed and closed their eyes again, and I waited impatiently, bouncing on the balls of my feet. The reply didn't take as long this time, though it was more disorienting. I was suddenly looking at myself, eyes scanning past my surprised face to the staircase over my shoulder. Then I was just as suddenly watching a different level of the staircase, before my gaze turned down a nearby corridor. Over and over the visions flashed in quick succession, especially by an Acediate's standards, my point of view jumping from spot to spot down a path upwards and through the palace, the trappings of the halls and landings around me getting fancier and more exquisite, until I was staring at a pair of double doors painted in white and trimmed in silver, that strangely familiar music carrying faintly through it. The next jump put me back in the auditorium, looking down at the stage, where a tall, leggy Luxuriate woman was running her hands over her bare thighs. "I was shaking at the knees," she crooned to the near empty audience, the line ending in a ragged groan. "Could I come again, please?"

And then I was back behind my own eyes and ears again, staring down at the Acediate sentry once more. "Holy shit, I was right," I said, breaking into a grin. "Thanks so much," I added to the Acediate as I rose up.

"Right about what?" Kriseia asked behind me, looking between me and the sloth demon on the floor in confusion.

I took her hand. "I know where to find the music I want," I told her. "Spire of Pride it is. C'mon, follow me." And I tugged her toward the staircase, the Acediate's directions still clear in my mind like a recent memory, like I'd already followed the route once before just a few seconds ago.

We climbed stairs, moved down long corridors, climbed stairs again, crossed an open indoor courtyard, and climbed more stairs, moving in a rough upward diagonal through the palace. After maybe fifteen minutes of walking, we arrived at our destination, the white and silver doors from the shared Acediate memory. The song that had caught my attention was long over by now, of course, and I opened the doors on an at-first unfamiliar song being plucked out on some deep stringed instrument that sounded somehow wet, like a bass guitar played underwater. Behind it, something was rattling like distant boulders rolling down a cliff, like an especially massive maraca. Even with the extra blubbing and grinding, though, the melody finally clicked in my head right before a broad-shouldered Superbiate stepped forward, head tilted back, and began singing in a powerful, resonant voice. "I'm a wheel, I'm a wheel, I can roll, I can feel," he belted with the refined gusto of a trained opera singer, "and you can't stop me turning."

Kriseia leaned in. "Isn't this one of your Earth songs?" she whispered in my ear between verses.

"Hell yeah," I said back, grinning ear to ear. A full demonic orchestra made for a weird cover, but I had to admit it was thematically awesome. And it was the first I'd heard my familiar tunes since I'd got here, if I didn't count my own amateur karaoke renditions, which I didn't. For being filtered second- or third-hand, she'd done a pretty good job with it.

"Lift my spirit *higherrrrr*," the Superbiate on stage bellowed, milking it. "Come and..." He trailed off, shaking his head while the music continued behind him. "Come and..." He frowned, snapping his fingers at his side, while the instruments petered out behind him.

I cupped my hands around my mouth. "Someone's screaming my name!" I sang out over the sparse audience, all eyes turning in my direction. "Come and make me..." I sucked in a deep breath. "HOLY AGAIN!"

Out of character, I know. I wouldn't have done it if I'd thought about it for a second, but I was at a concert, kind of, and this was my jam, and I had been starting to think I'd never hear my music again. I was psyched. The power of Dio compelled me.

"Excellent passion, dear, if a bit too unrefined," an expected, imperious voice called from above. I looked up and around to see Duchess Sidona descending a spiral staircase from an overhead balcony. She smiled as our eyes met. "Or perhaps just the right level of unrefinement?" She added, sweeping up to us. "You *would* know best, I suppose."

I smiled back. "You'd be surprised how unrefined the vocals are in some of the best Earth songs, Duchess."

"Oh?" she said. "Well then, think of the extra polish as my leaving my own mark on this artistic exchange of ours."

"Still, I'm surprised you could pull together this much of a performance out of one session of listening to me sing and make crappy instrument sounds," I said, gesturing toward the stage, where the performers milled about watching our exchange with curious looks.

Sidona tilted her head. "Is it so soon?" she asked. "If you say so. I've not been paying attention to such trivial details." Her usual haughty smile looked even faker than usual, tired. Hell, everything about her looked tired, from the slight slump in her normally ramrod-straight posture to the loose strands of white hair falling around her face to the dark blue circles under her eyes. Her legs were draped in another extravagant, flowing skirt, but over top of that she wore her paint-stained smock. There was paint smeared on the skirt too, and both garments look rumpled and unwashed.

My smile dropped. "Are you alright?" I asked, more quietly. "You look exhausted. Like you haven't slept in days."

"Why would I?" she asked, her own attempt at a smile also dropping. "Waste of time." She turned and strode through the theater toward the stage, waving an arm at the performers. "From the top!" she called. "Shakers, keep a slower tempo! And Lucifer's sake, man, remember your lines this time!"

The Superbiate singer crossed his arms with a deep, disapproving frown, but said nothing as the music started up from the beginning of the song. The half dozen or so audience members all turned back to the stage. I wouldn't have thought there'd be an audience of any size for what amounted to band practice, but it made sense for a Sidona production. Maybe they were super fans of her work. Maybe she just needed the validation, even for her rough drafts.

I was still incredibly interested with what she'd done with the songs I'd given her, of course, but the experience was tempered somewhat as I watched the duchess pacing back and forth through the theater aisles, attention fixed intently on the stage, her head never turning away. At one point the train of her skirt caught on one of the benches, but it didn't slow her. The beautiful fabric tore, a long rip now running down one side of the once-extravagant dress, impossible not to notice. She paid it no mind, only kept pacing.

The singer did remember the lyrics this time, and the performance finally ended with an uncharacteristic flourish of wet strings and percussion. The Superbiate bowed, and the small audience clapped, Kriseia and myself included. We'd taken seats in the back near the door, drawing no more attention now after my initial entrance, except for the usual curious glances at the new human girl that I was by now used to.

After a few seconds, the orchestra moved into a sudden flurry of music, the boulder shaker maraca things setting a quicker tempo, a whole row of Luxuriate musicians standing up and sawing away at thin violin-esque instruments that sizzled with an almost electric buzz. Another Dio number, I realized. The Superbiate vanished into the curtained back of the stage, replaced by lanky, sinewy Iriate man whose brown hair was shaved into a bristling mohawk. This new performer stomped up to the front of the stage, clenched his fists, and started outright yelling at the audience. "It's the same old song!" he screamed, the people nearest the stage quickly clapping their hands over their ears. "You gotta be somewhere at sometime! And they never let you flyyyyyyyy!"

Sidona may have taken my notes about the unrefined vocals a tad too far, I thought. Or maybe this guy was a virtuoso at Iria music and I didn't realize. Regardless, brute force singing aside, I was still digging it, though Kriseia looked a bit less comfortable with the cacophony.

We sat there for what had to be over an hour while Sidona's players ran through every song that the duchess had needled out of me that day in her music salon. Some translated better than others — I cringed through most of their rendition of "Comfortably Numb," which had been painfully slowed down to accommodate a plodding, pulled-apart Acediate style — but for the most part, the duchess had somehow gleaned enough from my rough, untrained renditions of every song to make something passably familiar and audibly interesting. When the last note died out and the curtain closed on the stage, what audience members there were all stood up and applauded as hard as they could, Kriseia and I among them, intensity momentarily making up for our lack of numbers.

As the clapping died down, I looked around for Sidona, expecting to see her mounting the stage to make some grand speech or other about her own brilliance. Instead, I finally found her hunched over in another bench seat further back, furiously scribbling onto a scroll of parchment stretched out on what looked like a long clipboard. She didn't look up at the applause or as her audience rose and began to disperse, chattering excitedly amongst themselves. When they'd all gone, with the stage curtain still closed, only the duchess, Kriseia, and myself remained in the room, and still she didn't move from her spot or take her eyes off the page in front of her.

"That was incredible!" Kriseia said beside me, rising to her feet and stretching her back. Somewhere in the performance, her appearance had switched back from the devil girl on my t-shirt to her usual lavender self. "Human music is so different from ours. I had heard a few renditions of songs that originated with His Majesty, but nothing like that before. This is the sort of music that you archived and traded back on Earth?"

"Hm?" I said at first, still watching Sidona. "Yeah, we sold all kinds, but this stuff was my specialty. What I played when I had control of the in-store radio."

There was no way she knew what a radio was, I realized, but she nodded and looked impressed anyway. "Thank you for bringing me," she said. "What shall we do now?"

"One sec," I said, then walked over to where the duchess sat. Her quill wasn't moving anymore, instead hanging limply in her hand at her side as she stared, eyes half-lidded and unblinking, down at the scratches she'd made on the parchment. Some kind of demon writing, I guessed, all sharp shapes and symbols that I couldn't make heads or tails of. "Sidona?" I asked.

No response.

"Hey, duchess," I tried again.

Still nothing.

I stuck a hand between her face and the page and wiggled my fingers. "Earth to Sidona," I said, louder this time. "You in there?"

She dropped the board and jerked so far back in her seat I thought at first she might fall out of it, hand clenching tight around her quill, and stared at me with wide, blinking eyes. "What?" she asked, confused. Her eyes darted around the empty room, going wider. "Damn it all," she muttered under her breath, then dropped her pen and scrambled at a pocket of her now-ruined skirt. "What?" she asked again, voice clipped and terse this time.

I took a step back, hands raised. "Sorry," I said, "didn't mean to startle you. I was just—"

"Quiet," she barked, pulling what looked like a brass compact from her skirt. "One moment." She snapped the compact open. Inside was a tiny silver spoon sitting in a mound of azure blue powder. I watched as she scooped a bit of the powder up with the spoon and brought it to her nose, sucking it up with a delicate sniff, her eyelids fluttering frantically afterward. She repeated the action for the other nostril, then a third time with the first one again, before closing the spoon back into the compact and dropping it back into her pocket.

Her demon cocaine medicine, I remembered. I'd only seen her take it once before in her art studio, something about preventing some kind of Superbiate Alzheimer's. Was that what was wrong with her lately? She'd snapped at me last time I asked, said it wasn't an issue and refused to talk about it further.

Suddenly, I felt very sorry for the uppity artist. If she was sick somehow, and too proud to talk about it, it was no wonder she was so aloof and bitchy, running herself ragged for her art.

Her medicine taken, Sidona rose to her full, intimidating height and tilted her head back, taking a deep breath before looking down her nose at me. "You were saying, my lady?" she asked smoothly, more herself now. In demeanor, at least — the powder had done nothing for the exhaustion painted across her face.

"I was saying, I was incredibly impressed with the performance," I said. "It was moving to hear some of my favorite music so far from home. You did an amazing job, especially with what little I could give you to work with."

"Hmph," she scoffed, but held her head a little higher regardless. "Of course I did. I would not allow any creation of mine to be anything less than impeccable, no matter the source or execution." She lowered her head to a less smug angle then, her smile growing a little less fake looking. "But I will admit, it is still gratifying to hear the praise of the Original Sin on my interpretation of Original Sin works. My thanks, Lady Morgan."

"If you…" I stalled, uncomfortable. There was no way to make this not awkward, so I abandoned trying. "If you need to talk about anything," I continued, quiet despite the fact we were all alone in the auditorium now, "I'm willing to listen, you know."

She quirked an eyebrow. "Are you reaffirming our artistic arrangement?" she asked. "Have no fear, my lady, I do not intend to stop picking your brain for new inspiration until that well has run quite dry."

"I'm talking about you personally," I explained. "Your mental and physical health. Sorry to say, you've looked better, and I'm kinda worried about you. I'd consider us friends, in a weird sorta way, so I wanted you to know—"

"Your concern is duly noted," she snapped, glancing around the auditorium as if searching for people who weren't there anymore. "It is also unwelcome. However I look is none of your nor anyone else's business. I am no preening pink performer obsessed with my appearance; I have higher aspirations to consider, grand works to complete, and no time to commiserate with those who do not comprehend the legacy I am building." Her hand whipped up, impatiently brushing stray hairs out of her face, and her glare softened a bit. "But if you have any more comments or criticism on the works themselves, I am willing to entertain them."

Even suspecting the worst about her health as I was now, she didn't make it easy to stay concerned for her. If that was her goal, I had to admit it was working. I bit my tongue on what I wanted to say. "You know how to find me, then," I said instead.

"Indeed," she replied, her eyes darting once again around the empty room.

"Everyone else really is gone now," Kriseia said hesitantly from behind me. "It's just us three left, ma'am."

Sidona's finger shot out like a spear, stabbing toward the exit door. "Get out," she demanded, glare returning in force and boring through my companion. "I have work to do."

The doors clicked closed behind us with an awkward finality. Kriseia stood close beside me, fingers playing anxiously with her hair. "I'm afraid I may have offended the duchess," she said quietly.

"I wouldn't worry about it," I said, draping an arm over her shoulders. "It's not exactly a hard feat to accomplish, even when she's not clearly going through some shit."

"Solitusia," said Kriseia, shaking her head. "I've seen it in person, just once, in Luciferis during an errand for my old Madame. There was a superbiate man walking in small circles on a street corner, glaring down the road in all directions over and over, muttering to himself. He couldn't find his way home, because he couldn't see any of the details on the streets he was on, because there were people in the way all around that he couldn't focus on. I wanted to help, but when I walked up to him, I just gave him one more me-shaped piece of the world he couldn't see, and that made him panic even harder." She shuddered. "I still feel guilty about that sometimes, when I remember it. I cannot imagine what it must be like to actually live in that world, where there are only holes where other people should be."

"Fuck," I muttered, concern for the duchess blossoming again despite her bitchy attempt to dispel it. "You think she's really got it?" I asked.

"I couldn't know," she said. "The duchess seems to believe she does, though, or that its onset is imminent. I do not begrudge her for her mood, either way — I don't think I could stay upbeat either if I was facing that."

I nodded as we walked away. "It sucks if it's true, but nothing we can do," I said. "I *do* still kinda like her, though. As much as I can like any self-obsessed Superbiate, anyway." My arm was still around Kriseia's shoulders as we walked. I gave her a nudge. "Why are you one of the only actually nice demons in this whole damn place, anyway?"

She smiled. "I was trained to be nice," she said, "and also, I really like you. Would I still be nice if it weren't part of my role to be so? I cannot know. Nobody regulates their behavior if they do not need to, if it is not required of them or will not benefit them somehow." She tilted her head. "Are humans different?"

"Hmm. Yes and no," I said. "Depends on the person, I guess." I squeezed her shoulder, smiling. "And hey, I really like you too."

She blushed fiercely. It was weird, I noted, the things she blushed at versus the things she didn't. "What should we do now, Morgan?" she asked.

I thought about it a second. Sidona's whole deal aside, I was feeling refreshed after all of that music. The prudent thing to do would be to go back to our room and keep working on what magic I could. That would probably bore Kriseia, though, whether or not she would admit to it; and natural recluse that I was, even I was starting to feel like I was spending too much time hiding away in that room lately. A longer break couldn't hurt, right?

"Food?" I suggested. "I'm not starving, but I should probably stop going so long between meals."

Kriseia nodded. "I could eat," she said.

We didn't sit down for a full meal, just got some snacks from the first cafeteria/dining hall/food court type of place we found and ate them as we walked. Kriseia had a cup of something creamy and layered with glistening fruit globs, like a fancy demon parfait. I had a bread roll filled with... something. Minced veggies of some sort. Beyond making sure there was no monster meat involved, I didn't ask questions about it. Better for my peace of mind that way, I thought.

We wandered the palace aimlessly as we ate, for lack of anything better to do. Stretching my legs and getting more familiar with the place seemed as good a use of my free time as anything else, though the more we walked, the more I became convinced there was simply too much palace for me to ever get wholly familiar with it.

We also chatted idly as we walked, and Kriseia told me more about herself, at my insistence. It was still strange for her, she said, having anyone interested in the minutia of her life or her personality — weirder still for that interest to be in the explicitly nonsexual details. The conversation still started out with her account of her favorite kinks (bondage, submission, genital worship, something called "salirophilia") and hardest limits (bathroom stuff, bestiality, vore in both theory and application) before I steered her toward more benign subjects. She liked to read, especially poetry or the epic ballads that Vambrace had brought with him from Earth. She liked dressing up even outside of the obvious sexy stuff. She'd had a stuffed doll of something called a "mearcstapa" when she was younger, and might have collected other dolls if she'd ever had the money or her own place for long enough. Her biggest fear was being eaten by a pisaca ever since one of the things had gotten into her dormitory at her luxuriate finishing school, prompting a long lockdown while city guards hunted it through the halls outside her room.

It was all incidental, menial, mostly unimportant conversation, and though she grew more comfortable with it the longer it went on, she never lost the impression that it was strange that I cared about any of it. For my part, beyond just being interested in getting to know my friend better, I welcomed the mundanity of taking a walk for no reason and talking with someone about nothing in particular. It felt a bit like my regular college routine, grabbing a quick cafeteria lunch and walking the quad, exchanging notes with classmates in between classes. My classmate in this case was a light-purple half-naked lady, and the class in question was magical study hall, and the lunch probably had unspeakable unholy ingredients that must not be named, but it was still nice.

We'd managed to find our way to some sort of ballroom/indoor courtyard, a wide space scattered with milling groups of different demons, and were halfway across it when a familiar voice called, "Ah, Lady Morgan!" I turned to find Prince Vambrace headed our way flanked by a dozen men and women, an equal mix of Iriates and Luxuriates, all of them mostly naked and glistening with sweat. Vambrace was still wearing his usual mail shirt, but my jacket was missing, and he too was sweat slicked beneath his metal clothing, black hair plastered wet across his forehead.

I stopped, wary and curious at the sight. He approached with a smile, breathing heavily, and Kriseia bowed low beside me. Still unsure what he wanted *me* to do in these situations, I just mimicked her actions, though only bowing about half as deep. Pure guesstimation on my part.

He didn't seem to care one way or the other. "I am pleased to see you about, my lady," he said, his sweaty entourage hanging back in a loose clump and watching the exchange. "Growing more comfortable with palace life, I hope?"

"Getting there, yeah," I said. "One day at a time." His eyes lit up at that. Happy to have someone else who understood the concept of "days," if I had to guess. His enthusiasm for the mundane still vaguely weirded me out, even if I understood where it was coming from. "Just come back from a workout, didja?" I continued, nodding past the winded prince at his equally winded hangers-on. "Another arena fight?"

"An arena exhibition, yes," he said, "and then an orgy. General Enkida is down there now, as I understand. If you wish to join the large crowds that she always draws."

My smile froze on my face as I worked for a reply. "I... uh... I don't think I..."

"Ah," he said, waving a hand, "no, I meant that she is fighting in the arena," he clarified. "Apologies, I should have been more clear. Enkida almost never partakes in orgies."

"Good to know, I guess," I said, glancing at his entourage again. There were some amused smiles there, a couple quiet chuckles, but mostly the usual curious staring. "Wait a minute," I said, waving a hand at them and looking at him. "You mean, *all* of you guys were just...?"

"Fucking, yes," he finished, tilting his head. "Was that not clear? Why do you ask?"

I counted off the group members again, reconfirming my suspicion. "Half of them are men," I said.

He looked over his shoulder at his entourage, then back at me. "... And?" he said after a second.

"And you're, like... from ye olden times," I said. "Older than that, even. Arthurian."

He looked confused for a moment, then nodded. "Ah, I think I see at last what you are getting at," he said, then held out a hand. "Come, walk with me a while, and I will explain. As it happens, I was just thinking how I was missing your company."

So I swapped Kriseia with Vambrace and we walked away together back into the labyrinthine palace corridors, while Kriseia went off with his orgy partners. It was a less easygoing atmosphere for a stroll this time, trading my servant gal pal for Satan, but he had a point; it had been a while since the two of us had been alone together, and we both still had plenty of questions for the other.

"I have mentioned already how permissive Arthur was with his subjects' and servants' personal tastes and choices," the prince said once we were out of earshot of the ballroom crowds. "You knew already that some women were openly sexual together in his Camelot. Yet you are surprised now at the idea that men practiced the same?"

"I guess I'm more surprised that you practice it," I said. "Though yeah, I don't know why I am, you make a good point. It's just kind of surprising to me still that that sort of thing was widespread and acceptable way back when. They don't mention it in our history books. Mostly it seems like the further back in time you go, the shittier it was to not be straight or male."

Vambrace sighed. "It saddens me somewhat to hear that, now," he said. "That any facet of Arthur's dream was overlooked or forgotten. At the time, though, there were many of us within Camelot and without who were of the opinion that the king was allowing too much. 'Unnatural fixations,' many said. Against the laws of this god or that. I was not without some amount of contempt myself for what I perceived as aberrations in normal behavior." He sighed again. "Then again, of the many points in my life on which I look back now in shame, that aspect is still toward the bottom of the list, I fear."

That was closer to what I'd expected, I thought. It seemed mean to say as much out loud to the guy, though. "So, what changed?" I asked instead.

"Need you ask?" he said, gesturing at the halls before us. "I came here. I absorbed this culture, reshaped it, added aspects of Camelot where I could, where I thought they would fit. Realized how ridiculous it was to try and enforce morals where they were neither needed nor wanted, where enforcement itself was nigh impossible. There were and still are many, many more important things to worry about than the individual paths to orgasm that every individual subject of mine takes."

"Cool," I said, "but I was talking about you. How'd you go from 'contempt for aberrations' to banging six girls and six guys all at once?"

"Oh." He looked for a second like he was thinking about it, then shrugged. "That answer is even more obvious, I think," he said. "I am

1,500 years old at least, according to your reckoning. Things get boring eventually, and then you try new things, until nothing is new anymore. Barring physiological differences, I would wager that I have more experience with every single type of sex act than even the oldest, most experienced, most depraved member of House Luxuria."

I cringed away from him at that. "What, *every* one?" I asked. "Even the really gross stuff?"

He gave me the side eye. "Do you want me to answer honestly, my lady?" he asked. "You will have to clarify what you consider to be the 'really gross stuff' first, of course."

Blech. "Yeah, no, never mind," I said. "I don't wanna know. You ask a question instead."

"Alright," he chuckled. "Were you ever able to re-energize the tiny lightning maze of the communication box?"

I let that word slurry slosh around my head for a second. No luck. "The hell are you talking about?" I asked.

"The hand-sized long-distance communication device which you took from my vault," he said. "The one powered by small cisterns full of lightning. You said that it lacked the energy to function, and I gave you a couple of soul crystals to experiment with it."

It still took me a few confused moments to piece all that together. "Oh, the dead cell phone!" I said when I had deciphered the riddle. "Yeah, the souls worked somehow, but it's bricked. Er, broken beyond repair. Turned on for a second, but completely unusable, and then died again."

He nodded. "Unfortunate, but I had not dared hope for more," he said. "I would like the artifact returned, then, if you have no further use of it."

"Yeah, no problem," I said. "I'll bring it by later."

We wandered like that for what felt like hours more, at a slow enough pace that my legs didn't get sore this time for all the time and distance they covered. Or maybe they were just in better shape by now with all the trips I'd been making all over Dis and back. The whole time, he plied me for more tales from Earth: What had happened to Britain after the fall of Camelot? What had happened in the rest of the world? How much rest of the world *was* there? Was I sure — really sure — that it was truly a globe? There was no edge of the world after all? How was such a thing possible?

So I put on my exam face and ran through a brief summary of human history and scientific discovery. As much as I knew and could speak of with any degree of certainty, anyway. There were big, big gaps in my knowledge there, of course, things I'd never learned or couldn't remember if I had. I still hadn't declared a major yet, but I knew history or physics weren't going to be on the table when or if I ever did.

To the prince of Hell, though, I might as well have been a divine oracle, a master storyteller, an encyclopedia of impossible, futuristic science fiction. He listened to my stilted, broad-sweeping, uncertain lecture on humanity in enraptured silence, except for the parts where he broke in to ask a breathless follow-up question, many of which were just repeated variants of "Holy shit, are you for real?"

I was digging deep in my reserves of human biology, explaining how the mitochondria was the powerhouse of the cell, when he stopped me and hurried a short ways ahead down the hall, looking for something. He waved me forward and led me through a door into a narrow library. The back wall wasn't very deep, but it curved away along the length of the outside corridor in either direction, disappearing around the bend on either side. The space was packed tight with shelves crammed full of books of all sizes, relatively blank spaces along the back wall here and there holding desks stacked with piles and rolls of parchment.

"This is all fascinating," Vambrace said, leading me to one such desk. He opened one of the drawers and pulled a pre-cut quill from the deep stack within, opened another and pulled out a stoppered pot of ink. He popped the cork on the latter, dipped the former, and handed me the pen. "Could you write it down, please?" he asked, pulling a piece of parchment from the desktop pile and setting it in front of me.

I looked between him and the quill in my hand. "What, all of it?" I asked. I hadn't expected a writing assignment.

"It is a lot, I know," he said, excitement still spilling from his voice. "The work of years, potentially, but you will have them. We have no human history books in this place, none that I know of, but you — you could write them yourself!"

No part of that suggestion sounded appealing to me. "I don't know," I said. "I'm no writer, and I'm not sure of a lot of the details of… any of this stuff, really. You're asking me to chronicle hundreds and hundreds of years of stuff across a whole bunch of civilizations."

"Any information at all, however fragmented and broadly painted, would be a highly valuable treasure, my lady!" he continued. "I am not asking for total accuracy, nor am I setting any sort of deadline. Just… when you have the time and inclination, if you would be so kind."

He was like a little kid reading his Christmas list to his parents, I thought. But, hey, what the hell; if I could buy his gratitude and favors with the occasional short essay on whatever I thought I knew about the world, why not cash in? There were worse prices the prince of Hell could demand. And besides — and this was the part I had to keep telling myself — if my own plans worked right, I wouldn't be here long enough to have to rewrite the entire encyclopedia.

"Screw it, I'll give it a shot," I said, and watched his face light up. It was heartwarming, in a way, and I smiled myself as I put the quill to the page, dictating my running monologue. "So, as I was saying," I continued, slowing so my writing hand could keep up, "the mitochondria… is the powerhouse… of the—"

"Wait," he interrupted again, suddenly frowning. I stopped, and he grabbed the paper from the desk, squinting at it. "I don't…" He sighed heavily, turning the page to face me. "I cannot read this language."

"You what?" I took the paper back and looked at it. I hadn't used the elfy script here — definitely not in front of this guy — just regular English/Latin/whatever they were letters. Basic ABCs. "But it's just regular English," I said, turning the page to him again. "You're speaking it well enough, but you can't read it?"

"English again?" he sneered. "I can speak some words of it, aye, but not happily. Regardless, that is not what you have written there." He waved at the paper in my hands. "And I am certainly not speaking it now."

"You're… not?" I asked, dropping the paper to the desk. "It's not? What are you speaking, then? What did I write in?"

"I am speaking the King's Brittonic," he said, in perfect American English. "And I do not know the name of the script that you just wrote in, but it is not the script of the Angles, nor is it Brittonic, though the letters do bear a passing similarity."

I chewed on that. "I think this might just be confusion over labels," I said. "English and British are kinda synonymous, where and when I'm from. Like, Britain is England plus Wales and… I wanna say Scotland? I've never actually been."

He looked horrified. "Synonymous?" he breathed. "But you… you told me that Britton became an empire that reached all corners of the world! Corners which you also claim are nonexistent, but still! Where and how can the Angles factor into that if Britton was able to grow so powerful?"

"I don't…" I scratched my chin, wracked my brain, all to no advantage. "I don't know that much European history that far back. Weren't the Anglo-Saxons the original people on the British Isles? Them and the Celts, I remember the Celts. Rome was there for a bit, at one point. And that whole mish-mash of people grew up into England and then Britain." I shrugged. "Sorry, that's all I know. My world history class started with Mesopotamia and didn't really get to Britain until the Middle Ages or so."

Vambrace leaned against the desk. Or fell against, more accurately, catching himself with one hand and burying the other in his hair as he stared, stricken, through the paper in front of him that had delivered such devastating news, apparently. "We were forgotten," he said, voice quiet and hollow. "We carved out our nation and our people, we finally had our identity, and it was subsumed in the morass and swallowed by history. As if we never were? What was the point of it, then?"

Okay, well, fuck me, I hadn't expected this big of a reaction. Concerned and confused, I walked behind him and laid a hand on his shoulder. I wasn't sure how to comfort him; I wasn't really sure what he was upset about.

He stiffened under my touch. "We… *I* did this, didn't I?" he asked. I was pretty sure he wasn't asking me. "We brought ruin to Camelot, and ruin to Britton by extension. Arthur dead, Excalibur gone, the knights scattered and warring, the people left unprotected in the middle. We practically handed the land to them. Now the invaders have laid claim to my mother tongue, to my people's destiny." His fist reared up suddenly, then crashed onto the desk and the offending parchment where I'd written in the wrong language. "I knew it," he growled. "I knew it would happen! I did not stay to see the aftermath, could not bear to, because I knew! Why am I surprised to hear it now? What right have I to feel sorrow over the history that I helped to birth?"

His shoulder heaved beneath my hand, and I looked around to find his eyes shut tight, welling with tears, his face crumpled and clenched against a sob.

Holy hell, did I just make the Devil cry? I had no idea how to handle this, except to squeeze his shoulder again and look away.

The prince pounded the desk with a fist a few more times, though without the same heat, then shrugged away my awkwardly comforting hand. "Go," he said without looking at me, voice thick with grief. "Leave me. I want to be alone for a while." He collapsed sideways into the chair and buried his head in his arms, his steel vambraces pressing against his face. "Apologies for this state, my lady," he continued, voice miserable and muffled by metal. "We will continue our conversation later."

I still hadn't thought of anything to say. Without a word, I bowed slightly at his back and left him in the library. I don't know what effect it would have on his careful image if one of his subjects walked in on him like that, but it would probably be worse trying to drag him teary eyed and snot nosed through the halls of the palace.

There was an Invidiate waiting in the corridor outside in a short, elaborate gown, like a scaled-down version of something Sidona would parade around in. "Lady Morgan?" he asked, as if it weren't obvious.

I pulled the library door shut quick behind me, before he could catch a glance of the crying archfiend. "Can I help you?" I asked.

"Forgive me," he said with a shallow curtsy, "I didn't want to interrupt your private audience with his majesty. I have a message for you from Alastaroth the 72nd. He would like for you to meet with him in the fields of Beelzebubis at your earliest convenience."

My heart leapt, the devastated prince momentarily forgotten. I hadn't expected this to happen so soon, but I was ready for it. "Take me to him," I told the Invidiate messenger.

He curtsied again. "Of course, my lady," he said. "Follow me."

It was forbidden relic time.

G.D. Burkhead

471

Chapter 29: Deception

I had passed by the Gulliate district a few times by now on my way into the city, but this was my first time venturing in. The Invidiate man in the fancy gown walked quickly ahead, his legs and stride short enough that I could keep up at a medium stroll, which gave me plenty of time and opportunity to take in my surroundings.

It was a good thing I'd just eaten not long ago, or I might have stopped my guide to duck into one of the many eateries we passed. Even knowing what kind of creatures were considered food around here, it was still tempting; there were a thousand smells drifting out onto the street we walked, and every one of them smelled delicious. Savory meat, sweet baked goods, sharp spices, ripe fruit, buttery sauces — my mouth was watering by the time we were only a few blocks in. All around us, demons of every kind lounged at outdoor patios or streetside tables, the conversational buzz of a lively street mingling with clinking dishware and the bubbling and sizzling of dozens of kitchens.

My Invidiate guide led me around a corner where a tall, burnt-orange Gulliate woman wearing a long apron and leather gloves stood behind a kind of wheeled food cart like a portable oven, the bottom of which housed a bed of burning charcoal, the top of which held a large, bubbling pot. I watched, curious, as she greeted an approaching Iriate customer, pulling a ceramic bowl from somewhere in her cart.

Then I watched, horrified, as she suddenly opened her mouth *wide*, way wider than her face seemed capable of supporting, her gaping maw stretching twice the width of the rest of her head. She reached an extra-long arm down her own throat, her gloved hand disappearing into the dark recesses of her mouth, then returning holding a thick, spikey, bright red fruit. Despite having apparently just been retrieved from the bottom of her esophagus, it looked fresh and dry, as if she'd plucked it from a grocery store shelf rather than her own stomach.

The Iriate customer didn't react at all, only watched as she cut the fruit into thick slices dripping with juices the color of hot sauce and dropped them into the bowl. She finished by ladling the thick, yellow creamy stuff from her boiling pot over the fruits until the bowl threatened to overflow, then handed it to her customer. He took it and handed her two sticks of soul crystal in return, then walked away sipping his food even as it kept bubbling and simmering in the bowl.

The Gulliate woman distended her mouth again and tossed the soul money down her throat, then went back to idly gazing at her surroundings, which now included a shocked and vaguely grossed out human girl staring at her from across the street. She grinned at me. "Hungry?" she called out. "Spiciest zaqqum bowls in all of Dis, right here!"

"Not right now, thanks," I called back, waving as I hurried to catch up to my Invidiate guide. All the appetizing smells around me had just gotten a bit easier to resist after seeing that.

The restaurants and bars and food stalls I had expected, here in the gluttonous part of town. What I hadn't expected was the extension of the bazaar, Avaritiate merchants standing in front of towering walls of colorful clothing or shimmering jewelry or beautiful artwork.

Or the multiple outdoor music pavilions, compact stages tucked away in nooks between buildings, Luxuriate and Superbiate musicians filling the air with background Gulliate melodies, each one spaced just far enough apart that the next band's songs didn't start becoming audible in front of us until the last band's songs were fading away in the distance behind us.

Or the brothels, Luxuriate men and women in gauzy outfits beckoning to curtained doorways or, in many cases, open air park spaces where every combination of demonic species and gender was plowing away with abandon in plain view of everyone who walked by. I even spied a few humans in some of those knots of bodies — Luxuriates taking their best guesses, some of them more realistic than others.

Beelzebubis so far was a microcosm of Dis as a whole, or at least all the fun parts. It reminded me of downtown on a Saturday night back home, but ramped way the hell up. There were no pedal taverns moving tourists from one bar to the next, just demons stumbling drunkenly down the road, swaying to omnipresent music and stuffing their faces with continuous snacks, until they fell face-first into the nearest gangbang.

After an hour or so of walking through all of this, the introvert in me was grinding her teeth, ready to call this whole escapade off and run home to her quiet room in the palace VIP hall. It was a relief when the urban hedonism suddenly gave way to a surprisingly large stretch of rural land hidden away inside this massive city. The cobbled street kept stretching forward and curving slightly to the left around the middle ring of the Gulliate district, but the buildings were replaced by fields of crops: golden wheat to our left, tangled bushes with thick, brown *dhari* thorns to our right. Gulliates and Invidiates moved among the wheat field and between the thorny bushes, tending the crops, the odd song or whistled tune drifting on the light breeze.

My guide led me further down the street through the city fields, the bustling noise of the debauchery district fading away behind us. The wheat eventually gave way to long trellises weighted down by what looked like grape vines; the *dhari* bushes turned into rows of short, spindly trees, the boughs weighed down by fat, red pomegranates. The cooking smells of the city were replaced by the smell of freshly turned dirt and the subtle scent of ripening fruit. Far away in front of us, over the tops of distant crops where the road curved away, I could see another chunk of Dis on the horizon, tall buildings too far off to discern any details.

And to the left, on the inward side of the curve of the road, Pandemonium still loomed larger than was possible over everything else, a dark spire keeping watch on the city as it disappeared into the cloudy red haze far, far above.

I had that same sense of unease I'd had days earlier, looking up at its imposing bulk while sneaking invisibly into the marketplace. Now here I was again, creeping off into the city on defiant, dangerous business, though fully visible and with a good surface-level excuse this time. I knew it was all in my head — it had to be. Still, I tried not to look over at it as we went.

Eventually the Invidiate leading me turned right off the road and headed through the dirt between rows of the short foliage of some kind of root vegetable. I followed, the demons working around us giving us weird looks but saying nothing as we walked carefully through their work. Now that we were headed straight for them, I noticed two new figures waiting ahead of us that stood out among the field workers around them: Archduke Abdeles and Alastaroth the Seventy-somethingth, both of them flanking what looked like a pile of square stones sticking out of the ground.

"My lady," the Superbiate said as we joined them, giving the barest tip of his massively horned head. "Thank you for coming on such short notice."

"Thanks for getting this trip together so quickly," I replied, casting a quick glance at the field around us. The workers were all giving us enough distance that I didn't think anyone could hear a regular conversation, but I lowered my voice a bit just in case. "So, where's this human ruin?"

The archduke inclined his head further. "We stand before it," he said.

I gave the fields around us another quick, confused glance before looking down at the stones at our feet. Fat, square bricks of gray brown, maybe three whole feet of them, jutting up at an angle from beneath the dirt. If I hadn't been looking for construction, I might have thought it just a big rock. As it stood, that didn't appear to be too far from the case.

"What, this?" I asked, nodding at the chunk of stone. "There's barely anything here. I came all this way for this little pile of brick?"

"The fact that there is barely anything here is our saving grace, Lady Morgan," Alastaroth said in his dry, dry voice. "If you were expecting standing walls and stately arches, it would have been discovered and torn down long ago with the rest of its kind. From the looks of things, it still was, yet a small piece remains. Perhaps more, beneath the earth; but to excavate it would draw attention to it. So we leave it where it is, and I visit only to study and speculate."

I squatted down, eyeing the dusty stone. The ground around it felt softer, like this thing had only recently been unearthed. It didn't look that old, but who knew with this place? "Fair enough," I said. "So, what am I looking for?"

"Here," said Alastaroth, kneeling across from me on the other side of the toppled bricks. "See the etchings on the cornerstone?" He reached out with a gnarled finger, running it through the rock dust at the cracked edge. "Mere scratches, I thought at first, a byproduct of its being torn down.

Now, though…" He pulled his hand away, his scarred, compound eyes all focusing on me. "Can you read it?" he asked. "Does it say anything?"

I squinted at where he had indicated, seeing the set of scratches that were carved deeper than those around them. "It's… hard to tell," I said, reaching out to brush more of the rock dust away. "It does just look like gouging on the rock, but… Maybe…"

There were a lot of real scratches overtop of the maybe-not scratches, along with a big crack running next to and nearly through the etching. It made concentrating on any one mark among the many difficult. But the longer I looked at it, concentrating on the marks that the Invidiate had pointed out, the more I got the sense he was on to something.

Then my eyes clicked, and I saw it. "Pen or paper?" I asked, thrusting my hand up without taking my eyes from the magic shape. "Anybody?"

Archduke Abdeles thrust a scroll of soft vellum rolled around a quill into my waiting hand, a small vial of ink dropping to the dirt beside me. I arranged the items with my periphery vision while I stared at the sigil, keeping it pinned, until I had the parchment unrolled on my thigh and my pen dipped and ready, dribbling ink over my pants in lieu of letting it mar the paper. Gaze shifting quickly now between the rock and the page, I copied the magic.

It felt kind of familiar, sitting there in my mind. A similar sensation to the shell glyph that Alastaroth had given me last time, at least at first. Where that one had lent a sense of expanding in all directions, this one felt more focused. Targeted. But targeted on what? And for what purpose?

I focused for now on transcribing the shape in exact detail. If I did it right, I could always puzzle it out later.

When I was finished, when I was sure I'd copied the whole thing and none of the extraneous scratches around it, I sat back in the dirt and looked at my transcription. I must have been getting better at this magical dictation, because the same sensation came to me instantly — stronger, if anything, now that there wasn't a bunch of erosion in the way of the writing. A bit of targeting magic, yes, but incomplete again, which explained why it felt so vague and grasping. Another modular glyph, like the shell spell from earlier; only this one was more of a funnel, shaping whatever came before it and declaring what came after, linking the verb of the spell with the subject. Simple and elegant, less a magic phrase than a magic punctuation mark.

No wonder it felt so familiar, then. I'd probably read this bit of glyph multiple times over in the *Morganomicon* back when I was studying it in my apartment. Hell, I'd probably read and written it myself in the spell notes I'd made since I got here. Extracted and isolated like this, it was just easier to define and understand.

"Any luck, then?" Archduke Abdeles asked from above. "What does it say?"

I rose to my feet, still staring at the parchment, and opened my mouth to answer — then paused. It was little more than a preposition, an arrow pointing from nothing to nothing on its own. I couldn't imagine there was any utility these two could get from it without knowing substantially more Old Elven first. As far as forbidden knowledge went, this was as harmless as it got.

But it *was* still forbidden knowledge, and it *was* still magic, even if only technically. And right now, I was the only living soul in this world that knew what it really was.

Which begged the question: Wasn't it better to keep it that way?

"Lady Morgan?" Alastaroth chimed in, stepping carefully around the ruin to stand beside the archduke.

Let's think this through for a second. These two were out here looking for illegal, taboo information purely for, they claimed, an accurate historical record. But accuracy was doomed from the start, because they thought these things were linked to humanity as the Original Sin — a factoid which was just another part of Vambrace's lies to keep himself in power. And beyond that, Vambrace had these sites destroyed and that knowledge banned for a reason. Whether or not I felt personally beholden to that edict, he felt that demonkind ought to be. Abdeles and Alastaroth were part of that demonkind. It was a lost cause on the prince's part forbidding me from knowing things that I already knew before I ever came here, but I would be breaking the law a lot harder and a lot more intentionally by sharing that info with anyone else.

"My lady?" the archduke asked, stepping forward and waving a broad blue hand in front of my face, above the scroll in my hands.

And what did I really know about these two, anyway? They were helping me right now, yes, but no demon helped anyone else without gaining something from it themselves. Even General Enkida's loyalty to Vambrace was grounded in the power and position she gained from serving him so closely, and probably in the opportunities it provided to beat the shit out of monsters and other people at his behest. Even Kriseia stuck by my side so closely in part, at least, because of sexual attraction and this weird submissive friendship-with-benefits thing we had going on now. There was no true altruism in this place; every interaction was a transaction of some sort, a game that you won by not losing more than you gained in the process. I had as much faith that Abdeles and Alastaroth had been completely honest and upfront with me as I had faith in my ability to fly — maybe not impossible anymore, but not a chance I was taking anytime soon.

Besides, they said they were only looking for snippets of old culture to reclaim and preserve. There had never been any assurances that useable magic was at stake here. And if the culture they sought was fake from the get-go, dishonestly attributed to my own species, then I should have the de facto say in its interpretation no matter what I claimed, right? Right.

"What?" I said, looking up at the two demons and shaking my head. "Oh, sorry, lost in thought there for a bit. Yeah, it's kinda hard to make out, but it definitely says something." I squinted at the vellum in my hand, turning it back and forth in my hands. "Something like… pillar, maybe, or… monument? Big… stony… chunk of rock… thing." I frowned and shrugged. "Maybe an inscription saying what the ruin used to be. It's hard to tell without the rest of it."

The two demons looked at each other, though Alastaroth kept a few of his pupils on me and a few on the paper in my hands. "Really?" he croaked, fingers stroking his chin. "Interesting…"

"Not what I expected," Archduke Abdeles added, eyes narrowing as he regarded the chunk of ruined bricks at our feet. Like he wasn't sure if they'd offended him somehow or not. "Still, that is the danger of assumption, I suppose. It seems we have even more to learn from these ruin sites than we thought." He stared at the rubble a few seconds longer, then turned and bowed his head to me. "Thank you for your assistance in this, my lady. Before we part, would you transcribe a copy of the text for our studies?" He pulled another roll of vellum from his coat pocket and held it out. "I assume you'll want to keep your initial copy for your own perusal."

"Yeah, no prob," I said, taking the scroll and squatting down again to copy my copy of the glyph. This one went faster now that I wasn't worried about nailing the fine details that made it readable. Better if it wasn't, in fact, though I couldn't make any sabotage obvious or I'd risk them catching on.

"Thank you," the archduke said as I handed him his copy. He regarded it for a moment before nodding and tucking it unrolled back into his pocket. "We will, of course, send word as soon as we have another ruin site to study. There are several that we know of already, so I expect the wait will not be long. We merely need find an opportune chance to visit them without raising suspicion."

"Awesome, thanks," I said, dusting the dirt and dried ink off my pants. "Looking forward to it."

"Would you like an escort back to Pandemonium, my lady?" Alastaroth asked, gesturing to the field behind him. My initial Invidiate guide stood a ways off, watching a Gulliate man bent down in the field, plucking vegetables from the ground and dropping them, still covered in dirt, straight into his open, distended mouth.

I watched the same worker for a few seconds, confused and weirdly fascinated, before snapping back to attention. "You know what?" I said to Alastaroth. "No thanks, actually. I think I'll take the scenic route, check out some more of the city on my way. Not like I have much else better to do."

The taller Invidiate nodded. "As you wish," he said. "Take care, Lady Morgan. We'll be in touch soon." Abdeles added a dismissive wave, staring down at the toppled bricks again as he did.

I smiled, held a hand up in an informal wave, and turned back toward the road through the fields of Beelzebubis, heading in the direction we had been going before my guide led me off into the vegetable patch. It was the opposite direction from the palace, but I hadn't been lying when I'd said I had little else better to do. There was still so much of Dis that I hadn't seen yet, and I hadn't had a chance to wander it at my own pace since the first time I'd snuck invisibly out of the palace. Who knows? I might find something or somewhere useful.

The fields changed crops every couple of blocks or so along the road, never repeating, almost never recognizable. Stretching away perpendicular from the road, though, the same crop extended for miles in either direction, rows upon rows upon rows of flourishing vines and orchards and vegetable plots, broken up only by the bodies working within them and the occasional low building that I assumed to be storehouses or tool sheds or something similarly farmy. Big as this agricultural district was, Dis was ginormous; between the city and the towering palace at its center, there had to be a million or more people living here. No way they were all being fed by these fields alone, right? There must be more somewhere, hiding in another district or just outside the wall or something.

I looked off at that same wall, way away on my right and high, high up on the rim of the bowl that held the city. Even at this distance, I could faintly make it out, just barely visible above the distant buildings of the outer rims. Part of that visibility was due to the fact that it was currently belching smoke, a dark black haze hovering above a faintly flickering line of dull red. The ovens were still firing, then; I remembered Vambrace giving the order after the garm attack, some kind of crazy city-wide safety precaution.

This was my first time seeing it, though; I'd been too lost in my own head after the attack to pay it any attention at the time. The spikey metal chimneys turned to glowing red smokestacks as the stone beneath and around it heated like a kiln. A kiln still full of prisoners and their guards. How the hell did any of them stand it? Either the wall was a marvel of demonic engineering, or everyone inside was being forcibly baked right now. Either option seemed just as likely.

As I walked, I passed the occasional cart full of the produce growing around me, each one pulled by Iriate workers rather than any kind of hellish oxen or horse. Did they not have draft animals here in Dis, or was it just easier to get roided-out demons to do it? I didn't know. After a bit more walking, the fields turned back into buildings, the traffic on the street picking up again as side streets and alleys joined the main thoroughfare. It wasn't the raucous bustle of the hedonistic part of town I'd passed through with my guide, though. Most of the buildings here didn't seem open to the public, with long stretches of stone or metal walls blocking off big portions of a given block, each tall enough to hide whatever was behind them from sight. I could hear shuffling and stomping behind most of the walls as I passed, and the air here held the faint but rank odor of lots of animals all gathered together: wet fur, musk and must, hints of dead fish, and here and there a sharper whiff of what I could only assume was assorted urine and dung.

I'd passed through the farming part of town; this must be the ranching part, I thought, holding my nose and breathing shallowly as I hurried through. No wonder it was less crowded here. Curious as I was to know if there were any normal animals here among all the hellish monsters I'd heard about, I wasn't about to linger to find out.

Unfortunately, it turned out I didn't have to go out of my way to meet the critters living here. I was passing by a thick brick wall topped with a heavy rope net when I heard stomping and snorting and looked up to find what looked like a giant horned ox staring down at me, its head poking through a hole in the net, chewing cud with a gormless look in its sleepy, bovine eyes. I started at the sight, but stopped and smiled up at it, slowly growing excited. I'd only ever seen real live oxen before in zoos, but any exoticism they may have held once was lost next to garm and harpies and man-sized bug monsters. And if they had oxen here, that meant they had beef and probably milk, both of them very cow-adjacent. I could finally get off my self-imposed vegan diet and have some real meat and cheese and —

Hang on, my brain interrupted. *How does a big cow climb a wall?*

The ox-thing mooed at me, loud and annoyed, and rose up higher, straining the ropes that held it. Big, thick, furry, jointed legs scrabbled at the net and wall, each one ending in a single claw that scratched at the stone and sawed at the ropes. I counted four that I could see, but I heard at least twice that number. The beast thrashed its big horned head, mooed again, then reared back and spit. I squeaked and fell backwards as a thick glob of ox-spider-monster spit splashed the cobbles where I'd been standing, viscous and sour.

"Hey, hey, hey!" a gruff voice shouted. A stocky Gulliate man hobbled toward me down the road, though his face was turned to the ox beast above us. "Settle down back there, ya big ornery idiot! Go on, down! Down, girl!"

The spider ox snorted, gave a last grumpy moo, and slowly slipped back down out of sight, clawed legs scurrying.

"Been meaning to get that gap patched," the Gulliate muttered, then held out a hand. I took it, and he helped haul me back to my feet. "Sorry about that, ma'am, she gets uppity whenever she sees me leaving," he continued. "Still haven't broken that habit. Her venom sac's been removed, though, so don't worry, no danger there except havin' the smell knock the breath out of ya." He laughed.

I didn't. "Venom sac," I repeated, my dreams of a normal-ass cheeseburger dashed once more. "Cool. Thanks."

"Hey, you're that human, ain't ya?" he continued, still holding my hand. "The new one living with the prince down in Pandemonium?"

"Yeah," I said, doing a quick check of my clothes for errant cow spit. No damages, thankfully. "Lady Morgan Amell. Nice to meet you."

He grinned widely, suddenly pumping my arm in a vigorous handshake. "Pleasure's all mine!" he beamed. "We don't get important folks in this part of town much. I'm almost embarrassed by it, to tell the truth. I'm sure your ushi-oni are kept much more in line back on Earth."

"Never been spit at by one before now, you got me there," I said, trying and failing to take my hand back. "But no hard feelings, you do what you can."

"That we do, that we do," said the Gulliate, nodding. "Must look awful backwards to someone so illustrious, but I sure appreciate the understanding, Lady. Care to take a look around while you're here? I was just headed to the market with a fresh batch of ushi sauces, but I don't mind sticking around a bit to give ya the tour of the place, if you're interested."

"Ah, thanks, but no thanks," I said, finally slipping my hand free. "I've got other business to take care of, but I appreciate the offer."

"Of course, of course, thank nothing of it," said the Gulliate, nodding again. "One moment, though, before ya go, if ya don't mind." He closed his eyes, tilted his head back, and had a sudden rippling, full-body spasm, his neck contracting at the base and convulsing upward. His mouth spread wide, wide open just as a glass jar came sailing up from somewhere deep inside him, arcing through the air and into one of his outstretched hands. He heaved again, this time spitting up a much smaller vial, and caught that one too before looking back at me with a grin. "Here," he said, thrusting both containers at me. "A small token of thanks, for your graciousness."

I stared wide-eyed at both of them for a second, wondering if seeing Gulliates do this kind of thing would ever get less gross. Nobody had tried to hand me anything they'd pulled out of themselves before now. "Uh, what are they?" I asked.

"Ushi-oni venom sauce," the Gulliate answered, shaking the larger glass jar. It was topped with a thick metal lid, the inside sloshing with a thick, green paste that looked like someone had poured tar into a wheat grass smoothie. "My own special blend. Sharp and smokey, but not too bitter. And the anti-venom, of course," he added, shaking the smaller vial. This one had a cork and was half-full of something cloudy and milky white. "One drop per spoonful of sauce should even ya out, let ya have the flavor without feelin' the sting. It's a slow-acting venom I've cultivated in my ushis, so you can wait 'til after the meal to dose yourself." He stepped forward and pressed both containers into my unwilling hands. "A small trinket of appreciation, and probably not a patch on the fancy cuisine they can cook up at the palace, but I'm proud of my work, and I'm sure you'll like it, m'lady."

"Yeah, thanks," I said, taking the jar and the vial. Not like I had a lot of choice at this point. They were thankfully dry, but still slightly, unnervingly warm. "Appreciate it. I'll, uh, remember this place next time I get a hankering for giant cow spider."

The Gulliate grinned wider. "Thank ya, thank ya!" he said, bowing his head repeatedly. "Norgoni's Ushi-onis, at your service, m'lady! Much appreciated, much appreciated!"

I grinned back, shoved the jar of poison gravy and the antidote into my pants pocket, and hurried away as quickly as I could without breaking into an outright jog.

Never mind, I was still vegan for the foreseeable future. Possibly forever, at this rate.

Eventually I reached the wide street that separated Beelzebubis from whatever the lust district was called. Amadeus or Apatosaurus or something — I only remembered that it was a mouthful. I'd crossed this road before on one of my trips, but I hadn't actually gone into the Luxuriate side of town. That one and the envy district were the only two I still hadn't visited. If I was showing myself the sights, might as well see something new, I thought.

I was maybe five steps down the street into Applepotamus when I heard a rough moan overhead and ducked, more out of skittishness at this point than any real instinct. Something splatted on the street beside me again, thankfully far enough away again that I didn't get splashed. Not a gob of spider-cow spit this time, and not as much fluid, but still a viscous, milky little puddle. And it still brought a smell with it.

I looked up. Leaning over a wrought iron balcony three stories above was a naked Avaritiate woman, her gold-green skin glistening with sweat, a ridge of short, bony spikes running between her scaled breasts. Leaning over *her* from behind was a long-haired Luxuriate man with a broad, muscled torso tapering to a thin waist. "Sorry, aim was off," he called down, breathless. "Didn't see you down there."

The Avaritiate woman's face rippled and changed, green shifting to pink, draconic maw shrinking to plump purple lips. "You're cute, though," she purred, now a Luxuriate from the neck up, though her glamour persisted the rest of the way down. "Nice human look. Wanna come up and join?"

I spun on my heel and marched back the way I came without a response. Envy town it was, then.

Chapter 30: Spite

Invidiate town was out near the edge of Dis, in the other half of the same ring as the rundown Acediate slums of Belphegoris, just across the river from the Iriate district of Amonis and the wall. It was a long walk down the wide dissecting street, over a bridge to the Avaritiate bazaar, through the thronging crowds, and up a steep flight of tall, tall stairs to the next highest rung of the crater. By the time I reached the main street between Belphegoris and whatever the Invidiate part was called, I was winded and my legs were killing me, so I found a low wall and took a seat to get my breath back and watch the crowds pass by. They watched me back, of course, though no one paid me too much mind; when she wasn't doing anything but sitting there, even the new human wasn't more interesting than whatever business the pedestrians passing by had going on, I guess. Nice to know that the fascination of novelty only lasted so long around here.

It was hard to tell how much time was passing without the sky changing at all to show it, but I also had no reason to keep track of it or care. I rested until I was rested, then stood back up and kept walking in the direction I felt like walking in, thinking briefly of General Enkida as I did. There was a real zen to time practically not existing in this place, I had to admit. I'd miss it when I finally left.

Side by side with the half-decayed, ruinous looking sloth district, the envy side of town stuck out like a sore thumb wrapped in a particularly garish band-aid. The Gulliate side of town had been jam-packed with all the different fun parts of demon society, but this district looked like an even more blatant mix. I walked past the looming splendor of a few Superbiate-style mansion-looking buildings, all columns and arches, polished stone and gleaming metalwork. On the same street were colorfully curtained tents and stalls that looked like they'd been lifted straight from the Avaritiate bazaar, bedecked with tapestries and ribbons and jewels all prominently displayed. Further in, I walked by a crowd of Invidiates all standing in the street and staring through the barred window of what looked like an Iriate smithy, the walls all metal and spikes, at the short stands of squat, scaled-down armor displayed within.

Maybe it was just because I was more familiar with the other parts of town by now, but it was a jarring mix of designs and functions to pass by so quickly in succession. It was kind of like going to Vegas and seeing the Eiffel Tower next to the Statue of Liberty next to the Sphinx — kind of impressive, kind of tacky. Nothing stood out as original here; everything was copying something else that had already been done before.

Thankfully, Beelzebubis was one of those inspirations. My appetite had been continually chased away by barfing Gulliates and spitting ox monsters, but now it was returning again, with no fresh grossness to scare it off this time. My stomach gurgled the first time I caught a whiff of food beneath the faint perfume smells that had permeated most of the streets so far. I followed my nose around a corner to find a short, skinny building wedged between two Superbiate-looking towers. An Invidiate woman with yellow lipstick and painted horns sat at a window counter in the front wall beneath a big sign flanked by lit torches. I couldn't read the jagged demon writing on the sign, but I could smell something grilling from within, that meat-and-sauce-and-smoke smell of a backyard barbecue. Hopefully there'd be something on the menu that didn't skeeve me out; it was a long and hungry walk back to the palace if not.

I walked up to the streetside window and stood behind another Invidiate customer, this one the same height as myself and wearing a full set of red-brown Iriate carapace armor that was a size or two too big for him, judging from how loosely it jangled on him with every movement. He pulled a small stick of soul from his breastplate and set it on the counter as the woman behind him handed him a steaming handful of some sticky, shiny, grilled bread thing in a cloth napkin.

It smelled amazing, hearty and sweet and buttery. My diet was far from balanced by this point, but fuck it, I was on self-imposed vacation. "Excuse me," I said, stepping in front of the armored Invidiate as he turned to leave. "Hi, sorry. What is that? It looks delicious."

He looked me up and down with all of his pupils before answering. "Mearcalum tart," he said slowly. Suspicious, clearly, but I couldn't imagine why.

"Cool, thanks," I said, then turned away, leaving him to stare weirdly at me as I went to the window. "Hey there," I said to the lady at the counter, "can you tell me what's in a mearcalum tart?"

She smiled. Behind her yellow painted lips, her teeth were also painted, each one a different color. At least I hoped it was paint. "Well, mearcalum, of course, thick sliced and grilled on a plank of suicypress bark," she said. "Then we dip 'em in kelpie butter and fold 'em in our fluffiest fresh-baked bread, drizzle it with a honey-butter marsh syrup, toast the whole thing again, and finish with a sprinkle of soul flakes."

I understood most of the words in that pitch by now, thankfully. Mearcalum were those marsh apples I'd tried with Kriseia, I was pretty sure. The earthy, alcoholic things. Marsh syrup was probably also apple based, because the alternative sounded gross and unnecessary. I think kelpies were some kind of Celtic fairy thing, if I remembered right; seals or horses or something, maybe. Which wasn't ideal for a foodstuff, but she said butter, so I was willing not to think too hard about it. "Suicypress" sounded the most suspect, but also minimally involved, so screw it, I was hungry. "Sounds good," I said. "One of those, please."

She flashed a rainbow-colored grin and ducked behind an inner curtain, replaced by the sound of sizzling and chopping and a fruity, honey smell. I leaned against the window counter, gazing idly around the street as I waited.

That same Invidiate customer in the oversized armor was still standing nearby, looking weirdly at me as the butter and honey of his mearcalum tart dripped down his hand. He didn't seem to care that I'd caught him staring.

"How's it going?" I asked to try and break the awkwardness.

His many eyes narrowed. "You're that new human, aren't you?" he asked, though it sounded more like an accusation. "The one living in Pandemonium."

"That's me," I said, smiling. "What gave it away?"

Joking didn't diffuse him either. "You can get a dozen-course meal with the snap of your fingers in that place, if you're important enough," he said. "Interesting that you're slumming it up here in Leviathanis instead, eating street food with the nobodies."

It was gonna be like that, huh? Guess I shouldn't have been surprised. "I don't know that I'm important enough for that," I said. "And street food's more my speed than fancy banquets anyways."

He frowned harder, but the lady in the window reappeared before he could complain any further. I turned away to find her holding a steaming, gleaming pastry wrapped in paper out to me. "That'll be one lesser soul," she said.

My hand froze halfway to taking the food from her. "Ah. Right. Shit, sorry, one sec." I made an exaggerated show of searching my pockets for the money I already knew I didn't have. I hadn't needed any until now, and the only souls I'd ever possessed so far were the impromptu batteries sitting back on my desk at the palace. "Well, this is embarrassing," I said with a sheepish smile as I pulled my empty hands from my empty pockets. "I seem to have forgotten my souls back at the palace."

"The palace, eh?" the Invidiate woman said, pulling the tart back through the window. "Been visiting at court, have ya?"

"No, I live there," I said. "Sorry about this, but I'm still new here. I don't know if you guys do credit, but I could write you an IOU, or you could send an invoice to the palace, maybe? Care of Lady Morgan Amell."

The woman in the window was eyeing me with suspicion now too. To be fair, she had better cause than the grumpy guy in the ill-fitting armor did. "Hang on," she said after a second, "are you that new human woman? The Archfiend's new pet?"

I scoffed before I could stop myself. "Uh, no, not his pet," I said. "Consort, I think he called me. Or that's what he told the archdemons, anyway. I'm more like a confidante. To be honest, we're still hashing out the details, me and him."

Her suspicion slowly melted back into a painted grin. "Well, damn my eyes," she said. "You're serious? Here I thought you were just a Luxuriate taking her glamour around public. But no, I see it now, lookin' closer at ya." She thrust the mearcalum tart at me once again. "Here, happy to oblige. I know you're good for it, if you're in the Archfiend's entourage."

"Really?" I said, taking the pastry from her. "Hey, thanks. I promise I'll remember my wallet next time."

"No problem at all," she said, quickly bowing her head a couple times. "Be sure to tell all your palace crowd about us, Lady Morganamel!"

I didn't bother correcting her, just smiled and nodded and turned away. I'd have to remember to talk to Vambrace about an expenses budget next time I saw him.

The grumpy armored guy was still glaring at me as I passed him, his mouth set in a tight frown. I kept eye contact with him as I bit into the tart and threw my chin up high in my best Sidona impersonation, hearing his low grumbling as I strode away. Maybe it was ignoble of me, but knowing that such an unpleasant guy was envious of me tasted sweet. Or maybe that was just the honey butter.

I wandered as I ate, watching the people and seeing what kind of places were around, just generally getting a feel for this part of the city. At first I stuck to the main road that I'd followed up the massive staircase, worried about getting too lost if I took too many turns in my walk. A quick look back at an intersection showed me how unfounded that particular worry was; even this far away from it, Pandemonium loomed impossibly tall in the distance, a jagged black nail driven into the horizon, a constant crack in the scenery. No sense worrying about losing my sense of direction, then — I couldn't hide from that thing's sight if I'd wanted to.

The marsh apples started kicking in before long, my head growing hazy, my legs going a bit unsteady. I'd thought cooking them would make the alcoholic part less potent, but if anything, it seemed to have made the effects stronger. Eating one whole apple with Kriseia had made me start to feel tipsy, but I was only halfway through this pastry when I realized that tipsy had come and gone when I wasn't looking, and now full-blown drunk was looming ahead. Well-known or not, important person or no, I knew better than to go stumbling inebriated and alone down unfamiliar streets. So I wrapped up the latter half of the tart for later, found a crowded and well-lit city square, and sat down on the edge of a fountain to rest and sober up.

The first deep breath I took turned immediately into a sudden fit of unexpected and violent coughing. I thought maybe I'd inhaled some soul flakes or bread crumbs or something, so I tried breathing through my nose once the coughing subsided. That was a mistake too; the air smelled foul here, rotten and smokey, and it set me off coughing even harder. I stood and tried to stumble away, back the way I'd come where the air was cleaner, but I'd barely taken a step when I tripped on something. A loose cobblestone, a piece of trash, I wasn't sure, and I didn't have time to figure it out as I went sprawling forward.

Someone on the street shouted, and then there was a splash. Somehow I'd managed to turn around and flop head-first into the fountain. How the hell had that happened? I'd literally just stood up!

I flailed, hands scrabbling through the dark water to find the bottom and push myself up. They broke the surface instead, waving in the air above as water rushed into my open, coughing mouth and down my throat. *If I drown in a foot of water in the middle of the street, so help me, God, I'll —*

Two strong hands grabbed me by the wrists and hauled me up and out of the fountain. I hit the cobbled street with my knees, hacking and spluttering, water streaming from my hair and nose over carapace-clad, black-taloned feet. "What happened?" a loud, masculine voice demanded, and I looked up, blinking through tears of exertion, into the white-bearded face of an Iriate soldier.

It took me another minute of coughing and heavy breathing before I could answer. "Too much apple," I croaked. "Got drunk. Fell in."

The soldier leaned down and sniffed, face contorting. "You don't seem drunk to me," he said, still too loud for conversation. "But you reek of miasma. You been hexed?"

I pushed myself up to my feet, albeit unsteadily. "I don't know what that means," I said, wiping wet hair from my face.

The Iriate soldier was only a head or so taller than me, but thick and stout, like a barrel in armor. He leaned in again, peering at me through my sodden bangs. "Don't know?" he asked, incredulous, then rose up, eyes widening. "You're that new human woman, aren't you?"

"Yeah," I said, wringing out my shirt. "I've been getting that a lot today."

He laid a meaty hand on my shoulder and spun me around, catching me with both hands when I threatened to keep spinning and fall over again. "Drink," he said, pointing at the dark waters of the fountain. "It'll help."

I might have brushed his hands off me, but my legs still felt woozy, and he was probably the only thing keeping me upright at the moment. "Think I've had my fill already, thanks," I said.

He tsked. "*Drink*, not inhale," he said. "Water from a soul spring will clear out any of that cursed shit you've already breathed in."

I still wasn't thrilled about the idea, but hexes and cursed shit sounded serious. With the soldier still steadying me, I knelt in front of the fountain and cupped my hands under one of the streams, then slowly and carefully sipped.

The effect was subtle, but definitely noticeable. After the first handful of black water, the world around me stopped spinning. Another handful later and the fog in my head cleared. After a third handful, the air freshened, that rotten smoke smell fading to an aftertaste in the back of my throat. I shrugged out of the soldier's grip and stood, and thankfully remained standing this time.

He stepped around beside me. "Better?" he asked.

I took a deep breath. "Better."

"Good." He turned to the onlookers in the square around us and swept them all with a glower. "Anyone want to fess up to that?" he barked.

The Invidiates we could see all quickly averted their gazes and busied themselves with not paying attention to us anymore. A couple of nearby Superbiate women snickered aloud.

The Iriate man turned back to me and sniffed again. "Some of it's cleared up," he announced, still a bit too loud. "Whatever little puffs of miasma our bystanders were contributing. The soul water helped take the worst of it off. Still too much around you to just be collected residuals from the public, though. Someone's hexed you deliberately." He put an arm around my shoulder and spun me to face back the way I'd come. "Come on, let's find the most likely suspects."

I was swept up with him as he strode off down the street. "I'm still confused," I said, stumbling along beside the soldier. "Someone put a curse on me? This is the first I'm hearing about it."

He nodded. "Recent, then," he said. "Good, that makes it more likely we'll catch the little scuttler that did this. You really don't know about Invidiate hexes yet?"

"I'm that new human woman," I reminded him. "Still figuring this shit out as I go."

He grunted. "They're not supposed to do it without authorized dispensation," he said, "but there're always some who conveniently forget that fact. Any Invidiates you can remember running into recently who might have cause to dislike you?"

"I haven't met very many so far who seem like they like anybody," I said.

He grunted again. "You're catching on. Most aren't easy to like. You being human, you've probably attracted the attention of a lot of 'em just by walking by. The miasma on you was pretty obvious, though, so whoever our culprit is, they're not very good at it. Probably taller than average for their kind. Anyone like that you can think of?"

I pulled the sodden remains of the mearcalum pastry from my pocket, now more a handful of mush than a tart. "One person comes to mind," I said.

We found him a few minutes later, walking toward us down the road, his loose-fitting armor jostling with every step. He froze as he noticed us, then turned and tried to book it.

"HALT!" the soldier beside me bellowed as he rushed forward, reaching into a leather pouch at his side as he ran. He pulled out a spiked metal ball, like a mace without a handle or a flail without a chain, and chucked it baseball-like at the fleeing Invidiate. The ball hit him in the back with a loud crack, the spikes lodging into his armor, and he shouted in pain as he fell forward and went sprawling into the street.

I caught up to the Iriate soldier as he was hauling the Invidiate man to his feet and wrenching his arms behind his back. It was an awkward stretch with his oversized pauldrons getting in the way, but the Iriate managed to yank them back enough to clap a pair of heavy black manacles over the smaller man's wrists.

"You want to dress like a guard, you ought to know better than to run from one," the Iriate grumbled as he yanked the metal ball from the

Invidiate's back. The armor beneath was cracked and dented now, a crumbling hole where the spike had lodged; still, ill-fitting or not, that armor had probably saved the guy from having his spine crushed, so I guess it wasn't such a goofy look after all.

The Invidiate twisted his head around to glare at me. "Uppity bitch!" he spat. "I've lived here my whole life, then suddenly you walk in and start siccing soldiers on people? Fucking humans, just *have* to throw their weight around!"

The soldier in question smacked him on the back of the head. "You sicced me on yourself, idiot," he said. "That hex was too big to be unintentional, and too sloppy not to be noticed. What did you think would happen?"

"I couldn't help it!" the Invidiate argued, thrashing weakly against the manacles. Or maybe he was just trying to get his weirdly bent arms more comfortable. "She waltzes in here, flaunting her human privilege, demanding special treatment, and I'm supposed to keep quiet about that?"

"That's exactly what you're supposed to do, yes," the soldier said, hauling him around to face me. "Now shut up and dispel it before I break your jaw, you little shit."

The Invidiate ground his teeth as he glared at me, but he said nothing else, only grumbled wordlessly from the back of his throat. All at once, I felt suddenly less fatigued, a haze I hadn't noticed lifting from my eyes, a chill I had thought was just the dampness in my clothes lifting from my bones. I took a deep breath, warm and refreshed, and stood up straighter.

The Invidiate man was still glaring daggers at me with a dozen pupils. "Thanks for that," I said, then held out the ruined mush of my leftover pastry. "You want the rest of this?"

He growled and kicked at me until the soldier smacked him in the back of the head again. "I'll take it from here," the Iriate said, dipping his head to me. "Take care, m'lady." He yanked the armored Invidiate around and shoved him forward, and the two of them marched off down the street, the prisoner still grumbling and growling as they went.

The food stand where this had all started was within sight, the woman with the painted horns and mouth leaning over the counter, watching the guard and her former customer walking away. She turned her attention to me as I headed over, the pastry mush still in my hand. "Sorry about all that," I said, then held out my ruined tart. "Do you have a trash can back there?"

She sniffed. "Ruined your snack with his little tantrum of a curse, did he?" she said, taking the soggy napkin from me and disappearing behind the back curtain with it. "Effects weren't very subtle, from the look of ya. No wonder the dullard went and got caught. Not surprised, given how tall he was. Sloppy hex work."

"That's the second time I've heard that," I said. "What does height have to do with anything?"

"By my eyes, you *are* new here, aren't ya?" she said with a chuckle through the curtain. "Us Invidiates stop growing once we come into our hexing abilities. That one was about as tall as you were, which makes him a late bloomer, talent-wise. Evidently he never got much better at it. Explains why he was overcompensating with that second-hand Iriate armor, I guess."

"Huh." I'd noticed the size differences in the Invidiates I'd met so far, but I hadn't realized they meant anything. "Is that why Archduke Aleviathan is barely two feet tall?" I asked.

She chuckled. "You got a powerful social circle, Lady. There's been a lot of Aleviathans through history, but if you're talking currently, yes, that's why Aleviathan the 43rd is archduke in the first place. One reason, anyway. I don't really got a mind to follow politics, you understand." She reappeared then, a fresh mearcalum tart in her hand, which she held out to me. "Here," she said. "On the house."

I pursed my lips. "I appreciate it," I said, "but I'm not sure that's a good idea, considering what happened last time I didn't pay for my food."

The vendor scoffed. "I ain't fool enough to hex a customer over a bit of bread," she said. "And I can't let someone who *is* fool enough keep my more sensible customers from getting fed. It's only a lesser soul, go on and take it."

I smiled and did as she asked. "Thanks," I said. "I didn't catch your name."

She grinned her multicolored grin. "Alhemerocallis the 98th," she said. "At your service, Lady Morganamel."

That one was a mouthful. "A lot of 'Al-something the Numbered' names, I've noticed," I said. "Is there something behind that, too?"

"No sense letting a good name go to waste, is there?" she answered. "You don't get to wear someone as prestigious as Leviathan's name without being archdemon-levels of important, but Hemerocallis was a renowned beauty in her time. That's an achievement I don't mind emulating, I'll tell you that for nothing." She smirked and ran a hand over one of her rainbow-painted horns.

I smiled and gave her a thumbs up. "You're crushing it, Alamoca…uh…"

"Alhemerocallis," she said.

"Alhemerocallis," I repeated.

"The 98th," she added patiently.

"Alhemerocallis the 98th. Got it." I backed up, waving the pastry in my hand. "Have a good one. Thanks for the grub."

"Anytime, Lady Morganamel," she said with a curtsy.

Right, that was enough excitement for me for one day. I headed back toward Pandemonium, nibbling on my drunken apple tart as I went, hoping my clothes would finish drying before I got there.

Chapter 31: Complacency

The next several days, or couple of weeks, or however long it was, they all passed more or less the same. I spent my days dividing my attention between Vambrace's company, Sidona's projects, and Abdeles' field trips, with my in-between alone time spent working on what I could manage of my magic notes between my own straining memory of the *Morganomicon* and what new tidbits of spells I gleaned from my excursions with the Superbiate archduke. It was, strangely enough, in its own way, a familiar and comfortable rhythm that reminded me of the mundane one I'd left behind: wake up, eat, go to class with whoever wanted to see me at the moment, a bit of free time, then studying and reviewing my notes before a bath and back to bed. The biggest differences were the lack of alarm clocks and time slots, and that I was occasionally casually fooling around with my dormmate.

Speaking of, Kriseia contented herself spending her time with me, whatever I was doing, whenever I wasn't meeting privately with someone or other. Part of it was no doubt her training as a servile companion, and part of it was her open crush on me — but a surprisingly large and still-growing part of it was her own continued fascination with Earth and its culture. Everywhere I went, it seemed, whatever other role I was playing at the time, I was always also a lecturer on human studies.

But where Vambrace was most interested in Earth history, and Sidona cared primarily for its art and music, Kriseia was more curious about the mundane details of daily life: What was college like? Where did I live? Where did I work? Did all humans learn as many different subjects as I did? How big was the city I'd come from? How big was my home town? How did we keep all the monsters out without giant spiked oven walls?

I felt more comfortable in my authority on these topics, at least. And also, unlike Vambrace or Sidona, Kriseia didn't seem to have any bigger picture idea she was hoarding this knowledge for, no grand performance or multi-volume historical encyclopedia planned. No, near as I could tell, she was just a huge Earth fangirl, and I was her enabler; so I regaled her with tales of term papers and family holidays and the plotlines of my favorite cartoons while we walked or ate or lay in bed together.

Those were the quiet, stress-free times. Less comfortable were my regular visits with Duchess Sidona, which had grown more frequent and more... awkward. That easy, if haughty, rapport she had was fading, replaced by a distracted urgency. Her hands never stopped moving whenever I was around, taking notes or playing chords or painting brush strokes, all the while demanding clarification on whatever lyrics I was repeating, or whatever melody I was trying to emulate for her, or whatever fashion trend we were discussing while I posed for her portrait of me. She tried a couple of times to teach me the basics of one of her simpler instruments, a kind of circular table thing with strings stretched beneath drum heads that sounded vaguely piano-like when I struck it — the better for me to communicate note progressions, she said, rather than with my amateur a cappella renditions. I'd just learned enough to sound halfway decent with it when, in a huff, she suddenly put a stop to the lessons one day. Too much time being wasted on trying to foster my amateur-at-best musical talent, she said, when it was quicker and offered more raw material to simply put up with my off-key warbling instead.

Despite these heightened levels of casual bitchiness, I found I had more patience for her sniping. Frankly put, she looked terrible lately; bags under her eyes, sunken cheeks, perpetual splotches and smears of dried paint in her fraying braid and on her fancy gown. It might have been the same gown she was wearing when Kriseia and I dropped in on her concert practice. It might have been the same braid. If she hadn't cleaned up or changed clothes since then, I couldn't tell; whenever she got close enough to be in my personal space, the faint, lingering odor of paint fumes and spicy perfume masked any B.O. she might have had.

I asked after her health once more during a session spent posing for her portrait of me. She dismissed the question with a glare and another snort of her cocaine medicine, then demanded I explain how the artist who painted my graphic t-shirt got the paint to adhere in such a way that it didn't wash off in the laundry.

Was she actually developing this solitusia thing? Or was her whole scare really to blame just on my unnoticeability spell? I wasn't sure anymore; she wouldn't talk about it, and I couldn't risk explaining my part in it, and this lingering, silent guilt went a long way toward my patience with her sour attitude.

The duchess wasn't the only one I was feeling guilty over. The next time I saw Prince Vambrace, he seemed to have bounced back from his depression at learning the fate of his homeland, though I could tell his enthusiasm for learning more about Earth history had waned somewhat as a result. I felt bad for having broken the news to him, and also because I wasn't sure that the news I'd broken was especially accurate. Whatever nuances of people and culture had existed in his time in his part of the world, the details hadn't translated clearly enough across 1,500 years or so to my modern, disinterested brain for me to be comfortable discussing them with someone who was there at the time. There was a possibility that I'd misspoken about something and bummed him out for no reason.

I said as much when I brought the broken cell phone back to his room, but he waved me off. "It is the ancient history of an alien world, my lady," he said as we rode the long elevator ride down to his subterranean vault. "I have no real stakes in its present or future, only bittersweet memories of its distant past. It was folly for me to behave otherwise."

"It's still your home, though," I said. "It makes sense to care about what's been going on there. I get it."

"I threw my homeland away long ago, willingly and knowingly," he said. "This is my home now. Your news was not what I would have preferred to hear, but I'm not surprised having heard it. If nothing else, it is nice to have closure of any sort — an end at last for Victor of Caerleon."

"Does this mean you're giving up on that whole recapturing chivalry thing?" I asked.

He sighed. "I don't know. I enjoy your company, and I like having a lady in my court to defer to on some level, even if only in private. One who isn't constantly grasping for power or influence, like all of my demonic courtiers. Speaking with you, remembering that feeling, those whispers of my first life — it is pleasantly nostalgic. But I am also never going to meet another human woman, I imagine, and I am never going to stop being the archfiend, so it is ultimately little more than personal indulgence." He chuckled. "A new kind of personal indulgence, granted, which is in itself remarkable to me after so many eons here. But still." He shook his head.

"My behavior toward you will not change, my lady, but I am no longer under any illusion that anything I may have lost is worth reclaiming."

That spiel, his attitude, his whole situation now, it all bummed me out. At the same time, there wasn't anything I could think to do about it, short of taking him with me when I finally figured a way out of here and showing him how modern Britain was doing. I didn't think he'd appreciate the gesture, though. He probably wouldn't like the state of modern Britain, either. Then again, my grasp of modern politics was only slightly better than my grasp of fifth century politics, so who knew.

On the plus side, his abandoning this particular dream meant that he was demanding less of my attention, and that my rewriting the entire encyclopedia was no longer on the table. That freed me up for more of my secret field trips with Archduke Abdeles.

The trips were still less frequent than I would have liked, maybe one every few days on average. Admittedly, that probably wasn't a bad rate of successful leads for hunting for ancient secrets, but it was the fact that each one bore fruit that made me perpetually impatient for more.

Each excursion ended up being pretty similar to the first. Someone brought me a message saying Alastaroth or Abdeles was requesting my presence, then escorted me to some private or innocuous location somewhere in the city: a tight back alley of Beelzebubis, a collapsed home in Belphegoris, the basement of an Asmodeusis brothel, the corner of a private garden within a Luciferis manor. Each time, whatever other people might have been around gave the three of us a wide berth while the two demon men explained what I was supposed to be looking at, until the rune came into focus and I made a couple copies — one for my own use, one to lie about to the archduke and his scholar.

My co-conspirators were growing more impatient the more we discovered as well, the archduke getting downright grumpy on more than one occasion, scowling at me the entire time I worked and dismissing me curtly after the new rune was catalogued. "Please understand, this research is more personal to his lordship than to yourself, my lady," Alastaroth explained after a particularly tense and uncomfortable trip. "This is the history of our people that we are unearthing and deciphering — a history which was purposefully erased by an outsider with no previous attachment to it, however much reverence that outsider went on to earn. His lordship is at times understandably upset that this research is necessary at all, but to vent that frustration aloud would be tantamount to treason. He does his best to keep it bottled, but even Superbiate nobility is not perfect, despite what they would have the rest of us believe."

I had to admit, it made sense. I felt another small pang of guilt for lying to the guy about what was actually written in these bits of magic we were finding. Just a small one, though, nowhere near the top of my current guilt list, and not enough for me to risk teaching these two actual magic, however piecemeal and probably useless it would have been.

Teaching myself, though? That's where I was making some big honkin' breakthroughs.

Despite all the sex and violence and luxury and literal hellishness around me, the most exciting parts of this new routine I'd fallen into was when all of it was over for the day and I was sitting quietly in my room, at my desk, doing my homework. My professors would have been proud to see me now, if they could ignore the pink woman quietly masturbating in the background, or the way my hands caught fire sometimes when I knew she was asleep.

Between the bits of magic I'd found on these field trips and the bits I managed to transcribe and dissect from the whole two spells I could remember on my own, I'd compiled quite the beginner glossary of witchcraft — enough, I realized, that I could pull apart both the heat spell and the unnoticeability spell into a series of individual steps, an order of swirls and symbols and loops of thought that each worked like discrete key words in a magical sentence.

Comparing the full spell to my rune glossary, that sentence went something like: Potential - gather; focus, hands; suffuse - skin, make shield (heat = nullify); focus, outward; potential = ignite; heat - increase, project; heat - increase, project; heat - increase, project; and so on, ad nauseum, until my burrito exploded or my hands caught fire or something else happened to interrupt my concentration and make the effect stop.

I'd made that breakthrough and called it a night, then woke up the next morning(?), took a bath with Kriseia, and reviewed my notes while she was busy polishing her horns. Coming back to my work with fresh eyes, I was confused at first at what I was looking at. This couldn't really be called a sentence, I thought. It looked more like a set of commands. Like a string of code.

That thought struck especially heavy. That was exactly what this was, wasn't it? It made a profound, simplified amount of sense: Magic was just a series of commands for reality. I was, just a little bit, editing the code of the world. Rewriting the program from inside of it.

I fell into my chair with a laugh, slapping my notes on the desk, just as Kriseia exited the bathroom. "What's funny?" she asked, horns gleaming in the lamplight.

I leaned back over my chair, smiling at her upside down. "I think I just figured out what major I'm gonna declare."

She pursed her lips. They were deep blue today, a sharp contrast with the bright orange skin of her current face. "That is… your main educational goal, yes?" she asked, leaning over me.

"You remembered?" I asked. "Good job."

"Of course I did," she said, holding my face as she lowered her lips to mine. "I remember all of your stories."

My own memory wasn't so iron clad, unfortunately.

It was my latest excursion with Abdeles and Alastaroth, this time in an underground caina berry farm beneath a Luciferis winery. The three of us were standing at the edge of a wide, placid, pitch-black lake, around which caina bushes grew in thick, concentric rows. The surface of the lake was broken every few minutes by small chunks of soul that fell from the pockmarked stone ceiling above, plopping gently into the water with a cascade of ripples. The errant soul-fall was what gave the lake its color and the nutrients that fed the thriving caina plants, as well as made the fog that rose like cold steam from the water's surface.

The whole damn cave was cold. It made sense this far underground, and it helped the caina berries grow healthy and ripe, but that didn't make it any more comfortable. I shivered beneath my new cloak — a gift from Prince Vambrace after he realized I only ever wore my t-shirt or that one Superbiate gown whenever he saw me. He'd brought me to a tailor of his after that, a thin Superbiate man whose long hair was braided with sewing needles and spools of colorful thread. Several hours of measuring and playing dress-up later, I was set free again; and ever since, new outfits in my size began showing up periodically at my door. The one I was in now was a sort of velvety jumpsuit of deep, shimmery purple, beneath the aforementioned cloak of brown, leathery fur.

Garm fur, Vambrace had explained proudly. Taken from the pack that had attacked us on the wall, of course. Even though I hadn't taken part in the fight, I nonetheless got to wear my opponent's skin like a trophy. A practical sort of revenge, he'd said.

I wasn't as enthused by the idea as he was. I still had the garm nightmare now and then, even weeks(?) later. But hell, it was a comfortable cloak, and super warm to boot. Real useful in a caina cave, even if the cold was still seeping up through my feet and fogging my breath.

We were standing on the bank of the black lake, a big slab of wet brick at our feet, having been dredged up and deposited as we watched by a handful of nearby Gulliate farmers that Abdeles had momentarily hired. They all flashed curious looks at the three of us as the archduke paid them, then waded away through the caina bushes back to their usual work.

I crouched down to examine the hunk of rock, not needing Alastaroth to point out where the squiggle language was this time. It was big and obvious here, a looping, branching pattern scraped deep into the surface running from one edge to the other, the lines still so clean and clear they might have been carved just yesterday. I ran my fingers over the carving, hmming aloud, but it was an act for my associates' benefit; I could read this shit in my sleep by this point. This rune especially.

It was the shell rune again, I realized instantly. The first one I'd pretended to decipher for them back when we started these field trips together, on the bricks buried in the fields of Beelzebubis. It was part of the code for both my heat and unnoticeability spells — kept me from melting my own skin off in the former, reflected attention in the latter. Super useful, this bit of squiggle.

Trouble was, I couldn't remember what I had told these two it meant.

"Difficulties, Lady Morgan?" Alastaroth asked from behind me. I held up a finger without looking away from the brick, really milking my "confused academic" face while I scrambled for a response.

He and the archduke had their own copy of this one already, along with my first mistranslation of it. Whether or not they remembered the pattern right now, they'd have to see the similarities when they added this new version they were waiting on. What would they think if the two didn't match? I couldn't think of any way I could just not give them their own copy for this trip's discovery. Was it too late to dismiss this one as a repeat that didn't need bothering with? I'd been staring at it in fake concentration for what felt like too many minutes now already.

With no better answer and no time left to stall, I stood up and cleared my throat. "We've seen this one already," I announced. "But the meaning can change depending on context. Do either of you remember what the translation was the first time?"

Alastaroth opened his mouth, but the archduke cut him off. "No," he said, "neither of us has memorized it yet, unfortunately. What does this version of it say?"

Alright, kinda rude, but not out of character. I turned back to look down at the damp carving. "In this context," I said slowly, "the closest translation I can think of is… 'sunken'?" I paused. "Yeah, 'sunken,'" I continued. Fuck it, in for a penny. "Or 'buried,' but in this context, it's more of a 'sunken.'"

Neither of them said anything for a long moment, but I didn't dare turn around and see why, lest my lying face choose that moment to give out. "'This context' being 'under a lake'?" Alastaroth finally asked.

I nodded. "Most likely, yeah. It's a very versatile character, this one. The nuance of its meaning can change in a lot of different ways," I explained, not even lying anymore. Good job, Morgan.

"Interesting," Abdeles said slowly. "Especially considering this lake would have been made artificially long after whatever ruin was here was destroyed. Caina farming didn't expand into Luciferis caverns until fairly recently."

Shit. Bad job, Morgan. "Yeah, that is interesting," I said, then cleared my throat again. "Well, who can say where this chunk of ruin originated or what this spot looked like way back then? I'd need a bigger picture to go off of to know the full story."

"Who can say indeed," the archduke grumbled. He sounded annoyed again, though whether at me or the repetitive rune we'd found, I didn't know.

Alastaroth handed me a quill and a couple sheets of parchment, and I made the usual two transcriptions, though in this case my personal copy ended up being extraneous. "Thank you for your help as always, Lady Morgan," the archduke said as I handed over his copy. "I will of course send word as soon as I have our next excursion figured out. It might be more of a wait than usual this time — I have a lead in mind, but it is not as solid as the others thus far. Still, I feel we are precariously close to an important breakthrough here."

"Awesome," I said, following the two through the caina bushes toward the winding path up and out of this cavern. "Can't wait."

I made a few minor breakthroughs of my own in the meantime, thanks to the glossary of new spell bits I'd gathered on these trips and my new perspective on reading magic as a series of command prompts. Not enough to even think about recreating the interdimensional travel spell yet, but enough to get a step or two closer. Probably.

My biggest advancement was that, with all these rune discoveries and my newly deconstructed heat spell, I learned how to put new spells together out of the pieces. It was hard to tell for sure at first — I had nobody that was safe to practice the attention diverting stuff on, and I couldn't do any heat stuff while Kriseia was watching — but the theory seemed sound, so I started playing.

When my roommate was asleep or out of the room, I tinkered with the heat spell, or at least the few variables I was pretty sure wouldn't kill me if they weren't invoked exactly right. That shell rune became my best friend, now that I knew it was the part that kept me from melting from the inside out whenever I cast this particular magic, so I left it where it was in the sequence; but I tried tweaking the heat, or the focus, or the area of effect.

I kept water in the tub while I tried all this, of course, just in case. I was curious and desperate, not stupid. Not yet.

One of the runes I'd found on my traitorous field trips looked like the part of the combustion spell that increased the temperature, but pulled inside out, and gave me an impression of diminishing or shrinking while I read it. Plugging that into the spell in the place where the heat usually started building didn't appear to do anything at first; but that was the part of the incantation that repeated ad nauseum at the end, so I sat there at my desk channeling in silence for a minute, in case something eventually happened.

With the shielding magic around my hands, keeping them safe, it wasn't until I started seeing clouds of my own breath that I realized what had been happening the whole time. Just to be undeniably sure, I stood, went to the bathroom, and plunged my hands into the tub of water, which immediately froze around them.

It really *was* that simple, then. Bitchin', I'd just increased my magical toolbox by 33 percent. I would have done a celebratory fist pump if my hands weren't currently trapped in a tub of ice. By the time I'd channeled the regular heat spell to free myself, the urge had passed.

That same "decrease" rune was also part of my unnoticeable spell, I realized shortly afterward — and from there, it was suddenly child's play to deconstruct that much more complicated sequence of magic, and my toolbox of runes ballooned with possibilities.

I didn't have time to play with any of them very much, though, before the next message came from Alastaroth.

I was attending a concert with Vambrace at the time, one of Sidona's small exhibitions of her work with the Earth songs I'd taught her. A full-blown symphony performance of modern Earth-inspired music was coming soon, she'd announced; but in the meantime, select practice sessions would be available to certain VIPs who couldn't wait that long to sate their curiosity. The prince was at the top of that list and the most curious by far, of course, and it didn't take much sleuthing on his part to discover that I'd had a hand in the duchess's latest musical endeavors; so there we were, sitting together in a private box seat over a mostly empty audience, the archfiend on the edge of his seat with his eyes riveted to the spotlit stage, where a Luxuriate man with a barrel chest and lungs to match belted out the words to "Don't Stop Me Now" to the backing of a string quartet and one of those wet drum instrument things.

It was a weird cover, but not a bad one, like most of Sidona's versions of the songs I'd been teaching her. It was better than I thought she'd do with a Queen track, at least, I had to give her that. I was getting into it myself, eyes closed and head swaying, when I felt a light tap on my shoulder. I looked up to see the Luxuriate attendant who'd brought us drinks at the start of the performance refilling my glass of marsh apple cider. She smiled as she finished, then leaned down close and whispered, "Your scholastic friend would like a word with you outside at your earliest convenience, m'lady."

I nodded and shot a glance at Vambrace, but he was too focused on the concert below to notice our exchange. I waited until the server had left again, took a sip of my drink, then rose from my seat. That caught the prince's attention. "Bathroom," I explained, hooking my thumb over my shoulder at the door. "Be right back."

He nodded and waved me off, and I ducked out the door to our booth into the corridor outside. I was expecting a messenger or someone with a note, one of our usual go-betweens that kept palace eyes from seeing the three of us together too much and getting suspicious. Instead, it was Alastaroth the Seventy-somethingth himself waiting for me, leaning on his staff while the pupils of his good eye swept asynchronously back and forth across the hall. They all focused my way as I exited the theater box. "Apologies for the interruption, Lady Morgan," he croaked after the door had closed behind me. "I would have sent word at a more convenient time, but we thought it prudent to give you this information as soon as possible, so that you could begin planning for it."

"Sounds serious," I said. "Everything alright?"

"Indeed," he said, smiling. "More than alright, though the news is double edged this time. Our next excursion will be taking us just beyond the wall — specifically, into the gulch from whence the most recent garm attack began. The beasts' activity there uncovered something fascinating, his lordship's scouts reported."

I already hated the idea. "Will that be safe?" I asked. "What if there are more garm hiding out there?"

"According to our scouting report, there aren't," Alastaroth answered. "With the number slain just outside the border of Dis, even if any of the pack remained, they would have abandoned the area for safer hunting grounds. Those his lordship employed to verify this fact have confirmed that, for all intents and purposes, the gulch is empty for the moment. Other monstrosities may move in, of course, so all the more reason for us to hurry."

I rubbed the back of my neck, only barely reassured. "I don't suppose you all could bring whatever it is you found back here for me to look at, could you?" I asked.

He shook his head. "Even if context and accuracy were not a factor in the translation, the discovery is simply too large this time to relocate or to adequately transcribe in detail, at least for our untrained perspectives. I'm sorry, my lady, but your presence will be required if we are to glean anything from this one. His lordship has arranged for a contingent of soldiers for our protection, but nevertheless thought that you might want to bring along a personal guard as well, just to be thoroughly safe."

"Personal guard?" I asked. "My personal guard lately is General Enkida, and I doubt I could convince her or the prince to change that on short notice, especially for a trip past the wall. Hell, I'm not even sure he'll sign off on me visiting the wastes at all, no matter how close by."

"Do you require his permission first?" Alastaroth asked, head tilting. "The law states that any other of his subjects is free to journey outside the city as they wish, though they take their safety into their own hands if they do so without first arranging for a guard. Surely with your elevated status, your situation should be no different."

"Maybe, maybe not. I'm not sure, honestly. I could try not telling him, but if I convinced Enkida to come with me, he'd find out anyway." I stepped closer and leaned in. "You sure about bringing the archfiend's right-hand soldier to this not-strictly-legal research trip?" I asked more quietly. "That seems like a real good way for all of us to get caught."

The Inviddiate sighed. "It is not ideal, you are right," he said. "But his lordship has taken precautions with the details of this excursion. She need not discover our true intentions if she comes; we can disguise our motive as curiosity toward the garm and their habitats and conduct our true investigation in secret. We may run the risk of seeming eccentric — yourself especially, Lady Morgan — but eccentricity is not against the law.

And as fascinated as the archfiend has been with your version of Earth of late, could you be blamed for showing fascination with our world?"

I frowned. "Probably not," I said. "This could all work, in theory. I'll be honest, though, I don't really like the sound of any of it. You sure this one's worth all the trouble?"

He grinned at that, wide and toothy. "More than sure, my lady," he said. "That is the good news. If our information is correct, we think we have found a fully intact obelisk this time."

My heart skipped a beat. "You mean…" I started, then stopped and pretended to clear my throat while I took a long, careful breath. "You mean like one with the interdimensional travel magic built into it?"

"That is our belief and our hope, yes," said Alastaroth. "Functionally useless to the modern demon, of course, without any practical knowledge of magic to make it work. But in terms of cultural archival, this is a potential treasure trove, wouldn't you agree?"

"Oh, absolutely!" I smiled and clapped him on both shoulders, grateful for the excuse to let my excitement off its leash for the moment. "It sounds completely fucking fascinating, you're right. When can we go?"

He grinned again. "My lady," he said, leaning in, "how soon can you arrange to be ready?"

Chapter 32: Imposition

On my way back to my room, I bumped into Enkida, who was also on her way back to my room. The accuracy of these psychic Acediate reports she was getting on my whereabouts was frightening at times — times like now, when I was in "conspiracy against the throne" mode.

We walked together in silence while I tried to figure out how best to broach the subject. With no options I liked readily apparent, I decided to go with blunt. "Hey, General," I said. "What would you say if I asked you to take me out past the wall for a bit?"

"I would say 'absolutely not,' my lady," she answered immediately, not even looking at me.

"Yeah, that's what I figured," I said. "But what would be the odds that I could convince you to do it anyway?"

"Slim to none." She glanced sidelong at me, which was progress, at least. "Is there a purpose to these hypotheticals?"

I hurried in front of her and stopped. She stopped too, one eyebrow quirked, as I took a deep breath and bowed my head. "General Enkida," I began in my most stately voice, "will you please accompany me out into the wastes just a very little ways, for a short time, pretty please."

"Absolutely not, my lady" she answered immediately again.

I sighed and rose up. "Can I try and convince you?"

"You can try," she said, striding by me. "Should be interesting, at least."

"It's not, really," I said, falling into step beside her again. "I just want to visit the big ravine where the garm came from the other day. Er, the last time. You know the time I mean."

She made one of those bark-laugh noises of disbelief. "Oh, is that all?" she asked. "Yes, I know the dogs in question. Why in Hell you would want to go there is the part I'm confused about."

I shrugged. "Why not? I—"

"It's a long trek, it's probably dangerous, failing that, it's boring, those garm nearly killed you, and they definitely left their stench behind."

"…Yeah, okay. All good points. But, also…" I took a deep breath. Time to lie some more. "Near-death experience aside, I'm really interested in the garm and their habitat. We don't have them back on Earth. Our biggest dogs are still smaller than me."

She frowned. "The beasts are really not that interesting, Lady Morgan. They're basic pack animals, driven mostly by hunger and territorial sentiment. They drool their own blood, which stains and crusts in their fur, marking packmate and prey alike. Their meat is gamey but not especially noteworthy otherwise."

"See, I didn't know any of that," I said. "I'm learning already. Imagine what else I could learn with a quick visit to one of their empty dens."

"I'm imagining, my lady," Enkida continued. "You could learn what the dried urine and feces and blood of a dozen giant dogs smells like, and not much else. Not exactly the most rewarding of lessons, I would wager."

"You don't know," I argued. "Maybe it could be. Maybe I'm into that kinda thing."

"You're not," she said. "Otherwise, you would have asked for a different Luxuriate a long time ago. Miss Kriseia doesn't oblige that sort of stuff, I've heard."

"No, not — ew, god! Not like that, jeez! I meant like in a studying natural biology kinda way!"

"You are a natural biologist, Lady Morgan?" she asked.

"I'm the foremost authority on Earth's natural biology in this entire world, technically," I said. "I've studied it before. Are you surprised?"

"I am perpetually surprised by you, my lady," she said. "I also don't believe a word of this so far. Why do you really want to visit an empty wasteland garm den, of all places?"

We were at my room now. Enkida posted up in her usual spot by my door. I stopped in front of both, staring at the floor between us. Lying wasn't working, but the truth was out of the question. Somewhere in between, then. "I'm not… I'm not over it yet," I said. "The attack. I keep having these nightmares. Garm chasing me across the wall, blood everywhere, and then…" I took a deep breath. "I know they're gone now. I've heard. But I think I still need to see for myself, to really convince my brain that it's safe and make the dreams stop."

She stared at me in silence for a moment, eyes narrowed. I assumed that meant she didn't believe me now either, until she asked, "Why did you feel the need to lie about that?"

I shrugged. "Why would I tell that particular truth if I didn't have to? I don't like looking weak in front of other humans in my own world. I doubly hate doing it in front of demons I'm still learning about in a world I barely understand yet."

She reached out a hand and laid it on my shoulder. I tensed, but for a change, her touch was surprisingly gentle. "You need the satisfaction of seeing that those who once threatened you have been crushed and driven from their homes," she said, smiling. "Perfectly understandable. Nothing weak about it."

"Well, when you put it like that," I said. "Thanks. Does that mean I've convinced you to take me out there?"

Her smile pinched. "Your odds just got better, at least," she said. "We'll see. I'd prefer to run the idea by His Majesty first."

Crap, crap, crap. "I'd, uh, prefer you didn't," I said. "If I'm still being honest."

Her smile disappeared entirely. "Lady Morgan," she said, "you must realize how that sounds."

"Yeah, I know," I sighed. "But he's... *him*, y'know? And if you tell him that his new pet human—"

"Royal consort," she clarified.

"*Pet human*," I continued, "wants to go outside the wall, for any reason, he'll either freak out and forbid it, or worse, he'll insist on coming along."

"Which would be... bad?"

"Not ideal, yeah. I don't want him knowing I'm still messed up from that day after he tried to protect me. And I don't want him feeling like he has to keep trying so hard to protect me in the first place."

Enkida's head tilted. "You think he's being overprotective?"

"He's got the literal general of Hell's army staring at the door to my room at almost all hours," I pointed out. "No offense."

She smiled again. "A valid point. So. You're trying to prove, to the archfiend and to yourself, that you're safer on your own than either of you give you credit for. Is that it?"

"Good summary, yeah," I said. "Thank you."

"And you're going to do this by continuing to lean on the services of the personal guard that the archfiend assigned to you to keep you safe?"

"Uh… I mean…" I stared at the floor again, fidgeting. "Baby steps, right? I've gone into the city by myself. Going into the wastes with a body guard seems like the next step. I'm slightly rebellious, not stupid."

"That remains to be seen," she said. "But… very well. I will consider your request, Lady Morgan."

I sighed in relief. "Awesome, thank you so much," I said, bowing deeply, then reached for my door.

Enkida's hand landed on my shoulder again as I passed, less gentle this time. "Would I be correct in assuming," she said slowly, not looking at me, "that, should I decline to go along with this plan, you'll attempt it regardless, without any guard at your side?"

I cleared my throat. "Hypothetically, you mean?" I asked. "Or are we still being honest?"

She *chuckled*, I swear. I heard it. "Rest well, lady," she said.

I went inside and went to bed. I wasn't sure how long I'd actually been awake, but I was tired and had nothing else to do, and Hell's "do what feels good when you feel like it" approach to scheduling was really growing on me, not gonna lie.

Enkida didn't have an answer for me when I woke up, but Vambrace had a summons. I got dressed and made my way toward the coliseum level, my head racing the entire way. If the general had told him about my request after all, I had no idea how I was going to talk my way into still making the trip without him tagging along.

But no, it turned out this was just another of his hangout sessions because he liked my company. Which was flattering, don't get me wrong; but with imminent magical victory on my mind, I couldn't honestly say I wasn't a bit annoyed at any distractions at the moment.

I stood in the arena stands with the rest of the crowds, drumming my fingers on the railing while I watched him dismantle two different Iriates, both of them nearly twice his size. He swung Excalibur in a dizzying dance between his two attackers, whirling to block the one's mace and the other's dual axes, batting away all danger with loud metallic clangs that could barely be heard beneath the excited roaring of his audience.

That sword should have snapped in half a dozen or so parries ago, I thought. Whatever blessing or magic was on that blade, it was incredible — and also kind of obvious, once I knew to look for it. Was nobody else watching right now suspicious that their archfiend's self-proclaimed invincibility was breaking physics around him? Was that real confidence in the smile he wore down there, knowing his enchanted weapon was still carrying him eons later? Or was that cocky grin a show for the audience, like the rest of him?

And — here was a new thought — if it truly was *magic* in that sword that made it work... was it *my* kind of magic, or something else? Were there other kinds of magic?

If I got my hands on that sword, could I learn more spells from it? Could I make *myself* an unstoppable badass too?

It was a hard question to shake once I'd thought it. Even if this next field trip with Abdeles was the one that got me home, I'd be going back with all this magical know-how I'd been acquiring still intact. I was a full-fledged witch now, whatever world I was in, and unstoppable badassery was nothing to sneeze at regardless of the setting.

My eyes stayed glued to Excalibur for the rest of the fight, which was pretty short despite Vambrace's grandstanding. Quick as it moved and as far down there as the arena was, though, it was a futile effort trying to examine it. It still shone faintly as always as it flashed through steel and flesh, chopping the axe blades and thick mace head to pieces before bloodying both Iriates with superficial slashes across their midsections that sent them sprawling to their backs in the hard-packed dirt. Vambrace turned and raised his sword to the adoring audience, almost all of which was now on their feet and roaring with cheers and applause. I clapped politely as I watched the torchlight glinting off the blade and noted that, somehow, there wasn't a trace of blood to be seen on the metal.

"Something on your mind, Lady Morgan?" the prince asked afterward when we were alone in the locker room/armory behind the combat arena. "You seem distracted."

He was in the middle of stripping down as he spoke, my jacket hanging on a rack nearby, his chainmail halfway over his head, his scarred abs peaking out from the shirt beneath where it lifted up. That wasn't what was distracting me, though.

Excalibur was stuck in the ground between his feet as he disrobed, the blade pierced several inches into the polished stone floor and, as I watched, slowly sinking lower. It looked as simple and nondescript as ever, faint starlight shining aside; but the longer I stared at it, the more I got the sense there was something hidden there. Some pattern going on, imperceptible, like light gray written on very light gray. I edged closer and squatted down to the sword's level, alternating between squinting and unfocusing my eyes, trying to coax whatever spell was hidden in there to the surface.

Above me, Vambrace cleared his throat. "Uh, Lady Morgan?"

I looked up from the blade to find his bare six-pack only inches from my face, then looked up further to find him staring nervously down at me.

"Sorry," I said, rising and stepping back. "Just admiring your sword is all."

"I see," he said, tossing his tunic aside and pulling Excalibur from the ground. "I didn't think you were interested in weapons, my lady."

"Yeah, usually I'm not," I said. "That one, though, I dunno. Sometimes when we're hanging out, I just catch myself staring at it. You ever do that?"

He chuckled and laid the sword carefully across both hands, staring at the blade himself now. "I do, actually," he said. "All this time later, I confess, I'm still astounded by it. I'd expected it would have abandoned me long before now, yet here we are."

"What, you worried it's gonna just stand up and walk off one day?" I asked.

He chuckled again. "Not as such, but something along those lines, yes." He held it aloft in one hand, the metal shining in the torch light, looking like a Frank Frazetta painting come to life with his scarred, bare muscles on display. "Despite my time with it, I admit, I don't fully understand Excalibur. It is powerful, yes, obviously. Is it also alive? I could not say. Does it have a will of its own? I would not fully discount it. But if one day it simply vanishes from my grasp, I would be disappointed, yes, fearful even, but not entirely surprised."

I nodded. "Want me to hold onto it for you while you're bathing, then?" I asked. "Y'know, just for a minute, free your hands up."

Vambrace's grip on the sword tightened. "Thank you for the offer, Lady, but no," he said, then pulled the sword's harness from the rack beside my jacket and slotted the weapon back into it. The catch was a complicated looking contraption that held the sword by the hilt and handle alone, leaving the naked blade untouched and hanging free — which made it all the more terrifying when he swung the thing around and slid it over his naked torso, the edge of the sword settling just above the relatively fragile flesh of his bare back.

I laughed as his intent became clear. "You bathe with that thing?" I asked. "Really?"

"I do," he said, sliding his pants down to his ankles and unsheathing his other sword. I probably should have been scandalized, but I'd seen way more explicit shit on the regular by now. Still, getting naked in front of an unmarried woman was definitely against some chivalric rule or other, but I didn't bother reminding him.

He gave me the side-eye, though, as I followed him from the locker room to the bath next door. Steam dominated the room, wafting from the massive pool at its center. Regular water in this one, not the shimmery black soul stuff. And just like the locker room, we were alone here.

"My apologies if I summoned you too soon, Lady Morgan," the prince said as he stepped down into the bath. "I didn't intend to make stand in this heat and watch me bathe. You can wait for me in the other room, or return to the stands to watch another fight, if you wish."

Vambrace faced away from me as he spoke, Excalibur still strapped to his back, the blade half submerged and still faintly glinting through the haze in the obscured torchlight.

An idea occurred to me. A couple weeks, a month, however long ago it was, it would have been unthinkable. Now, my hands were moving even before I'd finished considering it, because why the Hell not? "I do not wish," I said.

"Pardon?" he asked, and turned back to me just as I was peeling my shirt over my head. I heard a splash, then a "Lady Morgan! What are you — ?"

My t-shirt, already damp and sticking from the steam and the heat, finally slipped off. I dropped it between us and pointed my chin at his wide-eyed face. "Knights aren't supposed to watch their ladies undressing, are they?" I asked, channeling my inner Sidona. "Turn around."

He stammered for a few seconds, blushed visibly, then spun in the water, showing me his back once again. "My lady, forgive me," he said to the bath water, "but I distinctly remember you being highly averse to exactly this sort of situation. So, why… what is this, now?"

"That was then, this is now," I said as I sat and peeled off my boots. "I've gotten a lot more chill about a lot of stuff since I got here. You have too, haven't you? I thought, anyway." I kicked off my shoes and stood back up, grinning at the back of his head. "What's with the nervousness, Prince? You throw orgies on the reg, why is this suddenly a big deal?"

"On the what?" he asked, halfway turning before remembering himself and jerking his head back. "It is a big deal, as you say, because it is so sudden! I would expect this from almost any of my demonic subjects, but from an Earthly maiden—"

"Nope," I said, stepping out of my pleather pants. "From the Original Sin, you mean. Progenitors of all demonkind, we are, remember? I contain unpredictable, chaotic multitudes, you can't pin me down." I shoved my discarded clothes into a rough pile with my foot, dropping my panties on top for good measure. "Besides, that maiden ship done sailed already, you know that. Now step forward out the way, I'm coming in."

He obliged, still pointedly facing away. Bless his damned heart, he really was trying to be a good boy, wasn't he? "It would be remiss of me not to point this out," he began slowly, "but if I remember correctly, it is… unbecoming of a knight to have such carnal dealings with the lady to whom he has sworn fealty. Us two being where we are, however, and this being my kingdom, I confess I am not as averse to this circumstance as I might otherwise—"

"Let me stop ya right there, Prince" I said as I sank slowly into the steaming hot water. "Before you keep getting ideas, I never said anything about us two getting carnal. You're cool and all, but I'm still not interested in fucking you."

He turned partway back to me again, confusion in the one eye I could see. "Then what are you—?"

I reached up and pushed on his cheek, turning his face away again. "I'm gonna wash your back for you," I informed him.

"You what?" he asked. "That's all? Why?"

"Because it's a nice back," I said, carefully running my hands down his bare shoulders on either side of the blade hanging between them. "Because I had the urge to, so I'm acting on it. And because it probably needs it if you're bathing with your sword strapped to it all the time. I'm surprised there's still any skin to wash back here. How are you not constantly cutting yourself on this thing?"

"Long care and practice," he said. He didn't sound nervous or embarrassed anymore, only faintly annoyed. "You really think I haven't managed to properly wash myself in the past thousand and more years?"

"When you phrase it like that, it sounds even grosser." I cupped my hands and scooped up some of the water, pouring it over his neck to run down between his sword and his spine.

"I assure you that I have," he kept arguing. "And do you honestly think you're the first person to help me bathe in all that time? I am the archfiend."

"You're also paranoid where this sword is concerned," I said. "So yeah, I honestly think that."

"I have regular sex with a multitude of partners, you pointed out as much yourself. What do you think I do with my sword during those situations?"

"I'm actually morbidly curious about that now, yeah. Whatever the answer, I bet it's real weird and uncomfortable, isn't it?"

As we bantered and argued, I kept my hands moving slowly over his back. I had to admit, it really was pretty nice, that part wasn't a lie. Uncountable lifetimes of regular combat coupled with his unaging body had really honed all the muscles and contours to perfection. My fingers running over his skin, rewetting it and spreading the warm water around, it felt like I was massaging a marble statue draped in a layer of tight satin. Not the worst chore I'd set for myself, is what I'm saying.

Niceness aside, though, I really didn't give a shit about his back. As my hands roamed back and forth over it, my eyes were locked on Excalibur.

There was definitely something transcribed here, I was sure of it now. It wasn't in writing, though, no ink or cracks or ridges standing out against the flawless metal. It was more like… like trying to read invisible ink, maybe. Like trying to make out the edges of a source of light by staring straight into the blinding aura it was giving off. I focused on the unmarred sheen of the silver strip of metal until the world around it fell away from my vision, until Vambrace's voice was a vague hum of background noise, until the motion of my hands on his back grew lethargic and distant and monotonous.

I leaned in, and I stared, and I focused, and I willed whatever was hiding in there to show itself, and —

— And I felt that raw potential gather and build inside of me, the beginning of every spell I'd ever cast before, rising up unsought now like a reflex, and my fingers on his back weren't just rubbing idly anymore, they were drawing, tracing the runes I'd read a thousand times or more now against the contours of his muscles, writing magic against his skin —

— And I saw it.

For a flash, in an instant, I saw it burned like an afterimage into my eyes, glowing brighter than light against the backdrop of the world before me, a command prompt opened in front of the screen that showed regular reality, the lines already filled in with a graceful, beautifully simple sequence of pure willpower, an unignorable sliver of demand inserted with surgical precision right here amidst the rest of everything. It wasn't on the sword, or in the sword; it WAS the sword, the command was the blade itself, the metal forged of a tightly compacted sequence, a spell wrapping around and through itself.

Excalibur wasn't a weapon. Excalibur was an override command. Pure determination, unwavering and undeniable, in the shape of a blade. Too blunt and simple to be real.

"Lady Morgan? Lady Morgan!"

It was gone. As suddenly and strongly as the revelation had hit, it began to fade as the mundane world reasserted itself, starting with Vambrace's voice.

I blinked, and he was in front of me, staring down at me, his hands on my shoulders shaking me gently, water splashing between us. "Lady Morgan?" he repeated. "Are you alright? Answer me!"

"Wait!" I gasped, then shoved him away and spun, wading impatiently back to the edge of the pool. "Wait, wait, wait," I chanted under my breath as I collapsed over the rim of the bath. The marbled floor in front of me was slick with condensation. With trembling hands, I reached out, drawing frantically through the haze on the stone, writing dry on wet. The shape was nearly imperceptible even as it poured out of me, but it didn't matter; maybe my hands would remember the patterns if I just got them out, maybe my mind would internalize the thoughts if only I took a fleeting moment to examine them. Anything I could do, anything at all, that might help me remember something, anything, of the transcendental pattern I had just glimpsed, the earth-shattering knowledge that had flashed through my brain.

"My lady, please," the prince persisted, sloshing through the water behind me. I felt his hands on my shoulders again, felt him leaning over me from behind. "What is going on?"

I finished. Sort of. The desperate scrabbling in the watery film in front of me, it was... incomplete. Of course. There was no way I was memorizing such a masterpiece of pure cosmic rewriting after only one quick glance. Looking at it now, as the intensity and urgency faded, I could barely even tell what I'd drawn. It looked only like someone had quickly, aimlessly swiped away some of the condensation on the ground, which I guess wasn't far from the truth.

But I had the core of it. I knew. Somehow, I just *knew* it. This small segment of the full program, this one rune copied from an ancient enchantment, it was an integral piece of the whole, the bit that had captured my focus the hardest in the short time I'd had with it. I didn't know what it did — I didn't think it did anything on its own — but I had it.

I had it.

Rough, strong hands spun me around, pinning me against the edge of the bath. Vambrace's eyes bore down into mine, wide and worried, searching my face. "Morgan Samantha Amell," he said with quiet, strained patience. "Answer me. What has happened? Are. You. All. Right?"

I took a deep breath, my first in minutes. My head felt light and swimmy after staring past the veil of the world like that. Or maybe it was just the steam. "Yeah," I said, voice shuddering, then took another deep breath. "Yeah, I'm fine. Why?"

He sighed deeply as he released me and stepped back. "Thank Grannus," he muttered, then fixed me with a violent glare. "My lady, what, to borrow your phrase, the fuck?"

I was still catching my breath. "Yeah, that's fair. Sorry for that just now."

"What was 'that just now?' You went quiet, it felt like you were drawing on my back, then you were catatonic for a few seconds, then you were gasping and scrabbling at the ground. Are you well? What was any of that about?"

My head was still swimming. Part of that was definitely all these deep breaths of hot steamy air. I decided to lean into that.

"Yeah, sorry," I repeated, rubbing at my forehead and shutting my eyes tight. "I think I… climbed in too quick. All the heat and the heavy air… I got dizzy, then I got nauseous. I think I need to get out and cool off."

His glare melted back into worry and confusion as I hauled myself from the massive tub, then stumbled dripping and breathless to a nearby rack of towels. "I think perhaps you are taking my advice too far, Lady Morgan," he called as I toweled off in the corner with my back to him. "Keeping mercurial moods to flummox the demons around you is one thing; nearly passing out in the bathtub because you chased a fleeting fancy too hard is quite another. Especially when it is just the two of us, there is no need to be so performative."

That rune I'd managed to retain was still in the forefront of my mind, the pattern repeating over and over again as I tried desperately to cling to it until I could get it written down for real. "Good point," I called back as

I patted myself dry. "But maybe I'm trying to flummox you too, your majesty. Maybe I just like being unreadable in general."

I heard him chuckle amid the splashing of his bathing. "You are a rather strange creature, Lady Morgan."

"You don't know that. You've been gone for too long. Maybe this is normal for humans now and you're the strange one." It was impossible to get fully dry in all this steam, so I wrapped the towel around myself and called it good. "Hey, if it's alright with you, I'm gonna go back to my room and lie down for a minute until the spinning stops and all the steam's out of my lungs. Come get me there when you're ready for me."

Vambrace watched as I bent to gather my discarded clothing in my arms. "No need," he said, "this was enough excitement for now. Our conversations can wait until another time. Take as much rest as you need, my lady, and I'll call upon you again later."

"Hey, thanks," I said, flashing him a smile. "You know, for a Satan, you're alright sometimes."

He laughed. "I do try," he said. "Sometimes." Then he bent forward and dunked his entire upper body under the water, disappearing beneath the heat haze — except for Excalibur, which still shone faintly under the surface.

No way I was getting another chance anytime soon to study that thing that closely, not after the stunt I'd just pulled. The fraction of magic I was still reciting in my head would have to do for now.

I hurried from the bathing room, through the locker room and out into the public corridors, still wearing only my towel with my clothes bundled in my hands. The demons I passed gave me stranger, more lingering looks than usual, this being the first time any of them had seen a real female human this close to naked. If I had any shits left to give about that sort of thing anymore, they were preoccupied — my only thought, besides the Excalibur rune repeating again and again, was that I needed to hurry back to my room and record it before even a single detail got fuzzier.

Kriseia was there when I got back to the room, sitting up in bed with a coil of black rope in her hands. She tilted her head as I walked in undressed. I held up a finger as I dumped my clothes on the foot of the bed and stepped out of my towel, hurrying to my desk. I did a quick sketch of the rune first, then spent the next ten minutes redrawing it, refining the lines and angles, until I was sure that I had a copy that exactly matched the shape that had stamped itself across my brain. The practice sheets were swept into a pile in the bottom desk drawer while I examined the final sketch, double-checking my work. A faint hint of that same sense of blunt wonderment tickled the back of my mind as I looked at it; this was definitely it, or as close to "it" as I was able to comprehend, at least.

Satisfied, I tucked the page in with the rest of my magic notes and turned back to Kriseia. "Hey, sorry to snub ya like that," I said. "How's it going?"

"Well, thanks," she said with a smile. The coil of rope was wrapped loosely around her bare legs up to the thigh, with either end hanging loosely in her hands. "What happened with you?" she asked. "I've never seen you come in already naked before."

"Ah. Yeah." I left the desk and joined her on the bed, sifting through my clothes pile until I found my underwear. "The Archfiend summoned me again. I was in the bath with him before I left. Didn't wanna get redressed while I was still damp."

Kriseia whistled appreciatively. "Bathing with the archfiend," she said, somewhat wistful. "That's a small and prestigious number of people who can claim that honor. I think I'm a little jealous, if I'm being honest."

"It wasn't that kind of bath," I said, shimmying into my pants. "We just hung out for a bit, talked about some human stuff. What about you?" I gestured to the rope lazily wrapping her bottom half. "What's this you're doing?"

She pressed her legs together and cinched the rope tighter. "Just some bondage practice," she said, lifting up to make another loop under her butt. "I haven't been tied up in a while. I don't want to get rusty."

"Huh." I pulled my shirt over my head and finger-brushed my hair. "Need some help?"

"I'd love some, if you'd like," she said, smiling again as she wiggled the rope in her hands. "Are you also a fan of this sort of thing, Morgan?"

"I dunno. Never tried it." I took one end of the rope from her, rubbing my fingers over the weave. It was weirdly soft for rope, kind of fuzzy. "But hell, couldn't hurt to learn some knots and stuff. What do I do first?"

I had her halfway trussed up, her legs curled up to her chest and held there by some complex loop running around the back of her neck, when we were interrupted by a loud knocking. The prince again already? That was faster than I'd expected, given what he'd said in the bath. Kriseia took the rope from me with her one remaining free hand and held her half-finished bondage getup together as I opened the door.

Enkida stood in the doorframe, fully armored neck to toe in leathery red-brown chitin bristling with spikes, a viciously sharp spear of black metal standing a head and a half taller than her own height held loosely in one hand. She grinned — full-on grinned — down at me, bottom fangs jutting proudly up over her lip. "My Lady," she said, glancing over my head. "Busy?"

Behind me, Kriseia pouted and let go of her rope, her hogtie falling instantly apart.

I smiled at her apologetically before turning back to the general. "Not anymore," I said. "Why, what's up?"

The Iriate backed up and kicked the haft of her spear, sending the deadly point spinning lazily in her hand, sweeping the full height and breadth of the hallway. I leaned back from the door as she tightened her grip and stamped the butt of the spear on the floor, halting its momentum with a resounding clang.

"What's up?" she repeated. "What do you think is up? I gave your proposal some thought." Her grin widened, fangs flashing. "We doing this thing or what?"

Chapter 33: Betrayal

General Enkida, commander of Hell's army, right hand of the Archfiend himself, marched down the streets of Dis beside me in full battle attire, head held high, black spear spinning lazily in her hand as we went.

Cue every single set of eyes we passed turning our direction. We couldn't have been more conspicuous if I'd still been in my towel.

I followed along at her side, the one that wasn't occupied by a spinning blade, and tried not to worry about how I'd explain this to Vambrace when he inevitably heard about this trip. Was this her passive aggressive workaround to my request that she not tell him beforehand? No, probably not; it didn't seem like her to let any of her aggression be passive.

Which meant she really was this jazzed to be heading out into the wasteland with me. Given what I knew typically excited the general, that thought didn't bode well either.

Things got awkward as we neared the wall to find Abdeles and Alastaroth on our path, both of them surrounded by a contingent of a dozen more armed and armored Iriates. The Superbiate archduke spotted us as soon as we came into view, raising a hand to halt the slow march of his honor guard and smiling at us as we drew up alongside the group. "Lady Morgan," he said, amused. "General Enkida. What an unexpected pleasure."

"Archduke," Enkida said, less amused, as each of his guards clapped a fist over their chests and ducked their heads to their general. "Quite the retinue you've got there. Big plans?"

Abdeles gestured to Alastaroth beside him. "My scholarly associate here is interested in studying the abandoned garm den just beyond the wall. I offered him my personal guards to ensure his safety."

Enkida's eyes narrowed. "Offered him yourself too, it seems."

Abdeles chuckled. "I profess a certain amount of curiosity as well," he said. "And they are *my* personal guards, after all. I wanted to make sure they weren't shirking their duties. It would reflect badly on me as their employer, don't you think?"

"Hm." The general turned her narrowed gaze on me next. "Strange coincidence, isn't it, my lady?"

I shrugged. "I guess? People go past the wall all the time for a bunch of reasons, from what I've gathered. How am I supposed to know all the hows or whys?"

"Hm," Enkida grunted again, turning back to the archduke.

He laughed. "Pay no mind to our dear general's attitude, Lady Morgan," he said. "She's eternally suspicious of everyone and everything. All part of the job, of course. But do I hear correctly that you are also destined for the wasteland, my lady?"

"Yeah," I said. "Garm den. Personal curiosity. Y'know."

"Lot of that going around right now," Enkida muttered.

"And a lot more to come, I'm sure," Alastaroth cut in. "Any chance to study these beasts' habitats is enticing to some degree to a scholarly mind. This close to the eyes of the wall? It would be educationally negligent not to seize that opportunity."

"Speaking of," the archduke added, "if we've all the same destination in mind, it would also be negligent not to make the journey all together, don't you think? More bodies to guard Lady Morgan, and our formidable general to guard my scholar and I."

Enkida's spear kept spinning lazily as her eyes slowly swept the archduke's company. "I've got no reason to stop you lot falling in with us," she said. "Likewise, I also have no duty at the moment to babysit curious nobles, so keep that in mind."

Abdeles grinned. "Noted. Of course, just having you in sight without being the subject of your ire fills me with a profound sense of security, General. Don't concern yourselves with us, though, we'll be sure not to get in your way."

Enkida said nothing else, only stared at the archduke an uncomfortable moment longer before glancing at me and beckoning me onward with a sharp toss of her head. I tossed a wave at Abdeles and his group as I fell in behind her. A few seconds later, the sound of a couple dozen or so booted footfalls let us know they were following at a polite distance.

"You don't like the archduke, huh," I said quietly as we neared the towering wall.

"No," she said, less quietly. "But I don't like most people. He wasn't wrong on that point, I have to admit."

"Anything wrong with him specifically?" I asked. "I mean, if he's following us into the badlands…"

"Specifically?" she repeated, then snorted. "Pretty sure he wants the throne for himself, but then, that's most of the archdemons and nearly every Superbiate I've ever met. None of them have been stupid enough to try for it in a long, long while. Beyond that? His condescending attitude and smug, breakable face. But again, every archdemon and Superbiate."

"He's surrounded by a bunch of your soldiers," I pointed out. "That's something, I guess."

"Hmph." The butt of her spear struck the cobbled street mid-spin, splashing up sparks with a ringing clang that made me flinch. "Insecure little shits aren't *my* soldiers," she spat.

I glanced behind us at the dozen Iriates marching in step around their charges. "They saluted you like your soldiers," I said.

"Because they're not complete fools," she said. "Just spiteful cowards. The ranks of personal guards to self-important bureaucrats swelled after I rose to command. Some think they're slighting me. Most are just running from my influence."

"What, because you're a woman?"

"What?" She frowned at me like I was the one being foolish now. "Why would that have anything to do with it? No, because they think I don't deserve the position. That his highness only gave it to me to buy my loyalty after our public duel in the arena."

"Ah." We stopped before a massive gate of solid black metal at the foot of the wall, which slowly began to rise as we reached it. "Yeah, rude."

"They're right on that last point, of course," she added casually. "He was buying me, and it worked. Would've worked on any Iriate he made the offer to. But that he made it to *me* meant I was suddenly the superior of every sneering, snarling comrade I'd ever had, all of whom had told me throughout my entire career, from training to combat readiness, that I was defective, an aberration. I would never be a truly great warrior, never serve Dis well enough, with such a cold rage holding me back. I was destined to menial labor in construction or a smithy somewhere, and the fact that I refused to transfer was an insult to the military body I would inevitably drag down." She smiled out of nowhere. "Then I very nearly beat the unbeatable archfiend in single combat, and he gave me the perfect revenge as a trophy. Now, a majority of the army which I command continuously, openly hates me for commanding them, and some even resent my success enough to defect to the command of preening civilians like the archduke, choosing to guard banks and bedrooms rather than admit that they were wrong and that I won in the end."

She was still smiling, even after she'd finished speaking. I thought back to that day on the battlefield outside these same walls, after the last garm had been felled, where I watched the surviving Iriates around her turn on her, venting the last of their bloodlust on their commander and being driven to the ground for their audacity. A normal occurrence, Vambrace had said. Helped the troops take the edge off after the threat was gone, he'd said. Enkida's idea, he'd said.

"You like it," I said, nudging her.

Enkida's smile split into a wide, sadistic grin. "I fucking revel in it, Lady Morgan."

I looked behind us again. Abdeles and his group had nearly caught up, but for the moment, they were still out of earshot. Before that changed, I leaned into and up towards the general's face. "Did Prince Vambrace beat you fair and square?" I whispered. "Or did you let him win?"

She turned a sudden glare down on me. "That's a sentiment dangerously close to treason, my lady," she growled quietly. "Where did you acquire it?"

The archfiend has anxiety about it, I thought. Out loud, I just shrugged. "I can't say I remember," I said, still whispering. "Just a hushed rumor I picked up somewhere."

"Something 'they' say, is it?" she growled quietly again, gaze turning back to the rising gate in front of us. "Good."

She was still grinning as she said it.

A whole lot of Vambrace's subjects not-so-secretly wanted the throne for themselves, she'd told me. If anyone stood a real chance of taking it and holding it, I thought, it would be her.

The gate finally stopped rising about ten feet off the ground, just enough to easily admit the tallest Superbiate. Enkida and I stepped through, Abdeles's group following shortly afterward, into a long, dark gatehouse. We stood there in silence, Enkida and I near the far side, the other group near the opening, as the massive metal door slowly ground shut once more, the clank and rattle of unseen chains echoing in the enclosed stone space. Only after the gate behind us shut fully, casting us in total darkness with a final, shuddering thud, did the gate at the far end begin just as slowly to rise.

Enkida strode toward it, me following close behind, when it was just a few feet off the ground. She stopped me with a raised hand as she bent and ducked beneath it, disappearing from the waist up for a moment, before reaching under the enormous door to wave me forward. I followed suit, squat-walking further than I'd anticipated; this gate was thicker, more a slab of metal than a door, the inside-facing plane reinforced by long bands of thick black steel, the outer face covered in vicious spikes of various sizes and lengths, as I found when I finally emerged into the dull red of Hell's perpetual twilight. On this side of the wall, with dust floating on a warm breeze that I hadn't felt in the city, that sky seemed more ominous than ever.

I looked up, past Enkida, to see a familiar landscape from a new angle. No distant forests or canyons to be found down at this level, no. Nothing but dead, empty, bloodied earth as far as the eye could see, with the distant drone of stronger winds promising more of the same.

I had landed in this place when I came to this world, I suddenly remembered. Grum, the Acediate who'd found me, said he'd found me on this side of the wall, out here in the wastes and the dust. What would my reaction have been, I wondered, if I'd woken up here instead of in the crowded bazaar? What would I have done if I'd opened my eyes after that horrible spell to find dead emptiness and a distant monolith of blackness and spikes looming over it all?

I shuddered. For the first and last time, I felt a pang of gratitude for Dramoc and his seedy little shop. Confusion and anger had at least been a better introduction than barren solitude.

Enkida peered into that same emptiness, head turning slowly, until she hefted her spear and pointed. "That way," she declared.

We struck off, the gate behind us grinding to a halt as Abdeles's party finally passed under. A moment later, the ground shook with a thunderous crash that nearly knocked me off my feet, and I turned back to see a cloud of dust settling behind the group tailing us, the spiked slab of a gate shut tight once more.

We were officially cut off from the city now, alone together in the badlands of Hell, where even demons feared to tread. I gulped, wiped the dust from my eyes, and stuck close to Enkida's side as we began our hike.

Fear and unease gave way to boredom pretty quickly — it was a long trek, and every step was the same as the last, just flat dirt and dust broken by the occasional large rock or scrubby attempt at a tree. Early on, with the wall still looming over us, we also skirted large swaths of black muck where the garms' blood had mixed with the dry earth. I held my nose as we picked our way around this foul, rotten mud, the rank tang of copper and dog still thick and heavy in the air. No bones or bodies left, though; Dis worked quick and thorough when it came to salvaging anything useful from the monsters that besieged it.

The archduke's party stayed a respectable distance behind us out of, I guessed, a careful respect for the general's suspicion. Not that it wasn't warranted, given that all of us out here now were lying to her. I should have felt bad about that, I thought. In a distant part of my mind, I did. But with my goal feeling more within my reach than ever, I couldn't summon up too much guilt at the moment for all of the deception I'd been taking part in. I'd wait to wrestle with my conscience in the safety of my small apartment back on Earth.

We stopped to rest only once during our long march, after what felt like a couple hours of uninterrupted walking. Or rather, I stopped to rest, and Enkida obliged. No doubt she could've kept going without issue. Hell, she probably could've sprinted there and back by now.

The archduke and his party paused as well when they reached us, the bodyguards forming a loose circle around their employer. Alastaroth broke free of that circle to cross the distance between us, weathering Enkida's scrutiny as he approached the cracked boulder I was sitting on.

"Hungry, Lady Morgan?" he asked, holding out a hand. In it was a scrap of cloth wrapped around what looked like several scraps of meat.

I eyed it. "What is it?"

"Smoked harpy," he said. "Farm-raised, not the gamey kind you find out here."

Not my first choice, obviously. But I *was* getting hungry. "Which side of the harpy?" I asked.

"The flank, my lady," he said, selecting one for himself and popping it into his mouth. "Dark meat only, I assure you."

"Sure, thanks," I said with a shrug, one more of my fucks falling away.

"You trust this man, Lady Morgan?" Enkida asked from behind me as the Invidiate handed me a couple slices.

"You don't?" I asked. "He's had plenty of chances before now to hurt us if he wanted. Or, well, just to hurt *me*, I guess; you're invincible." I held the handful of meat out to her. "Wanna test it, just to be sure?"

She shook her head. "If it's poisoned or cursed, better you than me. Otherwise, you'd have no one to protect you or carry you back to a healer."

"Damn, harsh," I said. "But I guess you're not wrong." I bit off a mouthful of harpy. It tasted pretty much exactly like chicken, and probably not at all like human, I hoped and assumed.

Alastaroth chuckled. "Even if I wished to curse our general, shorter Invidiates than me have tried and failed miserably," he said. "And I hold nothing but respect for the Lady Morgan, I assure you."

Enkida's eyes narrowed. "You two know each other?"

I rolled my eyes at her. "Am I not allowed to have friends, mom?"

"We have spoken a couple of times, yes," Alastaroth answered. "Like his majesty, I too am intrigued by the culture and knowledge of the modern-day Original Sin. Is that an issue, General?"

She kept her glare on as she regarded the two of us for a quiet moment. "I suppose not," she said at last.

"Right. Well." The Invidiate scholar cleared his throat and bowed. "If you'll excuse me, then."

I waited until he'd rejoined Abdeles's group before leaning in to Enkida. "You're kinda extra suspicious of everyone today, huh?" I asked quietly.

"I am exactly as suspicious of anyone as always," she replied. "It's how I got to be invincible." She reached down and snatched a piece of harpy meat from my hand, tossing the whole thing into her mouth. "Are you ready to continue, Lady?" she asked before chewing.

I stretched my legs, stood up, nodded, and shoved the remainder of the meat into my own mouth. "O'war'," I declared, pointing to the horizon.

Enkida grabbed my wrist and corrected the aim of my pointing finger. "Onward," she repeated.

We walked, our only sign of progress the slowly dwindling wall at our backs and, eventually, the gradual rise of uneven terrain in front of us. Flat dust gave way to rocky, hard-packed ground, fissures and boulders littering the expanse before us. A short time later, the flat line of the horizon was broken by the first signs of the jagged chasm that was our destination.

Enkida stepped in front of me, her spear now gripped firmly in her hand. "If anything were going to threaten us, it would do so here," she said over her shoulder. "Eyes up."

I nodded and stuck like a shadow to her backside, some of my earlier unease returning with the warning. Two other emotions grew alongside it: excitement at the promise of what I'd find here, and anxiety at how the hell I was going to get away from the general long enough to study it.

The ground sloped gently downward at first as the chasm came into range. We picked our way down crumbled earth, part hill and part natural stairs, toward the lip of the drop, then stopped. It was indeed a literal drop; there was another rocky shelf maybe twenty, thirty feet below where we stood, another twice as far beneath that one. Deep gouges marred the rock here at the edges of the cliffs — claw marks where the garm had scrabbled out of the canyon to charge the city. I could faintly smell their lingering presence on the warm, arid wind, just the occasional whiff of rank dog and old blood.

I waved away the smell as I scanned the edges of the chasm. "There's a switchback over there, looks like," I said, pointing off in the far distance toward the faint, jagged line of a rocky slope. "It's a long walk around, but I don't see any other—"

Enkida's spear whistled as it spun in her hand, and I watched her casually lob it underhand over the edge and into the pit. She'd done the same on top of the wall, before she'd stepped off and plummeted down into the battle with the garm. It was badass then, granted, and it would be badass again now, but then how would I—?

She turned to me. There was a gleam in her eye that I didn't like.

"Wait," I said, backstepping as she opened her arms, "no, that's not—"

She lunged. It would have been comically fast, like a cartoon, if my anxiety didn't spike as she was suddenly on me, arms wrapped tight around me, scooping me up off the ground like she was snatching up a cat that really, really didn't want to be held right now. "Hold tight," was the only warning she gave me before she leapt, leaving my breath and my stomach behind.

I cinched my arms around her neck, dug my fingers into the shell of her armor, and screamed at the top of my lungs as we arced and plummeted.

There were a couple of jostling skips as we landed and leapt again, so at least she was taking the giant stairs instead of making a single drop. I kept clinging to her after we finally hit the canyon bottom and skidded to a stop, face buried in her armored chest. "We're here," she said. "You can let go now, Lady Morgan," she said again a few seconds later, when I didn't.

It took her physically prying my arms from her to detach me. I squatted and curled around my knees as she set me on the ground. "You colossal bitch," I breathed, voice shaking.

She shrugged and went to retrieve her spear, which was embedded point first in the dirt only a few feet away. "Your idea to come here," she said.

"We couldn't have brought a rope or something?" I demanded, slowly straightening again.

"We could have, but neither of us did," she said, plucking the weapon with ease. "Quicker and easier this way anyway."

"Easy my ass," I said. "I just about pissed your armor in fear there, General."

She glanced down at her still-dry armor and smirked. "Wasn't this trip about facing your fears, my lady?"

I caught the last of my breath with a deep sigh. "I'm scared of giant dog monsters," I said, "not falling off a cliff. Or I wasn't until now, anyway."

I started as another sudden thud nearby sent up a cloud of dirt, and one of the archduke's personal guards skidded to a stop. Then another beside him, with another ground-shaking landing, and I looked back up at the cliff we'd just leapt from to see it raining demons as each guard followed our approach into the canyon.

The biggest of them had the archduke slung over her back, his legs dangling from her arms like he was riding a living swingset, his cloak billowing dramatically behind him as they fell. Not the most dignified way to travel, yet Abdeles flashed us a haughty smirk as he disembarked from his extreme piggybacking. "Seems we're all just as eager to reach our destination, eh, ladies?" he called.

"No, I wouldn't have minded the long way around," I called back as Enkida scowled in his direction.

He just laughed. "We're not far from the beasts' lair now. Steel yourself and guard your nose, Lady Morgan."

Sure enough, the rank stench of blood and dog had settled over the canyon floor like an invisible fog, so sharp and obnoxious that it knocked me back as we walked into it. Enkida watched amused as I pulled the neck of my shirt up to just below my eyes before pressing onward. "It's not *that* bad," she said, her nose wrinkled, her eyes watering.

I coughed into my shirt, my own eyes stinging. "Yeah, sure," I said. "Is this safe to breathe?"

"Once the beasts themselves are dealt with, their blood is the only dangerous thing left, and that only if you drink it raw," she said. "You showered in the stuff and lived to be scarred by the experience, so you'll be fine."

"It stank then, but it wasn't this… pungent," I argued.

She nodded. "On the battlefield, it wasn't mixed with their piss and shit. Mind where you step, my lady."

I stuck close to her back after that, my attention focused downward more than on the rocky walls surrounding us. So I didn't notice at first when the corner we rounded opened up into a wide pit, until Enkida stopped and I carefully stepped out around her.

In front of us, the ground was that same mass of churned, black mud that it had been in patches near the wall where the garm had died. Here where they had lived, it was like a swamp slowly drying out, the earth stamped by innumerable giant paw prints, with the shattered and chewed remnants of bones of all shapes and sizes poking up through the morass. Piles of dung as big as houses intermittently lined the walls around the periphery, draped by clouds of some large, black insect that I definitely wasn't getting close enough to identify.

"Euggh…" I said into my shirt. Even so, the lingering odor that made it through my cloth barrier wasn't as biting now. Either the smell had somehow lessened here, which was unlikely, or else I was just getting inured to it, which was unsettling.

"Yeah, well, coming here was your idea," Enkida said, holding her spear in two hands so the butt didn't drag the muck. "So go on, wade on in there and get whatever closure you came to find."

"Aren't you coming with me?" I asked. "Bodyguard?"

"I can guard your body just fine from here, thanks," she replied, waggling her weapon. "Spears can be thrown."

"What if something happens, and you throw it, and you accidentally skewer me instead?"

She scoffed. "I would never *accidentally* skewer you, Lady Morgan."

"You know, you suck at reassurance." I looked from the muck to my boots and back, sighed, and resigned myself to the inevitable. Someone in the palace would probably be able to clean them when we got back, surely.

I'd taken my first fateful, squishy step onto the wet patch of garm mud when I heard someone hurrying up behind us, and Enkida and I both turned to see a lanky Iriate walking briskly our way, a scowl on his face, his leather armor bristling with jagged spikes. He stopped in front of Enkida and clapped a fist over his chest. "General," he said, then looked my direction with a sharp glare, lips curling. "Lady Morgan," he growled.

I confess I hadn't recognized his face until I saw it coated with irritation and disdain at me in particular. "Rezavix?" I asked. "What are you doing here?"

His scowl intensified. "Oh, so you *do* know my name."

I winced. Okay, yeah, I deserved that.

"The question remains, though," Enkida said. "You're no bluebrute lackey, last I checked. What are you doing here, soldier?"

"Looking for you, General." He glanced from me to her and back, then leaned closer to her. "Can we speak in private?"

Enkida's eyes narrowed. "We're private enough here but for the Lady Morgan, whose person I am currently guarding. Speak, soldier."

He growled at me before continuing. "We noticed a… possible security issue from the wall, General. Possibly heading this way. I was sent to inform you of the potential danger, and retrieve you to lead in dealing with it, if possible."

"That's vague as shit," the general replied. "I need details, man."

Rezavix glanced my way again before speaking. "I'm not sure that's wise at the moment, General," he said. "If you'll follow me to the top of the ridge, you'll see what we might be up against, and why we thought it best to keep it a matter amongst Iriates only."

Enkida turned to me with an expression that looked as confused as I felt hearing that. She said nothing for a moment, visibly weighing her options, then finally lifted a finger in my direction. "Do not leave this muck pile," she ordered, pinprick eyes drilling me with the severity of her direction before turning back to Rezavix. "This had better be suitably confounding, soldier," she warned.

He clapped his chest again as he turned to lead her away. "I hope we're wrong and it's not, General, but that's your call to make, not mine."

I watched with growing concern as they walked off, then turned back to the sodden expanse of the garm den. That's when I saw the blue arm sticking out of a crack in the stone between two towering piles of dog shit, beckoning me. Abdeles's head appeared for a moment, looking my way, and he beckoned more quickly before ducking completely out of sight once more.

I already had a foot in the mess. Watching my step as best I could, for what little it was worth, I made my way carefully and slowly over to the hidden crevice, the black and bloody ground sucking at my boots with every step. My shirt went back up over my nose as I passed between the two piles slumped against the wall to find a wide crack in the stone — barely wide enough for someone as big as the archduke to fit through, but I managed to squeeze through with ease. The ground beyond was thankfully solid and dry, a pocket of space in the stone about the size of my studio apartment back on Earth. The canyon walls slanted as they rose, culminating in a narrow crack of red skylight above that was all that kept this from being a cave.

In the center of the space stood Abdeles and Alastaroth, both looking my direction, and flanking a single wall of stacked stone as tall as the Superbiate archduke. It was the largest of any leftover relic we'd seen so far, and the magical phrase carved into its surface was clear as day, free of marring or damage in the dead center of the construction.

My heart leapt even before I knew what it said. A find this well-preserved was too good to be true.

"Lady Morgan," Alastaroth said, bowing his head and gesturing at the wall. "If you'd please enlighten us."

I took a deep breath and stepped forward. "Right, we should probably make this quick," I said. "The general's stepped away to look at something maybe dangerous. I don't know how long I've got without her or if we're under attack now or what."

The archduke chuckled. "No imminent danger on that front, my lady, I assure you," he said. "Distracting the general with that ploy was our arrangement."

I frowned at him. "It was a soldier, not a bodyguard," I said. "We thought. Rezavix works for you now?"

"Is that the soldier's name?" he asked, still smiling proudly. "No, not as such. Not directly, at least. Call it an exchange of favors."

I winced mentally. That poor guy had the worst luck. "He's gonna be in a heap of trouble when she finds out there's not really any security problems," I said aloud. "Hope whatever he's getting out of the deal is worth it." I held out my hand between the two demons. "Either of you have the stuff? I didn't wanna risk bringing my own with the general tagging along."

Alastaroth produced paper and charcoal from his robe and handed it over. I stretched up on my toes to reach the spell carving in the wall's center and began carefully, thoroughly taking a rubbing, not stopping until the stick of charcoal had worn halfway away and the paper was dark and black around the light gray leaving of the indentation. When I was finished, I handed back what was left of the charcoal, wiped the worst of the smudging off my hands onto my pants, and focused eagerly on the new magic in my hands.

Only… it wasn't new magic. No, this was a piece I already knew, a glyph that featured heavily in my unnoticeability spell. Roughly translated, it was the concept of awareness or perception, of how a mind might take in and interpret the world in front of it. It made sense that it would be a central, big part of a spell that tried to alter that very thing in the people around me. What didn't make sense was what it was doing here, alone, carved cleanly into a big wall in the middle of nowhere and devoid of any other sigils or context.

"Well?" Alastaroth asked, hands clasped tightly around his staff as he watched me intently. "What does it say, my lady?"

I had no explanation to give them. Hell, I didn't have one for myself, no sliver of arcane truth to hide since I didn't understand it either. Still, better not to actually teach any demons any honest magic, even if I was just as confused as they would have been. This trip, much as I was looking forward to it, was a bust for me, but I could let them dream.

"This one is… it means something like 'travel,'" I said slowly, twisting the paper this way and that for effect. "'Travel' or 'journey,' something along those lines. That's the best translation I'm coming up with, anyway. I dunno, maybe there was supposed to be more pieces to this wall, or the gate was actually just past it, and this part was just a sign announcing what it was for. Could be this bit was left standing just because it seems harmless by itself."

They looked at one another, both of their faces suddenly very tired. Alastaroth gently shook his head, and Abdeles sighed. "My lady," said the archduke. "Please. Enough of this."

My breath seized in my throat. "Enough of what?" I asked, only barely succeeding at keeping my voice from a panicked squeak.

"This pointless game and your continued deception," Alastaroth answered, his dry old voice pitched to a low hiss. "You lie to us. You're lying now. You've been lying from the beginning, haven't you?"

I had a fleeting thought about poor Rezavix again as I hoisted my chin and put on my best fake indignant scowl. "Last I checked, of the three of us, I was the only Original Sin one in the group. I'm the only one who can read this language. What makes you think—"

"You were!" Alastaroth barked. It was the first time I'd ever heard him raise his voice above a croak, and it threw me. "No longer!" He swung his staff and smacked it against the carving on the wall. "This bit, at least, I have decoded. It deals with awareness and understanding, not a journey. Not a simple signpost to mark a location."

I couldn't stop my voice from betraying me this time. "You've... you what?" I squeaked, panicked. "You can read this? But, then — okay, if that's true, why bring me all the way out here to read it to you?"

"Verification," said the archduke, glaring down his nose at me. "This was your last test. You, my lady, have failed it."

My veins turned to ice. I had to will myself to breathe as I held up the charcoal rubbing in my hands like a shield between me and their sudden, violent suspicion. "Look," I said, backing away slowly, "whatever's going on here, we can discuss it back at the—"

"You will be still and quiet!" Abdeles spat, and suddenly my legs locked, my jaw clamped shut so forcefully it made my teeth ache, and I pitched forward, landing on my knees on the stone floor. "You've said quite enough already, human, every word more brazen and deceptive than the last, while you stride about our home like you own it! You and that sniveling coward squatting on his stolen throne! No more!" He took a step forward, towering over me, but I couldn't look at him, only the ground at his feet. "Our culture lies in ruins, defaced and defiled, our history torn down and obfuscated and fed back to us only at your kind's convenience, while we dig through rubble and dog shit looking for scraps of the truth, of our sullied pride! And yet still you dare — *you dare* — to spew poisonous lies in our faces to cover for your own horrendously obvious flaws?"

The closer he got, the lower I bent, until my forehead pressed into the coarse stone hard enough to scrape, my every shallow breath mixed with dirt. I couldn't bear the weight of his accusations, the power of his indignation, the force of his words; they weighed on my spine and my conscience, pushing me lower, terrified of having been stupid enough to cross him, to try and outsmart him. I had never before felt this kind of soul-crushing, all-consuming guilt.

Except… yeah, except for that one time, briefly, in Sidona's salon. When I'd been modeling for her and that palace guard interrupted us, and she bore him down into the ground with her scorn and… and…

Oh, shit! This wasn't me, this was that Superbiate mind control shit! This fucking guy!

"Human!" Abdeles bellowed. "Are you even listening? Answer me, you worthless wretch!" His voice, his words echoing in my head, it hurt to listen to, and not just because he was shouting them directly above me.

But he was cheating. He wasn't this intimidating — it was just a cheap trick. Just some magic bullshit.

And he wasn't the only one here who could pull some magic bullshit.

I crawled toward him, belly dragging the dirt, until my hands landed on his booted feet. I pushed myself up from the ground — easier now that I knew what I was fighting against — and climbed my hands up his legs, hauling myself up until I was on my knees, head still bowed. "Lord Abdeles," I said quietly, voice trembling, and he didn't stop me as I groveled and climbed, until I was clutching the hem of his robes tight in my fingers, hoping this passed for reverence. "Archduke. Sir. I'm sorry, very sorry. You're right. This deal we made… it was a bad idea. I'm sorry." I took a deep breath, then forced my head up to look him in the eyes. "I don't want to work with you anymore," I said. "You're fired."

He seemed surprised that I could manage to look him straight in the eyes like that.

He seemed even more surprised when his robes caught fire beneath my hands and the flames shot instantly up the length of the garment. My first and best spell — I could cast that one near instantly now.

Abdeles jerked away, flailing and shouting, wreathed in fire and smoke. His concentration shattered, the weight of his disdain evaporated from my back and my lungs. While Alastaroth rushed to the archduke's side, both of them struggling to get his robes off, I shot to my feet and sprinted through the crevice and back into the open garm den, my boots sucking muck as I raced over the sodden ground, shouting for Enkida

I heard it before I saw it, the roaring of an angry crowd, the clanging of steel on steel, the wet thuds of steel on flesh, the screaming. Enkida was at the foot of the cliffs we'd jumped down from, surrounded — swarmed — by dozens upon dozens of raging Iriates, all of them violently, recklessly throwing themselves at her. She was the only one in the churning crowd not screaming or roaring, her face locked in a grim snarl as she ducked and weaved and danced, swinging and thrusting her spear, all with inhuman speed and force.

I stopped in my tracks, arrested for the moment. The first time I'd watched Vambrace fight in the arena, I'd been stunned by the impossible skill on display. When I watched the assault on the garm pack from the top of the wall, I'd been in shock at the amount of efficient brutality on display.

This scene suddenly before me outclassed both. Enkida was a whirlwind of determined carnage, a humanoid meat grinder with a ballerina's grace. Her spear whistled as it spun and stabbed, ribbons of dark liquid red trailing the flashing blade, arcing through the air, splashing against her dark armor, her white hair, her long, lithe limbs.

It was art; horrible, horrifying art.

But however morbidly impressive it was, whatever her skill, there were just too many Iriates screaming for her blood. Bodies pinwheeled off her spear, crumpled and fell at her feet; she was building a ringed wall of dead around her, but the crowd kept surging over it, hacking and swinging, every type of melee weapon I'd ever seen present and aimed toward her. She repelled them all, but not without cost: her face, her body, what glimpses I could catch of them through the surging throng, were streaked with sweat and blood and some noticeable wounds. Not all of that blood was her enemies'.

I stood watching, rapt and terrified, for only a few moments, and then a black haze descended into the center of the violent maelstrom, faint but undeniable. It centered on the general, and now it seemed she was fighting in a cloud of smog, her eyes widening, her grim snarl flashing with pain. Her movements slowed — still superhuman, still graceful, but less so than a moment ago. She was faltering, taking damage. Her wall of bodies was still steadily growing, but more of them were getting in hits before they fell.

I looked up at the cliffs surrounding us to see the edges lined with Invidiates, dozens of them, all of them staring down at the churning fight below, all of their attention focused on Enkida at its center. All of them cursing her at once, hexes stacked upon hexes until they grew into a tangible miasma.

Was this the danger Rezavix had warned her about? This massive ambush coming for her? But then, where was he? Off getting help? Or was he part of the crowd trying to murder her too?

This was too much. I'd watched Enkida pull off impossible feats before, heard stories that even other Iriates considered incredible, but she was still just one woman. One woman whose entire army had turned against her at once, it seemed.

She was going to lose. She was going to die.

The thought knocked the wind from me. I cupped my hands over my mouth and shouted her name, for what good it did. I'd run to her to protect me, but she was barely protecting herself. And if she fell here, now, where did that leave me?

Nobody noticed me before I shouted for the general. Almost nobody noticed me afterward, but Enkida's head turned my way, eyes wild. She took an axe to the chest for her moment of distraction, and my breath hitched, horrified that I'd just been the end of her; but no, she kicked out at the offending Iriate, bowling him into the wall of opponents on that side, and wrenched the axe from her chest plate. The next second, she towered above the crowd, climbing atop her wall of bodies, and her hand flashed as she crouched. The axe whirled a short distance into the mass of bodies and cleaved someone's skull; Enkida was already in the air, leaping clear over the horde of raging demons —

— and straight toward me.

I backpedaled, mouth gaping, and fell backward as she barreled down toward me from the sky, landing only inches from where I'd been standing. Her spear whipped back, her other arm shot forward. She grabbed me by the collar and hurled me up to my feet. Behind her, I caught a glimpse of the crowd turning our direction, surging toward us.

Then her face was in mine, blocking all else. I could smell the sweat and blood on her, the heat of her labored breath, the faint noxious tinge of the Invidates' lingering curse. Her eyes were eerily calm, though, as was her voice. "Get Vambrace," she said quietly, her blood-slicked forehead pressed to mine. "Tell him. Then run."

There were a thousand things I wanted to say right then, so many questions I needed to ask. I didn't get the chance to do more than open my mouth before both her arms were around me, her spear momentarily abandoned. For a fleeting second, I thought this was some sort of goodbye hug. It kind of was, I suppose.

Then she spun me off my feet, and spun again, and kept spinning, a sudden cyclone holding me tight. My body lifted further off the ground with the force of it, her grip on me shifted, and in the next instant, I was flying. I didn't have the time, the breath, or the wherewithal to even scream as I watched the canyon floor fall away below me, the bodies stampeding over and around Enkida growing smaller and smaller, before my trajectory slowly spun me away from the scene to stare up at the dull red sky above.

Real shitty last thing to see before I die, I thought in a brief moment of clarity, and then the spinning of the world sped up, the sky and the ground tumbling over each other as I began plummeting back toward the ground.

I hit it way sooner than I expected, given how long I'd been in the air. My left shoulder struck the dirt first, and I rolled through the shock and the rocky earth, feeling my clothes tear and my skin scrape away with each rotation. I tumbled for what felt like a mile before finally skidding to a halt, bruised and bloody but, against all logic, still alive.

As much as I wanted to do nothing more than lie there bleeding in the dirt until my head stopped spinning, the immediate horror of the last couple minutes was still fresh in my rattled mind. I forced myself to my hands and knees, took a deep breath, then retched a bit, but nothing came out. I counted to three, then pushed myself up onto my feet, swaying but standing, to get my bearings. The edge of the canyon was a good twenty feet or so in front of me, the edge of the ring of Invidiates even further. The closest few to me were staring my way between quick glances at each other, until a triumphant laugh from below — Enkida's laugh — turned their attention back to the fight inside the chasm.

I turned as quickly as vertigo would let me and limped away from the scene. In front of me was an expanse of barren wasteland and, on the horizon, the towering wall of Dis.

I ran toward it. Bloody, dizzy, and alone, I ran for my life.

Chapter 34: Treason

It had taken hours to walk from the wall to the garm canyon. Somehow, running from the canyon back to the wall felt like a much, much longer trip. The terror and the bleeding probably had something to do with it.

The screaming and clanging of Enkida's impossible stand faded behind me quicker than I would have thought. I prayed that this was because I'd run further from it than it felt like I had, and not because she had already lost.

I wondered if praying did any good in this place, and who, if anyone, could hear it.

I don't know how long I struggled onward with just the sound of my own frantic breathing and pounding footsteps for company. Sooner than I liked, I had to stop and catch my breath, hands braced against my trembling knees as I sucked in lungfuls of warm, dust-tainted air. Sweat ran freely down my face, mingling with the grime of the wasteland. I reached up to wipe away the worst of it and found my cheeks coated with tears as well. When had I started crying? Tangled ball of anxiety that my brain had become, I hadn't noticed.

Then I heard it again, distant clanging and roaring voices. Not from behind me this time; no, now it was in front of me, growing steadily louder. I looked up from my panting only to have my breath catch in my throat as, far out in the distance between me and the wall, a new group of Iriates was stampeding in my direction, weapons and voices raised.

Reinforcements for their general? Or for her attackers? If the former, how did they know she was in trouble? And if the latter, how fucking much of Hell's army was out for her blood?

I didn't know the answers, and I wasn't rolling those dice, not after everything that had just happened.

Both times I'd tried the unnoticeable spell before, it had taken a while, a lot of slow faltering, a lot of trial and error. I didn't have the luxury of that much time right now, but what I did have was a couple of amateur attempts under my belt already and a recent vocabulary reminder courtesy of Abdeles and Alastaroth's bogus relic site.

Time for a pop quiz on how well I'd been doing in my homeschooled magic course.

With a deep, steadying breath (as steady as I could be at the moment), I closed my eyes and lifted my hands, my fingers flexing while the rest of me went loose. The oncoming clamor grew louder by the second, and I had no way of knowing if anyone involved in it had seen me yet, but I forced my attention away from that as best I could, inverting my focus, letting the world around me fall away.

The incantation began familiarly enough. Just gotta feel my way through the meat of things. Potential - gather; focus, self; cover, body - make shield (awareness = decrease; if look, then awareness = other); shield, cinch - make skin; focus, outward —

An uptick in the encroaching noise snuck into my concentration, my focus wavering dangerously, my unexecuted spell flickering in my mind and threatening to erase. *They're too close,* warned a stray thought. *No way they don't see you yet. This spell only works on those who aren't already looking for you.*

I clamped down on that awareness, on rising panic, and pinned the magic back beneath my focus before it could evaporate. Either this thing worked as-is or it didn't; there wasn't anything else I could do.

Except… no, that wasn't true anymore, was it? I'd diagrammed these arcane sentences enough to see the rudimentary logic beneath them. If I was careful, I could ad lib this code. Couldn't I?

The spell wavered again, almost slipped away, but I flashed my mind through it once more and recaptured most of it. The last part few pieces I let evaporate; then I revised and started padding:

Cover, body - make shield (awareness = nullify; if look, then forget); shield, cinch - make skin; focus, outward; focus, increase; focus, increase; focus, increase; focus, increase; focus —

The sounds were too close. *They're right on top of me. Now or never!*

— increase; potential = activate.

The spell clicked. The unknowable force building inside me burst out in every direction, contracted, settled back down just outside of me. I'd felt this the first two times I'd done this spell, but never quite like this, never so strong or so clearly. Was that a good sign?

I was about to find out. My spell completed, my attention ricocheted back to the world at hand, and I opened my eyes to see—

FUCK!

—several dozen armed and armored Iriate soldiers sprinting toward me from only several yards away, screaming at the tops of their lungs, bristling with blades and spikes, ready to gore me, trample me underfoot, tear me limb from limb. I tried to scream but couldn't as I dove sloppily to the side, my entire body hitting the dirt with a heavy thud only a few feet away, nowhere near enough distance to save myself from the stampede. I wrapped my arms around my head, buried my face in the dirt, and braced myself for a quick, messy death.

What I got instead was coated in a spray of dust as the group of Iriates skidded to a halt only inches from my spot in the dirt, their battle cries deteriorating into confused, angry grumbling. I risked opening my eyes to peer at the pair of spiked boots stomping the ground within spitting distance from my face.

"Where is she?" the voice atop the feet roared. "Where did she go?!"

"Where did who go?" another voice in the mob demanded.

"The human girl! I saw her! We all saw her!"

"Trick of the wastes, maybe. An illusion in the heat haze."

"What fuckin' heat haze?!"

"Find her! Find where she's hiding!"

"Where in Hell could she be hiding on the barren plains, moron?"

The grumbling grew in volume again as they argued, then grew again as the argument grew physical and gained heat. Slowly, my eyes on the mob, I pushed myself to my feet and stood on weak legs that I was convinced by now would never stop wobbling ever again. I could have reached out and touched the nearest Iriate, but he wasn't looking my way, instead shouting back at his cohorts.

Another soldier behind him *was* looking my way, though, her eyes slowly scanning the horizon behind where I stood. Her gaze reached me and jerked past, flitting over me as if I were a gap in her sight.

My revised spell had worked. I could look down and see myself, but to outside observers, I was for all intents and purposes completely invisible.

For the moment, at least. How long would this version of the magic last? What were the triggers that broke it? How much noise and movement could I get away with before I was spotted through the enchantment?

These questions burning in my mind, I slowly, carefully backed away from the squabbling Iriates, sidestepping wide around the group as a fight threatened to break out in their midst. I had finally gotten behind them, the wall at my back, when someone shouted the order to spread out and search for me, and the cluster of soldiers broke apart as Iriates ran off in every direction except back toward the city.

My heart in my throat, I stood still and watched as my hunters dispersed, a small contingent of the group hurrying on ahead toward the canyon. Only when the nearest soldier was a good twenty feet or more away from me did I dare to breathe again. Safe for the moment and bolstered somewhat by my successful illusion, I turned back to the wall once more and ran like the armies of the damned were after me, because apparently they were.

If the sky ever bothered to change in this place, I might have had an idea how long it took to make this breathless journey. It felt like hours, but that might have just been because my lungs and legs were on fire the entire time, and I kept having to stop and catch my breath whenever the ground started spinning too much. Four more groups of soldiers passed by me along the way, but none came as close to catching me as the first; my supercharged perception spell was still holding, for now, at least.

Come to think of it, that might have been contributing to the crushing fatigue I was carrying, keeping a jury-rigged spell running the entire time. If that was the case, then I was on a tighter time limit than I realized. I tapped what few dregs of willpower I still had left and forced myself forward, toward the city and the palace, before I passed out or my magic ran dry.

After what felt like the better part of the worst day of my life, I finally, finally drew within sight of the wall — and the massive gate of spiked metal several feet thick that was the only way past it. I stopped yet again to catch my breath and to stare at the imposing slab of iron, wondering how the hell I was going to get through that now that I'd reached it.

How did anyone else coming back from the wastes get inside again? I can't imagine there'd be any mechanism for opening it on this side, cautious as the entirety of Dis was with everything outside its borders. Shouting up at the wall for entry, maybe? That would definitely break my spell, and I wasn't willing to do that until I knew I was back in friendly territory — or at least, less obviously hostile territory. If there was such a thing anymore.

I was still pondering the problem a minute later, and growing antsier by the second, when a deep, muffled clang sounded from somewhere behind the massive wall and the spiked slab of a gate began slowly trundling open. I would have thanked any god listening for the luck as I ran toward it, if I didn't know this also meant another batch of soldiers heading out in my direction.

It was a smaller group this time, at least, only half a dozen. I pressed myself against the outside of the wall just beyond the gate while I waited for it to finish opening, counting their numbers as the Iriates ducked beneath it and crabwalked through only a couple of feet from my hiding spot. Either they were running out of soldiers to send on this inexplicable errand, or they were getting more confident in the numbers they'd sent already.

The last demon had barely cleared the outside edge of the gate when the metal clang sounded again and the spiked hunk of door, still only barely halfway off the ground, stopped rising. For about half a second, I wondered why, before I realized what was about to happen.

One summer in high school, I'd worked part-time for a local grocery store. In the back room where the excess stock was kept, there was a machine for crushing all of the empty boxes down into a tight cardboard bail. Part of my job was feeding boxes to the machine and watching as the massive mechanical crushing arm slowly squished and mutilated everything beneath it into barely recognizable pulp. And every time I stood there waiting while the machine grinded through its tedious business, a little voice of anxiety in the back of my mind wondered what it would be like to be inside the thing, waiting to be slowly and inevitably crushed into a thin meat pancake.

A morbid thought, sure, but that's what was running through my mind as I sprinted the short distance to the barely open gate and dove beneath it, the grinding of unseen chains echoing in the tiny space as several tons of solid black iron pressed back down toward me.

At least this would be a quicker death if it didn't work than being torn apart by Iriates or collapsing in the wasteland. Would my invisibility spell stop when I died, or would it keep going for a bit? Would anyone notice the red smear on the bottom of the gate, or would soldiers be trampling through my giblets without realizing it?

I kicked and rolled away from the dull light of outside, toward the blackness of the wall's entryway, the rhythmic chunk of metal on metal spurring me forward. A sudden boom reverberated through the ground and my bones, the last traces of light disappearing as the enormous gate finally thundered shut. The fact that I still had bones left to rattle told me I'd made it, and I breathed a sigh of relief into the gritty stone beneath me. This was, what, the third or fourth time I'd narrowly avoided dying today? Whether I was having good luck or bad, I had to be nearly out of the stuff by now, right?

I pushed myself to my knees, then my feet, stretching out my hands to grope my way through the darkness. They met resistance immediately, about ten inches or so to my left. One of the inner walls of the gatehouse, I guessed, as I ran my hand along the hard, unbroken surface.

My blood froze in my veins. Nope, not a wall, this was smooth iron, solid and still vibrating from the impact. I'd missed being stamped into goo by less than a foot. Cool. I spun around and stumbled forward, adding being crushed, tight spaces, and giant honking slabs of metal to my growing list of new phobias, right next to great big dogs and accidentally eating something humanoid.

So, that was the terrifying outer gate dealt with. That just left the inner gate, which I remembered was also a slab of black metal, but not as impossibly thick or covered in spikes as the wasteland-facing one, and less likely to suddenly crash down and smoosh a person. There was still the issue of how to open it without giving myself away, of course; but after fumbling my way across the pitch black gate house to the other side, I felt along the far wall around the inner gate, and my arm bumped a chain thin enough to get my hands around threading down from the ceiling. It was secure on both ends from the feel of it, barely any slack, but this had to be part of some door-opening mechanism, right? I nodded to myself, planted my feet, and pulled.

Shouldn't have skipped arm day for the past twenty-one years, I thought when that didn't work. The chain didn't move an inch past its slack; I might as well have been trying to pull the entire wall apart. If this was the way to open the door, then it had been designed with an Iriate's strength in mind, not my twiggy human arms. I adjusted my grip and leaned my full weight into it this time, my feet eventually leaving the ground entirely as I swung from the unimpressed chain like the world's least athletic monkey. I think I may have felt it drop down just a bit for just a moment, or that might have just been blind optimism on my part. Regardless, I wasn't getting that second gate open this way anytime soon.

Resigned and defeated, I stumbled blindly toward the nearest wall to search for an inner door. Three steps in, I cracked my shin against what felt like a steel pole jutting up out of the ground and barked out a few quick, pained swears before I could stop myself. I rubbed my bruised leg with one hand and reached for the offending object with the other. Yes, it was indeed a big metal rod sticking up at an angle from the floor, thick and smooth and capped with a rounded edge. I leaned my weight on it, and it shifted downward another forty-five degrees or so with a deep clunk. The heavy chain nearby began slowly clinking as the inner gate crawled upward, the outside light revealing the gatehouse and the lever I'd just pulled.

I took a deep breath and hobbled into the city at last, feeling only a little foolish and chalking that up to the day I was having.

The outer wrath district of Amonis seemed the same as it had been when we'd left it hours ago, the air filled with a heat haze and the sounds of rhythmically clanging metal, guards and civilians walking the streets as if they had no idea about the treason the army was currently pulling at the moment. Either that kind of thing was comparatively normal here, or it was all focused on Enkida, and news hadn't spread inside the city yet. Regardless, I still had to get word to Vambrace as quick as possible.

I glanced up at Pandemonium rising from the center of the city and audibly groaned. The damn monolith was somehow immune to that hazy washed-out look that normally came with being a huge thing on the horizon, but the fact that its width looked almost like a reasonable size for a building from here reminded me that I was still miles and miles from the palace itself, to say nothing of how long it would take trying to stealthily hunt down the archfiend in its labyrinthian layers once I'd finally reached it. Even the implication of all that running still ahead of me made my legs nearly collapse again.

There had to be a faster way. If Enkida wasn't dead after this long, she definitely would be by the time I finished this next leg of my journey, to say nothing of the return trip. If only Hell had text messaging, or pay phones, or even a freaking telegraph! Any kind of long-distance messaging at all would really save the day right about —

Oh shit, that's right!

I scanned the street for the nearest Acediate that looked like they were alone. They didn't exactly stand out, even now when I was actively searching for them; but after a few moments of wandering down the street I'd found myself on, eyes darting from doorway to alcove to cranny like a methed-up squirrel, I finally spied a lump of gray fuzz slouched against the stone-and-sheet-metal wall of an open-air furnace, slowly eating lumps of something magenta and drippy from a soggy paper bag while they stared in my direction at the gate I'd just entered the city from.

I rushed forward and skidded to a stop in front of them. "Are you part of the archfiend's psychic communication network thing?" I asked. Not exactly the most subtle or coy approach, I know, but there was no more time now for clandestine wankery.

The Acediate paused with a handful of soggy magenta giblets halfway to their open mouth, staring slack-jawed into space around me without ever actually looking at me.

Right, shit, I thought, and reached my attention into the back of my mind to stop the magical thought loop that had been running these past couple hours or so, willing the invisibility spell away. It was kind of like trying to banish a song that was firmly stuck in my head, weirdly difficult despite the active effort it had taken to maintain it in the first place.

I felt the magic dissipating when I finally succeeded, felt it drain off of me like a physical sensation, like coming out of a pool and shedding water — and taking a good measure of my remaining stamina with it. That got the furry gray demon's attention at last, a sweat-stained and dust-covered human suddenly materializing in a slumping heap at their feet. I hit my hands and knees in a controlled collapse, the street spinning beneath me while, somewhere behind me, what few onlookers there were nearby gasped and murmured.

One of the Acediate's wet magenta globs slowly fell from their hand and splatted to the ground in front of me. "Who…?" they drawled. "Where did…?"

"No time," I breathed, suddenly winded once again. "Acediate communication network. Are you in it? Yes or no."

It was the Acediate's turn to scan the street now, head swiveling infuriatingly slowly. Whatever curiosity my unnatural appearance had drawn was already moving on, leaving nobody but the sloth demon in earshot of my question. Finally, they tilted their head and leaned down closer to where I knelt. "Yes," they said. "How did…?"

I waved a hand and forced myself to standing, then leaned in way closer than could be considered polite, planting my hands on their matted shoulders and nearly pressing my face against theirs. Their breath smelled like halitosis and fruit juice. "Can you get a message to the archfiend?" I urgently muttered. "He needs to meet me here, Lady Morgan, by this gate, as soon as humanly possible! Drop everything, come now, *right now*, holy shit, I cannot overstate how urgent and important this is, just, fuckin', *get your ass here, Vambrace*!" I shook the Acediate's shoulders for emphasis, barreling my gaze into theirs like I was staring into a camera. Then, when I realized I was doing all that, I cleared my throat and stepped back. "Can you tell him all that, please?" I asked, more subdued now.

They swallowed, then slowly nodded and turned to gaze further down the street toward the city, where another Acediate was sprawled across a roadside bench looking our way.

"Awesome, thanks," I sighed, then collapsed again, planting my butt firmly on the ground next to my new Acediate acquaintance. My rush was finally over, or at least paused for the moment. With luck, I might even have the energy to make the trip a third time once the prince got here, if I could get some intense resting done in the meantime.

Their message apparently sent, the Acediate turned back to me once again. "What are you…?" they began, then trailed off. A minute later, they shook their head and went back to slowly shoveling glistening magenta nuggets into their mouth, the juice dribbling into and staining their beard.

"What are those, anyway?" I asked once my breathing was back to normal.

They shook the soggy sack in their hand. "Pomegranate pickled hornets," they said, then held the bag out to me. "Want one?"

I considered the bag for longer than I would have thought. "Nah, better not," I realized a moment later. "I'm probably allergic. Thanks, though."

They said nothing, only resumed their snacking with the occasional side-eye cast my way.

No sooner did I finally catch my breath than my hours-long hurry turned to impatience. The ball was in Vambrace's court now, but every second he wasn't here in front of me was another second Enkida was fighting for her life without backup. I couldn't convince myself any of the soldiers I'd skirted in the wastes were rushing to her aid; the only hope she still had of not being dead already, at least in my mind, was the fact that she was only in that canyon in the first place to keep me safe. As soon as I was gone, maybe that had freed her to escape somewhere safer. Maybe she was hiding out from her attackers now, hunkered down and nursing her wounds. Maybe she was also making her way back to the city, where she could rally whoever was still loyal to her against the traitors. Or hell, maybe without me there in the way, she'd released her limiters and killed everyone else already, and now she was just sleeping it off.

It helped to fantasize while I waited. The only other options were stress and despair, and I didn't have any more room for those right now.

I don't know if it was a blessing or a curse that I had no way of counting time while I sat there. It could have been an hour, or less, or several — my brain was too fried to trust its accuracy in the matter. All I knew was that I had caught my breath, rested my legs, and was on my feet again, pacing back and forth across the street in front of my now-napping Acediate messenger, before Vambrace finally rounded the corner into view farther up the road, skidding as he came around the bend and then sprinting toward me, leaving concerned stares in his wake.

I rushed to meet him, but didn't get too far. He was faster than me, and right now, a lot more panicked. "My lady, what is the matter?" he demanded in quick, hushed tones, grabbing me by the shoulders as we reached one another and pulling me into a conspiratorial huddle. "I thought you were with Enkida, wherever you had gone. Where is the general?"

"In danger!" I whispered back. "In the canyon with the garm den, fighting the entire goddamn army!"

"What?" He released me and took a step back, puzzlement on his face. "Why is she...? Why were *you*...?"

"No time for that!" I shouted, then grabbed him by the wrist and yanked. "Come on, you have to help her or she'll die!"

That spurred him. I was the one pulling him along for only a couple of seconds, and then he rushed into the lead, dragging me stumbling in his wake. I shook off his grip so I wouldn't slow him down, running after his retreating back, my legs stiffly protesting that they were in sprint mode again so soon.

He reached the wall gate while I was still too far away to hear what exactly he was saying as he shouted at whatever unseen demons manned the gate mechanism. They heard him, though, wherever they were; by the time I caught up again, the gate was slowly trundling back open, the archfiend hurrying to duck beneath it. I followed suit.

"The outer gate!" Vambrace ordered in the shadowed gatehouse. "Open it, now!"

"But sire," a voice echoing somewhere above us answered, "security protocol has always been to maintain a buffer—"

"Now, damn you!" Vambrace shouted, tendons in his neck bulging with the volume. "Both gates open and stay that way until I give the order, or I'll have your heads! D'you hear me?!"

Not that I blamed the guy, but I'd never seen him this out of sorts before. All he had to go on in this situation was my word that Enkida was in dire trouble — no explanation yet, no details, no one else to back up my assertion — but he was absolutely losing it. While massive mechanisms clanked and groaned in the darkness above us, the gate behind us still rising, the giant slab in front of us now slowly shuddering to life, the archfiend paced a quick, tight circle in between the two, Excalibur gripped tensely in one restless fist, the other repeatedly clenching and unclenching as his head turned in his orbit to keep his frantic gaze glued to the outer gate.

He looked ready to pop, whatever that might entail here. To cry, or scream, or stab the next person to get within stabbing range. I gave him plenty of space while we waited for our door to open. Whatever specifics I had to give him, they could wait for now.

The outer gate clanked, and the giant slab had barely lifted off the ground when the archfiend rushed it. I watched him baseball slide underneath it, heard him scrabbling to clear the other side. After my most recent encounter with it, though, I wasn't in so big a rush myself that I couldn't wait for it to rise to a comfortable walking height before I followed.

Vambrace was pacing again just beyond the gate, and as soon as he saw me passing under it, he rushed in to grab me by the wrist and yank me out the rest of the way. "You said the garm canyon, right?" he asked breathlessly, eyes so wide I thought they might fall out of his head. "That's where you left her? That way?" He released me to stab a finger toward the horizon on my left.

"Right, that's where we were," I answered, rubbing the ache where he'd grabbed me. "I can't see it from down here, but I think that's the way—"

"Can you run?"

"I… think?" I said. "I've done it a lot today, so I'm not sure how long I'll—"

That apparently wasn't good enough for him, because next thing I knew, he'd scooped me princess-style into his arms and took off at a sprint in the direction of the canyon. I was being manhandled a lot today, I noticed. At least it was mostly for my safety, so that was something.

Fortunately for my legs, we didn't have to go as far as I thought. Not very far at all, actually: When the prince gasped and skidded to a stop, we could still see the wall behind us, still barely make out the figures high atop it as they rushed to cluster around the nearest edge.

That was the only thing fortunate about the surprise we were suddenly faced with. Because Vambrace set me down — nearly dropped me — in front of the mangled wreck of what was left of General Enkida, who lifted her blood-crusted face to us and smiled weakly. "Oh… good," she breathed, voice ragged and weak. "Made it after all…"

Vambrace said nothing as he dropped to his knees in front of her, hands hovering but unsure where was safe to touch. All I could do was stand behind him, hands over my mouth, shock and horror and guilt all warring for dominance in my churning gut.

Not all of that blood was hers, I knew. She had already been covered in the stuff when I'd left her in the bottom of the canyon, when she seemed to still be winning against the overwhelming odds. When she wasn't… missing pieces.

Now, though…

She still had her spear with her, the point of it jabbed into the dirt, her hand trembling where she gripped the haft. Her other hand — her other arm, up to the elbow — was gone, the skin ragged around the bleeding stump, the black bone sticking out of it jagged and splintered. It hadn't been cut cleanly, no, it had been ripped off. One of her horns was also gone, snapped near the base, the other one cracked and missing its tip, the wreckage of someone's eyeball impaled halfway down the length. A dozen arrow shafts sprouted from her back through her armor, and what looked like the warped chunk of some broken blade was half-buried in one of her thighs, the leg below it twisted and mangled. And behind her, a smear of blood trailed the ground back in the direction of the garm chasm, the path punctuated by a semi-regular line of holes, each about the size and shape of her spear head.

She had been dragging herself home this whole time, I realized with sickening awe. She really *had* beaten or escaped her innumerable enemies and was on her way back to Dis, just like I had foolishly hoped for. But it was a double-edged wish I'd made, and I was horrified to see it come true.

"Enkida…" Vambrace breathed, heartbreak audible in the quiet trembling of his voice. "No… How…"

"Traitors, sire," the general answered, lifting her head. "Lot less of 'em now, though…" Her long braid had also been hacked away in her fight, her now-choppy hair framing her wry grin through busted, bloodied lips.

One of her lower fangs was missing, and fresh blood was still seeping from one empty eye socket. Arms, legs, eyes, horns, fangs — she had left one of every piece of herself on the battlefield, along with two-thirds of her hair and at least as much of her blood, from the looks of it.

How had she pushed herself this far? How was she still alive right now? How much life was left in her? I didn't know much of anything about demon anatomy, but Iriates were supernaturally tough, right? Maybe she could still survive all of this damage if we got her help right now, I thought, maybe there was still hope —

But no. I watched Vambrace's trembling hands finally reach up to grip his own head. Watched him curl forward into himself. Heard his wordless, anguished scream carried off into the vast, empty expanse.

He knew, better than I did. Now I knew for sure too. There was no coming back from this. These were General Enkida's final moments.

"You told me you could handle your soldiers' animosity toward you!" Vambrace shouted into the ground. "You said they all knew not to take it too far! There is no advancement through murder, every Iriate knows this!" He punched the dirt with a dull thud. "To betray you en masse like this, to go to this extreme, it makes no sense! What the fuck is happening!?"

"No," Enkida grunted. Her broken smile dropped, but her voice and her remaining eye sharpened. "Not just soldiers… Invidiates too. Not after me… bigger than that. After… you too, Vambrace. The throne… Dis, all of Hell… and beyond…"

The prince's head snapped up at that. "That's… impossible," he breathed. "No, that can't… Nobody has been foolish enough to attempt a coup in, in centuries! It's pointless — everyone in Dis knows it's pointless to even try! How long has this… Why now? Why, what have I done differently to make anyone think —"

Vambrace was still breaking down, and I was still reeling from everything that was happening, so neither of us were ready when Enkida's only remaining arm shot out and grabbed the prince by the collar of my jacket. "Listen!" she shouted, her dying voice suddenly at full power again as she used Vambrace to haul herself up off the ground and right into his face. "It doesn't matter what shortsighted scum thought up this scheme or why. You face this treason, and you end it! Finish my duty, destroy this plot and everyone involved! Anyone, *anyone*, who dares to try and take our Hell from us, you find them, you rip them to shreds, you make them lament they were ever born! Understand?" She yanked again on the prince's collar with far more strength than half of a dying woman ought to plausibly have, pulling him in so their foreheads butted against one another, glaring straight down his eyes and into his soul. "Finish what I started," she snarled. "My wrath will not die with me! End this, and *avenge me!*"

The next moment, she slumped forward, leaning on the prince with her full weight. Her arm was still flexed, her grip still tight, her face still set in a furious grimace. But her eye slid slowly shut, and her last ragged breath slipped from her lips in a tired growl, and she moved no more.

General Enkida, leader of Hell's armies, right hand of the archfiend, and baddest of any ass I'd ever met, was gone.

"Enkida…" Vambrace whispered, voice breaking. "Enkida, no… You can't die on me, I need you! This doesn't work without you!" Now that there was no more damage that could be done to her, the prince wrapped his arms fiercely around the wreckage of her body, burying his face into the crook of her neck, heedless of the blood or her armor. "You can't be dead!" he sobbed into her shoulder. "I forbid it! Do you hear? You can't!"

The archfiend of Hell wasn't here right now, just a broken man mourning his closest companion. I no longer knew how long I'd been in this world, so I couldn't say for sure how long I'd known the general myself. Still…

I wiped tears from my stinging eyes, my own crying quiet and subdued compared to Vambrace's unabashed grief. She'd been nice to me; she'd vouched for me when even her boss, the only other human in this world, seemed like he might be an enemy. I'd thought her literally unstoppable.

And now she was gone, her last words warning of imminent danger. I was painfully hyperaware of how much I was to blame for her death, for that danger, and how I would never have the chance to apologize to her for leading her into that trap with me.

It was too much to deal with right now, after the rest of today; suddenly I felt that if I watched Vambrace breaking down for even a moment longer, I'd join him in a useless heap on the ground, and that would be the end of me. So I blinked back the rest of my tears, took a deep breath, and turned back to face the wall and give the prince some privacy in his mourning.

That's when it hit me.

"Hey, Vambrace?" I asked, loud enough to be heard over his sobbing. "We're within sight of the wall right here. And Enkida had been crawling her way toward it for what has to have been hours now. Why didn't anyone up there see her? Or help her? Why weren't you alerted before my message found you, or on our way through the gate?"

It took him a minute to calm down enough to answer me, but when he'd gotten himself under control again, there was a thoughtfulness to his silence. "Why?" he repeated, voice thick, as he slowly rose to his feet. "Yes. Excellent question." A second later, he'd ripped Excalibur from its harness on his back and spun to glare at the wall, teeth gritted. "And look, here comes our answer."

I followed his gaze in time to watch as dozens of Iriate soldiers rained down the side of the wall, kicking up a cloud of dust as they hit the ground and rushed toward us. My second time today facing down a horde of rampaging demons, and I have to say, the previous experience didn't exactly make the prospect more appealing this time.

"Think they're... coming to help now?" I asked, backing toward the prince. "It's too little too late, but..."

"Possibly," he answered, stepping past me. "But I doubt it. Odds are these are more of Enkida's traitors." His grip tightened on his sword. "Appalling that there are still so many of them, but she'd be happy to know her vengeance is in such a hurry to be done."

I made the mistake of turning to glance at Enkida's body, and had to fight down a pang of equal parts sadness and revulsion before I could speak again. "Are you... are we gonna be okay? With that many, and the general gone?"

"Not as okay as we'd be with her still alive, of course," he answered. "For all my reputation, it seems everyone still knew what a bulwark Enkida is... was to the power of my rule. These cowards no doubt think me helpless now, without her might backing me up." He hefted his sword higher into the air, a grim smile on his face. "But so long as I have Excalibur at my side, no matter the odds, nothing can ever—"

Neither of us heard the whistling of the arrow until it thunked into the back of his raised hand, the force jolting his whole arm forward. The arrowhead pierced clean through, knocking the sword from his grip.

Excalibur flailed through the empty air for a second before it was caught—

—by a tall, lithe Luxuriate man who hadn't been there a second before. He flashed us both a quick smirk before spinning in place and launching the sword, javelin-like, toward the onrushing Iriates.

"No!" Vambrace cried, shoving the man aside and sprinting after the weapon. He only made it a few feet before two more arrows stabbed into his back, sending him sprawling forward.

I threw myself to the ground, hands covering my head, anticipating the sharp bite of whatever arrows were heading for me. That seemed to be the end of the firing, though, as the Luxuriate scrambled away toward the approaching soldiers and Vambrace struggled to try and gain his feet. He forgot about the arrow in his right hand, though, and immediately collapsed again with a pained yell as soon as he put weight on it.

I couldn't see what had happened to Excalibur. I couldn't tell what the fuck was going on anymore, or why.

"Stop firing, you fool!" someone bellowed behind me as another arrow whistled overhead, going wide of both of us. "He's already down, and I want him alive!"

I risked twisting to look back. Once again, a Luxuriate had popped into existence where there was only empty wasteland just a few seconds ago, this one a woman holding a shortbow with a quiver of arrows dangling from her hip. And behind her, Archduke Abdeles loomed, glaring down at me from maybe fifteen feet away.

"That one, though," he sneered, pointing at me with his chin. "If she makes any sudden moves, pin her to the dirt. Nonlethally," he added as the Luxuriate nocked another arrow and aimed it down at me.

"Abdeles!" Vambrace shouted, finally struggling to his feet. "You addled, grasping viper!" As he spoke, he snapped the arrow puncturing his hand, barely a flinch registering on his enraged face as he yanked the shaft from the wound. His hand was coated with blood, the hole ragged on the edges, his fingers trembling. The arrows sprouting from his back must not have broken through his mail, because he was ignoring those.

"That's another of your Earth fauna, is it?" the archduke asked as he walked around and past us. "Please, tell us how monstrous and terrifying *this* creature is, your majesty. Ten feet tall, with rows of fangs and razor-sharp claws, no doubt. Oh, but you've surely slain hundreds of the beasts without breaking a sweat, haven't you?"

Vambrace glared like he wanted to leap at the Superbiate and throttle him, but with at least one archer trained on us, a horde of Iriate soldiers finally pulling up, and himself disarmed in two senses of the word, he only spun slowly to watch as Abdeles sauntered past.

"I have to wonder if you even realize how long ago your lies grew obvious and tiresome, Sire," the archduke continued. "Or perhaps, just maybe, some of those stories were true? After all, even an addled, grasping, lowly demon like myself could likely fend off thousands of impossible monsters if I were wielding *this*."

He reached a hand toward the assembled soldiers, the foremost of which stepped forward and laid a sword into his palm.

Excalibur.

"You…" Vambrace growled, taking a step back from the now-armed Superbiate. "You have no idea what—"

"No, I have a pretty good idea 'what,' human!" Abdeles interrupted, pointing the blade toward his prince. "Sidona's wretched propaganda plays often enough in our theaters, and you showboat in front of your adoring public even more often! Did you think you could force us all to watch your displays and not one of us would pay attention? Your soldiers learn multiple disciplines, but you yourself only ever wield a sword in your stories. And in person, you only ever wield *this* sword."

He swung the blade through empty air, a sudden slash of moonlight against the dull red dust and sky. Vambrace took another step back, nearly tripping over me.

"Not the most impressive blade at first glance, is it?" the archduke continued, holding said blade close and staring into the metal. "Sturdy, though, to have been with you through your unnatural eons. One might think it was indeed the skill behind it that made it so deadly. Unless one's eyes were opened, and they had learned what to look for to confirm their suspicions."

My heart leapt into my throat. The magic powering Excalibur, comprising it, the runes hiding just beneath the surface — could he see them too? Was he seeing them now? But even Vambrace didn't seem to know they were there. The only reason *I* could, I thought, was because I'd already been studying magic, because I'd had understanding of the language shoved into my head by the *Morganomi*—

No.

No…

This fucking guy, did he…?

"Let's test my theory, shall we?" Abdeles continued. "How will you fare without your crutch to lean on, human?" He snapped his fingers and stepped back as his Iriate lackeys swarmed us — slowly at first, but when all Vambrace did in response was grimace and glare and shrink back, they grew bolder. I was hauled to my feet alongside him, powerful hands wrenching both of our arms behind our backs. I felt rope winding around my wrists and breathed a quiet sigh of relief. If they'd been using metal shackles, I might have been screwed, but rope?

Rope burned.

"By Lucifer, this is sad!" Abdeles chuckled. "I knew ridding ourselves of our beloved late general would give us a clearer shot at you, 'Sire,' but is this really the only fang you had to pull?" He lazily spun Excalibur in his grip. "How in all Hell did you keep your position for so long with so little to stand on? I'd surmised that you were mostly smoke, but I thought there would at least be *some* fire underneath!"

Good, keep gloating. Really revel in your master plan, dickhead.

More importantly, now that the prince and I were subdued, the archer behind me had put her bow away. All eyes were on the archduke and the prince as one preened himself and the other seethed. The longer this lasted, the more I got to charge up.

I'd sped through the initial priming stages as soon as my captor's hands were off my bindings. Now I was just piling on the penultimate loop in my head, waiting for a chance to pull the trigger.

Heat - increase, project; heat - increase, project; heat - increase, project…

God, I hoped this wouldn't kill me.

"—stand before all the realm for every citizen to see what a parasitic charlatan they've been suckered into worshiping for all these eons," the archduke was still saying. He snapped again. "Bring them both. We're going to take a little parade through Dis on our way back to the palace. To *my* palace."

That seemed like as good a cue as any.

Potential = ignite

I heard the screams behind me before I felt the magic flowing down my arms and out of me — way out of me. The ropes tying my wrists practically evaporated, and I swung my arms forward in front of me, dragging tails of heat in their wake, scattering Iriates on either side of me.

Nope, wait, not just heat. That was full-on fire engulfing my arms and spewing out of my hands. I'd overcharged that spell so much, I was accidentally dual-wielding flamethrowers.

Fuck yeah, I could work with that.

I spun and sprayed flame at the soldiers encircling us, driving them back to give the prince and I more room. "Vambrace, duck!" I shouted, and swung my arm in a wide arc up and around him as he did, bringing it down again over the middle of his back, just close enough to scorch the ropes binding his own wrists, and maybe a few of his fingers, just a little bit. He yelped as the flames licked his skin for a second, but pulled his arms free as he ducked down further, the rope crumbling to ash and blowing away in the heat.

Both of us free now, I rushed up beside him, waving one fire-spewing hand in front of us and pointing the other squarely at Abdeles, who held Excalibur like a talisman in front of his wide-eyed scaredy-bitch face as he scrambled backward. All of them were scrambling backward, shock and awe visible on every face and in every panicked murmur.

"Yeah, that's right!" I shouted at the lot of them. "You still wanna talk shit about humans? Cuz this one has magic goddamn powers! Original Sin, motherfuckers!" I waggled my fingers, and it made the jets of flame wobble and flicker in new, rippling patterns, which was enough to make some of the slack-jawed soldiers flinch again. "Alright, Prince," I muttered as I backed toward him, hoping my voice was quiet enough not to be heard over the searing roar of my fire. "I can hold them off with this, but I've never actually been in a fight before. What's the plan?" I turned toward him.

He wasn't there.

I turned further. No, now I could see him. The back of him, anyway, as he sprinted off into the wasteland without a backward glance. With all assembled now focused on my sudden display of magic, nobody had stopped him, and nobody was chasing him, so he'd already fled an impressive distance.

"Vambrace?" I breathed, stunned. "Vambrace!" I repeated, shouting at the back of his head. "What the hell, where are you—?"

That was as far as I got before something crashed into me from behind. I hit the ground and my head hard enough to knock the wind out of me and send my vision spinning and blurry. There was a heavy weight pressing down on me, squishing me, more hands grabbing and yanking at my limbs. Distantly, I realized my fire was out, the muscles in my arms limp and fatigued as they were re-bound. Not rope this time. Chains? Felt like chains.

"Imbeciles!" Abdeles was screaming as the world pressed in on me. "Fucking useless incompetents, how could you let him escape! No, you idiots, stop shooting at him, I can't risk you hitting something vital! The filthy cur needs to be alive to confess his lies to the rest of demonkind!" There was stomping, then a boot on my neck. "Take this one back to the palace and throw her in the dungeon, maximum security, no compromises, am I clear? And inform Alastaroth the 72nd what happened here! He's to hold Pandemonium and proceed with the next step while I take a more *competent* team to hunt down that wretched human and drag him back to justice!"

Maybe I'd done too much magic in too powerful a burst and run out of whatever energy powered it. Maybe the stress and trauma and exhaustion of the day had finally, finally caught up to me. Or maybe it was the archduke kicking me in the back of the head that did it.

Whatever the reason, that was it for me. There was dust in my eyes, ringing in my ears, and dread in my heart as the blackness slipped over and swallowed me whole.

Chapter 35: Resentment

Everything hurt when I woke up. My muscles ached, my body felt bruised and beaten all over, my head was throbbing, my throat burned, and from the pressure inside my skull, I surmised that my eyes wanted to push themselves out and roll away. What little light there was as I blinked groggily awake stabbed hatefully into my brain when I looked toward it, so I kept my eyes scrunched tight as I slowly pushed myself to sitting.

This wasn't my room, that much was obvious. The floor beneath me was hard and rough and uneven, and there was a slight breeze blowing from nearby, the only sound besides my own groaning. Gradually, I dragged my eyes open and took in my surroundings. Rough-hewn obsidian floors and walls with thin hairline veins of red etching through them told me I was back in Pandemonium. The small, empty room they comprised, and the thick bars that made up one whole wall, told me this was that dungeon Abdeles had demanded I be thrown in.

Fucking Abdeles. I'd known he was a pompous prick who made no secret of not liking humans, but I hadn't imagined he'd go this far, or that he'd even be able to. But he was the one who'd had Enkida murdered, and now he had Excalibur, and the prince—

A wave of indignant rage shot through me. I used the momentum of it to shove myself up to my feet, my groans of pain morphing into angry growling as I did.

The prince, that *gigantic goddamn asshole*, took the first chance to run clear the fuck away and leave me on my own in the middle of a crowd of human-hating traitors. I stuck my neck out for the guy when we were both in a pinch, and he just threw me to the fucking wolves.

My hands clenched so hard at my sides they were shaking. I hoped Abdeles and his cronies had caught the bastard already. I hoped he was rotting in another cell nearby somewhere. I hoped they shoved Excalibur up his ass when they got him.

The heat pricking at my eyes is what clued me in that I needed to calm down. I took a deep breath, sat back down on the floor, and let the tears flow.

I hoped he would come back and help me figure a way out of this mess. I hoped there *was* a way out of this mess. I hoped I wouldn't die in some dark pit of Hell, alone and forgotten in some hateful alien dimension a zillion miles from home.

It had been, to put it lightly, a real fucking bad day. Couple of days. Whatever it was. It took a long time of sitting and sulking in the dark before I was finally finished crying. I couldn't even tell what the tears were for anymore, fear or stress or exhaustion or grief. All of the above, probably. I'd been off my anxiety meds the entire time I'd been here; frankly, it was a minor miracle that I'd been functioning at all lately.

When the crying was done, fatigue set back in. I laid down in as comfortable a spot I could find on the black stone floor and attempted a nap, but it wasn't coming, no matter how soul-deep tired I felt. Eventually, hunger grew to be a bigger concern, and I gave up and sat up again when my stomach started growling.

There was a metal tray sitting on the floor near the cell bars. I hadn't noticed it before, but I walked over to it now and picked it up. The classic prisoner meal: a hunk of crusty bread and a cup of black water. Okay, maybe not so much that second thing. The black water had soul in it, I remembered — full of nutrition, good for curing Invidiate curses. So scratch that, I had the *fancy* prisoner meal here. Well, good to know my title still counted for something.

I drained half the water cup in one gulp to wash the dust and dryness of the wastes out of my throat, then munched on the bread while I paced my cell and took stock of where I was. As much stock as I could take, anyway; the flickering torchlight in the quiet hall outside my bars only told me that I was in some underpopulated part of the palace where they didn't spring for the steady crystal lights. If anyone else was locked up here with me, they were being remarkably silent about it. Given what I remembered of the raucous prison cells in the wall, it was probably safe to assume I was alone.

The only other feature of note was the barred window on the back wall, the source of the low breeze I'd been feeling. I stood on my toes and peered through it at every angle I could manage, but all that was visible in any direction was splotchy red sky with dark gray clouds scudding through it. I must have been in one of the towers, then. I pulled myself up to the sill and looked downward as much as I could, but I couldn't see even the outer rim the giant bowl that was Dis. I must have been really, really, *really* high up one of those towers.

I'd never clearly seen the top of Pandemonium before, no matter how far away I got before I looked back at it. Clouds and distance always obscured it after a certain point. Depending on where in that massive monolith I was, there was the possibility, at least, that I was currently miles and miles above ground.

I lowered myself from the window and backed slowly away after that thought.

"Lord Abdeles was hesitant to give you a window cell," a voice behind me rasped. I spun around to find Alastaroth hunched over his staff outside my cell, every one of his remaining eyes watching me. "Afraid you would melt the bars and fly away, or something similar. I had to convince him how unlikely it was that you knew any kind of flying or levitation magic, given that we've read no evidence of such yet, and that you failed to use any earlier when it would have been more prudent. Far more important, I said, to give you a cell with thicker inner bars. We don't know how much control or precision you have over that magical fire of yours, or how hot it can get, so better to make melting through them a longer and more arduous chore, just in case." He smiled and bowed his head slightly. "You're welcome for that."

I stomped over to the food tray on the floor, snatched up my water cup, and threw the remaining contents in his face. "Don't you fucking monologue at me, you dusty old shit," I spat. "I've been through enough hell today because of you, I don't need the cute speeches. Get to the fucking point and tell me what the hell is going on here."

He blinked water from his eyes and slowly wiped his face, his beard dripping as he gazed silently at me. "Interesting," he muttered a moment later. "Not the reaction I was expecting."

"Yeah, I'm fucking full of surprises." I threw my arms out at my sides, then dropped them. "But hey, humans are tricky, right? And what the hell else have I got to lose at this point?"

"Besides your life, you mean?" he retorted. "But, no, your point stands. Every privilege you had before, you've lost, my former lady. Only bars and silence and bread now." He rapped on the bars with his staff, the dull metal thud echoing off the stone. "But you could reclaim some of the comforts you've grown used to, if you wanted. Depending on which direction you choose to take this conversation we're having."

I crossed my arms and glared. "Ooh, so generous of you."

"Better than the current alternative, I'm sure you'll agree," he said. "And you did ask what, I quote, 'the hell is going on here.' Do you want to hear my answer? Or shall I leave you to sulk alone for a while longer first?"

I took a deep breath and closed my eyes. As much as I wanted to roast this guy alive right now, he was making a point; this current situation absolutely sucked. And anyway, with the bars between us, he could probably run away before I could get a good cook going. "Alright," I sighed. "I'm listening."

"Help us," he said. "Willingly, and without the lying this time, of course."

"Help you with what?" I asked. "Your coup? Taking over Hell? Because Vambrace is gone and you got his sword, so you seem to have that part well enough in hand without me."

The Invidiate shook his head. "Seizing power is a means to an end, not the goal itself. Though admittedly, for Lord Abdeles, taking the throne might be the most important step in the process. For the rest of us, what comes next is more interesting and substantial."

"What comes next?" I repeated. "What could top 'seizing the throne of Hell' as an endgame? You gonna storm the gates of Heaven now or something?" I froze. "Wait. Are you, though? Is *that* a thing too?"

Alastaroth frowned. "Who or what is a Heaven?" he asked — a sentence which opened up some weird theological doors coming from the mouth of a demon. "But, no," he added, holding up a gnarled hand. "Questions for later, perhaps. No, my former lady —"

"Stop that," I snapped. "Stop that right now."

He glared at me and cleared his throat. "No, Morgan, what comes next is, we finish this grand magical project that we were working on before our little falling out. Without any of the deception this time." He reached into the deep pocket of his toga and pulled out a book thick enough that he could barely get his hand around it, with a battered gray-brown cover that looked like some combination of leather and tree bark —

My head nearly clanged off the bars between us as I rushed forward and reached a hand out of my cell. Alastaroth took a quick step back, his fangs peeking through his lips in a coy smile as he clutched the book — *the* book, *my* book, *that damn* book — to his chest.

The *Morganomicon*. It wasn't dead after all. It had just turned against me, like every other goddamn thing in this place.

"Give me that!" I demanded, my arm still stretched hopelessly through the bars, reaching toward it. "That's mine, you have no idea what you're dealing with there!"

"Funny," said the demon, "our former archfiend said much the same thing about his sword, didn't he? And yet, you've both been proven wrong."

"Alastaroth, I swear to —"

"Alastaroth the 72nd, please," he interrupted. "So long as we're insisting on proper names and titles. And if you'll calm down and listen, Morgan, if you'd been paying attention this whole time, you'd realize that I know exactly with what I am dealing here."

My reaching hand balled into a fist. His face was right there, it would be so easy to chuck a fireball at it… but the *Morganomicon* was also right there. My ticket home, miraculously undestroyed after all. I wanted it now more than ever; I was reluctant even to take my eyes off it.

But I was also in jail. *Play along for now*, I told myself, trying to tamp down my rising, impotent frustration. *Play nice, listen to the villain scheme, wait for the first opportunity to grab the book and run.*

I stepped away from the bars, crossed my arms, and held onto my own sleeves for dear life to keep my magical arson hands from doing what they itched to do. "Fine," I spat, unable to hide my venom. "I'm listening."

"Pleased to hear it," the envy demon cooed. He held the book more loosely in the crook of his arm, leaning his staff against the wall to run his other hand gently over the cover.

I felt a sharp pang of envy myself at that, but held back this time.

"Cards on the table, then," he continued. "No more lying, no more withholding information. For either of us. Agreed?" He gazed at me expectantly.

I nodded at him with my chin. "You first."

"Hmph." He held the book aloft, as if showing it to me for the first time. "I can read this," he said, and my heart sank. "Or I nearly can. Bits and pieces, here and there, which I am slowly, painstakingly, maddeningly deciphering," he added, and my heart unsank a bit, not gonna lie. "From the moment Lord Abdeles placed this book in my possession, I have been picking my way through it, forcing understanding where I could, with only the scantest scraps of remaining pre-human magical relics as my guide. Indeed, it was sheer luck that the Avaritiate from whom my lord purchased this item didn't realize the full extent of what he was selling, what a treasure trove of dangerously illegal knowledge he had in his shop."

"Gilderos?" I muttered. Tracking down that name had been such an intense obsession for such a painfully delayed time there, I'd probably never forget it. "Even luckier for you that you got the book out of that shop before it burned to the ground. Until you started waving it in my face just now, I thought it had been incinerated."

"Yes, that was rather the point," said Alastaroth, condescension creeping into his tone. "With such a valuable and potentially fatal relic, we had to cover our tracks. We couldn't have the merchant realizing what he'd had, after all, or telling anyone whom he'd given it to."

"Cover your tracks?" I repeated, a second before what he was saying clicked. "Son of a bitch, *you* burned that shop down? You killed Gilderos?"

"I did no such thing myself, of course," he said with a sniff. "Lord Abdeles sent another agent of his for that task. I'm a scholar, not a criminal."

"Fuck you, you know that doesn't make you better!" I argued. "You killed an innocent merchant, and another innocent man died in prison because he took the fall for it!" Dorgagovek. My last tenuous hope after Gilderos, another desperate name I'd probably never forget.

"Of course," he said. "Not just the Iriate suspect, but his entire cell block as well, just to be safe. We were lucky the garm attacked the wall when they did; we weren't sure how his lordship's agents in the prison were going to carry out their orders without raising alarm, but the wastes provided the perfect distraction."

My anger flared high enough that I could feel the heat from my palms through my sleeves, threatening to set my clothes on fire. I wrenched my hands away to my sides instead, fists clenched so tight they trembled. How that nightmare of a day could be good news for anyone made me sick. "You and your whole group of whoever," I growled, "you're all real fuckin' scumbags. Surely you realize that, yeah?"

"Don't presume to lecture me, human!" Alastaroth growled back. "What revolution ever succeeded without some degree of bloodshed? Your beloved Vambrace murdered his way to power the same as any archfiend before him, however much he liked us all to pretend he was simply predestined for leadership. Human superiority is a falsehood that has done irreparable harm to demon culture and history for eons, and if we want to reverse that damage now, of course it will require drastic action and sacrifice! Your arrival here, with your book of lost magic and your wide-eyed ignorance of all the lies we were fed about what made your kind untouchable — perhaps that was the spark that lit this flame, but make no mistake, we have been building this pyre for untold generations!"

His hand flew back to his staff, and for a second, I thought we were about to come to blows through the cage bars after all. Instead, he seemed to catch himself, and took a deep breath as he stuffed the *Morganomicon* back into his toga.

"But if you truly do balk at our methods," he continued, "if you sincerely wish to avoid unnecessary violence and this isn't just a show of false primacy, then you will aid us now. Our plans are succeeding with or without you, but your assistance would speed them along. And the sooner this transition is finished and our new age begins, the sooner the situation in Dis will calm down to something like normal once more."

"My assistance," I said. "With teaching you magic, I assume. Just like our fun little field trips we all took. It was never about studying history or preserving culture, was it? It was always about trying to trick me into showing you how to read my spell book."

Alastaroth inclined his head. "No more deceptions, as I said. In truth, it was always about both goals. We have more plans in mind for this knowledge than simply cataloguing it, of course; but do not doubt the sincerity of my anthropological work, or the deplorable state of the past that we must scrounge in to do it."

"Were any of those old relic sites real?" I asked. "Because some looked weirdly fresh, and what was actually carved into them didn't usually make sense in context."

He shrugged. "We were limited by time, location, and what we could do in semi-public spaces without drawing too much attention. It was hazarded that you would be too culturally ignorant to see through the fabricated archaeological finds. Whether or not the phrases and symbols we applied to them would be appropriate in their circumstances, we obviously could not predict without first learning enough of them to begin our own decoding efforts more heavily. Efforts which, again, you failed to adequately assist in given that you were lying on your end as well."

"Yeah, I don't exactly feel bad about that now, given recent events." I threw my arms out, gesturing to my cell and the general situation. "But why, though? Why do you need to learn magic at this point too, if you've got a literal army of conspirators behind you and you've already ousted all your major opponents?"

"Besides strengthening and consolidating martial and sociological power, you mean?" he asked. "Because if my theory is correct, then somewhere in this book is the key to intra- and interdimensional teleportation. If we're going to locate and bind the Original Sin, or re-establish contact with other worlds, I need to know how to read it."

"Other worlds?" My breath caught. I hurried forward and pressed my face between the bars. "You mean Earth," I said. "Why? You hate humans, why would you want contact with more of them?"

Alastaroth scoffed. "We hate one human in particular. You, though, have shown us another side of humanity, another point on a potential range of what humans can be. One that is less... imposing, let's say."

"I turned my hands into flamethrowers earlier today," I reminded him with a glare.

"And I made Luxuriates imperceivable while they stood but a few feet from you both," he said, patting his pocket. "And we both have the same source for those marvels, don't we? One that is, crucially, outside of us both. One that can teach its secrets to anyone." He scoffed and leaned forward, and I backed up again to keep us from butting faces. "Between your book and Vambrace's sword, it has become clear that any advantage your kind may seem to hold, it is borrowed. It can be lost, taken, redistributed. On your own, you are nothing special."

"Then why try and, what did you say, locate and bind us?" I pressed. "Is this some sort of 'conquer and enslave Earth' plan you're doing? Because I can tell you right now for free, spell book or not, that plan would fall to shit immediately."

"Bah!" The demon snatched up his staff and banged it against the bars. There wasn't a lot of strength behind those scrawny arms, but the sudden venom was still surprising. "Your kind, you humans, you are *not* the Original Sin!" he spat. "You take our founding ancestors' names in vain, you wear their mantle undeservedly, but you will sully their legacy no longer! No, you ignorant savage, I speak of the *true* Original Sin, the cardinal perfection of all demonkind!"

I held my hands up in a "chill the fuck out" motion and waited for his quick, raspy breathing to calm down. "Buddy," I said, which sent him glaring again, "if it's been a lie for this many eons, what makes you think it's suddenly true somewhere else now? If you're all descended from some superpowered demon species, why aren't there any real ones around? If they still exist today, where did they go, if they're not here with the rest of you?"

To my surprise, he actually did seem to calm down, stroking his beard again as he stared at me. "Fair questions," he said in his inside voice. "And while I have my theories, I confess that I do not have concrete answers. But," he added, patting his toga pocket again, "I know how to find them. If our glorious past is still alive somewhere, hidden from us, then all I need do to prove it is summon it before us. With your help, of course."

I put on my best poker face as I took a deep breath. "And how do you know any spell to do that even exists in that book, if you can't read it yet?" I asked.

"Because I can read a little of it, as I've said," he answered. "And because you're here, Morgan. Humans don't stumble in and out of this world regularly; you came here somehow, with this book in tow. And if you could get home without it, you would have done so by now, wouldn't you?"

My poker face failed me. I had to look away before it cracked, but that was just as damning.

Alastaroth grinned. "So, the secret to crossing worlds is in its pages somewhere," he continued. "And you know where. You will point me toward this magic, you will assist me in deciphering it, and when we are finished, I will conjure the true Original Sin to Pandemonium. We will show all of Dis the truth about our heritage, the extent of your human lies and propaganda; and to make sure this truth is never lost again, we will reestablish the link between Hell and its neighboring worlds — Earth included — and allow demonkind to truly flourish across dimensions once more. We will spread out from this cramped little crater, we will leave the dangers of the endless wasteland behind, and we will colonize the multiverse."

"Colonization's not really fashionable on Earth right now, gotta warn ya," I muttered while, inside my mind, my thoughts raced.

So, point number one: Demons coming to Earth, definitely a bad idea. True, turns out most demons I'd met here were mostly just regular people, plus or minus a few quirks, but it was the shitheads among them that wanted to come over, and Earth had enough shitheads of its own already. Interdimensional culture shock wouldn't be pretty for either side at the most diplomatic of times, much less so with anti-human radicals leading the charge.

Point number two: There was no way Abdeles and Alastaroth, even with an army of sturdy rage demons and a rudimentary grasp of magic, had any actual hope of conquering anything or anywhere significant like they thought they would. Earth had tanks and guns and drones and stuff. If even General Enkida could be brought down by enough stabbings, then Hell's armies were one well-aimed missile away from being converted into a cloud of angry dust.

But, point number three: Stopping them on that side of the dimensional barrier would do a lot of damage to wherever they marched out, however doomed the invasion was. We were talking medium-scale interdimensional terrorist attack — lives and livelihoods would be lost. And Hell had worse than racist demons. If a garm pack got through, or a flock of harpies, or one of those flesh-eating flesh-suit pisaca things? Whole different set of wrinkles.

No, it was definitely, objectively best if this plot didn't happen.

However, point number four: They had the *Morganomicon*, Vambrace fucked off without me, and Enkida was dead. Anyone or anything with any power I may have had in my corner was gone. No one on Earth knew where I was or what was happening. Nobody back home would be able to do anything about it even if they did.

No help of any size or sort was on its way for me. If there was any way out of this situation, any way whatsoever, I had to make it myself.

And that was easier to do when I wasn't stuck in a dungeon cell.

I took a deep, slow breath and sighed, dramatic and defeated. "Fine," I said. "Alright, fine. You got me. No use pretending otherwise. I can't get back to Earth without that book. Nobody can. So, you're right. Lies and massive treasonous assholery aside, we still need each other." I walked up to the bars, pressed my face between them, and turned on my serious glare. "I want to make a deal."

Alastaroth wore the smuggest smirk as he stroked his chin at me. "I'm listening."

"I want no part of your plots except the part that opens up travel between worlds. Don't try and get me to kill anyone for you, don't use me for no political maneuvering. I tutor you in this magic, I help you find and unlock this spell, I give you the keys to the interdimensional part of this plan, and as soon as that first door to Earth opens up, I go home through it. Back where I belong, out of your hair, wash my hands of all this demonic bullshit. Deal?"

"Hmm…" He pursed his lips as he mulled my words. "Well, we're definitely going to be using you for political maneuvering," he said. "You're human. Until we get Vambrace in custody, you're our symbol of the false tyranny that's been holding demons back for millennia. But we can play that card without having to parade you in chains through the streets or anything, if that's what you're worried about."

Well, it is now, I thought, but elected not to share.

Alastaroth smiled again. "Very well," he said. "If it guarantees your docile cooperation. Once the gateways are reopened, you will be permitted to return to Earth along with the first wave of our expansion — preferably to never return to Dis again. No hard feelings."

"You absolutely meant some hard feelings there, you dusty shit," I said, reaching a hand through the bars. "But yeah, deal."

He reached for my hand, immediately caught himself, and narrowed his eyes as he prodded gingerly at my palm with one finger. I smirked. The thought had definitely crossed my mind, but no, I needed to play along for now. "Deal," he repeated, clasping my hand firmly in his.

"Cool," I said, shaking once and then quickly pulling away. "So I think you said something about getting my room back if I cooperated? I'd like to go back there now, please."

"In due time," Alastaroth croaked. "We are finishing other preliminary preparations at the moment, securing the palace, rearranging key forces and players. A successful coup is a complicated set of moving parts, you understand." He snatched up his staff and turned away from my cell. "Don't worry, you will be brought back to your quarters as soon as it is safe to do so. In the meantime, relax and enjoy the view and the fresh air."

After he'd disappeared down the hall and around the curve of the walls, I sat on the floor with my head in my hands and resisted the urge to scream in frustration. I wouldn't give him the satisfaction. But fuck, man, what was I supposed to do now? I could barely plan a semester schedule, much less an escape from political imprisonment. What was my game plan supposed to be? For that matter, what even were my options?

A counter-coup seemed unlikely with Vambrace and Enkida gone. I didn't know who all Abdeles and his lot had on their side, much less who might be against what they were doing. And just killing the big blue bastard, even if that was something I could do, that probably wouldn't fix things, right? Alastaroth or someone like him would likely just slide into his place, keep their plan going. I don't know how many people in their chain of command had to die before the whole group of traitors gave up, but I had nobody I could order or convince to do that kind of thing, and I *definitely* couldn't handle doing it myself. Even if I had the means to do so, I didn't have the stomach. I felt mildly guilty squashing bugs; no way was I working up the moxie to squash a person.

So the whole leadership of Hell thing was screwed and well above my pay grade. That just left escape. Somehow, I'd need to find a chance to steal the Morganomicon back without being immediately caught, then I'd need a place to turtle up long enough to find and cast the interdimensional travel spell on just myself. Maybe I'd even find somewhere in the text of the spell where I could tell it *where* to take me, instead of just blindly hoping it was a two-way street from here to Earth and I didn't zap myself to, I don't know, Purgatory or something and had to have this whole isekai adventure shit all over again.

A lot of "somehows." A lot of "ifs." A lot of "hopefullies." I didn't like it. I didn't like much of anything right now.

With a sigh, I pushed myself up against the wall and went back to eating my allotted hunk of prison bread. I still liked the bread, at least, even if I had nothing left to wash it down with thanks to Alastaroth's stupid face.

I wondered where Kriseia was right now. Was she okay? She better be okay. If these coup assholes tried to mess with her too, then—

"Attention all citizens! Urgent news from the new leadership of Dis!"

I nearly choked on my bread at the sudden shouting, then scrambled to my feet and over to the window. What the hell were they doing now?

"The human archfiend, Prince Vambrace, has been deposed! All hail the new archfiend, Lord Abdeles of House Superbia!"

The voice wasn't coming from outside, I realized. It was inside my head. How the hell did they—

"Behold, the turning point of history! An end to humanic tyranny!"

The view outside my window disappeared, suddenly I was standing on a parapet atop the wall, looking down at the dusty wastes just beyond. Far below, but close enough for a clear view, a crowd of Iriates interspersed with a handful of Luxuriates were swarming around three figures standing off in their midst: Abdeles, Vambrace, and myself.

"Witness: Lord Abdeles, fed up with the lie of human supremacy, challenged the archfiend for his throne in fair combat! But rather than meet his lordship's challenge, the human Vambrace fled the field! Like a coward!"

As the booming voice narrated, the distant Abdeles took a single confident step forward, sword raised high in his hand. Across from him, Vambrace quailed, his own sword held tight in both hands, his legs shaking. Another step from Abdeles sent Vambrace backing up, and the next moment, he'd dropped his sword and shoved me aside, turning and sprinting away through a surprised crowd of soldiers. Abdeles thrust an authoritative finger after the fleeing figure, and the bulk of the Iriates gave chase, a red tide washing the prince out into the wastelands. I watched my legs buckle as I fell to my knees, hands clasped in supplication before the Superbiate archdemon. With a flourish of his cloak, Abdeles snapped his fingers and strode past where I knelt. Two more Iriates hauled me to my feet, and I was marched away back toward the wall as Abdeles followed his forces chasing Vambrace away from the city.

"Our new archfiend hunts the spineless human tyrant throughout the dangerous wasteland as we speak! Vambrace's consort and co-conspirator, the human invader Morgan, sits imprisoned in our custody! And General Enkida, of House Iria, traitor to her own kind, lies dead in the field for her complicity in our subjugation!"

The vision shifted, and now I was sitting on a clifftop at the abandoned garm den, staring down at the crevasse below where Enkida, battered and bloodied, squared off against half a dozen other soldiers. As she lunged toward one with her spear, another ducked under the blow and rammed his sword through the center of her chest. Enkida staggered, coughing blood, and —

No, I thought — my own thoughts this time, not this intrusive mind being forced into my own. *No, I don't want to be here, I don't want to see this. This isn't real, these aren't my memories, this isn't where I am, this isn't how it happened!*

My head throbbed as the vision blurred and the booming voice narrating the action slurred. With an effort, I pushed the broadcasted sensations out of my mind, wrenching back control of my senses.

I stood in my cell again, staring unfocused at the floor, the only sounds now the soft and distant wind outside my barred window. Several confused moments later, I realized that this wasn't a new sensation.

Acediate mind-sharing. I'd only been on the receiving end of it a few times, and never this loud or forcefully. So, either the conspiracy had taken over Vambrace's network of sloth demon communication, or they'd organized their own. Neither would be surprising, or good news for me.

The voice in the visions hadn't been addressing me, but "all citizens," so this must have been some sort of mass-announced public propaganda thing, presumably beamed into every mind in the city. Which also explained why the memories I saw didn't match what had actually happened. Luxuriate actors playing me and the prince, most likely, to stage events in a more positive spin for Abdeles.

I'd noticed they left out the part where I'd briefly menaced his forces with twin streams of fire — cold comfort to know that I'd behaved too competently for their liking, for a second there at least.

Still, here was Abdeles railing against his people's history being erased and then immediately releasing a doctored version of what happened. Big blue hypocrite bastard.

But wait, how had *I* gotten hit with that broadcast? Acediates had to have line of sight to share their thoughts and memories with someone, I'd been told — and a quick look around my immediate surroundings assured me there was no one else hiding in my cell with me, nor any visible sloth demons just outside the bars to peek on me. And beyond just my circumstances, there was no way every single denizen of Dis was within eyesight of a conspiracy Acediate right now. How were they sending their message to those people? Was the sight rule not a rule anymore if they got enough Acediates together around the same memories? Or did some just have a juiced up version of the talent?

That second option seemed more likely. Enkida's wrath had been overpowering and unbreachable for most other Iriates, after all, and Kriseia had a weaker version of her kind's glamour than most other Luxuriates, by her own admission. No reason other demon talents couldn't also come in different tiers. Maybe this unseen broadcast was the work of a few especially talented individuals, or even just one. But with a juiced-up type of power like that, you'd think this demon, whoever they were, would have to be some sort of big-shot in Acediate circles.

Like an archdemon? my brain supplied.

I chewed thoughtfully on my prison bread, rolling the thought around and not liking the weight of it. Archduchess Bargryf, ruler of House Acedia. I hadn't had any dealings with her aside from Vambrace's fancy dinner gatherings, but I knew the archdemons weren't chosen by political acumen alone. Demons may not have had much magic left to them, but they flaunted and celebrated what innate talents that Vambrace couldn't decree out of them — the leader of each House, on top of whatever leadership skills they had, also had to be impressive with their Sin's given talents to command respect. So if any Acediate was going to be able to transmit their thoughts as far and wide as this broadcast had been, it would be her.

Which meant that Abdeles wasn't the only archdemon involved in this coup, even if he was the one leading it. And if we had at least two archdemons involved, where did that leave the other five? They wouldn't be able to sit this power shift out, right? If they weren't actively on the conspiracy's side, then they were probably in the same situation that I was in — blindsided by events and locked up out of the way.

I might have potential allies in whichever of them weren't on board with Abdeles's plan, but would that matter? Could they help me if they were imprisoned like I was? *Would* they help me if they could, if it meant sticking their necks out and upsetting the new de facto ruling body of Hell?

Something to think about and feel out during whatever happened next, but I wasn't letting my hopes rise too much. The only ally left that I knew I could count on was Kriseia, though what she might be able to do to help, I didn't have a clue yet. Moral support, of course, sure, but without any clout or social status, there wouldn't be much she could —

I shot to my feet, revelation propelling me to anxious pacing once more. There *was* still one person left who was ostensibly in my court. The self-proclaimed jewel in the crown of House Superbia, whom I may have accidentally tricked into thinking she was losing her mind.

Duchess Sidona. She could have been an archdemon if she'd wanted, and the cultural scene of Hell bent to her whims, according to her. If nothing else, she was nobility without being in the way of Abdeles's power grab. More importantly, we kept owing each other favors, and by now I knew how to win her interests and buy her assistance. Also, if I wasn't trying to hide the fact that I was a witch anymore, then I suddenly held a powerful card up my sleeve, vis-a-vis her mental faculties being healthier than she realized. That had to count for something, right?

Right. Well then, the good duchess had just shot up to the top of my priority list. Time to see if her ego lived up to its reputation.

Chapter 36: Perfidy

It was a long march back to my room, and the guards escorting me made sure we took the scenic route. I'd agreed to cooperate, but Alastaroth had still ordered me shackled for this part, for the optics. The people we passed definitely took notice, murmuring to one another or openly pointing me out as I was led down the halls and through crowded gathering spaces.

If he wanted me to look defeated, tough shit. I kept my head up and glared back at every pair of eyes that landed on me — not too dissimilar from the first time I'd been escorted by guards through this palace. The difference was, this time, it wasn't a brave face I was putting on as a bluff to mask my terror. I'd been here long enough to recognize some of these faces from frequency alone, and I knew now how most of them operated, how they thought and perceived, what they were capable of.

No, this time, it wasn't an act. I was pissed off and genuinely daring someone to start something. Any sign of resistance one way or another, any opportunity to see a crack in this plot that might herald the beginning of a plan.

No such luck, sadly. None of the shocked or concerned faces we passed challenged my guards or raised any kind of fuss. Most of them were already deep in their concerned murmuring even before I was paraded past; that propaganda broadcast had been quick and thorough, and things were progressing swiftly. How long this conspiracy had been lying in wait, how many people had been onboard before, how many were signing up now — I didn't know any of this, but from what I was seeing, it was more coordinated than I'd hoped. No obvious fighting, no audible shouting, no backup coming to storm the stolen palace — if Vambrace had any loyal forces left willing to fight for their absent archfiend, they'd already lost.

Cool, so it was all gonna be up to me. No pressure.

I did still have one loyal, outspoken ally left spoiling for a confrontation, and she was waiting for us downstairs before we'd even reached my front door.

As I was marched around the slow curve of the lower halls, Kriseia hurried into view in front of us. She skidded to a stop with a gasp as she saw me, horn-heeled feet scraping the floor, then rushed forward and threw her arms around me. "Morgan!" she cried, the Iriates on either side of me halting at this new intrusion. "Oh, throne below, I'm so glad you're safe! I saw those memories with you in them and I, I didn't know what to think, I was so worried! Are you hurt? Are you okay?"

I smiled despite our predicament, and as I couldn't hug her back with my shackles, I settled for resting my hands on her hips between us. "Missed you too," I said. "Glad you're okay as well. Am I hurt? No. Am I okay?" I lifted my chained wrists between us and couldn't keep the edge from my voice when I replied. "Also no."

Kriseia ran her hands over the chains, disbelief passing over her face, then… anger? Was that it?

She turned to the nearest guard, a barrel-chested wall of a man with thick, bulging biceps, and slapped him across his chiseled face. "How dare you!" she huffed. "How dare both of you! Don't you know who this is?"

She gestured at me. I gaped at her. Yeah, she was angry. I'd never seen this side of her before, hadn't even been sure it existed.

Not gonna lie, it was kind of hot.

It was also ineffectual. The guard's face hadn't moved an inch under her slap, but it did morph into a scowl. "This is an upstart human saboteur and a political prisoner of the new regime," he growled. "And you aren't authorized to—"

"You're the upstarts!" Kriseia shouted, spinning to the other Iriate. "Lady Morgan has done nothing to warrant this kind of treatment, and you should all be ashamed of yourselves! I thought House Iria was supposed to stand for justice! There's nothing just about what you're doing now!"

"Uh, Kriseia," I said, laying my hands on her back as she seethed at my escorts. "Hey, love the fire you got here, but maybe tone it down? You're outnumbered and a lot smaller than these two."

"I don't care," she argued, which was another first. "You said I should speak my mind more often, right? Well, here I go." She planted her feet, set her hands on her hips, straightened her spine, and glared up at my towering escorts. "Prince Vambrace was chased off, and now Morgan is in chains, and why? Because you're all mad at humans?"

"The Original Sin is a lie," the barrel-chested Iriate rumbled. "Have you not been paying attention? Humanity is the enemy of demonkind, and Archfiend Abdeles will—"

"Enemy my tail!" Kriseia interrupted, stabbing a finger into his stomach. "Morgan has been nothing but kind and accommodating since she got here! And if Prince Vambrace was trying to kill us or whatever, he's had plenty of time to do it by now, and we're all still here!"

The barrel-chested Iriate's teeth were audibly grinding by now. "That pretender has stifled demon society and blocked our expansion into—"

"Why are you wasting time arguing with this slut?" my other Iriate escort, this one lithe and long-limbed, interrupted. "Take the human to her chamber, I'll deal with this one."

"Deal with how?" I demanded as they released me and their stocky companion pulled me closer. "Wait, deal with how? Leave her alone, she's not—"

Their hand clamped over my mouth, dangerously tight. "Enough out of you!" they shouted, then spun and grabbed Kriseia by the horn, wrenching her closer as she squealed. "You're under arrest for defying the throne and conspiring with the enemy. Now move it!" They released my face to grab Kriseia's instead, their other arm wrapping tight around her torso and pinning her arms as they hoisted her kicking into the air.

"Get your hands off my—!" I screamed before my remaining guard clamped my mouth shut once again. My hands flared to life on instinct, the shackles on my wrists quietly hissing against my white-hot skin.

"Keep giving us trouble and we'll do worse than arrest her, human," my escort growled into my ear. "No glamour that House Luxuria's ever seen will be enough to hide the damage we'll do to your pretty little friend if you don't cooperate."

If looks could kill, then the side glare I turned on this motherfucker would have blown his head into chunky salsa. But if that spell existed, I didn't know it yet. Instead, I went carefully, hatefully still in his grasp, my fists balled so tight that I could hear my blood sizzle in my palms as my nails dug in and immediately cauterized the wounds. It went against every instinct screaming inside me to turn the heat down again, but I forced the magic to dissipate as best I could.

The last I saw of Kriseia was her still kicking and yelling into the other guard's hand as she was hauled away around the curve and out of sight. Our eyes locked again a moment before she disappeared. She looked as angry and scared as I felt.

Alright, fuck just escaping. I was saving my friend too before I left this world behind. How dare Hell give me someone to care about and then steal her away from me! I was the Lady Morgan Goddamn Amell, goddammit!

When we finally reached my room, I was shoved inside, shackles and all, and the door slammed shut behind me. The heavy clunk of a padlock let me know I'd have some time to myself now, so I took a moment to rage: I slammed my chained fists against the door, screamed obscenities at the walls, completely wrecked a couple of the pillows I'd been left, that sort of thing. By the time I'd gotten the worst of it out of my system, every surface was strewn with feathers, the door had a few new scuffs and dents in it, and one of the wall sconces lay in a shattered rain of glass shards on the floor.

With a series of long, deep breaths, I sat down on the bed, grabbed the chain of my shackles in my hands, and began the slow process of melting it while I tried to think but mostly just seethed. It had been a while since I'd had this space to myself. Once upon a time, that would have been a welcome change, but it had been a long while now since I'd welcomed any of the changes that were happening.

Eventually, the focus of my ire turned to the shackles around my wrists. Melting these chains was taking forever. A voice in the back of my head told me this probably wasn't a feasible task I'd set myself to, but a much louder and more prominent voice was shouting screw that, we didn't have anything else going on right now and we needed a win, no matter how small. So I sat there and squeezed the chains in my hand like I was throttling Alastaroth's scrawny neck and ran the heating spell on an escalating loop in my head, damn the consequences.

Heat – increase; heat – increase; heat – increase; heat – increase…

I wondered how long could I keep this up before it got dangerous. The first part of the spell shielded me from the effects, but given enough time, maybe I could hit nuclear levels of heat, and then who knew what would happen.

It didn't take quite that much to finally see results, but I did end up sitting there for what felt like an hour. Metal doesn't melt easily, who knew? Eventually, though, the chains began feeling softer in my hands. As I shifted my grip, the iron shifted under my hands, slipping like clay between my fingers. I glared at it as it slowly shifted from black to brown, to orange, to red, whereupon a dollop of it leaked out of my palms and splatted against the marble floor with an angry hiss. That was my cue to get off the bed while I finished this, lest I set it on fire; somehow, I doubted the anti-human conspirators would let me have another mattress if I burned the room down with this one. In the relative safety of an empty corner on the other side of the room, I gave the chains a final twist and a yank and pulled the gooey strands of molten metal apart at last.

Alright, I'd accomplished one good thing for myself since all the shit had gone sideways. On the way up at last; good job, Morgan.

I was working on melting the bands off my wrists when my door opened again and two Iriate guards stomped in, one holding a tray with food on it — a hunk of bread, a leg of meat that was probably harpy given its size and shape, and a glass of some kind of blue juice or wine. More than I'd gotten in my jail cell earlier, so here was one more way I was moving back up in the world, hot damn.

The two froze when they saw the ragged ends of chains hanging, still red hot, from my now-useless shackles. I glared at them as one of the wrist bands warmed to orange beneath my fingers, silently daring either of them to say something about it. The empty-handed Iriate looked like she wanted to, but her partner with the food took the initiative to walk over to my desk and set the food tray down. "Do you understand our writing system, human?" he asked.

"No," I answered, "why?" The orange metal under my fingers was slowly shifting red. I gave it an experimental rub and smeared the top layer off onto my fingertips, wiping the residue on the marble floor beneath where I was sitting and dripping iron.

The guard recoiled visibly, just a little, as he watched. I added another tick to my "minor wins" column. "Lord Alastaroth the 72nd has ordered that you transcribe the contents of his magical text in preparation for his grand undertaking," he said. "But if you cannot chronicle your studies in a comprehensible manner, then you will have to dictate your findings to him personally during these sessions."

I didn't bother hiding the distaste I felt at that. I'd told that dusty little shit I'd help willingly, but that didn't mean I had to pretend to like him. "Don't suppose anyone in this palace can read the English alphabet, huh?" I asked.

The guard's expression was blank. "I don't know what that is," he said.

"Didn't think so," I said, my attention back on my shackle bracelets again. "Vambrace thought he did, but turns out we were on different wavelengths, and he had some kind of British vs. English hate boner getting in the way on top of that." The guard didn't reply. I wiped another layer of iron against the floor and sighed. "Fine, if that's what it takes, I'll meet with the piece of— with Alastaroth the Whatever-his-number-was."

"The 72nd," the guard supplied.

"Yeah, him. Most of my time here has been spent helping bigwigs with their pet projects, might as well keep up the trend." My head snapped up as I remembered. "Speaking of, what's Sidona up to during all of this coup business? She had a lot of irons in the fire that needed my help. Mr. 72nd might need to check with her for a custody schedule that doesn't get in either of their ways."

The guard shook his head. "Duchess Sidona's activities are none of your concern any longer. Focus on your duties toward the new regime instead."

He turned to leave, but spun back cautiously, one hand on the hilt of his sword, as I clambered to my feet. "All due respect, I'm gonna need her to tell me that herself," I said. "I was invested in a few of those projects of ours too. Can you bring her here?"

"No," he barked, hackles finally rising. "Uninvest yourself. You will have no contact with anyone else without his lordship's approval." He turned away again, his partner joining him as they both headed to my door.

"Then tell him I want his approval for this!" I shouted after them, but they were already out the door before I finished the sentence.

Figured. Still, if talking to Sidona was off the table without special permission, maybe that meant they were worried she'd be sympathetic to their human captive. That gave me another crumb of hope; if I could swing a meeting somehow, I might still have a duchess on my side, which would mean… something, presumably. More options to do something other than play along with the bad guys, but what I didn't know yet. Still figuring that part out.

In the meantime, I focused back on my damaged iron wristband until I'd melted and scraped away a big enough gap to slip my wrist through, then tossed the shackle with its dangling bit of chain into the iron-smeared corner where I'd been working. One hand free and unencumbered at last, I set to work on the other shackle with one hand while I ate my prisoner's rations with the other, careful to eat around the bits where I was leaving iron goop fingerprints on the food.

Time passed. Slowly. I finished the food, then finished unshackling myself, then squatted in the corner with my hands splayed over the floor and radiating heat until the last of the iron stuck to my fingers dripped off, my hands now magically clean. I took a long bath, then another nap, then woke up and just laid in bed for a while, staring at the ceiling and wondering if Kriseia was okay, what Sidona was up to, if Abdeles and his cohorts had found where Vambrace had fled, if the only other human on this entire plane of existence was lying dead in a ditch in the ass end of nowhere or not.

Eventually, once being in my own head with myself started getting too stressful, I got up and got dressed and went over to the small collection of books on the shelf by my desk. Mixed in among whatever demonic offerings had come with the room were the few books the prince had loaned me at my request so long ago, written in whatever archaic version of English it was that kept setting him off. I hadn't given them much thought since realizing they weren't what I had meant to ask for, but now they were something to take my mind off the boredom and anxiety.

The letters inside almost looked familiar, spelling words that almost looked like something I could pronounce and understand. Still, that near-familiarity just made it more annoying that I couldn't actually glean anything from the writing. After a few minutes of pointless scrutiny, I set the book aside and grabbed one of the demon ones.

This one was even worse. Just like I'd remembered, demon writing just looked like a bunch of angry stabs and slashes and claw marks in ink, not one of which looked like any letter I was familiar with. Any words they may have been spelling were all crammed together without any spacing, which meant each page was jam packed edge to edge with intense, cramped, angry doodles I had no hope of comprehending.

Two attempts at reading down, only one left to go. I pulled open my desk drawer and reached for the only thing I knew how to read in this room, my old elvish magic flashcards — which weren't there.

"Fuck's sake," I muttered aloud as I yanked the other drawers open. Nothing. None of my notes, none of my pages from our faked field trips or my own work in private here in this room. They hadn't even left me blank paper or anything to write with to recreate my work; the only thing not missing from my desk stash was the jar of complimentary spider cow gravy that one random farmer had given me during my wanderings through Dis.

Well hot damn, at least I had something to spice up my next prison meal with. "Alastaroth, you piece of shit!" I shouted, standing up and kicking my desk in frustration. It did nothing to make me feel better.

In desperation, I reached into the pockets of the demon dress I'd put on after my bath, just on the off chance I'd stuffed some notes in here and forgotten about them. If I had, though, Alastaroth's and Abdeles' people had taken those too whenever they'd ransacked my room. A cursory inspection of the other outfits I had in my wardrobe turned up the same results, each one of them painfully empty. They'd probably all been that way before the coup, but I was still cursing those bastards' names with each pocket I searched.

As a last-ditch effort, I went back into the bathroom and rummaged through my Earth outfit, which I'd left in a pile by the tub. Here, too, each potential crevice turned up as empty as the last — until, already defeated,

I slipped a finger into that tiny pocket within a pocket on one side of my pants and, surprise, felt the faintest tickle of a fold of paper shoved deep inside. I nearly tore the seam open as I desperately fished out the note and, with a quick glance over my shoulder at the closed bathroom door, opened it up.

What I was looking at wasn't immediately apparent. It was definitely a magic rune of some sort, but more complicated than most of my notes had been, a long scrawl of particularly decorative script written vertically. I knew I could read it before I knew what it meant — a detail about some of the higher concepts in old elvish that still threw me on occasion. It was familiar, though, and definitely my handwriting.

I focused on it, trying to find the words for the concept it was giving me. Something about... force of will, maybe? The impression was absolute, the parameters vaguely defined. It was success, the realization of an endeavor — certain victory, certain achievement. Uncontestable. Unstoppable. A force beyond force, wrapped in a skin of a phrase of an attitude that rebuffed any further interaction, so contained and removed from any other ruleset as to be immune from logic, an intangible entity that near shone with actualization—

Recognition knocked me back on my ass from where I'd been squatting over my own clothes. The paper in my hand shook as my fingers clenched harder on the edges, my breath quickening.

Excalibur.

I was holding, I was reading, the very essence of Excalibur, the soul of the enchantment that I had glimpsed once, fleeting but starkly unforgettable, while in the bath with the prince. The rune I had frantically copied into the condensation on the floor, then set down in ink as soon as I'd been alone again. I'd stuffed it down deep in my inner pocket as soon as it was transcribed, more paranoid at this scrap of magic being discovered than I'd been even for the rest of my notes. Then I'd gotten distracted by all the other craziness going on and forgot to ever add it to the rest of my illegal knowledge hoard.

I ran a reverent finger over the page, reading and rereading it again and again there on the bathroom floor, committing it to memory. I didn't know yet what, if anything, I could do with this, but holy mother of fuck, this felt like a big deal.

Could I cast this on myself somehow? It wasn't an instruction set like the other spells I'd managed to pull off; it was more like a complicated and elegant variable, something to be plugged into a spell, something to define whatever it attached to. Not a spell, I realized — an enchantment. Magic as infusion, as definition, rather than action. A spell coded into something else, a self-contained program that ran on a loop rather than relied on the caster for execution.

My mind whirled with possibility, with potential. More than anything, I wanted that damned book back in my hands again. I wanted the knowledge and the skill to put this enormous find to use, to understand what I had, what I was doing. Ambition surged inside me, consuming and impatient.

Witchcraft had been a curiosity at first, a mistake shortly afterward, and a hidden tool for all my time so far in Hell. Now, holding absolute power in sentence form in my hand while my mind opened in front of it, it became an obsession, a driving urge, a siren song that stuck and echoed in my head.

Up to now, I had been an accidental novice in magic. That was going to change. No more need to hide what I was learning or what I already knew, and no more trepidation in my research going forward.

I was going to become the best godsdamned sorceress in modern history, in Hell or on Earth. If it took the rest of my life, however long or short that may be, I was going to make myself a fucking legend.

By the time Alastaroth finally deigned to grace me with his presence, my attitude had done a complete one-eighty. I was already sitting at my desk as he walked in, the Excalibur rune securely squirreled away once more but still burning in my mind. He had the *Morganomicon* tucked under one arm, his walking staff in the other, and two Iriate guards trailing him — one with an armful of parchment and quills and bottles of ink, the other with his hands gripped firmly around the twin swords at his hip. All three of them stopped in their tracks as I smiled at their approach.

"Took you long enough," I said brightly, patting the desk in front of me. "Let's get started, partner."

G.D. Burkhead

Chapter 37: Importunement

Working with Alastaroth was as academically satisfying as it was emotionally intolerable. I'd kind of only been expecting the latter to be true, though, so I guess this was a welcome surprise? A little bit?

I tried to tell myself that, anyway, as he flipped casually through the *Morganomicon* — *my Morganomicon* — just a few well-guarded feet away from me, cross-referencing the pages in the book with the sheets of parchment his Iriate assistant held in front of him for his perusal. After several long minutes of watching him quietly read to himself and fantasizing about burning his stupid face off, he selected a sheet of parchment and handed it to his other guard, who brought it over to where I sat at my desk, blank paper and quill ready and waiting.

"This section," Alastaroth ordered. "Explain its purpose. And know that I have a passing understanding of how it reads, as well as the context from which it comes." He patted the *Morganomicon* for emphasis. "If you try any of your little misdirections again, I will consider your usefulness to our cause terminated." The guard who'd handed me the parchment flexed his arms, unsheathing his blades just a couple of inches. "Do I make myself clear?" Alastaroth asked.

"Yeah, you're not exactly being subtle," I said, eyes already scanning the parchment I'd been handed. "Don't worry, I told you I'm in, didn't I? We made a deal."

"We did," the Invidiate croaked. "I am merely reminding you, human."

"Loud and clear, boss," I said, turning away as fully as I could manage. Then it was their turn to watch me quietly reading, the flexing guard hovering near the desk as I set to work.

The parchment was Alastaroth's version of my notecards, a scrap of a spell copied out of the *Morganomicon*. I had hoped they would be shortsighted enough to let me study straight out of the book itself, but no, they were being maddeningly careful with how much magical leeway I was getting at any one time. The competent bastards.

Still, circumstances aside, this was a step up from trying to study magic from memory and experimentation alone. I had a textbook now, even if it was only being fed to me half a page at a time, and out of order. So long as I could keep myself in the "just get better at being a witch" headspace, I could consider this another small win.

First, I stared at and through Alastaroth's transcription while making my own, copying the lines and strokes of his symbols as best I could. The excuse I gave was that this was part of my learning process to help understand what I was looking at, which was partially true. The ulterior motive was that I was hoping my hands might remember the motions even after my written notes were inevitably taken away again at the end of this session.

Any little trick to help memorization. Any attempt, no matter how slim, to add another weapon to my internal magical arsenal, no matter how small or ultimately useless it might be.

"This one… is like an identity tag?" I slowly reasoned aloud. No point hiding my inner monologue or playing for time anymore; if Alastaroth had been bluffing, I wasn't calling it, not after the disaster that was the last time he'd caught me in a lie. "Anticipatory declaration. See this bit?" I waved my quill around the end of the section of sigil, where the looping smoke lines had widened to frame the start of a more angular symbol, some half-started, open-ended hedron. "The construction around it has a feel like something vague solidifying into a more concrete definition. Like it's starting a sentence but leaving the subject blank. I think it's the opening measure of something bigger. You declare in whatever comes next what the object of the action will be. There's no apparent effect happening yet in the runes so far." I set my quill down and turned my own transcription over in my hands. "Is this a self-contained effect? It seems like it could be versatile enough to plug into other spell codes. And there's a… a kind of slow curve going on in the overall construction. Like a segment of a circle. You don't notice until your eyes are deep in the lines and your head starts tilting a bit…"

Alastaroth's two Iriates looked lost and bored, but the old Invidiate was stroking his chin and staring intently at me when I looked up again. With a snap of his fingers, the guard nearest me snatched the note I'd made from my hand and brought it over to him. He flipped through the book in his hands again, half his pupils on its pages and the other half on my transcription, and slowly nodded. "Impressive," he rasped. "That makes a sense, in context. Yes… Thank you for being truthful, for once."

"Yeah, if you and your cronies could remember that I'm cooperating now, I'd appreciate it," I said. The paper had been taken from me, but my hand dangling at my side behind me was still moving through the motions of the rune I'd just copied, my fingers quickly tracing and retracing the shape in the air out of sight of the demons in the room. "Got another one for me?"

They did. The *Morganomicon* is a thick book with cramped pages, and for a while, it seemed Alastaroth wanted me to translate the entire thing piece by piece. I sat there for what felt like hours, my first full day of school since I'd gotten here, playing telephone with the contents of the spellbook: Alastaroth made notes, handed the notes to the guard who handed them to me, who made notes of the notes and handed them back to the guard who handed them back to Alastaroth, who made more notes.

It should have been extremely dull. It *was* extremely dull, judging by the slowly deteriorating mood of the two Iriates involved. But inside, my mind was glowing.

Growing up, I'd always had pretty good grades. The only way my family could afford to send me to the city college I was at was because of the small handful of academic scholarships I'd qualified for. Exams, essays, reports: I was good at learning things and retaining them long enough to pass a semester. But throughout my academic career, I'd never really found any subjects that called to me enough to make me think, "This is what I want to do for the rest of my life." Skill didn't translate to passion. I passed all my classes, but none of them excited me.

This was exciting me. At some point in the process, the room around me and my house arrest status drifted away from my awareness as new magic whirred through my brain, a cloud of possibilities expanding and solidifying.

Solid spatial partitioning. Planar target location. Temporal parameter declaration. Impossible sounding high concepts materialized in my understanding with just a few lines and shapes contemplated for just a few minutes, and the part of my mind that was still somewhat grounded puzzled through them and translated:

Barrier. Clairvoyance. Time fuckery.

If I could get a handle on just one of these things, I could be *terrifying*.

So I was actually taken by surprise when, after handing off my latest notes on a symbol that either reconstituted or imploded inorganic matter (the jury was still out), Alastaroth closed the book with his notes in it rather than hand me another one. "That will be sufficient for now," he said, handing off the full load of *Morganomicon* and his papers to his stand-by Iriate. "Thank you for your cooperation, Morgan."

"Yeah, no problem," I said as the guard that had been hovering near me for hours scooped up the leftover parchment and paper from my desk. "So, how about that audience with Sidona?"

Half of Alastaroth's eyes swiveled in my direction. "Come again?"

"That other guard didn't tell you?" I asked. "I need to speak with Duchess Sidona again as soon as possible. I was told you had to sign off on that, though, so if you could pass the word along, that'd be great."

He turned his full attention on me then, both hands on the staff planted in front of him, smug superiority radiating from his face overtop it. "And why, pray tell, would I allow that?" he asked.

Of course things had been going too smoothly today. Of course I needed another obstacle added to the pile. Of course.

"It's not just me that's concerned in this," I argued. "Duchess Sidona had a few different ongoing projects that I was involved in, that she needed my help with. Ask her about them if you don't believe me."

"Duchess Sidona's attention has recently been otherwise directed, as I'm sure you can imagine," Alastaroth answered. "We're in the middle of a new start for Dis, human. No sense dredging up outdated concerns now, is there?"

"Outdated?" I asked. "Why, what's she doing now? What did you lot do to her?"

"So suspicious even still?" the demon croaked, his tone sickly sweet with condescension. "My lord and I, and the rest of our 'lot' as you put it, we have only the best intentions for all of demonkind in our sights. Why do you think we would do anything untoward with one of our brightest creative minds?"

"All her human-centric art, maybe?" I said. "It wasn't really a secret

I'd been helping her with some projects. And she'd wrote at least one play about Vambrace, painted that big portrait of the guy. I don't suppose you'd hold a grudge over that, would you?"

He snorted. "An eccentric fascination with the novel and with the deep lie being fed to us," he said. "No, Morgan, we do not begrudge a brilliant artist over her taste in muse. Inspirations change. Priorities shift. Sidona has outgrown your influence, don't worry. Her sights are turned to bigger things now — things that will not require your input."

"Then get her to tell me that herself," I argued, but he was already leaving, the Iriate woman with her arms full of supplies falling in behind. "Why is that so big an ask, huh? Hey!" I took one step toward him, only for the other Iriate in the room to clamp a heavy hand onto my shoulder and shove me back down into my chair. I shared one last parting glare with the guard before he too turned and left. Alastaroth didn't even bother looking back at me again, but I heard his amused chuckling before the door to my room was shut and locked once more.

Son of a bitch, I thought I'd been getting somewhere. One step forward, two steps back, every fucking time. And now that they'd taken Kriseia away, I didn't even have anyone to vent to.

Kriseia. I hoped she was alright, wherever she was. Hell had a couple different prison systems, as I was well aware, so she was most likely sitting in a cell somewhere. Right?

This was a violent coup that was happening now, though. They'd only kept me around because I was useful. There was no guarantee anyone else would get the same treatment, was there? Did Dis have guillotines?

No, bad Morgan, don't go down that route! I took a deep breath and forced my nerves to calm down again. Someone had said something about using her as a bargaining chip, hadn't they? So long as I behaved, she ought to be alright.

Of course, there was no way they were going to let me verify that, was there? The way things were going, I probably didn't have any better chance at seeing Kriseia than I did at seeing Sidona.

Sidona. What the hell did he mean, she'd moved on? She was obsessive when it came to her projects, that was like one of her key features. Had they locked her up or worse, and they were just lying to me?

But what would they gain with a lie like that? Not like they were trying particularly hard to spare my feelings so far.

Had she bought into their coup? Alastaroth talked like she was amenable to it. Honestly, I couldn't envision her caring too much about politics outside of how it influenced her artistic pursuits. Even still, if she was on their side, that was one more reason it should be fine to let us meet, not a reason to turn me away.

Unless she really had moved on completely and didn't want to finish our work together? That would make the most sense for anyone else. But I'd seen the gleam in her eyes when I was feeding her inspiration, and more recently, the desperation as she succumbed to the belief that her mind was leaving her. If anything, that combination should make her more eager to see me again, not less.

I felt another quick jolt of guilt at that thought — which, frankly, surprised me that I could still feel guilty about anything given the situation. But Sidona's false belief that her faculties were failing was due to her witnessing my faltering, fumbling first attempts at magic. I didn't dare explain before and put myself at risk, but now the point seemed moot. If nothing else, that was one more reason I needed to force a meeting with the duchess, to explain myself and set her mind at ease. I owed her that much, at least, whatever else the balance of our personal debts may be.

And so I went to bed again more determined than ever to find a way to force an audience with the duchess. No new ideas on how to accomplish that presented themselves, granted, but maybe blunt force and repetition would win out before I'd outlived my usefulness and they killed me. Or maybe some brilliant new tactic would reveal itself. Either way, all I could do now was wait and watch and bide my time.

It was easier said than done. Magical study time with Alastaroth may have been more academically stimulating than I'd expected, but it was also the only thing that happened to me anymore besides meal delivery and sleeping. If I'd had any grasp of time beforehand, it was long since lost now; my new routine was waking up when a guard came in with food, eating, then brooding and plotting until Alastaroth and his personal guards came by to have me study and transcribe and translate for him. Each time, I brought up my insistence that I be granted an audience with the duchess. Each time, I was rebuffed with decreased patience.

"Kriseia, then?" I argued after one such attempt. "My Luxuriate companion you guys took away. Can I at least see that she's alright? That you didn't dump her body in a ditch or something without telling me?"

"Don't worry, Morgan," Alastaroth snapped, "if we did such a thing, I would be sure to tell you all about it in great detail. Your companion is being kept somewhere suitable. Duchess Sidona is where she needs to be, doing what she needs to be doing. As are you. As are all of us. Trust that our new system is working as intended — or, barring that, at least stop pestering us about it."

That was after our fifth or sixth such translation session, and the wait until the following one was longer than usual. I was getting under the raspy little asshole's skin, I presumed.

Was that good for me? Or was I digging myself into a hole? I couldn't tell anymore. I had no other plan, no grand scheme, no way out of this. I'd taken to pacing circles around my room, resisting the urge to just bang my head against the wall until something useful happened.

After eight or nine or ten visits from the Invidiate lordling, my worry grew even more. I'd been loading up my brain with disorganized snippets of spellcraft, but without my own way of organizing them, without my own copy of the work to record or revisit my discoveries, the new knowledge I was gaining was starting to leak out again. It didn't help that most of the sigils I deciphered were connective tissue, things that seemed useful in the right context but didn't seem to do much on their own.

Maybe I could have started to assemble them into something useful, some functional magical sentence of power, but the fine details were growing too fuzzy in my mind to reliably string together. I'd attempted a few times to cobble new spells together in my downtime, or to alter the spells I already knew with my latest findings; but it was like being handed pieces of a machine one gadget at a time with no instructions or framework to hang them on, and now the gadgets were being taken away again as my mind failed to hold onto them. I didn't know what it was possible to build yet, and now whatever possibilities may have existed in front of me were slipping by.

I still had the secret Excalibur rune, my hopeful ace in the hole — but no clear way to deploy it yet. If I could just find a clear opportunity to bust it out, I knew it would get results. But how? It was undeniable willpower in a transcribable, actionable form, but it wasn't a complete action on its own. It was like a noun, or a modifier to a noun, but it wasn't a full clause in itself. Maybe I could weave it into a spell to make it unfailable, but it needed to be the *right* spell, because I only got one chance to whip it out against my enemies before the surprise wore off. And if I didn't wield it just right, that would be the end of me, and probably Kriseia too.

It was a magic bullet. I had to be careful where I aimed it. And before that, I had to build the right gun for it.

These new magical studies had presented my best chance at doing just that. But Alastaroth, damn him, was doing too good of a job compartmentalizing the data I was feeding him so that I couldn't feed it to myself as well. Did he plan these sessions that way? Did he have that much competence with the *Morganomicon* already? Or was he getting lucky?

It didn't matter. It was working. I was losing. I was running out of time.

Desperation was dangerous. The ideas I was getting lately, the closest things I was formulating to plans, were getting more and more unlikely and self-destructive. I lay in bed, staring up at the canopy, wondering how my captors would respond if I threatened to harm myself if I didn't get my way. It would be inconvenient for Alastaroth's purposes, sure, but I couldn't convince myself it would be worth the risk. "Go ahead," I imagined him sneering at me.

It would be a bluff, and he'd surely call it. Scared and worried as I was getting, I wasn't so hopeless that I was willing to risk my own life on a last throwaway chance at success. I wouldn't give them the satisfaction. There were people still relying on me here, people back home wondering where I'd gone. No way was I leaving everyone I cared for hanging like that.

Also, I really, really didn't want to die. That was honestly motivation enough not to do anything too crazy.

That said, if this pattern kept up for too long, it wouldn't be up to me anymore. Alastaroth had agreed to let me go back home once I'd helped him master spellcraft enough to invade Earth or whatever, but I didn't exactly trust him to keep his word there. And even if he did, I don't imagine my prospects back on Earth would be too great as the person that helped facilitate a demonic invasion.

I was screwed. I was well and truly screwed. And the certainty of that fact was maddening.

It came to a head in the bathroom one day. I had just finished toweling off and was staring at the mirror, jar of some turquoise cleaning goop that I'd been using as shampoo in my hand, and the absurdity of what I was doing hit me all at once. Here I was still trying to condition my hair while my own doom marched closer and closer with each passing minute. I wasn't even sure that what was in this jar was soap-related at all, that's how little clue or control I had left.

The jar was shattering against the wall before I realized I'd thrown it, glass and blue goo exploding with a cathartic crash. It was petty and pointless, but it was an action I could control, one with a noticeable result.

I stomped over to the shelf of colored containers, grabbed another at random, and let it fly. It was a more delicate smash this time, a vial of thinner glass, and the contents that splattered against the wall were a clear and aromatic light green, with a smell like sweet lemons.

Still felt good. Calmly, wordlessly, I chucked another jar, then a bottle, then vial, on and on, steadily running through the contents of my bathroom shelf and making beautifully colored music.

It was impotent rage that drove me, yes, but my nerves felt strangely placid while I rained destruction against the wall. Was this how Enkida felt all the time? It was an oddly comforting thought. It might have worried me how enjoyable this methodical violence felt if she hadn't made it look so cool.

My hand paused with a new jar cocked beside my head, ready to go. I stopped and looked at this one, curious. Something about it was off.

It was heavier than most, the contents brown with a sickly green tint. There was a label affixed to the front of it, the handwritten demon words unreadable to me. I unscrewed the metal cap; inside, submerged in the center of the thick brown sludge, another vial poked through. I pulled it free to find what looked like a test tube of thin, milky gray liquid, the glass stopper sealed tight with wax. The brown stuff, now disturbed, wafted it's strong, pungent scent up against my face, smelling faintly of smoke and strongly of… meat?

I sniffed again. Yes, smoky, and faintly bitter, and weirdly savory, like roast meat. A very red roast meat. Was this gravy? Why did I have bathroom gravy? With an included milky chaser? Who the hell —

Oh shit, I knew what this was! My walk through Dis by myself, the Gulliate farmer with the spider cows! I didn't remember his name, but I remembered his marketing ploy now, and the weird ass gift I'd brought back from the encounter.

Ushi-oni poisoned gravy. The deadly venom gave the flavor an extra kick of danger. It was perfectly safe though, he'd said, so long as I also took the included antidote after the meal.

I'd forgotten I had this novelty condiment, and somewhere along the way, either I or Kriseia or whoever came in to search my room after the coup had gotten it mixed up with the other jars and bottles of self-care fluids sitting around the place, and presumably that's how it ended up on the bathroom shelf.

I couldn't believe I was having this thought, but hell yeah, I could use this gravy.

The next time Alastaroth showed up, I was already sitting at my desk with the open jar in my hand. "Hey," I said, raising it to him in a toast. "Bring me Sidona for a minute or I'm drinking this."

The invidiate and his guards paused in the entryway. "A strange ultimatum to start with," Alastaroth said, eyes narrowing. "The more you insist on this pointless line of inquiry, the less inclined I feel to acquiesce. And I began with zero inclination."

I spun the jar so the label faced him. "You know what this stuff is?" I asked.

Several of his pupils flicked across the face of the jar. "You're threatening me with a condiment?" he asked with a sniff. "Not your most intelligent move, if I'm being honest."

"I'm all out of intelligent moves," I said, which was almost the truth. "I'm also all out of the antidote, so things are about to get complicated if you don't cave and do me this one favor finally."

Alastaroth regarded me for a tense moment. "You wouldn't," he said, predictably. "You'd be knowingly throwing your life away for no—"

I didn't let him finish, or give him time to sic an Iriate on me before I could commit. I just knocked back the poison sauce like I was doing a particularly high-stakes shot.

One of the guards did snatch the jar from me then, but it was too late, I'd already gulped down a mouthful. Honestly? Kinda tasty.

Alastaroth was staring wide-eyed at me, and with the number of eyes he had, it was an impressive expression. I smacked my lips at him. "Tangy," I said. "Got a cool, tingling aftertaste. Yeah, I can see the appeal now. Put that on some ribs and—"

"Give me that!" the Invidiate snapped, stomping forward and taking the jar from his guard. He frantically read the label again, peeled it off and looked at the blank back, peered into the jar, and finally fixed me with a glare. "You have the antidote," he declared. "You wouldn't be this foolhardy if you didn't. Not now, not after waiting this long to pull a stunt like this."

He wasn't certain. I could hear it in his raspy, shitty voice.

"If I had any," I said slowly, leaning forward, "it would be hidden somewhere only I knew about, masked by magic that you haven't learned yet. Along with the other servings of ushi-oni poison that I set aside in case you didn't want to take me seriously. Now..." I sat back in my chair, elbows on the desk behind me, and crossed my legs in one of those girl-boss power poses. "I admit, I don't know how long the venom takes to kick in and do damage. If you want to race the clock on it, you can toss my room and try to find an antidote that may or may not exist. Or — and this seems like the quicker and easier route to me — you can go get Duchess Sidona and bring her here, and I'll take this hypothetical antidote myself to save you the trouble. And then, this is the best part, we can put this argument behind us for good and get on with the research without any further drama, which is what you'd really, *really* like to do at this point."

Alastaroth glared and fumed and said nothing. I coughed for emphasis. "You filthy, scheming, underhanded human parasite," he grumbled at last, fingers clenched tight around his staff. "If you think your leash is tight now, after a stunt like this, I swear—"

"Tick tock, Al," I interrupted, pointing at a nonexistent watch on my wrist. "Oh, right, that probably doesn't mean anything to a demon. I'm dying slowly, is what I'm trying to communicate. You should hurry."

He took a deep breath through his nose and loosed it in a wordless noise of frustration, then spun to the furthest of his guards. "Fetch Duchess Sidona immediately, by order of Archfiend Abdeles!" he ordered. "She'll be in her tower quarters. Drag her down here bodily, if need be." The Iriate hurried off, and the Invidiate spun back to me. "And you," he rasped, "you will live to regret this, human."

"If you follow my instructions for a change, yes, I will," I answered. "I'm blaming you for such a simple request escalating this hard, though, just so you know. This meeting really could have been an email, Al."

"Shut up," he snapped.

That was it for our conversation until his guard returned, Sidona in tow. She was resplendently dressed in an ostentatious gown with a foot-tall collar and a tail that trailed a full three feet behind her, bejeweled charms hanging from shimmering threads tied around her horns. And as had become the norm with her lately, beneath the fancy clothes and accoutrements, she looked like shit: deep bags and dark circles beneath tired, dull eyes, her high cheekbones accentuating how sallow her face had gotten of late. She looked bored and detached as she was escorted through the door, and her expression didn't change as she looked at or through me.

"There," Alastaroth spat. "Now say whatever piece you need to say and let's be done with it."

"That's the plan," I told him. "Once you get outta here and give us some privacy."

His fist clenched around his staff again. "You're either joking or pushing it."

"No," I said, "I'm dying. Get out or I'll keep dying."

"You're what?" Sidona asked, snapping back to reality at last, concern and anger replacing her dead-eyed expression. "No, you'd better not be. That wasn't part of our deal, insect," she added with a haughty glare at Alastaroth.

The Invidiate grumbled under his breath and waved his arms at his guards, who filed out of the room. He followed, pausing beside the duchess. "She *has* the antidote somewhere, I'm sure of it," he said. "Make sure she takes it before you're through with whatever is going on here."

"You stunted little gremlin," the duchess responded with even more venom than I'd just ingested, "if you've done something to endanger my muse…" But Alastaroth, ignoring her, was already out the door. With him gone, she turned her ire on me. "What is this?" she demanded. "What did you do?"

I held up a finger. "One sec," I said, then hurried into the bathroom and pulled the antidote vial from its hiding place inside one of my remaining unsmashed bottles of cosmetic jelly. It was a makeshift hiding spot at best, I'll admit; the first bluff that Alastaroth had called hadn't been a bluff, but a lot of what I'd said afterward was. Maybe I should take this new poker face to Vegas when I got back home.

Sidona watched with crossed arms and a cross look on her face as I came back with the vial and took a shot of the antidote. It was cold going down, with an invigorating vapor that wafted through my sinuses as a chaser, chilly and cleansing. I shook my head and blinked hard as it burned through me. "Damn," I said aloud, "it's like shotgunning mint extract. Am I supposed to drink the whole thing? I only had a mouthful of the poison sauce."

"The antidote-to-sauce ratio is equal across containers, if you bought from a legitimate supplier," Sidona said. "If you consume half the jar of poison, you need half the vial of antidote, and so forth. Also, what the fuck, you poisoned yourself just to talk with me? I am equal parts flattered, confused, and annoyed."

"Thanks, I'm making it all up as I go," I said, tucking the rest of the antidote vial into my pocket. "He wasn't gonna let us meet if I didn't do something drastic. Said you were too busy for me, focusing on more important projects."

"He wasn't exactly wrong. Now, what's so important that it could possibly merit such a response?"

"I dunno, how about everything everywhere right now?" I gestured wildly with my arms at the room, the palace, generally all of Hell. "There was a coup, Vambrace is gone, I'm a political prisoner. Did you notice? I know you like to keep your nose buried in your work if possible, so you can say you didn't notice if you need to, it honestly wouldn't surprise me."

Sidona sighed. "Rather a lot of change all at once, yes. Nobody has the luxury of not noticing, least of all me. My current work concerns the shift in our societal zeitgeist. I'm sorry for you if this is hard to hear, but it's true, the projects that you were consulting on have been postponed for the time being. Don't worry, your portrait is finished enough that I can use a luxuriate doppelganger to smooth out the last of the —"

I grabbed her by the front of her gown, staring up at her with my best serious stare. "Sidona, I am going to die before all of this comes to a head, unless you help me out. That's why I pushed so hard to talk to you like this. I have nobody else left that I can turn to."

She rolled her eyes and placed her hands on mine, pulling them off of her outfit. "You're not going to die, Morgan," she said. "Not now, and not once Abdeles' little interdimensional plan is finally realized either. You're going to be given to me as a gift, much like your little Luxuriate companion was to you. I was very insistent upon that fact."

"What?" I asked. "That's not what they told me. Nobody told me that." I backed up, brow furrowing, considering the possibility. It was an unexpected loop, for sure. "The agreement I'd made with Alastaroth was that I'd be sent home to Earth once the door was open, but I doubt he'd actually go through with that deal once he's got what he needs from me. Those guys hate humans. Why would they agree to let me not only live but stick around the palace? I know you're a celebrity duchess and all, but how'd you swing that?"

Sidona crossed her arms and shrugged. "That was the price I'd named for my help in recent events. Well, one part of many prices I'd named. I was always going to be a very busy and influential cultural figure for the rest of my life, but now that body of work will span two whole planes of reality. The least I'm owed for that is an assistant and advisor on the new world we'll be conquering."

"So you're… on board with the invasion plan, then," I said, heart sinking. "Shit. Wait, prices? Plural? And what help?"

"You are rambling, my lady," Sidona replied, pinching the bridge of her nose. "I feel for you, I do, change is always stressful. But we will have all the time in the world to work together once Abdeles's portal is successfully opened and the invasion of Earth kicks off. Your work for Alastaroth the 72nd and his cohort will be over, and ours can begin again.

Until then, however, I really must be — "

"You don't just approve of the plan, you're *helping*," I said, thinking aloud as the full scope of what she said settled on me. "Why, and how? What could possibly be worth letting these assholes use you like this?"

She rallied at that, drawing herself up to her full height, the pride that was her House's namesake filling up the room. "Use me?" she accused, advancing a step toward me. "Excuse me, *use* me? My lady, if I did not know you better, I would demand satisfaction from such a crass insinuation! Nobody *uses* the great Duchess Sidona! Not an archdemon, not an upstart new regime, not even a fledgling new archfiend too incompetent to seize power on his own! You think *Abdeles* had the spine to kickstart such a momentous event on his own accord? You think his bootlicking little scholar shadow has enough brains in his withered head to see the opportunity laid before them and craft such an efficient, ambitious plan on his own? Any success those two fools have had, any they still stand to gain, they owe *entirely* to me, to my generosity at allowing them to capitalize on the scraps of my genius!"

I took a slow, deep breath and closed my eyes. The magic was already weaving around me in anticipation of what I was afraid I was about to hear, but it was a subtle spell, a quiet one, and I think both of us were too deep in the moment to notice any visual signs of it. "Sidona," I said slowly, opening my eyes. "From the top. Just to be crystal clear. What. The *hell*. Did you do?"

She shrugged, as if it were the simplest thing in the world. "Everything," she said. "Everything that required any modicum of thought or talent, anyway. Abdeles was terrible at hiding that little book of yours that he found in Mammonis, or the fact that he had no idea what it was or how to go about deciphering it. But when you showed me your own notes, my lady, those songs you claimed to be writing, I realized it was the same script as was in his contraband book. And once I approached him with *that* tidbit, and he gave me the book to peruse myself, I realized he'd stumbled upon something far bigger than he knew. So, in that respect, I suppose I do owe you an apology for being the first one who outed you as a practitioner of magic."

"Can't help but notice there was no actual apology in there," I said.

Sidona smirked. "Given how things have turned out so far for me, it's hard for me to actually feel bad about it yet. So I suppose that I'm sorry that I'm not as sorry as I should be."

I clenched my fists. I wasn't done weaving my spell yet, though, so for now, I had to keep her monologuing. "So, you can read the *Morganomicon* too, huh?" I asked instead.

She chuckled. "Is that what you're calling it? Cute. But yes, it was a... strangely enlightening experience, all of that jumbled squiggly nonsense suddenly coalescing into a language. The translatory potential for such a language is staggering, and I'm sure I'll need to explore it in the near future when it's time to introduce my written works to your people. Still, one thing at a time. Oh, and don't let the Invidiate know that I can read it clearly; I didn't tell him, and I don't have the time to translate for him or teach him what he's looking for. Far too busy."

"Did you plan everything?" I asked. "The fire, the assassinations, the ambush on me and the general? Are you the reason Enkida is dead?"

She sighed. "No, the fine military details were left to Abdeles and his allies in the army," she said. "I can't make you believe me, and I suppose it doesn't matter either way; but for what it's worth, I do regret what had to happen to our dear general for the plot to come to fruition. She was a fascinating exception to the norm, but she was clearly also the lynchpin in Vambrace's power, so I understand why she had to go."

"Bitch," I spat quietly. "Smug fucking cunt. Why would you do any of this? For the 'inspiration?' Are you really that desperate for a bigger audience? Are you really so out of ideas that you need to start whole cataclysms just for something new to do?"

"Ideas, no, but I *am* out of time," she snapped back. "So yes, Lady Morgan, thank you for getting to the heart of the matter — I am desperate. Desperate and, I'm loathe to admit, terrified." Her gaze turned to the floor, and sure enough, fear almost completely replaced the smugness in her expression as she spoke. "You have no idea what it's like," she said, almost mumbling now. "You can't know, you're not one of us. Solitusia is worse than death when it finally manifests in full. I watched some of the greatest minds of my youth succumb and go mad; the songwriters and artists and writers that inspired me to become who I am today, too many of them ended their lives stumbling through crowds and their own homes, insensate to the world around them, crying out for recognition they could no longer feel."

She started pacing, one of her hands gripping the front of her gown, the other fiddling with a string of gems hanging from one of her horns. "It saps the world from you until you're alone in your own mind, the only person left in a void of darkness and silence. And you know still, on some level, that others are around you, that there is a world of people and things just beyond your grasp, watching you lose everything, maybe even reaching out to you; but more than that, you know, you *know*, that none of that matters, because to you, there is only loneliness, pure and complete, for the rest of your future. And the only release from that living terror is to make the end official and remove yourself from the void as well, and you go to your grave a shell of the person you clawed and scraped your way into being, any past accomplishments rendered meaningless in the agonizing wake of being the only person left in your entire world."

She stopped pacing then, raising her eyes to stare through the wall at the far end of the room — like I wasn't even here anymore, appropriately enough. "But I will not go quietly into that looming prison in my own mind," she continued, more heat in her voice now. "Maybe I can't stop its encroach, but by every devil living or dead, I will leave such a mark before it claims me that nobody, in this world or the next, will ever be able to overlook me, to ignore that I was here and that I triumphed! And when Abdeles and his cronies have finished playing their parts in my plan, I will have the inspiration of two whole worlds to draw upon, and an audience spanning multiple dimensions to appreciate my work, my life, my legacy!" Her voice was growing, and she actually raised both her hands in a dramatic flourish to an imagined crowd. "The biggest, the most important, most life-changing event in the history of both our dimensions, and I, Sidona of House Superbia, will be its key chronicler, the voice and vision of a legendary time, capturing every event and emotion and happenstance in music and marble, on canvas and the stage!"

I gave her a moment. She was lost in the grandeur of her soliloquy, breathing hard and, for the first time in a long while, eyes shining. It would have been a heartening sight maybe an hour ago, before her bombastic villain reveal.

"That sounds terrible, Sidona," I said flatly after a moment. "It really does. And I would feel horrible for you, if you weren't spouting complete bullshit."

"Hmph." She spun back to me, her haughty mantle resumed. "Maybe you can't appreciate the brilliance of my machinations, but I assure you, it will—"

"Not your evil scheme, dumbass, your pointless crisis! You're not losing your mind, that was me!"

That visibly knocked the wind from her smug sails. "What?" she hissed.

"I'm magical, idiot! You know that now! You couldn't perceive me because I didn't want you to!"

"You..." Her shoulders slumped, her gaze on the floor again. "But... when I looked harder, I could..."

"Yeah, then you could see me, cuz I wasn't very good at it at the time. We're both stumbling fuck-ups who keep coming up with bad ideas. Mine was trying to sneak out of a palace I didn't know my way around and ending up in your room. Yours was getting confused for a minute and orchestrating a *goddamned interdimensional invasion about it*!"

"I'm not...?" Sidona mumbled, honest to goodness tears welling in her eyes. "I'm not going to...? Oh...!" She collapsed to her knees on the floor — weirdly elegantly given how far she had to travel to reach it. "Oh, thank the devils! I have so much still to do!"

"No, you shortsighted asshole, you don't," I said, squatting down beside her. "Because you're about to start a massive, massive war, and now you're stuck living through it. Maybe humans aren't the Original Sin like Vambrace had been claiming, but you know what we *are*? Really good at finding new and efficient ways to kill each other. And if you kick in the door and march into Earth with a literal demon army, you're going to get absolutely stomped. You have swords and spears and bows and shit? We have guns and bombs and tanks. Maybe you don't know what those words mean right now, but you'll find out *real* fast. How close can a pissed off Iriate get to an explosion the size of this whole city before their anger armor doesn't matter anymore, do you think?" I leaned in closer for emphasis. "Whatever you think this new era you're bringing will look like, the truth is that it will be incredibly violent and incredibly short lived, and demonkind is going to be on the losing side."

The duchess took a deep breath and rose to her feet, with me following. "Fair points, Morgan," she said. "Fine. Let's assume you're correct, that my mind is sound and our armies are not. The importance of the moment will still remain. There will still be great works to be done, events to document. There is still merit in allowing this to happen."

She wasn't looking at me as she spoke, though. She wasn't sounding so sure anymore in her words. I'd shaken her. If I kept shaking, maybe she could fall.

"And is it really any difference to the work if the audience for it at the end is human or demon?" she continued. "Perhaps humanity would even be preferable. Fresh eyes and ears and minds, who can appreciate it all the more for being new to it. And if there is no place for another great demon artist to arise after me, then… all the more security for my legacy, yes?"

"No," I said, "because no human will give a shit about your artistic merit, they'll just want you dead and this place destroyed. All of it, including everything you've ever done. You will disappear along with all of your own history, and demonkind as a whole will only be a conglomerate footnote in ours as a threat that came out of nowhere and was crushed back to nothing just as quickly. It's a dumb plan, Sidona, and you will lose everything if it succeeds. Which is why, instead, you're going to help me make sure it never gets that far."

"Help you?" she repeated. "Help you undo all of my hard work? That's a bold request, my lady, even given recent revelations."

"It's not a request," I said. "It's an order." And I pressed play on the spell I'd been building around myself.

"An order?" she repeated with a sneer, drawing herself up again. "You have the gall to think to *command* me, Morgan?" The pride was back in her countenance, then spilling into the room — her Superbiate power, raw intimidation and awe radiating out from her like the heat of a roaring fire suddenly burning in her gaze. "I am fond of you, human, make no mistake, but how *dare* you speak to me like that! Misled or not, I am *Duchess* Sidona, and you are a prisoner out of her depth right now! Why would I deign to take orders from you?"

The waves of her intimidation plowed into me, washed over and around me — and didn't touch me. Shell magic, the basis of shielding myself from specified effects, was the first trick I'd learned, even before I knew I'd learned it. It was the part of my heat spell that protected me from hurting myself, and the part of my unnoticeable spell that protected me from others' perception. With the right variable plugged in, it could theoretically protect me from any number of things.

And, as it turned out, with the enchantment magic from Excalibur plugged in, it guarded my will against hers, and let me cut through her psychic onslaught like the prow of a ship plowing through the waves of obedience she was unleashing.

I kept my feet and stared her down, unmoving, until I saw the confusion cross her face. "Because," I answered then, "you know now what I can do to you if you don't."

Her glare intensified, the force of her power doubling. "Is that a threat?" she asked slowly in a low, icy tone.

Double nothing was still nothing. I raised my hands and, with the ease of long practice, lit them on fire with a thought. "It's a goddamn promise," I growled.

Our impasse lasted only a few seconds while we stood there and glared at each other. My glare was better; I had a willpower buff, and I was holding fireballs. It didn't take long.

Without another word, Sidona spun on her heel and bolted toward the door.

I honestly didn't think that was the tack she would take. But I knew it was a possibility, and the closest thing she had to a smart move if she was still going to resist. So I was ready.

She hadn't made it two steps before I flung myself at her, tackling her around the waist and sending us both sprawling to the ground. Even then, she might still have gotten away, except that the train on her fancy-pants gown was so ridiculously long. I clung to it and dragged myself up its length to her, the fabric singing and smoking with every handful. I paid it no mind.

Sidona did, though. "Are you crazy?" she wailed beneath me. "Let go of me, you savage witch! Ah!" She stopped trying to crawl away, twisting to instead swat desperately at her smoldering dress. "I will not be killed like this!" she shouted. It still sounded like a demand. "I will not burn at the hands of an uncouth—"

I reached her face and clamped a hand over her mouth. I'd turned the fire off on this one first, but I made sure it was still nice and warm against her lips, as a helpful reminder. "Shut up and listen to someone else for once in your life, Sidona," I growled, straddling her waist and keeping her pinned — more out of momentum than actual force, since lord knows I wasn't going to crush seven feet of demon with my five-foot ass. "You're going to help me for the same reason you've ever done anything in your life — because it's in your own best interest. Because you can do it without getting found out, and it will make you look good. Make for a more interesting story, too, since you seem to care so much about that. But you're also going to help because, if you don't, Lucifer as my witness, I will burn you and everything you've ever created to the fucking ground before they catch me. I've got nothing left to lose at this point, thanks to you. But we both have everything to regain, if you play nice and *do what I fucking tell you to*. Got it?"

God help me, but the fear in her eyes at that moment was so incredibly satisfying to see. I couldn't even muster an attempt at feeling bad about it, not right now. I just watched and drank it in while I waited for a response.

It took her a while to give in entirely — she had her reputation to think about, I suppose — but after a minute, she nodded against my hand, her breathing still quick and panicked.

I smiled. "Good girl," I said, letting go of her mouth. "Now, here's what I need. Alastaroth wants to summon something before he turns the portals to Earth back on, yeah? He said something to that effect, I think, but I've heard so many evil plans lately, it's starting to run together."

Sidona nodded again. "The Original Sin," she said quietly. "The real one. If any member of that race still exists on any plane, he wants his hands on one, as a figurehead and a rallying point for demonkind to fall in line with the new regime. And to satisfy a lifelong academic obsession of his. Probably more that latter one, honestly. It would be a symbol, not a necessity."

"It's necessary now," I said. "Where's this happening? How do I get in on it?"

"The bottom of Pandemonium," she answered. "The Abandoned Throne. We've seen it now, with Vambrace gone, and it is…" There was a moment when the stress of her situation melted away, wonderment replacing it. "It is glorious," she breathed. "A testament to our fallen greatness. To be in its presence was a religious experience that I am still trying to capture—"

I smacked her, but gently. "Focus," I commanded.

That brought her back with a sneer on her lips, but a quick flash of warmth from my hand cut off any snipey comment she was preparing to make. "It's also the closest site we have to a convergence of other worlds," she continued, "even moreso than the abandoned and destroyed gateways scattered throughout the city. Even without any magical awareness, it's evident once you're near it how flimsy your sense of reality can be. Also, if the Throne itself is any indicator, it's the only space in the palace large enough to house a member of the Original Sin, if the summoning works."

"Ominous," I said. "I'd be scared of that, but the summoning won't work."

"How can you be sure?" she asked.

"Because I'm going to fuck it up," I said. "I need you to get me Alastaroth's blueprint for whatever sort of spell he's prepping to do this, so I know how to hijack it. And if I get any indication that you're not going to bring it back to me, or you're going to try and rat me out, or really any bad vibe at all about this, I'll pull the trigger on my promise and start burning my way toward your tower."

"Not necessary, my lady," Sidona said quickly, bringing her hands up palms out in surrender. "You've made your point abundantly clear. In fact, I admit, if whatever *you're* planning works, that would add a dynamic new angle to the narrative of events. Maybe I could—"

I slapped her again. "Art later, redeeming yourself now," I said. "I also need you to get me in the room when the summoning happens."

"You won't need my assistance for that part," said the duchess. "Alastaroth is going to require your presence, by force if necessary, for your assistance and your inevitable supplication once he succeeds."

"Ugh. Did he really say that?"

"In more flowery language, but yes, it was heavily implied."

"Well. Cool." I rolled off of her and rose to my feet, dusting myself off. "Duchess, I'm looking forward to working together again. Now get the hell out of my room and get me results. I've got to start getting ready."

Chapter 38: Temerity

"Getting ready" was mostly mental prep at this point — and for a day or so there, most of what I was prepping for was Sidona's inevitable re-betrayal. It was nerve-wracking watching her walk out the door right after our confrontation, and though she said nothing to the guard just outside, I didn't let myself fully believe I was in the clear at first. So I mostly ran through scenarios in my head of what I was charitably calling battle plans, flicking the fire on and off in my hands like an arsonist with a nervous tic.

I had a heat rune, a shielding rune, a perception blocker, and Excalibur's mega-buff. When they came for my head, I could probably take a good amount of them with me first. Maybe if Alastaroth was among them, I could also self-destruct the whole invasion plan as I died. Not a comforting thought, but it would be kind of heroic, which was something, right?

No. No, if I was being honest with myself, dying for a good cause still sounded like a worst-case scenario. I could understand where Vambrace's cowardice had come from, angry though I still was with him over it.

Miraculously, though, the next time my door opened, it was just Alastaroth and his usual two guards, plus a third one to hover even closer to me and glower down at my progress, as punishment for the poisoning stunt I'd pulled. I'd been kind enough to have the remaining poison sauce and antidote ready to surrender when they got here, but they still tore through my room before translation began. They didn't find any more contraband lethal substances, but they did commandeer several bottles from the bathroom, just in case. It hadn't occurred to me to threaten to eat soap, but better safe than sorry, I suppose.

They still didn't find the tiny scrap of paper with my Excalibur rune on it. Since finding it myself, I kept that thing closer and more secure than my own heart. At this rate, I'd be equally dead without either.

"See, Al?" I said once the search was completed. "I kept my word, like a good girl."

"Lord Alastaroth the 72nd to you, human," he croaked. "And if you're looking for praise after your insubordination, you're more addled than I believed."

"Not praise, just an understanding. You have the upper hand here, yes, and I'm playing nice, but I'm not going to roll over for you every time we have an argument. We're on the same side here, remember? You want to go to Earth, I want to go to Earth, we need each other's help to get there. Maybe next time I have a simple request, you remember that and we won't need the added drama."

"I hate you both on principle and, now, personally," he replied. "But if this truly was the extent of your tantrum, then perhaps you have a small, warped point. I must ask again, what in Hell occurred during your meeting with Sidona that was worth the immense trouble?"

"She didn't tell you?" I asked. "I was confirming the status of our work together, just like I said. And, yes, you were telling the truth, I'm not too proud to admit. Her previous projects that involved me are on hiatus while she pursues more pressing issues. We talked about possibly resuming them if there's time before I return to my own world." I didn't bring up Sidona's confession that Alastaroth had no intention of letting me go home. I remembered it as a strike against him, sure, but we didn't need the complication of that argument so close to go time.

"Hmph," he hmphed. "Then maybe the next time I give you an answer that doesn't suit your whims, you'll believe me instead of flying off the handle with your stubbornness."

I smiled sweetly. "Maybe," I said. "Looks like we both have trust issues. You know any good couples therapists?"

"You are being glib and obtuse again, and I don't care for it, human," Alastaroth grumped as he snatched a rolled paper from his Iriate valet. "Now, it's time we both got back to work. Prove your sincerity with your actions."

The second Iriate ferried the page over to me along with my writing tools, while the new third stood just outside my personal bubble and flexed silently. "I always do, Lord Al," I answered before focusing on the magic transcription.

Back to work, back to waiting. More translations that weren't quite usable. Still, I tried my best to ingrain each session into my own memory, just in case, and hope that nothing important was being overwritten without any notes of my own to reinforce them — and all the while, the make-or-break final exam was looming ever closer in the indeterminate future.

I couldn't get a break from school stress even during a fantasy adventure in another world. What a crock.

Days (I assumed) passed. They'd taken my MP3 player when they'd tossed my room, so I couldn't measure time anymore outside of my own anxious and restless perception of it. And since Alastaroth only showed up for my help sporadically as he needed it, meals and sleep became my only benchmarks for how long I'd been here. I stopped counting even those pretty early on; there was no guarantee they were feeding me on a set schedule, after all. I mean, I know my sleep schedule was shot all to hell with nothing to enforce it but my own boredom and mental fatigue.

Even worse, during all that time waiting, Sidona was nowhere to be seen. Had I put too much faith in how persuasive I'd been to her? Had she double-crossed me? Triple-crossed? But nobody was kicking in my door to put me under arrest even harder, so it didn't seem like she'd sold me out. Alastaroth and his cronies were acting the same level of disdainful as ever. Had she just quietly bailed, then? What was going on? Every hour that passed without her returning added to my mounting mountain of unease.

And then, finally, it happened. The door opened, and it wasn't the duchess or Alastaroth and his usual buddies walking through, but a whole mess of armored Iriates filing in to surround me. The time had come, ready or not.

I sighed as one of the Iriates produced a pair of metal shackles. "Are you serious?" I asked. "We're still doing this? After everything?"

"Apologies," the lead guard said. Maybe even meant it. "But yes, it's a necessary precaution. I'm sure you understand why."

"Breaking out of amateur bondage was literally the first thing I did when I got to this world," I grumbled as I held out my arms. "But fine, whatever gets this over with."

He seemed nervous as he slapped the cuffs on. But cuff me he did, and then I was marched out of my room and away amidst a ring of silent security.

I didn't realize that we were heading to Vambrace's quarters until the door opened and I saw the familiar furnishings. Or, most of them: the massive portrait of the triumphant human archfiend was gone, replaced by a smaller but still grandiose painting of Archduke Abdeles glowering down his nose at the room, surrounded by kneeling demons of every color on one side and kneeling humans of also every color, even a few that humans didn't come in, on the other.

"Subtle," I remarked aloud as we marched through the room. "The style looks different from the old one, though. Not one of Sidona's, is it?"

The lead Iriate, the one who'd apologized for shackling me, grunted. "The duchess has never painted any of the archdemons. 'Too pedestrian,' she says."

"Sounds like her," I said. We entered Vambrace's former bedroom, crossed through to the elevator in the back, and I squeezed into a closet-sized space with half a dozen burly Iriates all at once as their leader spun the handle and dropped us down into the depths of Pandemonium.

"Nobody fart," I said after a moment. "I'm the shortest one here, I'll get the worst of it."

None of them replied, but a couple turned to look at me. One looked offended. The other looked confused.

"Sorry," I said. "Just trying to lighten the mood. It feels a bit like I'm being marched to my own funeral."

None of them replied to that either. *Awesome. Just breathe, Morgan, we're almost to the end of it. For better or worse.*

I said "almost," but I'd forgotten just how long the elevator ride was to get to Vambrace's treasure vault — and even that was on one of the earlier sublevels, he'd mentioned. We were on our way to the capital-T Throne, the one we weren't allowed to talk about, that nobody but the archfiend was supposed to be allowed to see. Who knew how far down that was.

The Iriate cranking the handle did, apparently, because he spun the thing as fast as his arm allowed without any concern or any slowing down. Eventually, he let go, and for a moment I thought we were finally there. But no, he just switched arms and kept cranking while he shook out his first, cramping hand.

"This thing does have an end eventually, right?" I asked at that point, after what felt like fifteen minutes straight of descent. "We're not riding down to, like, the center of the world, right?"

"Pandemonium is the center of the world," the lead Iriate said. "No, we are headed to the bottom of the world. The ride does end eventually, yes."

"The deepest, darkest pit of Hell," I said with a strained smile and a shackled double thumbs-up. "Awesome. Love it."

"It's not dark," he replied, a gleam coming to his eye. "Not at all. It is… glorious. You'll see."

"Believe it or not, that's somehow even more ominous," I said.

With that thought hanging in my mind, and the ride still stretching on seemingly interminably, I could feel my anxiety building with every passing floor. Every minute crammed in that box was another minute of anticipation stretched and stretched and still not breaking.

Eventually, the Iriate on the handle switched out with another, who also wore out one arm before swapping. I felt like I'd been standing here for an hour already, the resonant swish of wind and stone outside the room not abating. We'd been dropping at full speed this whole time and we still weren't there. How was that possible? How was any elevator ride this long? How was any hole this deep? Were we even going anywhere, or was this all some elaborate, torturous prank at this point?

I took a deep, slow breath that tasted like the same breath I'd been breathing and rebreathing for an hour. "I think I'm going to scream," I said quietly, calmly. "This is getting ridiculous. How much further could we possibly —"

There was a clank from the elevator handle that nearly stopped my heart, the change was so sudden and so long coming. The Iriate working the lever let go and stepped back, and I watched as the spinning began to slow on its own. The shift in velocity was mildly stomach churning as we decelerated, the floor of the room finally hitting some sort of slight resistance. We were sinking more than plummeting now, the handle spinning down slower and slower like the hand of fate finally running out.

The moment the room clunked to a final stop was almost transcendent at this point. We all breathed an anticipatory sigh of relief before the door cracked and slid open — and light poured in.

All of us gasped, even the lead Iriate who'd clearly known what to expect. "Beautiful," he breathed, voice wavering. "It's so damned beautiful…"

Outside was another rough-hewn, uneven cavern stretching away in front of us, much like I'd expected, much like the last time I'd been to a lower level of the palace. But this far down, the red-veined black guilt that made up most of the walls and floor and ceiling of Pandemonium had been replaced — or maybe "subsumed" was the better word. There was no black to these walls, not anymore; instead, the tunnel before us pulsed with a bright, living crimson, a geological artery leading down into the heart of this place.

I could almost swear I heard breathing in the distance, and all around us, from above and below and beside. Pandemonium was *alive*. It was the only thing that made sense at this point.

My stunned reverie was broken by the cold, but calling it that was another disservice. The first sublayer, where Vambrace's vault was, *that* was cold, the all-over chill of a subterranean cave. Down here, this was beyond freezing, a platonic cold that felt like an invasive, smothering assault rather than just a total lack of warmth. My bones hurt, my eyes stung, my skin did nothing to shield me from it. It felt like every liquid in my body was about to seize up.

One massively miserable moment of that was more than enough; the warming spell flashed through my thoughts almost unbidden, but extremely welcome. I clamped my now-toasty hands close to my chest and consciously added the shielding sigil, extending it across my entire body and letting the warm magic flow across and suffuse me. The unnatural cold retreated, but I could feel it hovering just outside the edge of my spell, waiting for another opening.

I neither knew nor cared in the moment if my Iriate entourage could tell I'd just done some unauthorized magic; their disapproval was nothing in the face of potentially flash-freezing. But when I looked up at them to check, I realized it was a moot point. Every one of my escorts was staring forward at the sight before us, rapt and unblinking, a few frozen tears hanging in the corner of a few eyes. Was it their super tough biology keeping them from noticing the oppressive air, or just the force of their rapture? I couldn't tell.

It took me stepping through the door first to break the spell, my guards shaking themselves back to the present task at hand as I walked unaccompanied a few feet into the pulsing red tunnel.

Way, way up where Vambrace kept his human garbage museum, I remembered the constant tinkling of soul crystal dropping out of the ceiling and sinking down through the walls and floor, like a light drizzle of gemstones on a journey to somewhere deeper. But this deep, here at the bottom, there was none of that, not even a trace of stray soul breaking up the complete uniformity of living crimson. No distant light tinkling of stone on stone, only the faint sound and even stronger sensation of the rock around us breathing.

I shivered despite my heated magic shell. "What is this place?" I whispered aloud. "And what the hell is down here with us?"

The lead Iriate sighed heavily and happily as he walked up behind me. "You'll see," he said as he laid a hand on my shoulder — and then immediately yanked it away, staring at his palm as if he'd just touched a hot stovetop, though I knew the warmth I was outputting was nowhere near that level.

I shrugged. "It was either do some magic or freeze to death," I explained. "Figured you didn't want me dead just yet."

He only grunted. "Follow close," he said as he stepped past me, not touching me this time, and his crew fell into place around me.

We walked down a widening, uneven corridor of slowly pulsing red, like something out of a psychological horror flick. After the long, long standstill in the elevator, I welcomed the chance to stretch my legs again, at least. The ceiling and walls slowly, gradually pulled away the further we went, the semi-claustrophobic tunnel soon stretching into a spacious cavern that was growing even more spacious still with every step, until eventually, the walls spread so far apart on either side of us that they could have built an interstate through the tunnel, and the ceiling above would have seemed to disappear entirely if it weren't for the constant, thrumming red glow.

Unfortunately, every step deeper we took, that breathing sensation also intensified. Before long, I could feel the breeze on my face with every exhale — and the breeze on the back of my head with every inhale. In my peripheral vision, I could see strands of my own hair swaying back and forth with each alternating wind.

No bad breath smell, though. Maybe it really was just a weird wind? It was nice to pretend that was probably the case.

My honor guard continued to say nothing as we marched, but this time, it was less out of a professional disconnect and more out of reverence. I could tell when I looked up at any face around me and saw that same familiar glassy-eyed gleam in every eye. No anxiety there, only anticipation. Must've been nice.

Then, all at once, the distant walls around us disappeared entirely, opening into a stadium-sized space. The floor in front of us fell away as well, down into a bowl-shaped pit like a miniature replica of the city above us — and hanging from the center of the room, suspended over the pit, was what looked like a twisting, braided stalactite of pure soul crystal, impossibly thick at its base at the top, but tapering drastically to a sort of corded tree-trunk width before it disappeared over the edge of the cliff, like a mystical geological drill piercing down through the earth.

Or like a root ball, I realized. We were deeply and directly below Pandemonium right now. Was I looking at the tower's guts? Its arteries? Was this the *palace's* breath I was feeling washing over us?

We marched to the edge of the cliff, and every Iriate around me sucked in a rapturous gasp. I pushed past those in front and followed the flow of soul down into the center of the bowl, where they terminated in a massive obelisk of soul crystal with a raised platform jutting out from its bottom in the front, two thick walls rising up on either end to about half the height of the main obelisk. The slab, the platform, the walls, all of it shone with the milky, starry gleam of concentrated soul, so much so that a faint haze of a glow flickered at its edges like an aura of power. The base of the whole construction was embedded deep in the pulsing red floor, which climbed up round the edges of the thing in violent ripples like water frozen in time, like the soul obelisk had crashed down into the sea of red, and the floor was still mid-splash.

As I stared, I swear I saw the floor moving against the obelisk, suckling at the intrusion like a thing alive, like angry gums sucking tight to an implanted tooth.

"What the fuck is this?" I breathed as I stared at the alien scene before us.

"The Throne!" the Iriate beside me breathed in reply. His hands rose at his side, reaching toward the obelisk, shaking and grasping at the air. "The Abandoned Throne! Seat of power the first archfiend, the womb that birthed the Original Sin and all of demonkind! Is it not... *glorious*?"

He wasn't wrong, I had to give him that. The thick veins of glowing crystal, the massive chair-shaped shining structure they connected to, the great crater that housed it, the pulsing floor, the frigid gusts of breathing: this was some cosmically transcendental shit I felt like I was witnessing. Something larger than my comprehension was happening here. Something majestic and terrifying.

"I want to go home," I said aloud. Nobody around me heard or cared.

Down into the crater we went, descending steps that were way too regular and even to be natural, and way too deep down and massive to be demon-made. The Throne loomed, breathing at our approach. Or maybe it was the soul roots above it, or the gently writhing pit that it was sunk in, or the room itself, or some unseeable and incomprehensible presence nearby, I didn't know. I didn't care. The plan I'd had seemed like such a tiny folly now, and my mind struggled to recall it as I stepped closer and closer to the beating heart of Hell itself.

The ambiance was jarred somewhat, though, when we got close enough to see the crude rope ladder hanging down the side of the impossibly large seat of the Throne. And standing beside it at the bottom, a familiar face: Duchess Sidona.

I didn't know anymore if I was happy to see her or not.

"Lady Morgan Amell," she called out, smiling, as we approached. "Here at last. Magnificent, is it not? We here assembled are the first and only beings in eons uncountable, besides our past archfiends, to gaze upon the Throne of Hell. A momentous moment for us all."

I couldn't tell if she was putting on an act or if this was her genuine fervor. She had that same semi-glazed, faraway look in her eyes as my escorts, but this wasn't the first time I'd seen it on her; it was the same look I'd seen a few times before, when she was getting swept up in ideas for her artistic possibilities. So maybe this was just her being normal.

"Duchess," the lead Iriate guard said as we drew up, "shouldn't you be above, assisting Lord Alastaroth the 72nd?"

"I was, until I saw your approach," Sidona answered. "I wanted to welcome the lady of the moment in person. She is of course every bit the celebrity here as myself, wouldn't you say?"

A few members of my escort snapped out of their trance for a second at that, passing surprised glances at one another. I couldn't blame them; it was a weird sentence, coming from her.

"Thank you all for ensuring her safety on the trek down here," the duchess continued, then turned to me with a polite smile that was shockingly free of any obvious condescension. "Shall we, my lady?" she asked, gesturing at the ladder beside her. "After you, of course."

"We weren't…" the lead Iriate started. He paused to stand at attention and clear his throat. "Apologies, duchess, but there seems to be a misunderstanding. We are not an honor guard for the human here, we're to keep her in line and under surveillance during the ceremony."

"Nonsense," the duchess scoffed. "Is that what that stooped brown-noser led you to believe? She is instrumental to the plan and a willing participant like the rest of us. What need would there be to coerce her here?" Her frown deepened as she looked at me, her gaze landing on my shackles. "And what are those doing on her?" she demanded. "Remove them at once, you misguided fools!"

The Iriate leader had the same harried look of a part-timer being ordered by a belligerent customer to go against store policy. I could sympathize. "But… she is a human, and a practitioner of magic," he argued. "She is dangerous."

Doubt was creeping into his voice, though, and Sidona pounced on it. "We are about to open a doorway to an entire world full of humans," she said. "If you are so afraid of just one, however will you deal with whole settlements of them? Or are you still under the illusion perpetuated by our last archfiend that a single human is by definition more powerful than every other race of sin in Hell? An illusion which, I will remind you, we have all witnessed to be proven false."

"I…" He looked down at me, mouth drawn in a tight line. "Well…"

"If it makes the decision easier," I said, holding up my shackled wrists for inspection, "I can't climb with these on, so they gotta come off anyway. Unless one of you was planning to carry me up there."

"Absolutely not!" Sidona interjected. "Our distinguished ally, the only human shown to truly be on demonkind's side, and my own personal muse, hauled bodily into the Throne's glory like a sack of potatoes? I will not abide by that!"

"Wait, you have potatoes here?" I asked. "Holy shit, why hasn't that come up sooner, that would have made food so much easier! I didn't think they grew in Hell!"

Sidona quirked an eyebrow at me. "Are you serious?" she asked. "They're potatoes; they grow anywhere."

The Iriate leader, meanwhile, apparently gave up trying to follow along or fight back. Instead, he produced a key from somewhere in his armor and took the chain of my bindings in his other hand, unlocking and removing them, albeit reluctantly.

"Thank you, finally, someone listens," Sidona sighed. "Now, no more delays, we have history to make and a new age of enlightenment to usher in. Come, after you, my dear." I stepped past the surrounding Iriates toward Sidona's outstretched arm. She clasped my hand and pulled me gently the final few feet to the bottom of the rope ladder. "Careful with the first step now," she said, "the ground is a bit strange here at the edge of the world."

With her uncharacteristically proffered help, I stepped up on the first rung of the ladder and found my balance. The duchess smiled again as she released my hand and stepped back, leaving me to lead the climb to the top.

The small objects that she had surreptitiously passed to me with the gesture made grabbing the first wrung above me a little difficult. I didn't take the risk of even looking to see what they were, only quickly tucked them away into my outfit once I was sure my hands were out of sight of those below and behind me. They nestled, hard and small and slightly warm, against my skin as I clambered up the ropes, Sidona and the Iriates coming up after me.

I smiled as I climbed, a slight relief settling over me even as my heart still nervously pounded in my chest. She hadn't brought me what I asked, but she'd brought me… something, at least, which was more than I was beginning to hope for. For once, I was glad to find the duchess's priorities and loyalties as capricious as ever, even if I didn't know yet what form that was taking.

Two more guards were waiting for me at the top of the rope ladder, ready to help haul me the rest of the way up to the platform. As I crested the edge, it was hard to think of the view in front of me as the seat of a giant chair; the Throne stretched out in front of me, a plain of shimmering crystal, with the towering face of the back of the seat jutting up several stories above it, and a kaleidoscope of solid soul erupting from the top into the distant ceiling.

In the center of the seat stood Alastaroth, *Morganomicon* in hand, directing half a dozen other Invidiates who were all scratching at the ground in a wide, loose circle around him, leaving faint but legible marks on the Throne's surface. Further out from them, another dozen or more Iriates stood at attention, weapons at their sides. I headed toward my nominal co-conspirator to get a better look, stopping at the edge of the massive group art project in progress.

"It is safe to walk on," Alastaroth croaked at me from across the remaining space. "Only guilt can mar the surface of soul, and only soul itself can wipe the markings clean once again."

With that blessing telling me I wouldn't immediately be jumped or impaled, I walked across the crop circles in progress toward the diminutive demon standing at their center. All around us, his flunkies were doodling the familiar curves and whorls of old elven script across the surface of the Throne with sticks of red-black guilt, each one holding little reference papers for their section of the spell. Alastaroth must have trusted whatever instructions he'd written for them, because he kept his face buried in the *Morganomicon* as they worked.

"A summoning circle, huh?" I thought out loud. "Cool. Got a real classic, old school magic feel going here. I never got the chance to play with these myself."

"You summoned yourself to our world, did you not?" Alastaroth asked, looking up at me with a few of his pupils over the edge of the book. "How, then, if not through this method?"

"It was kind of a blur, honestly," I said. "And an accident. Maybe I should have done one of these? Maybe I would have, if I'd been careful enough to get that far before I tried it out." My gaze was wandering as I spoke, as I examined our surroundings, trying to absorb every detail for what had to happen next. As I was staring up the immense height of the back of the seat we were on, though, another thought struck. "Hey, Al," I said, "uh, real quick, if we're standing on a bigass chair right now... how big is this Original Sin you're summoning gonna be when it gets here?"

"Too much knowledge has been lost to be sure," he said, irritable again. "The Throne, the Original Sin, the origins of either, all of that is a lost and distant past, as has been explained countless times by now. We will know the details shortly."

"But are we about to be flattened under a massive demon ass, is my concern," I continued. "Should we, maybe, perhaps, move?"

"Enough!" he snapped. "The time for questions is over, Morgan. Now is a time for answers. *You* may move, and leave me to the work."

"You got it, boss," I said with a salute and a placating smile, then headed toward the outside of the circle toward the back of the Throne. If his intent was to summon something big enough to make this underground pit seem like a sensible size and crush us all, then that was one more reason I couldn't let him do it. As if I needed more.

As she watched me leave, Sidona broke off from where she was admiring the work over the shoulder of one of the laboring Invidiates to intercept me. "A grand achievement and undertaking, is it not, my lady?" she asked, loudly, as she looped her arm through mine. "You are certainly proud of your part to play in it, I'm sure." She smiled, leaned in closer, and, under her breath, said, "I couldn't get the blueprint to this without arousing suspicion. Don't take it personally."

"I believe you," I whispered back. "I'm just not happy about it."

"Do you have a backup plan?" she asked. "Because *I* can still save face, if not."

"Not without me, you can't," I said, tightening my grip on her arm. "We're sinking or swimming together, Sidona, so keep your head in the game. You cut and run, I start throwing fireballs."

Her rictus smile stayed plastered on her face as she sighed impatiently through her nose. "Fantastic. So, about that second plan that you definitely have?"

"I have a goal, is what I have" I whispered back. "Now that I'm here, I have better information. As for a plan..." With a quick check to make sure nobody who was looking our way was close enough to see, I tugged open the neck of my dress and peeked down inside at the small objects Sidona had palmed to me on the ladder.

A small lump of soul and a sliver of guilt nestled where I'd left them, the former's sparkling white reflecting the latter's dim red glow against my skin.

I paused in our walk, turned around, and looked at the whole of the summoning circle once more. The Invidiates were very nearly finished with copying it down, most of them already finished and waiting on the edge of the incantation. At a glance, the writing had looked familiar; looking over the entire thing stretching out away from me, I got a clearer impression of what it was meant to do.

And looking down at my feet, at the intricate designs traced beneath them, I recognized the details. The words themselves, the individual spell runes, the distinct synonyms that made up the magic. The same bits and pieces of magic I had been translating and transcribing, piecemeal and out of order, for Alastaroth during my house arrest, of course. But now they were assembled correctly, in sequence. Now they made sense.

Now I could read them.

I patted the little lumps hidden in my clothes — one an eraser, one a pencil. "Yeah," I said, and took a deep breath. "Holy shit, yeah. I have a plan. Here, walk me around the summoning circle. I need... I need to read."

The duchess smiled, made a sound of amusement, and tugged me toward the perimeter of the writing. "Imagine," she said loudly, proudly, "such a resource was so arbitrarily off-limits so soon ago, and now, after having access to it for barely a moment, we are ready to use it to usher in a new demonic golden age! And if a mere gathering of Invidiates can pull off this feat, imagine how much more powerful must our exalted progenitor be, once it successfully arrives?"

It was a good cover noise. It sounded like her; hell, she might even believe it, on some level. Myself, I was nodding along dutifully while I tuned the rest of it out and studied the notes beneath me like my life depended on it. The make-or-break exam was minutes away, and I was cramming harder than I'd ever crammed before.

It really was just one big note card written on the ground, I realized immediately. As fancy and elaborate and intimidating as any magical circle of gibberish I'd ever seen in a movie or video game, but I could comprehend this one, and it was little more than written instructions. The beginning of what amounted to this page of directions was in the center, at the foot of Alastaroth. The symbols that detailed how to tap into and gather the potential of the change to come. From there, the instructions spiraled around him, growing wider and further out as they went, functions nested within functions, key variables defined in the margins of the script as they entered the equation and became relevant.

Scratch note card, this was an entire cheat sheet, arranged so that the person casting the spell could stand at its center and just spin around to read it in full as need be. He was still holding the *Morganomicon*, but that must have been either out of protectiveness or habit or lack of confidence, because he didn't need it anymore. Everything he needed was written plain as day around him, in an easy to check spiral; even if he couldn't hold the entirety of the magic in his focus at once, he just needed to turn his head and he'd have it. Wouldn't he?

Wait... was he still bad at this? Or, more pertinently, was he at least still worse than I was? I had used a very similar spell to this to get here, after all, and I hadn't gone to this much effort to do it. Granted, I *had* been using the book to check at the time, and it hadn't worked right, so maybe I should have used a circle after all, but...

My eyes scanned every inch of the notation we passed by, the specifics growing more and more familiar in the re-reading. This wasn't just similar to the spell I'd accidentally cast on myself, it *was* that same spell, at its fundamental level. In my newfound hubris, I had left key variables undefined; here, now, in this version, every possibility was being carefully considered and detailed. But it was the same basic incantation, as every new step around it made more and more apparent.

This was the spell I needed to leave here. My ticket home. I had cast it before, alone, as a mistake, and now here it was again, with most of the work done for me already.

And I was better at this than the demon about to use it. I had more experience. I had a better grasp of the mechanics. I was the better magic student.

I could copy his answers. I could steal his work.

"…no doubt echo down eons untold," Sidona was still vamping. "Can you imagine the incredible achievements to come? The art, the music, the — oh, looks like it's starting now." She tugged me aside, off the summoning circle and toward the edge of the Throne, where Invidiate servants and Iriate guards alike were standing expectantly, watching Alastaroth in the center. He raised his hands, *Morganomicon* still held aloft in one of them, and, with half his eyes on the pages and half on the floor, began chanting something indistinguishable under his breath.

"Fuck!" I muttered, eyes skimming the spell between us. There wasn't the time or opportunity right now to rearrange all of this into something to send me home, but at the very least, I had to interrupt it. Sabotage it somehow, to keep him from trying this again after I was done. But how to do that without getting myself killed?

Frantically I read through the spell ahead of Alastaroth — potentiality, spatial weaving, output targeting, search parameters — looking for a change I could make with the time I had, something small but integral, some pivot point in the ideation somewhere that would work, something —

My eyes landed on a new symbol right in the middle of the process. Or, not exactly a new symbol. I had seen it before, references to it, in the design elements of Pandemonium, in the artwork displayed around the palace, a repeated background motif — seven concentric, interlocking rings all inside one another, an eighth wrapping around the middle fastening and binding them together. In context here on the floor, in a place of distinction, in a rune defining a subject and a goal, it made perfect, obvious sense.

The Original Sin. A transcription of the idea of it, anyway. Filling in the blank of the question being posed by the spell: "What are you trying to summon?"

"I've got one shot at this," I said, grabbing Sidona's arm and prying it from my own. "Cover me."

Without looking at her, without taking my eyes from the key rune in front of me, I stepped away from her and queued up a spell of my own.

Potential - gather; focus, self; ccver, body - make shield (awareness = nullify; if look, then forget); shield, cinch - make skin; focus, outward; intensity(total); potential = activate.

The magic weaved around me, the heating shield I'd had on before dissipating to make room for it. I shivered at the sudden, violent influx of cold air against my skin but pressed on.

The change in my actions, or maybe the change in temperature around me, or maybe some imperceptible sense that reality was being prepped to change around me — one or all of these things caught the attention of the Iriate guard standing nearest to us. "What are you doing?" I heard them demand from behind, growing closer. "Stand back and stand down, or else—"

"*You will not!*" Sidona's words cut through the air like an icy blade, startling me but cowing the soldier she'd interrupted. "How dare you attempt to embarrass me or my muse at this pivotal moment! Return to your place, dog, and stand still and silent, or Lucifer help me, I will see your miserable life ruined for your disrespect!"

Superbiate intimidation. I was used to the feeling by now, even if it wasn't directed at me. Useful and appreciated, for sure, but now her hand had been tipped. If this failed, she was going down with me, no question.

I won't say I wasn't surprised that her help extended this far. Well, better make the most of it.

The shield against perception clicked into place around me, bolstered as hard as I dared to make it given the urgency. It would buy me time, at least. Hopefully, it would buy enough.

I sprinted out across the summoning circle, toward the Original Sin glyph. Alastaroth hadn't reached this part of the process yet. There was still time — whole seconds, maybe a full minute, if my luck didn't run out before then.

I slid to my knees and skidded to a stop on top of the rune, the fabric of my dress tearing beneath me, then yanked out the two thin chunks of rock, one in each hand. My fingers scraped the solid crystal beneath me as I raked the soul chunk in my hand over the glowing symbol, wiping it out like chalk off a blackboard. Once most of it was cleared, I dropped the soul and paused for half a second with the guilt held just above the now empty space.

What to replace the summoning subject with? There was only one real answer available to me, only one that might have a chance of working. I took a deep breath and closed my eyes as I drew, recalling the new rune in question, focusing as hard as I could on its exact details.

Somewhere in front of me, Alastaroth's chanting faltered and stopped. "What...?" I heard him mutter. "Why can't I...? What is going on? Hey! What's happening over there?" I didn't dare look up until the rune was finished. When I did, I saw the Invidiate lord waving his hand at me, though he couldn't make his eyes land on me. "Guards! Investigate that space at once!"

The Iriates rushing toward him were searching frantically, but none of them were managing to focus on my position either. Unfortunately, I couldn't do the next part of this plan from this safe of a distance.

With a fearful voice in my head screaming not to do what I was doing, I stood and ran — directly at Alastaroth and his gathering guards. I needed to be where he was, after all.

Their heads jerked aside as I closed in, driving their attention aside like a wedge. But as I ducked past them, the spot where I had been was left open to scrutiny at last, and the guards rushed forward to where I'd been. Alastaroth stayed in place, angry and perplexed, sweeping the circle with his many different gazes.

I parked myself directly behind him and did the same, holding onto my unnoticeable shield for as long as I could while I fed a newer, heavier, more complicated slab of magic into my focus on top of it.

Potentiality, spatial weaving, output targeting, search parameters — all the new information of the past several minutes, but in order this time, actionable, not just understanding the process but enacting it. Deja vu shot through me here in the early stages of the spell, and for a moment, it was like I was back home, standing in the quad on campus, a mix of excitement and incredulity bubbling inside me, the nagging sense that this wasn't going to work and I was making a mistake playing with forces I didn't understand and shouldn't be controlling.

No floating feeling this time, though, no spikes of heat and chill as the magic kicked in. I wasn't the target of it this time. But that also meant I had no evidence it was working yet beyond gut feeling, beyond whatever confidence in myself I already felt and brought to the exercise with me.

It wasn't a lot, honestly. But it was enough.

Power settled over me, inside of me, like an infusing fog filling me up. I felt it, felt the change, the growing tide. Felt the world immediately around me loosen, felt reality slacken, just a bit, in preparation for a change. It's impossible to put into words that aren't the words of the spell itself, but… right there where I was, in that Morgan-shaped bubble of time and space, I felt a sense of permission from existence itself, an expectation, a waiting to see what I would do. What command I would give it.

The sensation, the moment of change, it demanded all of my focus and attention. Distantly, around me, I felt the perception shield melt and fall away as all of its potential for being funneled back through me into this next moment. I heard Alastaroth's cry of "You! Stop!" Felt hands grabbing me, hauling me away, trying to stop me.

Too late.

I commanded.

And the world obeyed.

Chapter 39: Abdication

Once again, Vambrace awoke in a panic, groping at his side for a sword that wasn't there. Same as he'd done every morning since fleeing Dis.

With a groan and a curse muttered under his breath, he planted his hands beneath him and levered himself halfway up into a hunched over sit. It was the most he could do in the tight, damp space of his latest bedroom, which he was generously telling himself was a cave but which could more accurately be described as a rocky burrow in the side of a muddy hill. Probably belonged to a junior mearcstapa, if he had to guess. Which meant he needed to be on his way before it or its mother came back and found him trespassing.

He maneuvered himself around in the cramped space until he could poke his head out through the opening of the burrow and peek around his immediate surroundings. Nothing in sight but the muck and haze of the bog, gnarled and stunted trees reaching like snaggled claws from the brackish brown waters. No sounds but the distant screech of harpies and the low rumble of thunder approaching from somewhere.

Satisfied in his relative safety for the moment, Vambrace wriggled one of his arms up through the opening past his head to grab a wet handful of solid, damp earth, then clawed and clambered his way out into the muck. Once he was free, he took a deep breath, picked a direction at random that wasn't back the way he'd come, and mentally prepared himself to face another day on the run from his own subjects.

How long had it been? Days? Weeks? He'd long ago lost the habit of paying attention to time, outside of it as he was. Morgan's arrival had briefly rekindled an interest in measuring the moments, for old times' sake, but now…

A pang of guilt lanced through him. It was almost nostalgic, the emotion; he'd felt none of it for literal eons, but once, in another life, guilt was all he'd been able to feel. Now here it was again as he was driven from yet another kingdom he'd called home, an old scar long healed that had suddenly been ripped open.

Had she made it out alive? He hoped so. Even though her arrival had been the crack in his eons-old bluff that had eventually pulled him down and led him here, even given that she'd brought treacherous magic into his kingdom like her namesake before her, he couldn't bring himself to wish her ill. Whatever her intentions, whatever the results, she was the only other human on this entire godsforsaken world, and his confidant for a time. The only person he could drop his facade around.

Which, in hindsight, might have been a mistake, considering where he was now. Still.

Breakfast was a couple of marsh apples he managed to scavenge from the healthier trees along the route of his silent, trudging trek. The fact that many of the trees around his hiding hole were barren added weight to the idea that mearcstapa were nearby, so he picked up the pace as he ate. The apples themselves were half-rotten already, but the nice thing about marsh apples was that it was hard to tell, and the alcohol content probably kept them safe to eat, he thought. If nothing else, he doubted fate had kept him alive this long just to die half-drunk on bad apples in a swamp.

His stomach was still growling once his impromptu meal was over, but he couldn't afford to be on the run while drunk, so it would have to do for now. Maybe he could find something more substantial once he was out of the bog. This wasn't his first time needing to forage for his meals, but it was his first time doing so without a weapon at his side, and he'd grown accustomed over the last thousand years or so to having feasts made ready for him at the snap of his fingers. Those survivor's instincts were still in there, but they were groggy at being woken up after so long. Try as he might, he couldn't help fixate once more on all that he'd lost as he hiked deeper into exile.

Slowly, step by step, the marsh beneath his feet began to firm up. The haze thinned and disappeared as the stunted trees grew sturdier, more sure of their footing. Behind him, in the distance, he heard the angry, near human wailing of a mearcstapa — the rightful owner of his sleeping burrow, if he had to guess, discovering his scent in its territory. It would be unlikely that the beast bothered to track him this far, but even still, he hastened his steps into the encroaching forest.

Tangled undergrowth, murky darkness, and hanging, grasping vines replaced the muck and the haze as his constant companions now. With no blade to hack a path through, Vambrace's pace slowed again as he was forced to clamber under and around the foliage. More than once, he bumped into vegetation so tall and thick that it startled him momentarily into thinking he'd found another person here in the woods; but no, it was merely the person-sized and vaguely person-shaped growths of a suicypress, one of the bent and gnarled trees native to Hell. Mossy pods hung from their wide-reaching branches like dead bodies, swaying in a passing breeze that carried their seeds across the forest.

It had been probably decades since he'd last encountered one such tree, and they still creeped him out now like they had the first time he'd stumbled across one back when he'd first arrived here. The lumpy growths that stretched up their trunks like agonized faces trying to burst free didn't help matters.

Still, at least the woods tended to grow sparser where the suicypresses took root, given the amount of space they needed for their canopies to grow thick and wide enough to support their macabre burdens. The hiking became easier as the underbrush thinned and the trees spread out, the dappled red skylight growing brighter as the murk of the dense forest gave way.

He trudged a meandering path around the trees, deeper into the woods, where at least there might be better foraging. Hunting anything larger than a wolpertinger was out of the question right now without a weapon, but maybe he could find something small's burrow and lay a snare or something. Or maybe find a branch sturdy enough to fashion a crude spear. Pausing to do either meant staying still for longer than felt safe, but collapsing from hunger wouldn't help him either, so maybe it would be worth the—

Something crunched further into the woods, directly in front of him. A snapped twig, or a crushed shell, he wasn't sure. Vambrace froze, ear cocked, breath held, and listened.

There, faintly. The rustle of leaves, the shifting of dirt under a step. Some sort of creature. Possibly a monstrous one. Very unlikely, but not impossible, a person — an exile, an eccentric, a desperate renegade, there were any number of ill-advised reasons some demons chose to take a shot at living outside the safety of Dis.

Would such a person be safer or more dangerous than, say, a far-ranging mearcstapa, or a hungry wendigo? There was no way to know without encountering it first. But the least likely possibility of them all was that one of his pursuers had somehow circled around ahead of him, so whatever or whoever it was shouldn't be expecting him or even know he was here yet.

Slowly, and with all senses on high alert, Vambrace crept forward toward the noise.

They weren't bothering to be stealthy themselves, from the sound of it. The closer he got, the surer he became that the source of the noises was at least person-sized, if not a person themselves. Anything small enough to be prey in this environment wouldn't be so carelessly giving away its location like this. He stooped to pick up a fist-sized rock on his slow way toward his quarry, arm half-cocked, ready to throw if necessary.

And then he peeked around the side of a particularly wide tree and saw it. In a small clearing ahead, where the canopy of two suicypresses entangled, one of the hanging pod sacks was rustling and trembling as if it really had come alive and was trying to free itself from its gruesome fate. Vambrace thought at first that this anomalous growth was the source of the noises he'd heard, that his disturbed impressions of the plants had finally been proven right; but then he saw the bare feet on the ground behind where the mossy pod hung, saw a brief glimpse of an arm as the growth shook and shifted violently to the side for a second.

It was a person after all, then, digging noisily in the corpse-like foliage. Suicypress nuts were edible in a pinch, it was true, but far from tasty or filling. Vambrace himself never saw the treat worth the morbid digging before, but evidently this person, whoever they were, was either more desperate or at least less squeamish than he was. Behind his trunk, Vambrace crouched down lower, watching and waiting to see who and what he was dealing with. Ideally, whoever they were, they had a settlement of some sort nearby, some spit of civilization where he could barter for assistance or supplies.

A few seconds later, the forager let loose a frustrated, wordless growl and ripped the body-sized burden down from its branch, moss and vines and wet leaves showering the ground as the person holding it tore it to shreds and flung the pieces about the clearing with wild abandon. *An Iriate, then*, the ex-archfiend thought, though that immediately didn't add up as the wreckage settled around the angry perpetrator and Vambrace got his first good look at them. Their skin seemed to flash red for a moment, but a strangely shiny red, which shifted to orange and then purple as they turned their body.

A Luxuriate, then? An unusually strong and angry one, if so; but no, they didn't have the proportions of any Luxuriate Vambrace had ever seen. They were as tall as a Superbiate, for one, well-muscled but skinnier than seemed healthy for either race, and so androgynous that he couldn't place their sex. Their skin shifted again as they crouched, glossy blue flashing to dark, shiny green. The way that color kept shifting — it wasn't something they were doing consciously, Vambrace realized, it was some sort of natural iridescence.

As the being in front of him scooped up the half-rotted, skull-sized nut that had fallen from the destroyed tree pod, Vambrace risked creeping out a foot or so around the tree to get a closer look. Was that… scales they were covered in? Like an Avaritiate? No. Maybe. As whatever it was lifted the nut to its face for a tentative sniff, with the motion of its arm, it looked more like they were coated in a thin, tight weave of… were those feathers? Or another trick of the light?

And the face; he hadn't focused on it yet, but looking at it now, this creature, this person — they were beautiful, he realized. Strangely, eerily attractive in a way many Luxuriates he knew would kill for, with high, sculpted cheeks and a strong, slender jaw. Thin lips pulled back in a fanged grimace as the being growled again and crushed the rotten nut in its powerful grip, flaring a nose that… well, it was more like two curved slits than a nose, almost snakelike in the middle of its handsome, sallow face, beneath golden, glowing eyes that seemed to flare with an inner light like some sort of fire burning just inside its skull.

What in all of Hell was he looking at? He shook his head, confused and a little dazed — and in that brief puzzlement, lost just enough of his grip on the tree at his side that he slid an inch forward. His breath caught, his weight shifted, and he managed to catch himself, but not without the quietest rustle of the grass beneath him.

The strange being's head whipped up, and it locked eyes with its human observer, and those eyes burst to life. Its hair, a messy curtain of silver gray hanging limp behind its head, flared up like plumage around its head, bright and white and wispy. Its horns, which sprouted from the back of its head and curved around the crown to nearly touch in the front, flashed warm and golden and dazzling. Its skin shifted in a blink through every color to a blinding combination of all of them, shining like the Earth's sun itself. In an instant, it was up on its feet, standing at full height, arms spread, shining, radiating, filling up the clearing, the entire forest with its presence, which bore down on Vambrace like the cosmos come down to meet and crush him, and all he could see, all he could register, was the light and the majesty and those burning, staring eyes.

He felt himself rising to his feet as well, though he hadn't meant to. He felt himself walking slowly toward the strange being in front of him, though he hadn't given his feet the order. And then he simply stood in front of it, transfixed and watching, waiting, outside of himself, disconnected from all that was happening, all that he was or had been before.

The creature made another wordless sound in its throat like a curious grunt, lowering its arms as it walked up to meet him, though the light and the overwhelming presence flowing out of it remained. Locked away somewhere deep inside himself, Vambrace could only watch with an uneasy detachment as it reached out to poke and prod at him, no caution or fear in its beautiful, alien face as it inspected him. Its hands ran slowly, unconcerned, over his body, through his hair, inside his jacket. He felt the touch, but distantly, like recalling an old memory even as it happened in the moment. He felt the thing's breath on his face as it stepped in closer and awkwardly pulled the jacket off of him with a difficulty that told him this thing had never encountered clothing before.

But mostly, he only felt the light from this thing pouring into him and filling him until there was no room for him anymore. It would have been terrifying, if there was any room left for terror.

The thing, the creature, the being, whatever it was, it turned its attention to the jacket now in its hands, sniffing at it and rubbing the strange material between its fingers. It gave the sleeve a hard tug that strained the denim without breaking it, cocking its head at the durability, before finally bringing the same sleeve to its mouth and sinking sharp fangs into the elbow. The material tore at last then as the thing took a bite, chewed pensively for a moment, then scrunched up its face. With a disgusted snarl, it flung the jacket behind itself into the dirt and spit the mouthful of denim at Vambrace's feet.

Then it was the human's turn. Vambrace stood docile and waiting while the thing leaned in to sniff at his neck, down his chest, across one of his arms. It grabbed his wrist and yanked his arm up, leaning in to run a long, pointed tongue along the iron mail covering it. Its grimace returned, but nevertheless, it bit down anyway. Somewhere, he registered the soft pinch of its jaws as it tried and failed to pierce the armor with its teeth. He no longer had the capacity to feel relief at the failure, or panic as the thing instead turned its attention on his unarmored hand. The pain of its fangs chomping down on his middle finger was distantly registered, but he gave no reaction whatsoever as the thing's teeth tore through skin and muscle and met his knuckle. It gnashed and bit again and again, fangs clicking repeatedly on exposed bone, and it likely would have succeeded in biting the digit off entirely if it hadn't once again gotten annoyed at how inedible everything around it was being.

In a fit of pique and with another unintelligible bark, the thing flung Vambrace's bloody hand away, then slammed a fist into the human's chest. Though his mail absorbed the brunt of the blow, he heard the crack of one of his ribs breaking before he sprawled and landed face-first into the dirt, his head bouncing off an exposed root as he went limp. Even with his face pressed against the ground and only grass and soil in his sight, he could still feel the light of the thing inside him, still see it behind his eyes, burning away his thoughts, his will, his sense of self.

He lay there twitching and lurching as the creature kicked and stomped him repeatedly, another rib snapping, dirt flying as his assailant growled and grunted with incoherent anger. He didn't know how long the abuse lasted, or when it stopped, or when the creature finally turned and stalked away. He still felt its glow even as its footsteps and its grumbling faded into the distance, still felt the warm, obliterating light inside him as he lay in the dirt in the stillness and silence.

Finally, much later, or perhaps after only a few moments, the sensation of its presence ebbed ever so slightly, just enough for his mind to reestablish the most tentative of footholds — before the light vanished completely, swift enough to shock his entire system, as everything that was Vambrace rushed back into himself all at once to fill the cold void left behind.

The pain registered immediately, all at once. He screamed against the forest floor, the dirt muffling his cry and filling his mouth, but the sound still echoed off the trees all around him. He'd filled his lungs with another choked breath and was halfway through screaming again when coherent thought returned and he realized what a bad idea it was, but it was too late at that point to do anything but curl up around his broken ribs and cradle his bleeding, mangled hand in a weak, shaking grip.

The horrible, beautiful being was gone now, long gone, and his interactions with it already felt like old, fuzzy memories — but the consequences, the sensations and reactions and the racing thoughts that came with them, were raw and sharp and fighting for attention all at once, and all he could do was lie there and whimper and fight for breath through the pain and panic and confusion.

When he'd at last acclimated to the ache in his chest and the stinging in his hand, when the initial rush of selfhood and sensation had passed and his conscious mind had reestablished some semblance of where it was and what had happened, a new theory occurred to him, one that made his breath hitch all over again.

That monster, that person, it had looked like a demon, but not one he could place. There was an intelligence behind its burning gaze, but a strange lack of recognition — a simple mind with nothing familiar to grasp at. It handled him with the same disregard as the foliage it had torn from the trees, but it had to realize that he was another thinking being, right? Or else why use its strange light to subdue him?

Too smart to be a mere monster. Too savage to be a familiar Sin. A mesmerizing appearance that evoked bits and pieces of the demonic races he knew, and a seemingly innate power that dwarfed all of them.

He knew with a deep, sudden certainty exactly what sort of entity he had just encountered, and he shuddered. Demonkind didn't realize how lucky it was that they'd vanished into myth, presumed extinct; if the one he'd just met was any indicator, there was no place for beings like them in any sort of functioning society.

Surprising and upsetting as the realization was, though, he had bigger concerns now that the thing was gone. None of his injuries were life threatening, but they still hurt like fuck and needed tending.

Gingerly, carefully, Vambrace pushed himself up to sit against a nearby mossy rock, gritting his teeth against a cry of pain as his ribs screamed in agony. His gored, bloody hand thankfully looked worse than it was. It was just the one finger that the beast had savaged; if he could get to a healer in time, it wouldn't necessarily be —

He groaned. No, that wouldn't be an option anymore. He was his own doctor for the foreseeable future, wasn't he? Alright, so he'd probably end up losing that finger, but it could easily have been much worse. Might as well try to bandage it, at least; no sense letting it get infected if it wasn't already.

Getting his mail off to reach the shirt beneath was out of the question in his condition. His pants might work for bandages, but he had nothing to cut the coarse cloth with, and he doubted he had the strength right now to rip the fabric with a single bare hand. Maybe the leaves that demon had scattered in its anger would be clean enough?

He was reaching for just such a pile when he heard rustling in the trees once more and froze. Ye gods, was it coming back? No, it had vanished further ahead into the woods, and the noise was coming from the opposite direction — the direction Vambrace himself had come.

He cursed viciously under his breath and tried to drag himself behind his rocky seat, but it was too late.

Two Iriate guards stepped into the clearing spears-first, immediately spreading to a flanking position when they spotted him. "Don't move, human!" the one on his right commanded, shifting his grip on the weapon to ready a throw.

Vambrace held up his bloodied hand. "I couldn't if I wanted to," he replied. It was a bluff, however ineffectual; it would hurt like shit to do so, but he could, technically, scramble to his feet and book it just far enough to get speared through the back rather than the front. A useless card to hold onto, maybe, but every little lie helped now.

The one to his left kept her gaze and spearpoint leveled at him as she craned her head back toward the forest. "Sir!" she shouted. "We've got him!"

"Excellent," Abdeles answered as he emerged from the trees, a dozen more Iriates surrounding him and a single Avaritiate trailing behind him, looking out of place. "And about damned time, too. Hello again, false archfiend."

"Hello, Abdeles," Vambrace said as brightly as he could manage. "You're looking especially pompous."

"Am I? It must be my swiftly approaching victory." He smiled his smuggest smile as he held Excalibur aloft and brandished it toward Vambrace. "Quite the long and futile chase you've led us on, human, and where has it landed you? Weary and bloodied in the mud at my feet, right where you belong. How appropriate."

"Hell, so we're doing *this* now, are we?" Vambrace grabbed the rock beside him with his good hand and leveraged himself up against it in a less awkward position. The soldier with the cocked spear hoisted it higher, but the human ignored him. Now that Abdeles was here with the prince's own weapon, any threat from his lackeys was empty; the Superbiate wouldn't brook anyone but himself the satisfaction of a killing blow. Might as well die comfortable.

"Hmph. You, of all people, do not get to complain about someone lording an undue amount of authority over you, human," Abdeles said with a sneer as he slowly advanced. "You, who hid behind stolen and unearned laurels, who—"

"How did you even find me so quickly?" Vambrace interrupted. "My path was far from intuitive by design, and I know I was doing a fairly skilled job of covering my tracks at every stage. Whoever your tracker is, they deserve a raise."

Abdeles glowered at the interruption, but it melted back into smugness when he was handed another opportunity to gloat. "Oh, you can thank your other human pet for that," he said, half-turning back and gesturing with his free hand. The unarmed and unarmored Avaritiate in his group dutifully stepped forward, grinning literally from ear to ear.

Vambrace sniffed. "Morgan got uglier while I was away, it seems."

Abdeles chuckled. "The witch is either locked away in the tallest of Pandemonium's prison towers, or else assisting my subordinates in the next phase of our plans," he said. "No, I was referring to this." He held out a hand, and the Avaritiate dutifully plucked the discarded denim jacket from the dirt and handed it over. "One of your precious pieces of Earthward detritus," the Superbiate continued, holding the garment at arm's length like a foul rag. "Had you been less foolishly sentimental, we would have had a much more difficult time finding you, I'll grant. Instead, we needed only to find the Avaritiate who owned the thing in between the girl bringing it here and you becoming so attached to it."

"A most singular garment," the Avaritiate chimed in, drumming their fingers together. "Hard to forget. Very easy to scry for."

Vambrace looked between the jacket and the grinning Avaritiate, chagrined resignation settling over his face. "Right," he said flatly. "Well… fuck."

"I couldn't have put it better myself," said Abdeles. "Here." He tossed the jacket over Vambrace, who grabbed it and pulled it down off of his face in time to see the Superbiate rear back with Excalibur. "Since you love the thing so much, let it be your burial shroud."

"Abdeles, wait!" Vambrace shouted, clambering backwards up the rock behind him. "You don't—"

Too late. The sword plunged into him, through him, into the stone behind him, buried until the hilt slammed against his mail and stopped it.

It wasn't the most powerful or graceful stab. Abdeles was no warrior. But he didn't need to be. It was Excalibur.

And it had turned on him at last.

Strange, Vambrace thought, as the Superbiate pressed down on him with a vicious smile and the blade shifted inside him. *It should hurt more than this.* He'd been stabbed plenty before — not straight through, not with magic, but still — and the pain had been unbearable. Excalibur, by contrast, only felt like a weird pressure swelling in his abdomen, just below his lung.

His blind scramble up his rocky seat to escape had spared him the stab to the heart that Abdeles had lined up. He clung to that rock now to keep himself slipping back down and bisecting himself on the blade.

"Yesss," Abdeles growled with more glee than the prince had ever seen on the Superbiate's dour face before. "Squirm, human! Your death will not be quick nor painless, I promise you that."

Vambrace grit his teeth as his mangled hand slipped in its own blood and his hold with it gave way. He caught Abdeles' wrist, pain screaming through his finger the way it wasn't through his gut, and fought to push himself back up. The demon in front of him gave no ground as the human's blood leaked down through his own grip on the weapon, and the glow coming from the sword lit his exultant face from below like a sick pantomime of —

Wait, what? Glow? Why was Excalibur glowing?

The two of them noticed the anomaly at the same time. From pommel to blade, Excalibur was diffused in a silvery, shimmery light that poured slowly out from somewhere deep within the weapon's core, shining like a moonbeam through the demon's grip and the hole it had opened in the human's mail.

"What is this?" Abdeles demanded under his breath, either to Vambrace or the sword itself. "It has never done this. Has it done this before?"

It catches the light unnaturally, Vambrace thought (for there was no way he could speak anything at the moment), *but this is something different.*

The slight breeze, lighter than a breath, that gradually began pouring from the sword then was also unusual. As was the charge in the air, the heavy static pressing in from all sides around them. The slow sensation of sliding: upward, inward, he couldn't tell, just *elsewhere*. The air around them primed itself — gently but inexorably, and stronger by the moment — for *something*. Some change. Some indescribable shift.

And the next moment, Vambrace realized what was about to happen, pulled from an ancient memory, long gone but never far from his mind. He had felt this exact same phenomenon exactly once before, ages past and in another life.

With a steadying breath and the last drops of his strength and courage, Vambrace leaned forward, pressed his forehead against the demon's, and grabbed Excalibur by the pommel with one hand and the hilt with the other, holding on for dear life — holding the blade inside of himself like a human sheath.

"What?" Abdeles barked, all triumph gone from his face and voice. "What is happening? What are you—?" He yanked on the sword, now humming in an impossible pitch, and tried with all his strength to pull it from Vambrace's abdomen.

His strength could not match that of a squire of the Round Table, even a bloodied and perforated one. Vambrace laughed, actually laughed aloud, at the realization, even as the sword jostled inside him and widened the hole.

A cry of shock and confusion went up from the soldiers somewhere behind Abdeles — somewhere already distant, already out of reach. The space between them flashed and darkened, empty air swirled, as the ground below and the forest around gave way like shapes in a mist. A low keening, a high thrumming, somewhere nearby, as senses blurred and stumbled over themselves.

Vambrace laughed again as he shut his eyes against the torrent, aware now only of the sword in his hands and the stone at his back, and at the demon pressed against him howling in panic and fear.

The present dissolved with an inverted clap and a discordant, ringing rumble, and all flashed white then black then white again as Excalibur and everything attached to it tumbled through what-if into another possibility, obeying a command deeper than logic.

And amidst the tumult, Vambrace clung on and laughed through the pain and the chaos and, for the first time in his impossibly, unnaturally, sinfully long life, thanked any god listening for bringing a witch to his court.

Chapter 40: Upheaval

The crack was near deafening, the localized thunderclap of empty space being obliterated to make way for sudden substance out of nowhere. It rocked all of us within the sigil, sending us sprawling across the hard, icy crystal of the Throne. Me, Alastaroth, his guards who'd rushed me — and two other figures who came tumbling through from nowhere.

I was the only one expecting this, so I was the first back on my feet, desperately scanning the scene for what I'd summoned. A clattering nearby grabbed my attention, an oblong shape sliding to a stop a few feet away. I dove for it, giddy with triumph as my hands firmly grabbed hold of —

Wait, this wasn't Excalibur. It was some kind of silvery metal tube, wide and flat and, weirdly, warm to the touch. Not hot, but pleasantly, comfortably warm, especially down here in the frigid depths of Hell.

Screw it, I raised it up like a sword anyway while I took in what else was going on now. There were definitely more new changes than there should have been. I'd asked for a sword, why did I get a tube and… two guys?

The echo of the summoning thunder had died out by now, replaced by the loud, confused muttering of the Iriates still standing guard around the circle, none of whom seemed inclined to move from their spots. I heard a few repeated refrains of "What happened?" and "The archfiend?" as I realized that I knew these two summoning stowaways.

"Morgan!" Prince Vambrace's voice cried out weakly from the bottom of the unexpected tumult. "Quickly! Kill him!"

The figure on top unfolded upwards, a giant wrapped in a fine cloak over fine armor, horned head whipping around in confusion. "Where are we?" Abdeles thundered. "What happened?"

Stray light flashed silver between them. Excalibur. Dammit, I was hoping the spell would just suck it out of his hand, but the Superbiate lord still held it in a tight, bloody grip. And Vambrace —

Oh, shit, Vambrace was holding it too, in a sense. Fuck. I was still mad at him, but I didn't particularly want to watch him die today.

Abdeles's gaze settled on me, an angry grimace splitting his face. "You!" he roared, then ripped the sword out of Vambrace's midsection and swung it around to point it at me. Funny, I would have expected the sword to be bloody after that, but it gleamed immaculately like always. Vambrace, unfortunately, couldn't say the same as he clutched his open wound with both hands while the puddle of blood beneath him bloomed. "I knew keeping you alive would be more trouble than it was worth," Abdeles continued. "No more! *On your knees, human!*"

The unignorable command in his words hit me, and I ignored it. The power of his Sin washed over and around me like the smallest, gentlest of breezes, evaporating.

No idea yet what that was about, but I'd been rolling with weirder things for a while now, so I rolled with this as well, standing up straighter and glaring at him, metal thingy in my hands held higher. "That's not how this works anymore, Abdeles," I called back with as much bravado as I could fake. "It's over. *You* kneel."

It would have been nice if he'd taken the bluff, because I had no way left to back it up. But no, the head Superbiate was done being bluffed at by humans; his only response was to snarl and rush toward me, Excalibur raised for a killing blow.

I stepped back and raised the flat metal thing in both hands before I realized how incredibly useless a gesture that was. No time left for another idea, though — the unstoppable sword swung down at me, and I prayed rapidly that at least it wouldn't hurt, and then —

The unstoppable sword hit the metal tube I held, and with a melodic, chiming clang, it stopped.

The physical shock sent the demon stumbling back. The mental shock showed on both of our faces, and our eyes met briefly in a shared look of confusion, both of us clearly thinking the same thought: *That shouldn't have happened.*

Desperate, out of options, staring down my own death, I lunged and swung the silvery bar I held like a club, driving Abdeles back again. He recovered and slashed at me again, low and from the side, at an angle and speed that was impossible for me to block in time.

The sword clanged beautifully again as I blocked in time, my magic club thing whipping down of its own volition to intercept Excalibur just before it cleaved through my waist. Silver blade bounced off silver metal without a chink or scratch on either.

I swung for his face. Abdeles, stunned and beginning to panic, barely raised the sword in time to avoid being clobbered across the temple. With another ringing chime, our weapons canceled out, and the Superbiate backed quickly away. "What is—? This is not—!" he stammered, looking wide-eyed from Excalibur to me and back. "How are you doing this?!" he shouted at me at last.

Good question. With no sword waving inches from my face for the moment, I turned my attention on my savior stick, looking for a clue. It was still just clear, clean, unadorned silver, that same forged moonlight-looking metal that Excalibur was. Same dimensions as Excalibur too, now that I was looking for it, and…

…And there was something else. Something… deeper, familiar. Nothing was etched on the metal, but if I looked hard enough at it — really focused and drilled down and *looked* at it — then I could almost swear I saw, deep in the reflection of way too much ambient light, a pattern of sorts. Symbols. Writing. An idea, a concept, perfectly articulated.

The same as the one I'd used to hijack this summoning spell. The same that lived inside Excalibur, but with a different… context?

No, a different *tense*. A confirmation and a denial. Matching variables. A paired set of commands.

A sword, and a sheath.

I laughed, actually laughed aloud, as I raised Excalibur's lost sheath high above my head. "I told you, man!" I shouted exuberantly. "It's over! You can't kill me, Abdeles — *nothing* can!"

That got our audience buzzing like nothing else. Sheath still raised, I turned and swept my gaze across the assembled demons on the Throne with us. The Iriates were wavering, some still gripping their weapons, some having already given up on the idea of being any help here and dropping them. Behind me, Alastaroth stood a safe distance away inside the summoning circle, every single one of his working pupils fixed on me as he leaned on his staff and visibly trembled. And behind him, Duchess Sidona clasped her hands together and stared with open-mouthed rapture at the scene playing out in front of her. Well, good for her, I guess.

"You!" Abdeles barked. I turned to see him snapping his fingers at someone behind me and to the side, and only realized he was ordering someone else to try attacking me when an arrow pinged harmlessly off of the back of my head. Or, rather, off the empty space just outside the back of my head, as the sheath in my hand pulsed warmly, protectively.

I turned, slowly, to stare deadpan at another Iriate who half-heartedly, half-assedly chucked a spear at me. The sheath pulsed gently with power once more, and I didn't move as the spear struck the barrier just above my skin and skidded, stuttering, away from my chest. It should have stabbed me through the heart. Instead, it bounced along the ground at my feet and rolled to an anticlimactic stop.

I let the spectacle sink in a moment longer, then turned back to a slack-jawed Abdeles. "I win," I said. "I won. You sonofabitch, you tried so hard, you and your cronies and this whole godforsaken world just kept throwing shit at me, and I'm *still standing here*, and I *fucking won*, do you understand? So… I don't know, bow down or something!"

That shook him out of it. "No," he growled, angry grimace returning. "No, not yet, I don't think so!" He backed up until he'd almost tripped over the prone and bleeding Vambrace, then bent down and hauled him up. Vambrace grunted in pain (good, still alive for now) as the demon got him in a one-armed grip and pinned the human against his chest, then pointed Excalibur at his face. "I will never bow to a lying human usurper ever again, do you hear me?" he shouted. "None of us will! Now, surrender, or our former archfiend dies!"

Vambrace grabbed at Abdeles' arm, smearing it with blood. One of his fingers was mangled, I realized, all exposed bone and ragged meat that was hard to look at. His midsection was still bleeding beneath his mail too, from the look of it. Jeez, the poor guy was a mess. I'm not proud to admit that I was, a little bit, kind of pleased he'd been having a bad time after abandoning me like he did.

It was about to get worse for him, though. Sorry, prince.

I took a step forward. "Abdeles," I said, slowly. "Serious question: Why do you think I would care?"

The demon waved Excalibur threateningly in front of Vambrace's face, the human flinching back. "Don't play coy with me!" he said. "You two have been conspiring against demonkind since you arrived here! Do you think I've forgotten?"

"I think you've bought into your own propaganda," I said with another step closer. "And I think you've forgotten the part where you sprung your trap on us both and *that* asshole," I added, waving the sheath at the prince, "ran away and left me to die. So, yeah, sorry, your hostage thing isn't working on me."

"Morgan!" Vambrace rasped as loud as he could, pausing to cough on his own blood. "You cannot... be serious, surely! Save me!"

"Oh, I *am* serious!" I shouted back. "And don't call me Morgan! What happened to 'my lady,' huh? What happened to standards?"

"Selfish witch!" Vambrace gurgled angrily again. "I took you into... my palace! I protected you—"

"Excuse *you*?" I demanded, still slowly approaching. "Oh, *you* don't get to yell at *me* about being selfish, you goddamned coward! Your first setback in thousands of years and you immediately bail? You didn't protect me from shit, you shit!"

Truth be told, I meant everything I was saying, but even I couldn't tell exactly how much I was bluffing. And neither could Abdeles, I gathered, from the look on his face and the slight waver in his sword arm as it drifted ever so slightly down from Vambrace's face.

Vambrace noticed it too. "Look, I'm sorry," he rasped, "I didn't—" And then his arms shot up, his bloody hands grabbing hold of Abdeles' horns. The Superbiate grunted in surprise, but before he could make good on his promise, the prince yanked his horns down, hauling himself up by the demon's head, and rammed his skull into Abdeles' chin hard enough that something audibly cracked.

Abdeles floundered and stumbled, his grip loosening further. With a pained yell, Vambrace snapped a leg out and kicked viciously at the Superbiate's hand.

Excalibur went flying.

"No!" Abdeles shouted, rallying. Vambrace was quicker, slipping down and out of the demon's loosened grip on him, collapsing at the Superbiate's feet and tripping him up. The demon sprawled forward. The human dove for the sword. I rushed forward toward both.

The scramble on the floor wasn't exactly an epic battle to inspire further songs and plays and artworks, but it worked. Vambrace grabbed hold of Excalibur just a second before Abdeles could, rolled about a foot away, and flailed, frantic and inelegant and no less lethal for it.

Abdeles roared in pain and fury as his reaching arms were sent flying in haphazard chunks across the floor, his blood splashing in every direction. "Stop this!" he howled, still stretching desperately for the sword and the frantic blender it had become in Vambrace's hands. "No, I was so close! I was so—!"

Vambrace heaved himself up on his hips just long enough to give himself the leverage to lunge forward with something like an aimed strike. Excalibur plunged unceremoniously into the julienned demon's jugular, silencing him with a sickening gurgle, seconds before the sword ripped upward and through his skull. A portion of Abdeles's head went flying across the Throne, one massive horn bouncing off the crystal seat and rolling to a stop, bits of brain like ground meat dribbling out onto the floor.

"Jesus, dude, you can stop now!" I called out to the still grunting and flailing Vambrace. "He's dead, you got 'em! Oh, fuck, I think I might hurl…" I turned away from the grisly sight before I made good on that promise. This was, what, the third or fourth time I'd seen someone or something get violently mutilated in Hell? You'd think it would get easier to look at after a while, but nope.

After a couple deep breaths, I looked up to see Alastaroth and Sidona both still staring in my direction, with what Iriates remained for security arrayed behind them. There were a lot fewer guards now than there were a minute ago, though. Sidona still looked rapt and enamored with the proceedings, despite the clumsily gruesome turn they'd taken. As for Alastaroth…

As soon as he realized I was looking at him, he backpedaled several panicked steps, bumped into the duchess behind him, and almost fell on his ass. "G-guards!" he squawked as he regained his footing, then turned and fled as quickly as his hobbled gait would let him, his staff clacking swiftly against the floor as he levered himself away with it. "Stop her! Stop them! Insurrection!" He stumbled at the edge of the Throne, then threw his staff over the cliff and dropped out of sight onto the ladder, clambering down while still shouting. "I need backup! Soldiers! Stop the humans! Stop them!"

God, what a gratifying sight. I waited with a smile on my face until he'd stopped shouting, somewhere down the ladder there, then swept my gaze across the Iriates that were still standing and waiting. "Well, you heard him," I called out. "Who wants to come and get the humans?" I hoisted the scabbard in my hand and waved vaguely back in the direction of the other human with Excalibur and the pile of giblets that used to be all of these demons' boss.

I'd barely finished speaking when the first two Iriates dropped their weapons in unison and held their hands up in surrender. More followed suit as the first pair sidled cautiously toward the ladder, all of them keeping their attention in our direction. In under a minute, all remaining conspirators had excused themselves and left, leaving me, Sidona, Vambrace, and the remains of Abdeles alone on the Throne.

The duchess was positively vibrating with excitement as she rushed forward. "Marvelous, Lady Morgan!" she said as she beamed and grabbed my shoulders — or grabbed the barrier just around my shoulders, anyway. The scabbard didn't take chances, I guess. "Absolutely stunning performance! Inspiring, unprecedented, incredible! Ah, I could kiss you right now!"

"Thanks," I said, holding up the scabbard between my face and hers. "But no thanks."

"Of course," she said absently, eyeing the scabbard like it was the most beautiful thing she'd ever seen. "And this — what manner of instrument is this? Where did it come from? How does its power work?"

"Later," I said, slipping from her grasp. "I'm not finished yet."

Vambrace had calmed down as I approached, his breathing deep and ragged and pained, but even. His wounded hand clutched tightly at his wounded abdomen through his mail, all of which glistened with blood, both his own and Abdeles's. His good hand clutched Excalibur in a white-knuckled death grip, his eyes still staring intently down at the ruined corpse of the Superbiate in front of him.

I knelt down next to said corpse, careful not to look directly at it, as I examined the ex-prince. "Soo," I said slowly. "How are you feeling? Think you're gonna live through all this?"

His head whipped around to me, eyes wild, and he swung Excalibur around to point it at me. "Is that a threat, witch?" he grunted.

"Alright, calm down," I said in as soothing a voice as I could manage, gently batting the sword aside with the sheath. "We've all been through a lot today. I'm just worried about you, is all, alright?"

He took a deep breath, composed himself, and lowered the blade. "Are you?" he asked, sounding suddenly, incredibly tired. "Why?"

"Because I'm not an asshole," I said. "Or I'm trying not to be. I don't know anything about stab wounds, though. How bad is that one?"

Vambrace patted the bloody mail and winced. "Bad," he grunted. "Probably not fatal, though, if it gets attention. Nothing vital punctured, I don't think. Might lose this finger, though."

"Yikes. That sucks. Sorry." I rose to my feet and held down a hand. "Alright, let's get this all over with. Give me Excalibur."

He grunted in pain again and used the hilt of the sword to lever himself back into a sitting position. "I'm sorry," he said, hoisting the sword again, "what was that?"

"Hand me the sword, please," I repeated. "I need it for a bit."

"You… need it," he repeated, eyes narrowing. "Why do you think you need it? You have the king's aegis, you have your own magical power — thank you for keeping that horrible secret the entire time we've been acquainted, by the way — why would you possibly need Excalibur as well?"

"Okay, one, my 'horrible secret' just helped save your life, buddy," I said. "Two, you of all people don't get to be mad at people keeping secrets. And three, what use would you be with it right now anyway?"

Without breaking eye contact, he waved the blade at the diced chunks of Abdeles.

Without looking at them, I nodded. "Alright, fair point. You flail most excellently. Now stand up and walk out of here and do that with something more like skill, hm?"

"It is my —" he began heatedly. Too heatedly, because it devolved into pained coughing. "It is my sword," he continued, calmer and raspier, once he had his breath back. "It has been my sword for eons. My constant, vital companion. Everything fell apart when it was stolen from me. I finally have it back in hand. And you would take it from me once more, now, in my darkest hour?"

"Jeez, you're dramatic," I muttered. "Look, I get it, you suck and you're scared without it. I understand. I feel for you. But I'm also, and this is important, still *fucking furious* with you for the way you ran away and left me to die back there. And with no help at all from the great and mighty Prince Vambrace, I had to survive and stop a violent coup against *you* all by myself—"

"Ahem," Sidona interjected from behind me.

"Shut up, you know what you did," I shot back at her. "So, by my count, you owe me fucking big time at this point, Vambrace. Your life, your throne, the biggest fucking apology you've ever given. And you can start by letting me have my turn with the unstoppable magic sword for a little while, so I can go out there and keep cleaning up *your* mess that you fucking *left* me here with, while you sit there and bleed and think about what you've done. Does that sound fair to you?"

He grit his teeth and grimaced, and for a second, I thought he was about to get confrontational again. But this time, when he finally swung Excalibur around again, he held it out carefully by the hilt with a deep sigh. "You swear entirely too much for a lady," he muttered, eyes averted.

"Yeah, I've gotten worse about that since meeting you. Go figure," I muttered back as I took the hilt and held the sword carefully aloft. It was slightly, pleasantly warm to the touch, just like its scabbard was; like it had been recently bathed in sunshine, despite shining like the moon.

Unstoppable force in one hand, immovable object in the other. Logically, I knew, this should have felt like a transcendental moment for a mere mortal like me. Mostly, though, I just felt tired and cold and resigned to finally putting all the horrible days behind me to rest at last.

I slid Excalibur home into its sheath with a ringing chime that echoed in the vast cavern like the toll of fate, took a deep breath, and spun on my heel. "Sidona, could you see to his wounds, please?" I asked as I walked past the duchess. "Make sure he doesn't bleed out, take him to a doctor or something, if you can, if you've got one of those around here. Thanks."

"As you wish, my lady," the duchess simpered, giddiness still evident in her voice. "But, if I may ask, where are you off to?"

I held up the weapon of legend in my grip and wiggled it. "I'm going to go find what's mine and take it back," I called back over my shoulder. "And take a few more things while I'm at it, I think."

I sounded badass to my ears. I felt badass in that moment.

I felt substantially less badass by the time I'd reached the bottom of the ladder and walked all the way back to the elevator that was the only way in or out of this massively subterranean literal hell hole. Especially once Sidona caught up, a wounded Vambrace draped over her shoulder and bleeding onto her fancy gown, while I was waiting for the little room to make the journey all the way back down here again.

"We meet again, my lady," the duchess said with a smug smirk. "Didn't think this first part through, huh?"

"I haven't thought a single thought through in so long, Duchess," I sighed. "And this is my first counter-coup; I'm learning as I go."

The elevator finally arrived after an interminably long wait, opening at last to disgorge four more armed and armored Iriates, who rushed forward maybe two whole feet before stopping short before our little group, hands wavering above their weapons.

"Oh, cool, he sent help," I said, and waved back toward the Throne with the sword in my hands. "Could three of you go collect what's left of Abdeles from the Throne, please? I'm guessing we shouldn't just leave him up there. I'll need one of you to stay and work the elevator crank, though."

They looked uncomfortably between themselves before one of them, a towering brick wall of a woman with arms nearly as thick as my entire torso, stepped forward, both hands wrapped around the haft of a spiked mace as thick as a cinderblock. "Humans!" she barked. "You are both under arrest by order of Lord Alasta—"

I yanked the sword free before she finished speaking and swung, chopping cleanly through the center mass of the mace head. Spiked steel fell to the floor and clunked impotently against the dimly glowing guilt ground.

It was like cleaving through empty air, the act was so effortless. No wonder Vambrace had gotten so cocky over the years. That badass feeling was returning already.

"Alastaroth and his buddies aren't in charge anymore," I said as I sheathed the blade again. "Breaking news, I know, I don't blame you for not knowing yet. Start spreading the word, though, if you don't mind."

The massive Iriate paled for a moment, then rallied, swinging what was left of her weapon with an angry grunt. I held up the sheathed Excalibur in one hand and marveled along with her as the half-mace bounced harmlessly off the sliver of silver, no impact whatsoever traveling down my arm from the blow, only a slight pulse of warmth.

I sighed as the woman and her cohorts backed away, wide eyed. "Right, look," I said, "I don't want to hurt anybody I don't have to, but I *am* kind of in a hurry, so if we could focus?" I waved the sword back toward the Throne once more and pointedly lifted my eyebrows at the big woman. After another moment, when nobody seemed inclined to make a move, I sighed again. "Duchess Sidona?" I asked over my shoulder. "If you would please?"

"Of course, my lady," Sidona said, then lifted her chin and, in a tone that echoed deep down the chasm, commanded, "*Do what the human woman tells you to, you slackjawed simpletons!*"

That moved them, finally. With a group shudder at the words that drilled straight through their wills, the group of Iriates rushed forward and around us, hurrying down the tunnel at our backs. All but the lone Iriate left in the back of the elevator, who dropped the handaxes they were holding and grabbed tight to the wheel crank with both hands.

"Thank you, Duchess," I said as we piled inside the elevator. "Thank you, soldier. We're going up, please. Whichever floor they're most likely to keep political prisoners on, if you know the one."

"Yes, ma'am!" the Iriate barked with a quick salute, then stared straight ahead at the wall as they began spinning the wheel so quickly that their hands blurred. We rocketed up the shaft so suddenly that Sidona and I nearly fell over before we found our footing and braced against the speed of the rapidly climbing room.

"Political prisoners, huh?" the duchess asked after a few minutes. "Gathering a small army to assist you in what comes next, Lady Morgan?"

"That's not a bad idea, actually," I said. "That wasn't my first plan, though. I just want to check on someone in particular before I do anything else, see how vengeful I have to be before I'm done."

"Oooh, excellent!" Sidona said, grinning hugely. "Damn, but I wish I had my sketchbook right now! Some way to capture these exact moments in history before any detail slips my mind!"

"What of the other archdemons?" Vambrace muttered against Sidona's shoulder. He seemed tired, on the verge of passing out, but he raised his head enough to turn his unfocused eyes on the toiling Iriate in here with us. "Abdeles betrayed me. What's become of the rest? Where do the Houses of Sin stand now?"

"Archduchess Cinaedemis and Archduke Aleviathan the 43rd both threw in with the new regime immediately," Sidona answered him. "Cinaedemis was swayed by the promise of the new riches and wealth that an invasion of Earth would bring, while Aleviathan saw a chance to rise to the prominence of his namesake by being a key figure in the creation of a new interdimensional paradigm. 'Perhaps the second most influential Invidiate to have ever lived,' was his phrasing, I believe. Archduchess Bargriff, unsurprisingly, had no particular stance on the matter and was content to let events happen — though she did sign off on the use of your Acediate broadcast network for the regime's communication and propaganda needs."

She paused to kneel and set Vambrace down against the wall, taking a seat beside him herself. "Archdukes Grodon and Melchius are both under house arrest in their personal quarters — Melchius because it was believed he would object to the takeover, and rather than take any chances, Abdeles thought it best to lock him away until his rise to power was cemented completely. Grodon, though, I think they just distracted him with feasts and sex and entertainment. He might not even realize how much of an uproar has been going on. Or he might be dead of some form of overindulgence by now, I can't say."

Vambrace grunted in both pain and disappointment. "Such flimsy allegiances," he muttered. "I shouldn't be surprised, yet I am. Are you two truly my only allies?"

"Well, Archduchess Pyressa was also a pretty big obstacle, as I understand," Sidona continued. "She didn't take kindly to the news that our General Enkida was so thoroughly betrayed and assassinated, and you know she never liked Abdeles."

Vambrace sat up a little straighter at that. "Pyressa fought for me?" he asked. "Truly?"

"Fought and died," Sidona confirmed. "Sorry. House Iria has been running with blood of late. More than usual, I mean. Any Iriates left who actively dislike the new order have either been imprisoned or outnumbered enough to be cowed into obedience. Honestly, though, most of your subjects don't seem to notice or care one way or the other who holds the throne. It's been a novelty and a point of gossip, but unless or until Abdeles actually opened the gates to other worlds again, the city at large has been content to go about its usual business."

"Hmm." Vambrace took a deep breath, sighed heavily, and rested his chin against his own chest, eyes closed. "Oddly reassuring, I suppose. At least your own loyalties have remained with me, Duchess. Thank you."

"Yes, about that," Sidona said slowly, side-eyeing me. "I suppose… well, we can discuss that matter once everything has settled down again, sir."

I wasn't coming to her rescue there. Not yet, anyway. I also hadn't made up my mind about the duchess and what to do about her "loyalty." Instead, while we climbed higher toward the palace, I was busy focusing on a new spell idea, weaving the barrier shell of the anti-perception sequence with the protective warding of the heating spell, and layering potential triggers on top of both within a weave and a repetition I would never have dared experiment with if I didn't have the invulnerable protection of Excalibur's scabbard with me.

My companions in this little room noticed what I was doing after a while. I could see it in the nervous glances that our Iriate attendant kept flashing at me, in the concerned staring of Vambrace, in the visible anticipation on Sidona's face. By the time our elevator ride finally slowed to a stop, the little space was practically humid with the buildup of magic ready to pop off, just as soon as I pulled the trigger.

The door opened onto a long, dark stretch of hall, the heavy concentration of vibrant red in the guilt from below replaced now with walls of darker black guilt only sparingly shot through with thin veins of red. Lamps hung far apart from the ceiling, with spaces of oppressive shadow thick between them. Definitely the kind of atmosphere I would expect from a dungeon floor.

That impression was deepened by the spear-wielding soldiers standing at attention further down the corridor, who immediately turned toward us as we arrived and began slowly advancing. "Who goes there?" one of them called as the two approached, spears leveled at us. "State your name, clearance, and business!"

I turned to our conscripted elevator attendant and nodded down the hallway. "This the way?" I asked.

The Iriate saluted again. "Yes, ma'am!" they said, standing at attention. "This entire floor has been sectioned off for political dissidents, ma'am! Down the hall and down the stairs to the main cell block, ma'am!"

Sidona's command powers had worn off a long time ago, but you couldn't tell it by their demeanor. "Thank you, soldier," I said, stepping out of the elevator. "Next, can you take Duchess Sidona and Prince Vambrace to a doctor, please? And don't let anyone lay a hand on them or try to stop you — you've been granted full authority to carry out that mission, understand?"

They saluted a final time. "Yes, ma'am!" they said, and the doors slid shut once more before the elevator trundled off further up the palace.

Alright, moment of truth. Like I'd said, I really didn't want to have to hurt anyone if I could avoid it, but I'd seen too many dismemberments around here to be confident I wouldn't have to also use that trick to get what I wanted. Not unless I could shock and awe people enough to stand down before I even got to them.

"Hey!" one of the guard Iriates shouted as they stopped maybe fifteen feet away from me, weapons readied, blocking the hall with their bodies. "Did you hear us? Answer or die!"

Shock and awe was the entire point of this new spell of mine, if it worked. I pulled the trigger on it.

Potential(outer shell) - ignite, all

A loud, dull *whoosh* rocked the corridor as my enchantment burst to life, blowing the Iriates onto their backs with the force of the ignition. Magic roared into bright, hot flame that poured off of me and lapped against the hallway walls, climbing up to the ceiling, swirling and dancing with new life. The dress I was wearing burned immediately to ash, evaporating off my frame like tissue paper in a bonfire — but Excalibur, the sheath, and most importantly, my body remained undamaged at the center of the blazing maelstrom.

Through the waving flames, I watched the Iriate guards scrabbling backwards, sheer terror on their faces, as they tried and failed to gain their feet. It was like looking at the world through a gauzy, shimmering curtain of orange and yellow and light. But if I could still see them through it, then they could still see me.

I gripped Excalibur tight and raised a hand. Around me, the roaring flames also lifted a hand — an inferno given shape and something like structure thanks to the tightly wrapped bodily shell at the base of my spell.

I stepped forward, clothed only in a twenty-foot-tall firestorm in the shape of myself. "I heard you," I decreed loudly through the roar of the fire (given the circumstances, I could only speak in grand decrees at the moment). "My name is Morgan Samantha Amell, I have as much clearance as I decide that I have, and my business is not with you. Move aside or die, but I won't be stopped any longer."

I took another step forward. The Iriates both finally scrambled to their feet, turning tail as they rose, and ran screaming in the other direction.

Perfect. If anybody died to me now, well, that would be their own fault.

Word was already spreading as I strode down the corridor, the light fixtures on the ceiling melting in my wake, molten metal dribbling down behind me. More guards rushed up to meet the approaching threat that was me; just as many skidded to a terrified stop, then spun and fled as soon as they saw me. Ahead, shouting and chaos and confusion grew.

By the time I reached the bottom of the stairs and looked out across the cell block proper, a grid of corridors with barred doors every few feet, I had invoked a pretty impressive crowd. Guards and prisoners alike stared in horror from afar, through cell doors or from huddles at the safe ends of hallways. More than a few guards had even decided the safest place to be was inside the cells with their prisoners.

I raised my head and smiled benevolently, basking in the attention while, in my mind, I fiddled with the metaphorical knobs of my spell until I managed to crank the blaze down to just a ten-foot flaming replica of myself. Didn't want to burn anyone to death in their prison cells as I walked by, after all.

"Thank you all for being here today," I called to the prison. "You can stop panicking quite so much, I'm not here for a killing spree. But I will need one of you to point me toward a certain prisoner of yours." I scanned the cowering guards nearby and pointed to one at random, a short, wiry man with a trim beard who was trembling harder than any of his associates. "You," I said, and crooked a finger as he yelped and jumped up. "Do you know where I can find a Luxuriate woman, name of Kriseia?"

The short Iriate swallowed visibly, then violently nodded.

"Cool," I said. "Take me to her." He rose up slowly, approached me cautiously, but stopped again when I added, "Oh, yeah, and if she's been mistreated too badly, then I *will* consider a killing spree after all. So I hope for your sakes that you've all been playing nice down here."

The Iriate whimpered, violently nodded again, then slowly slipped past me with a much wider berth than was necessary before taking off at a sprint down a side corridor. I followed, a lump of worry building in my throat that I tried to suppress. I hadn't seen my roomie in what felt like weeks, but I had thought of her every day since she got arrested trying to defend me.

Now that I had been here for a minute or more without killing anyone, the shocked murmuring was starting up, confusion and fear and disbelief on every voice I passed. The bars of cell doors warmed to a sizzling red if I passed by too closely, their lock mechanisms softening and giving way; a few swung gently open in my wake, their occupants freed incidentally by my presence.

Nobody dared escape yet, though. Nobody moved except to track my actions as I followed my guide and scanned the faces inside the cells.

At last I found the face I was looking for. At the end of the main corridor, down a right-hand branching hallway, and tucked far away in the back, I saw her again. "Open it," I commanded before we'd fully reached the cell, and the terrified guard leading me scurried to obey, flinging wide the bars and then shrinking dutifully back into the hall corner out of the way.

I braced myself for the worst and stepped into the doorway. "Kriseia?"

Her arms were strung up by chains to the ceiling, a short metal bar hobbling her ankles, and she was covered in some sort of baggy gray burlap-looking material. Like an oversized onesie made of cheap sweatpants fabric, hanging loose on her down to her shins. Some sort of weird prisoner uniform, maybe? I hadn't seen anyone else wearing one, though.

At the sound of her name, she lifted her face. The tracks of long-dried tears streaked her cheeks, and her eyes were dull, the skin around them red and puffy. "Morgan?" she asked, her voice faint and breathy, as if just now waking from a daze. "Is it… really you?" A life and energy returned to her previously dead expression, and she lurched forward as much as her chains would allow. "Oh, Morgan, thank the devils! I was so worried about you!"

"*I* was worried about *you*!" I replied, looping through another ad-hoc spell addition to turn down the flames and the heat enwrapping me. I didn't want to shut them off entirely — putting them back on would be too much of a wait and a hassle now that I was on the populated levels of the palace. Once the danger was significantly dialed back, I stepped into the cell and swung Excalibur, cleaving through her hobble and her chains. "Stay back from me for now, I don't want to burn you," I explained as I quickly back-stepped and she crumpled to the floor. "Kriseia, are you okay? What did they do to you?"

On her knees on the ground, Kriseia sniffled. Her posture and the big, drab bag she was clothed in made her seem especially small and pitiful. "Do to me?" she repeated, voice cracking. "They… they didn't do anything!"

My heart dropped at the rawness of her voice, the choked-back tears. "Kriseia…" I said softly. "If you can't talk about it yet, that's alright, but I want you to know—"

"No, I mean—" she interrupted, head whipping up. Never mind, she didn't look sad so much as pissed. "Nobody did *anything* to me!" she repeated, then grabbed at the rough fabric hanging off of her and yanked, angrily and impotently. "Nothing! Nobody's touched me, spoken to me, barely even looked at me since I got here! It's, I'm, I—!" She made a wordless sound of frustration and gave up on her clothing, instead raking her fingers through her hair, over her horns, down her neck, arching her back with another annoyed mewl. "Aahhh, it's worse than unbearable, it's so *boring* here, I hate it!"

My heart undropped. *Of course*, I thought, *she's too kinky to punish any other way.* "Alright," I said, "well, I'm… sorry about that, but glad you're not hurt. It's good to have you back. Now, c'mon, let's get out of here."

I stepped back out of the cell, retraced my mental steps on the spell cloaking me, and reverse engineered the commands that had cranked down my initial heat. The air in front of me grew wavier, brighter, as the flames rose higher once again.

"Morgan?" Kriseia piped up behind me, voice breathy once again. I turned to find her on her feet, one hand to her mouth, her teeth bit down on one of her fingers. Her other hand was, predictably, occupied somewhere further south. "Um, I don't know what's going on with you, or what's been happening out there, but you're…" She pulled her hand from her lips long enough to wave it at me. "This is, um, new, isn't it? It's surprising, but…" Her fingers returned to her lips, tracing the lines of her growing smile. "It's kind of doing it for me, if I'm honest."

I got the feeling just about anything would do it for her at that moment, but rather than say as much, I grinned. "Yeah, it's doing it for me too," I said, hefting Excalibur in its sheath over one shoulder. "I'm trying some new things. Speaking of which, can you lead me to the throne room? The regular one, not the big forbidden one in the basement. I'm still fuzzy on a lot of the directions in this building."

Kriseia shot a glance at her jailors, but the fear and deference they'd all adopted as they watched for my next move seemed to quash any hesitancy she still had about her sudden freedom. "I can do that," she replied, stepping up as close to me as the flames would allow. "Does that mean the coup didn't work? I can't imagine they would let you walk around doing… *this* for any reason."

"Long story, but short answer, yeah, they lost," I said, backing up to give her room to slip out ahead of me. "Or they're about to. I'll explain on the way."

Kriseia grinned, then turned and snatched a sword from the limp hand of an Iriate still too awestruck and unsure to stop her. With careful impatience, she pulled the coarse sack of her outfit out far enough to stab through, sword point downward, and rip away the confining garment, letting cloth and weapon both drop to the floor with a deep, blissful breath. "Let's go, my lady," she said with a wide, excited grin.

Thus did the two of us proceed, naked and unstoppable, through the halls of Pandemonium, kicking up plenty of the palace's namesake in our wake. Guards we approached tried a few more times to challenge me, nearly all of them giving up and stepping aside after they saw that charging me or chucking a spear at me only resulted in burned skin and the useless bouncing of sharpened steel off of my invincibility.

The last Iriate to make the attempt, to his credit, committed enough to try and tackle me, which didn't work and didn't hurt, but also didn't align with my current PR goals. It was the first and only time I had to actually pull Excalibur and stab someone — not fun for me, sure, but the enchanted blade slid into flesh so remarkably smoothly that it didn't feel like the viscerally violent act I was dreading. My conscience was surprisingly clear as I shoved the erstwhile attacker out of the radius of my fire, leaving the man screaming in pain and lightly smoking in the hall behind me, singed hands clutching the gash I'd put in his leg.

"Get him to a doctor, would you?" I asked the guard he'd been paired with, who had been smart enough not to rush the towering inferno with an armed woman at its center. "I was going for a nonlethal wound, but I'm not used to stabbing, so I'm not sure how good a job I did."

The more sensible Iriate nodded vociferously and hoisted his yowling comrade over his shoulders like a sack, jogging away down a crowded corridor.

All the corridors were crowded now, actually, most of that crowd falling in behind my passage and marching with me toward my destination. Morbid curiosity, a sense of impending import, fear of missing out: I can't speak to the motivation of every groupie I added to my entourage, but it was convenient that the palace was assembling for me.

The throne room itself was already bustling before I ever got there, demons of all sorts and across the entire spectrum of fancily dressed all shouting and recoiling at my entrance. I stood in the doorway behind the throne for a minute and raised my hands dramatically to give them something to wonder at while I unwound the flame spell around myself. When I dropped my hands, the fire died with a whooshing suddenness that sent a breeze roiling through the room.

I pointed to a nearby Superbiate woman as I approached the dais. No idea who she was or if she was someone of note, but she was short for her Sin at only about six foot, which made her the closest person to my own size I had on hand. "Cloak," I said, holding out my hand. "If you please. You'll get it back."

The room fell dead silent at my voice, and with the attention at least partially on her now, the woman complied all too readily, unclasping the purple satin hanging about her shoulders and handing it to me with something almost like a bow. Cool, she could read the room.

I smiled benevolently as I took the garment and wrapped it around myself. Maybe demons didn't care at all about nudity, but if this next part was going to be immortalized in portrait or statue someday, I wanted them to have at least a modicum of modesty, for my own peace of mind.

All eyes watched as I stepped up to the empty throne, sword in my hand, purple cape trailing the ground behind me. I turned my head to find Kriseia at the head of my entourage behind me, eyes wide and sparkling, and held out my hand again. She vibrated in place for a moment before eagerly rushing up and taking my hand, then my whole arm, pressing herself against me at my side, head lolled onto my shoulder, rapturous anticipation shining from her face.

There we go, that should make an impressive enough image. I squared my shoulders, thrust out my chin to the crowd, and raised the sheathed Excalibur in the air.

"Hear me, City of Dis, and all of Hell beyond!" I shouted to the audience. "My name is Morgan Samantha Amell, human, sorceress, and scion of the great and powerful Original Sin! And, starting from this moment—"

I ripped Excalibur from its sheath and plunged it a full foot into the ground at my feet. A quick heat sequence repeated silently in my head sent a small plume of flame traveling from my hand down the pommel to the blade, where it hit the ground and erupted in a short but dramatic backsplash, framing me for one more moment in fire as I smiled at my enraptured subjects.

"—I am your new archfiend!"

Chapter 41: Authoritarianism

Running Hell was probably a lot harder than Vambrace had made it look. Back when he'd been making it look possible at all, I mean, before this shitshow I had just inherited the end of. Meanwhile, the most governmental experience I had under my belt was helping make flyers for a friend in high school who was running for class president. And she didn't even win.

But if I'd learned anything here in Hell, it was that I was damn good at doing my homework. First step, I figured, was to work out what all needed doing and make an organized list based on timeliness and importance.

Item one: *Get that damn book back.*

Before the crowd could disperse from the dramatic declaration of my new rule — before I explained anything or checked to see if Vambrace was still alive or even put on clothes — I ordered the apprehension of Alastaroth, wherever he'd fled. Abdeles was dead, his secret backer was firmly in my pocket, the coup attempt was over, and we were mopping up now, so fall in line or face my wrath.

It seemed to go over well, as far as proclamations went. I got bows and salutes and other shows of deference from the audience before they broke apart, abuzz with fresh gossip and clamoring for my attention. The palace guards that had fallen in behind my march to victory rushed off to follow my command. All in all, it was a pretty gratifying moment.

It was also a lot to take in, here at what I decided was the end of a very, very long day. I waved off anyone attempting to gain a further audience with me and walked doggedly back down the familiar halls toward my usual room. Anyone still hanging on beside me that wasn't Kriseia stopped once we reached the well-guarded entrance to the archfiend's private chambers, blocked by the firmly crossed spears of two very stressed Iriate guards who were still processing the news of their new allegiance. By the time we reached my bedroom door, the din was a distant murmur far off down the halls.

"If you're the archfiend now," Kriseia said as we stepped inside, "then doesn't that mean you can have the bigger suite further down instead?"

"I like this one," I said as she closed the door behind us and I let my borrowed cloak fall to the floor. "Feels familiar now, y'know?"

She smiled. "I do know," she said. "I've missed it."

We fell into bed, and I was asleep almost instantly. A little bit later, I wasn't — and then about an hour after that, we both fell back asleep even harder, freshly exhausted, but in a much nicer way than I had been before.

I'd missed that too, I realized. I'd missed Kriseia, her company, her warm and stabilizing presence. The more, uh, *extracurricular* activities she came with weren't as important to me as they were to her, but I'd even missed those too by this point. They were fun, and I hadn't realized until we were on top of each other how severely in need of something fun I had been.

Fuck it, I was ruler of Hell now, the queen of sin, commanding legions of demons. Shame was for regular mortals, not me anymore. I had hot, sweaty, passionate, toe-curling sex with my lust demon familiar, and I was proud of it. There.

By the time we'd both woken up, bathed, and I found something to wear (in this case, the same T-shirt, leather pants, combat boot outfit I'd arrived in, which felt like an appropriate bookend), news came that Alastaroth was in custody, ready for my judgment.

"Excellent," I told the Iriate who had delivered the news. "Take me to the nearest empty sitting room we have, then chain him and bring him to meet me in it."

The guard bowed. "You don't want to deliver his judgment publicly in the throne room, your highness?"

Ooh, "your highness" felt better than I thought it would. I smiled. "Not yet," I said, "we have some things to discuss privately first. Lots of baggage between us to work out still, me and him."

The guard bowed again. "And will you require an armed escort as well, highness?"

I hefted Excalibur in its sheath in one hand. My other, I held up and set it on fire. "No," I said, still smiling, "I think I'm good without it."

Things got done quick when you were in charge. Within minutes, I was sitting in a lavish chair in a lushly appointed office, feet propped up on a low, beautifully carved table, idly admiring Excalibur while I waited for my prisoner. Not fifteen minutes later, said prisoner was marched in and dropped on the couch on the other side of the table, glaring at me with cold contempt over his shackled hands, saying nothing even after the guards had bowed to me and left once more.

I let him sit for another few minutes in that angry silence as I examined the sheath in my hands. Maybe I was power tripping, but I'd earned it.

Finally, I set Excalibur across my lap and met Alastaroth's many gazes. "So," I said. "Where is it?"

He sniffed. "I'm sure I don't know what—"

"No, don't do that," I said, flatly, drumming my fingers on the sheath. "We're past that now. Produce the book, or tell me where it is, and I'll go easy on you."

The Invidiate grinned. "And if I refuse? If you kill me, you'll never find it, human."

"You're really gonna go right down the checklist of predictability, huh?" I leaned my head on my fist and gave him my most dismissive stare. "Al, I know you think—"

"Alastaroth the 72nd," he interrupted through grit teeth, no longer grinning.

"Not right now, you're not," I said. "Allie-boy, I know you think you've got me over a barrel here, but let me make my position right now crystal clear. I want my book back; I do not, however, *need* it back. There's a difference." I held open my other hand and conjured a small fireball, which drew his attention before he could think to ignore it. "When you took it from me, you forced me to adapt. It sucked, but I did it, through trial and error and a lot of educated guesswork. I am a self-taught sorceress now, thanks to your schemes. I have stared into the language of creation at its source and learned to bend it to my will through sheer effort and cleverness alone. You, meanwhile, have had the manual in your hands this entire time, and you still couldn't do anything with it without tricking me into helping. What possible hope of using it to your own ends do you think you have now that you are well and truly without help?"

He had no retort or smug expression for that, only sat with his lips curdled as he stared hatefully at the fire in my hand.

I pushed. "Your summoning circle down on the capital-T Throne was what sealed it," I continued. "I'll admit, piecemealing the work for that had me blind for a bit, but seeing it in person filled in whatever gaps I had left in my understanding. I can leave this world or come back to it whenever I feel like now. I can summon in other allies, if need be, as you've seen. I can flood Hell with an army of humanity if I feel like it. And you couldn't stop me if I did."

His face paled. It was hard to see in Invidiates, but he made it obvious enough. I smiled as I leaned forward, holding the fire before my face and staring at him over top.

"I don't feel like it, though," I said. "And if you cooperate, I won't feel like it. I also won't feel like having you violently executed for making my life suck this past however long it's been, to say nothing of what harm your plan has actually done to Dis and the people in it. No, Al, if you give me back my book, I will be in a very good mood. A good enough mood to have you comfortably imprisoned. You won't have any more influence or any chances to try this 'let's overthrow Hell and invade Earth' plan ever again, but you'll be alive. Best of all, you won't even have to hear from me for the rest of that life — as soon as I have my book back in my hands."

The flame I held flared violently, a dull *fwoosh* sending it up in a puff of fire that nearly reached the ceiling before I closed my hand and snuffed it out. Alastaroth flinched back in his seat at the display.

Yeah, definitely power tripping, but definitely not feeling bad about it. I leaned back in my chair and drummed my fingers on Excalibur again. "Deal?" I asked.

He gulped, took a deep breath, sighed, and grumbled. But in the end, he said, "Deal."

Truth be told, I wouldn't have had it in me to actually have him killed, despite what he'd done. But he didn't need to ever know that.

Within short order, I was standing with four palace guards in Alastaroth's personal quarters high up in House Invidia's sub-spire, watching him rip open a pillow and fish out a small iron key, which he stuck inside an unseen hole on an inconspicuous wall sconce nearby. With a twist and a click, a flush panel of obsidian guilt wall slid aside to reveal a small, locked iron door. After fishing another key out of a potted plant in the next room, Alastaroth opened this as well, and pulled from the cubby beyond the only thing currently in there: the *Morganomicon*, which he reluctantly, but dutifully, handed over at last.

A thrill passed through me as my hands finally closed once more around the leathery, leafy, tree barky cover. That was less to do with any magic than with the satisfaction of finally, *finally* having the damn thing back, alive and unharmed. I flipped through it just to be sure; I hadn't actually read very far into the thing, but it felt as thick and heavy as I remembered, seemed to have the same amount of uneven, anachronistic pages inside. I smiled as I found the page that detailed the heat enhancement spell, followed soon by the section on sensory redirection wards.

Man, I thought, *if only I'd read past the first chapter before I sent myself here, this whole trip could probably have been over inside a couple days.*

I snapped the book shut and cradled it close. "Thanks for everything, Al," I said with a smile. "It's been mostly horrible, and I sincerely hope I never see you again, but I'll keep my promise not to have you killed. You three," I added, pointing to the nearest three of my guards, "guard him for now. Make sure he doesn't leave, make him stop if he tries anything sneaky or suspicious." The three clapped a crisp salute while Alastaroth scowled and ground his teeth. I turned to the fourth guard. "You. Do you know where the former archfiend is?"

Her brow furrowed. "In pieces, deep under the earth, from what I understand, your highness," she said.

That was worrying for a moment before I realized my mistake and shook my head. "No, not that one," I said. "Vambrace."

"Vambrace is back?" she asked, eyes widening and awe evident in her voice. "He still lives?" A hopeful look slowly suffused her features as she said this, which I was surprised but happy to see. If nothing else, his still having fans after all this boded well for my plans.

"He is, and I hope he does," I said as we left Alastaroth's rooms. "By that response, though, I'm guessing you don't know where he'd be if he was, say, nursing an all-the-way-through gut wound."

The Iriate's eyes widened again. "He was skewered through and still made his way back to us? By Amon…"

I wasn't going to correct the misconception in those words. Instead, I nodded. "Power of the Original Sin, remember," I said smugly.

She whistled. "No wonder he commanded General Enkida's respect so easily," she said, then paused to salute. "My lady, I don't know where my former lord is now, but I know how we can find him, if you'll please follow me."

"Thank you, soldier," I said. "Lead on."

Which brought me to item number two of my master itinerary: See if Vambrace was dead or not. I'd have a lot of rethinking to do if he'd kicked the bucket while I was away seizing his throne.

Thankfully for him, and for me and my schemes, Vambrace was indeed still breathing when at last I was brought to him, albeit with a kind of pained gurgling. But he was lucid, and the Superbiate doctor seeing to him assured me that he would recover from his injuries in time. Most of them, anyway — he was going to end up losing that finger after all. Still, considering everything that had happened to him, that was small potatoes.

He was lying beaten, bloodied, bruised, and bandaged in bed in a private room off the main recovery lobby of the hospital ward I found myself led to, and both my guide and his physician left us alone at my urging, closing the door behind them as they left. I took a seat near the head of his cot and listened to him rasp wetly through the pain for a minute before he finally sighed and rolled his head to look at me with half-lidded, barely focused eyes. "Well?" he asked.

"Well," I repeated. "Good news, weird news, and better news. Which do you want first?"

He closed his eyes and rolled his head back to face the ceiling. "In order, please."

I leaned forward. "Alright," I said. "Good news, the rebellion is over. You killed Abdeles, Alastaroth is under house arrest for the moment, and the whole conquest and invasion scheme they had planned is dead in the water."

Vambrace grunted. "Good," he said, "but I dare not believe it's that easy. Until the matter of the archfiend's throne is settled, their allies may renew their push for power once they've recovered."

"Yeah," I said, "that's the weird news. The matter *has* been settled. It's me."

Once more, his head lolled over to me, and he fixed me with the most exhausted stare.

"Archfiend Morgan Amell, at your service," I said brightly. "Or you're at mine now, I guess. I'm still learning."

"Hm." He smiled weakly. "I cannot be entirely surprised. Not after you seized Excalibur and marched away with it. It was probably the smartest move to make."

"Plus I'm human, plus I'm openly doing magic at everyone now," I added. "Everyone's falling into line real quick and neat so far, it's kind of amazing."

He sighed again. "So," he said wearily, "what does the new queen of Hell want of her broken and humbled predecessor?"

"Well, first off, I'm gonna need you to drop the weak and humble thing," I said. "Because what I want you to do is get back to work as soon as you're well."

His brow furrowed, and then he levered himself slowly and awkwardly up onto one elbow in his bed. "Elaborate, please."

"I've never held an office or been anyone's manager before," I said. "Probably I could learn, but I don't particularly want to. Doesn't speak to me as a career path, y'know?"

"I would have thought you'd considered that before you claimed a literal throne for yourself," Vambrace said. "What is your plan, then, as a ruler with no intention to rule?"

I grinned. "That's the better news," I said, rising from my seat. "Send me word as soon as you're feeling well enough to stand up and walk around. I'll fill you in at the same time as the rest of Dis."

"You can't fill me in now?" he asked as I opened the door.

"I could," I said, pausing in the entryway, "but then I'd have to repeat myself. And I also don't want you talking me out of it if you don't like what I'm gonna do." I turned to give him a grin and an over-the-shoulder finger gun. "You just keep on not dying and everything will work out great."

He sighed and flopped back down into his bed, but he didn't argue. Excellent. I closed the door and moved on.

Item number three: Lock down security on the Big Ass Throne downstairs. Now that I had the *Morganomicon* again, I didn't strictly need the summoning circle that Alastaroth had made; but if he'd already done most of the work for me, why squander it? Editing his sigil would be safer and easier than attempting the interdimensional spell by hand again anyway. I didn't need another adventure in another different world so soon after this one.

Thankfully, with my new super archfiend powers, getting that task accomplished was as simple as ordering the nearest guard I saw to pass the message on to whoever they reported to. It helped that the deep down bottom of Pandemonium had been considered sacred and off-limits until just recently; I got the feeling from those Iriates who received the order that a return to a "No non-archfiends allowed" policy was both expected and, on some level, appreciated.

That led smoothly into item number four on my list: Repair whatever damage I could that Abdeles and Alastaroth had wrought on this place since they sprang. What exactly that entailed and how deep it went, I didn't really know. But while I was waiting for Vambrace to get back on his feet, I figured I had the time to at least take a stab at it, if for no other reason than to give my own conscience whatever placebo it needed for being involved in the whole thing, even if that involvement was largely involuntary.

This being my first actual attempt at anything governmental, I decided the easiest thing to do was to gather the people who actually knew how that stuff worked and had been doing it already: the archdemons of the various Houses.

If memory served, half of them were traitors and at least one of them was dead, but it was a start.

It was also extremely awkward once we had all gathered around the long table of a swanky boardroom near the main audience chamber. On one side, Archduchess Cinaedemis sat beside Archduke Aleviathan the 43rd, both staring tight-lipped and nervously at the table directly in front of them, pointedly avoiding looking at me. Across from them, Archduke

Melchius fumed silently at them beside the empty seat that would have sat Archduchess Pyressa, were she still alive. And at the end of the table, Archduchess Bargryf sat slumped and half-awake across from Archduke Grodon, who had pulled a bottle of wine and a haunch of some dark red meat from deep within his gullet and busily munched and slurped away while everyone waited for me to start the meeting.

I gazed evenly at all of them over steepled fingers, trying to look more sure of what I was doing than I was. "Where to begin?" I mused aloud, and noted with a petty smugness that the Avaritiate and Invidiate nobles flinched slightly. "A lot has happened quickly around here, huh? I'm hoping it was all too quick for any ill effects to ripple out too far, but I don't have a clue yet. That's what you're all here for." I turned to Melchius. "You seem like the most eager out of everyone here to speak your peace, Melchius. How's House Luxuria been during all this craziness?"

He loosed a deep breath through his nose and sat up straight. "My lady, as you know, I was forcibly contained as well when Abdeles began his nonsense," he said, looking at me without any hint of a leer in his eyes for the first time since I'd met him. "'Loyalties uncertain,' I was told. 'Could go either way.' Honestly? I think the stuck-up prick just didn't like me personally and saw a chance to make me suffer for his bad taste."

"I can see that from him, yeah," I said. "Does that mean you don't know the state of your House either, then?"

"I know the broad strokes," Melchius said. "He and his lackeys weren't sure enough in me to have me killed, just confined, so I was afforded the courtesy of having my inquiries mostly answered. From those reports, and what little I've gathered since you ended the fool plan, my lady, I'm under the impression that the rogue element within House Luxuria was minimal, and has now entirely disbanded and surrendered with the news of your ascension."

"Entirely?" I repeated, brows rising. "That seems… quick and convenient."

Melchius shrugged. "We weren't exactly linchpins in the grand scheme, from what I understand. A small cohort was swayed by the idea enough to work directly with Alastaroth. I'm told he taught them some sort of invisibility magic that he stole from you, some twist on Luxuriate glamour that was necessary to steal power from our previous Lord Vambrace before the conspirators could act further."

"Ahh, yes," I said, "I was there for that." I'd almost forgotten about the Luxuriates that had appeared out of nowhere around General Enkida's body to nab Excalibur and train arrows on us. "That means magical knowledge has disseminated further than just Alastaroth himself, then," I added, rubbing my chin. "Hmm."

"Depending on who that group talked to and how easily taught the skill was, we may have an issue going forward with invisible Luxuriates, yes," Melchius said. "I'll keep an eye out, as it were. Beyond that strike team, though, House Luxuria was only involved insofar as there were standing orders to gather whichever talents we had that were best at impersonating humankind, presumably for infiltration purposes once the invasion began." He raised his hands and shook his head. "Honestly, though? Most of my House that was involved at all was being hired for their services, same as most any other client. Apart from fringe cases seeking some radical new excitement, I'm willing to wager that they were just professionals readying for a big job for a large group. We don't exactly tend to have huge stakes or interest in big political maneuvers, House Luxuria. We're entertainers and lovers of the pleasurable, not soldiers and revolutionaries."

I nodded as I stared at the table in thought. How much did I trust or believe Archduke Melchius? More than I distrusted him, I supposed. If he was hiding anything or glossing over important details, that could be dealt with later. For now, it was a satisfying answer, and I chose to accept it.

"Alright," I said, "good. Next." I laid my chin in my hand and turned my stare on the Avaritiate. "Archduchess Cinaedemis," I said coolly. "Time to explain yourself."

Melchius's glare returned as we both watched her squirm in her seat before sighing. "Little enough to explain, honestly," she said, meeting my eye at last. "An invasion of the human world would bring in unimaginable new riches and wealth if successful. And if it wasn't, well..." She threw her hands up and cast a guilty glance at where Pyressa should have been sitting. "It wouldn't be our House that got destroyed first, but it would be up to us to finance the rebuilding and defense if the plan failed. House

Avaritia either got first pick of the spoils or a massive loan contract with the new archfiend as the client. It would have been irresponsible of me as their archduchess to *not* agree to the deal."

I pursed my lips. "And if humans invaded Hell right back and stomped out all traces of demon society, razed Dis to the ground, and killed everyone who lived here, where would the profit be, Cinaedemis?"

She shrank in her seat. "Well... I mean, that would have happened with or without our help, right?" she said, more quietly now. "The invasion plan wasn't *our* idea. You can't let the threat of societal collapse get in the way of a good business opportunity."

"Can't you?" I asked. "I bet you could, if you tried hard enough, or at all. But more to the point, how is your House at large doing?"

"In quite the uproar, my lady," she answered. "A lot of investments changing hands to ready for the coming storm, a lot more trying to change right back or falling through now that it's been averted." She groaned, her fingers moving to toy fretfully with one of the bigger, shinier earrings hanging off her head. "I despise the very concept of business sanctions, but given what stands to happen to the economy at large if we don't take some of the more ambitious contracts into oversight, it may be a necessary evil. Just this once, at least. Though I doubt my station within House Avaritia will survive the backlash, if indeed I am forced to make that call."

"Quite serious and quite horrible, I'm sure," I snapped. "But I'm less concerned with the money than the people involved."

"The people?" Her bejeweled brow furrowed for a moment before she waved a hand. "Oh, the people themselves are fine, even if their finances are not. A few were borrowed for consultation of key items that Lord Abdeles wanted found, and one prominent merchant of Mammonis was conscripted to a confidential mission far beyond the wall. That one almost certainly died, but overall—"

"Got it," I interrupted, "thank you, you're done talking now. Aleviathan?"

"...the 43rd," he muttered.

"You know who you are," I said. "You also know the question. Answer."

He sighed. "Our strongest hexers were drafted to assist rebel Iriate forces in subduing loyalist elements within the army and guard. We suffered heavy losses in those campaigns, but were promised compensation, both monetary and honorary." He shot a pointed look at Cinaedemis.

She snorted. "Well, we're obviously not paying that out *now*."

"That's not your call anymore," I said. "We'll revisit that later. Continue, Mr. 43rd."

He grimaced. "That's about it," he said. "I mean, if you want a list of Invidiates who would love to see an archfiend knocked down, that list is 'every Invidiate,' but it wouldn't be personal. Nobody with any amount of power or influence appreciates what they have until they lose it."

"So you turned traitor out of a general distaste for power?" I asked. "Is that it?"

It was his turn to squirm where he sat now. "Yes..." he said. "And, well... because Abdeles promised a more prominent position for House Invidia in his new regime. For me specifically, an advisory position at his side as well."

"In other words, more power," I said. "Not surprising, I guess. Forty-three, do you know what a 'cliche' is?"

His small, clenched fist pounded the table in a rare moment of heat. "Don't you understand?" he asked. "I would have been the most influential Invidiate in demonic history since our founder and my namesake! Archdukes and duchesses following in my wake would be clamoring for the name 'Aleviathan the 43rd the 1st!'"

"Then thank goodness we dodged that algebraic bullet," I replied. "No offense to Invidiate culture, I guess, but yes offense to you personally, you understand."

He grumbled some more and turned his many gazes back to the table. "That's all," he said glumly. "If you want an inquest to unearth any remaining sympathizers for Abdeles's plan, well... it won't be easy, but it would be manageable. Eventually. With time."

"Maybe," I said. "I'll settle for a 'We won't do it again' for the time being. Sound fair?"

His shoulders rose, then slumped. "More than, my lady," he answered.

"Good," I said. "Archduke Grodon?"

The Gulliate held up a finger as he finished chewing and swallowing his latest mouthful, then leaned back with a creak in his chair and patted his ribcage just above his prodigiously absent gut. "Oh, I'm fine, Highness, and so is House Gullia," he said. "All in all."

My brows rose. "That so?" I asked. "Nothing worth mentioning after all that happened?"

"Oh, plenty worth mentioning!" he laughed. "I believe I spent almost the entire time drunkenly feasting and inside a procession of some of the most talented beauties of House Luxuria!" He raised his wine bottle to Melchius in toast, and the archduke smirked as he bowed back over the table. "Much more lavish than my standard reposes, and much longer lasting as well. I wondered several times what the occasion could be. Now, well, seems that mystery has been solved."

I took a deep, slow breath before responding. "You didn't even notice the coup going on all around you, then," I said. "You just… drank and ate and fucked your way through the most volatile period of your history in centuries without looking up?"

"I know, right?" He laughed deep and loud, then took another swig from his bottle for good measure. "If only all insurrections were so grand! But, no, I have nothing out of the ordinary to divulge other than that. And House Gullia's business, as a whole, had not and has not changed as a result. If I have rebel elements in my domain, the worst they were likely to do was stockpile resources in preparation for a siege or an invasion, neither of which will be happening now."

"Hm." I drummed my fingers on the table, but no issues with what I was hearing sprung immediately to mind. "And out of curiosity," I added after a moment, "if you *had* paid enough attention to realize some political upheaval was afoot, which side do you think you would have thrown in with?"

Grodon chuckled again and licked a dribble of wine from his chin with an impressive display of way too much tongue. "Why, the winning side, of course," he said with a smile. "Which seems to be you, Your Highness. I would have been on your side, if it came to it."

My eyes narrowed. "That is the squirmiest, weaseliest answer I've heard from any of you yet," I said.

He shrugged lankily. "Nevertheless," he answered.

"Nevertheless," I repeated. "Archduchess Bargryff? How you doing down there?"

The Acediate leader's face was hidden beneath her curtain of hair, which fluttered as she sighed. "Tired," was all she said.

"Oh yeah?" I asked. "I hear House Acedia was on the insurrection's side. All the aiding and abetting wear you out?"

She sighed again. Or maybe that's just how she breathed. "No," she answered. "Abdeles wanted secret surveillance network access. Wanted to also broadcast citywide. I just gave permission."

"Was that before or after the last archfiend went missing?" I asked.

Bargryff shook her head. "After. Before was illegal. Classified. After?" Another tired sigh. "Just following orders."

I pursed my lips. "If you didn't want to be a part of his plot, then Abdeles would have just been your colleague, not your boss. You didn't need to follow his orders if you didn't agree with them."

She nodded.

When she did nothing else, I sighed as well. "Didn't occur to you to argue?" I prodded. "Or, no, it probably did, but that would be harder. You were just going with the flow, right?"

She nodded again. "Easier," she said. "No fuss. No conflict."

"Not for you, you mean," I said. "Plenty of conflict everywhere else, though. Nothing *but* conflict for House Iria, I have to assume; but with their leader *and* general both dead, there's nobody to tell me just how severe it is on that front."

Bargryff just nodded again, face still obscured.

I slapped the table, making Melchius and Cinaedemis both startle. "Bargryff," I commanded. "Look at me."

Now that it was a direct order, she did. I don't know what I was expecting to see in that face. Guilt, maybe, hiding behind the eyes. Sadness for Pyressa's absence. Nervousness now that she was sitting here under my judgment. But no, she really did just look deeply, completely tired, her gaze more bags than eyes.

It struck me, then, just how much I shared the feeling. Everything had been exhausting for so long, and the closest thing I'd had to real rest was a change in the kind of stress I was under.

I leaned back in my chair, irritation evaporating. "You look like you feel like shit," I said to the Acediate archduchess. "Alright, let House Acedia know in no uncertain terms that the archfiend's classified psychic sloth network thing is restricted to just the archfiend's use once again. Whoever you let have access to it, that's revoked starting now. Starting yesterday, I'd say, if that meant anything here. Understood?"

Archduchess Bargryff nodded again, the corners of her weary eyes crinkling in what might have been the first step of a smile.

"Good," I said, "you're dismissed. From this meeting, and from your position as archduchess." I cast my gaze sternly around the table. "Aleviathan, Cinaedemis, you're both dismissed from your posts as well. Go to your rooms and stay there until further notice. We'll sort out your replacements later. Grodon, learn to pay attention to things better going forward, if you're supposed to be a leader. Melchius... uh, I don't know. Nice harness, I guess."

The luxuriate archduke flashed me a leering smirk that looked more at home on his face than his earlier anger did. Cinaedemis looked heartbroken. Aleviathan was visibly, silently fuming in his seat. Grodon raised a thumbs up as upended the last of his wine into his mouth. And Bargryff just sat there staring at the table again.

"Right," I said, rising from my seat, which sent everybody else rising too. "Council adjourned. This has been... eye opening, I guess. Thank you for your time, ladies and gentledemons."

I left ahead of the rest of them, striding alone down the short corridor toward the doors that led back into the front throne room. The Iriate guards posted at the end there saluted and threw the doors open for me, and I stepped out onto the dais behind the lowercase-t throne.

Kriseia was waiting for me there, leaning against the seat with a thick parchment book in one hand and a quill in the other, scribbling something furiously. She didn't seem to notice me approaching.

Until I tapped her on the shoulder. "Whatcha got there?" I asked.

She squeaked and snapped the book shut as she whirled. "Oh! Nothing," she said, holding the book behind her. "Just, uh, a diary, of sorts. I figured, with everything new happening and everything you're doing, I should write down my part in it. For posterity."

"Chronicling this moment in history, are we?" I asked with a smile.

She chuckled nervously. "Something like that, yes," she answered. "You're kind of a bigger deal than ever, Lady Morgan."

"I've told you," I said, "we're friends, you can drop the 'Lady' part."

"I know," she said, face flushing purple. "And I will again, if you prefer, but… I kind of like calling you 'Lady,' Lady Morgan."

"Ah." I recognized that flush, and the little twist and squirm her hips did as she spoke. "Like that, is it? Alright, 'Lady' me all you want, if that's what you like." She twisted in place more prominently at that, and I leaned to peer around her as she did. "Still, must be a scandalous chronicle of me, if *you're* embarrassed about it."

"Um…" Her purple deepened. "It might be mostly my own thoughts on the matter, if I'm honest. My own deep, very detailed thoughts." She brought the book in front of her to hide her face, peering over the top at me. "You've never acted this dominant before, Lady Morgan. I like your confidence very, very much."

My turn to flush now, though not nearly as hard or as purple. "Yeah, well, I'm wallowing in it while I've got it," I said. "But you know, I can't read demonic, so you don't have to hide it from me. Or even confess to what it really is; I wouldn't have known."

"I suppose," she said, then froze for a second. "Wait. What do you mean, 'while I've got it,' Lady Morgan?"

"Shit. Said that out loud, huh?" I sighed, then waved for her to follow me as I turned toward the main hall out of here. "I'll have to explain that when I know we have total privacy again. For now, I need to find Sidona again. Let's go."

Chapter 42: Escapism

Sidona didn't want to leave her room. I could have demanded it, I guess, but it seemed quicker to meet her on her own terms for now, hopefully catch her in a happier, more amenable mood. Also, by now, I just wanted to get this business over with.

Kriseia accompanied me up the duchess's tower but hung back in the halls, admiring the art, while I talked with Sidona alone. Maybe I was doing the duchess a favor that way, maybe I was saving Kriseia from getting further involved with potentially dire political machinations. As I entered her salon, I didn't really have much of a plan beyond "Deal with it somehow."

Sidona sat in the middle of the room amid what looked like the aftermath of a very fancy hurricane, parchment and instruments and open books brimming with bookmarks scattered in a chaotic mess across every surface. The Superbiate herself was on the floor bent low over a long, thin, tapering table with strings running along the top and metal plates hanging off the sides, her fingertips sheathed in what looked like wooden claws, plucking discordant, experimental melodies, her face hovering barely an inch over her instrument as if the right tune would emerge if she just stared hard enough.

I cleared my throat as I stepped carefully over a pile of papers, half-finished sketches of Iriate armies and burning spell circles. "You got a minute?" I asked.

She plucked out a four-note riff, smacked a rattling cymbal beat on the metal side of her instrument table, then pulled a notebook from underneath and started furiously scribbling with a stick of charcoal. "You know I don't know what that is, your highness," she said, not looking up.

"You can use your context clues," I said as I knelt in front of her opposite the instrument. She reached out to pluck the strings again, but I laid my hand on them first. The muted, impotent tune that followed finally snapped her attention up with an annoyed curl on her lips. "Take a break for now," I said. "We need to talk."

She exhaled a sharp, short breath as her lips pursed, then reluctantly sat back, rolling her shoulders with a deep pop and shaking stiffness from her neck. "As you wish," she sighed. "What would my archfiend ask of me?"

I sat back as well, and we regarded one another over our boardroom table of this recumbent guitar thing. "By your own admission, you enabled this entire power grab situation we're still settling," I said. "You gave Abdeles the idea to invade Earth, and you tipped him and Alastaroth both off that it was my spellbook they'd found and that I could help them read and understand it."

She sighed like the list of her treasons were the most boring topic in the world to her. "I did," she said. "I thought my mind was going. I wanted to leave the biggest cultural imprint possible before that happened."

I nodded. "But that was a misunderstanding brought on by my magic. And when I explained that to you — and then threatened your life and your legacy — you turned around and helped me put a stop to the very plan that you'd started."

"Well, I was wrong, and you were being very scary at the time," she said. "My liege, I must ask, is there a point to retreading this ground that we've both already been over?"

I stroked my chin and stared at her for a moment, looking for any sign of guilt or smugness or deception or, I don't know, anything illuminating. But she just looked politely irritated that I was interrupting her work. "Perspective, I guess," I said. "I'm thinking out loud. Reviewing the facts. Trying to figure out what I'm going to do with you now."

"Oh, is that all?" She smiled, then brought her notebook back up and started scribbling again. "I heard Alastaroth and the turncoat archdemons are all under house arrest for the time being. That punishment suits me just fine as well, if you're looking for input."

"The archdemons weren't involved as deeply or integrally as you were, Sidona," I said. "And Alastaroth is under house arrest for the moment as part of a plea deal while his ultimate fate is finalized. I agreed not to have him executed, but beyond that... well, I'm waiting for Vambrace to get well enough that I can get his input on the matter."

That caught her attention, and her scribbling stopped as her eyes snapped up over top of her notes. "Oh?" she cooed. "Do go on, please. I've been *dying* to know what will become of your dear predecessor. Keeping him on in an advisory position, it sounds like?"

"He's been keeping this place going for a literal eon, and I've been doing it for I think maybe two days so far," I said. "Yeah, I'm gonna use that resource. Don't worry, you and everyone else will find out my plans for him very soon. Right now, though, we're figuring out what my plan for you is gonna be."

She tilted her head with a smile. "We are together, are we?" she asked. "I'm touched, highness, honestly. Why not confer with his ex-highness on that point as well, if you're struggling?"

"Because he doesn't know how guilty you are yet," I said. "He only knows that you helped me save him and stop his enemies. And… I'm still debating how much of the truth I'm going to let him know."

Her smile widened. "Oh, juicy! You may have a better head for politics than you think, my lady."

"That doesn't feel like a compliment." I sighed and leaned back on my elbows. This was already as tiring as I'd feared it would be. "So, where do we go from here, Sidona? Because you've really muddied the waters for yourself, but I don't think you've broken even, as far as culpability goes."

"Hmm…" She tapped her lips with her charcoal stick, leaving a black smudge overtop her green lipstick. "And you really want my input on this? You trust me to help appropriately punish myself?"

"Not exactly, but your reluctant change of heart at the eleventh hour bought you this meeting, I suppose," I said. "Although, as narratively minded as you apparently are, I do kind of trust you to self-judge slightly more than I would otherwise." I rose back up, steepled my fingers, and studied her overtop of them. "What's an appropriate end to the story arc of Sidona's short-lived but powerful treachery?"

Her smile split into a wide grin. "You are the most interesting muse I have ever been blessed with, dear, human or not," she said, then rose to her feet and began to pace the room, heedlessly trampling papers and books as she went. "I confess, I do love that neither side in this little spat would have gotten anywhere without my help. It feels deliciously appropriate. I would worry that I'm too close to the story to tell it well, were it not for my practiced and obvious brilliance. But for my final act in this play?"

She strode another lap of her side of the room, then stopped, rigid, and snapped her fingers, her eyes lighting up. "I've got it!" she gasped, spinning toward me. "Exile! To Earth!"

It took a bit of rapid blinking to process what she was saying. "Absolutely not," I said a moment later. "Try again."

"No, but think about it!" she continued, dropping down to her knees again and leaning excitedly over her instrument. "Maybe I helped pose a danger to the human world, but then I turned around and saved it! What better fate after that than to actually see it with my own eyes, to walk among it and absorb it in all of its myriad and exotic—"

"You just want the ideas and the audience," I said, waving her back. "It wouldn't be a punishment, or even a good idea."

"And why not?" she demanded. "Are you worried that humanity won't be able to handle the incredible Duchess Sidona, jewel in the crown of House Superbia?"

"That's exactly my worry, yes," I said. "Bringing back one demon won't cause exactly the same uproar as bringing an army of them, but you would still be a big, *big* deal, and not in the way you're thinking. We don't have seven-foot-tall blue horned people on Earth, Sidona. There would suddenly be a whole lot of questions that I don't think Hell is ready to answer yet. More importantly, *I* don't want to answer them."

The enthusiasm stilled in her as her eyes slowly narrowed. "And why would you need to deal with any of the repercussions that happen on Earth," she asked, "if you're staying here to be our new archfiend, Archfiend?"

"Don't be coy," I said. "You've already guessed what happens next, I'm sure."

"Oh?" She paused for a thoughtful moment, then deflated. "Oh. Boo. That's not nearly as exciting, my lady."

"I don't want exciting anymore, Sidona," I argued. "I've had plenty. I want comfort and normal and rest now."

"And I'm one of the last things standing in your way of that, am I?" She sat back, crossed her arms, and sighed. "Honestly, that feels like punishment in and of itself. Why not reconsider? Stay with us, my lady, and craft for us a new epoch that will reverberate throughout—"

"I don't want to reverberate!" I groaned. "I want my life back! Don't worry, everything's changed plenty after I landed here, for Dis and for me. I'm sure you'll have plenty to do and plenty to inspire you from here on. You don't need me to stay here for that."

Sidona huffed, then shrugged. "Not like I can stop you, highness," she muttered. "So… when?"

"Soon," I said. "You'll hear about it. You won't be there, though, I don't think."

"What? Why can't I—"

"Because now I'm worried you'd try to jump into the spell and follow me home." I shot her a pointed glare.

She pursed her lips. "Fair point," she said. "Fine. But so you know, Morgan, I *will* miss you when you're gone."

That touched me, actually. It was a complicated feeling, given everything she'd done, but it was a feeling nonetheless, and the barest hint of a lump formed in my throat. "Y'know, crazy as it seems, I think I might actually miss you a bit too, Sidona," I replied. "I'm never going to trust you ever again, but I'll miss you, in a weird way."

She smiled. "I never needed your trust, my lady," she said. "Only ever your inspiration, and you delivered on that more than I could ever have hoped for."

So… that was that.

In the end, I did put her under house arrest, and stripped her title from her for good measure, though I let her keep her studio and all its amenities. If the loss of her nobility and privileges hurt her at all, she didn't show it — she had too much work to do, too many songs and stories and artworks burning in her to be thought of and finished, for something as inconsequential as her social status and legal freedoms to matter. Honestly, I think the only punishment I could give her that she would even notice would be to forbid her from creating anything going forward, and I just couldn't find it in myself to hate her enough to destroy her like that.

Kriseia was sullen on our trip back down from the Superbiate tower, rubbing her arm and staring at me until I noticed her doing it, at which point she turned her attention to the floor. "What's up?" I asked, though I think I knew the answer.

I did. "You're leaving, aren't you?" she asked quietly. "Going back to Earth."

I sighed. "I am, yeah," I said, wrapping an arm around her shoulders. "I'm sorry, it's just, I have a whole life already, people who probably miss me—"

"I know," she said, turning into the hug and pressing her face to my shoulder. "I understand, but… you're the archfiend now, right? If you leave, who's going to — oh."

"Yeah," I said, stroking her hair. "Look, I'd be a shit archfiend in the long run, trust me. I don't know the first thing about running a place like this."

She sniffled. "You could learn?"

"Eventually, yeah. Probably. It wouldn't be great for everyone else while I worked through the growing pains, though. But all that aside—"

"I know." She wrapped her arms around me and squeezed me tight. "But I'm going to miss you."

A lump was rising in my own throat now as I returned the gesture. "I'm gonna miss you too," I muttered into her hair. "But hey, once I know more about the traveling spell and how time works between here and home, maybe I can come back and visit sometimes. Y'know, on purpose, instead of trapping myself here by mistake."

Her sniffle turned into a laugh. "You'd do that?" she asked. "I thought you hated it here."

I chuckled. "Yeah, well… I don't hate everything here, as it turns out."

It was a long elevator ride, but even after the room reached our floor, we didn't leave until the doors opened from the outside and a couple of janitorial Invidiates loudly cleared their throats. If they knew who I was to them now, they didn't care, and I found I didn't either as I disentangled myself from Kriseia's arms, fixed my shirt, and walked out with her hand in hand.

By now, thankfully, Vambrace was well enough to leave his bed, and could even walk around on his own, albeit slowly and with a pained limp.

Not the best optics, considering the damage that had just been done to his undefeatable image, but it was good enough.

I offered him my arm as we walked together to the audience room, but he refused, stubbornly wincing as little as possible with each step. "So," he asked along the way, "what's the occasion, your majesty?"

"Do I detect a hint of jealousy, good sir?" I asked back with a smirk. "Seems unbecoming."

He grunted, and I couldn't tell if it was from amusement, pain, or both. "It's not," he said. "Envy is but a facet of the Original Sin; it would be less becoming if I were immune to it. But no, I wasn't trying to be particularly snide, my lady. It just feels weird to call somebody else by that title after so long."

"I bet," I said. "Well then, I've got good news for you, my lord."

"'My lord?'" he repeated. "Now *that* is unbecoming of an archfiend. But could it be that this good news of yours is the reason you have so mysteriously required my presence without explanation?"

"Yup. Sorry," I said, "didn't mean to keep it this secret-y, but I also didn't want to risk you knowing what I had planned too soon and spreading the news early or talking me out of it or anything."

"Because my social life has been so rich and lively from my hospital bed where I lay bleeding until now," he scoffed. "But very well. I suppose I of all people have no right to complain about such a ploy." We walked in silence after that, barring his occasionally audible wince or grunt. "What is the ploy, though?" he asked again after a minute.

"First," I said, "I'll need you to show me how it is you call for an official royal audience when nobody in Hell understands what a schedule is."

"Easy," he said. "Acediate network."

"Oh. Yeah, I guess that makes sense," I said. "Honestly, even knowing about it, I forget those guys are there."

"That's part of the design, yeah," said Vambrace. "Honestly, if you're going to be archfiend now, I can admit: most secrets about how I do things boil down to the secret psychic Acediate network. Or the power of Excalibur. Or..." He trailed off with a pause and a sigh, his face falling.

"Or Enkida," I finished for him, then laid a hand on his shoulder. "Yeah, I miss her too. Speaking of, with her and Pyressa both gone, we gotta get the Iriates' entire deal sorted sooner rather than later."

"I've been thinking on that," he replied. "Wait, 'we?'"

"Royal audience first," I said. "Then I'll explain."

Sure enough, it was as easy as pulling aside the curtain in the alcove behind the dais and telling the slouched Acediate napping there to call all the major and minor nobles to the throne room for an important announcement. The Acediate nodded, turned their attention to a slitted peephole in the wall nearby, and presumably relayed the message to whichever sloth demon they could see that made up the next node in the chain. Then we sat and waited, me on the throne and Vambrace on the edge of the dais in front of me.

It took maybe an hour for everyone important enough to show up to get there, the wide hall slowly filling with bodies until we looked out over a multicolored lake of expectant faces all muttering and speculating to one another.

"How do we know when everyone's here?" I quietly asked the only other human in the room.

Vambrace was busy not acknowledging the confused stares he was getting from his former subjects, many of whom were no doubt surprised to see him still living, much less perched on the step before the throne that used to be his. Must be awkward for everyone, I thought. "When you tire of waiting for more people to show up, is how I always decided," he answered.

Fair enough. I stood from my seat and walked to the edge of the dais, a move which made the entire room fall silent. My eyes scanned the crowd for a minute before I saw Kriseia in the press near the front, smiling sadly. I smiled back with a nod, then cleared my throat and turned my attention to the room at large.

"Thank you all for gathering here so promptly," I began. "No doubt my presence up here won't come as a shock to most of you; it's been a chaotic past few… well, days, yes, I know that word doesn't mean much to most of you, but it's been several days now since the former Archduke Abdeles failed in his coup attempt and paid for it with his life. A lot happened all at once, a lot's happened since, but just to summarize the important part: yes, I, Morgan Samantha Amell, a human and practicing magic user, am your new archfiend."

I paused for effect, which here meant a bit of murmuring in the back of the crowd and some general clapping all around. I held a hand up before it could swell into full room-filling applause.

"I'm told there are no demons alive today old enough to remember the last time the title changed hands," I continued. "My predecessor, Vambrace, has led you all well for eons from this throne. Given that Abdeles failed to actually be here doing anything useful after he tried to claim the title for himself, I don't think we'll count him among the distinguished ranks to hold the title. So, from one human to another, Hell has been ruled by a member of the Original Sin for thousands of... well, nobody here knows what years are either, I realize, but for a long fucking time, let's just say."

I strode across the front of the dais, tapping Excalibur in its sheath against the floor as I went. "Now, as this recent batch of unrest and scheming and power grabbing has shown, not everybody has been completely happy about that fact the entire time. Still, it's worked for this long, it can continue to work going forward — with a few changes, to make sure we don't repeat these recent mistakes. Well, one major change in particular. Vambrace?"

I stopped beside where he sat and offered my hand. Confusion flashed briefly across his face before experience stepped in and he schooled his expression, then took my hand and rose to his feet. He let go, but I didn't, instead lifting our joined hands up above our heads for the crowd.

"I will not rule this realm alone," I declared loud enough for the demons in the back. "From this moment forward, Hell will have two archfiends, and be further united and strengthened under the guidance of the last remaining two Original Sins!"

The gasp that rose from the crowd at this announcement nearly sucked the air out of the room. If anyone applauded, it was drowned out by the shocked and confused din that suddenly arose, loud enough to hurt my ears.

I banged the sheath in my hand against the floor, three loud, ringing clunks. "Hey!" I shouted to the room. "Shut up and pay attention!"

That worked. Everyone's faces stayed stunned, including Vambrace next to me, but the room was silent and all eyes were on me once more. It was weird how used to it I already was.

"Let me explain," I said. "Hell's disconnection with Earth has clearly been going on for too long. Our worlds have forgotten too much about one another, and what little we all think we know keeps proving to be wrong. Abdeles sought to change this through force with an ill-equipped invasion that would have seen Dis reduced to ruin and Earth thrown into disarray in response. We cannot have that again, but we also cannot continue as we have, ignoring or blindly speculating about our neighbors just on the other side of a thin interdimensional border. So, here's how we're going to solve this issue."

I released Vambrace's hand, gripped Excalibur by the sheath, and held out the handle for him to take. He caught on surprisingly quickly, schooling his face into a resolute mask and nodding as he gripped the sword between us. "I leave my partner, the Co-Archfiend Vambrace, here to keep Hell running as it had been, to oversee its daily needs and enact our laws and judgments as needed," I said, then yanked the sheath off the sword, leaving Vambrace holding the naked blade as I flourished the aegis. "I, meanwhile, will return to Earth to spread the influence of demonity and reawaken diplomatic channels between our worlds. I will help lead you all remotely, my will enacted through the archfiend I leave here in the palace, while I establish a New Dis on Earth, a colony and embassy that will lay the groundwork for interdimensional cohabitation through peaceful, sustainable alliance rather than the blind and ignorant warmongering that our enemies would have had."

I banged the sheath against the floor once more, then grabbed Vambrace's hand again and raised both high in triumph. He hoisted Excalibur in the same moment, both of us smiling. "Let there be no more infighting, no more warring factions, no fracturing or division over the perceived majesty or threat of the differences between the Seven Houses of Sin and we, the Original Sin that preceded them!" I declared. "From this moment forward, let us instead all walk hand in hand, together, into a brighter future, all of us the stronger and more prosperous for our newfound unity! For we are all of us siblings, the children of Sin!"

The room erupted in deafening cheers. Vambrace and I held our poses, pumping our respective components of Excalibur and smiling. He was still smiling as he leaned sideways toward me and, without taking his eyes off the crowd, mutter-whispered, "What the hell was any of that?"

"Good, right?" I mutter-whispered back. "I stayed up pretty late figuring out that speech and going over the key points over and over again. Do you think the 'children of Sin' thing was too much?"

"Not what I was talking about," he replied. "Co-rulership with me? With you back on Earth? That's a tall order, and one I would have greatly liked to know about at least a little ahead of time."

"Yeah, but I didn't want to give you the chance to say no," I admitted. "Because whether or not you wanted your old job back, I really, really want to go home."

"And now I suppose I'll have to give a speech on the spot to my former, now renewed subjects, all while pretending I'm not as surprised and confused as they are?"

"Yup." I risked a sideways glance to see him scowling openly at me now. I grinned back. "In my defense, I'm *still* not totally done being angry at you for running off on me. But we can call us even after this."

He sighed but didn't protest further. Not right here, at least. So, with a companionly pat on the back and a thumbs up, I left him between the throne and the crowd to say whatever he felt he needed to say. For myself, with this announcement out of the way, I was finished with my pre-flight checklist, except for gathering up whatever I was taking with me and making my final goodbyes.

That first part was easy, since I hadn't shown up here with much and didn't exactly make any big purchases during my stay. Besides the *Morganomicon* and the clothes on my back (minus my denim jacket, which I let Vambrace keep to remember me by, since he was so fond of it), all I was taking back with me was the fancy Superbiate gown I'd worn whenever my Earth clothes were dirty, my bundle of all the magic notes I'd made for myself, and a few soul crystals plus the pandemoniumite chunk I'd used to save the day, as souvenirs.

Oh, and the scabbard of Excalibur. I hadn't had time to study the invulnerability enchantment on it yet, and Vambrace had lasted this long without it, I figured. Plus, it was just good optics for the co-leaders of Hell, one holding the unstoppable sword and the other holding the immovable aegis.

My long-dead mp3 player I left as a surprise gift to be delivered to Sidona after I was gone — something to help her musical studies in my absence, and to hopefully keep her too busy and behaved to think of disrupting things too much for a while. It was an old enough model that I could upgrade and replace it pretty cheaply once I got back home, and of course I still had all the files on my computer and the CDs in my apartment.

I also decided to leave the ushi-oni poison gravy behind, for obvious reasons.

By the time I was packed and arriving back down at the Abandoned Throne, with a sad and somber Kriseia in tow this time, I found I had more luggage waiting for me after all. Vambrace was waiting for me at the top of the massive seat of crystal soul with Archdukes Melchius and Grodon beside him, and a pile of stuff just behind them. "Honored Highness, Princess Morgan," Melchius began with a shit-eating grin plastered across his face. "In this most momentous and auspicious of moments, let us offer as tribute the gifts of our Houses, to assist in the establishment of the majesty of New Dis—"

"You guys," I interrupted, walking past them to the pile of stuff. "I'm flattered, but I can't take all of this with me. Moving even small objects alongside myself with this spell is dubious, a small mountain is out of the question."

"Yes, we figured," Melchius continued, sullen. "But we had to try, at least. You are our beloved new ruler, after all, my lady."

"That, and high-protocol deference to authority gets him off," Archduke Grodon added, ignoring the elbow to the ribcage that got him from Melchius. "Worry not, though, your highness, as anything you do not want, I will gladly requisition."

"We're all shocked, I'm sure," Melchius drawled.

It *was* an impressive pile of gifts, I had to admit, as I walked a wide circle around it. Trunks of fine clothes and fancy cloths, crates of various pastel-hued ointments and lotions and other bottled liquids, a whole cask of wine nearly as tall as I was, baskets of baked goods and fresh fruits, pots of flourishing exotic plants, and a few gleaming swords and polearms and shields propped against the side of it all.

"Well, it's the thought that counts," I said with a smile. "So, thanks, you guys. I'll miss, uh, some of you." I turned toward the center of the wide seat, paused, then turned back to the pile of presents. "Actually, on second thought," I said, and snatched up a jar of deep purple-red caina berry jelly and a bottle of golden-brown mearcalum wine. "A little bit of tribute wouldn't hurt."

And so, with everyone else I'd met and liked here in Hell either under arrest or dead, this was my farewell party: Kriseia, Vambrace, and the two archdemons I had the least reason to dislike. Not exactly a grand crowd, but a bigger one than I might have had.

Melchius and Grodon stayed a polite distance away as Vambrace and Kriseia followed me to the center of the summoning circle that I had altered to unsummon me back to where I came from. "I don't know how much of what you announced to the realm was a white lie to get out of here," Vambrace said in a low whisper, "but just in case it wasn't all blowing smoke, you should know." He slipped an arm over my shoulder, and I paused as he gave me a quick, firm side hug. "If you ever do want to return here someday, my lady, we will welcome you back with open arms and the greatest fanfare. I'll even make sure your room stays clean and ready to receive you."

My smile was genuine as I turned and hugged him back properly. "Thanks," I said into his mailed chest. "That means a lot. And if *you* ever want to come back to Earth and check it out... well, I don't know how you'd do that without me coming to get you, but if you manage, I'll have a futon ready for you in my apartment."

He hugged me back tight and smiled. "I don't know what that is," he said.

I was ready, when he released me again, for Kriseia to fling herself into my arms one last time. She'd been morose ever since learning of my plans, but had quickly managed to accept it and keep herself together. Not so much right now, though.

"I'm going to miss you, Morgan," she sniffled into my shoulder. "Gift or friend or whatever I am to you, I've never been closer to anyone before. Moving on is going to be the hardest thing I've ever done, and that includes the deprivation torture in prison."

I laughed, and my voice hitched a little. "I'm sorry," I said, tears welling. "I'll miss you too. If I ever do come back to visit, it'll be to see you again most of all."

She sniffed again, then took my face in a firm grip and pressed her lips tenderly to mine in a searing goodbye kiss. "Thank you for everything," she said as she pulled away.

My tears fell at last over her hands on my face as I reached up and cupped them. "You too," I said. "I'll never forget you, Kriseia. As long as I live."

That was that.

I'd wiped my tears and composed myself again by the time everyone had retreated to the periphery of the summoning circle. With a nod and a smile to the four of them, I took a deep, slow breath, turned my eyes to the beginning of the spell at my feet, and began.

The first time I had cast this spell, long ago and far away in my apartment, it had only been a series of meaningless hand movements and thought patterns, intrusively etched into my attention span but otherwise inscrutable beyond the function that the book promised me should I perform them correctly.

The second time I cast this spell, just a few days or so ago as far as I could tell, I was hurriedly skimming, running on instinct and adrenaline, powering through the motions before I was caught and everything fell apart, with no time or chance for deeper comprehension.

Now, this third and final (for a while) time, I at last had the opportunity and the experience to understand what it was I was doing.

As I turned in place at the circle's center, gaze tracing the flowing runes and intricately curling shapes, I felt my hands moving subconsciously at my sides, fingers flexing and curling and tracing the same old elvish language as I read it, supplementing my eyes by interpreting the lines that hovered at the edges of the main story that the spell weaved. When my mouth began moving as well, I realized it had never been words that I had chanted, it had been the same shapes, the same curling and twisting and spiraling through perceptions around me that my mind and hands and attention were flowing through. The whole was a pattern that I absorbed with everything I had, that absorbed me in turn, sight and thought and sound and movement, the magic building and twisting and flowing out of and simultaneously into and through me as it formed and weaved and executed.

Reality is perception, and perception is malleable, controllable, imperfect, and so the world around me is forever open to interpretation, to translation, and what can be translated can be edited, and what can be edited can be rewritten, and what can be written can be unwritten, can be read aloud, can be absorbed, can be understood and internalized so deeply that the reading changes me, changes what I perceive, changes where I am and when, changes the world I know, changes everything I thought unchangeable, if only I concentrate, if only I focus, if only I comprehend hard enough to forget and misremember and change my perspective on perspective, change myself, change everything—

The wind and the wailing and the heat and the cold and the long endless tumble through everything and nothing are distantly familiar, like a bad dream remembered much later, but now I am awake in my dreaming, and I understand what I am and where I am going and how I am getting there, and the swirling chaos maelstrom of light and dark and everything everywhere all at once make perfect sense in the momentary forever of their passing and of my passing and of what and where and when is happening around me, and with a steady mind and a surety of purpose and intent, I reach out through the infinite possibility with myself and reach for where I want to be and what I left behind and where and when I will be again and—

—and just before I reach it at last, I am ripped sideways at the last possibility and tumble against another will that is not my own, and with my goal still firmly in my sight and my will, I roll and flip feel a pause rushing forward to meet me, a cosmic interruption that wears a smile like wind chimes on a rainy night and eyes like distant silver stars that peer through the infinite expanse of space millions of years removed and pin me to the spot I am and say —

"Ah, yes, there you are. Excellent work, very impressive; but before I let you finish, let us chat, you and I."

And all at once, I am — I was — still and present and stable once more. But not where I should have been.

Chapter 43: Revelry

Where I found myself was dimly but warmly illuminated, a cozy gloom like a low-burning fire, lit by hanging lanterns that looked like black filigree cages holding entire tiny stars. The walls around me pressed in close, each and every one overstuffed with shelves that were themselves overstuffed with so many jeweled and detailed knickknacks, so many shimmering bottles and flasks, that I found it impossible to focus on any one object or detail.

So instead, I focused on the chair I was sitting in, a soft and plush thing of crushed leather that I sank so deeply into, it was like I had always been sat here. In my hand was a dainty green saucer of porcelain leaves, sporting a blooming glass flower of a teacup filled with warm, steaming tea that smelled of sweetness and the feeling of coming home after a long and stressful day. The *Morganomicon* sat closed and secure in my lap, Excalibur's sheath laid overtop like a safety bar on a rollercoaster. The jar of jelly and bottle of wine I'd taken off the tribute pile sat upright and safely on a low wooden coffee table in front of me.

And across from me, on the other side of the table, sat a familiar woman in the same sort of chair as me, sipping the same tea from the same cup and saucer, her high cheekbones raised higher still in the most self-impressed smile I'd ever seen on anyone who wasn't Sidona. Stray leaves and bits of crystal adorned her night-black hair like a crown, and she still carried the same faintly musty smell of her secondhand store.

She took a single sip of her tea before she spoke again. "Morgan, Morgan, Morgan," she crooned in her honeyed windchime voice. "My, my, what *have* you been up to?"

I took a sip of tea before leaning back in my seat with a tired sigh. "Hello, Other Morgan," I said. "How's the shop?"

She chuckled, the room around us tinkling along with her laughter. "You're in it now, dear," she said.

I looked around at the shelves again. They were packed enough, but my eyes hadn't glazed over looking at the clutter in her store the way they did here. "Huh. Back room, then?" I asked, sipping more tea. "Employee break lounge?"

"Back room, of sorts," Other Morgan answered. "In a dimensional sense. You have not quite made it to Earth yet, if that is what you mean to ask."

"You still know what I mean to say without my having to say it, I see," I said. "That remains slightly annoying, you know."

"I know," she answered. "And yet, I suspect your threshold for what you are able to endure has increased dramatically of late, has it not?"

"Alright, if this is what we're doing," I sighed, leaning forward to set down my tea and pick up the wine bottle. The cork was removable by hand, thankfully. I popped it out and took a swig of that warm honey-apple-dirt mearcalum flavor I'd developed a taste for, then held out the bottle to the witch across from me. She shook her head. "Cool, I only have this much of the stuff," I said, sitting back again. "Alright, so how much do you know already?"

That amused, tinkling laugh again. "I know where you've been," she said. "I can imagine who you've met while you were there. And I know how quickly you must have grasped the craft, to make the trip there and back again under your own power. Not to mention that the King's Aegis vanished from my possession not long ago, seemingly of its own accord, only to return now with you. The book has done you many favors, it seems."

"You'd be surprised how little it helped while I was there, actually," I said. I took another swig of the wine, then reached for the tea again and took a drink of that too. They paired surprisingly well together. "Yeah, so, Vambrace. He was a squire in King Arthur's court, one of the traitors who helped dethrone him, then he stole Excalibur and disappeared into Hell." I watched her face as I spoke, and it didn't move a millimeter. "I'm guessing you helped with some or all of that. You're Morgan le Faye, aren't you?"

Her head tilted. "Do you need clarification," she asked, "or is there a specific reaction you're looking for?"

"I've honestly kind of washed my hands of fully comprehending what your deal is," I answered. "Other worlds exist, some of our myths are actually history, magic is real, and reality itself is frighteningly delicate. I'm trying to keep my eyes on the prize that is returning to my ordinary life, because without that anchor and the promise of something solid and familiar, I think I might go properly insane."

"A common and sensible reaction for an initiate to have," Other Morgan said, nodding. "Sensible enough to keep hold of into mastery, even. What if I were to tell you that I am, and that *you* are, both that same Morgan le Faye? That I am your future, and that you will one day travel back into history to become me?"

"I'd call bullshit," I said.

There was nothing weird or mystical about the laugh that got from her, just her throwing her head back in amusement. "Solid indeed!" she laughed. "Yes, I think you will be quite successful in your studies to come, Young Morgan. You and the book chose one another well."

"Who says I'm going to keep studying anything?" I asked, hefting the *Morganomicon*. "What if I'd rather have a refund?"

"Did you keep the receipt?"

I paused. "Did you give me one?"

"Doubtful," she said. "But as you say, I call bullshit. Look me in the eyes and tell me that a true reversion to total normality lies in your future, dear. Tell me true that, having tasted this power, having begun to grasp its workings, you are not hungry to delve deeper."

I drummed my fingers on the book's cover. "This is a weird conversation," I said. "But yeah, no, you caught me. Magic is cool and I'm good at it, so I'll be keeping the book."

"Of course," she said. "And the King's Aegis?"

I hefted the scabbard between us. "I mean, I had planned to keep that too?" I said. "But it didn't occur to me at the time where I'd summoned it *from* — I didn't mean to actually summon it at all, that was more a happy accident." I looked over it at her and held it out. "If it's yours, do you want it back? I was going to study the enchantment on it, but I wasn't trying to steal from you, if that's what I did."

Her eyebrows rose as she slowly set down her tea cup and crossed her hands in her lap. "You would surrender it willingly?" she asked with the cadence of a trick question.

I pursed my lips as I regarded the thing. "I mean, I'd be bummed," I said, "but I also get the feeling you're not the kind of person I should steal from, accidentally or not. And that if you wanted this thing back, I wouldn't really be able to stop you having it. So I thought I'd be civil about it."

"Hm." Another enigmatic smile spread across her lips, some mixture of impressed and amused. "Yes. Quite successful indeed. Enough to warrant my own involvement? Remains to be seen, I suppose. It *has* been ages since I directly involved myself with anything."

She wasn't talking to me at this point, but I nodded anyway. "Great ominous mutterings," I said. "Very mysterious, somewhat spooky. So, do you want the sheath or not, then?"

Other Morgan chuckled and waved a dismissive hand. "You may keep it," she said. "For now. One day, I am sure, I will remember that you have it and come to reclaim it; until then, study its workings well, and enjoy the nigh-invulnerability. I would also caution you to be wary of dramatically altering balances of power on a historical level while you have it in your possession, but it seems that ship has already sailed."

My grip on the sheath tightened as I nodded again. "I'm not planning on overthrowing any Earth governments," I said. "Not anytime soon, anyway. After recent events, I'd really like to just take it easy for a long while. Speaking of, can I go home now, please?"

She made an airy motion to the side of the room. "Of course, of course," she said. "There's the door."

I leaned forward in my seat and stared at the wall she was waving at. Sure enough, nestled in between a shelf of glowing insects in jars and a hanging tapestry that looked like it was woven out of stained glass, there was a seam in the solid wood of the wall that I hadn't clocked before.

I stood and gathered my things. "And I just walk through that into… what?" I asked. "Your shop? Some sort of interdimensional bus station?'

Other Morgan laughed her tinkling raindrop laugh. "Into wherever you meant to go when you left," she said. "I didn't disrupt your carefully planned spell, merely inserted myself into it. This space is a liminal pocket I set up to catch any intelligences moving from Hell to Earth. Once I realized what you'd done and where you've been, it seemed the smart move."

"Right," I said, moving toward the door. "Well, it's been... fun? Kind of. Interesting, at least. Thank you for... Actually, I don't know if I should be thanking or blaming you, if either."

"Yes, I get that a lot," she replied. "Relativity, my dear. It's an important keystone. I'll be seeing you around, young Morgan. Take care."

I wasn't sure how much I liked that insinuation, but it wasn't up to me. Either way, I was done here. With a deep breath, I pushed my hand against the crack in the wall. It swung open on unseen hinges, and I stepped through.

Into my apartment.

By the time I'd recovered from the disorientation and turned around, all that was behind me was my own front door, which hung open onto the same hallway it always had.

I poked my head back through just to be sure. Sure enough, to my right, there were the stairs leading down to the ground floor. To my left, one of my neighbors — one of my fellow *human* neighbors — was just coming home and unlocking his front door. He smiled and gave an awkward wave when he saw me staring. I returned it, and we both ducked back into our own units.

I rushed to my kitchen table and dumped the book, the sheath, the gown, the bottle of wine, and the jar of jelly, then stood in the center of my one-room home and stared. There was my cheap couch, my used TV, my twin bed, my bean bag chair, my desk, my laptop — all of my mundane stuff, all where I'd left it. The dirty dishes I'd left in my sink were even still there, and still dirty.

But not disgustingly so, given how long they must have been sitting here unwashed. I opened my fridge, and while it was still nearly empty, the food inside didn't look like a moldering nightmare. My half-gallon of milk even passed the sniff test.

That... didn't seem likely. What was today's date? How long had I been missing?

I found my cell phone half buried in my unmade bed, steeled myself, and hit the power button. It lit up immediately to show 53% battery and no missed calls.

Well, that part kind of stung, to be honest. Nobody had even tried to get in touch with me while I was vanished from the Earth? I would have suspected my parents at least to blow up my voicemail demanding to know why I wasn't answering.

And then I noticed the date in the top right-hand corner. That couldn't be right. I powered it off and on again to let it reboot, then checked again, but it still showed the same date. Just to be extra sure, I flipped to the calendar app and opened it to check what year it thought it was.

No change there either. According to all evidence around me, today was the day after I'd accidentally traveled dimensions. My entire adventure in Hell had taken less than 24 hours.

That was flat-out incorrect. I knew it in my heart, in my mind, in my bones. Maybe demons didn't measure time, but time had passed, dammit. I'd eaten, I'd slept, I'd grown hungry and sleepy again later. I'd dealt with boredom and impatience and, and… and life! I'd done stuff! So much stuff! Not that I wanted to return to a full-scale manhunt and have to explain where I'd been, but this made the whole thing seem like one night's bad dream!

But no. I had just as much evidence it hadn't been, most of it sitting on my table right now. I uncorked the wine and took another deep swig, and it had the same marsh apple flavor I'd remembered. I unfolded the gown and held it up, and it had the same fancy tailoring and exotic style as I'd seen on plenty of Superbiate women and not a single Earth one.

So somehow, my spell was so successful, it not only brought me back to *where* I wanted to be, it brought me back to *when* as well. Time was evidently just as flimsy and rewritable as space and dimension if you knew the language.

I should have rested then, fallen into bed and slept straight through the next three days at least. Instead, I changed my clothes, grabbed my phone, wallet, and keys, strapped Excalibur's sheath to my back with a belt, and walked out the door. I needed a walk. I needed to move and breathe and think.

The world outside was extremely, blissfully mundane. Normal and familiar and boring, or as boring as a world could be once you've discovered you can change it on a whim. I walked down sidewalks I'd walked down a thousand times before, past the first humans I'd seen in months, and watched the traffic go by with a soaring heart. The sounds of honking cars and roaring buses and someone's overly loud stereo rattling their shitty four-door sedan with too much bass was music in my ears. The sky above was a blindingly vibrant blue, even if it was mostly, objectively more of an overcast and muddy gray at the moment. I found the sun behind a cloud and stared directly at it for a couple of seconds before the glare overpowered my nostalgia and made me look away, blinking tears from my eyes.

I was home. I was safe. It was the most underwhelming, unglamorous, beautiful homecoming I'd ever had, and I found myself grinning unstoppably as I walked, wondering at every familiar sight.

I reached the bus station nearest to my apartment just before the bus itself and climbed aboard eagerly. There were a few curious stares at the girl wearing the empty sword scabbard as I took my seat. I would have been anxious about that before, ducking my head and trying to shrink from the scrutiny; now, I just couldn't care anymore. I smiled back at anyone whose eyes caught mine as I found a seat, and found myself humming a tune as the bus pulled away.

It was still packed and stank, and I hadn't magically learned to love the crowd of strangers, but it was such an outdated and quaint problem to have now, I almost laughed.

I got off at my school's campus and strode through the gate, then wandered aimlessly up and down the quad. It had the scant, unhurried traffic of a weekend afternoon, which leant more credence to what my phone was telling me was today's date. Which also meant I didn't have any classes right now, which meant there was no reason for me to be here except the sheer contentment of being here.

I found a covered swing between one of the dorms and the English building and laid down in it, twisting the scabbard around to cradle it like a body pillow as I watched the birds flit between the trees. Normal birds, and normal trees.

Normality. Once upon a time, it was the only ambition I'd really had, and somehow, I'd thought it was out of my reach. I didn't fit in enough in too many spaces, I didn't know where I was going or what I was doing with myself, I didn't know how to act around people, how to be comfortable in my own skin in my surroundings.

And now here I was again, surrounded by all of these normal things, and I was about as abnormal as a human being could get. I knew magic, I had traveled between dimensions twice, I was the literal queen of Hell, and I was snuggling a powerful, invaluable artifact from ancient myth.

And none of it felt uncomfortable at all anymore. It felt right. I was where I wanted to be, and so far beyond who I was meant to be, and if at any point I decided I didn't like either of those things, I could pull them apart and put them back together however I liked.

And I realized then that I hadn't been telling white lies to Kriseia and the other demons I'd left behind. I really could — really might *want* to — return to Hell someday. If and when I ever got bored with Earth, I had other options, whole other worlds open to me. Such a trip even sounded nice, if I were consciously choosing to make it this time.

I was Morgan Samantha Amell, part-time lord of demons and retail employee, full-time student and world-striding wonder witch. And I really liked the ring of most of those.

I didn't realize I was falling asleep until the chatter of passing students woke me up again, and I rolled up to a groggy sit on the swing. The sun was lowering toward evening, and the air had gotten chillier.

Invincible aegis or not, I didn't really want to be out in the city after dark. Not tonight, at least. With a yawn and a stretch, I stood up and headed for the campus main gate, and from there back toward home.

On my way, though, I swung by Old Sound. This late on a Sunday, it was already closed, but that was fine. My real interest was in the junk shop next door.

Or lack thereof. The windows were empty, the inside was dark, and a closer peek through the glass showed nothing but empty shelving and bare floor space. Morgan's little shop of adventure hooks had already moved on.

I was a little confused, but not surprised — and I had no purchase for the confusion. Whatever the point of her brief stint in my world had been, I guessed it was over, but I couldn't guess at what it was. Unless the whole thing was just a ploy to offload the *Morganomicon* on some unsuspecting fool. That would be a convoluted plan with no immediate benefit as far as I could see, but even still, I couldn't put it past her. Or maybe Excalibur's sheath disappearing from her trove spooked her and she'd changed direction with whatever her plans were.

Or maybe she just got bored quickly and moved on. Any explanation seemed as likely and as insensible as any other. However expanded my mind was now, comprehending Morgan le Faye's was still outside its wheelhouse. I sighed and shrugged and moved on.

It wasn't until I was back outside my apartment door that my first worry of the day finally sprung. As I was slipping the key into the lock, I heard a noise from inside: faint, but unmistakable, a soft yelp followed by something clattering. Somebody else was in my home.

This would have called for a full panic attack before. Now, I was just irritated. With Excalibur's sheath still fastened firmly around me, I finished unlocking the door, then readied a white-hot heat in my other hand as I shoved the door open and stomped in. "Alright," I demanded in my deepest voice as I strode to the middle of the room, "who the fuck thinks they can—"

A gasp and a happy squeal interrupted me as the intruder bounced up from where they were sitting on my bed and rushed toward me. I planted my feet, but registered the horns and the lavender skin just in time to dismiss the heat on my fist before it caused any damage.

Kriseia threw her arms around me in a hug so tight, it might have hurt had it not been for the aegis. I was too stunned to return it, or to do anything but stand there with my mouth agape while she crushed herself against me.

When at last she pulled back, there were tears in the corners of her eyes — her gem-shining, fully turquoise eyes. She took a step back on those spiked stripper heels she called feet, her tail still swishing forward to brush my hip as she clasped her hands and beamed, her smile reaching almost all the way to her horns.

This was a full-ass demon standing in front of me, no doubt. *My* demon, even. I hadn't expected to see her again so soon, if ever, but here she was in my entryway looking the same as when I'd left her earlier today/months ago/whenever the hell.

"…What?" was all I could offer in the moment. I turned and quickly slammed the door shut before anyone else passed by, then tried again. "How? Kriseia, what are… how and why are you here, holy shit!"

She bounced giddily on her feet before holding her hands out to me. There was a crumpled piece of velvety parchment held there that I hadn't noticed before. I stared in wonderment and confusion at her face as I took it, and had to force my eyes down onto the paper after a moment.

There was a short note scrawled on it. An Old Elvish note. One of my study cards I'd forgotten to bring with me? Even so, it wouldn't be enough on its own to send her interdimensionally. Had someone turned the circle on the Throne back on somehow just to deliver some of my lost homework?

I shook my head and made myself focus on the actual words, such as they were.

Dearest Morgan,

I trust you made it home safely. I had not planned to meddle in your life once more so soon — and it must seem very soon after indeed from your perspective, if I've done the calculations correctly — but you can see why I felt compelled to, I am sure. This poor thing found her way into my waypoint space, only the second being after yourself to make that particular journey in that particular direction in eons. An unexpected occurrence, and perhaps cause to leave this liminal checkpoint functional for a while still, if this ends up becoming a trend.

But back to matters at hand. She explained to me that she was trying to find her way to the human world, in search of her Morgan. Benevolent creature that I am, I've sent her along in your wake. She seems quite taken with you, so my advice is that you take good care of her. Every good witch has their familiars, after all.

Oh, and before you ask: Yes, I could have woven an enchantment across her to make communication easier, but I think you'll find things are more fun this way. Finding a solution will be a good lesson in and of itself. Think of it as your first official assignment from me, and do with that what you will.

Eagerly watching from just beyond the veil,

— Morgan

I turned the paper over, but the other side was blank. "This raises so many more questions than it answers!" I said, dropping the note to the ground. "Kriseia, holy… I mean, I'm happy to see you, but how the hell did you get here? How did you get to Other Morgan's pocket dimension first?"

She grabbed both my hands in hers and, beaming, said, "⌃⛢⥁⍨⚵⇰§!"

It sounded like a garbled, made-up Eastern European language of only consonants and grunts, chopped up and remixed in random order. It sounded like nothing approaching any comprehensible speech I had ever heard before.

"Demonic," I said after a moment, snapping my fingers. "You're speaking demonic right now, aren't you? Fuck, whatever weirdness helped us all understand one another in Hell, that must have been part of the traveling spell, or something innate about that plane, maybe? But if it was the spell, it's not working on this side of things. Some detail in the execution language I overlooked? I'd have to go over the entire summoning ritual again with a fine-toothed comb to make sure, but…" My hands flew up to grip my hair in frustration. "Ah, this is what Morgan was talking about in her note! Is this a test, then? I never told her I agreed to—"

I paused in my ramblings to look at Kriseia again. She was still standing patiently in front of me, radiating happiness and excitement and not an ounce of comprehension at what I was babbling about. "◍⊢⧾⚖⊶⋏⋎∈⌇⫶!" she said.

I sighed and wrapped my arms around her. "This is a lot," I said. "An amazing surprise, but a lot. I'm sorry, if I'd known you were going to find a way to chase me anyway, I would have tried to bring you along when I left after all, but…" I slid my hands up to cup her face and returned her smile with my own. "Alright, I guess I already have my next magic project figured out, then," I said. "How the hell am I going to talk to you like this? How will either of us understand each other while you're here?"

She pressed her lips against my own in a desperate, searing kiss, her hands tracing light, ecstatic lines up my sides and underneath my shirt. It was a sensation even more familiar to me now than the sights and sounds of the walk I'd just taken, and I found myself returning it on instinct, pulling her tight against me as we both sank wordlessly to the floor.

Alright, never mind. Figuring out what she was thinking was going to be about as easy as it ever was after all. I could work with this. I could work with anything.

My life was going to be fucking amazing from here on out, I could feel it.

About the Author

G.D. Burkhead is a speculative fiction author living in Chattanooga, Tennessee, with his wife and their various critters. He has a BA in English with a creative writing emphasis. He and his wife self-published their debut dark fantasy novel in August 2017 titled *The Black Lily*. He also has published numerous short stories and poems. His hobbies include writing, reading, playing video games, and TTRPGs. You can find him on Facebook, Instagram, and Bluesky @burkshelf and visit his website at www.burkshelf.com.